ANN

THE LIVES OF OTHERS

'An outstanding novel: compelling, compassionate and complex, vivid, musical and fierce'
Rose Tremain

'A devastating portrayal of a decadent society and the inevitably violent uprising against it . . . It is ferocious, unsparing and brutally honest'
Anita Desai

Neel Mukherjee was born in Calcutta. His award-winning first novel, *A Life Apart*, was published in 2010. This is his second novel. He lives in London.

BY THE SAME AUTHOR

A Life Apart

The Lives of Others

NEEL MUKHERJEE

Chatto & Windus
LONDON

Published by Chatto & Windus 2014

2 4 6 8 10 9 7 5 3 1

Map drawn by William Bragg. (This map is a representation only and makes no claims of
authenticity or accuracy with respect to the external boundaries of the country.)

First published in Great Britain in 2014 by
Chatto & Windus
Random House, 20 Vauxhall Bridge Road,
London SW1V 2SA
www.randomhouse.co.uk

Addresses for companies within The Random House Group Limited can be found at:
www.randomhouse.co.uk/offices.htm

The Random House Group Limited Reg. No. 954009

A CIP catalogue record for this book
is available from the British Library

ISBN 9780701186296

The Random House Group Limited supports the Forest Stewardship Council (FSC®), the
leading international forest-certification organisation. Our books carrying the FSC label are
printed on FSC®-certified paper. FSC is the only forest-certification scheme supported by
the leading environmental organisations, including Greenpeace. Our paper procurement
policy can be found at www.randomhouse.co.uk/environment

Typeset in Plantin by Palimpsest Book Production Limited,
Falkirk, Stirlingshire

Printed and bound in Great Britain by
Clays Ltd, St Ives plc

Christopher

How can we imagine what our lives should be without the illumination of the lives of others?

James Salter, *Light Years*

It's a poor sort of memory that only works backwards.

Lewis Carroll, *Alice in Wonderland*

. . . things are the way they are and when we recognise them, they are the same as when recognised by others or indeed by no one at all.

Daniel Kehlmann, *Measuring the World*

In historical events what is most obvious is the prohibition against eating the fruit of the tree of knowledge.

Leo Tolstoy, *War and Peace*

CONTENTS

THE
GHOSH FAMILY

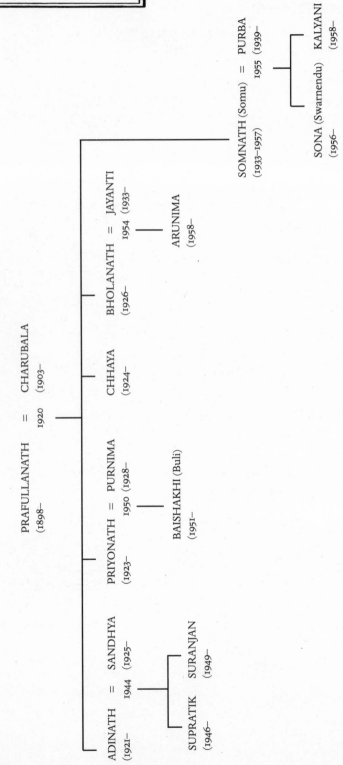

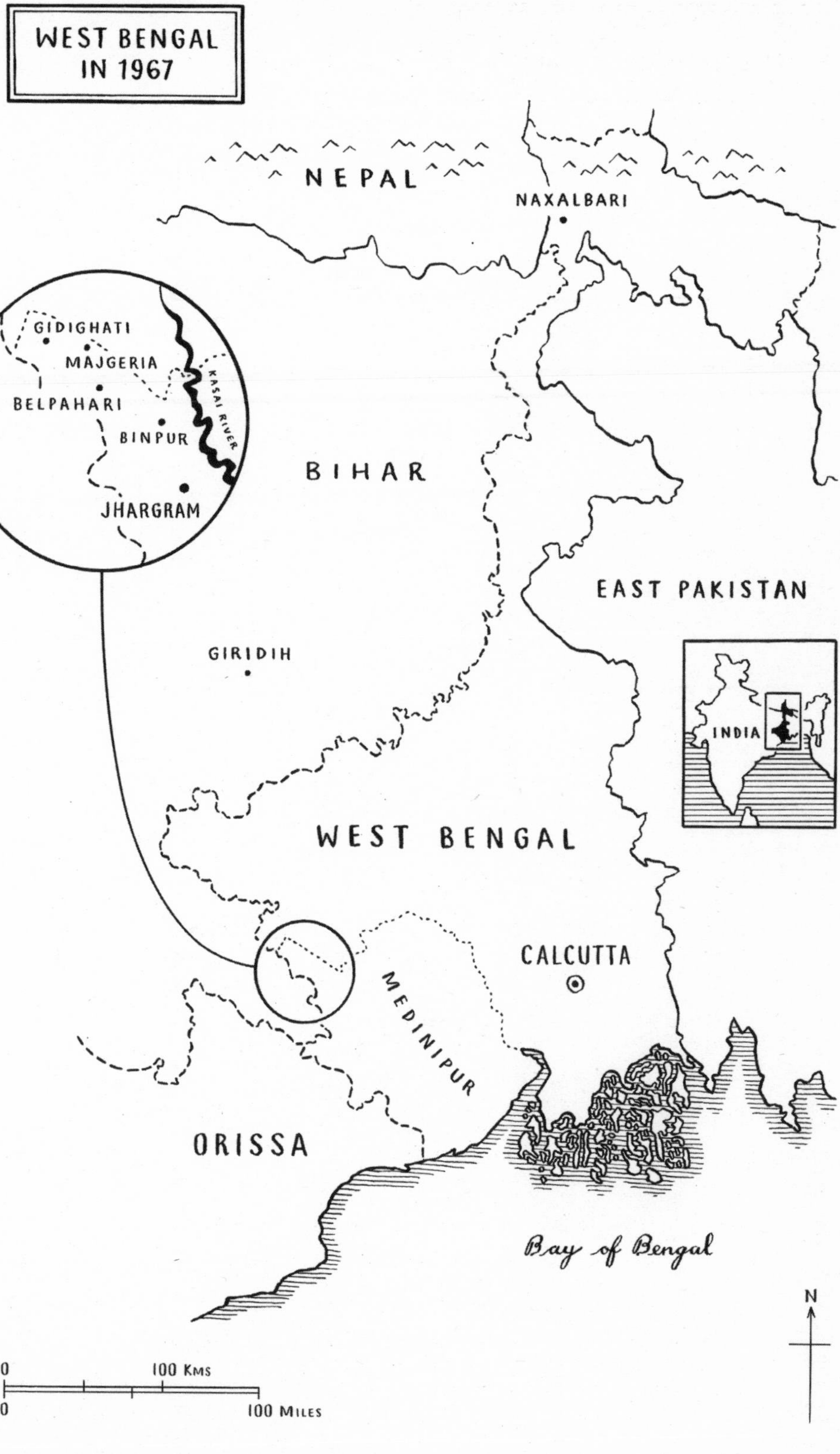

WEST BENGAL
IN 1967

NEPAL

NAXALBARI

GIDIGHATI

MAJGERIA

BELPAHARI

KASAI RIVER

BINPUR

JHARGRAM

BIHAR

EAST PAKISTAN

GIRIDIH

INDIA

WEST BENGAL

CALCUTTA

MEDINIPUR

ORISSA

Bay of Bengal

N

0   100 Kms

0   100 Miles

PROLOGUE

May 1966

A third of the way through the half-mile walk from the landlord's house to his hut, Nitai Das's feet begin to sway. Or maybe it is the head-spin again. He sits down on the lifeless field he has to cross before he can reach his hut. There isn't a thread of shade anywhere. The May sun is an unforgiving fire; it burns his blood dry. It also burns away any lingering grain of hope that the monsoons will arrive in time to end this third year of drought. The earth around him is beginning to fissure and crack. His eyelids are heavy. He closes them for a while, then, as sleep begins to take him, he pitches forward from his sitting position and jolts awake. Absently, he fingers his great enemy, the soil, not soil any more, but compacted dust. Even its memory of water has been erased for ever, as if it has never been.

He has begged all morning outside the landlord's house for one cup of rice. His three children haven't eaten for five days. Their last meal had been a handful of hay stolen from the landlord's cowshed and boiled in the cloudy yellow water from the well. Even the well is running dry. For the past three years they have been eating once every five or six or seven days. The last few times he had gone to beg had yielded nothing, except abuse and forcible ejection from the grounds of the landlord's house. In the beginning, when he had first started to beg for food, they shut and bolted all the doors and windows against him while he sat outside the house, for hours and hours, day rolling into evening into night, until they discovered his resilience and changed that tactic. Today they had set their guards on him. One of them had brought his stick down on Nitai's back, his shoulders, his legs, while the other one had joked, 'Where are you going to hit this dog? He is nothing but bones, we don't even have to hit him. Blow on him and he'll fall back.'

Oddly, Nitai doesn't feel any pain from this morning's beating. He knows what he has to do. A black billow makes his head spin again and he shuts his eyes to the punishment of white light. All he needs to do is walk the remaining distance, about 2,000 hands. In a few moments, he is all right. Some kind of jittery energy makes a sudden appearance inside him and he gets up and starts walking. Within seconds the panting begins, but he carries on. A dry heave interrupts him for a bit. Then he continues.

His wife is sitting outside their hut, waiting for him to return with something, anything, to eat. She can hardly hold her head up. Even before he starts taking shape from a dot on the horizon to the form of her husband, she knows he is returning empty-handed. The children have stopped looking up now when he comes back from the fields. They have stopped crying with hunger, too. The youngest, three years old, is a tiny, barely moving bundle, her eyes huge and slow. The middle one is a skeleton sheathed in loose, polished black skin. The eldest boy, with distended belly, has become so listless that even his shadow seems dwindled and slow. Their bones have eaten up what little flesh they had on their thighs and buttocks. On the rare occasions when they cry, no tears emerge; their bodies are reluctant to part with anything they can retain and consume. He can see nothing in their eyes. In the past there was hunger in them, hunger and hope and end of hope and pain, and perhaps even a puzzled resentment, a kind of muted accusation, but now there is nothing, a slow, beyond-the-end nothing.

The landlord has explained to him what lies in store for his children if he does not pay off the interest on his first loan. Nitai has brought them into this world of misery, of endless, endless misery. Who can escape what's written on his forehead from birth? He knows what to do now.

He picks up the short-handled sickle, takes his wife by her bony wrist and brings her out in the open. With his practised farmer's hand, he arcs the sickle and brings it down and across her neck. He notices the fleck of spit in the two corners of her mouth, her eyes huge with terror. The head isn't quite severed, perhaps he didn't strike with enough force, so it hangs by the still-uncut fibres of skin and muscle and arteries as she collapses with a thud. Some of the spurt of blood has hit his face and his ribcage, which is about to push out from its dark, sweaty cover. His right hand is sticky with blood.

The boy comes out at the sound. Nitai is quick, he has the energy and focus of an animal filled with itself and itself only. Before the sight in front of the boy can tighten into meaning, his father pushes him against the mud wall and drives the curve of the blade with all the force in his combusting being across his neck, decapitating him in one blow. This time the blood, a thin, lukewarm jet, hits him full on his face. His hand is so slippery with blood that he drops the sickle. Inside the tiny hut, his daughter is sitting on the floor, shaking, trying to drag herself into a corner where she can disappear. Perhaps she has smelled the metallic blood, or taken fright at the animal moan issuing out of her father, a sound not possible of humans. Nitai instinctively rubs his right hand, his working hand, against his bunched-up lungi and grabs hold of his daughter's throat with both his hands, and squeezes and squeezes and squeezes until her protruding eyes almost leave the stubborn ties of their sockets and her tongue lolls out and her thrashing legs still. He crawls on the floor to the corner where their last child is crying her weak, runty mewl and, with trembling hands, covers her mouth and nose, pushing his hands down, keeping them pressed, until there is nothing.

Nitai Das knows what to do. He lifts the jerrycan of Folidol left over from three seasons ago and drinks, his mouth to the lip of the plastic canister, until he can drink no more. His insides burn numb and he thrashes and writhes like a speared earthworm, thrashes and writhes, a pink foam emerging from his mouth, until he too is returned from the nothing in his life to nothing.

CHAPTER ONE

1967

Around six, the zoo starts to shake itself up from its brief sleep. Lying in bed, wide awake, Purnima hears the stirrings of life, each animal, each part of each animal, becoming animated in slow succession. Under the mosquito net the September humidity is already beginning to congeal into the suffocating blanket it will soon become. The fan, running at its top speed of five, battles away, unmindful of its futility. The only thing it circulates around the room is the sound of the fluttery pages of the Ghosh Gold Palace calendar hanging from a nail on the cream-painted walls. That calendar is a sign of her defiance; by some silent understanding reached a long time before she arrived in this house, all tokens of Ghosh Gold Palace are forbidden here, so she has made a point of having their calendar on the wall in her room.

Beside her, Priyo sleeps the sleep of the sinless. His early-morning snore has a three-toned sound to it – a snarly growl in the inhalation, then a hissing during part of the exhalation, completed by a final high-pitched insecty whine. She hears the scouring sound of a broom sluicing out with water some drain or courtyard. Someone is cleaning his teeth in the bathroom of a neighbouring house – there is the usual accompaniment of loud hawking, coughing and a brief, one-note retch. A juddering car goes down Basanta Bose Road with the unmistakable sound of every loose vibrating component about to come off – a taxi. A rickshaw cycles by, the driver relentlessly squeezing its bellows-horn. Another starts up, as if in response. Soon an entire fleet of rickshaws rackets past, their continuous horn shredding what little sleepiness remains of the morning.

Now she can hear other vehicles: the toot of a scooter-horn, the bell of a bicycle. This is how this world begins every day; noise is the way it signals that it is alive, indomitable. The sparrows send up a chinkless wall of manic cheeping. The doleful remonstrations of the pigeons, shuffling about on windowsills, sometimes tumble over into an aggressive chorus; they have the same merciless presence. The sound of water loops like a liquid thread through the other sounds; someone is beating their washing against the stone or concrete perimeter around a running tap. The clatter of metal buckets; uninterrupted cawing of crows; wrangling stray dogs; a distant conch-shell being blown three times in the prayer room of a house nearby . . . Here, up on the first floor of 22/6 Basanta Bose Road, all sounds converge as in an amphitheatre. Had she, her husband and their daughter, Baishakhi, lived on the top floor, where her parents-in-law and their favourite son, their eldest, Adinath, and his family have their quarters, it would have been so much less noisy, she knows. And away from the onslaught of mosquitoes, which would never have been able to ascend to the third floor. And, of course, more distant and safer from the troubles in the streets, bombings and murders, the terrifying stuff she hears about, that have started erupting in the city. Who can say that their street will not be the scene of such action?

From the thought of that one minor instance of preferential treatment of Dada to the real cause of all the rankling is a negligible distance. Dada, her elder brother-in-law, had been groomed to enter the family business, Charu Paper & Sons (Pvt. Ltd), from his school days and had obediently followed the path set out for him by his father, a trajectory as natural as the cycle of seasons. If family stories and reminiscences are to be believed, her husband, Priyo, however, had never shown any interest in the business, despite receiving the same training and indoctrination that his older brother had. If this had once caused ructions and displeasure, they are long vanished now, or almost vanished, for it is so obvious and accepted that Adinath is going to inherit the greater share of the family wealth in all its forms – business, money, house – that it is, like the air one breathes, not noticed, not remarked upon.

Despite the pervasive chatter of how the Ghoshes have fallen on hard times, how the business has been doing badly for years now, resulting in the selling-off of most of their mills, even most of her mother-in-law's jewellery, Purnima has never quite believed these crafty, convoluted North Calcutta people. Well, maybe they don't live there any longer, Purnima concedes, but her parents-in-law were originally from North Calcutta and these traits are difficult to eradicate and, she's convinced, even passed down the generations, irrespective of location. Everyone knew what a big gap existed between what they said in public and what they did in private.

On paper, Priyo appeared to have equal standing with Dada, certainly as far as the burden of work went, but it was Purnima's unshakeable belief that Adinath drew a significantly bigger salary than her husband. While she had a fair idea of the amount Priyo brought home, she was still in the dark about her elder brother-in-law's takings; this ignorance was not for lack of trying on her part. It was made even more maddening by too much information from another, opposite side: Priyo's contributions to the running of the household, which kept rising. Over and above paying the electricity bills for the entire household, which had been his responsibility for as long as Purnima had lived here, and paying some subsistence money to Purba, his youngest sister-in-law, he was now expected to increase his regular contribution to the family purse. The rest of his salary was deposited in a State Bank of India account held jointly by Purnima and Priyo. Part of this balance was cashed and kept by her in a locked drawer of their Godrej steel almirah, to dispose of and use as she deemed fit.

Despite being wholly in charge of this subset economy, Purnima felt that neither the money for her use nor the sum in the joint bank account was enough. She never reconciled herself to the fact that an increase in one meant a proportional depletion of the other. She wanted both to go up, and the mathematical impossibility of it irritated her so much that she often fell back on haranguing her husband. This, however, did not take the form of direct complaints about the meagreness of his income – it was not meagre – but about the inequitable nature of the levies imposed on her husband's salary. Why did he have to shell out so much? Adinath practically owned the family business, so he should shoulder most of the costs. Besides, being the eldest son, it was his duty to look after the younger ones. Did he, Priyo, *know* for certain that Dada's share of the costs was significantly larger or did he simply believe what he was told? How naïve was that? And what about her younger brother-in-law, Bholanath? He was the sole director of Charu Books, an entire company in itself. All his income seemed to go on the expensive education of his daughter in a fancy English-medium school. Where were his contributions? Exactly how much were they? And talking of dependants, shouldn't Dada have the sole responsibility of looking after that hapless widow, Purba? If all the brothers contributed equally, why should Dada get preferential treatment in the family? It was still the case that no meal could begin without Dada taking a big spoon to the virgin mound of cooked rice and breaking it, yet another irritating North Calcutta affectation.

These and other related questions had accumulated over the course of their seventeen-year marriage and now found expression in ever-longer sessions of nagging. If Priyo had tried, in the past, to answer a few of them with reason and accuracy, he had long since given up, faced with the proliferating queries; now they went in through one ear and left through the other. And yet this is not the nub of Purnima's dissatisfaction. That lies in the future.

It is evident that after the deaths of Baba and Ma, her parents-in-law, Dada will become head of the family. But who will the house, this big, four-storey house with a rare back garden in the heart of Bhabanipur, be left to? Will the entirety of it go to Dada or will it be divided amongst all the brothers? If divided, how? Equally or commen-surate with the differential treatment they have received?

Years of trying to extract solid information from Priyo had yielded nothing. He was either evasive and lackadaisical in his responses, saying, 'Let's wait and see', to which she always said that that would be too late, they couldn't do much *after* the division; or he sided with his family. 'We've all lived together happily in this home, sharing everything; the question of dividing it into units for the use of one and not another does not arise. We'll continue to live like this. Everything belongs to every one of us,' he'd say.

Purnima took this badly. A threatening cloud would settle over husband and wife until its inevitable precipitation into tantrums and shouting. 'I'll see who looks after you and your daughter when you're left with nothing,' she'd rage. 'They'll take everything, counting each and every brick of the house, each and every single brick, you mark my words.' The 'they' remained nebulous and unspecified.

The seven o'clock siren from a distant factory now adds its wail to the symphony outside. Like another clock, the blind beggar and his daughter begin working this particular patch of their beat, the sound of small cymbals accompanying their devotional duet, 'Let my soul blossom like the hibiscus at the feet of my mother-goddess'. Purnima reluctantly gets out of bed to begin another day in her prison.

Late that afternoon, Adinath, sitting on a tired cushion – battered and leaking dirty greyish cotton – on his favourite planter's long-sleever in the seldom-used drawing room on the ground floor, nervously contemplates the edgy story that the slim sheaf of papers left at a careless angle on the cane-and-glass coffee table is trying to tell him. Samik Sarkar, head of the State Bank of India, Eastern Region, had come in with the papers in the afternoon to guide him through that story; Adinath asked him to leave the documents behind. He fingers the packet of Wills Filter – several rungs down from Rothmans and Pall Mall, his brands of choice during easier days – but decides not to light up another one. The room is blue with smoke. Samik-babu had switched on the tube-lights before leaving and, in their depressing white glare, Adinath can see the oily iridescence of the film that has formed on the remains of the milky tea in the cups on the coffee table.

An extreme tiredness, seemingly from nowhere, suddenly clings tight to him; he lowers his head, takes off his glasses and passes his fingers through his salt-and-pepper hair, once, twice, three times. He is happy to have the papers sit in front of him, unyielding with their slow, poisonous information. Numbers never lie; one can make them, of course, as one can make anything speak another story in another tongue, but they do not have the inherent falsehood that words carry. The moment he looks at the figures, whatever little scrap of peace there is in his mind, trying to hold on to some fragile ledge, will be dislodged into an abyss for ever. Suddenly the taste of exhaustion changes and modulates into fear: he almost feels that swift somer-saulting of taste on the sour-bitter fur coating his tongue. Samik-babu had brought himself to utter the word 'repossession' and then quickly skated over his own embarrassment by suggesting that both outfits be sold to some Marwari buyer at whatever price they were willing to pay. The creditors won't be put off for too long now: that will be the pointed truth at the heart of the thicket of numbers waiting by his side, resilient and impatient at the same time with their dangerous, whispery story.

The botched modernisation of technology at one of the factories, all that high-risk borrowing against capital – what enormous reach they had into the future, like those she-ghosts in the stories they were told when they were little, ghosts with nasal voices and long arms that could traverse fields and houses and ponds and grab your neck. There is labour unrest and unionism in the mills and, given the fragility of the coalition government and the way the left party is strong-arming, where will they be if the Communist Party, the CPI(M), actually comes to power? Which could be any day now, he suspects. Charu & Sons will have to accede to every demand of the unions; their contacts with the rapidly attenuating Congress Party will not be of much help in troubleshooting; the prospect gives him the gooseflesh of terror. But for how much longer can they continue hanging on to a factory locked up for two years now? The business with Dulal last year, that unthinkable gherao, all those workers swollen in numbers by lumpens brought in from the outside, all of them shouting, chanting, *You must, you must, you must listen to our demands. Break and crush the black hands of the owners* . . . There, another ripple of that gooseflesh rakes over him.

He hears his brother Priyo's wife, Purnima, upstairs cry out to her daughter, 'Buliiiii, come inside, don't stand on the verandah at this hour, everyone can see you.'

He knows what he needs now, while the siren numbers wait. He needs protection, insulation, someone, something to shore him up and whisper another provisional truth to him: that the world can look different, kinder; that it won't always be a merciless landing on a bed of nails, but sometimes a silky easing onto a lawn of down feathers. He needs a less vulnerable eye with which to see the world. He gets up from his long-sleever with some difficulty, his knees sending out an audible crack (his father's arthritis, could it be? is arthritis heredi-tary?), picks up a hollow terracotta Bankura horse standing on the coffee table, removes its detachable ear and upends it. A little key clinks out. With that clutched in his slightly shaking hand, he makes his way across the room to the glass-fronted book-cupboard. He unlocks it, reaches for the topmost shelf, which houses the collected works of Rabindranath Tagore nestled tightly against each other, a uniform brown-spined army, and deftly removes volumes five to seven. The gap created by the removal of those three soldiers from their ranks reveals his pint-bottle of Johnnie Walker.

He hears the front door open, then the sound of his younger son, Suranjan, entering the house: that erratic, charmless clatter could belong to no one else. The boy would now thud his way up the stairs and shut himself in his room for the . . . But no, before he can complete his thought, the loud advancing footfalls alert him that his son's destination is no place other than the ground-floor drawing room. A nervous hurry ruins the ephemeral grace for which Adinath had reached out his hands.

On the second floor, Chhaya sits on the low stool in front of the dressing table in her room, looking into the gloom of the heartless mirror. She opens the drawer on her right and takes out a pair of tweezers, her heart beating out a hot tattoo of shame: what will everyone think if they find out that she plucks her eyebrows?

She nearly jumps off her stool when she hears Purnima's loud summons – 'Buliiiii, come inside, don't stand on the verandah at this hour, everyone can see you' – reach her, muffled and diluted, one floor up here. That coarse, vulgar, low-born woman, she thinks; braying all the time, not a whit of class about her, typical of her South Calcutta origins. Her voice is like a split bamboo. You can take the girl out of Behala, but you can't take Behala . . . Her familiar thoughts run along the runnels made deep by the ceaseless flow of these very sentiments for the last seventeen years. She gets up hastily, shuts the door to her room, turns on the light and sits on the stool again. The open drawer, a tongue stuck out in shame, mocks her. The crowd of cosmetics on the table – face powder, creams, snows, skin-whitener, lotions, eye-pencils, perfumes, lipsticks, even, improbably, a tiny pot of rouge – didn't quite carry, collectively, the single charge of . . . of . . . *immorality* that the tweezers sent through her fingers.

After years of plucking and shaping her eyebrows, she still feels this heat of shame flushing through her. Oddly enough, no single act of her elaborate evening toilette – before she sits on the front verandah of the second floor for an hour or two until the light gives out, a ritual she has followed for seventeen years now, with only a brief interruption at the beginning – fills her with the kind of self-reproach that this does. The application of snow or cream to her face followed by face powder, then the painting of her lips and eyes, placing a beauty spot on her chin, wearing jewellery and an expensive, dressy sari, spritzing herself with perfume – none of it carries that sting. She wishes her face were a blank canvas on which she could compose her features anew every day, but she has been given, instead, an almost indelible painting, which she tries to paint over, brush out, erase and correct in order to have a more pleasing picture; every afternoon she fails and is left contemplating the unbending stubbornness and tenacity of the original.

She ruffles her brows, letting the unruly hairs stand out. Like weeds, they're going to be rooted out. She steadies her trembling hands, leans forward towards the mirror and brings the tweezers up to her face. Her hands won't be still and obedient, so she waits while she lets the old poison of her low sister-in-law surface again. It is best to think of something else while she plucks out the refractory hairs, and hatred is an ever-reliable friend.

Her hand inches closer to her right eyebrow, *for seventeen years she has had to, the whole family has had to, put up with that woman, that serpent,* one, there, the first one out, with that pricking twinge; two, the pain isn't negligible, it all depends on how toughly they are rooted in; three, ouch, *perhaps no one really knows the true depths of her evil, that crow pretending to be a cuckoo, but she has known, from the very beginning;* four; five, easy enough; now her left, *anyway, what does one expect, from a low-caste family, a Saha, all charm on the outside, 'Didi this, Didi that' on the surface, sticking the knife in afterwards* one, oh god, this is going to set her sneezing. She drops her tweezers, her face a comic mask in the first moments of being seized by an imminent sneeze, mouth open, jaw turned down, eyebrows furrowed, face lifted in expectation, as the sneezes arrive, one after the other, racking her short, pudgy frame in their cathartic succession.

Suranjan walks into the seldom-used drawing room on the ground floor, the LP held in his sweaty hands, almost clasped to his thin chest, as if he were guarding the elixir of immortal life. From the entrance to Basanta Bose Road he has heard Boro-kaki call out to Buli to come in from the verandah. Hopefully, at this time of the day, about to fold into evening, the drawing room will be empty and he will be able to listen, uninterrupted inside the still centre of concentration, to this album, *Revolver*, borrowed from his friend Bappa-da after weeks of begging, wheedling, cajoling, even offering money as security against damage by scratching or accidental loss. He is going to have to guard it with his very life. Not that that is going to be a problem, for ever since he heard the mournful strings of 'Eleanor Rigby' and the jubilant harmonies of 'Taxman' he has felt as if he has watched his own rebirth into a new being. The record in his hands is not an LP, it is his beating life itself. It is where all the soiled trade of human life passed through and emerged as prelapsarian truth.

Enmeshed in purple rhapsodies, Suranjan takes a while to identify the sharp bouquet of spirits in the drawing room as he enters. Part of the reason for his slowness may be because he is thrown by his father's presence there. It seems Adinath has been waiting for his son, looking expectantly at the door, almost willing him, or anyone, to walk in. Frozen for a few moments by this unexpected and wholly unwelcome encounter, both father and son fall back on a default embarrassment – staring at the floor, mumbling, groping for excuses – until the smell of alcohol brings Suranjan back his presence of mind. It embarrasses him further and releases a sudden squirt of fear and shame in him, as if it is he who has been caught doing something illicit.

Muddied in his mind are two strains of thought; first, if he can smell the tang of alcohol in the room, does that mean that his father can detect the occasional whiff on him when he returns home after a bout of furtive drinking with his college friends? The second, even more disturbing, is the question of whether his father is going down some slippery slope; it is one thing to indulge in the forbidden pleasures of alcohol at the age of eighteen, quite another for that eighteen-year-old to discover that his father drinks too. What for him is both pleasure and transgression, a matter of guilty delight, can surely not be the same for his father? In the older man it is almost certainly a sign of dissolution. He looks at his father with hooded distaste, the

LP in his hand, its promises of a transporting salvation lost in the very quicksands of family that he had been seeking to escape.

Arunima, seated on the floor, restlessly arranging books according to size, sharpening pencils to points capable of stabbing a small creature, cannot rid her mind of the image of the pencil box Malvika Tiwari brought to class that day. Meanwhile, *her* sharpened Flora and Apsara pencils, ranging from 2H to 2B, are all going into the old, dented, lustreless Camlin pencil box. Malvika's shiny new pencil case, brought all the way from Singapore by her father, had a picture of a wide-eyed, golden-haired girl standing in a field of closed yellow buds, but if you tilted the box the girl winked and all the buds bloomed into a blaze of unfurled flowers. Ever since she had seen that, everything had flown out of Arunima's head, as from an open window, to make space for only one thing: desire. While the other girls had sat oohing and aahing, and some had even been transparent in their envy, she had fallen into a trough of silence, sad that such a thing existed, but not in her possession.

The only way she can have it is to ask her father to buy her one. But it has to be done without the knowledge of her mother. If she ever finds out that Arunima wants a flash pencil box, she will go out of her way to ensure that her daughter doesn't get it. She will tell her husband that his contribution to parenting consists solely of spoiling their child: *Before the words have left her mouth, you go and get her whatever she wants. You are eating her head. Can't you see what she's going to grow up to be, how much trouble she's going to cause all of us?* She can practically hear her mother's snapping words. Then she will add the clinching detail, a final, shaming cut, like that from paper and as annoying: *And in these straitened times, too. Do you think money grows on trees?* Her father will then sheepishly tell her, *Without Ma's permission, I cannot do anything.* That is what it always comes down to: her mother like an unassailable wall between her and everything she ever wants.

It seems to her nine-year-old mind that her mother had her so that she could have someone to punish, scold and thwart. And to stand between her and her father. Now, sitting arranging pencils in descending order of size, from left to right, in her unlovely pencil box, irritated already at the sure prospect of them changing their assigned places during the journey to school tomorrow morning and upsetting the beauty of the ranking she has given them, she reaches inside herself and feels for the ever-present crystal of anger, commuting effortlessly between the minor pique with unruly pencils and the bigger frustration with her mother, and finds herself moved to a bitter joy at the hardness of that gem. She breaks the sharpened graphite points of each of the pencils, one by one, and starts sharpening them again with a rigorous fury.

The swish of sari, the rattle of keys tied to her aanchol, and the tinkle of bangles heralds the approach of Jayanti.

'Is your homework done?' she asks. 'Arunima, I can only see tools of study, but not a single open book or exercise copy. You think I won't notice?'

Arunima does not bother to look up.

Jayanti raises her voice: 'Arunima, I'm talking to you, look up. Why don't you have a book open in front of you? Don't you have home-work to do? Am I to believe it's all done by half-past six? Where is your Bengali book? You got four out of twenty in your Bengali spelling test last week. Shameful, shameful! You can't seem to get your head around the difference between the short and long 'i' sounds. And you're now sitting here wasting your time sharpening pencils.'

Arunima has this all sorted out in her head, including the trump card she slaps down in front of her mother. 'There's no Bengali class tomorrow, Ma, only homework for Eng. Lit. and Drawing. I was sharpening the pencils for drawing class. You know how angry Sister Josephine gets if our pencils are blunt.' Pause. 'If you want, I can start on the Eng. Lit. homework instead.'

Arunima knows, with the confident cruelty of a child, that her mother increasingly fears all her subjects except Bengali, because everything else is in English and, therefore, outside her reach; the downside of sending her daughter to the English-medium Carmel Convent. Only after she has said that does she look up to note the hesitating deflation of her mother, then she lowers her eyes, seemingly absorbed again in preparing her pencils exactly as Sister Josephine likes them. The jewel inside her flickers and gleams.

Jayanti, the wind taken out of her sails, aims for a swift rebuttal that would save her face, but all she can come up with is, 'Well, then, *after* you're done with Drawing and English, I want you to go through "Shiladitya" from *Raj Kahini*. I'll be back to test you on it.'

Feeling a sense of bathos at what she has just said, Jayanti adds, 'I don't want you sneaking out of the room before you're finished with your lessons. No inattentiveness' and huffily leaves the room.

Sitting on a battered rush mat on the floor of the dingy room, which she shares with her mother and her brother, Kalyani looks at the open book in front of her with a familiar mixture of bafflement, indifference and boredom. That dreary, unfathomable story again about those two impeccably good children, Hashi and Tata, and their strange relationship with a king with a toothsome name, Gobindamanikya. For all that she can make out, the lines in front of her could be the effect of a swarm of insects, their legs dipped in ink, let loose on straight, closed tracks on the pages; the letters and words, one after the other, make no more sense to her than that. She has difficulty reading on the very basic level of individual words. If she fails again this year, she will be thrown out of school. For two years running she has remained in Class Three of their local school, Katjunagar Swarnamayee Bidyapith. Without the help of her elder brother, Sona, she would have been expelled last year, for she had failed in every single subject. But Dada is busy preparing for an exam that will help him move, if he is successful, from the government school, where he is now, to the better, more prestigious Calcutta Boys, and it has been decided that his fees are going to be paid by Mejo-jyethu, so Sona is putting in extra hours after school at his friend Sougata's home.

Which is just as well, because if he stays on late enough he is at least going to get a proper meal there, with most likely two kinds of vegetable dishes, fish, even mutton or chicken if he gets lucky, not the unchanging watery dal-rice-mashed-potatoes that they have every evening, unless someone from upstairs sends something down. By some unspoken agreement their dinnertime has been pushed further and further back, even within Kalyani's short living memory, so that they eat after ten o'clock now; perhaps in the hope that salvation in the form of leftover cauliflower-and-potato fry or egg curry or even stale, old food that the people upstairs won't eat any more will get sent down. Often, that does not happen.

She hears the call – 'Buliiii, come inside, don't stand on the verandah at this hour, everyone can see you' – in her aunt's ox-bellow of a voice, and the residue of guilt and fear that is left in her, pricking her to apply herself to the insurmountable nature of her school work, vanishes, replaced by colourful dreams of all the cosmetics that Buli-di has and which Kalyani so cravenly desires. Lipstick and nail polish are magic words to her: they can make the entirety of the known world disappear. As far as she can ascertain, Buli-di has one shade of lipstick – a pomegranate-flower red – and two bottles of nail polish: hot pink and scarlet. Buli-di isn't allowed to wear lipstick – Kalyani saw her hastily and brutally removing it from her mouth one evening last year during Durga Puja, standing at the corner before entering Basanta Bose Road; she had been out with her friends, doing the evening tour of the different pandals of South Calcutta – but nail polish, while not exactly endorsed by her mother, does not carry such a flagrant charge. She is not even sure if Buli-di owned the lipstick or was wearing one of her friends'. If the former, she would certainly have to keep it stashed well away from the prying eyes of her mother. If only Kalyani can discover where that secret place is . . . But she is not even allowed to go to any of the floors above without being looked at as if she were a mangy dog that has strayed indoors, so rooting around in Buli-di's room on the first floor is a wild dream, no more. Besides, if Kalyani's mother finds out that she has been upstairs without her permission, she will be 'beaten to the shape of a plank', as her mother never ceases to remind her.

They have to stay hidden away, all three of them, in one room on the ground floor of this big four-storey house, as if they were servants and not what they really are, true family, she and Sona first cousins to Bor'-da and Chhor'-da, Buli-di, and Arunima. Each of the brothers and their families got a whole floor to themselves, while she and her mother and brother had to remain cooped up in what was nothing more than a hastily emptied-out junk storage room, with one low bed and a cracked, smoky mirror, both rejects from upstairs, a rusting metal wardrobe with doors that did not stay shut and a rolled-up mattress and folded-up mosquito net that sat in one end of the room and were spread out for her and her mother before bedtime every night while Sona, being the son, had the pallet.

Not that Kalyani has ever thought this set-up to be unfair, in the sense of assigning it that particular term and being consequently moved along the path of enquiry on causes and reasons. The situation is as it is, she has known no better and she has unconsciously imbibed, from her mother and from the very air circulating in this nether region of the house, not to ask questions or even think of them in the first place, so the incongruence in the conditions of the families of the three brothers upstairs and her mother's hardly ever strikes her as anything other than an ineluctable fact, as given as the fact of a tree rising upwards from the soil or of rain falling in the direction of the earth.

Or the fact of the fawn-coloured lizard edging closer and closer, with utmost furtiveness, towards the cockroach perched under the tube-light on the wall she faces. The sight freezes her; fear mingled with a repulsion that gives her the sensation of a whole forest of tiny hairs along her spine and back rising to attention. Her stomach heaves, yet she cannot take her eyes off the atavistic scene unfolding two yards in front of her: the cockroach seems unaware of the predator inching closer, or is perhaps hypnotised by the prospect of imminent death. Suddenly, so quickly she thinks she has imagined it, the lizard flicks out its gummy tongue and swallows the cockroach whole.

She has started shivering now: the hind legs and the wing-ends of the insect still stick out of the reptile's mouth and then disappear as the peristaltic movements within the lizard, something she can clearly see as a slow ripple of convulsions, convey the prey inside. A dry heave goes through her, as if in answer to the motion she is witnessing. Another heave. The lizard stays still, bloated at its centre, its skin so thin, almost to the point of translucence, that she thinks she can see the struggling cockroach – or is it dead by now? – inside. Then, in an unimaginable moment, the reptile ejects the brown wings of the ingested insect through its mouth. As the wings float down to the floor, Kalyani, paralysed as a creature in a malign myth a few seconds before, throws up all over her Bengali textbook. At that exact moment her mother, barely able to suppress her sobbing, storms into the room.

Three floors up, in the bedroom of her parents-in-law, Kalyani's mother, Purba, is making their bed as her mother-in-law, Charubala, stands by, watching her as a falcon watches a quivering rabbit. Purba has done this, every single evening, for the last eleven years, but she knows that the possibility of slipping up is infinite. A pleat not smoothed down, the sheets on the bed not pulled tightly enough before being tucked under the mattress, the bolster and pillows not fluffed up perfectly . . . it surprises her that these ambushes can still trip her up. Today, the slowly ticking silence in the room since she has entered it makes her prepare herself for something worse than the usual corrosive nagging. God alone knows from which direction it is going to come. She hears her Mejo-jaa call out to her daughter, 'Buliiii, come inside, don't stand on the verandah at this hour, everyone can see you', weakened and muffled in its passage two floors up, and as if on cue the barrage begins. And, as always, it begins with finding fault with the task at hand.

'Cataracts!' Charubala barks, 'have you suddenly developed cataracts in your eyes? Can't you see the dustball in that corner, or do I need to point everything out to you? Who is doing the cleaning: you or I, hyan?'

Purba dutifully takes up the broom, resweeps the corner of its imaginary dustball and resumes making the bed. But before she can touch the sheets, Charubala shrieks, 'Touching my bedsheets directly after touching the broom? You sewer-witch! Go wash your hands immediately. Use soap.'

Purba, silent, head bowed as always, enters the bathroom, runs the tap at the sink and stands watching it, without washing her hands, for what she considers a seemly duration, then turns off the tap, counts up to five, comes back into Ma's room and carries on with making the bed. She knows that Charubala's outburst has been only a prelude, a kind of clearing of the throat before the real singing begins. She continues lifting and tucking, waiting for the inevitable; what makes her jittery is not knowing the particular form it is going to take.

'Have you gathered the dry washing today? It's getting dark, I have no idea why you leave it till so late. The evening dew will make it damp. You can't be trusted to do anything properly nowadays. What's got into you?'

Purba cannot work out where this is leading, so she hesitates before replying.

'What, someone's put a lock on your tongue?'

'I was going to do it after I'd made your bed,' Purba bleats, her head still lowered. If she so much as dares to look up, she will be accused of being disrespectful and intransigent.

'To time it with Shobhon Datta's cigarette break on his terrace next door. Do you think we're blind?'

Purba reddens instantly. The accuracy or incorrectness of what her mother-in-law is accusing her of is irrelevant; the fact that it has been articulated means that a certain set of assumptions has been made about her character and given public existence in the form of an utterance. It is in the nature of flung mud that some of it sticks.

Charubala takes her youngest daughter-in-law's blushing as evidentiary proof of a guilty soul. There is no stopping her now. 'Chhee, chhee! Aren't you ashamed of yourself? You are a widow, a mother of two. You'll bring shame and scandal on our family, more than you've already done . . .'

'But, Ma, this is not true,' Purba manages to speak out, before Charubala cuts her short.

'So you're accusing me of lying? Oh god, I had to live to see this, accused of being a liar by a girl from another family. Was this what was written on my forehead?'

Purba hastens to negate this, but knows it is pointless. If she does not choose her words carefully, she will dig herself in deeper, but if she remains quiet, locked in the incredulity at what is being thrown at her, she will condemn herself equally.

Charubala, on the other hand, is on a roll. 'Shame! Shame! I see that I shall have to keep a sharper eye on you. God knows what's going to happen if anyone finds out' – Purba knows that she is going to make sure that everyone does – 'the good name of the Ghosh family will lie in the dust. Haven't you done enough to make us suffer? I knew from the very beginning that you were trouble, I told your father-in-law, when the match was being made, *Listen, she comes from a lower-caste family, her father is a mere postal worker, it's not right that such a girl should come into our family*, but he didn't listen. Now we are all reaping the cost.' Charubala, of course, was mindful that the Ghoshes were not perched on a high rung of the caste-ladder, so she was grateful to have a few upon whom she could look down. The gratitude expressed itself as venom for those below.

Years of this kind of unceasing torrent have somewhat blunted but not eliminated, not by any measure, the keenness of the hurt and humiliation Purba feels when faced with it. She wants the ground to open up and swallow her. She shuts her eyes, hoping that when she opens them, she will discover all this is a bad dream, but the trick fails her yet again.

'If I see you on the roof in the evening, I will have to take other measures. I shall see then how much appetite for secret love you have when you're starving.'

If she had any residue of dignity left, she would have long run out of the room, Purba thinks, but she has fallen far, far below that. Even anger at being treated like this has been burned out of her. What remains is a dead weight of darkness. Her eyes rest on the powder-blue sheets and pillowcases and the stripy blue and yellow tasselled bedcover. If she looks up, she knows she will see the rolled-up mosquito net, a large, crumpled, brooding bird, above the bedposts, but she cannot move her head or her eyes to glance upwards. There is no salvation to be had from the objects in the world.

Supported by his silver-tipped cane, Prafullanath hobbles to the room adjacent to his bedroom, towards his daily ritual of early evening tea, unchanged for the last twenty years. It is the second and last time he leaves his bed during the day, for an hour, to sit, imprisoned in the hardened angularities of his pain, staring at the Charu Paper & Sons (Pvt. Ltd) calendar on the opposite wall, a cup of unsweetened, milky tea in his hands tilting slowly to spill out half its tepid contents onto the saucer and sometimes onto his pyjama.

Prafullanath waits for Madan to bring his tea and a couple of Marie biscuits and with them, invariably, he notes with mounting dread, the compulsive jabbering. Ever since the upheavals involving Madan's son, Dulal, last year, it has been deeply uncomfortable for Prafullanath to be alone in a room with him; and these teatimes, where Madan, in blithe denial, has not eased off his habitual pointless chatter, as if nothing in the recent past has happened to make him as uncomfortable as Prafullanath in each other's presence, have been especially excruciating. The old man has toyed with the idea of asking Madan to stop jabbering, has spent months appearing to be conspicuously restless and impatient and distracted, often cutting him short and changing the topic, but the cook has persisted with such terrier-like tenacity, apparently oblivious to the signals being given out, that Prafullanath has accepted this small defeat and has locked himself away deeper inside his own head, while Madan has wittered on about chicken stew and how fish in mustard sauce gives you hyperacidity and about Patit, the driver, drinking, and Gagan, the general dogsbody, being caught gambling at shatta in the slums across the railway lines . . . Does Madan seriously think that Prafullanath, at the age of almost seventy, arthritic, diabetic, with an ischaemic heart and two heart attacks already behind him, is interested in these paltry nothings? Besides, domestic servants are the women's domain; he does not remember if he has ever had a word with Charu, his wife, about this excess in Madan, now grown so trying. He must remember to talk to her tonight and see if she can arrange for it to stop; Madan has always been her creature, while his role has only been to pay his salary.

Madan walks in, teapot, cup, saucer, milk, sugar, plate of Marie biscuits all on a tray, sets it down and proceeds to pour while beginning his daily bulletin. 'Chicken ishtu for you today. Light like water. Ma's orders. With toast. No butter. The rest are having deep-fried aubergines, dal, spinach balls stuffed with cottage cheese, fish fry. Soaking the pieces of bhetki in marinade now, have to take them out in the next hour. Said to Ma, one or two pieces of fish fry won't do Baba any harm, she wouldn't listen to me. Well, we are poor, illiterate people, what do we know, but since when have people died of eating, I ask you? They die of hunger. But if Ma says it's bad for you, then it must be. But what harm can a couple of pieces do? Want some with your tea now? Could quickly sneak in a couple for you, no one would be any the wiser.'

Prafullanath blows on his tea, thereby avoiding answering the question.

Madan continues, 'So it's Durga Puja next month. I will be going to the country after Kali Puja for twenty days, as usual. That Gagan will be bringing you your tea. Will probably forget it half the time, not bring it on time, you'll have to keep nagging. Said to Ma, whatever gets done, or doesn't get done more likely, see that they don't slip up with Baba's afternoon tea and bishkoot. Gagan's mind is like a sieve, nothing except bad habits stays in it, that and finding money for cigarettes and god knows what else, wouldn't be a tiny bit surprised if it wasn't just cigarettes. Even saw him whispering to Suranjan-da by the stairs that day, very close they were too.'

Prafullanath coughs, shifts around on the sofa as far as his creaking body will allow, shuffles his feet and starts pouring out the tea onto his saucer to cool it faster. The tea dribbles out and drips into a small brown puddle on the low table; a few warm drops fall on his pyjama and, in trying to avoid more of them falling and staining the white cotton, he moves his shaky hand quickly, only to have the drops now fall on the floor, on the edge of the sofa, on a different spot on the table, on the tray that holds the tea things.

Madan pounces at once and starts mopping up the spilt tea with a dishcloth that he always carries, slung on his shoulder. 'Eeesh, eeesh, let me, let me, I've got it.' With that only concession towards what he knows to be a deliberately engineered distraction, he reverts to his monologue. 'Don't get me wrong, but Suranjan-da is at an impressionable age, and Gagan such a ne'er-do-well, such close whispering under the stairs; and then that other time on the terrace, I swear I saw something pass hands, could have been I saw wrong, but as they say, a poor man has four eyes and four ears.'

Prafullanath sips his cooling tea, coughs and tries to say 'Achha, achha' dismissively, but it comes out as a pathetic croak.

'Saying this to you and no one else, he doesn't earn that little, thanks to your generosity and Ma's and Bor'-da's, but where does all that money go? Don't think he sends any to the country, doesn't have a wife and children to support, but every month, without fail, *Ei, Madan-da, can you lend me ten rupees, can you lend me twenty rupees, will return it the very minute I get paid, swear on Ma Kali.* I say, where does all his money go?'

This time Prafullanath manages a gruff, 'All right, all right' before beginning to dip his fingers for the dregs of the biscuit, which has become too soggy after being dunked into the tea to make it to his mouth and has dropped instead into the cup. Madan notices the mishap, feels a small surge of joy inside him and continues without a pause, 'But anyway, who am I to say anything? To each his own. My interest is to look out for Suranjan-da. Nowadays people of many hues seem to be all over the place. Take the Datta family next door, their maid, Parul, Parul this, Parul that, there was no end of talk about her endless virtues' – he notices Prafullanath getting fidgety, being overly fussy about dunking his next biscuit in his tea, clearing his throat to prepare himself to say something to him, but paralysed in the attempt – 'and then one day, right in the middle of the street, at two in the afternoon, in full view of the world, there she was, screaming her throat cracked, tearing out her hair in clumps and shoving them into her mouth, handful by handful, swallowing it all. They had to send her back to the country.'

He pauses to inhale the odour of small triumph that has suddenly suffused the room. The old man will not try to send out hints asking him to stop again this evening; maybe tomorrow, but that will be a new battle. Today, he has broken the old man's back, he has won. Again.

He resumes his recounting of the scandal with the insane maid-servant next door. 'Much whispering, much talk about how a young woman could go mad suddenly like that. So many people said so many things, I kept my mouth shut, as always, the wise never talk, only listen, all this gossip about something that may have happened to her in the Datta house, after all with that young man there, I didn't say anything, of course . . .'

Prafullanath fixes his eyes on the tattered, yellowed calendar opposite and attempts to shut out the low babble in the only way he knows: by concentrating on the fact that the year it is from, 1957, was the year his life began to turn to rubble.

'C-o-n-j-u-g-a-t-i-o-n,' Dibyendu-da writes on Sougata's exercise book. Sona copies it diligently, awaiting an explanation. 'From the Latin *conjugare*, meaning "to join together",' Dibyendu-da adds and Sona writes that down too, as if he were taking dictation. He hopes that this will ease his path towards mastering it; at the moment, it is an impenetrable forest from a particularly malevolent fairytale. Standing at the edge of that darkness, where 'be' becomes 'am', 'is' or 'are', depending on who one is talking about, and thorny thickets of 'has been', 'have been' and 'had been' – where does this 'been' come from? what does it mean? – Sona is stabbed momentarily with despair that he is never going to reach the illuminated freedom on the other side: English *is* going to defeat him. But a pluckiness, born from that very despair, reasserts itself: if there are rules, as there are in mathematics, then he will master those rules, and their exceptions, and the truth will reveal itself. He just has to concentrate and a world different from numbers will unfurl slowly and invite him in.

The private English tuition had been the idea of Mala Saha, Sougata's mother. News of Sona's preternatural mathematical abilities – at the age of eleven he had already mastered differential calculus and was champing at the bit to get to integral calculus – had spread quickly in the closed world of Basanta Bose Road. It was she who had suggested to Sona's Boro-jyethima that the boy should look in a couple of evenings a week to help Sougata with his mathematics homework; Sougata was not the brightest of students in his famous English-medium school, St Lawrence, especially in arithmetic, and the prospect of starting algebra and geometry next year was terrifying. The matter could have been idly mentioned, within the course of aimless chit-chat, and could have died an equally idle death, so how exactly it managed to translate into action remains a mystery to Sona, to a large measure because he has not grown up with good or favourable things happening to him, from new clothes and proper meals to fancy, fee-paying, English-medium schools and private tuition. They happen in the lives of the lucky ones, like all his cousins, but he and his sister, Kalyani, have not been born into it. The world is as it is, and Sona makes do with Suranjan's hand-me-downs, and Chhoto-jyethu's algebra books from his college years (nearly twenty-five years old, saved from a clearout sale to the bikri-walla), and scraps of leftovers sent down irregularly from upstairs, and Khastagir, the free government school down the road, on Mahim Halder Street, where the teachers have trouble solving elementary quadratic equations and the pupils have to sit cross-legged on the floor, being cooked in the heat in the summer because there are no fans. Such is the way his world is configured and he cannot yet put a shape to the lineaments of his desire to escape it, let alone articulate the desire. Not yet.

Someone has done some bargaining behind the scenes so that Sona is expected to give maths tuition to Sougata, his thick neighbour, in exchange not only for dinners, but also for tuition in English, his weakest subject; the flimsiest subject in his school, in fact, for the English teacher in Khastagir hardly knows how to transpose a sentence from the simple present tense to, say, the past continuous, such is the state of government schools. But Sona has been asked to soak up the lessons passively, not actively participate; just an audience of one witnessing the English classes between Sougata and his tutor.

The English tutor, Dibyendu Majumdar, a second-year undergraduate in the English Department of Presidency College, does not think that the deal is as good for him as it is for his employer. A stereotype of the Bengali *aantel* – the word, with ironic appositeness, is a bastardised form of the French *intellectuel* – Dibyendu has all the appurtenances to go with the role, straggly beard, glasses, khadi kurta, jute shoulder-bag, and resents being made to be on the giving end of the two-for-one offer. He takes out his resentment, in so far as he is intrepid enough to do so, in pathetic dribs and drabs, on Sona, the added extra. Dabbling in fiery left-wing politics in college has clearly made him more sympathetic to the lot of the have-nots further afield than the one right under his nose. Instead of resenting Mala Saha, which would have been the logical thing to do, since it is she who foisted Sona on him without increasing his pay, he diverts it to focus on the wrong person; money breeds a lot of attitudes in men and a particular stripe of obsequiousness is high on the list for people of his kind.

So Dibyendu takes pains to explain a point over and over again to Sougata, but a rare question or request for clarification from Sona – rare because he has been told obliquely but repeatedly, so that there can be no ambiguity in his own mind about it, that he is only a watcher – will be met with silence, or with an expression of irritated reluctance, sometimes even a mocking 'I see your head is full of cow-dung.' Dibyendu puts petty obstructions in the way of Sona, such as not allowing him to share Sougata's textbooks, or setting Sougata homework while making it obvious that Sona is not going to be given any.

Sona, electrically alive from the earliest time that he can remember to being excluded to the margins, from where he watched everyone else get their share while he only looked on in silence, has sniffed this politics of mean-mindedness in the air from the moment he walked in on his first class.

Already hobbled by the sense of obligation this exchange tuition entails, he is further humiliated by Dibyendu-da's gratuitous cruelties and, as always, recoils deep inside himself to nurse the word so frequently used of him, 'beggar', as if it were a talisman, in a prolonged, introspective agony, his soul's equivalent of pushing his tongue cease-lessly against a wobbling tooth that hurt. And then, suddenly, over the course of a few weeks, he crosses the line as he knew he would, an invisible fence beyond which it does not hurt him any longer, or even touch him: he is deaf and blind to it. All that remains within that insulated self are his mother's words, the words that have been embossed on his impressionable soul – 'If you study hard, very, very hard, and do nothing but study, and do well in school, be the "first boy" in class every year, there will be an escape from this, escape for all of us.'

The words save him yet again from an intractable situation. He knows he has been invited to Sougata's to give, not to receive. He bites down hard on the fact, steels himself and takes all the barriers in the way to his one chance of acquiring English as challenges, much as getting his head around trigonometry or logarithm had been. Once framed that way, he knows he will keep at it, with the doggedness of a switched-on machine, until he gets the better of it; in this, algebra is no different from the cheap exclusionary politics that the world plays against him. After Dibyendu-da leaves each evening, when it is Sona's turn to teach maths to Sougata, he deliberately sets problems well above Sougata's ability to solve. While the other boy is thus occupied, racking his brains and chewing the end of his pencil, Sona borrows his English books and concentrates on the lesson recently finished with Dibyendu-da with such ferocious will that he has his jaws locked tight and his temple throbbing by the end of it. He knows he is racing against the great winner, time.

In four weeks, Sona has wrestled to the ground all forms of tenses, including the supremely eloquent and difficult future perfect continuous, has begun to get the hang of clauses, and has started grappling with the capricious and illogical absurdities of English prepositions.

As eldest daughter-in-law of the Ghosh family, married to Adinath, Sandhya has a set of elusive duties no less binding for their status as tacit and unformulated. They lie in a nebulous notion of tradition, of the way things are done and have been done for generations, of the overweeningly important idea of what the world thinks, especially if that world consists of her elders. Of the several of these duties, one is being in charge of the prayer room (a miniature temple, really) up on the terrace, and all the rituals of daily worship – cleaning out the room in the morning, giving the deities fresh water, cut fruits, crystallised-sugar sweets and flowers, watering the tulsi plant, then repeating the same chores in the evening, except then it is a more ceremonial affair involving the ringing of a big brass bell, sprinkling of water from the Ganga (kept in a frog-green plastic water-bottle), more flowers, the lighting of incense sticks and copra and frankincense, which fill the whole room with dense, aromatic smoke, lighting small terracotta lamps, carrying the brazier of copra into each room in all four storeys of the house and sanctifying it with the holy smoke . . . The rituals have their own shape and place and rightness, and over her twenty-three years in the Ghosh family, Sandhya has devolved and delegated a lot of tasks to the other daughters-in-law, but this she keeps to herself, although she is beginning to find the business of climbing up and down the stairs to take the brazier into every room of the house laborious and harsh on her legs and tightening knees.

This evening she has been uncharacteristically late with the evening worship, but her jaa Purnima's call – 'Buliiiii, come inside, don't stand on the verandah at this hour, everyone can see you' – has elbowed her out of her reverie. The prayer room has a white marble floor, a large bell suspended from the ceiling and a whole fleet of statuettes, framed pictures and figurines of a dozen gods and goddesses and saints arranged along two raised stone daises set against the wall. Her older son, Supratik, at the age of fourteen, had once impudently said, 'Ma, there are thirty-three crore Hindu gods and goddesses. You seem to have a fair few of them here. How do you know that sending up prayers to all these different deities won't cancel each other out?'

At the centre of the wall facing east a niche has been carved out, with symmetrical ascending curves on either side that join in a final point at the top. Inside, in a blaze of red silk and gold, is housed the reigning deity of the Ghosh house, the gentle goddess of wealth, Lakshmi, with her faint, inscrutable almost-smile, her sheaf of paddy and her docile barn-owl. Sandhya had heard long ago that in her father-in-law's family home in North Calcutta – there is very little mention of that chapter in his life – the goddess was stripped of her clothes after the puja and left naked throughout the year so that she couldn't run away.

The conducting of the annual puja on a full-moon night in late October was the most honourable duty that had been bestowed on Sandhya when she married into the Ghosh family. In time-honoured fashion, this is really the eldest daughter-in-law's investiture as the earthly, domestic symbol of the goddess. It is she who channels Lakshmi's blessings on the family. In her is vested, by an understanding of priestly transference, the household's economic prosperity, well-being and harmonious daily life. Beside it, her other daily chores as eldest daughter-in-law – supervising the cook and cleaners and servants and household accounts, caring for her elderly parents-in-law, looking after their meals and medication, deciding which tasks can be ceded to the wives of her three brothers-in-law, keeping a family of twenty (including the servants) ticking over without hiccups or mishaps – all these appear as milk-and-rice, as uncomplicated, bland and digestible as infant fare. Now that Lakshmi Puja is a little over a month away, she can feel the gathering thrill again.

But something is clouding the excitement this year and she already knows its name: Supratik. Over the last year he has lost so much weight that the shadow he casts, in all light, is nothing more than a thin line. She can swear that his eyes have grown bigger as he has started to look more cadaverous; set deep within his bony face, all sharp angles and a luxuriant black beard, they make him look like a starving mystic, a Naga sanyasi on the banks of the Ganga in Gomukh. He has certainly grown as quiet and uncommunicative. Never the most garrulous of children, Supratik, now a young man of twenty-one, barely speaks and, when he can be bothered to, it is only in monosyllables as if he is conserving all the energy he needs to hold on to his cage-like frame. There is an incandescence about him: the large, blazing black eyes are devouring in their intensity, and the opacity of his inner world, its unknowable resilience, makes Sandhya fear far more for him than any mother should for her child. When had the change begun? She cannot put a time to it. Does that make her a bad mother? Where does he disappear to for days on end? Where is he, out until so late at night that she has long lost any handle on when, or if, he returns? Why has he become like a furtive ghost? How can one's own son, her flesh and blood, nurtured in her womb for nine months, become such a stranger? Who is he?

Sandhya's hands shake as she refills the terracotta lamps with oil and she spills some of it onto the marble counter. She has the cast of mind that sees omens in the number of birds congregated on telegraph wires and portents in a child's killing of a scurrying spider or touching food with the left hand – nothing falls outside a predestined design – and the small spill grips her heart. Is Ma Lakshmi trying to tell her something? Is she offended? Has she, Sandhya, not done something right in the daily ceremony or in last year's big puja? The very contiguity of her worries about Supratik and the oil spill makes her think of the minor accident as heaped with meaning about some imminent evil related to her son, maybe some danger that is about to befall him. As she mulls on this, a cold fear rises in her and she forgets to ring the bell that announces the evening in auspiciously.

I

I want to set down an account of all that has happened and is happening. When you hear different voices chattering away afterwards, all with their shadows and half-truths and lies and fiction, you can come back to this and think that you and only you have the truth. That is all I can give you. But after you've read it, burn everything. On no account must a shred of these letters and journals be found on you or in the house. You will soon find out why I'm asking you to do this.

Did you know that Calcutta was the capital of British India until 1912? The English built this city by bringing together mosquito-infested swamps and marshes and mud. Today, walking down Chowringhee, with its rows of palatial buildings and arcades and shops on one side, the huge Maidan on the other, the towering Monument off Mayo Road in Esplanade, can you tell that this was just a vast expanse of silt? The British left our country twenty years ago, but their handiwork will remain for ever.

You may never get a chance to walk up and down Chowringhee, so let me try and put it into words for you. The grandeur of the Great Eastern Hotel alone would make you slack-jawed with awe. On the street level of this part of Chowringhee, it's one long colonnade, sometimes interrupted by cross-streets: the paved footpath gives way to Chowringhee Road and Bentinck Street on one side; on the other you have shop after shop selling jewellery, fancy goods, liquor, clothes, luxury items, imported food, watches, shawls, carpets and rugs, chandeliers, lights and candelabra, carved wooden boxes, antiques . . . whatever money can buy you can get in these shops. An endless fountain of things. They can dazzle and blind you. Left off north Chowringhee, on the colonial splendour of Old Court House Street, sits the Great Eastern. The first floor of this blindingly white building is above the colonnade, as if to lift its elite guests and residents a few feet above the torrent of ordinary life outside.

I have never been inside its rooms or to the restaurant, the ballroom, the bar, the shops that still display the sign of the British crown and the words 'By appointment to HM the King Emperor and HM the Queen Empress', the tearoom where waiters in full regalia – cinched waistband; high, pleated headgear; sash; brass buttons; cuffs; starched uniform – bow low and bring in tea that you and I will never drink. But you can walk around – if you're properly dressed and do not attract the suspicion of the uniformed guards and staff – and see the gravelled drive, the blue swimming pool, the stone and marble and glass of the building, the gardens, the well-tended lawns, the flowers . . . even Nature seems to oblige the moneyed.

But my concern is not with the inside. I have tried to give you the tiniest glimpse of it, so that you can better imagine the world that is my concern – the world beyond the walls of the Great Eastern Hotel, the world immediately outside, at its doorstep. If you walk down the colonnaded arcade below the hotel at dawn, just as the dawn chorus has started, long before the luxury shops have opened or the mad bustle of life in Chowringhee and BBD Bag has begun, you will see a very different view. Here, lying on their gamchha, a jute sack, a piece of tarpaulin or plastic or whatever scrap of cloth they can spare after wrapping their bodies, is a row of sleeping men curled up like foetuses. Those who have sandals use them as pillows, otherwise they will be stolen. Those who don't, do without, resting their heads on the concrete. Their vests are full of holes, they wear dirty, threadbare lungis that ride up while they are asleep, exposing their shame to the world, the soles of their feet are so cracked that they look like parched land during a particularly bad drought, they have nothing to protect them from the morning drop in temperature. Extreme exhaustion clings to their faces and the shadows under their eyes, even when they're sleeping the sleep of the near-dead. Only ten feet separate them from the world of extreme wealth. Inside-outside: the world forever and always divides into those two categories. Inside, the amount of water used daily to keep the lawns and gardens so lush could provide drinking water to each of these men for a month. Outside, these men have to walk miles sometimes to get to a public hand-pump. On the way, if they collapse of thirst, even dogs won't piss into their mouths to slake their dried tongues and throats. These men piss on the road, shit behind a bush or by a railway track, eat one meal of muri or chhatu a day, if they are lucky, rummage in the footpaths and drains surrounding New Market to see if someone has left a stub of banana in its peel or a corner of a shingara in a sal-leaf plate. They fight off the swarm of beggars who are also looking for food thrown away by the sated rich, they wash in the muddy brown water gushing out of broken standpipes. Do you remember that poem I read out to you? 'Poetry, I bid you goodbye today. / The world is prosey with hunger / The full moon is like a piece of singed bread.' You might see the pale bronze-coloured full moon, but they see, in its round shape, something to eat.

Who do you think they are? They are not beggars, and they are certainly not the worst-off in our country – they have the clothes on their backs and the physical ability to work, at least for now. They haven't yet found a foothold in a slum, but the lucky ones among them will. A slum will offer them a roof made of sheet plastic, maybe of bundles of hay held together by wooden stakes to form a tent. They won't always have to sleep in the open like this. But, in a few years, most of them will contract a disease – TB, cholera, dysentery, malaria – and die like animals. Do you know what happens to their dead? To take them to a crematorium would mean paying the cremation fee, registering the death. That means a death certificate and money; in fact, more money than they earn in a week. It means a name, an address, a next of kin, a date of birth. They have nothing. So they are slipped into the Hooghly in the dead of the night. There the corpses rot and bleach and bloat, wash up ashore, get half-eaten by dogs and foxes, rot on land for a while, then get pulled back into the water during high tide . . . even in death their blighted lives won't let go of them.

They come from the suburbs, the villages, the mofussils, to look for work in the big city. From Uluberia, Bansdroni, Ghutiarishwari, Medinipur, Birbhum, Lakshmikantapur, Canning. The lucky among them will become rickshaw-pullers, balloonwallas, streetside snack-sellers. The less lucky will dig ditches, carry bricks, sand, cement, stone chips on their heads on construction sites. Some will be reduced to begging. You may ask: why don't they go back to where they came from, if this is what the city holds for them? I will answer with another question: do you know what life holds for them back home? We don't see them, so we don't think about them. But I have seen their lives, I have lived with them. For a while. I will tell you all about it.

But a small digression before that. You come from a lower-middle-class family from a small town. You've told me about the overstretched resources, the pinched lives, the relentless calculation of making ends meet going through your parents' heads, the need to think long and hard, say, before you could be given five paise to spend on jhalmuri. You've talked about the look of fear in your parents' faces when you came down with a cough or fever: where was the extra money for a doctor, to buy medicines, going to come from?

What did I know of such lives, sheltered, bourgeois boy that I was, living in the cushioned vacuum created by my grandfather's temporary boom of minor-mode prosperity – four-storeyed house, cars, many servants? Nothing. Yes, I was a communist activist from my very first year in Presidency College, but there is a large gap between being an activist out of the idealism that comes from books, conversations, the fire of youth, and being one because you have lived through the depredations that life has thrown at you.

Last year, I witnessed riots outside a ration shop on Beniatola Lane on my way to college. Had you heard of food riots erupting everywhere in the city? Food prices rising like a baneful wind, no jobs, no prospects, no future – how could we not have heard the pervasive murmur outside our walls? And when the murmurs turned to shouts and slogans and angry processions and bus-burnings and violent demonstrations, did they impinge on our world at all? Yes, but as other people's stories, as gossip, as tales told to fill the time.

One day on my way to college I had to get off the bus near Pataldanga Street because a huge procession was making its way down Harrison Road. 'We want jobs, not diplomas!' they shouted. Trying to avoid the big road where that giant, angry river in spate, a river of black heads, was inching its way, taking up all space, I started walking down side-streets. On Beniatola Lane there was another angry crowd, more shouting, furious tussling and stampeding. Occasionally, from that jostling clot, a man carrying a huge jute sack peeled off and tried to run away, hampered by the weight of his load. It took me a while to realise that a ration shop was being raided. The line between spectators and participants had been totally erased: anyone entering the street would have taken me, in the first few seconds, as part of the angry crowd too. Apparently the ration-shop owner had opened the shop, only to announce to the restive queue outside that he had no rice, kerosene or wheat to sell, only jaggery. Someone had shouted out that the shopkeeper was stockpiling staples to sell on the black market, and the idea had caught like a burr to soft wool. The people who had been waiting for hours every Thursday and Friday for over a month, only to go back home empty-handed, their food supplies depleted to practically nothing, had reached the end of their patience. A couple of local mastaans had leaped over the low gate in the front and started ransacking the shop. Others had joined in, distrustful of the mastaans, suspecting them of making off with the grains themselves to sell on the black market.

Ordinary, middle-class people, like you and me, scrabbling like dogs over food. How did we get to this?

Yes, as a student in Presidency College, I was 'doing politics', as the slightly shaming, slightly dirty expression would have it. I was, briefly, a member of the

Students' Federation, the student wing of the CPI(M), the Communist Party of India (the Marxist wing, as they like to think of themselves), and while I was their bright, short-lived star, I cut my teeth doing the usual. If posters had to be put up, if slogans had to be painted on walls, I provided copy ('Exploited peoples all over the world are waking up today', 'Change the world, change yourself', 'Today is the day to burn like fire, to repay the debt of blood with blood', 'Poor, landless peasants have given their lives and blood to build this country. It's our duty to repay that debt'). I decided who among us was going to work in which segment of the college or the city, I worked out the most favourable time to do it, safe from a possible crackdown by the police or Congress foot soldiers. If a procession or a sit-in needed to be organised, or a road-blockade or a bus-burning, I planned the route and logistics and exact manner of its execution, complete with fallback options, working out the possible weak points and allowing for those eventualities. There were class boycotts, and marches to the American Embassy to protest against the war in Vietnam, chanting, 'Break and crush the black hand of American imperialism' or 'Your name, my name / Viet-nam, Viet-nam'. Another popular one was 'Blood-bright Vietnam is Bengal's other name'.

Coinciding with these standard issues of student politics there erupted the troubles in Presidency College over the expulsion of students from the Hindu Hostel. I was an active participant in the movement that rocked Presidency and genteel Bengali society in those six months in '66 and '67. Chucking a few young men out of the Hindu Hostel seems like such a small stone to have caused such endless ripples. The Food Revolution agitations in the city in '66 morphed seamlessly into this front of our war: the gherao of the college Principal, the subsequent lathi-charge by the police against the students standing guard at the gate of the college (since the police had no right to enter), the arrest of 150 of them, the angry ransacking of the science laboratory by the agitating students. Yes, I was part of the group that shut down all of Calcutta University for one and a half months and Presidency College for four. Unprecedented, this. All of these events, or their telling as stories, seem just a spark now, a tiny one; in time that spark will appear even tinier, dimmer. The blaze it lit, however, will far outlive the originary ignition.

I played a similar role here too, but with a difference, as you'll see. All our actions, initially, were under the aegis of the CPI(M). I devised plans to get around Section 144, under which all of College Street had been placed during that period, meaning that the police could arrest you if they didn't like your face. How to avoid them during processions? If they were stationed on Harrison

Road and near the Medical College, I decided that going down College Street in one big crowd wouldn't do. So the marchers were divided into two groups: one would start from the gate of Hare School, the other from College Square. If one set was obstructed by the police on this side, then the other could proceed past Eden Hostel towards Colutolla.

It'll become clear shortly why I wasn't part of that group of twenty-two, including 'names' such as Kaka and Biman Basu and Ashoke Sengupta, who picketed the college, sitting at the gate on mats for a month. Members of the Chhatra Parishad (CP), the student wing of the Congress Party, a synonym for the Establishment, threw a bomb at them from the roof of the Coffee House to scare them away. In the early days of our agitation, when it became a badge of honour to be arrested and beaten up in a police cell in Sovabazaar, a thought struck the less volatile among those of us who were planning strategy on a daily basis: if everyone is arrested, especially everyone in the leadership, who is going to continue the movement? On the day of the gherao, at 10 p.m., seven hours after it had begun, three of us were smuggled out of the police cordon surrounding the college. We knew its nooks and crannies, the porous bits of its boundaries, better than they did. It was done before the lathi-charging began, so we escaped untouched.

As for the twenty-two recalcitrant strikers who took to sleeping on the college lawn – yes, I attended to them, sat with them, spent hours in their company, as hundreds of others did, but from the beginning it was clear that it wouldn't do for me to be part of them. An invisible shadow separated me from the rest. I had severe misgivings about it, as did several others, who taunted me about how safe I had kept myself, how unbloodied my hands were, how full my stomach when they were having to eat their six-anna meal in the slums of Kalabagan, or in Bagbazar, where the beggars of North Calcutta paid thirteen paise to eat bread, vegetables, onion and pickle. Some of these criticisms were spoken to my face; most of the murmuring was behind my back. Trained as an economist as I was, I held on to the lifeline of pragmatism and efficiency: would you, I asked them, damage your head or your fingers? In a war, as this clearly was, would you sacrifice a pawn or the king? How would you find your way in the densest of forests if you lost your compass?

I didn't think of myself as the king or the compass, but I knew I couldn't extinguish myself in the fray of student politics. This was a side-show, a diversion. It was one of the biggest lessons I learned; the inevitable end of innocence, you could call it, so necessary to growing up. All these strikes – student strike, tram strike, bus strike – all this great ferment to close down all of Bengal, to search for alternatives . . . with what immense hope we began, that we could change the world, not one little thing at a time, but in one great unstoppable propulsion, as if we could stand outside the whole planet, put a giant lever under it and set it rolling in a different direction altogether. Throughout my two years in CPI(M) student activism (embarrassing now, in hindsight, and amateurish), one thought became steadily inescapable: we could only poke the government into a kind of low-grade irritability, but never scale that up to something life-changing, something that would bring the system crashing down. All this hurling of bombs, burning of trams, headlines in newspapers – to what avail? The condition of the people remained unchanged. Life carried on as before, restored to its status quo, like the skin of water after the ripples from a thrown pebble have died away, as if the surface retained no memory of it.

And what drove home that lesson? The short answer is: the impossibility of staying within the fold of the CPI(M). When the general election was called in 1967, the Party tried to rein in the more militant and idealistic amongst us, for fear of losing the chance to be part of a power-sharing government. Orders arrived from the Party head office that we had to call off these strikes; it was of greater importance to win the elections, to wage our war softly-softly and by the rulebook written by the Establishment, by the powerful. So it boiled down to that dirty thing – power. To be part of government, of the established order of things, on the side of institutions, those very ones we thought we were taking a giant wrecking-ball to.

But things have their own momentum: union leaders who tried to follow orders and call off the strikes were beaten up by their supporters. Those of us who didn't want to be designated as traitors, as unthinking servants of the Communist Party, which was rapidly becoming every bit as power-hungry, as establishmentarian, as compromised and complicit as the rest, decided to continue with our sit-ins, our roadblocks and bus-burnings.

I spoke little, and silence is always taken to be a sign of strength. As my fellow revolutionaries raged and shouted and talked blood and fire, my coldness seemed somehow more solid, more reliable than banging on tables, burning trams on the streets, lobbing bombs, shouting slogans.

Where to source the raw materials for our bombs, where to buy the cheap pipe-guns that were beginning to appear on the market after the war with China, in which warehouse or garage or back room of which house in a tiny alley to assemble explosives without anyone becoming suspicious, where to lob them at CP activists and at what time and at what stage of the clash, where to hide in any given area once the police vans came speeding . . . I became very good at these details, so good that it was decided I should not be visible. This was as much protectiveness on the part of the breakaway, truly left movement as clear, strategic thinking. I was valuable to them, therefore I couldn't be exposed to the dangers of the frontline. (All this makes it sound as though we sat around in a circle in College Street Coffee House or some tea-shack in Potuatola Lane and worked it out over endless discussions. No, it wasn't like that. It just came about. Events fall into a pattern that we can only discern retrospectively. We credit ourselves with far more agency than we actually possess. Things happen because they happen.)

I have come to think of all this ferment as boring and inconsequential compared with what I really had in mind – armed peasant rebellion, an entire and comprehensive rehauling of everything, of land reform, food production, wealth distribution, of realising the full meaning of 'The crop belongs to those who cultivate it'. Placed beside this aim, all this student unrest was like flies buzzing around a horse: the irritation caused was so ephemeral, it could be dispersed with one lazy swish of the tail.

It became clear to me that the last thing the CPI(M) was interested in was radical change. I tested how much dissent against this sell-out would be tolerated by articulating my unease as innocent questions. None, it emerged. They even quoted Chairman Mao to justify their betrayal: 'Battles are waged one by one and enemy battalions are destroyed one at a time. Factories are built one at a time. Farmers cultivate one plot after another. We serve ourselves the total amount of food that we can consume, but we eat it spoonful by spoonful; to eat it in one go would be impossible. This is known as the "piecemeal solution".' Their argument went something like this: a small presence of the leftist parties in government may appear to be insignificant, but this will give the opportunity to manoeuvre for more power and that, in turn, for more, until the nation will be run by a government that is wholly communist. India will become Vietnam.

Towards the end, hearing these words and arguments, especially quotations from Chairman Mao, issuing from the blind mouths of these self-interested, power-hungry, corrupt Communist Party flunkies set fire to my blood. Not a single one of them was truly interested in the revolution to which they paid such assiduous lip-service. All they wanted was power, the rest of the nation could go to hell.

While the spectre of erstwhile revolutionaries becoming Establishment figures within the folds of that great betrayer, the CPI(M), was painful and intolerable, something else was taking shape, something that was going to explode like a thousand suns in an unsuspecting sky – Naxalbari. For those of us who had been reading Charu Mazumdar's electric writing in <u>Liberation</u> ever since we joined university, the events of May 1967 themselves were not a surprise so much as the fact that they happened.

Being a Bengali, one is surprised when all the endless spume and froth of talk suddenly reveals itself to be the front of a gigantic wave of action.

CHAPTER TWO

1967

The autumn mildness is just beginning to set in. The blue sky is dotted sparsely with cottony white clouds. Children are on holiday and the skeleton of the puja pandal – a wondrous structure made of bamboo and planks and coir ropes and coloured cloth, stretched and ruched and concertinaed across the bones of bamboo, covering them decoratively in furls and drapes – has already been constructed in the piece of land that abuts the Durga temple of 23 Pally. This cathedral of fabric will house the goddess Durga and her four children, Lakshmi, Saraswati, Kartik and Ganesh, two on either side of her, for nearly five days. On the final evening, the clay effigies of the goddess and her children will be immersed in Tolly's Nala or the Hooghly at Outram Ghat, marking the end of the biggest festival in the Bengali calendar.

For the last six weeks volunteers organised under the banner of '23 Pally Sharbojonin Puja Committee', consisting mostly of teenagers and young men of the neighbourhood, have gone from door to door, collecting donations for the festival. The intricate, sometimes baroque, light displays have started going up along the street, on trees, on the water tank on the roof of number 11/A/2. This year, the most numerous of them, along the whole length of Basanta Bose Road, all the way to Jogamaya College, are in the form of a fountain tree: a tall column of yellow fairy lights exploding in a six-veined fountain, three on each side, parted in the middle like a child's drawing of a palm tree. The coloured lights of the cascading head, green, blue and red, blink on and off, as do the yellow lights of the column, and the whole thing gives the magical impression of an upward-flowing capital of water spewing into a polite fountain at the head. This is the *pièce de résistance* of the lighting display. These displays are competitive affairs between neighbourhoods, but this year everyone in Basanta Bose Road looks smug in the knowledge that they have the edge over their rivals' parsimonious offerings of coloured fluorescent tubes and strings of fairy lights hung on trees and across balconies. The lighting will be turned on in three days' time.

A welcoming arch at the entrance to the pandal spells out in lights 'Sharodiya shubhechha', autumn good wishes, and the fixture, again made out of lights only, on the water tank on the top of the Dasgupta house features an animated boy kicking a football. The football appears in staccato stasis in three different points of its parabolic trajectory, then reappears, in a slightly Sisyphean manner, at the foot of the kicking boy, for him to start all over again. There is also the light-installation marking the twentieth anniversary of Independence: the Indian tricolour, flanked by one freedom-fighter, Netaji Shubhas Chandra Bose, and one poet, Rabindranath Tagore, has been made to do an impression of stop–start fluttering. Gandhi is, of course, pointedly left out and the light-manufacturers have not tried to simulate a breeze waving Tagore's long beard. Words of light on top say 'Twenty Years of Independence 1947–1967'. But everyone agrees that although this has its novelty value, it is nothing compared to those flowing palm trees of light.

In the brimming light of the early morning a gauzy mist lies on the ground in shreds and patches, a mist so thin that you have to look away and then quickly back to perceive it; gazed at for too long, it disappears. The garden at the back of the Ghosh house is full of fragrant shiuli, some flowers having fallen on the grass in the night, making that small section of the garden look like a green shawl flecked with white in one corner. If you look minutely, you can pick out the orange stalks of the flowers; a subtler, more delicately patterned shawl.

There is the smell of puja in the air: a crisp, cool, weightless sensation. In the collective Bengali imagination, fields of kaash phul, with their enormous plumes of satiny cream flowers, bowing gracefully to the clement autumn breeze, are easily visualised, although there are no patches of pampas grass to be seen anywhere, not in this part of the city anyway. And to the collective ear the sound of the dhaak, beaten to a whole complex repertoire of rhythms and syncopations by the dhaaki, is already veering on the air, phrasing a sudden sentence in the mind of someone here, a group of words spoken by someone there, to follow the beat and curve of its percussive line. With one voice, the choir made up of the grass, the drum, the sky, the dew sings out, 'Holiday, holiday, holiday'.

Knowing well that there will be a possessive rush to grab the puja special autumn issue of *Ultorath* between Ma, Pishi, Boro-kaki and herself, Baishakhi picks up the family copy, which has arrived that very morning along with bumper issues of *Nabokallol*, *Anandamela* (for the children, she thinks derisively) and *Ananda Bazar Patrika*, and smuggles it to her room. She has a quick flick through it – novels by Ashapurna Devi, Bimal Kar, Bimal Mitra, Shankar. Two years earlier the serialised novels in *Ultorath* and *Nabokallol* would have been forbidden reading for her, on the grounds that they were for adults, and she would have been asked to stick to *Anandamela*, but those rules have now been relaxed somewhat, although she is not wholly confident that her mother or Pishi will not tell her off if she is caught with her head buried in either of these magazines. She hides the copy under her pillows and decides to avoid any possible impediment to her reading by taking it up to the roof terrace after lunch and reading it there, away from the traffic of people in the house, while sitting with her back to the sun, drying her long hair. Possibly with a bowl of mango pickle by her side. Thrilled at the prospect of the treat she has just planned to give herself, she skips to her parents' room to consolidate her joy by going through the new clothes she has received for Puja, which is only ten days away.

A similar thought may have occurred to Chhaya, for she decides to take out her new Puja clothes from her almirah and arrange them in order of the five days of the festival. But what should have been gloating joy quickly topples over into a restless bitterness as she contemplates the saris laid out on her bed: two pure silks, one tangail, one tashar, one kota, one for each of the five days of Puja. Last year she had had seven, the year before that, eight. She does not take into account the two she has bought herself: those do not count; only the things given one as presents truly matter.

This year her brother Priyo has given her one sari. One only. The tangail. Admittedly it is from Adi Dhakeshwari Bastralaya on Rashbehari Avenue, but Purnima, his wife, has been given four saris. That is four times what Chhaya has received from him. And it is only by guesswork, with a bit of judicious snooping, that she has arrived at that figure. There are only four that she has been able to ascertain; in reality it could well be more, say, seven or eight. The truth will be discovered only over the five days of Puja. She will be watching her sister-in-law's outfits like a hungry vulture.

As if this were not enough, Buli, her niece, has boasted of ten – ten! – sets of new clothes, including two ghaghras, which are all the rage, and four saris, which Chhaya thinks the girl is too young to wear. No doubt most of them are from her father. They, or to be more accurate, she, *she*, the mother, has spoilt the girl rotten. Chhaya can already discern the incipient signs – a defiance somewhere in Buli's eyes, an immodesty in the way she holds herself, a growing tendency to answer back and a complete indifference to her studies, a fact corroborated by her school reports: she barely scrapes through each year. Her secondary-school results are due shortly after the Pujas. It is Chhaya's belief that the girl will perform so miserably in her first public examination that she will be asked to leave Gokhale Memorial and join an inferior school to continue for the school-leaving certificate. This is exactly what happens when one has an uneducated mother, Chhaya thinks. She has been honing and sharpening the words she will let slip at a family dinner one evening, after the proof of the girl's failure arrives. She rehearses the tone and inflection every day, perfects the pauses, moves one word here, two words there. She is waiting to pounce. Lately – and Chhaya cannot put her finger on it – there seems to be a . . . a . . . an air of furtiveness about Buli. She needs watching, that one.

But that is not Chhaya's business. She has evidence of something rather more urgent right under her nose, in the form of that mocking tangail sari. If Priyo can buy his wife four saris – *at least* four saris – and his daughter ten outfits, then giving her one sari is like a slap to her face. She feels the familiar pressure in her chest, the pressure of dammed-up water pushing against the sides that contain it. Her throat closes up, she lets herself go and prepares for a great deluge. But after several minutes of coaxing and trying, her eyes remain uncompliantly dry, which maddens her even further. She sits on her hands to prevent herself from tearing into strips of ribbons the poisoned tangail sari given by her brother.

Even Madan-da and Gagan and the other servants have got *one* article of clothing from her brother for puja. Has she now been demoted to their level? Is this the lot of the unmarried sister who has overstayed her welcome at her parents' house? Has she become unwanted because they have not been able to marry her off? This time the tears oblige, although only for a short while: it is a momentary light drizzle rather than a downpour and, instead of feeling relieved, something coils and loops and knots and reknots inside her.

In the time she would come to remember as her two years of blazing brightly, Chhaya had received, on average, one marriage proposal a month. Much later, after the steady parade of suitors had fallen from ten a year to eight, then to four, and finally to one every two or three years, as the clock had ticked on and time had raced and rushed, it was openly said that being a graduate, having a BA degree, had harmed Chhaya's chances of finding a husband. She did not know if it was in defiant retaliation or for consolation that she embarked on an MA after the flow of suitors had thinned to a trickle with all the volume of a newborn's piss. Priyo had announced that he would not marry until someone was found for his sister first. That resolve, it transpired, had clearly not been set in stone, although, to be fair to him, he got married only when Chhaya had reached the age beyond which the issue became irreversible. Next, it was the turn of her younger brother, Bhola, to make a similarly rash promise. He had reneged the year his sister hit the point of no return: thirty.

It had all started off with not insufficient promise. Chhaya was the only daughter of the wealthy Ghosh family, so the dowry and attendant gifts such as jewellery, consumer durables, kitchenware and clothes would have been very attractive; she was reading for a degree (at the initial stages this had been a positive thing, something to be proud, even boastful, of); she had 'Spoken English'. More importantly, she had the right sun-sign with the right planets in alignment – Pisces with Venus ascendant in the fifth house of Jupiter – to make an auspicious bride.

But the dizzying, whirling, magical roulette of matches, so rich and teasing with possibilities, had proved to be a slippery wheel. The laws of probability, while seeming so amenable to providing not one but a whole suite of matches, seemed disobliging when it came to achieving that one crucial hit of success and had somehow always tricked and wrong-footed her so that she remained outside the circle of the favoured. Some element in the whole set of required or desirable qualities had either not been satisfied or had been lacking. If the family of one prospective groom approved of everything and the marriage deal seemed almost closed, suddenly the question 'And do you cook?', or the demand that she would be forbidden to work once she was married, would have the effect of a ghost entering the room, chilling everyone to silence, ushering in the instant end of that particular match.

On a couple of occasions some incongruence during the matching of Chhaya's horoscope with the suitor's, discovered at quite an advanced stage of the matchmaking process, had finished off things. Charubala had raged, 'Why did they not bother to find out earlier? Why did they get our hopes up, leading us on this merry dance? Low people, I say, low, common people! Good thing that our daughter didn't go to the home of such lowlives.'

In moments of tremulous, private introspection a shadow of an admission flitted through her mind that it was not such a good thing after all, that on the balance of things it was better to have a daughter married than to carp about such hair-splitting on the part of the suitors' families. It also struck her that circumstances had so tumbled over to their opposite that *they* were now the party with the suit, they were the real and true suitors, not the steadily diminishing stream of men who came to see Chhaya.

The family was forced to set their sights lower once they realised that the high noon of matchmaking had inexorably passed. First, they relaxed the category of the groom's profession. In the beginning, nothing but doctors and engineers would do, particularly with the parenthetical word 'London' or 'Edinburgh' after FRCS or MSc, but a while later that 'London' or 'Edinburgh' clause was silently dropped. Then they relinquished their hold on FRCS and MSc; an ordinary MBBS or BSc would suffice. Soon, those requirements too fell away as the search was broadened (diluted, some said) to other professions – lawyers, lecturers, businessmen. From here, it climbed down further to white-collar worker, bank-teller, government employee, school teacher, even, at the final, desperate stages, clerk.

When even this didn't produce a husband for Chhaya, other variables were tinkered with and revised. The dowry money climbed up by a factor of 1.5 with every rejection; to a refrigerator and cooking range were added a gramophone, a flat in Purna Das Road. Then the age of the candidates was relaxed – it had to be, Chhaya was not getting any younger – followed by an attendant loosening of criteria in the looks department. The words 'fair', 'young', 'handsome' were all deleted from the matrimonial ads in the newspapers. Ads put exclusively in the matrimonial columns of the English dailies – *The Statesman*, *Amrita Bazar Patrika* – started migrating furtively to the Bengali broadsheets, *Ananda Bazar Patrika*, even *Jugantar*. Charubala had a new set of portrait photographs taken of her daughter by Robin-da, the neighbourhood's professional photographer. It emerged during these sessions that her face had looked too polygonal in the previous pictures, her chin and jaws too prominent, her forehead too broad. Quantities of make-up and snow and powder were applied so that the fact of her dark complexion would not be revealed to the groom's family, at least not right at the beginning. The lighting was ramped up, cruel suns were shone on Chhaya's face and she was made to look very slightly away from the lens, as if something was just beginning to catch her attention outside the frame, so that the camera would not be able to capture the fact that she was cross-eyed.

Herein lay the rub. Chhaya had been born preternaturally dark and with a squint that was not immediately noticeable – it depended on the light and the angle of her head and how obliquely she turned her gaze on something – but once it was detected it was impossible to unknow it. All those crucial final questions, such as 'And do you cook?' or 'Will you stop working once you get married?', were really an occluded reaction to that detection; an irreversible decision had already been made.

Her very name, which meant 'shadow', was a backhanded acknowledgement by her parents of the undeniable and omnipresent fact of
her complexion. Through her girlhood and adolescence the less well-
behaved girls in her school and the less decorous people of Basanta
Bose Road had called her by several derogatory names, *Kali*, *Kelti*, all
to do with her skin colour. Never to her face, of course, but they also
did not make a great secret of it; a stage-whisper, a catcall, an overheard remark as she passed the loafers gathered outside Bhawanipur
Tutorial Home: all these brought home to her, relentlessly, the ines-
capability of her skin colour. Stringent regimes of applying to her
face ground red lentils, the cream top of whole milk, and dried orange
peel made into a paste with cream had not wrought any change. The
patented and unpatented whitening creams and lotions available in
the shops had proved equally deceitful. Throughout all this, Charubala
consoled and encouraged and empathised, holding out dark-skinned
women who had made it in public life as role models, trying to over-
turn familiar habits of thought by making her daughter aware of
some of the positive associations with negrescence – 'Have you seen
a cloud that is not dark? It is because of dark rain clouds that life
thrives on earth', or 'The kaajol that women wear around their eyes
is always black, never white', or rhyming *kaalo*, black, with *aalo*, light.

Ever since Chhaya had learned to identify the face looking back at
her from the mirror as her own, she had been intimate with the fact
– hard, unchangeable as fate and as merciless – of her own ugliness
and, harder still, with the awareness that the world outside shared the
knowledge too. To know that you are ugly is one thing, but to grow
up with the imprint that it leaves on others' thoughts, facial expressions,
murmurs, talk, gossip is quite another; the former is a reckoning with
one's self, the latter an instilling of that most adamantine knowledge
of all: that the world is as it is, and knocking your head against its
hard shell is only going to break you, not dent the world.

So the storm-fronts of girlhood – tears, capricious cruelty, tantrums,
envy, brittle self-consciousness – had seemed to pass eventually after
an unseasonably prolonged stay, but more intractable, more sustained
damage was left behind in their wake.

After five years of the drama of diminishment that was her
matchmaking were played out, the neighbours started talking. Like

all such examples of this genre, there was a great deal of histrionics about protecting the subject of gossip from unkindness, but drama, that is, fiction, was what it was, for it was seen to that Chhaya came to hear of what was being said about her via some circuitous route or the other. The usual, predictable things: she would die a spinster; the Ghoshes would never be able to get her off their hands; she would bring bad luck; that kind of dark skin ('black, really, coal-black, ink-black, soot-black') surely pointed to a dark fate; if the first face you saw after waking up was hers, your day was certain to be ruined; maybe there was something else wrong with her, something other than her dark complexion . . . and so it went on. Several kind-hearted people made ameliorative gestures: there were regular remarks along the lines of 'What if she is so dark, she is remarkably well educated' and the gradual currency of euphemisms for her skin colour – *warmly glowing, a radiant darkness* – that they thought shielded Chhaya from the misfortune she was born with. But all this was as leftovers from a small dinner party offered to a region ruined by famine: the gesture was noted, but the effect was nil. In the eyes of her suitors and their families, Chhaya had seen the instant knowledge, shocked, flickering, imperfectly repressed, as soon as she had walked into the drawing room. Beside that knowledge, everything was like her name – just a shadow.

○

Armed with comb, *Ultorath* and a small stainless-steel bowl of mango pickle, Baishakhi stealthily runs up the stairs to the roof terrace. Lunch is just over, so most of the household is getting ready to go to bed for a light snooze. She is fairly certain that no one has seen her coming up here. Still on tiptoe, she makes her way to the west side of the prayer room; here she is sheltered from the eyes of any casual visitor to the terrace – someone coming up to hang out the washing, or clean out the prayer room. They would have to know she is up here to find her. She positions herself so that her back catches the October afternoon sun, loosens her still-damp hair and settles down with *Ultorath* in front of her. It is nearly three o'clock and her mind is very far from reading. It is almost time for Shobhon Datta, who lives next door, to come out onto his roof for his sneaky post-lunch cigarette. This is what Baishakhi has been really waiting for: the book, the bowl of pickle, even her comb and damp hair are just props in a pre-emptive drama of deception. If anyone finds her sitting here, with Shobhon on his terrace, the suspicion that she is romantically entangled with him will alight instantly on her. The props will then give her performance of wide-eyed innocence some credence.

Without this deception, perpetrated by daughters and inevitably discovered by parents, aunts, servants and neighbours, played out, it would seem, since the very beginnings of family and society, the entire fabric of Bengali family life would be marred by a huge hole. There are 'arranged marriages' – the real, respectable, acceptable form of union between a man and a woman – decided by parents and families, *not* by the people getting married, and sanctioned by centuries of tradition and practice that say the daughter is her father's property, to dispose of as he sees fit. A marriage is a social transaction; individuals come into it later, if at all. And then there are 'love marriages', where two people conduct their romance with the furtiveness of a shameful, sinful act, then take their hearts in their hands and decide to break the news to their families. They are transgressive, discordant, with all the desirability of the ruptures and havoc that a cyclone creates. They are also forbidden, and such a huge force of morality is brought to bear against them that they are practically irresistible. Baishakhi has taken the first steps in sowing the storm.

Shobhon, twenty, reluctant BCom student at City College, only son of the Datta family, which has made money recently in the catering business; Shobhon, who wears his hair long, wears a gold chain around his neck, has a reputation of being a Romeo, and leaves his shirt unbuttoned nearly down to his stomach so that the chain can be seen nestling in his chest hair like an iridescent snake in dark grass, duly emerges on the terrace of the Datta house. Baishakhi, who has been staring unblinkingly at the green-painted wooden door through which Shobhon will make his entrance, instantly looks down and pretends to be so deeply absorbed in her novel that she is oblivious to the sound of the door, to his appearance a mere fifteen or twenty feet away. Shobhon, a seasoned player, pretends too that he has come to the terrace merely to have a smoke away from the eyes of the elders in his house. The acts of lighting his Capstan Gold, of cupping the match in his hand to shield it from the breeze, of flinging the spent match away all seem to be done with a slight excess of movement, more than the actions themselves demand. He starts walking up and down the terrace, Baishakhi still apparently unnoticed. Baishakhi, breath held, blood pounding in her ears, eyes fixed unmovingly on the meaningless black scrawl of letters on the page, can hear his footsteps pacing back and forth. And then, without any prelude or warning, he comes over to the side of his terrace that she is facing, places his elbows on the parapet, leans forward and whispers, 'Ashtami evening, eight o'clock, behind the puja pandal.'

Baishakhi jumps out of her skin at this sudden violation of the tacit rules of the game. On no account are they supposed to look at each other in public, let alone speak. She stares at him, then gathers her wits about her and hisses, 'What *are* you doing? Someone will see us. Don't stand on this side of the roof.'

He answers back, still whispering, 'Who will see us? If anyone appears on your roof, I'll see them before you do, I'll move away immediately. They'll never know.'

'We can be seen from Mala-mashi's roof, from Namita-di's, Sunil-mama's . . . If they look up, they'll see you. Please, please don't stand here.'

'How will you love, if you fear so much?' Shobhon asks, neatly inverting the opening line of a popular Hindi film song. He is given to such smart wit at moments of great risk. As a result, Baishakhi finds him almost unbearably attractive. She colours furiously at the word 'love', floating so openly, so publicly, between them – a secret thought suddenly embodied and exposed by being spoken aloud – and cannot find a way to answer him.

'Don't forget, eight on ashtami evening, behind the puja pandal,' he repeats, debonairly blows out some smoke rings, blue and fragile, and leaves the terrace through the green wooden door.

Throughout lunch Chhaya has watched the movements and actions of everyone, like an undercover surveillance agent. Purnima has, as usual, eaten as much as a Bihari guard or a rickshaw-puller, almost up to her wrist in the mound of rice and dal and vegetables and fish curry; Baishakhi has, uncharacteristically, toyed with her food, her mind altogether far away; it seems that Arunima, monosyllabic but jumpy and lit up somewhat dangerously from within as if plotting grand arson or regicide, is following her older cousin into a private no-man's territory too. It never crosses Chhaya's mind that others could be thinking similar thoughts about her unnatural silence: where is her relentless carping, her flurry of barbs let loose at everyone, the measured drip of acid from her tongue?

Chhaya had started off being unusually animated, asking everyone, nicely for a change, what plans they had for the rest of the afternoon, whether anyone would be interested in joining her for a few rounds of Ludo afterwards. When she had established what everyone was going to be doing – no one was remotely interested in Ludo or snakes-and-ladders – she lapsed into silence and let the viscous plan move up and down in her mind like the meniscus of an exotic poison.

Malati, the maidservant, comes rushing upstairs from the kitchen just as lunch is ending and says excitedly to Purnima, 'The knife-and-scissors sharpening man is going down the street now.' Purnima gets up, energised and active, goes to the kitchen downstairs and orders, 'Quick, quick, gather all the stuff, don't forget the bonti. And all the scissors – all of them, they're all blunt. Call Gagan, ask him to carry the stone mortar. Quick-quick, I don't want to miss the sharpening man this time, he's been quite elusive, we keep missing him. The sheel has lost its friction. Call Gagan, what are you waiting for? Here, I'll take the rest downstairs, let me first wash my hands. Call out to the man to stop.' And in a whirling vortex of activity, Purnima thud-thuds out, carrying a clattering, clinking armoury of assorted knives and scissors.

Now that the sudden frenzy has blown over, Chhaya can hear the raucous cry of the dharwala cycling down the street, his call so stylised over time that you have to know what it is in the first place in order to identify it as the knife-sharpening-man's call. An opportunity sent by Ma Kali, she thinks, as she too rises from the table and announces calmly, 'I'm going to wash my hands now, I'm done. Arunima, if you're going to watch all this sharpening, don't stare at the sparks for too long, you'll go blind. I know you like watching it, but be careful.'

She leaves the table and goes to the sink in one corner of the room to wash her hands. Then she goes to her room one floor up, picks up a bottle of red nail polish and walks out again. Moving calmly and confidently, she takes the stairs down, back to the first floor, then goes to Purnima and Priyo's room. New clothes are strewn on the bed lavishly. A quick look tells her that they are both Purnima's and Baishakhi's. She empties the bottle of nail polish on as many of the garments on the top layer as the small volume of cosmetic will allow. Then she returns upstairs to her room, the empty bottle held in her hand. The burn in her is still unassuaged.

A small fear begins to form: she has to dispose of the empty bottle; what if they find it in her room? She lets the fear grow to the point where the accusing bottle glows with reproach. She picks it up and, calmly again, makes her way up to the roof. She is going to fling it far onto someone else's roof and run away from the terrace as soon as the deed is accomplished. When she reaches the top landing, before she can push open the door to the terrace, she hears Baishakhi's unmistakable voice, 'If they look up, they'll see you. Please, please don't stand here', followed by something unintelligible in a man's voice. She begins to turn back to escape downstairs, but some knowledge gives her pause. She stands still for a while and the embers of the burn inside her suddenly flare up into flames of unexpected joy.

Earlier that day, while Purba had been filling up a bucket from the tap in the corner of the courtyard, the maid, Malati, had surreptitiously given her some Vim, which she had smuggled from upstairs in a small newspaper pouch.

'You do your washing-up here with ashes and charcoal, seeing that makes me feel small, I do their washing with Beem, so I bring some down. Hide it, hide it, if anyone finds out, I'll be kicked out,' she whispered to Purba, slipping her the packet of powder. Noticing Purba's hesitancy and fear, Malati added, 'Take, take, quickly.' Both women looked upstairs with guilt and fear.

Touched by this gratuitous act of kindness from a servant, Purba's eyes pricked with tears. But sentimentality was a luxury, she knew, and fear had the upper hand. She whispered, 'Come into my room. If anyone sees you standing here talking to me, you'll have a lot of questions to answer.'

The two women scuttled into Purba's little room. 'You'll get into trouble one of these days,' she said to Malati.

'Only if I get caught. But I'm careful.'

'Why take the risk? I manage fine with charcoal,' Purba said, trying to keep her voice steady; she felt soft, malleable.

'What can I say? We are servants, illiterate, poor people, it is not our place to open our mouths. But we too have eyes and ears, we can see and hear what goes on.'

Purba could only remain silent in the face of such empathy.

'Do you think we don't know that Boro-boüdi secretly sends down used clothes and other stuff for your son and daughter? They're growing up on leftovers and bones, those two; they'll come good one day, you mark my words. Those who suffer, win.'

At the mention of her children, Purba couldn't restrain herself. She covered her mouth with her sari to hide her trembling chin, her twisting mouth.

The timing for doing the washing-up has been calculated by Purba with the utmost deliberation: late afternoon, when everyone upstairs will be deep into their siesta, so there is no chance of getting caught using Vim. She will have to be very quiet too; no clanging and clattering pots and pans that could wake up her mother-in-law.

While doing the washing-up, Purba hears a commotion break out upstairs. A few minutes of straining to listen – and it does not require much effort, for Purnima's voice carries for miles – establishes the main facts: Baishakhi has spilled a bottle of nail polish and ruined three saris and two salwar-kameez sets. Alight with rage, Purnima has mercilessly thrashed her daughter. Everyone in the family is now assembled on the first floor to witness the show and contribute their two-anna worth of opinion.

Kalyani comes out of Purba's room and listens, wide-eyed, thirstily soaking up the sounds of the circus upstairs until Purba shoos her away: 'Go inside, someone will see you gaping and grinning.'

Perhaps Purba is only trying to protect her daughter from the knowledge of how many new items of clothing the people upstairs have received and given, a knowledge that will extinguish the joy her daughter is clearly deriving from the drama. For the three of them, a separate household really, have received only one set each, the obligatory one bought at the last minute, from cheap shops and hawkers in Gariahat: Sona, a short-sleeved shirt and a pair of trousers two sizes too big for him; Kalyani, a salwar-kameez set; and Purba, a block-printed cotton sari. They will shrink, their colours will run, they will look like floor-swabbing cloths after the first wash, then they will start falling apart at the seams; you can predict all this by taking one look at the garments.

Washing-up completed, Purba crosses over to her side of the courtyard and enters her room. She feels like a nap, but there are a hundred and one things to be done – darning the holey mosquito net alone will take up the rest of the afternoon. She decides instead to fold the dry washing and put it away.

'Kalyani, why don't you give me a hand with folding the big things?' she asks her daughter.

When all the folding is done, Purba starts putting the clothes away in the small wooden cupboard that houses practically all her earthly belongings. In it, tucked carefully under a bedsheet so that it does not stick out egregiously, is a flat parcel wrapped in paper and string. What is it? she thinks; how did it get here? She takes it out and, in her impatience to open it, knots up the string, so she lifts it up and holds it to her mouth to cut the string with her teeth. A piece of paper flutters to the floor. She picks it up and reads the austere note that does not give much away: *Didn't have enough money to buy you a puja sari, forgive me, but here's something for Sona and Kalyani.* She opens the package with trembling hands, barely able to swallow the growing lump in her throat. Inside it are a shirt and a pair of short trousers for Sona and a frock for Kalyani. She turns to face the cupboard, pushing her head inside, pretending to be busy sorting clothes, to hide her wet face from her daughter.

From seven o'clock on ashtami morning, the priest has been conducting half-hourly public prayer sessions at the pandal. The PA system, which has been rigged up for the loud dispersal of music day and night from the two ends of the road and from the pandal through the five days of puja (a mandatory practice, this), is used for the purpose of worship only on this day. Flocks of residents, all got up in the finest of their new clothes, go in family groups or with friends and neighbours to congregate in orderly rows inside the pandal, face the stage where the statues of the goddess and her children stand looking at them and, led by the priest's chanting, repeat the Sanskrit slokas and throw tufts of flowers to the deities in worship. Those who cannot go, such as the infirm Prafullanath, sit on their balconies and hear the priest's voice, intoning the verses, issue from the PA system and feel comforted and consoled.

Baishakhi goes with her parents to the pandal for anjali around noon. She sees Shobhon, an ardent worker in the Puja Committee, as busy as clockwork with some other young men, and looks through him. She has known that she will see him and, though she does not give the slightest indication of having done so, he knows that she has clocked him and she knows that he knows. As she stands at the bottom of the stage, between her parents, trying to gather her mind to the gravitas of communal worship, she notices that Shobhon has taken it upon himself to distribute the flowers for anjali to the people gathered for worship. The sudden thudding of her heart is raucous to her own ears: what is he *doing*? She imagines every eye there in the pandal on them. She is certain Baba and Ma, flanking her closely, almost touching her sides, can feel the heat radiating off her. When Shobhon reaches them, she can barely bring herself to put her hand into the big basket of flowers to pick out a small handful of marigold petals. She imagines a spectral brush of his arm against her fingers as he moves on to her mother, and then to the next person and then the next along the row, perfectly composed, cool and unruffled, as if she were only just another familiar neighbourly face. Baishakhi keeps her head resolutely down. Her face is burning. Coursing through her heart and mind is a seam of a delicious mixture of outrage, fear and awe at Shobhon's foolhardiness.

What is said about the darkest spot being directly under the light is nowhere more true than of the area behind the puja pandal: all that crammed symphony of festival lighting barely a few yards away does not have much effect on the dark here. Here the jutting ribs and carcass of the pandal have not received the care of being covered up with yards of coloured cloth; here you have the feeling of being in

the wings of the makeshift stage of a travelling theatre company in
the provinces, all bamboo, old tarpaulin, discarded nails, coiled snakes
of rough ropes, damp earth, patchy clumps of tough, unruly grass.
Here Baishakhi stands, on ashtami evening, quivering with fear that
someone has spied her slipping into the shadows at the back of the
pandal. If someone has noticed a young girl negotiating her way
through the narrow gap on the side of the big tent, they would
indeed have been alerted enough to ask themselves why she was
heading for the back, the discarded side as it were: a tryst with
someone perhaps?

Chhaya has lured Priyo into sitting with her on the balcony on the
first floor – *Let's go and look at people from the verandah before we go out
later in the evening, the crush of people will be terrible now, it'll certainly
ease* – and from their vantage position they have an unimpeded view
of the milling crowd, the pandal, the sea of faces and heads where
the known mingle with the unknown. The PA system airs songs from
the hit film *An Evening in Paris*. Chhaya chatters on, 'Look, look, Rupa-
boüdi is wearing a parrot-green silk-tangail. Gorgeous! Pity her face
is so scarred by that terrible teenage acne. O ma, Pushpa-babu has
come out too, he's using his cane, someone's helping him. Priyo, isn't
that Pushpa-babu? Not very considerate of them to have let the old,
ill man out at this peak sightseeing hour.'

Priyo gets up and peers. 'Yes, it is. His first time in years, no?'

'First time since we heard he was not well. We should persuade
Baba to go out too.'

Then the meandering aimlessness of all this ends as the grail swims
into view. Chhaya tugs at Priyo's sleeve and says in a voice pitched
perfectly between surprise and uncertainty, 'Priyo, look, isn't that Buli?
Why is she trying to go to the back of the pandal? Quick, quick, she's
about to disappear.'

Priyo asks, 'Where? Where?' before he manages to pick out the
flash of an orange kurta, which, like a rare visitation from a species
of butterfly assumed to be lost, disappears almost as soon as it has
been spotted. 'Couldn't make out anything, it's so dark. Are you sure?'

Chhaya, with measured casualness, then says, 'Now look, isn't that
our next-door neighbour's son, Shobhon, going there now?'

Priyo, suddenly alert, sharp, looks again, this time with more focused intent.

Yes, it is.

Baishakhi, after much coaxing, has laid her head on Shobhon's chest. He has clinched the embrace with an apposite line from a new film, *Aamne Samne*, starring Shashi Kapoor and Sharmila Tagore. He holds her close to him, trying to move, as subtly, as imperceptibly as he can, from stroking her back to stroking her sides. All he wants to do is fondle her breasts, but he will have to be very, very slow and cunning. Baishakhi, beginning to feel as if she is free-falling towards a floor that isn't there, has at last relinquished her nervous attention to all kinds of sounds that could announce an intruder.

A sudden crashing, like a miniature stampede, and rapidly advancing voices make them spring up, but, frozen by utter panic, they remain entangled when Baishakhi's father and mother appear like vengeful, unappeasable gods.

To the background music of *An Evening in Paris*, distorted ever so slightly by the volume of its amplification, thrilled neighbours see a weeping Baishakhi being frogmarched home by her parents, both of whose faces are black and brimful with imminent thunder.

Severe weather rips through the Ghosh home and, when not inflicting damage, it sits brooding, umbrous, threatening, a pall over day-to-day activity. The frenzy first. Several rounds of immediate disciplining follow the discovery of Baishakhi: intense interrogation by her mother, physical punishment in the form of generous slapping during the questioning sessions, locking the girl in her room. All of these are accompanied by hysterically raised voices. Crueller measures follow. A lock is added to the door to the terrace. It remains shut day and night, and Purnima holds the only key to it. Baishakhi is forbidden to leave the house. When school reopens after the puja holidays, she is to be accompanied there and received at the gates after school is over and chaperoned back home. She cannot meet any of her friends unless they come to see her at home. These visiting friends are questioned fiercely by Purnima and asked if they are carrying letters or acting as go-betweens in any capacity. If she could, she would have frisked them. There is a clotted silence in the house, pulsating with reproach and judgement; Baishakhi feels she is being treated like a pariah, which indeed she is. All eyes are upon her, the elders' dark with accusation that she has brought shame upon herself and the name of the Ghoshes; the children's awed, embarrassed and a bit frightened, because they know she has done something terrible, but what exactly they have not been told. They are shielded from the whole truth in case it corrupts their morals. There is nothing new or unusual in all this; it runs along the well-ploughed furrows of middle-class Bengali life.

Chhaya seems to be the one who is most eloquently upset. She speaks of it at every mealtime and will not let the topic drop off the conversational horizon. 'Eeesh, how shaming the whole thing! What are people thinking about us? Being caught with a loafer . . .' and lets the silence carry the rest. At other times, she tries another tack, her voice modulated to the articulation of sympathy: 'But I hope the girl is all right. Who knows what advantage has been taken of the poor flower by that immoral man?' The silence after this is even more damning. No one notices how animated she has suddenly become, how buzzed, as if a hidden ecstasy is exerting her to too keen and bright an enthusiasm.

As a consequence of this unfolding drama, bijaya, two days after Baishakhi is caught, is a muffled affair. But tradition has to be upheld at all costs, so the annual practice of buying quantities of assorted sweets from Girish Ghosh and Putiram is observed faithfully this year too. Adinath is driven to North Calcutta and back by Gagan, the boot of the Ambassador full of terracotta pots and paper boxes and cartons. Certain things cannot be done this year, such as allowing Baishakhi to go to the puja pandal to watch the enormous statue of the goddess being transferred by the young men of the neighbourhood from the stage to the lorry that will take it to Babughat for the immersion ceremony. Not a single person stays at home during this dismantling; it is the one event of the festival that comes close to a spectacle. This year Purnima stays indoors with Baishakhi, guarding her with the vigilance of a trained dog. They do not go to their balcony to watch the preparation for the final immersion, in case Baishakhi and Shobhon catch sight of each other. The rest of the Ghosh family stays in too, and misses seeing off Durga and her offspring on the three tempos

hired for the occasion, because they are apprehensive of the neighbours' acute curiosity, their weighted, probing gaze. They watch from
their respective verandahs.

The tempos, packed with scores of men and children holding onto
the effigies, leave Basanta Bose Road at a crawl. They are preceded
by an entourage of people, a band, and a group of locals who dance
along to the music the band plays as the pageant makes its creeping
progress to Babughat. When this farewell crowd departs, bijaya is
officially declared. In the Ghosh house, wives bend down to touch
the feet of their husbands with their right hands and bring the hands
forward to their foreheads and then to their chests in the gesture of
pranam; sons and daughters do the same to their parents and elders,
younger relations to older, and the men embrace each other three
times in quick succession. The sweets are distributed and the stricken
looks resulting from Baishakhi's intransigence two days ago – it is
difficult to estimate where the genuine strickenness ends and its self-
conscious enactment begins – are relaxed enough to allow the usual
bijaya practices to proceed.

Purba, on the one evening she is suffered to come to the grand
living room on the first floor and mingle relatively freely, so that
everyone else can have the desirably short-lived luxury of playing One
Big Happy Family, is, in reality, on menial duty, as always; she stands
in a corner and hands out plates of sweets, clears away empty cups
and saucers, refills glasses with water, even though there is a small
fleet of servants to do these chores. For once, Charubala does not
bark at her, but files away, for later use, the fact that she gives two
pantuas each to Sona and Kalyani when she knows she is not supposed
to give them more than one. Charubala chooses to ignore that it is
Supratik who insists that Purba gives extra sweets to her children; she
does not have to, thinks Charubala, just because someone is persis-
tently asking her to do it, does she? Purba could have been equally
obstinate in not giving in. A hot flash of irritation blooms inside the
old woman, but now is not the time. She cannot even have the satisfaction of baring her teeth at Sona and Kalyani; Supratik is teaching
them a game that involves paper and pen and they are absolutely rapt.
It will have to wait.

On the morning after, a few minutes into her matutinal duties in the prayer room, Sandhya discovers the following note in a sealed envelope at the foot of the statuette of the goddess Lakshmi:

Ma, I feel exhausted with consuming, with taking and grabbing and using. I am so bloated that I feel I cannot breathe any more. I am leaving to find some air, some place where I shall be able to purge myself, push back against the life given me and make my own. I feel I live in a borrowed house. It's time to find my own. Trying to discover my whereabouts won't get you anywhere, so save that energy; you might find you need it for something else. I'll write periodically to let you know I'm alive. Forgive me. Yours, Supratik.

II

I left the city to work with landless peasants, the sharecroppers, wage-labourers and impoverished tenants who were the backbone of our movement. My job was to go to the villages and organise them into armed struggle.

That was the only way – to seize power, one field, one village, one district at a time. 1) Formation of armed squads in every village; 2) collection of arms by seizing them from class enemies and the police; 3) seizure of crops and arrangements for hiding them; 4) constant propagation of the politics of armed struggle – these were our aims, outlined by Chairman Mao first and then Charu Mazumdar. We went to indigent agricultural areas where feudalism was still the order of the day, where the exploitation of farmers by jotedaars and moneylenders and landowners was at its inhuman worst. Along the Bengal–Bihar–Orissa borderlands this feudalism was supplemented by the plight of the tribal peoples whose ancient lands had been taken from them and who had been reduced to a form of slavery. Or else they had run away into the forests, hoping for some kind of life in hiding.

Of the people I knew, three groups went to the Gopiballabhpur area in south Medinipur, near the border with Orissa; another two, where Purulia edged into Bihar. I formed a group with Samir and Dhiren. Samir, from Naktala, was a Part II Bengali Honours student at Bangabashi, a budding poet and short-story writer, also reputed to be the brightest student his department had seen in the last twenty-five years. He had got record marks in his Part I exams last year. How he had pulled off that trick, given that all his time was devoted to 'doing politics', no one knew, but it seemed unlikely he was going to be able to hold onto his first in Part II. Or even sit his exams. How could he? He had abandoned all that and thrown in his lot with the roving revolutionaries. A classic rice-eating, timorous, creature-comforts-loving, head-in-the-clouds Bengali, you'd think, to look at him, and he was all those things, but behind that there was a core of steel. It took me a while to discover that.

Dhiren, on the other hand, had the toughness of someone who had known only want in his life. Mind you, Samir didn't come from a particularly well-off family – his father was a clerk in the Electric Supply Corporation – but he and his family lived in a house built by his grandfather, so at least they had a roof over their heads that they could call their own. Dhiren came from Uttarpara. His father worked in a light-bulb factory, which had seen its entire workforce go on strike against its owners' decision to fire nearly a quarter of them; the factory had been shut for three years now. The family had been without an income for that period. Meanwhile, Dhiren, the eldest son, on whose BCom degree course in City College the family's hopes of sustenance rested, had barely attended college, choosing to change the world instead of adding to its aggregate of unquestioning petty-bourgeois invertebrates.

'What good will the degree do?' he had once said to me. 'There are hundreds of thousands like me, graduates who are sitting twiddling their thumbs because there are no jobs. I'll be joining that great herd of unthinking cattle. The thing is to get to the heart of the sickness, not tinker around with the symptoms, do you understand?'

Of course, I did.

I headed towards the westernmost region of Medinipur with Samir and Dhiren, towards its border with Bihar – past Jhargram, past Belpahari, near Kankrajhor in the Binpur area. Sometimes the places were so small that they didn't have a name, they called themselves by the name of the nearest village. We operated in Baishtampur, Gidighati, Chhurimara (what a name! 'knife-stabbed'; still haven't been able to find out the history behind it), Majgeria, Chirugora.

There were jungles on the near horizon everywhere, dense, dark forests of kendu and sal. It was not accidental that most of our comrades worked in or near areas under the cover of trees. The jungle provided protection, obviously. In our line of work, the ability to go into hiding quickly was a matter of life and death. Literally. These were the forests that received the tribals of the area when their land was grabbed by a landlord, a moneylender, a coal or iron company. There were mines nearby – coal, iron-ore. Jamshedpur and Bokaro were just a short hop across into Bihar. And north, across Purulia and Bankura, there were the big dams, Maithon, Massanjore, and the mining towns of Dhanbad and Jharia. All these had been built on the lands of tribal peoples, flooding or displacing them. Who was going to listen to 100, 500, 1,000 or even 10,000 dark-skinned, backward, jungle-dwelling adivasis, the so-called 'scheduled tribes', over the collective might and muscle of Steel Authority of India, Tata Steel and Hindustan Cables?

These areas had been seeing agitation for some time now. We decided to begin here because, in some sense, our work had a ready, if somewhat basic, foundation in the region. Naxalbari happened in North Bengal because unrest at tea plantations there had been brewing for a long while — the labour movement, agitating for rights, better working conditions, better pay, rights over the land. The beginning of our revolution there didn't come out of thin air. Similarly, here too there was a continuing history of great wrongs. We could build on that.

Have you seen how I cannot keep away from talking shop? Awful, I know. There I was, trying to tell you the story of my journey to Medinipur and, without being aware of it, I got pulled back into politics. I'm sorry. I keep thinking of you reprimanding me gently, saying, with so much laughter held in check in your voice — There goes the parrot again, reciting its textbooks.

Yes, our journey. That was what I really wanted to write about. From Gidhni Junction the railtrack became a loop-line, my first time on one such. Nature seemed to change its looks and personality as the loop-line separated from the broad-gauge. The earth had turned dry, dusty and red. The distance between the large trees became greater and greater. Instead of those big ponds, surrounded by coconut and palm trees, we saw little ponds — large puddles, really. The density of everything, vegetation, human habitation, people, thinned out. Huge fields of rice, then a few dots of thatched mud houses. Some dwarf date palms, that was all I could recognise.

Actually, to tell you the truth, I thought they were betel nut trees until Dhiren laughed and said — You're such a dyed-in-the-wool city boy, you don't know your betel nut from your date palm; really, what are we going to do with you? We're going to be living with peasants and you'll stick out like a pylon in a flat, empty field and embarrass us all.

More laughter. Because he was not from the big city, Dhiren fancied himself as a bit of a Nature man, at one with trees and birds and flowers and such things. He was always playing this game of one-upmanship with me; his way of reducing the distance between us, I suppose. There had been several times in the past when I'd had to bite my tongue to stop myself from saying — Dhiren, it's Uttarpara you're from, the mofussil, hardly open countryside and the very heart of Nature, is it?

Then Dhiren pointed out simul trees — not in flower, so I wouldn't have been able to identify them anyway. I can hear you laughing and ganging up with

Dhiren, saying — He's right, you're a through-and-through city boy, you can't even put a name to the simul tree? To which I can only say that this is the tyranny of you rural folk . . .

When the train left the main railway line and went over the cutting, the music of the wheels changed. The people at the stations were taller, darker than city people. They had curly hair. The women who boarded the train were much shyer. They did not want to sit on the benches, but sat on the dirty floor of the carriage.

At a tiny station we bought tea in small terracotta cups. Dhiren said — Have your fill, there's no tea where we're going, and it wouldn't do to drink tea anyway when we are with the farmers, because they don't have any and it's considered an urban luxury. Where would they get money to buy tea?

Ufff, Dhiren did talk so . . . jabbering away constantly: squad formation, methods of warfare, teaching class politics to farmers, how there was no transport where we were going, we would have to walk scores of miles . . . unending, his chatter. No wonder he was the de facto leader of every activity that required talking — speeches in assemblies, canvassing votes during elections, student-body meetings . . . anything you could think of. I kept looking with suspicion at everyone in the carriage. Whose ears were picking up on all this? I made a sign to Dhiren to stop. It took some time before he caught on.

Then, suddenly, scrubland. And the promise of forest beyond the horizon. I didn't know how I had sensed it.

Red earth. Have you ever seen it? The dust that catches in your hair, in your clothes, when you walk over the dry soil, is red. I had never seen red earth before.

We got off at Jhargram. Samir said we should look out for police at the station, we should get off the train and walk out singly. From Jhargram to Belpahari in a bus. Right at the other edge of Belpahari, from where you could see the forests of this corner of Medinipur spreading out in all directions, was the home of Debdulal Maity, our contact in this region. He ran a cycle-repair shop and we put up in the shed where the cycles, tools, spares, tyres and all manner of jumble were kept. It wasn't a good idea to stay at his home. First of all, there wasn't much space there. Besides, it wouldn't do to implicate his wife and children. What they didn't know, they could neither confess to nor reveal.

So his shop it was: mats on the floor, no mattresses, only a few layers of folded-up shataranchi, mosquito nets. Only one hurricane lamp — he could not afford more kerosene — sooting up rapidly. The little flickering yellow light that it cast seemed like a timid, jumpy prey, which knew that the darkness around it was going to get it soon.

— Only four hours of electricity every day, Debdulal-da said, and that too after paying 500 rupees' bribe to the man who had come to connect it. And the four hours that we get are so weak that it's not worth the name of electricity. All these villages: not a single one has electric power.

— But you are in dams territory, there's so much hydel power in your back yard, I protested.

— That's hardly for us, he said, that's for the cities and the big companies. We are little villages in the backwaters here, mostly full of tribal and lower-caste people and harijans and scheduled tribes. Who cares about us? We've been forgotten.

Samir opened his mouth to say something, but stopped himself. I knew what he was going to say: that the land for the dams and the mines belonged to the tribals and lower-caste people. It was their villages that got submerged, their livelihoods that got destroyed, they did not get even a minuscule fraction of the resettlement money; in most cases they got nothing for being kicked out of their homes and their land.

Why didn't he say it? It wasn't as if we hadn't talked endlessly about it. Maybe that was the reason . . . There had been too much talk.

Dhiren had a tired but tense look on his face. He watched me take in the arrangements. I didn't even blink. Before Dhiren could say anything, could say what I thought — feared — he was going to say, I said to Debdulal-da that the shataranchis could go, mats on the floor would be enough for us. I didn't want his family to have to do without rugs because some boys from the city had to be made comfortable. The tension left Dhiren's face. I felt I'd scored a point.

Samir lit a bidi and said — Let's see if the smoke drives the bloody mosquitoes away.

Mosquitoes everywhere, whining away, clouds of mosquitoes. There didn't seem to be much energy or enthusiasm to talk, but we had to hang the mosquito nets and get inside and talk from our beds if we wanted to have a conversation.

Then Samir, breaking the silence that seemed to be solidifying around us, said — Erm, guys, can we keep the hurricane lamp on? I mean, turned down very low but burning, so that we're not completely in the dark?

Dhiren, laughing loudly — Oh, I'd forgotten, you're afraid of ghosts, aren't you?

I was too amused to be surprised by this revelation. I started laughing too – Afraid of ghosts? At your age? This is too good to be true . . .

I couldn't make out Samir's expression – it seemed to have become darker in the room – but I hoped he was looking sheepish. He sounded it when he said, almost laughing himself – Okay, cut it out, bravehearts. Stop pretending that you don't have any irrational fears.

Dhiren – But come on, fear of ghosts? That's ridiculous! I can imagine Supratik not having any fears, least of all irrational ones, but, Samir, you loser, only children are afraid of the dark. You are twenty-one. Nearly a quarter of a century, that is.

Samir, huffily – All right, all right. The question is: are we going to leave the lamp on or not?

I wasn't keen on talk of such things – fears, feelings, emotions, they're all irrational, right? – so I opened up another line of teasing.

– Listen, you know the outhouse is a few yards outside . . . we'll have to walk there in this pitch-dark and walk back. What are you going to do, Samir?

Samir, sounding really pathetic, weepy nearly – You think the thought hasn't crossed my mind? That's why I've been holding everything in for so long.

This made me and Dhiren erupt into loud, hooting laughter.

CHAPTER THREE

1968

Decorously Suranjan passes the chhillum to the man on his right, holding it in his right hand, as he has been taught to do, while keeping the lung-stretching volume of smoke he has just inhaled from it still locked inside, so that his blood can absorb the maximum amount of tetrohydrocannabinol. THC, he has learned to call it; he has all the lingo now. He lets out the smoke in a rush of dispersing cloud: there seems so much of it inside him. Six months ago, when he had first graduated from smoking grass in reefers to the chhillum, the native terracotta pipe made especially for it, his chest had found it difficult to accommodate the huge inrush of smoke flowing in like a geyser in reverse. He had spluttered and coughed and coughed and spat, embarrassed and ashamed at such a betrayal of his status as novitiate in Bappa-da's cool circle of friends, until one day, shortly after his experiment with the chhillum, something had happened in his chest while he was inhaling, some expansion, as if a valve had opened or a secret panel had slid away to make for a vaster room. He had actually felt that lowering of the floor, that inner expansion.

Now, sitting around in a circle of seven men, with his back to one of the walls of the gymnasium, a few metres away from the student canteen in Presidency College, he thinks with great pride on his casual professionalism as a seasoned smoker as the tendrils of the hit hug him tighter and tighter in its delirious embrace. Sounds come closer and edge further away simultaneously in an imperceptibly choreographed movement shuffling background and foreground. Now he can feel the pulse of his heart in his throat. He knows his eyes have become smaller: he feels a tightening around and behind them, as if an army of ants were pulling at them with delicate, spider-web threads.

Nikhil, sitting across from him, has a fixed, foolish, serene smile on his face, and Suranjan assumes that he must too.

'Hey, Nikhil, far out, man,' he says but so softly that the sound does not reach Nikhil.

All along his nerves and his spine and the base of his skull elusive blossoms are blooming and breaking up in ripples. The sounds outside, on College Street – of car horns, the clatter of trams, babble, music, shouts, a bell somewhere, commotion – all these flow in a harmony, recede, then flow back in again. He smiles. Debu is trying to say something to him, but he is too relaxed to ask him to repeat it; if it is important, he will hear it, the still-yet-turning chakra at the centre will ensure that he becomes a part of everything around him.

'Where have all the hmm hmm hmm, / Where have all the people hmm hmm / La la la la . . .' Debu sings softly.

'Grateful Dead,' Suranjan checks. Two months ago Bappa-da had introduced them to the first album of a group from San Francisco. The epiphany of the music had exploded in Suranjan when, riding the gently sinuous curve of some very good grass from Mazhar-i-Sharif, he had deciphered the cryptic words on the record sleeve, a vision bestowed by the drug itself, without which all knowledge was but information, incomplete and crass. 'In the land of the dark, the ship of the sun is drawn by the Grateful Dead.' Bappa-da, after weeks of research, had turned up its source – *The Egyptian Book of the Dead*. The revelation had catapulted Suranjan into the top bracket: here was a real stoner, one whose perception was so cleansed by smoking that he could read what was opaque to the clouded eye. He had arrived.

Suddenly the embrace of the pot tightens to something more tentacular, more menacing, as a procession of unwelcome intrusions start their march through his head: abysmal attendance record in his English BA (Hons) class, professors unhappy with his continued absence. No sooner has it begun than others, from hidden byways and side-lanes of his life, start joining the marchers, swelling its ranks. His missing brother, now gone for nearly one year, with only two postcards to show that he is still alive, god alone knows where. His mother, almost an invalid, bedridden from the moment Dada had disappeared, with all interest in life gone overnight. In college there are rumours everywhere that Supratik is a Naxalite, but if he is that, then why is he not around in the city, where all the action seems to be?

When Suranjan had joined Presidency College last year, it was still reeling from strikes and the agitation by the communist students who had been expelled from college and the adjoining Hindu Hostel. The college authorities had called in the police and there had been clashes between the rioting students and police on College Street almost every day: lathi charges, petrol bombs on several occasions, bloodied men on both sides, brutal beatings of the students, angry processions. At one point his mother, already consumed by worries about Supratik, had urged her younger son to apply to other places, or consider not going to university until the troubles had blown over. When she is not in the puja room, praying incessantly that Supratik might be kept out of harm's way, she sits on a chair on the verandah all afternoon and most of the evening, waiting for the sight of his tall, gaunt form to appear around the corner of Basanta Bose Road.

Suranjan hardly ever thinks about his brother and, when he does, it is not really as another, separate presence. Like the air he breathes in, his brother is only noticeable to him when he is absent. And now that he has disappeared – well, not really, but as good as, because no one knows where he sent those two postcards from; the postmarks said Ballygunge – Suranjan starts the train of a correlational algebra in his head, bringing into proximity the fact of the disappearance and the suspicion of his brother's involvement in the student political activism. Dada was so preternaturally quiet and secretive, so unyielding with any kind of response or reaction, that no one ever knew what he was up to.

But buzzing hornets of questions swarm into Suranjan's mind now. Not a day had gone by in the winter of '66–'67 without the circulation of fevered news: 'The Students' Federation are lobbing bombs at the police', 'The Superintendent of the Hindu Hostel has been gheraoed for thirty-six hours', 'There are buses burning on College Street', 'The police have opened tear gas on the student protesters'. If Dada had had anything to do with these conflagrations, wouldn't the distant heat from them at least have been felt by his family? No sooner have some suspicions begun to join up together, like links in a chain, than other countervailing arguments break them apart and separate them until, racked by this dance of tmeses, Suranjan's algebra stands in ruins.

Something starts pressing against him, as if some invisible walls are inching closer, trapping him, truncating his vision: surely this is the cannabis user's typical paranoia? Suranjan tries to brush off the feeling that he is in a narrow well, and concentrate instead on where he really is: sitting with his friends and getting high in a secluded corner of Presidency College. Patchy grass, weeds, straggling, spindly plants, a big tree, earth, a small pile of orange-red bricks, a big drain, the new canteen to his left, one wall of the gym behind his back. He tries to hold onto something more than this solidity outside him and settles invariably on the liberating knowledge of this evening's promise: smack, in Bappa-da's house on Ironside Road. His very first time. He has heard so much about brown sugar, all in excited, slightly frightened whispers as if the talk was about *the* forbidden fruit. Bappa-da has done it half a dozen times and has told him it is a necessary gradua-tion if Suranjan wants to have the doors of his perception cleansed and see the world in a grain of sand. The ritual was apparently called 'chasing'; yes, the pursuit of the vision that reconfigured everything in its real contours, that showed not things but the design behind things, unmediated meanings. This had been what Blake chased, and Aldous Huxley, and what Allen Ginsberg, the new poet Bappa-da has introduced him to, was after. He will be their acolyte and disciple.

The Ghosh and Datta families talk formally and agree on Baishakhi and Shobhon's marriage to go ahead next year. Both Priyo and Purnima are dead set against the marriage before Baishakhi finishes high school. They want it to be deferred until she is twenty-one, until she has finished university and acquired a BA degree, it doesn't matter in which subject. Of the many things that exercise them the most pressing is the necessity of her being a graduate. But the Dattas think five years to be an immoderately long period of engagement, so the compromise of 1969 is reached. The Ghoshes try to extract a promise from their prospective in-laws that Baishakhi will be sent to college, but they know they are defeated right at the beginning of their entreaty, not so much by what appears to them, rightly, it will turn out, to be empty and perfunctory assurances from the Dattas, as by their own daughter's placid indifference to any such concerns. The home side lets them down.

Her thinning and now greying hair spread out in a pitiful swathe across the bank of stale pillows on which her head rests, Sandhya runs the indelible film of her son's two postcards in her head. She had taken to her bed ever since Supratik left a year ago, only very occasionally leaving it to perform the bare minimum of tasks that would keep her from puncturing a vital divisive membrane and slipping from the world of humans to that of something less-than-human. Overnight she had dropped out of her life and become a spectre, giving up on all her duties and privileges as the eldest daughter-in-law at the helm of the family ship and letting it drift, keelless and rudderless; she didn't care any more about anything. The images of the two postcards burn through her: six inches by four inches (yes, she had measured them with a ruler) of light-beige ordinariness, the imprint of the head of the Royal Bengal Tiger, along with the denomination, fifteen paisa, on the top right-hand corner, just above the ruled space for the address . . . She knows every atom of those two postcards now.

She has stared at them so hard, willing them to release the imprisoned meanings from behind the cursive cage of the words, the *real* meanings that would communicate something special to her beyond what its surface said. She has handled them, stroked them, slept with them under her pillow, all with the wish to touch what he had touched, a kind of communion of distance, of air. And she had done it so often that even she was prepared to admit, had she been faced with such a requirement, that she had erased all traces of his touch from the postcards by now. There were times when she had wanted to ingest them, chew them into a bolus, swallow them and assimilate their essence into her blood. That would have been a way of holding on to his presence.

Two postcards in a year: that was all a firstborn owed his mother.

The first one, dated 19th April 1968 – it was her mother-in-law who had pointed out, over the weeks spent dissecting and anatomising it to its very elementary particles, that the date was the New Year – that first postcard, addressed to her, contained only five sentences:

Respected Ma, I am well, don't worry about me. I hope all of you are too.
The postal services where I am are a bit erratic and infrequent, so I'm getting
someone to post it to you from Calcutta. I will be in touch again. Give everyone
my love. Supratik.

It was his hand, confident, elegant, neat, there was no doubt about
that; Sandhya would have been able to identify it as her son's with
her eyes shut. The second one, sent five months after the first, was
even more parsimonious and ungiving:

Respected Ma, Hope all your news is well. I am in good health and spirit.
Truly. Don't worry about me. Again, this postcard is being mailed to you from
Calcutta. My love to everyone, Supratik.

The arrival of the first one had created such a huge jag in expectation that for the ensuing month or two Sandhya had left her bed and
taken up an almost immovable position in an armchair on the verandah
in the daylight hours, willing the postman to arrive with another letter
from her son. That hope had turned to ashes slowly and Sandhya had
taken to her bed again. Over the year that Supratik had been absent,
the harsh calculus of hope and despair, juggling with the usual variables of 'Where is he?', 'What is he doing?', 'Is he still alive?', 'Who
else knows of his whereabouts?', always regressed to that one irreduc-
ible question, 'Why?', and came to a halt. Was her love not enough
to keep him at home? Did nothing, no one, matter? How iron-hearted
did one have to be to walk out on everything so suddenly, so quickly?
And as easily as stepping out of stale clothes? How could she have
given birth to someone like that? Who *was* he?

At times a different light fell on the boulder weighing down on
her and it blazed into a burden of outrage: she wished she had
cracked open his skull to read his brains, riced with the maggots of
his secret thoughts, and prevented everything that followed. But that
light, too, dimmed, and she was left with the weight of the darkness
again.

In her head, she conflated several conversations she had had with
Supratik, few and far between though they were, since he had joined
college. With a mother's intuition, she had noticed that he was

changing, changing swiftly and radically, yet she could not tell in which direction or for what reasons.

'You've become very quiet. Is everything all right?' she had asked once. It was late at night; she had waited dinner for him, as always. Everyone else had eaten and gone to bed a long time ago. She broached the topic while serving him reheated rice.

'Why should everything not be all right?' he had countered.

'Such silence nowadays . . .'

'Would you like it if I jabbered away non-stop like Boro-kaki?'

'No, I'm not saying that. When you were young, you wouldn't shut up. Tearing up and down the stairs: *Ma, Ma, it's Independence Day next week, I'm going to play the bugle and lead the Balak Sangha boys in a procession down the street, will you watch me from the verandah? Ma, Ma, you will sit in the front row on Sports Day in school, won't you? Ma, Ma, look at all those lights on that house, is that a wedding? You must cover our house with fairy lights on my wedding.* What a lot of talking!'

'I'm not a child any more.'

'To me, you'll always be a child.'

'Achchha, if I have nothing to say, should I still keep chattering? People will think I've gone mad.'

'Is it true that you have nothing to say? Why? There's so much you can tell me: what you do in college, who your friends are, where you spend your time with friends, where you stay out until so late . . . My mother's heart, it'll always worry.'

'Ah, so you don't really want me to talk to you, you just want information of my whereabouts at any given time.'

'Ufff, we can't really cope with the twists and turns of your argumentative ways.'

A long pause.

'Are you angry with me?' he asked.

'No, what's there to be angry about? You'll understand when you are a father yourself.'

Another pause.

'Why do you wait up for me? I've asked you several times not to. And it's not good for your health to have dinner with me so late.'

'You don't have to think about my health. If you're so concerned, why don't you return home at a more civilised hour?'

'Ufff, I can't really cope with the twists and turns of your argumentative ways,' he rejoined, breaking into an unabashed grin.

Her heart swelled. She tried to accommodate it by changing the topic. 'You're eating like a sparrow nowadays. You've hardly touched your food.'

'You give me so much. There are so many dishes.'

'Where so many? One dal, one fry, one vegetable dish, a bit of fish, that's it.'

'And you don't think that's a lot?'

'You've eaten like this all your life,' she said, baffled.

'Don't you agree we eat too much?'

'Who, you and I?' she asked, still puzzled.

'No, no, by "we" I mean all of us, everyone in our social and economic class. Don't you think we have lots, that we could afford to lose a bit?' The grin had disappeared and all its traces too. Those big eyes flamed with a different kind of light now.

'I don't understand what you say nowadays. We have always been like this, what's wrong with our way of eating? Everyone eats like this.'

'No, not everyone eats like this, Ma.' The words were cold and heavy, like stones. 'Gagan, Madan-da, Malati-di, the other people who work for us, do they eat like this?'

'Tsk, but they are servants, they eat differently.'

'Can you explain to me why the servants eat differently while they live in the same house?' There was something else in his voice now, something cold and coiled.

'This is the way it is. It has always been like this,' she repeated, conscious now that she was failing to give him the right answer, the answer he was looking for. It was as if she had been forced to participate in an opaque game, the rules of which she didn't know. The knowledge of her failure made her even more hesitant.

'And what has always been must remain that way, must always be for evermore, right?' Again, that edge of something like menace.

'I . . . I . . . don't understand what you're saying.' Pause. 'I don't understand you any more.'

'No, you don't.' Delivered like three stabs. Then he had got up and left.

He had not spoken to her for weeks after that.

In the frenzied first two or three months after his disappearance, before she surrendered wholly to this lassitude, she and Supratik's father, aided by Priyo and Bhola, had done everything within their power to trace him. They had talked to the police, who could not or would not help because he was technically not a missing person; he had pointedly left a goodbye note. Her father-in-law's and Priyo's contacts in the Congress Party and in the Calcutta Police had not yielded much. They had paid the police under the table to turn up information on Supratik's whereabouts, even to locate, talk to and, if necessary, threaten his college friends who might have some knowledge. If anything had come of those lines of enquiry, Sandhya did not know or had not been told. She had got Gagan to drive her to Presidency College so that she could plead with the professors in the Economics Department to part with any news they might have, or anything he might have told them. She went there to find students who knew him, who were his friends – surely he must have had friends in the years above or below him – or even casual acquaintances who could throw her some scrap to sustain her diminishing life. Each time she returned home empty-handed.

Or not exactly empty-handed; the first impression she carried back with her was of dread. In the recent aftermath of the student unrest and the violence on the streets, there was a reluctance to give up information, however innocent, even to benign parties. No one knew the loyalties, affiliations or politics of anyone else: in such times it would have been foolish to open one's mouth. Accordingly, the faculty in the Economics Department professed ignorance. Amidst the usual 'There are so many who come and go every year, it is impossible to remember each and every student' and 'We teach them at this college. We do not become friends with them or gather their personal data', there was one that astonished Sandhya: 'He hardly ever attended classes. He failed his Part I exams and did not resit them.'

She stood outside classes, waiting for them to finish, and when the students streamed out, she randomly grabbed hold of some of them and asked about her son. Most of them did not seem to know Supratik and those who knew someone who might have known him redirected her. She went from pillar to post – someone could not be found, or had not come to college that particular day, or had already left – until, dizzy and weak, she returned home, swinging between hope and that familiar plummeting feeling. Day after day she went to his college, chased up elusive students, begged for names and addresses, until Supratik's father found out and put a stop to it.

'Have you gone out of your mind? What do you think you are doing? There are people already looking into this. Your weeping, pleading presence is only going to muddy matters,' Adinath raged and reasoned. 'Why don't you believe me when I say that we're doing everything, every little thing, to trace him? Isn't he my son too?'

'I am a mother,' Sandhya argued. 'How will you ever understand a mother's heart?'

Before Adinath forbade her to do her own private digging in Presidency College, Sandhya had managed to piece together a nebulous story, but one potentially so sinister that she felt she had to pass on some of the burden to her husband.

'Did you know Supratik was involved in all this student politics?' she asked Adinath.

'How do you know that?' he asked in return.

It was rumoured that a lot of students who went missing during the student violence had either been taken into custody and beaten up by the police, or had gone up to North Bengal and joined the militant Maoists in Naxalbari. He didn't know which was worse. He tried to console himself with the fact – was it a fact? – that if his son had been picked up by the police, he would have found out, sooner or later, through all the connections they had with the police and the Congress Party. As for Naxalbari, the rebellion had lasted a short four or five months: the cadres and miscreants had been rounded up, imprisoned, beaten, tortured, shot. A cold wave of fear bore him up and flung him down: surely he would have heard if something had happened to Supratik? Besides, there were two postcards to prove that he was alive, he thought, grasping desperately at anything that would keep the unmentionable at bay.

'I talked to his friends in college,' Sandhya said. 'Some say that he was an important figure, a student leader or something, although no one seems to be certain about anything. A young man called Partha said that Supratik had been expelled from college for fomenting student action; a girl called Bolan contradicted him and asked, if that was the case, why did so few people know him around college. My hands and feet turned cold with fear as I listened to them. They were very nice, they called me Mashima and gave me tea in their canteen.'

'You found out so much and didn't tell me?' Adinath asked, incredulous.

'I'm telling you now.'

'But if he was involved in student politics, wouldn't we have known?'

'How? He was always so quiet, so secretive. Just before he disappeared, he had become even more so.' Sandhya covered her mouth with the corner of her sari draped over her shoulder and neck.

Adinath tried to console her, without feeling a shred of conviction. He heard the thinness of his voice as the weak banalities – 'He might not write frequently, but at least we know he's alive and well. When he returns, we'll find out that he was up to something quite innocuous, like social work in a village, or travelling or something. Don't you worry, it'll all come good' – tried to smother the question looping and turning inside him: was his son a Naxalite?

Sandhya, on the other hand, could not bring herself to articulate the fear, even inside the privacy of her mind, and endow it with form and shape by giving it a name. That fear remained frozen in her, a vast, solid sea, but, unknown to her conscious self, she kept feeding it with the fuel that would one day combust and set it in unstoppable thaw. She read every single item in *Ananda Bazar Patrika* on the Naxalites – they were tucked away deep inside the paper and only infrequently got prominent coverage – and secretly got Arunima to translate the English articles from *The Statesman* and *Amrita Bazar Patrika*. She put dates to the violence in Naxalbari, to the eruptions of peasant violence in different parts of the country, to the Naxalite leader Charu Mazumdar's declaration, a week or two before Supratik disappeared, that hundreds of Naxalbaris were smouldering in India, that Naxalbari had not died and would never die. But, instead of teasing out the only design possible in this bunching of events, portents, rumours and facts, she smothered the cluster, pregnant with meaning, in a blanket of denial and turned her frightened self to what she did best: she became an even more ardent supplicant to her gallery of gods and goddesses.

She fasted three days a week now instead of her usual Thursdays. She found newer, more minor deities and saints to worship, each with her or his own specialisation: Santoshi-ma for lost things (her son was lost, was he not?); Manasha, so that wherever Supratik was, he was not bitten by snakes; Baba Lokenath, so that he would not come to any harm in wars, forests, rivers or seas. She awoke from dreams that her son was ill and got it into her head that he was going to be afflicted by pox, so she found the nearest temple of the goddess Shitala, whose weapons of choice were the smallpox and chickenpox germs, and lay prostrate in front of her statue for twelve hours. While she lay on the floor of the tiny temple on Abhay Sarkar Lane, just along from Jadu Babu's Market, yet another conversation, the last proper one she had had with her son, unspooled in a repetitional loop in her head.

She had been trying to tidy up his room and make his bed. 'Paper, books, more books, in all four directions. God, what a mess! Can't you be a bit tidier? You will drown under all this one day. What you read and scribble all day long cooped up in here, god alone knows.'

'Ma, do you like the life you're in?' he had asked out of the blue.

'What kind of a question is that?' She felt that sinking fear again, that anxiety, and started to steel herself.

'All this well-heeled comfort, this house, this large family, nothing wanting, no lack, no troubles, don't you find it a bit sealed off from the big world outside?'

'I have no idea what you're saying. Where do you see no lack, no troubles? Do you run the family? What do you know of how it works? Do you know what bad times our business is going through? We've had to sell off two cars, and even' – she was not sure she should be saying this to anyone, not even her son – 'some of Ma's jewellery to repay part of the bank loans. The business is on the brink of folding up in its entirety. The mills are all gone, shut. We cannot even sell off the last remaining one. Your childhood's days of ease – those are gone. Have you not noticed? But, then, how would you? You have no time for all this, all your time is devoted to your scribbling and reading and . . . and the stuff that you do when you stay away from home.' She smuggled in the final addition in a headlong rush of daring.

'Don't you ever think that we have too much, and others have too little? Take, for example, the Food Revolution agitations going on outside our four walls: do they affect us in any way?'

'By god's will we're lucky that all that unrest doesn't involve us. The one above looks after us.'

'Clearly only us, and not everyone else. You think it's the one above who looks after us? Don't you think we look after our own? Cushion our own corner and let others rot?'

'What on earth are you talking about? I don't understand you any more. It is not up to us to look after everyone in the universe. The rule of the world is to look after your family, your elders, your children, and see that you do the best you can for them all the time.'

'The rule of the world? Okay, let us assume it *is* the rule of the world, then do you think it's *right*?' He had started speaking in a way that made the italics all too obvious to her ears.

'That's . . . that's what we've believed all our lives. What . . . what we've been taught to believe.'

'Do you ever think that that's *wrong*? That what you've been given is wrong and that you have to make the world from scratch again?'

'What is all this you're talking about? I'm beginning to fear for you. You're not doing Red politics, are you?'

'Let's leave out politics for a minute. Are you happy with the inequalities of our family? Of the power-on-top-ruling-people-below kind of hierarchy? Do you think it's right? Has the thought ever crossed your mind that the family is the primary unit of exploitation?'

'Inequalities? Power on top? Hierarchy? Exploitation? What are you saying?' she found herself repeating like a slow learner.

'Fine, stay inside your bubble for as long as you can, because you won't be able to for much longer, the clock's ticking.'

The persistent rubbing against what she perceived to be her own stupidity in her son's presence, now something of a predictable pattern of things, suddenly ignited a rasp of rebellion in her; even the slowest learner in a class occasionally lets his idiocy tumble over into rage at the cleverness of others.

'All this book-learning, what good is it going to do you? We may not be learned, but we are content with our lot. I don't understand your mighty knowledge, and I don't want to,' she cried, then felt the flame of her anger snuffed out as Supratik refused to respond.

Thinking of that last exchange before Supratik disappeared, she had moved her initial focus on the mysteries and puzzles in his words – there could be no solution to those – to the regret, wringing her now, at her brief flash of temper. Was that what had driven him away, upset and hurt at her impatience with his ways of thinking? Surely that must be the reason, for what else could it be? There was only one way left for her to atone for her intemperance and that was to punish herself.

Her self-devised sumptuary rules became more and more refined: no meat, no fish, no eggs, no onions or garlic. She lost weight and had dizzy spells, seconds of blackout when she stood up too quickly from a lying or sitting position, so she took to lying down most of the time except when she had to brave the stairs to go up to the worship room on the terrace. By the time she gained it, her head spun and she had to cling to the banister in order to keep herself from falling. There were comments made about her visible debilitation, and concerns were voiced, sometimes forcefully, but she remained obdurately immured in the purity of her pursuit.

In the midst all this diminishment, she let go of her role as the eldest daughter-in-law of the Ghosh family, the person who had held it together with her efficiency, kindness and understanding. All her interest in what everyone would be fed every day, orchestrating the servants, the cook, the maids, the driver, everything withered away: she felt it was a play in which she had acted for thousands of perfor-mances, and now she had suddenly become an unengaged spectator of the repetitive drama, unable to sustain any regard for it, bored, removed, absent.

Purnima took on her role with gusto. Occasionally Sandhya heard her ill-tempered orders issuing from the kitchen downstairs – 'The mustard paste in which you cooked the fish yesterday was so bitter that we couldn't bring ourselves to eat it. How many times have I told you to grind black and yellow mustard together and put a dried chilli in it, then strain the paste? How many times, eh?' – her voice rising with every subsequent word. She found fault with everything the serv-ants did and reduced Malati to tears by scolding her for not having shelled perfectly enough the tiny shrimps that Kamala had added to a dish of arum leaves. Haranguing the servants at last gave Purnima a point of convergence for all her diffuse days and energies to focus on, and she took to it like a spindly, undernourished sapling to rich loam.

Lying in bed, Sandhya now overhears Purnima barking at one of the boys who does the trivial, miscellaneous domestic chores, and feels nothing, absolutely nothing.

On the 30th of every month Priyonath makes his way by bus from the southern boundary of Barabazar to Chitpur, over Bagbazar Khal, to a dingy alley through the godowns and slums off Kashipur and Dilarjung Roads. This humid and choking late afternoon in September is no exception. It is a long journey, and he has to change buses, but a taxi wouldn't do for these trips, and certainly not the one private car that is still owned by the Ghoshes. On these days he dresses ordinarily, even shabbily: untucked shirt, sandals instead of shoes, no briefcase. He could be an ordinary state government official.

Over the last few years, instead of excitedly anticipating what lies ahead, he has fallen into the enfeebling habit of returning in his thoughts to a juncture in his recent past that he identifies as a turning point. But every time the hope for a neat, single locus, where the bend marks the before and the after, defies him, and what he had hoped was going to be apparent as a clear turning point dissolves into something resembling an estuary, the unitary flow of events fracturing into a prodigal multiplicity of streams of cause and effect, so that he can no longer identify what or who to blame for everything that followed. And every instance of this sieving of his recollections begins with Dulal.

Madan's son, Dulal, had been a rickety teenager from the darkest depths of Orissa when he had been brought over by his father to Calcutta to be given a job by Madan's employers, the Ghoshes, at their factory in Bali in '51. When Priyo first met him over fifteen years ago he was a boy who kept searching out corners and shadows and walls so that he could hide. It had given him a little tingle of pride that Madan-da's son had since done so well. Dulal had a peasant's capacity for physical labour, so unexpected from the frame that generated it, and, it soon emerged, an even more surprising gift: an inherent talent for working with tools and machines and understanding them. Crowning these two abilities was the trickiest art, a knack for getting on well with people across all manner of divides. He was friendly, warm, caring, and everyone on the factory floor looked up to him as a kind of protective leader, a man of their own, someone who would take care of their interests. Those interests rarely clashed with those of their paymasters, as they did elsewhere in West Bengal.

When 20 per cent of the unskilled workforce in Bali had to be laid off only five or six years after Dulal's arrival, because of integrating the factory and bringing the pulp- and paper-making together under one roof, it was Dulal who had defused the potentially explosive confrontation with the union, which could otherwise have resulted, all too easily, in an indefinite shutting down of the factory. The management called him a safe pair of hands; the workers, their banyan tree. One less thing to worry about, the Ghoshes had thought and moved their attention to problems that needed fixing.

Then one day Ashoke Ganguly, the manager at Bali, had come in to see Priyo to deliver some astonishing news. Behind the scenes Dulal had been working as a CPI(M) stooge; he was the de facto union leader. He was rallying the workers in preparation for a strike.

'What are you saying?' Priyo asked. 'Are you sure about this?'

Ashoke-babu nodded vigorously, ingratiation and emphasis compressed into that one movement.

'I'm not lying, sir. You can visit and make your own enquiries,' he said. 'This is how the Party expands its supporter base and vote-bank. They send their cadres out to villages and small towns, to factories, mills, fields, farms, everywhere, and get them to join, promising them all kinds of things. Do you know, in the '54 floods, I saw this with my own eyes. The Party cadres in Bangaon, they went around in boats, doing relief-work, distributing sacks of rice and lentils, but they would give them only to people who had voted for them, not to Congress supporters. One of their biggest power bases is the unions in factories, shops, offices – every workplace you can imagine.'

'Yes, yes, I know all this,' Priyo said dismissively. What did it matter to him, this *modus operandi* of the Communist Party, as long as they were in a world far removed from his? Even then, he had trouble adding it all up and reading correctly that sum – that it *had* reached his world already.

Dulal had approached Ashoke Ganguly, demanding to know if a significant percentage of the workforce was going to be slashed because of the grim financial outlook; if yes, things might get troublesome at the factory. Things were not looking great, and because Dulal had saved them once did not mean that he could do it again.

Was Dulal threatening him?

No, not at all, but it was wise to be aware of consequences before embarking on any course of action.

Well, Ashoke-babu was going to ask for Dulal's advice when he needed it. Meanwhile, where had he picked up all these baseless rumours of redundancies?

No, he, Dulal, was just mindful of that possibility, given that times were bad. Besides, the integration and the new machines had cost people their jobs. Everything was getting mechanised nowadays, which surely meant that manpower would be less in demand. Or so people said.

Which people?

No answer.

'And are you sure he wasn't threatening you?' Priyo had asked Ashoke-babu. 'We were all under the impression that he was a force for good, you know, holding everything together. So competent and so amiable. You've brought really disturbing news.'

'No, his tone was not threatening at all. But the content . . . I decided to come to you straight away because, if there is anything the matter, then it should be nipped in the bud.'

'You've done the right thing. Definitely. And, as you know, we may soon have to discuss some reduction of the labour force there. Not just because of mechanisation, but because of . . . of other problems. It won't be possible to keep all the mills running at full capacity. But how do you think he knows? What is he going around *doing?*'

'How else but from Party HQ?' Ashoke-babu had answered. 'They know that you've had to close one of your mills' – the words had come out of an unthought momentum and he had visibly and audibly regretted them immediately afterwards – 'er . . . I mean . . . times are bad, we know . . . What can one do?'

Priyo had flinched inwardly at the correction, but had not allowed it to mark his face. The gist had been this: the CPI(M) were combing the countryside, recruiting, canvassing, and one of their policies seemed to be to target potentially troubled outfits under the same ownership. It stood to reason that if the Ghoshes had had to shut down one mill, others could be in similar danger, so the CPI(M) fanned across the provinces, looking to stir up trouble and add to their numbers. And trouble, as even a child knew, was the vivarium of politics.

A picture was coming into focus for Priyo. All the praise and endorsement and support for Dulal, which had slowly built up after he had been given a job at the mill, was turning out to be that old trick Nature used to hide poison or danger – camouflaging it in beauty; the more virulent the toxin, the more captivating its vessel.

Who could have known that behind the pleasant, reliable surface a different drama had been churning away? The soothing pictures from the past were slowly revealing themselves as optical tricks. The annual celebration of Bishwakarma Puja every September at the factory was not really the joyous congregation of factory workers and their friends and families come together in kite-flying, ceremonies, distribution of blessed offering and public feasting, but the amassing of foes for a future strike, a mobilisation of forces. That thin, pitiful face of Dulal, in which they had read, no doubt encouraged by their regard for Madan-da, a story of deprivation and blight, was, in truth, the lean and hungry look of the ever-resentful poor, trying to wring more from the people they considered infinitely rich and, if that was obstructed, then to bring them down. With the milk they gave him the Ghoshes had reared a snake.

'But does Baba know?' Priyo had asked Ashoke-babu. Prafullanath had started coming to work again, although on a part-time basis. The old man was not innocent of the knowledge of union activity in his mills, but the Ghoshes had always managed to avoid the worst of it, partly through luck, partly through Prafullanath's canny and far-seeing management policies. This new piece of information spelled setback in more than one area.

'No, not yet,' said Ashoke-babu, 'I thought I should tell you first.'

'You've done the right thing. Sit on it for a while. Baba is a bit . . .

fragile still, as you know. His health . . . We don't want anything to upset him again.'

'No, sir. Yes, sir. Absolutely, sir.'

A different line of thought opened up in Priyo's head. If union trouble did rear its head in Bali, then Ashoke-babu, as manager, had the most to fear since he would be directly in the line of fire, even physically so. Workers rarely had access to their employers, if at all; the conducting wire between labour and capital was the manager. This implied that Ashoke-babu could well be looking to sow, for whatever reason, the seeds of suspicion between Dulal and the Ghoshes. His motive remained opaque to Priyo. To protect himself? Yes, that seemed axiomatic, but only in the case of friction with the union. He was back to where he and Ashoke-babu had begun. And the futile nature of that circularity had made him decide to forget about it for the time being and watch what developed. What else could they do? Confront Dulal? On what evidence?

Barely two years after this meeting there had been some kind of a blockage at the pulp-feeding end of the Fourdrinier machine and the foreman of the factory, Sujan Hazra, had inserted his hand inside the funnel to clear it. Another worker, who had not known that this operation was in progress, had seen the machine switched off and had taken it upon himself to rectify that oversight. Sujan Hazra's right hand had been first chewed, then sliced off. The trouble, at least for Ashoke-babu, and, by extension, the owners of the factory, had not been the incident, which had been only a mishap that had befallen a stranger. The Ghoshes had paid for Sujan's initial hospital care and had assiduously circulated, in tones of great regret, the hard-nosed consolation of the doctors' supposed words – 'Only god can sew back a severed hand.' The trouble had begun a few months later, when Ashoke-babu, with the consent of his paymasters, had decided to let go of Sujan Hazra and hire someone else to replace him. Without his working hand, Sujan was not very useful; his salary was an unnecessary waste.

What unfolded next followed so exactly Ashoke-babu's forewarning that in his more deranged moments – and there were several in the months that followed – Priyo thought that the manager had somehow scripted the whole thing and then willed it into being.

Or had known about it all along because, cunning schemer, he really belonged to the other side. The union, led informally by Dulal, had reacted to the foreman's dismissal with unbending recalcitrance. The strikes began: at first, one working day of the week, but when that did not make Ashoke-babu or the ownership relent, Dulal instigated a gherao of Ashoke Ganguly in his office adjoining the mill. More than thirty workers surrounded the room, with Ashoke-babu inside, and refused to let him leave, even to go to the toilet. They chanted slogans: 'Our demands *must* be heeded, *must* be heeded' and 'Crush and grind the black hand of the owners, *crush, grind*'. They wanted the fired foreman reinstated, otherwise the entire factory would go on strike indefinitely. Nothing – threats, incentives, reasoning – could shake them from their position.

Ashoke-babu remained imprisoned by this human cordon for fifty-eight hours; his captors clearly worked on a shift-and-rota basis. At the end of the ordeal, when Ashoke-babu collapsed, the men were still unwithered, shouting out their mantras with undiminished vigour. When Dulal showed no inclination to call off his men after twenty-four hours, Adinath stepped in and requested Police Superintendent Dhar, a family friend of nearly twenty years' standing, to talk to his colleagues at Bali and have the local police deployed to break up the gherao. The arrival of the police and the crumpling of Ashoke-babu almost coincided. It was later said that if the police had not arrived, the factory workers would have happily continued until Ashoke-babu died.

The police presence was deemed intolerable by the workers, the breaking of an adamantine contractual code, something sacrilegious. Before Adi and Priyo, on the brink of firing the entire fleet with the explicit consent of their father, could make any move, Dulal ratcheted up the conflict by sanctioning a complete lockout of the mill. The long stalemate began. Posters went up everywhere, signed 'Charu Paper Mill Workers' Union', abbreviated to CPMWU. Every available external wall space was covered with angry slogans. In the bristling thicket of painted signs, all screaming imperatives, the letters CPI(M) were easily smuggled in. Priyo noticed it and knew that Ashoke-babu had been prescient. A new set of workers could be hired, theoretically, but how would they cross the picket lines that had been set up? This time the police dragged their feet about intervening because, presumably, orders had come from above, from a power higher than the informal networks of string-pulling that was the motor of Bengali life. The Ghoshes knew this or that minister, or could grease so-and-so's palms, but this economy of personal favours was less than nothing compared with the infinitely more potent arithmetic of consolidating vote-banks. Would a tiger be distracted by a toy-replica of its prey when it was following the smell of the real thing?

So the striking workers, feeling intrepid, and confident of remaining undisturbed by further police action, stayed on, beginning as a furiously boiling mass and then, over time, under the assault of the seasons and their self-willed impoverishment, simmering down until, all their heat leached, they were nothing but a thin, raggedy slum, their posters and placards faded and feeble, their numbers reduced to single figures, the huge locks on the factory gates and the threatening words on the walls mocking them as much as the evil capitalists who had brought them to such a pass.

The Ghoshes knew that bypassing them to hire a new set of workers to resume production in the mill was not a possibility, because the lockout men had the might of the CPI(M) behind them. Their visibly waning presence on the outskirts of the factory was an illusion. They might look like a tiny handful of people on the brink of beggary, but their numbers could be swelled instantly if provoked or offended; the Party would see to that. The Ghoshes' most productive factory – an output of seventy tonnes per day, down from 130 TPD in its heyday – lay fallow, an impasse so intolerable that Prafullanath swallowed his rage and humiliation and decided to confront Dulal in a private capacity and work out some kind of compromise.

If the Ghoshes had thought they had seen the worst, what with Dulal's betrayal, and the resignation of an ill and terrified Ashoke-babu, and the closure of their only profitable mill, the one that mitigated a fraction of their losses, they soon recalibrated their notion of the nadir.

When everything began to detonate in a way that seemed both unstoppably fast and yet somehow prolonged, Priyo was to persist in thinking that he had done the right thing by ignoring Ashoke-babu's early warning. His only mistake, he would grudgingly admit, and that only to himself, had been in not apprising Adinath and their father soon enough. He was back to that estuarine domain again, causality, responsibility, blame, all forking into a dizzying number of streams of 'what ifs', and he did not know which would carry him to some kind of consolation.

There is a good ten-minute walk after Priyo gets off the bus. This tributary of Nawabpatty Street is all open drains and squalid houses, densely clustered together along the lane, with rust stains from leaking drainpipes down their fronts. Plants take tenacious root in the cracks in the façade and the walls, clothes hang on lines or over railings on the verandahs. There is crumbling and broken masonry everywhere, and peeling plaster and paint, and the ubiquitous darkening presence of wrought-iron grilles and railings makes the windows and balconies look like the cages and penning coops of battery-farmed poultry. The sound from a radio left on in one of the houses drifts out into the murkiness outside and seems to contribute to the gloom, as if it has been endowed with the special quality of sucking in light. Although darkness is falling from the air and dim, naked yellow bulbs or white fluorescent tubes have started coming on, one by one, in the houses, Priyonath wonders if the lane is, even in the daytime, ever unenshrouded. It seems to him that this place lost its battle with shadows and darkness long ago and, in the uneasy treaty devised in the aftermath, the dark retreated only insufficiently into corners, waiting impatiently to flow out and take over entirely again.

Lately, the straggle of whores outside the slum-dwellings, in dim doorways like open, toothless mouths, and on the lane have begun to leave him alone and let up on the catcalls and lewd addresses. They know where he is headed and, he supposes, his particular predilections, so they almost welcome him as a regular or an old familiar. When he reaches a decrepit two-storey building, an amphibious thing between a brick-and-cement house and a makeshift slum-shack, he hesitates for a second or two before walking in. Someone has scratched the number 12/A with a piece of flint on the right-hand wall of the entrance. Inside, the dimness is exacerbated by the single strip-light burning in the front room and the pitiful attempt at papering over the squalor with framed, cheap reproductions of art, probably torn from magazines, all featuring naked women, in a move to add erotic charge to the place. Priyonath cannot identify any of the paintings, but they are conspicuously Western; of that he is certain. There is one of a nude woman, with her back to the viewer, and a winged boy holding a clouded mirror to her; another baffling, objectionable one of a little boy tweaking an older woman's nipple while standing almost behind her, the woman's smiling face turned back so that their mouths just touch. Covered with dust, the pictures hang crooked on the wall, unnoticed pieces of junk that have forgotten the role foisted on them. The place reeks of sewage overlaid with cheap incense and kerosene, and something more elementally biological for which he cannot quite find a name, something that suggests putrefying animal matter.

He walks through the front room into the inner chamber. Nandita had said she was sixteen when he first visited the place more than two years ago. She had looked a lot older, not because of her trade, or the company she kept, or the fact that she had tried to cake her face with cheap snow and powder and colour her dry lips in an attempt to look alluring, but because her eyes had not been those of a sixteen-year-old. The flash and spark, the quickness in an adolescent's eyes, had settled into a calculating lethargy, a caution that was also a hopeless inertia; they were not out of place in their turbid surroundings. After that first visit, he has tried never to look at her face.

In her room, with its meagre pallet, the grimy plastic curtain on the window and, hanging off a rusty, bent nail in a pockmarked and peeling wall, a Jay Ma Kali Jute Trading Co. (Pvt. Ltd) calendar, with its eponymous image of the fearsome black goddess made to look somehow smiling and benign, despite the garland of human skulls and her bloody red tongue, Nandita is waiting for him. He knows she is expecting him because she has a thin pile of newspapers at the foot of her bed. With a curt, 'What, ready?' he starts to take off his clothes. He fishes out a small paper packet from the pocket of his trousers and lies down on the bed in his underwear only. Even after more than a dozen sessions with him, Nandita has lost none of the hesitancy that seizes her at this stage of spreading newspapers in layers on his torso.

He chivvies her along with a gentle, 'Come' and watches her take off her cheap, glittery petticoat and blue blouse. She has dressed up for him, although that blue, easily the colour of some chemical effluent, could induce an instant headache. He says 'Come' again as she gets up onto the bed and tries to perch herself in a squatting position on the newspapers she has spread on his chest. It is just as well that she has a bony bird-like frame, otherwise it would have been difficult to have her squatting on him, her feet planted on his ribs, rather than the (to him) useless position of having himself straddled with her feet on the bed, on either side of him.

She now has her back to his face.

'Done it today?' he asks.

She takes off his briefs and says, 'No'.

'Good. So you're ready and full, right? Good girl. Try then.'

Nandita sits on him and waits for a bowel movement. None comes. Priyonath tumesces at the sight of the puckered stitch of her arsehole, its dark stain of a mouth now relaxed to let loose her uncoiling shit onto him. He starts playing with himself, but soon notices that although the lips of the hole are flexing and unflexing, nothing is emerging from it.

'What's the matter? Why are you taking so long?' he asks, his voice hoarse with arousal.

'Going to happen, wait-wait,' she says. The red glass bangles on her outstretched arms jangle thinly as she gestures to him with her hands.

A minute passes, then two. Priyonath is on his way to a full erection now, but there is still no sign of the gloriously emerging turd.

'Try a bit harder, go on. Put some pressure.'

'Just keep quiet. Rush me like this, it will go up to my head.'

After another minute of watching, Priyonath starts losing his three-quarters of an erection, but he does not want to make the girl more anxious, so he stays quiet and keeps getting limp.

Suddenly Nandita starts to strain and grunt. 'Gnnnnh, gnnnnhhhh!' – the sounds are punctuated by forceful expulsions of breath from her mouth.

Priyonath gets caught up in the exertion too. 'Once more, try once more, go on,' he eggs her on. 'I've got glycerine suppositories with me, do you want? I thought they'd come in handy.'

'What are they?' the girl asks, flushed now with all the arid effort to evacuate.

'If I put one up your arse, you'll be able to shit easily. It'll just slip out.'

'Nooooo!' the girl whinnies loudly. Her voice turns shrill and panicky: 'Last month a man showed up, a gentull-man like you, and buggered me. It was really painful and I bled afterwards, blood and blood. No way you're sticking anything up my arse.'

'Arrey, no, no, it's a small, slippery pellet. You push it up children when they have constipation. It dissolves inside and makes the resistant shit slip out softly,' he explains patiently to calm her down.

'Nothing doing. And now you jabber-jabbered so much, I lost it, it was coming down before that.'

They have also talked away Priyonath's excitement: the sleepy curl of his flaccid penis now rests against his thigh.

'Why don't you try again?' he coaxes.

Nandita compliantly grunts and strains and huffs, but Priyonath hears the excess of an empty performance, not the real thing.

'But you said you hadn't shat today, so where is it? You could have saved up from the day before – you knew I was going to come.'

At this, the girl breaks her position and gets off the bed. 'You telling me what? I deliberately holding it in?'

'No, no, I didn't say that, I was just pointing out that it might be a good idea to build up some pressure inside for a few days, in preparation for my visit.'

The girl appears to take this badly. 'You know how difficult it is to shit on demand like this? You say *Shit!* and I shit, hyan? It is that easy?' Her voice becomes louder and louder and she starts preparing her face for a bout of crying: her mouth quivers, her eyes start watering. Priyonath thinks: This is all to squeeze an extra fifty rupees out of me, the old waterworks.

What he has not reckoned for is that the brief mizzle will turn into a squall. Nandita begins by rehearsing, a bit amateurishly, a few sobs, but then gets carried away by her performance and modulates to loud, unstoppable wailing. Before Priyonath can ask her to calm down, three whores fling the door open and barge in.

'What's happened? What's happened?' a short, cylindrical woman demands. She has a face so round and fleshy that it looks as if she has got sweets tucked on the inside of each cheek. It is devoid of every single trace of benignity or kindness; she looks the sort to lead a rabble to arson, robbery or vigilante violence.

Another woman, clad only in petticoat and blouse and exposing a generous stretch of her cushiony midriff, envelops Nandita. The girl begins to sob on her shoulder.

The stout woman, clearly some sort of self-appointed leader, now takes charge. She puts her hands on her hips and turns to Priyonath, who has managed to struggle into his underwear and has moved from being supine on the bed, but only to a reclining position.

'Ei je,' she barks, 'so much the gentull-man on the outside, what you have done to this little girl, hey, what you have done?'

'Nothing,' Priyonath says, trying to put the situation into words by way of explanation inside his head, but the unconventional nature of the purpose of his visit inhibits him and prevents the words from being spoken.

This laconic reply is taken by the shouting woman as a sign of incontrovertible guilt; she pounces on her prey. 'You think we don't know what you're coming here to do, hyan? You think shirt-pant on the outside are fooling us? You think gentull-man on the outside-outside is fooling us, you son of a whore?'

Priyonath watches, frightened and aghast, silenced by the way this furious woman is whipping herself up to a pitch of such shrill rage, as more women troop into the room to watch the unfolding entertainment.

'We throw you out onto the street naked,' she shouts. 'Ask your sister or your mother to shit on you. You not coming to us for this dirty stuff any longer. We're seeing all this gentull-man stuff on the outside-outside and low dog on the inside-inside for many years, we're knowing what to do with your types.'

A supporting murmur ripples through the gathered crowd. Priyonath can see faces of children outside the window, lifting up the curtain and peering in.

'But . . . b-but . . . I've . . . she has . . .' he stammers.

'What you asking her to do, hyan? What? Why you quiet like a thief?' the pack-leader screams. She turns to Nandita and commands, 'You tell everyone here what he asking you do all the time.'

Nandita, by now whirled up in the excitement of the drama, has forgotten to continue crying. After a few nudges she sheds her coyness and reveals to everyone the services demanded of her by Priyonath. Another murmur goes through the crowd, different in tone, timbre and intent from the earlier one.

Priyonath, fearing a public beating in this insalubrious area of the city, decides to defend himself. 'She's done it before, many times, over ten times. I paid her well over the going rate. Ask her, if you don't believe me,' he says, moving his hand in a gesture that takes in everyone assembled, as though in appeal to a trial jury.

'Money?' the woman shrieks. 'You showing us the heat and dazzle of your money? We seeing it all, sister-fucker. You can buy everything with money?'

With a jolt, Priyonath notices that she has descended into addressing him as *tui*, the irreverent version of 'you'. Amidst diffuse paranoia about whether this is a set-up, one feeling isolates itself, a sense of mild indignation, so he says forcefully, 'Yes, here you can.'

He can almost see her combust into a burning column. She lets loose a jet of abuse. 'You son of a foolish fucker, I have your teeth broken with beatings. Then I plant the broken teeth in your mother's cunt, you son of a whore. When your father come to fuck her at night, he sees her cunt grinning.'

The incipient outrage at the indignity that Priyonath has fleetingly experienced now disappears, replaced swiftly by fear; it is his bowels that seem on the brink of release. His madly palpitating heart reminds him of his blood pressure. Where are his Amdepin tablets, he thinks in a stab of panic, and lifts his hands to his chest to look for the pills in the pocket of his shirt, only to realise that he is not wearing one, that his hands have touched the hairy bulge of his breast. The gurge of a new fear now adds itself to the spinning inside him. As he reaches for his clothes, the berating woman moves closer to him and demands, 'Where you think you going, hyan? Where?'

The crowd of spectators has thickened. The flapping and beating in his chest becomes more urgent. He grabs his trousers. As he is trying to get into them, a cracking slap lands on his left cheek; he has been hit by the screaming harridan. The shock freezes him for a few seconds, then the fear surges in again: what if he were beaten by this gathered crowd of prostitutes out in the open street? These things are all too common in the city, he knows. As if to stem the shame that such an event would bring about – being thrashed in public by a bordello of whores, imagine that – he looks around for the presence of a man, any man, a pimp or someone; somehow a beating administered by a man would be easier to bear.

'Give money. Give all money you have,' the woman screams, inches from his face. A sour stench gusts out from her twisted mouth. Priyonath involuntarily moves back his head. 'Give your shirt-pant. Right now, give your shirt-pant,' she orders, then snatches the trousers from his hand. She turns the pockets out: side, front, back. One hundred and seven rupees, eighty paise. The hundred-rupee note was for Nandita, payment substantially above her standard fee. Even in the middle of this thuggery, Priyonath feels a small thread of relief course through him: he has been wise in leaving his wallet back in his office, bringing only what was necessary for this visit.

The prospect of possibly no more money hidden away turns the fury even more fractious. 'Only this, byas? Where you hide the rest, hyan? Where, arse-fucker?'

Priyonath answers, 'That's all I have with me. You've checked my pockets. There's nothing in the pocket of my shirt.' He reaches out for it, shows it to her, then puts it on. The Amdepin is not in the pocket of his shirt.

'You tell me you have no money and I believe, hyan? What you take me for? That milk comes out if you squeeze my nose, hyan? Wait, I show you fun,' she says and, picking out someone from the crowd, commands, 'Go call Badal.'

There is a rustling as a few of them peel off to fetch Badal. In all probability a strongman-pimp-goon figure, Priyonath thinks, now jolted out of all residual inertia.

His cock has shrivelled to the size of a pea. He debates whether to go on the offensive, threaten with names of police and politicians, or be meek and retreating, in the hope that perhaps that will somewhat abate their concocted fury. But either stance can backfire.

A short, lean young man, with dark skin, his face pitted from a bad case of childhood pox, and oil-slicked hair combed flat over his head and ears and curling to a well-maintained wave right at the nape of his neck, walks in. He wears a tight, short-sleeved white shirt, a golden chain around his neck and a green lungi. The shirt is unbuttoned almost to his stomach, showing off his hairy chest.

Priyonath closes his eyes in terror at the thought of the physical pain awaiting him. Through the fear runs one dark thought: how is he going to explain his bruises and wounds when he gets home? Then another thought: is he even going to get home?

III

We walked the twelve miles to Majgeria. Walking will be our chief, indeed only, way of travelling from one place to another. Bus no. 11, Dhiren calls it.

We had a list of the villages in this block of the district, places that would be receptive to our mission. That particular piece of groundwork had been done for us by our All-India Coordination Committee of Communist Revolutionaries (AICCCR) cadres. Samir and Dhiren, especially Dhiren, were not new to the business of large meetings, public speeches ('fire-in-the-mouth' addresses, as they were called). I, as you well know, have no gift for the work of eloquence to move and activate. Samir was from the southern suburbs of Calcutta, Dhiren from the mofussil; both were attractive candidates for the CPI(M) since it was well known that the party recruited mostly from the provincial working- and lower-middle classes. They had been inducted to the Party early and had been doing this for longer than I had, in any case – a meeting in Sonarpur, an assembly at Bansdroni, at Chunchura, at Srirampur, swelling the numbers at a students' strike in Kanchrapara, constantly on the move: this was the real legwork. I'm not cut out for it. Maybe I grew disillusioned with 'communist' politics faster than they did. Maybe I realised earlier where the real politics lay – in the countryside.

Did I imagine it or was there really a slight distance between my friends and me, a small, cold gap that could never be bridged? That they took me as someone not quite belonging to them, despite the equality of comradeship, because I hadn't gone through the apprentice years in the CPI(M) with them? I don't know.

Sometimes, in the great silence of the nights here, when I couldn't sleep, or in the minutes before sleep took me, it was one of the many thorns that I became suddenly conscious of. But what could I do? I was made this way. Training myself to become an orator-activist would have had the end result of making me look like an animated puppet, never the real thing that Samir and

Dhiren and Biman and Badal and Rathin and Debdulal-da and others so clearly were.

I remembered a recent comment made about me at one of our secret meetings in Calcutta. These 'cell meetings' were set up in an interesting way. You went to a tiny, narrow, dense lane in Santragachhi and realised, while looking for the number that had been given to you, that no such number existed. A boy of eight or nine, playing marbles in the alley, came up to you and asked which number you were looking for. Only after he led you to a completely different number, in a different lane, did you realise that the deliberately wrong number that you were initially meant to look for functioned as a kind of password. The boy was part of the game. Anyway, all this by way of saying that at one such meeting, full of young men my age, mostly, and a couple of more senior men, one of these older leaders had asked the assembled activists, barely hiding his contempt and speaking of me in the third person – Will he be able to last the race? After all, everyone here is of a certain kind of background, we've all led tough, hardbitten lives, we know about life's difficulties . . . whereas . . . he is from a different world altogether. A prince, really. Will the prince be able to become one with his subjects?

There were some muffled titters after that.

Those words came back on sleepless nights and rang repeatedly in my soul's ear.

Sometimes I felt I was behind the curve, missing out on the crest of the vital activities. I had sat in the city and devised elaborate theoretical strategies for: 1) building a village defence force in every village to protect the residents from police attacks, and attacks from the lumpens paid by class enemies; 2) directing crop production; 3) arbitrating disputes among farmers; and 4) setting up people's courts to judge and punish class enemies and their agents and flunkies. Others, meanwhile, had been the ones to work actually in the villages, with the farmers, watching them sow and harvest, talking to them day after day, listening to the problems they had with the village head or landlords and moneylenders. What do I know of crops?

Well, I found out. And alongside knowledge of agriculture came also the knowledge of how much was being done by my comrades.

This is what Samir said – When we first came here a few months ago, in the summer, they thought we were another party looking for votes. If they could have brought themselves to do it, they would've set upon us with their lathis. First of all, they vote for whoever the village head asks them to cast their vote for: either for the twin-bullocks sign or the hammer-and-sickle sign. The head is paid in kind for this, you know, his food grains taken care of for a year, or a parcel of land suddenly made out to his name. No such rewards for the farmers, mind you. And there's a lot of murderous rivalry going on with acquiring these vote-banks, as you can imagine. Two years ago, during the drought, CPI(M) cadres were doing some relief work here, distributing sacks of grains to hard-hit villagers, but on the understanding that they would be casting their vote for the hammer-sickle-star. The aid relief was received only by villages that have always voted for them. There had been some mistake: some people in Changripota had already received some rice from the relief people when it was discovered that they had voted for Congress in '62. The cadres went back and took away the rice from the starving farmers.

So it wasn't easy for us to convince them that we hadn't come for their votes. One of them spat at us, an old man, thin, wiry, a bit stooped, white moustache on a black face. He said, 'Twenty years we've been independent of foreign rule, but things have remained the same for us. No, they've got much worse. At that time we used to be told that the sahebs are sucking our blood dry, the sahebs are taking our land away, our crops away, the sahebs have stolen all our possessions from us, but the sahebs have long gone now, why are things still the same? We're foolish, illiterate people, we can't read, we don't understand much, but we understand at least this: the bloodsuckers are still there, their skin colour has changed. That's the only change that has happened.'

– Later I found out that this man, Mukunda Mashan, used to be the tenant of four bighas of land. His father had been the tenant on it before that. Under the Land Tenure Act, Mukunda was eligible for occupancy because his father and he had rented it for so many years. When the government officials came to measure the land in this area, the jotedaar gave Mukunda a choice: if Mukunda wanted to register as a tenant, he would be evicted immediately; if he didn't, he would be kept on as a tenant. What would he feed his family, what would he eat, how would they live if he got evicted? And in these times? And you know how people like to say that listening to what the landlord says, obeying him, is hard-wired in these classes of people. But the landlord and his legion of supporters and yes-men have other ways too: arbitrarily increasing rents, say, from half the yield on the land to three-quarters; or killing the tenant's bullock so that he cannot work the rented land efficiently enough, thus falling behind with the rent; a son or a daughter or a wife threatened . . . these are probably some of the more benign methods of intimidating him. Fear is a much more reliable tool than hard-wiring, no?

– And then there's good old deceit: the jotedaar didn't tell Mukunda that if he registered, he <u>couldn't</u> be evicted, because of the number of years that had passed in their tenancy. They were illiterate people, so they didn't, couldn't, find out more. Mukunda thought that things had ticked along without registration for two generations, so what did it matter now? On top of that, Mukunda belonged to a lower caste, so it was not in the interest of the village head or any official to enlighten him. Soon after that the jotedaar evicted him anyway, and Mukunda had no recourse to the law because he was not the officially registered tenant.

So the jotedaar pushes a family down, a demotion really, from tenants to wage-labourers, a demotion from year-round work to work for a quarter of the year. We know what that means for the family. And all for what purpose? To add four bighas of land to his existing 250.

This was something about human nature I'd never been able to understand. Why did words such as 'sufficient' or 'enough' have no meaning, no traction in our lives? Greed ate the soul. Sometimes I felt that the haves in our society became giant magnets and, following some law of physics or astronomy transposed to human affairs, sucked in more and more, enlarging their states. You know that Arunima goes to a missionary school, so she has to study the Bible. I have occasionally browsed through her copy. One day a sentence leaped out and hit me between the eyes: 'For everyone who has will be given more, and he will have an abundance. Whoever does not have, even what he has will be taken from him.' This was the way the world was, so why did I refuse to acknowledge and accept this truth? Why did I keep pushing against it and fighting it as if it were the greatest wrong in the world? Not as if; it <u>was</u>. That was why the only way to live was to battle its great error.

Teaching the small farmers, the daily-wage labourers and the sharecroppers the politics of class was not my duty. Samir and Dhiren were seeing to it. They said that class analysis was something they found easy to get across. The day-labourers had an intuitive understanding of it. All over the villages here our comrades have fanned out, taking on the task of first educating the farmers, giving the examples of peasant revolutions from the last twenty years – Tebhaga and Telengana and Naxalbari – to encourage and enthuse. I was beginning to think that the basic work, a belief that things could not, need not, remain the same for ever, had been achieved.

A little politics lesson now (I promise to keep it short):

These regions had seen, in the last few years, a radical solution to the reduction of enormous landholdings by greedy jotedaars. Landless peasants, organised under some leftist party or another, have marched on Congress-supporting jotedaars, carrying knives and spears and lathis and axes, have driven out the landlords, planted red flags on the four corners of his illegally acquired (and illegally consolidated) land, distributed their hoarded grain, seized their crops. What were the police doing in all this? you may ask. Nothing. Orders had come from up high, from the CPI(M) headquarters, that this was legitimate, this was the true democratic struggle, the first step towards land reform and the ultimate abolition of private ownership of land.

Was it?

No.

At first I too thought that it was. As Harekrishna Konar, the then Land Minister, put it: abolition of large-scale landholding → distribution of land to the landless → education of peasants in the disadvantages of cultivating small landholdings → peasants voluntarily adopt collective farming → END OF PRIVATE LAND-OWNERSHIP. Five easy steps, and the first two were already under way, the second one with the support of the police.

How wrong I was. How innocent I was not to have understood the vote-bank calculus of the CPI(M). By appearing to be on the side of the landless peasant, they added nearly five lakh of them to the party in a clean, swift stroke. You had to admire them for their far-seeing chicanery. They had no intention of pursuing real and radical land reforms, as envisioned by Charu Mazumdar. They only wanted enough votes so that they could come to power in West Bengal as a majority, not in a coalition, as they are now, in the United Front.

Their mask slipped when Naxalbari happened. They had not reckoned for this – they had wanted the peasants to stay within the boundaries set by them. They underestimated what would really happen if the landless were given a taste of their own power. So when that began to happen, the CPI(M)'s true colours were revealed – every bit as reactionary as the Congress, every bit as supportive of the Establishment, as fearful of upsetting the apple-cart, as ingratiating to the central government . . . If they alienated the central government with their tacit, even open, support of all this militancy and land-grabbing, they would never come to power in the state. So they had to trim their sails to that end.

We had decided early on to avoid the villages that had seen this kind of state-sanctioned land-grabs. Admittedly we would have had an advantage if we'd gone there – we would have had far less work mobilising, because farmers would already have been organised and militised (up to a point). But there were disadvantages too: 1) we were the erstwhile radical wing of the CPI(M), some of whom had been expelled from the Party in June last year, so any CPI(M)-led farmers' movement to redistribute land and kill landlords, however much our aims coincided (again, up to a point), would not have been sympathetic to our invitation to move even further to the left towards guerrilla action; 2) we worked in units of three to seven in each village, so we were nothing against the might of the bigger, better and more centrally organised CPI(M) cadres; 3) landlords were not stupid people. Wherever the CPI(M) had organised peasant-led forcible land redistribution, the landlords had quickly sworn allegiance to the CPI(M), paying protection money to the Party's local leaders, so that the land they held far in excess of the ceiling wouldn't be grabbed by the landless peasants marching against them. Classic CPI(M) politics, it has to be said; petty-bourgeois revolution-mongering.

There wasn't enough space in one farmer's hut to put up the three of us together so we went to different places – I was billeted in Kanu Mahato's, Samir at Anupam Haati's, Dhiren at Bipul Soren's.

Early winter afternoon: green and brown everywhere under a white-blue sky. And much cooler than in the city. There was a constant breeze that was very enjoyable in the sun, then it gave us goosepimples after the sun went down. Flocks of chirruping birds flitted above. The fields were parcels of straw-coloured gold where the paddy was almost ripe. Occasionally, tiny pairs of frantically gesticulating hands emerged from the top of this uniform gold sea, their position in it changing rapidly. I realised that there were children, entirely hidden by the crop, running around inside.

– They're chasing off babui pakhi, Dhiren said.

So this was the weaver bird.

Something happened to me when I saw the children going about this job as if they were playing. Well, they <u>were</u> playing; they were running across the fields and wheeling their arms about and shouting at the birds and waving them away. They used a scarecrow as a post that marked either a beginning or an end to their game. Something happened to me and I wanted to run into the fields and join them, waving my arms over my head, copying the children. What looked graceful when they did it, in me, I was sure, was going to appear ungainly, making me resemble some kind of lunatic on the run. I would explain to them that I was a scarecrow, a live scarecrow, as big as the rag-and-stick-and-earthenware-pot one they had in the corner. Soon we would all be shouting and running about in the golden paddy, the flocks of birds above us dispersed.

The fantasy too flitted away like the birds.

I asked Samir and Dhiren to accompany me in two reconnoitres of our hamlet, once while there was still daylight and the other in the total darkness that was the village night. Some of the plots were tiny, say, about four or five times the size of our garden. How much rice would each yield? Not enough to feed one person for a couple of months. My head spun when I tried to think what the peasants ate for the remainder of the year. The breeze set the paddy swaying. It gave out a sound somewhere between rustling and rattling.

Dhiren said — We'll have to learn how to use the sickle soon.

A meaningful look passed between the three of us. We had our eye on three huge acreages on the other side of the village, beyond the outer edge. Three enormous fields belonging to the three big jotedaars of the village — Haradhan Ray, Kanai Lal Kuiti, Bhaben Sinha.

At our end of the village, the Mahato and Santhal end, there were banana and palm trees all around us. I pointed out possible exits and escape routes. The crop-filled fields might shelter us now, but after the harvest they would be open stretches of pure danger where we would be completely exposed.

Samir said — We'd never make it.

Nervousness was something all too easy to activate in him. I said — Look around you. Don't you see the forests?

— But they're some distance away. We'd have to cross these bare fields to get to them.

Dhiren said — It'll all appear different at night. They won't be able to make out one person, dressed in black clothes, running across these fields in the dark.

Samir wasn't convinced. He said — But there'll be many of them and only three of us. And they'll be armed to their teeth: sticks, axes, knives . . . They'll hunt us down.

He had that familiar wobble in his voice that made Dhiren and me erupt into laughter each time we heard it. But not this time. This time we were in the field of action, not in the safe luxury of imagining it while sitting in Calcutta.

Dhiren said — You know the line, no more than three to five people in a squad.

The words were meant to instil determination, but they came out hollow.

Everyone went to sleep around seven or seven-thirty. It was the rhythm of life in the hamlet. During the growing and harvesting season, the farmers were too exhausted after a day's toil in the fields to stay up for longer. Besides, kerosene, or any other oil, was in short supply and to stay awake would mean burning already-tiny rations.

Being on the outskirts of the village, we weren't far from the jungle: bamboo groves, a pond, little copses, fields, another small pond, the burial grounds of the Santhals, then forests of sal, mahua, kendu. The effect of moonlight on the trees and fields, with no sound or other light to dilute the experience, was startling and pure. I'd never seen anything like it, or rather, what I'd seen so far now struck me as having been a very adulterated version of the real thing. It silenced us. There was only the sound of the breeze. The night was cold, and clear as glass. We had many things to talk about – where to hide our weapons, which route to take when walking all night to the next village, how to go about getting together small groups of farmers without arousing anyone's suspicions – but this bath of silvery light made those discussions appear as small violations.

Dhiren broke the silence by starting to hum a tune under his breath, very gently and with feeling. It sounded so familiar that for a second or two I was fooled into thinking that it was a revolutionary anthem, until I got it. It was as far away from revolution as that moon was from this hamlet. 'The smile of the moon has spilled over its banks' . . . that was the song. I knew it because I'd heard Pishi sing it on moonlit summer evenings on the terrace. I was filled with – with what? An affectionate contempt? A sense of ridicule? Shock that Dhiren, the earthy, self-styled tough guy, had any truck with the kind of music he'd consider effeminate? Tagore seemed to be carried inside all Bengalis, regardless of class or social background, like some inheritable disease, silent, unknown, until it manifested itself at the unlikeliest of times. How irredeemably middle-class all this was: The Little Red Book and On Practice on the one hand; on the other hand, the poetry of Jibanananda Das in his cloth sidebag and a coy, cloying Tagore song almost involuntarily on his lips. There really was no hope of escape for us.

I wondered if I should say something about the absurdity of this. Could I get it across with humour and warmth and lightness? I decided to hold my tongue. Then, all of a sudden, I was blurting out – For god's sake, Mao by day and Tagore by moonlight?

Dhiren didn't miss a beat. He put his right arm around my shoulders and said – That's the quintessential Bengali soul for you. Did you think that because I come from a poor, lower-middle-class set-up, my kind wouldn't have been touched by culture?

I couldn't see his eyes in the dark, but I could certainly hear the big, teasing smile in his voice.

I said – But that particular song is such rubbish! It's supposed to be about a full-moon night and he brings in blue skies and flying birds . . . which just goes to show that the quintessential Bengali soul is both confused and inconsistent.

And I almost forgot to tell you one big reason why we were in this corner of West Bengal: this was the hamlet where Nitai Das killed his family – his wife, his son, his two daughters – and then swallowed poison last year in May.

CHAPTER FOUR

Not all family bonds are equal. The lie so assiduously propagated by mothers – 'How can you ask who is my favourite? They are all my children, I love all of them equally. Are you partial to one finger of your hand over another?' – is disbelieved by everyone, yet it is quite astonishing what pervasive currency it has in the outward show of lives. Everyone is hectically denying the existence of favourites, of special affections and allegiances and alliances within a large group of siblings, or between parents and children, while, just under the surface, the empty drama of equality is torqued to its very opposite by the forces of conflicting emotions and affinities.

The Ghosh family unwittingly followed this paradigm with slavishness. The existence of four brothers and one sister, with a gap of twelve years separating the oldest from the youngest, meant that the siblings, with the exception of Somnath, were close in age. Priyo and Chhaya were born almost back-to-back, within a year of each other. If a reason had to be found for their extreme closeness, this could do for the moment. It was said that the first word Chhaya uttered was 'Dada', even before 'Ma' or 'Baba'; no one really cared that this was not a very robust proof, especially since, defying the laws of appellation in a Bengali family, Chhaya called Priyo by his first name and reserved 'Dada' for Adinath.

As children, they had formed one unit, slightly separate from the other two. In any game, Priyo and Chhaya could be relied upon to gang up with each other against Adi and Bhola. They helped each other cheat in hide-and-seek even if they were on opposite sides: Chhaya gave away the hiding places of Adi and Bhola if Priyo was doing the seeking, and Priyo kicked up a fuss if Chhaya was made the seeker, wanting to join her instead of hiding with his brothers. In a game of 'Blind fly buzz-buzz', Priyo left subtle clues for the blindfolded Chhaya to locate the others. The real game for them was the inset one, the one of how not to make their collusion transparent, rather than what they came to consider as the framing game; in that, they had little or no interest. It was the embedded core of duplicity and coalition that got them going. The effect of this was the inevitable withering away of the assumed game to a boring charade, and it took Adi and Bhola years to understand why all the games they played between the four of them turned out to be so wet, so unexciting, when those identical ones with their other friends retained their element of fun and spark. They shouted, 'Cheating! Cheating!' at their middle siblings, because they instinctively understood that some vital element was missing, but could not put their fingers on what exactly was undermining everything.

Before long, Priyo and Chhaya were left to their own devices, which was what they had desired all along. They designed games no one else could understand. Even their mother started to comment, 'You are like twins, you think each other's thoughts and say each other's words.' They sat next to each other in the back seat of the car, or on a train or bus. Other members of the family took to leaving a seat beside Chhaya vacant, for they knew it was marked for Priyo.

At an enthusiastically planned function on a summer evening on the terrace of 22/6, a sort of informal private variety show, with the children and other members of the family and friends from the neighbourhood acting in skits, singing, miming, and a clothes line with two or three huge bedcovers serving as the curtain separating the 'stage' from the audience, six-year-old Priyo sang, 'There's a game of hide-and-seek between the sun and the shade in the paddy fields today / Who has set afloat boats of white clouds in the blue sea of the sky?', while Chhaya danced across the concrete, gracefully miming the words: here covering her little face with her tiny hands and uncovering it again, there joining her hands to form a boat and lifting them up above her head, fluttering her child's fingers to indicate the expanse of the sky . . . She knew the song well: a music teacher, Shipra-di, had just been engaged to come to the house and give the little girl singing lessons, and this was the first Tagore song that she had been taught. The applause was deafening. In the audience, Charubala and Prafullanath beamed and looked triumphant.

For months afterwards, whenever anyone saw the boy and the girl, they went into raptures about the pair's magical performance until it became a kind of local legend, sticking, with increasingly piteous glamour, to the lives of Priyo and Chhaya like the residue of a lingering illness. Even when they started going to college, elderly men and women of Basanta Bose Road, whose lives consisted only of chewing the cud of memory, reminded them of that performance, drawing from them strained smiles that never quite managed to reach their eyes.

Seven years after that memorable evening on the terrace, the connection between Chhaya and Priyo edged, more by chance than natural progression, into a different territory. At that time, Charubala and Prafullanath occupied the first floor with their daughter and youngest son, while the three older boys lived on the second floor. At around noon one Sunday, Charubala was harrying all her children to have a bath and get ready to sit down for lunch. Priyo, discovering that the bar of soap in the bathroom upstairs had been worn down to a tiny nub, ran to fetch a fresh one from a bathroom downstairs. The door was closed, as always, but not locked, so he pushed it and rushed in.

The rest happened in increasingly suspended time, moving from fast to very, very slow as if the events had been rolled into a small ball and shot with force through a tube of viscous liquid. Chhaya was squatting on the latrine built into the floor, letting out a large, dark cheroot of turd. Before the shriek from Chhaya's horrified open mouth could become sound, Priyo raised his index finger to his lips and, in one seamless movement, reached back his hand to slip the shutter into its catch and lock the door. There was a quiet, calm majesty in his gestures, as if he had rehearsed this episode numberless times in the recent past, that settled Chhaya. Priyo leaned back against the wall, silent, watching with a devouring intent. As the convergent point of that gaze, Chhaya became a pliant puppet, almost with no will of her own, carrying on her unspeakably private hygiene activities as if she were all alone. The silence in the bathroom, punctuated by the drip-drip-drip of the tap onto the water's surface in the full bucket under it, conducted Priyo's supplication, and Chhaya's instant granting of it, in a way that would only have been ruined by language.

Priyo watched Chhaya sluice her arse, pour four big mugs of water down the latrine to flush the shit away, then wash her hands with soap. There was no trace of shame or inhibition in her, just the abiding fluidity of something routine done without thought. Very oddly, the threshing that had taken over Priyo's insides served only to calm and slow him down. He watched his sister, oblivious to any potential discovery, oblivious to any sense of wrongdoing, of shame, a statue of solid desire.

From outside came the frantic symphony of everyone going about their busy Sunday routines: the clatter-and-hiss from the kitchen downstairs; the chaotic bass of footsteps of people running up and down the stairs; music from the gramophone in his parents' room; and, as the top line above all this, Charubala's barrage of instructions and commands – 'Madan, if you leave grinding it till late, no one will be able to eat poppy-seed fritters with their dal'; 'Adi-i-i-i, have you had your bath?'; 'Chhaya-a-a-a-a, are you still hogging the bathroom? Do you think no one else needs to use it?' – while she thud-thudded around the first floor.

At the sound of her name Chhaya panicked, but only briefly because Priyo stepped forward and turned on the tap. The water ran; added to this sound was the one of water overflowing the rim of the bucket, splashing onto the floor, running and gurgling down the drain. More time passed, although neither could have guessed how much. This dent in the normal perception of things was nowhere more apparent than in the continuation of the trance-like state brother and sister found themselves in, even when their mother came to the bathroom door and hollered, 'Chhaya, I can hear running water, there are five others in the house needing a bath, if you finish all the water the pump will have to be turned on again.' Once again, the arc of private, silent language welded Priyo and Chhaya together as she replied from inside, raising her voice, 'Ma-a-a-a, forgotten to get my chemise, will you fetch one for me? The yellow, floral one. It's on the clothes-horse.' From outside, an irritated response from Charubala, 'Ufff, unbearable all this running around, serving . . .', receding further. Stillness for the measure of one-two-three beats. Then, in a movement that could be missed in a blink, Priyo opened the bathroom door and slipped out and Chhaya locked it again. Madan-da and the servants were in the kitchen downstairs. From Baba and Ma's room came the raspy wailing of the Atulprasadi song Baba was listening to on the gramophone: 'Fill me right up to the brim, fill up my life'.

The incident was never repeated.

Somnath was nearly four at the time. Born seven years after Bhola, he had, at first, seemed like an afterthought, added distractedly after the main story. But the coda became more important than what preceded it. The deeper, more recessed locks of the dams of affection were opened for the baby in the family; he was everyone's *golden moon*, the *iris of their eyes*, the *radiant prince*. Where Madan and the other servants had entertained the children with cautionary tales and stories that sent a tiny current of fear through them – stories of snakes biting children, children falling off trees or drowning in ponds, children tumbling to their deaths while flying kites from terraces without raised boundary walls, children tailed by evil spirits or possessed by malicious devils – for Somnath only the loveliness was ever distilled. There were stories of beautiful princes on their beautiful white, winged steeds; the prince always bore the name 'Somnath'.

With his head of glorious loose curls, his fair skin, his chubby cheeks that dimpled when he smiled, his huge brown eyes, the term 'prince' seemed to be something he had a natural right to. Even Charubala, whose closeness and partiality to her firstborn, Adi, had by then ceased to be an open secret and become more of a much-narrated family story, even she felt the beginning of a new season in her. He could only be a blessing. Her husband's business moved up several gears after the birth of Somnath; he was clearly an auspicious child. Prafullanath, who did not bother himself with the bringing up of children, considering it wholly women's domain, Prafullanath, who did not go in for displays of fatherly affection or demonstrations of love or the occasional playing with his children, singing to them, telling them stories, whose onward narrative of life was not temporarily slowed by the parenthetical presence of the silly, playful, giddy expressions of love between parent and baby, even buttoned-up, costive Prafulla had his head turned by his new son. Like a bad comedian, who elicits laughter of derision and not the laughter resulting from successful comedy, the noviciate Prafullanath hit the wrong notes when he tried to do the traditional things with his baby. While throwing Som up in the air and catching him, an act that had the boy almost choking with delight, Prafullanath's mouth became a rictus of tension, his face a pinched, nervous mask, as if he knew he was performing badly at an audition for the role of easy, happy father. His songs were strained, off-key and tuneless, his recitation of children's rhymes strangulated, his dandling of the toddler on his knees stiff and regimented, the silly nothings and baby talk embarrassed. He appeared to be a marionette playing the role of father in a puppet play. The awkward matter of his heart would not animate his limbs and eyes, and yet that unaccustomed heart swelled with love and a kind of seduction, of bewitchment. This was a child, he knew, to whom he could not say no, one who would escape the strictures of discipline, of the tiniest of harsh words or irritated looks; an angel cannot offend.

This behaviour stood in marked contrast to his attitude towards his other four children. Always a stern and distant yet dutiful father, Prafullanath, because of his private history, would have been opposed to a notion of fatherhood that could consist, as well, of intimacy with children, of becoming a child with them, yet he would have been surprised if he had been told that he was not a loving parent. Mollycoddling was the mother's duty; the father's lay elsewhere. As a consequence, his four older children feared and respected him, as they had been taught to do, and the love they professed to feel, had they been asked and had they answered truthfully or even had access to that truth, was of a duty-bound, obligatory kind too, a love issuing from commandment and tradition and the notion of family, not one from the tides of the heart or the unbridled, inexplicable pull of feelings. If painted, that love would take the form of a polite and manicured wash of pleasant colours, not the hurl-and-splatter of impastoed reds. But having been the victim of the unintended consequences of his own father's love for him, Prafullanath had been unconsciously moulded by forces in a way that had resulted in him becoming a fair if unpassionate father, or at least one who was undemonstrative with his fatherly feelings. Probably some deep instinct for protecting one's offspring from internecine relations, from being exposed to the depredations of rivalry, as he himself had been, dictated to him that cast of personality. Yet with Somnath, the workings of this instinct slid into his blind spot; just as he did not know that he was not an expressively affectionate father with his four older children, he also did not realise he had become exactly that with his youngest.

When Adinath was born, Prafullanath had been cheered that his first child was a son because he could hand over, in time, the reins of the small paper business he had built from scratch and close his eyes in peace. That is what a son was for. Accordingly, the special place that Adi held in his father's regard was almost exclusively connected to his future role as helmsman. But by the time Adi turned one, Prafullanath's ambitions had swelled; he wanted his son to start a construction business, while he would consolidate the paper one, which could provide Adi with the start-up capital necessary for his scheme. He and his son, or sons, could run at least two, if not several, business empires together, not be confined by having to pass the baton of one trade down the line, as his grandfather, his father, his half-brother – and he too, had he not decided to disrupt the relay – had done to such baneful effect. Once again, an instinct, which had germinated in the turbulent soil of his past, led him to insure himself and his sons against any such possibility resulting from following a monadic trade; thus, the branching out. The idea of several different pieces joining up to form a pied world appealed to him. He had experienced the opposite paradigm, of one family business growing and becoming bloated and sick down the generations, leaking its toxins to those who inherited it, and he did not want that for his sons.

So, from a very early age, Adi was groomed by his father, trained in the language and texture and details and workings of the construction business. As a boy, Adi had heard from his father how houses were built: how concrete was mixed; what the functions of the various components of concrete were; how a collection of tall iron rods provided the spines of a building; how foundations were laid. This complemented, often substituted, the stories children are usually told, stories of djinns and fairies, of a prince whose life was tied to a gold chain that lived in the stomach of a giant carp in the pool of the palace gardens, stories from the *Mahabharata*, of Abhimanyu who had learned, while he was in his mother's womb, the secret of breaking into an impenetrable phalanx, but not the secret of emerging from it. Adi assimilated the fundamentals of construction in stories. When he started going to Ballygunge Government High School and, like all children at a certain age when they are unstoppable with their questions, he too spent the entirety of his talking time asking endless whys and hows, Prafullanath channelled this curiosity to focus on buildings, on the strength of materials, on bricks, mortar, lime, sand, cement. The foundations were imperceptibly laid.

Prafullanath, on returning home in the evenings from the office he still retained where he had started up, in Old China Bazar Street, used to holler out 'Adi-i-i-i' as soon as he crossed the threshold. The boy, stationed on the ground-floor verandah, already on the lookout for his father's return, would rush to him only after that deep, elongated call. Out would come something from the pocket of his father's panjabi or his black Gladstone bag: a dozen A.W. Faber coloured pencils or a roll of discarded planners' drawing paper.

'Look what I've got you,' Prafullanath said.

Adi nodded, too happy to speak.

'Come, let's have our tea in the sitting room and you can draw your Baba something with this. What is it going to be today?'

'The house that I'll build and we'll all live in,' the boy answered, not one whit of delight diminished from the game father and son had played dozens of times before.

'Well, well. Let us see how grand this house is going to be and whether we'll all fit in. You have to build a big, big house. Right, tea now.' Another holler – 'Mada-a-a-n.'

As Madan came from the kitchen at the back of the house with fried diced coconut and other savoury snacks on one tray and a maid, following, with the tea paraphernalia on another, Adi was already on the floor, pages strewn everywhere, busy erecting his house on paper. Over three or four years he had perfected his vision. From crooked lines and scribbles he had moved on to the basic shape of a house, a tall rectangle with a mouth-like door and the two eyes of windows, every single line at an angle or slightly wobbly, but the whole discernible as a diagram of a basic house-like structure. The lines had become straighter, stood at sharp right-angles to each other, the door had acquired a knocker, the front of the house a garden and steps leading to the door. Then, as Adi and his competence grew, the ideal house became proportionately detailed and mature. He kept a running commentary going as he carefully moved his hand about, his face radiant with effort and concentration, the tip of his tongue sticking out from one corner of his mouth, a habit his father found adorable.

'One storey . . . two storeys . . . three storeys. Now, a front verandah on each floor. Round verandah or straight verandah, or a hanging one? Ummm, let's try a round one this time . . . How many windows on the front? Eeesh, my hand shook a bit there, the line's not quite straight . . . Now, the garden. Here, a bed of roses. Let's keep the shiuli shrub, a lot of fireflies sit on it at night – I like them. What about a fountain? Or a pond, in which golden fish will play? Shall I put a dovecote on the roof?'

He talked to himself while the pencil in his hand moved over the space of the sheet of paper in a slow, cautious dance, smearing on it the geometry of his dreams. Prafullanath and Charubala, who had come downstairs to tend to her husband, let him chatter on. Once or twice, the boy's father would intervene.

'Bah, first-class! Excellent. It looks grand. Now what about the interior?'

'Interior?' Adi repeated, baffled. What did his father mean?

'You've drawn how our house is going to look from the outside. But what about the inside – the different rooms, the staircase, the courtyard?'

How could these be shown in one drawing? Adi wondered. 'You mean, draw each room, one by one?' he asked hesitantly.

'Aha,' said his father, his eyes gleaming. 'There is a way of showing the whole house from the inside in one drawing.'

Adi, now even more confused, asked, 'But how? There are walls . . . and floors and . . . well, floors and ceilings between storeys. How can . . . how can *one* drawing show all the rooms on different floors?' The boy didn't have any notion of or terms for isometric projection, perspective and three-dimensionality, and his mind was trying to stretch itself around that lack.

'We'll have to learn that,' his father said. 'But not now. When you're a little older, you'll learn how to do it. But it won't look like your house from the outside; it'll look different, not like a house at all. But enough. Why don't you go and share your pencils and paper with your brothers and sister?'

Priyo and Chhaya had been waiting upstairs on the balcony that ran the inner perimeter of the house on each floor, circling the courtyard in a squarish formation. As Adi ran up the stairs, Chhaya advanced towards him excitedly, 'Show us, show us what your father's brought you today.'

Many years later, an unbidden memory of that casual, unpremeditated possessive adjective, 'your', before 'father', was to give Adi another lesson in perspective and the layout of the interior world. But now it did not strike him at all. The three of them oohed and aahed over the pencils, admired Adi's drawing, then decided to give a few of the pencils and some paper to Bhola, who was only three at the time, to see how he would delight in them. Off they went.

At school, Adi slowly started picking up how to represent three dimensions in two, the elementary rules of perspective, the difference between photographic representation and stylised diagrams. He was not formally taught all this, but found his way in slow degrees. Then Somnath was born and things got further deferred. The baby grew, gathering to himself all the skeins of love and attention in the house, and wrapped himself in a tight cocoon with them. The diagram of the interior of the house remained untaught by Prafullanath and undone by Adi, at least for now.

Somnath's birth was like the sudden appearance of a blazing comet or a new planet in a known alignment of heavenly bodies: a previously understood system was now dented by a new presence and had to be subjected to a recalibration, a new set of calculations. No one could predict how the alliances and balances of different forces that kept everything in a stable equilibrium would now respond.

Initially, it was all jubilation at the birth of a baby brother. Adi, at twelve, was growing too old to find it such a thrill, although he appeared to participate in the general festal mood, at least until eighteen months or so down the line, when he began to discover the facts about human reproduction, and the proximal nature of the two, the recent baby brother and birds and bees, filled him with distaste, embarrassment and, at times, a physical sense of revulsion. He stayed up thinking uneasily about carnal intimacy between his parents, such *recent* sexual congress between them, and felt a mild nausea. He could not look at the curly-haired, cooing toddler without the shadow of shame falling over his own self. He became parsimonious and stilted with the expressions of affection – almost paternal, given the age difference – expected of him.

He saw his father trying to catch fireflies for the four-year-old Som and the initial, momentary enchantment, during which he even toyed with the idea of running out to pick up the little boy and get him closer to those magical, flickering points of living light, suddenly become soiled by that familiar cloud of queasiness. He watched the whole family caught up in a huge song-and-dance to feed his little brother (a fussy eater) – Madan-da distracting Som by pointing out pigeons in the attic of the house next door and singing 'Come, come, o long-tailed bird', Chhaya shaking rattles and belled anklets and doing peek-a-boo with a shiny scarf, their mother making little patties of Som's food and planting tiny florets of cauliflower on top, in an effort to convince him that they were little wooded hills and wasn't he a brave giant to swallow them one by one – and Adi felt a cindery taste on his tongue that was nothing but pity and a hooded distaste for his mother. But not for a moment did these unaccommodated intrusions impinge on his relations with the child, for whom he was bound by the bonds of family to feel the protective love of a much older brother.

When Bhola had his plum position as the family's youngest child usurped by Somnath, he was only seven years old. In one of those wholesome surprises that a family can occasionally throw up, Bhola, instead of grudging Som the privilege that had been his for so long, took his baby brother to his heart. He stared and stared, in the beginning, at this tiny, warm, quick thing, no bigger than a large toy, then took to devouring him with his eyes when he was asleep; when he was blinking and awake, bringing up liquid ropes of curdled milk from the corner of his mouth; when he was wailing with all the might of his tiny lungs; when he was gurgling at nothing at all, engaged in some frolic of his own, unknowable mind. Bhola watched the baby being rubbed with Nardelli olive oil and washed in a shallow plastic basin of warm water. He took to propping him up and chattering to him while his mother poured small mugfuls of water over the boy's hairless head. He loved watching the baby gasp for breath as the water streamed down his face. He watched his mother put kaajol, from a tiny tin, with her little finger under his eyes in a fat curve. 'Makes the eyes brighter,' she would say. Then she put a big, fat circle of kaajol on his forehead or, sometimes, awry, almost on his temple, to one side. 'To ward off the evil eye,' she said. Then she mimicked biting his nails, followed by a mimicking of spitting on him. 'Thhoo, thhoo,' she said. Bhola watched, transfixed.

'Did you do that to me when I was his age?' he asked his mother.

'To all of you,' she replied.

'Why?'

'So that no one gives him the evil eye.'

'But why would they do that?'

'Because he's looking lovely.'

'Did I look lovely too?'

'Yes, you did. Now run off, I have a hundred and one things to do, I can't spend all day chatting to you.'

Then Bhola innocently asked the question that had the effect of a blow to her chest.

'Did Didi look lovely too?'

This was the first time Charubala was brought face-to-face with the nature of the way the outside world saw her daughter. If Bhola could ask such a question, did that mean that others had similar, or even more merciless, thoughts going through their heads? Or was it her own guilt, the unnatural cruelty and small-mindedness of a mother thinking that her own daughter was ugly, that this child had read and reflected back at her? Could he have asked the question in all innocence, without the injurious implication she saw lurking behind it? Before she could decide, the answer tumbled out and, along with it, her refusal to engage any longer.

'Yes, she did. Lovelier than all of you. Now, don't you have anything to do? You're keeping him from falling asleep, jabbering away non-stop. Go, go!' she said, practically shooing him away.

Minutes after he left, she felt a cloudy sense of melancholy at having compared all of them unfavourably to Chhaya; the overcompensation was neither going to transform the truth nor make Bhola feel better. If only two lies could add up to one truth, she sighed to herself and concentrated on feeding the baby. Her milk flooded through the clamping gums of the infant at her breast. She decided to send Madan out for those reddish-black hot-and-sour boiled sweets Chhaya loved so much. And let her eat the dried raw mango with black salt that she wanted all the time.

It was around this time that Bhola developed a habit that was, in a more modified form, to mark him for life. It began with him baby-talking to Som – idle, nonsensical chatter, strings of pure sounds that were only a simulacrum of words, opaque, meaningless, not just a distortion of adult speech through the glass of the perceived aural understanding of a baby with one or two nonce-words thrown in. It seemed to be an entire vocabulary, giving the impression at once of being spun out on the hoof and of being a fully limned and realised world, which Bhola had had inside him all the time and had been waiting for another creature from that undiscovered planet to appear and spark him off into communication. A sea of private language, with intoned waves riding up and down, the surface a mesh of movements and agitation of inflection, song-like points of expressiveness, of ascendants and descendants, walls of thick-stacked sound-cascades in motion. It was like hearing any language, of which you did not understand a single word, being spoken. It gave the hearer the feeling of listening to pure abstraction, like music, except that this language had no meaning under the surface of its words; it *was* pure abstraction of a kind.

Bhola returned from school, the local Mitra Institution, in the afternoons and rushed to his little brother the instant he was through the door. Som gave a smile of room-filling radiance when he saw Bhola and they launched into their world of nebulous music, now lit up here and there by an occasional word or phrase of Bengali. It was a wonder to watch: the toddler wide-eyed, rapt – you could even imagine his ears, delicate as sea-shell, pricked to catch every note – while his elder brother set him in the middle of the torrent, cut off the rope tethering him to his life of meals and sleep and children's rhymes and mollycoddling, and set him wildly adrift.

'What you say, ashes and cinders, I cannot understand a word,' Charubala complained; half-heartedly, because she was secretly pleased to have such a ready tool for calming the toddler. Instead of Madan,

Bhola was now summoned to deal with the more refractory moods of the new child. And Bhola was so effective that Charubala's initial wonderment at his powers gave way to an uneasy sense of being spooked.

'What if he grows up speaking that nonsense-language?' she asked one day.

'I'm not teaching him anything. Anyway, I speak to him in Bengali too.'

But at the age of two years and seven months Somnath, to the anxiety of his parents, had not spoken a single word, not even basic things such as 'Baba', 'Ma', 'Dada'. He stared and heard everything and the way his huge eyes took on the look of attentive stillness meant that he understood some things, if not all, but speak he could not or would not.

Charubala badgered Bhola. 'Does he speak when you're alone with him?' she asked.

'No, he only listens. And laughs.'

'Do you expect me to believe this? That you spend so much time with the boy, eating the worms in his ears,' she exclaimed in pique, 'and he doesn't even open his mouth?'

'No, he doesn't. I'm telling the truth.'

'Lying again?' she threatened.

Bhola, intimidated, said, 'You can come and listen if you don't believe me.'

'Fine, that's what I shall do. But what if he sees me and decides not to speak?'

'But he doesn't speak anyway!'

Charubala was on a roll now. 'I know what I'll do. I'll hide outside and you carry on as you do. If you tell him that I'm outside, I shall punish you severely.'

Charubala alerted Madan; no one was to go into the room and no one was to pass outside it for the duration of her spying. She heard Bhola constructing walls of sound with the ease and fluency of a wizard. They seemed to flow out of him and, once in the common world, they remained there, of their own magical accord. On their surface Bhola occasionally stuck a window or two of comprehensible Bengali words – 'bird' featured more than once, and she noted 'monkey' and 'glow-worm' – but those came as mild shocks to her, embedded as they were in such a huge, furled fabric of strangeness that the familiar became the exceptional, the odd. She could not bring herself to peep in case Som caught her watching, and all she had was this strange music to go on, but for the quarter of an hour that she listened with intense concentration she only heard Som let out a carillon of laughter twice. That was all.

The experiment failed.

Som was now taken by his father to a renowned paediatrician in Shyambazar. The doctor tested the child's hearing, asked him to open his mouth, stick out his tongue, say 'Aaaaa' – Bhola was taken too, to make Som comply – and finally said to Prafullanath, 'Nothing wrong with him. He'll speak in time.'

'But he is nearly three years old and he hasn't said one word,' Prafullanath said.

'Have you ever come across an adult who doesn't speak unless he is dumb? And the child isn't a deaf-mute, I assure you. Take him away, he'll start speaking soon.'

And he did. Shortly after the visit to the doctor, Som exploded into speech – ordinary, Bengali speech, halting, part-incomprehensible as a child's speech usually is, but with not a single element of Bhola's private language adulterating it. Charubala was relieved of a worry that was beginning to become burdensome.

She called Bhola aside and said, 'You must not talk any more nonsense to Som. He's learning how to speak, I don't want you to hamper that.'

Bhola felt crushed. Did this mean his special claim on Som was over? Would he not be his little brother's favourite person any longer? Something settled on him; he began to feel heavy.

'But . . . but he . . . he seems to like it,' Bhola said.

'Never mind like. You listen to me. I don't want to catch you speaking all that rubbish to him. Is that clear?' she warned sternly.

He nodded his bowed head once. His eyes began to prick, but he was determined not to cry, at least not in front of his mother. He felt more baffled than sorrowful; why did Som abandon him so capriciously?

Madan-da slipped into the room. He came up to Bhola and whispered, 'Ma's scolded you?'

Bhola nodded. He was not going to be able to hold back the tears, definitely not if he had to speak.

'Come with me to the kitchen, I have something for you,' Madan-da said. 'But you mustn't tell anyone.'

Bhola couldn't look up. What if Madan-da saw his tears?

'Come on, quick. We don't want to be seen, do we?'

The boy followed him to the kitchen. The betrayal was still smarting, but it felt somewhat less keen now that a promise of something – what could it be? – had been held out to him.

In the kitchen Madan-da stood him in a corner and said, 'Close your eyes. Hold out your palms in a scoop. And no cheating, no opening your eyes while my back is turned.'

Bhola, eyes squeezed shut into tight crinkles, shook his head vigorously. Suddenly, in the bowl of his hands, the touch of cool, solid things. He opened his eyes. It took him a couple of seconds to work out what they were: aniseed lozenges and sour-hot-sweet boiled sweets. His face shone with joy.

And then, unknown even to himself, something in the substance of his chatter with Somnath, so irksome to his mother, changed. His opaque communication with Som started filling up with light, becoming translucent with meaning: he started spinning new worlds in Bengali.

It happened like this. On a bright, rain-washed afternoon in October, Bhola stood on the three steps to the garden and watched Som, who had somehow managed to escape Madan-da or Uma-di's supervision, bewitched by dragonflies hovering in the air, flitting about from bush to shrub to unkempt grass. Bhola saw Som freeze for a few seconds, then start to move on the tips of his toes, one step after one careful step, stalking a dragonfly that had landed on a leaf. From a window on the first floor, their father too had his attention caught by the sight of his youngest son creeping up on something in the untidy clump of sparse vegetation under the guava tree. Bhola and Prafullanath watched, immobilised, as if the tiptoed, alert unbreathingness of Som had transmitted itself like an electric current to his watchers, binding them hushed as one. Som edged forward, inch by inch, magically in touch with the atavistic hunter gene in humans, closed in on the unsuspecting insect, his right hand reaching out, his forefinger and thumb brought forward in a pinch, his breath held . . . then he had it. A dragonfly, curled up in an inverted C, was now captive in the tweezers of Som's little fingers.

Prafullanath could not see from upstairs what Som had caught, only his look of amazement. He felt a slight tightness in his chest, but the residue of the hypnotic scene still kept him immobile. Bhola, downstairs, shared the remainder of the same transfixion. A delayed thought was about to take shape in Prafullanath's mind – what if the boy had caught something that could give him a nasty sting or even a poisonous bite? – but it was still held in abeyance.

The insect, caught by its folded-up wings, had instantly curved and grasped Som's finger with all the thread-thin limbs in its head and thorax. This caused an unpleasant, rough sensation, and the little boy, somewhat afraid now, loosened his fingers. The dragonfly flew out, free but dazed, and in that instant a brown mynah, which had, in all probability, had its beady yellow-rimmed eye on the captive insect all this while, swooped down from the roof of the house in one graceful arc, caught hold of the dragonfly in mid-air and, without a break in its flight curve, a miraculous hyperbola, ascended back to where it had taken off from, insect clamped in its beak, the crumpled bits of wings and the thin line of the abdomen poking out of that bright-yellow vice. Everything happened in a minute flash of time, but it played out to all three of them, slowed down and stretched.

Som turned his astonished head to follow the bird's flight-path, wheeling around to see it perch on the terrace. The look on his face was such a roil of reactions that Prafullanath's heart turned; all he wanted to do was to rush down to the garden, swoop his little boy up in his arms and make him forget whatever upset he had been caused. Bhola, on the other hand, was in the grip of a twofold marvelling: at the smooth, predatory art of the mynah, so swift, so unerring, and at Som's shock at witnessing this god-knows-how-many-in-one chance of the freak yet perfectly poised hunting and his role in it as a facilitator. It was as if Som were the servant who had been duped into capturing the prize that his master would consume regally; it was the deception that hurt.

Spell broken, Bhola ran towards Som, who could only point to the air, in the direction of the opportunistic bird. Then the little boy burst into tears.

Bhola gathered him in his arms, kissed his cheeks and consoled him. 'No, no, my kushu pushu, it's all right, it's all right.'

Som howled and said something that was more garbled by the sobbing than his usual clotted child's speech, then howled some more.

Bhola tried to divert his attention by extemporising on a story, an old trick, but so far an effective one. But, for the first time, the words that emerged were not in the shared private language; the world began to be spun in children's Bengali, ordinary, comprehensible, reassuring.

By the time Bhola was about five minutes into his telling, Somnath was a figure carved in stone.

A shout came from inside the house: 'Bholaaaa, Sooom, what are you doing outside? Come in right now. I'm making bananas-milk-puffed-rice for you. Come in quickly.' Their mother.

Som clung tighter to his brother's neck and shook his head forcefully. Bhola put a finger to his lips and said, 'I'll come with you too.' The hold on his neck relaxed somewhat.

And so Bhola's logorrhoea began to mutate into story-telling, the transparent, sense-filled words now a clear pane of glass between sound and meaning, offering a view of a fantastically confabulated world of wood-fairies, incarnations and metempsychosis, of imaginary beasts and birds and their magical powers, of mangoes so sour that a whole forest of monkeys was struck dumb after eating them off the trees . . . and so it went on, over the years.

One day Adinath overheard, in passing, a particularly colourful story about speaking fish that could transform themselves into malignant spirits residing in tamarind trees and remarked, 'Arrey, you are not half-bad at spinning tales. When you grow up, you will be a writer.'

Bhola, who saw his eldest brother as an adult really, and accorded him appropriate respect, felt himself puff up with pride. The stories got wilder.

His mother reacted differently. 'All day you talk rubbish. Where do you pick up these monsoony tales? Really, I sometimes wonder if there is madness in store for you. Your father used to say that there was madness in his family, some uncle or aunt. Why can't you concentrate on your studies instead? I can see that your relationship with your books is nearly over.'

Bhola's school reports had seen a proliferation of marks in red ink. He had scraped through Classes Five and Six, just, struggling chiefly with his English. The English teacher at school, a brown saheb, pointed out repeatedly that his 'native tongue' got in the way of English acquisition: Bhola's spelling was appalling; he read aloud in a ridiculously Bengali-accented English, confusing the 'z' sound with 'j' and short accents with long; his grammar was parlous; his sentence-construction still at the level of a seven-year-old's. English was a key subject in school. If he did not pass his English exams, he would have to repeat the year.

Meanwhile, he was more than happy to recline on the easy chair on the front balcony, watching the shapes of the white clouds against the blue sky: a crocodile with its mouth slightly open, trying to swallow a fluffy dog, which was heading straight into the fall of the veil on a woman's face . . . Now, how did that configuration happen? Was there someone behind the blue of the sky, drawing out the shapes with a giant pencil that had white clouds in it instead of lead? There, there was an idea . . .

IV

Nitai used to live on the periphery of the neighbourhood of his caste, one circle inwards from where we were. There seemed to be some taboo about speaking of him, or at least referring to him directly. But his ghostly presence and the story of his fate were just under the surface of all our conversations with the villagers. How could it not have been so?

I fought my urge to bring up his name in my usual daily chit-chat with Kanu and Bijli until one night I gave in. I asked Bijli, while she was serving me food, if she knew Nitai or his wife.

— Nitai's wife used to come sometimes. In the beginning she couldn't bring herself to ask for food, but I could tell. She used to bring the baby and the girl with her. Dry and thin, all of them, like jute sticks. I felt very bad for them. Sometimes I gave them what I could, not much, a handful of rice, another of dal, maybe some waxed gourds or ridged gourds. Shame held her back from asking for food, but I knew. And then that shame went when the hunger became too much. It filled my soul with pity. Poor thing! The almighty gave her a burnt forehead at birth. Towards the end she stopped coming. Maybe out of shame — she had been reduced to a beggar. Maybe she didn't have the strength to come here. But it's not as if we had a lot to give away. I gave her as much as I could. The drought over the last two, three years had been so severe . . . Many people died here, around this area. Eeesh, I see her shrunken face in front of me now . . . One afternoon I came out and found that she had fallen asleep just outside the door. I didn't understand then that it was because of weakness, I thought she had been working hard, sowing or collecting kindling in the forest, something. My heart bursts, thinking of those silent, downcast eyes now . . . god gave us stomachs to punish us — the punishment of hunger is a great punishment. Nitai's wife too used to say that all the time. Then she stopped coming . . . Eeesh, if only I had tried to find out, maybe all this wouldn't have happened.

And here is the 'all this' that happened. In this aman-rice-producing area, a small farmer like Nitai, who didn't have any land of his own but worked as a sharecropper or, when times got really bad, as a wage-labourer, had work for only three to five months of the year. Majgeria was not close to the river, so it wasn't a double-cropping area, which would have meant nine months of work. The meagre money that he got as wages from labour, and the tiny percentage of the yield that he got as a sharecropper, rarely stretched to enough sustenance for a family of three, and then, killingly, four. And there were very few opportunities of employment outside agriculture – what else could he do? Break bricks and stones by a road under construction? Dig? Physical labour at a factory somewhere? Who would look after his wife and children if he left the village and went wherever such work was available?

He had a tiny vegetable patch next to his hut, the size of a bitten nail, no more, and on that he grew some gourds and onions. He had to pawn even this apology of a plot to a moneylender when he desperately needed money to feed himself and his family.

Kanu said – You're desperate then, and the moneylender knows he can get anything out of you at that point. If he says, I'll give you two kilos of rice, but you'll have to return three kilos to me in a month's time, you don't think then: Where am I going to get three kilos of rice in a month? You think: I don't care what you want, give me the rice now, my family is starving now, I'll think of what comes later later. And they've got you then.

That was the time-honoured way they got Nitai. He couldn't pay the interest on the loans he took out in desperate times, loans of money and rice, and had to sell that scrap of land of his, the land that could have kept his family just about surviving until times improved. The interest accumulated. Nitai had to service it with labour on the land the moneylenders owned, but this time it was labour for which there were no wages, not even, sometimes, the subsistence meal given to the daily labourer working someone else's land.

Kanu again – The last two years have been so bad with droughts and starvation and crop-failure, but it's like an opportunity for the landlords and moneylenders; they use these things as an excuse to lower our wages and not give us the daily meal when we work on their land. Bad times, they say, we can't afford to pay you so much or feed you. They think that we poor people don't see what's really going on, that they are using this shortage of food grain to hoard it in their barns and warehouses, then sneak it out in lorries and trucks in the dead of the night to the cities, where it's sold at a huge profit on the black market. And they tell us that they can't afford to give us our daily meal when we work for them.

While Kanu was saying all this, I was reminded of the food riots in Calcutta last year: middle-class people behaving like wild dogs, looting from ration shops, fighting to grab what little was entering the public distribution system. If the middle classes were not getting enough to eat, what hope for these invisible people? They call themselves munish, or labourers; they have climbed down from manush, humans. They cannot imagine even <u>thinking</u> about food – even that is a luxury to them.

Do you know, I was reminded of something else too, a childhood memory surfacing, aided by Kanu's words. I was seven or eight years old and all the adults in the room forgot that I was there, or thought I could be ignored, that I wouldn't understand what they were talking about. The thing that has remained with me was Pishi and Boro-kaka recounting something they had seen: a woman lying dead on a narrow side-street and a crow pecking out her eyes, while her child, near-dead with hunger, watched the scene. This was during the famine of '43. It struck me, listening to Kanu, that it was mostly the starving people from this very district, Medinipur, who had flocked to Calcutta in the hope of getting food in the city and had died like flies on the roads.

Nitai's physical weakness: that was what I couldn't get out of my head. Starving for days at a time, but having to work – back-breaking physical labour – double, three times his normal effort because whatever he earned, the rice that he harvested, say, belonged to the moneylender, who had secured it at a price below the market rate. I supposed his creditors gave him enough to keep him working: what use was a dead labourer to anyone? What was it like, having the last drop of your blood (and your land) squeezed out of you and there was nothing you could do about it? Was it like getting trapped in quicksand: the more you struggled, the more you sank in? How quickly did it break the frame of the man – the physical frame, I mean –. as it would break a pack animal worked like that on a fraction of its food rations, and that too given intermittently? What had Bijli said? 'He couldn't bear the torments of his stomach any longer.'

The nights were getting colder. I longed for a sweater or a woollen shawl, I feel ashamed to admit it. But not to you. We had to live with the farmers as fish in the sea, Chairman Mao wrote. But who knew of these daily, minute changes in life as we adapted to swim in those seas? Some we were not prepared for before we jumped in. We had to adapt while in the water. This threadbare green chador will have to do.

I can see the Milky Way. It's like the smudge of a cosmic giant's fingerprints on the inky black sky. And stars — so many millions and millions of them that, if I let my eyes unfocus for a bit, they too become a smear in the sky. You never see this kind of a sky, living in the city. These stars, all revealed now, hide themselves from urban eyes. My heart hammers audibly every time I see a sky like this; yet another thing I didn't know existed, this sheer density of pinpricks of light. And sometimes I see your face in the stars, just for a brief moment, as if they have arranged themselves in the shape of your face and nose and eyes and mouth and eyebrows. Then it disappears and I'm unable to find it again, however hard I try. At other times the stars seem to arrange themselves into spelling out your name in that infinite sky. Again, it's an optical trick — the moment I become conscious of it, it's gone, and the stars return to being themselves.

Samir raised it first — Ei, what's that you scribble in your notebook so secretively?
 — Hardly secretively, if you know all about it.
 — But what is it that you write?
 I felt panicky, so I tried to turn the tables against him — It could be the kind of revolution-tinged poetry that you scribble away yourself in small pieces of paper hidden inside The Little Red Book. Everyone thinks you're reading Mao, but actually you're practising to be a cross between Jibanananda and Sukanta.
 A mixture of anger, embarrassment and sheepishness from Samir, some of it feigned — What?? You've read my notebook? You've been going through my things?
 — No, no, don't be stupid. Don't you think the rest of the world has eyes? It's obvious even to a child what you're up to.
 — Really?
 He was most surprised at being caught out and, while I could understand a mild embarrassment at being discovered in this rather sweet and adolescent act of deception — no, too strong, that word, but you know what I mean — I couldn't fathom the acuteness or depth of this discomfort. He had been caught writing poetry surreptitiously, not doing something unspeakable. At last he gave a sheepish laugh and it blew over.
 In relief he began to play-attack me — And you? What do you scribble away? Poetry too, I bet.
 — No.

– What then?

I told him a partial truth – Nothing very important. Just a record of our times here. A sort of diary.

Now Dhiren said – Careful! If it includes names and whereabouts of the people in the various regional cells and committees, it could be a godsend to the police. They're dragging comrades away to jail if they so much as find poster paint and brushes in their homes.

Yes, I had thought of that. Which was why I decided that I wasn't going to post you these pages. It wouldn't do to have them discovered in your room, in the event of a police raid. Word reached us that the blacklisting of our comrades had begun. It was only a matter of time before our names reached that list. But, then, what was the point of noting all this down, having you in my head as its only reader, if it never reached you?

Then Samir, after some hesitation and hemming and hawing, came out with – All this writing business . . . you know . . . among people who are, almost without exception, illiterate . . . Isn't it . . . isn't it a bit . . . you know . . . Mao said we have to be like the fish with the fish in the sea . . . This writing business is . . . is . . .

I put him out of his misery – Conspicuous?

– Yes, yes, conspicuous! That's what I was thinking.

Another long and hair-splitting discussion of Chairman Mao's words until I silenced him with – Don't you think Mao himself wrote, when he was being one with the Chinese peasantry?

Samir wasn't quiet for very long – Yes, that may well be true, but the Chinese peasantry is not illiterate like their Bengali counterpart, so writing amidst them wouldn't have stood out so much.

CHAPTER FIVE

1968

On a monsoon day loud with downpour, during the short break at ten-past-eleven before the beginning of the English period, Arunima is summoned to Sister Josephine's office on the ground floor. Here, she is grilled about the short essay, 'A Day in the Life of My Mother', she wrote and submitted as her homework two days earlier.

'Is this true? Are all these terrible things you've had the cheek to write about your mother true?' Sister Josephine asks.

The exercise copy sits on the glass-topped table between them. Arunima, head bowed, remains silent.

'LOOK UP. Why have you written these awful lies about your mother?' Sister demands. 'Do you not know that lying is a sin? And lying about your mother, who has given birth to you, who has fed, clothed, loved, protected you, does this not make you feel ashamed? Do you not see what a big sin this is?'

Arunima lowers her head further, hoping that the posture conveys her wish to become the vessel for any punishment Sister deems fit for her sins; the ready humility could then go some way towards mitigating her anger.

Perhaps the performance works; there is a sudden diminishment in Sister Josephine's ferocity as she says, 'Come up to my desk. I want you to take this letter back home and give it to your parents. I'm going to keep the exercise book for the time being.'

Arunima is overthrown by this wholly unexpected turn of events. A severe scolding, punishment, these she had expected, and had steeled herself for, but this? Never. What is she going to tell her parents? And how will they cope with a meeting with the Sisters, her mother with no English, not the barest minimum, and both Baba and Ma intimidated into subservient silence by those who speak the language; how will they ever bring themselves even to consider a meeting with the Sisters of Carmel Convent? A worm of anxiety bores through her. Her face flushes with the imminent shame of this unveiling of her parents as rustic 'natives', as Sister Claire has it, unsophisticated, 'uncultured' – that accusation she has heard levelled by her aunt Chhaya at armies of people. The fear and tension looping through her are more to do with this than with being exposed in the eyes of her parents, or being punished at school and at home as a consequence.

By the time school ends at 3.35, the rain has abated but has left behind the usual damage: the road on which the school stands is a battlefield of umbrellas; rolled-up trousers and pyjamas; wet, bedraggled people looking like crows; an infernal soundtrack of vehicle horns punctuated occasionally by a timpani-roll of thunder; traffic jam; crowds, crowds and crowds. The press of parents, almost exclusively mothers, and drivers waiting outside the gates to collect their charges resembles the early stages of a gathering stampede. From here only chaos can take over as girls scan anxiously for drivers or parents delayed by the flooding and traffic disorder, and car-shares and lifts are organised with something bordering on neurosis. Some school buses have made it, others not.

Arunima has spent all afternoon trying to figure out when and where she can destroy Sister Josephine's letter. It cannot be done on the school bus, obviously, or anywhere in school, for she is paranoid about the torn-up pieces of paper being discovered and then put together like pieces of a jigsaw. But the same kind of problem would obtain at home too: what if her mother, forever ferreting about, forever enquiring and suspicious, comes upon the fragments and subjects her to an interrogation?

In the mayhem she sees a chance to become inconspicuous: she runs up the stairs to the bathrooms on the second floor, shuts herself in a cubicle and takes out the sealed envelope. Then she sets to tearing the page in half, then quarters, eighths and sixteenths. Each sixteenth she tears into two or four, shoving the tiny bits of paper into her white socks as her hands become full. She is careful to distribute these more or less equally between her left and right legs. All the while she is aware of god's eye watching her in the act of compounding her sin, seeing through walls and barriers straight into this cubicle, straight into her heart. As she leaves the bathroom she is intensely conscious of the area between the elastic top of her socks and the edge of the black shoes around her ankles. Her gait changes. The paper feels as if it is burning her lower legs, turning them into glowing columns of light.

On the school bus, which arrives ninety minutes late, Arunima swings between sitting immobile, like a statue, afraid that moving might give away her secret, and fidgeting, but in a slowed-down, staccato way, nervous that natural movement might lead to the hidden objects spilling out and leaving an accusatory trail behind her. When the Don Bosco School bus passes theirs, the girls lean out of the windows to shout in chorus, 'Donkey Boys, Donkey Boys', to the boys' combined retort of 'Camel Girls, Camel Girls', but today Arunima, usually an enthusiastic participant, sits in silence.

When she is set down at the crossing of Basanta Bose and Bediapara Roads, the stretch towards Hazra Road is still flooded. She waits for the bus to go a few metres north, up its usual route, then bends down to retrieve the paper stuffed in her socks and strews the confetti onto the puddles in the road. There, she thinks, no one will ever know. A few remaining bits have gone into the space between her instep and socks. A different problem nags her now: what if the goddess Saraswati is offended by her deliberate and prolonged flouting of the rule that forbids the touching of study materials sacred to her – paper, pen, books, pencils – with the feet?

At home, things continue with the grey pallor they have worn ever since Bor'-da went missing. Dread and the tighten-relax routine of the grip of anxiety have now given way to the settled, monotonous drone of a dull ache. Boro-jyethi, who has been most affected by it, naturally so, has become a ghost in the house she used to hold together. She is hardly ever seen and the children are not allowed to go to her room, where she lies in bed day and night, wasting away. Then there is Arunima's ill grandfather, also on the third floor: something terrible happened to him a few years ago, the details of which had not been discussed in front of the children, but from what she had pieced together it had been something involving his work and bad people who worked in his paper factory and somehow Madan-da had had some role to play in it and it had all resulted in her grandfather's second heart-attack and he has been mostly bedridden since. Arunima has been told off so often for being loud while playing or talking, for showing any signs of joy or life or frivolity, a constant 'Shhhh' from the adults, accompanied by a furrowing of the brows and a finger to the lips, that her life seems conducted under the cover of a tarpaulin that will never lift to show the sky again.

Jayanti, like everyone else, has used Supratik's disappearance to wring whatever advantage she can get, mostly in the domain of the superficial. When her daughter, while packing her school satchel for the next day, had lifted a book in a way so careless that the dried wad of marigold petals from Saraswati Puja in February, pressed between its pages, had fallen out, she had immediately pounced upon it.

'Have a care, have a care,' she had scolded her daughter. 'Dropping sacred flowers like this, eeesh! No wonder all auspicious influences have departed from this house.'

The unspoken hint at the tragedy hit home. The guilt that Arunima may have had anything to contribute to Bor'-da's disappearance worked its way through her, to silence and intimidate.

The feel of dark curtains hanging everywhere in the house, in thick, unbroken folds that one has to keep dodging, is inescapable today too. Previously, on returning home from school, she would be summoned to the third floor with, 'Come, come. Quickly. Look what I've got for you.'

Arunima would rush to their Boro-jyethi.

'I got Madan to make coconut shapes,' she would say. Or 'Your face looks dry and shrivelled. They must be working you very hard in your English-medium school. Come, let me get Madan-da to mix up spicy puffed rice for you.'

No such pampering now. Even the memory seems attenuated by the darkness in the house. At dinner Arunima feels the yawning hole around which everybody is walking, trying not to fall in, trying especially not to acknowledge it by talking about it. At times, adults fall silent as she enters the room, the air still rippled by whatever they have hastily stopped discussing; it could only be Bor'-da. She has become very good at sensing these ripples because she has been given, inadvertently, just the slightest glimpse of the unmentionable: adults being reliably ignorant of the depth of how much children understand or can imagine.

Take the conversation overheard when Arunima was in the room as Jayanti was folding clean laundry and putting it away, Bholanath sitting there, not doing anything particular.

'What is going to happen, then?' her mother asked, a frequent question for her, worried as she was about the worst possible outcome of anything. It was a question asked in fear, with hope that someone would contradict her and allay her jitters.

Bhola answered with peevishness. 'How am I supposed to know? *What will happen, what will happen?*' he said, mimicking her cruelly. 'Am I a clairvoyant?'

It was the rasp of irritation, so unusual in Baba, that made Arunima prick up her ears. Hoping that her father was going to win this round, she settled in for the fight, concentrating on looking totally uninterested and making her face take on a far-away gaze.

'My hands and feet turn cold when I hear these things,' Jayanti whined.

'Your hands and feet have a tendency to turn cold whenever the breeze changes direction,' Bhola said.

'What can I do? I can't suddenly become brave, like all your brothers,' Jayanti said, trying sarcasm. 'One of them seems not to have noticed that his nephew has been missing for nearly a year and a half now, such is his attitude. Even the father seems to be resigned, behaving like a saint who has renounced the world. This is not natural.'

Bhola, not to be cowed, not this time, said, 'What good will it do any of us, your feeling afraid? I don't think you should be poking your nose into this business at all. This has reached some pretty unpleasant and dangerous quarters.'

'But what if something happens to *us*?' The sarcasm had been short-lived.

'What do you think will happen, eh, what, what?' Bhola was not going to let this one go.

Arunima silently cheered her father on. Let him crush her with his heel, she thought.

'There's lots happening already,' her mother flared into anger again. 'Do you think I don't have eyes? How long can you hide fish with greens? There are bombs in the city, people being killed . . . All this chatter about Supratik . . . some of it must be true.'

At the mention of Bor'-da's name some kind of alertness was restored to the adults. A look passed between them, one that took into its arc Arunima as well. She understood that the conversation was over, at least in her hearing. She also had more support for her suspicion that something terrible had happened to the missing Bor'-da.

This afternoon Jayanti has worried herself into pacing up and down, from second-floor verandah to bedroom to verandah again, because her daughter is late returning from school. Arunima's arrival soothes her somewhat. Now there is only her husband to fret about.

'Is Baba back?' Arunima asks.

'Is this the normal time for Baba to come back?' Jayanti answers. 'He'll be late this evening, the roads are all flooded.'

Arunima does not bother giving her mother any information about the current state of the roads. A sudden visitation of fear, as if the horrible face of a ghost has peeked at her from behind a pillar then removed itself again, unsettles her: what if the school discovers that the summons has not been delivered and gets in touch with her parents without her help or knowledge? Best not to think about it, she decides, willing it away. The thought of feigning illness and not going to school for two or three days begins to take shape in her mind. Surely by that time Sister Josephine will have forgotten the whole thing? The nuns have so many things to think about . . .

A Friday afternoon gathering at the offices of Basanta, a small publishing house, on West Range. Bhola has been in charge of this small subsidiary of Charu Paper ever since its inception in 1952 and has tried, of late, to extend its narrow remit of publishing only educational books to branching out into poetry and fiction, which is where his real interests lie. These Friday-afternoon addas brought together friends, friends of friends, aspiring writers and whoever someone who knew Bhola brought along, and amidst much talk of politics and how best to run the state and the world and how everything was going to hell and how the Bengali was never going to roar again, some scribbler read out a story or a section of a novel or a handful of poems to the assembled company in the hope that Basanta Publishing Co. was going to take to it enough to consider bringing it out. These addas had started acquiring the comfort and reliability of ritual amongst the small group of people who knew about them; and even if putative writers wanting to change the very course of Bengali literature – an ambition they shared with Bholanath Ghosh – found that Basanta did not always do the right thing by giving their dreams the fixity and immortality of print, they could get soft loans and handouts from Bhola.

Bhola saw himself as the centre of patronage in this fledgling court. Whenever he could, he helped out struggling writers and poets with money and, often, publication; how could he not support the pursuit of literature? That would be a betrayal of the very soul of Bengaliness. Besides, these Friday afternoons had another typically Bengali underpinning: it was not crassly purposive, or a means to an end that was commercial and material profit. It was, instead, an end in itself, a celebration of conviviality and the art of conversation and the sparklingly playful things one could do with time. He felt dismayed and besmirched even thinking about adherence to a business model or vulgar things like that; money was such a dirty, downright polluting thing.

Today there are six of them, including Bhola: his printer; the editor of a 'little magazine' and author of the fiery experimental novel *Endnotes for a Beginning*, recently published by Basanta Publishing Co.; Bhola's colleague and employee at Basanta; an out-of-work theatre director; and today's writer, an unemployed graduate of Bangabashi College earning a pittance from private tutoring, brought here by the editor, who has published a few of his revolutionary poems in his 'little magazine' named after a Sanskrit verse-form, *Mandakranta*.

There is a mild running joke in the circle along the lines of how Bhola lives up to the scatty forgetfulness that his name embodies. There is also great affection for the wild raconteur in this slightly distracted, slightly unanchored, slightly off-kilter man. Today, though, there is something more in the aura about his normally dispersed personality.

The printer asks, 'Everything all right?'

Bhola answers, 'Yes, yes, fine.'

'Just thought you seemed a little more distracted than usual.'

'Hmmm' comes the frugal reply. That is eloquent enough to most of the company; in ordinary circumstances Bhola Ghosh would have seized on that calculated 'more' and spun a giant castle from it. '"More"? What do you mean "more"? Have you known me to be so distracted that I have walked into ditches or got on the wrong bus? Talking of which, did I ever tell you of the time when . . .' it would begin.

Now, however, Bhola dodges, 'No, no, it's nothing. The buses and trams are so crowded nowadays . . .'

The theatre director and the editor are slightly puzzled by this reduction in Bhola Ghosh's usual volubility; maybe it is nothing, maybe they are reading too much into it. But the greater matter of the adda awaits; the scribbler's story, with its scalpel-like finger on the dying pulse of the terminally ill times, is sure to set a thaw in motion, of that the editor is sure.

He signals to his protégé to begin. The writer stubs out his Charminar, takes a sip of lemon tea and begins, 'The story is titled "Prehistoric". It's set in the present time.' He pauses to let the witticism register, then emphasises it, in case someone has not got it, by emitting a short, ironic snort.

PREHISTORIC

Eleven-thirty on a Tuesday morning. Writers' Building is a crackling, buzzing hive of activity. Bechu Sarkar of the Housing Ministry has just arrived at work, a quarter of an hour later than usual. He puts his cloth side-bag on his chair, sits down, greets everyone in the office with his time-tested general bulletin – 'Don't even ask, it was murder on the number 74 this morning, I came here hanging from the door, I tell you, hanging from the door, like a bat' – then hollers for tea, 'What, is there a tea-strike on? Where has the tea-boy gone? Where's my tea?' As if on cue, a grubby boy with a huge blackened kettle enters and pours out milky tea into a smudged greenish glass.

Bhola's mind is elsewhere today, on his own far more pressing situation, but he must force himself to listen to the reading, if only to save himself:

A crowd of people sit outside, waiting, hoping to get some work done by the officials inside – have a file traced or moved to another department, have papers signed and attested, enquiries answered, bureaucratic mazes unlocked, puzzles elucidated. One such petitioner, a shuffling, creased, dusty, creaky, bent man of about sixty-five enters and takes in the scene of smoke-wreathed business of the government before hobbling his way to Nakshatra-babu.

But Bhola's attention soon drifts away from the dull, predictable hell of others to his own consuming one. It had been his own unpreparedness, his lack of all the necessary information, that Bhola had found so difficult to cope with while the Sisters had talked to him in their office; lightning in clear skies. Obviously he was going through some serious bad times, he mused, and when times were bad, even buggery resulted in pregnancy, as the salty theatre director never ceased to remind everyone who came within his orbit. The thought of the director forces him again to concentrate on the proceedings under way right in front of him:

Mr Das returned to the Employment Ministry, where the relevant PA, sighted only once, declared hurriedly, 'The Minister is in Burdwan, he'll be back tomorrow,' and disappeared, not to be seen since. The following day the underlings and hangers-on in the PA's office said that the Minister had gone to Siliguri; the day after, to Delhi. A polyphony of gossip, informal advice, chatter, loose talk, suggestions, the tabla keeping the taal to his eighty-two visits, kept sounding its infernal accompaniment throughout.

Bhola interrupts, 'Achchha, this is all very well, but . . . but isn't this, how should I say, isn't this all a bit *familiar?*'

The young man's face falls before he can rearrange it into a mask of defensive contempt. He is still trying when Bhola's colleague seconds his boss, 'Yes, yes, right, right, we know all this stuff. So much time to state the obvious . . . I'm sure there's a twist coming?'

The magazine editor begins to defend the writer, 'It may be familiar to us, but maybe it's not familiar to a lot of people who have no first-hand or even second-hand experience of *all this stuff.* It's new stuff to them.'

The theatre director says, 'It opens up a more philosophical point: should stories be about the familiar world or should they show us something new each time?'

The young man, who has had some time to swallow his disappointment, now argues, 'If you look at the work of the German writer Franz Kafka, you'll find that what I'm trying to do is not dissimilar: the hellish nature of bureaucracy, the labyrinth from which man cannot escape, the going-around in circles . . .'

The director adds excitedly, 'Yes, yes, Kafka, Kafka, we're going to put on a play by him, it's called *Insect*. Do you know that play, where a man becomes an insect? Masterpiece, masterpiece! We are all insects.'

Insect, thinks Bhola; that's about right, that's what he had felt during the incident at Carmel Convent yesterday, when he found himself facing two Christian nuns. Dressed in impeccably starched white blouses, grey skirts, grey wimples, with chunky crucifixes cradling on their shelf-like chests, Sister Josephine and the headmistress, Sister Patience, had throughout addressed him as 'Mr Gauche'. Their English had seemed opaque, probably because authentic; accordingly, Bhola's deep fear of the English language and those who spoke it well had taken the form of abject deference.

'Mr Gauche, we are a bit worried about an essay Arunima has written,' Sister Josephine said in clipped tones.

Bhola grinned in incomprehension, then, realising it was an inappropriate reaction, shut his mouth and tried to look serious.

Sister Patience took the baton now. 'Would you say you were having problems at home?' she asked. Not wishing for it to be construed as an unhealthy curiosity about domestic matters, she hastily added, 'Problems with Arunima, I mean, of course.' The severity in her voice was notched up to compensate for what she saw as an unfortunate slip.

Bhola quailed at the stentorian tone of the headmistress, even while straining to follow this alarming flow of *echt*-English, but he identified the repeated word, 'problems', and clamped onto it.

'Problems . . . heh-heh . . . yes . . . I'm meaning no . . . heh-heh . . .' he began. Perhaps they meant that his daughter was having problems with her English lessons, and he had been called in to be made aware of the glitch so that he could ask her to pull her socks up and get her to improve her performance? Yes, that must be it.

'I asking my brother and . . . and brother's son for helping in English all the time,' he said, 'but they . . . they busy.' This last word he pronounced 'bi-ji' – his old problem of distinguishing between a palatal and a sibilant fricative – and set the Sisters' stern mouths twitching.

Years of dealing with parents who had no English, but aspired to better for their daughters – thank the Lord for that – had made Sister Patience adept at recovering the real meaning from behind the fog of Benglish, so she replied, 'No, Mr Gauche, I'm not referring to the quality of Arunima's work. With that, we're all satisfied. I mean this.' With that she passed him an exercise book covered in brown paper, with a Sulekha ink label on it indicating name of owner of the copy, class, section, subject, school. He remembered bringing back from work sheets of brown paper, the regulation cover for his children's textbooks and exercise copies, at the beginning of their school year. He had a slight tightness in his chest, seeing them in their correct use now, at imagining this aspect of his daughter's life to which he had no access, to which he could never be a daily, present witness: her small hands opening the pages of the book in a classroom, writing in it, putting it away in her bag. It was as if this object was the bridge to a corner of her life that would increasingly become separate from his. He felt an invisible hand squeezing the inside of his chest again. Then the words of Sister Patience dissipated that momentary sensation.

'If you could please read the piece that is on the last page that is written on. We are dismayed, too, that Arunima did not give you the letter in the first instance.'

Bhola, who was settling into his terrified state and therefore beginning to comprehend the Sisters' words better, took the slim book and opened it on the requisite page. Two pages of his daughter's rounded, cursive English hand under the title 'My Mother'. His eyes began to smart at the evidence of her flourishing competence in the language; was it true that it was *his* daughter who had written so fluently in that treacherous language, which had eluded him with such obstinacy?

'We'll wait until you finish reading. It's not going to take you long,' Sister Josephine urged.

Bhola obliged; he was much better at reading than at aural comprehension. But before long, a lag seemed to be opening up between the signs on the page and the meanings behind them and a corresponding one between meaning and sense. Acutely conscious of two pairs of judgemental eyes riveted on him, and also of his own deep anxiety brought about by a sense of lack, he nevertheless found himself forgetting them, ensnared by the peculiar nature of Arunima's essay on Jayanti. What on earth had she written? This was not the Jayanti he recognised. What were all these wild fictions?

My mother's name is Jayanti Ghosh. She is short and black and has hair till her waist. She gets up in the morning and shouts at me and my father to get ready to go to school and office. In my tiffin-box she gives a banana and a boiled egg, sometimes insects and worms.

She burns the food for my father and throws down the plate in front of him. Then she takes all the money from him and says, 'I want to see your dead face today.' Then I come to school and she spends all day beating the servants. One day she hit the maidservant so much that she went to hospital with broken arms and legs.

Then she eats lunch, all nice and delicious things that she does not give to me and my father – mutton, fish, chop, cutlet, sweets. After lunch she waits until all my aunts are asleep. Then she goes into their rooms and steals their saris and jewellery.

In the afternoon, I return back from school. She shouts at me and beats me with a wooden stick and sometimes with the handle of a hand-fan. Then my father returns back and she shouts at him. She gives him rice and water and salt to eat. Sometimes there are eggs of cockroaches and spiders in our food.

Then she sends my father and me to sleep on the floor at the bottom of the stairs. One day Jesus Christ will burn her like the thornbush.

He looked up at the four eyes watching his every nerve-twitch and eye-flicker then lowered his baffled face to continue reading. He switched back to the cover to read Arunima's name on the label on the front, hoping that the Sisters had made a mistake, then wondered if there were two girls with the same name in the class despite the evidence of his daughter's handwriting.

Then, shocking himself and the Sisters, he started giggling uncontrollably at the absurd nature of Arunima's imagination.

For a startled few seconds Sisters Patience and Josephine dropped their masks and stared with incredulity at Bhola, until an even pricklier disapproval took over.

'Why do you laugh?' Sister Patience demanded. 'Is it true what she has written? We are of the opinion that these are all terrible slanders. What do you have to say?'

The clear note of haranguing in her voice tethered Bhola somewhat. 'Erm . . . yes, ma'am . . . no . . . meaning Sister . . . this is very laughing matter. No, I mean, writing funny,' he said and halted. The Sisters heard the substitution of the fricative with a plosive in 'funny', but they were too far gone in their perplexity and outrage to find it even mildly amusing. Now barely concealed disdain took its place.

'We, on the other hand, do not find it a laughing matter, Mr Gauche,' said Sister Patience in her coldest, hardest voice.

Bhola made a swift calculation in his head: he did not have enough English, or nerves steely enough, to explain to the Sisters that the stuff Arunima had written was all fabricated, because he would then have to field further questions – whys, whats, wherefores – which would lead to larger stretches of communicative quicksands, so it might be a wise strategy simply to look apologetic, even outraged, and let the tide of the Sisters' displeasure and disciplinary prescriptions for his daughter wash over him. Tussling with this decision was a more amorphous shame: what if the Sisters thought that Arunima's essay was true? What kind of an idea would it give them of his domestic life, his family, his marriage, his general ineffectuality? This counter-feeling made him want to speak out, but he did not have the right words. Not for the first time in his life he felt himself fall into the gap between feelings and their articulation in language.

So relieved was he to step out onto Gariahat Road after his ordeal that he nearly forgot how he would be quizzed by Jayanti as soon as he returned home. She was fretting herself to dyspepsia. The English sentences Arunima had written would make little to no sense to her, so how was he to summarise the events of the morning? What *could* he say? Walking down to the bus stop on the other side of the road, he felt suddenly weak-kneed with pity: pity at Jayanti's ignorance of English; pity for the incomprehension and then the puzzled sadness that would be her reaction, were she to be told the entire truth; compassion for the unknowable emotions that would be going through her in her private moments when she worried at the episode, trying to parse some kind of sense out of it.

He lit a cigarette from the burning tip of the braided coir rope hanging beside the narrow paan-bidi shack adjacent to the Ucobank building and inhaled deeply. He decided to weave a different tale altogether for his wife when he got back home, something along the lines of a new order they were trying out in Carmel Convent, which had to do with calling parents in at regular intervals throughout the year to keep them apprised of their daughters' academic progress. Then he would make up something for verisimilitude and density: how they were satisfied with Arunima's work, although there was room for improvement in some subject or the other. The prospect of lying calmed him instantly, more than the nicotine.

But far more treacherous were proving to be the currents running under the complicity that united him and Arunima now. He could barely bring himself to look her in the eye; he knew that she knew of his deception, knew also that some uneasy coalition into opposing camps across a dividing line had occurred. While this made him feel disloyal to his wife, and the screw of an odd discomfort now and then turned and turned inside him, Arunima seemed to have developed a silent, intentful intensity, refusing to let go of her pinning gaze on him, searching his eyes out, wanting something ungiveable. Her child's heart knew that he had protected her, but its susceptibility to magnified fears and anxieties seemed, perhaps, to want also a kind of reckoning about the content of what she had written, an acknowledgement from him of the spirit and life under the surface of those words. This she would not get because he did not know it was demanded of him and, had he known, would have found it impossible to endow it with a form in which things of the soul or heart are given. What shape does collusive understanding take? What her innocent mind could not comprehend was that it was not her that he had shielded; that knowledge would have been reckoning enough. But that was not to be, not yet.

Although the events are recent, to Bhola it appears that the clouds, which have begun to settle across the sky of his heart, have acquired a tenacious staying power. Bhola is unsettled by this new, growing grain of – of what exactly? This is what he cannot put his finger on, and the inability distracts him significantly enough to bleed into other areas of his life; he cannot safely shut it away in a room to be revisited in the silence of introspective solitude.

Sitting at work now, it continues to gnaw at him; nothing major or disruptive, nothing painful or upsetting, just a kink that will not go away. The debate around him is in wild spate; he has not heard a word for a long time. Where are they? Someone is saying agitatedly, 'Let me tell you, the Shakti-Sunil-Niren crowd will become a shrine, a shrine!'

V

Samir said – Do you know how Debdulal-da referred to you?

– No. How?

– Pratik-da. The 'Su' prefix to your name has been – here he made a cutting movement, but with his hand held sideways, so probably indicating a sickle – chopped off.

Much laughter from Samir and Dhiren.

I asked – Did you not correct him?

Samir answered – Arrey, at least six times, but it was like a dog's tail: the moment you let it go, it curled back again.

– Not a bad change, what do you say, from Supratik to Pratik?

Dhiren said – Not bad at all. From 'auspicious symbol' to 'symbol' only. Who wants to be auspicious? Bloody cant of the bourgeois ****ers!

I, too, thought: Not bad, this loss of weight in the name. I could happily live as Pratik, as pure symbol only . . .

I had been handed a sickle and shown how to cut the paddy stalks at the base, about three inches from the soil. Each of us went to the plot that his host was working. Kanu, mine, was a wage-labourer, on the lowest rung. This, I realised later, had its uses: a number of class enemies could be pointed out to me – owners of small plots who overworked and underpaid day-workers; the subset of yes-men of big landlords among these; the absentee jotedaars' managers who cracked the whip . . .

The plot didn't look big when I saw it, but twenty minutes into disciplining myself to maintain the required inverted-U shape sent my neck and back screaming silently. The field seemed like a sea now and I had to swim across it. Already I was well behind Kanu and his wife, Bijli, and the three other munish working with us. They advanced with the choreographed grace and rigour of dancers, leaving me behind, standing alone, the bad student who couldn't master the movements. How did they do it? I knew those tired lines about practice and acclimatisation, but didn't their backs and necks and shoulders hurt too? In the beginning at least? I began to count small blessings: the fact that it was November (the thought of doing this in April was unthinkable) although my vest was stuck to my skin with sweat and the fatua over it was beginning to show signs of damp too. The sun was not strong enough for my head to be covered, not yet.

I bracketed the sickle around the base of a sheaf of stalks and cut using the 'towards me' motion that they'd taught me. The sickle was very sharp and there was no effort involved in the actual cutting. The cut stalks fell over my head. This was the thing I was failing to master, the way the left hand gathered the cut plants into a bundle, the bundle increasing in girth and the hand adjusting to accommodate that as you moved forward, cutting more stalks, until you had enough and you turned around and threw the harvested sheaves behind you and moved on. Even that flinging backward of the sheaves – even that required the mastery of a trick, a particular motion of the hand and wrist so that the stalks all fell with their bases aligned to the bases of the others already harvested, the tips to the tips. Mine fell in a fanned mess. How was I ever going to reach the end of the field?

And then I noticed: my palms and fingers were a mad criss-cross of little cuts from the sharp, dry edges of the rice leaves and stalks. Shame rose in me like bile. Hands that revealed instantly that I hadn't done a day's honest work in my life. The only thing I could do was ignore the sting, grit my teeth and keep cutting and advancing with all the strength and endurance I had. I wanted to make the cuts worse, deeper, my hands really bloody. It was the only way I would learn how to harvest properly and the only way my hands could stop being the shamefully middle-class hands they were now.

'Change yourself, change the world.'

When you look at a field full of ripened grain ready to be harvested it's a uniform brown-gold-sand colour. But as you cut with your sickle you notice that there's still some green inside, hiding within the larger brown, a few long partially green leaves, a little green fraction of a stalk. And as you cut these down, a tiny cloud of insects hiding in their massed density flies out; some wriggle away into the thickets not yet harvested, some scurry into the grass and sheaves and earth around you. And yet another thing: the sound of the paddy plants as you enter the thicket and cut them down. That rustle and rattle, louder, much louder now, accompanied by something between the snap of an almost-dry stalk and the wet snip of cutting through a twig that's still partly green. I can't explain very well. Taken together, this swishing of dry, dense vegetation fills your ears. You can hear it at night, resounding in your head, before you slip into the total silence of sleep.

My hands were sore in the morning after a night's sleep. I couldn't make a fist. So I made myself make a fist ten, fifteen, twenty times with each hand. The cracks reopened and beaded with blood. Some were tiny red threads, the red smudging when I touched them. And speaking of sleep, I'd never known sleep like this before – a total wiping out of all senses, all consciousness. I hadn't known exhaustion like this before either, a bone-breaking, bone-aching tiredness. That little revelation again, granted to an outsider, of the hidden inner cogs and wheels of the lives of others: now I knew yet another reason why everyone in the heart of rural Bengal went to sleep so early. When you worked in the fields from six in the morning to four in the afternoon the tiredness resulting from it stunned you into silence. You went from being a human, animated by a mind and spirit and consciousness, at the beginning of the day, to a machine without a soul at the end of those ten hours, moving your arms and legs and mouth because you felt some switch hadn't been turned off. Then it was, and the machine was dead, or just a stopped machine.

The next step was beating the sheaves in bundles against a sizeable boulder, which was placed on a large expanse of gunny cloth or jute. The impact loosened the ripe paddy grains, which collected on the cloth. After ten or fifteen minutes of work, the accumulating matt golden grains looked like a giant colony of insects or insect eggs, thinning out towards the peripheries in an untidy scatter. This was a much more exposed activity: you worked in the clearing where there had been dense plantation before. While harvesting, you were hidden by the tall paddy in front of you and sometimes to your left and right, but here, as you raised your hands above your head and brought down the sheaves of rice on the stone with all your strength – and it had to be done with all the force that you could bring to it; this, too, was a skill you had to acquire – you were the solo performer on a stage. Here you stood out, there was no help for it.

In my first hour of doing this, I kept interrupting my work to pick up bundles of spent sheaves to check if all the grains had really come off. I had heard that Nitai Das, and others in his situation, used to secrete some of these grainless stalks in their clothes, or steal them later, in the middle of the night, as the sheaves lay outside, drying, before being tied up into cylinders of hay. He would boil and eat them in the hope that a fleck or two of tenacious grain had clung on to the stalk-tips here and there. This is what they did in times of famine. This is what Nitai did here last year.

The paddy was taken away to be threshed. I could hardly move my arms and shoulders when I woke up the next morning.

Kanu took me with him wherever he was engaged to work this season: two sharecropping plots, and two where he worked as wage-labourer in the plots of the two big jotedaars here, the Rays and the Sinhas, part of the upper-caste inner-core neighbourhoods of Majgeria. He told me that it was less than half the work he did during harvesting time in a good year; now it had dwindled to this. From sharecropping he got, as his wages, one eighth of the husked weight of rice from each of the fields that he had worked. From the daily work in the absentee landlords' bigger plots, he got money.

In the wealthier parts of the village, the inner core that is, there were sumptuous harvest festivals with mass feasting and giving of gifts. Here, we gave the first new grains to crows, which were believed to be the reincarnations of the farmers' ancestors.

It was a breathless time of the year. These were part of the ninety or so days of guaranteed work that Kanu and others like him had, and they passed in consciousness-obliterating labour. Rice left overnight in water was eaten in the morning with a couple of green chillies and salt, before we set out for the fields; coarse-grained rice and a vegetable or dal given at the end of a day's work by the stewards of the farms where we harvested or threshed, then the walk back to Kanu's hut — that was it. In the evenings, no serious talk of land reform, of putting Mao's policies into practice in this particular context of a small Medinipur village with a population of 400 people, of debate on the relative virtues of 'economism' versus militancy, of rhetoric and corresponding action, of planning and consolidation and uniting the actions of various regional cells . . . none of that intense conversation that brought the foam to our mouths. No small meetings with the farmers who lived on the outer edges of the village, that is, the lower-caste and Santhal landless labourers. (I'm going to spare you the contents of past meetings. They'll bore you; they bore me sometimes. You'll say, 'Ufff, that same old chewing of the cud of politics.' Quite.)

Tonight the exhaustion has crossed a barrier — I feel I'm too tired to sleep, if that makes any sense to you.

Until now it has been all right sleeping on what I can only call their verandah, the narrow raised space between their threshold and the two steps leading to the general earth. The weather was cool, and it was getting colder, but it hadn't started biting yet. When we first came to Majgeria, Kanu said that I could share their one twelve-foot by ten-foot room, sleep in a corner, with him and his wife and their little child (six months old) and his wife's old father, but something in me could not assent to that arrangement. The room was spick and span – washed with red mud; what few possessions they had were in their places, the little dung-cake-burning oven in a corner, one dented aluminium rice pot, the jointed tongs, two plates, one terracotta vessel for drinking water . . . not much, as you can tell. But everything was neat, there was no mess. The low coir-and-wood pallet was for the old man, who lay or sat on it all day and all night long, wheezing but otherwise silent. Beautiful drawings, done with quicklime, of gods and goddesses, rising from the floor to nearly three or four feet up the walls on all four sides. The straw and palm-leaf thatch on the roof came down low and protected my 'verandah' from the sun and the rain.

The thatch was compact but sometimes, when I lay awake at night, or when something had woken me up, I didn't know what, and there was a breeze, I imagined I could hear the loose ends at the edges stir up in the barest whisper of a rustle, as if it was trying to say something secret to me. It was at those moments, when there was nothing between me and the secret sounds of the inanimate world, that I asked myself – Why didn't I accept their offer of sharing their tiny space inside? I had a ready answer: because one more person in that tiny space, bringing the number up to five, would have been difficult for them, yet they wouldn't have been able to say no. It was a true answer; I didn't want to add yet another small difficulty to their already hard-bitten lives. But at this hour of the night, with a silence only deepened by the occasional rustle in the thatch, I wondered if it was the entire truth or even the only truth. Could it be that I was going to be more inconvenienced than they by sharing their small space? This 'verandah', after all, was bigger in the sense of person-to-space ratio. And it was all my own. I had come here with my comrades, inspired by Charu Mazumdar's words, to become one with the lowest, the neediest of rural people, to eat with them, to live with them, to live as them. 'Like a fish with the other fish in the sea.' Then why did I pick the 'verandah' over the room? Did it not, by emphasising, even making literal my apartness, give the lie to our most basic principle, the very soul of our movement: oneness with those who had nothing?

The doubt was like a breach in a dam. Other thoughts rushed in, all to do with the awareness of my separation from those with whom I wanted to be at one. Quite often, for example, I had some difficulty understanding the dialect of the Santhal people. One day Kanu said something about how sleeping on the 'verandah' now, in winter, might be all right, but once summer, and especially monsoon, came along, I might like to rethink because – then he said something short, two words or three, that I couldn't quite decipher. After some questioning, he mimed it for me with his hands: the palm cupped and held upright, the inside facing me, then a swift movement of that cupped palm coming down.

Ah. Snake. Snake-bite.

Some more details emerged – in the monsoon the rains brought out a lot of snakes, not all of them poisonous, not the ones that lived in the flooded rice fields, but some certainly. Sleeping outside then was not such a great idea. I nodded. I was about to say that moving inside was hardly going to protect me since their room was not exactly insulated from the entry of snakes, but I bit my tongue.

Kanu said – A lot of snake action around these parts in the rainy season, lots of cases of snake-bites.

Something else made sense to me then. Throughout the village we had noticed tiny shrines housing amateurish clay figures of many-headed snakes, all poised to strike, sometimes accompanied by a figurine of Manasha, the goddess of snakes. Now I understood why the propitiation of this particular minor goddess was so universal here.

Much later Samir pointed out to me that the more numerous of these shrines did not hold either snakes or the goddess of snakes. They were to Shitala, the goddess of smallpox, chickenpox and other fatal and contagious diseases. The reason? In my naïvety I had thought this was the usual rural overdependence on religion and superstition, but Samir corrected me. He pointed out that this was the district that had been struck hardest during the 1943 famine, the very district from which hundreds and thousands of people had fled to Calcutta in large exoduses, only to die on the streets in the capital. And they had thought that appeasing the goddess of epidemics would spare them, so the shrines to Shitala had proliferated everywhere.

The picture kept getting muddier. From the convoluted measures Kanu gave me, I did a swift calculation to work out what his share from sharecropping each plot, one of 1.5 bighas, the other slightly over three, should be. Kanu received eight ser of rice from the first plot and twelve ser from the second, a total of half a mon of rice. Under several rules, not a single one enforced or enforceable in this country, he should have received slightly more than double the amount, just over one mon. Half-mon rice will feed him and his family one square meal a day for two months. The two plots where we worked as wage-labourers earned us five rupees a day for each plot. We should have ended up with a hundred rupees each, but the manager of the bigger piece of land decreed that because of an unusually low yield this year, only six mon per bigha on average, the labourers would get only three rupees a day. Thirty rupees for working a ten-hour day for ten days in which even breathing seems a luxury.

Kanu said that when the midday meal was given while harvesting this plot, they discovered that the portion of rice served to each labourer had been halved. Four other workers confirmed this. There were murmurs. Then there was an answer from the masters — How could you have the cheek to ask for more food in a straitened year such as this, when the effects of the past years' drought was not quite over and when it had depleted previous years' yields so drastically? Where was the extra food going to come from? From the air? They should be thankful for what they were getting; the alternative might well be no work and, therefore, starvation. Wasn't half a plate better than nothing on the plate?

I told Kanu that I was going to deal with them. He looked ill with fear and said — Babu, then what we are getting is going to go too. Don't make that mistake. Half-stomach is better than an empty stomach, they're right. If you cause trouble, you'll be marked out and then you'll never get work again.

His calculation, however destroying, was shrewder than mine. Besides, despite being called 'Babu', I was here to be one of them, not to tell them what to do. Except for our ultimate business when the time came.

I hear Bijli shout at Kanu — What are you going to eat? Why did you give him only your money? Why not give him your rice as well? Take it, go on, take it and give it to him.

Then her anger ends in her voice breaking into choked sobs. From what I can piece together, she's aghast that Kanu's entire earnings had to be given away to the moneylender to repay a fraction of the interest on the loans they had taken out.

The next day I give Kanu my thirty rupees. He says no, but he can't look me in the eye. His gaze is fixed on the notes in my outstretched hand.

— Take it, I say, I eat your food, I stay in your home, take it as my contribution to your family expenses. Your brother or your son would have done the same, no? Wouldn't you have taken it from them?

He takes the money from my hand and closes his fist around it, not to secure it in his grasp, but as if he's hiding something shameful and dirty.

At night, the muffled sound of sobbing again from inside . . .

I retold the story of 'The Foolish Old Man Who Removed the Mountains' from The Little Red Book to Kanu and Bijli one evening, but stumbled when it came to the ending, with god sending angels and all that rubbish, so I had to improvise quickly. Any reference to god would only have fed their natural fatalistic bent, so while explaining the story I laid special emphasis on the real meaning of god, repeating over and over the Chairman's sentence, slightly tweaked, 'Our god is none other than the masses of Indian farmers.' I changed the two mountains of imperialism and feudalism to the two mountains of poverty and feudalism, then I explained, yet again, the evil that was feudalism in plain, simple language, referring constantly to their present situation in this village.

I felt the session had gone well when Kanu said to me – Babu . . .

I flinched.

– Babu, you will have to come inside, it's getting colder, it's winter now . . .

I said – If you keep calling me Babu . . . Then I tried to laugh to make light of the barter I was trying to reach with him.

Kanu gave a shy and embarrassed smile, lowered his eyes and said nothing.

I pushed it – Go on, say Pratik. PRA-TIK.

He shook his head and cringed with shyness.

– Pra-tik, Pra-tik, I kept repeating.

– Per-tik, he said, at last – Per-tik babu.

Maybe I heard it because I was outside, sleepless and anxious with unbegun business. The sound was unmistakable, especially in a tiny village that saw a big motor vehicle only rarely and that too during peak times, such as harvest, which had just ended. Then, I don't know how, I put everything together. Of course, how obvious. I got up, wrapped the two pieces of chador around my head and body and ran to Anupam Haati's hut, where Samir was, and from there, three huts away, to Bipul Soren's, to rouse Dhiren, who, when we got there, was already waiting for us. The identical thought had gone through his head, for he greeted us with a whisper – Did you hear it?

A lorry, maybe two, maybe more, shaking noisily on their way through the dirt tracks, the sound progressing nearer and nearer, too loud in the silence of the cold night, then cutting out, followed by the slamming of the doors of the vehicles.

The night was as chinklessly dark as hell.

Samir whispered – We must separate, each of us follow the sound on his own.

This was the man, who, in ordinary circumstances, was afraid to visit the outhouse in the dark. I told you, didn't I, that he had steel in him, deep down?

There were trees and bushes and groves all around us and we could slip behind these at any time. There were proper brick houses in this neighbourhood, walls behind which we could crouch or against which we could flatten ourselves.

Sticking my head out from behind a huge tree near a pond, I observed what was going on less than a hundred metres away. The proceedings were illuminated only occasionally by hurricane lamps and torches, but what I could pick out in the dark was this: from the granary of the Ray house, the biggest house in Majgeria, as befitted the absentee landlord of more than 250 acres of land in the area, a string of three or four men came out, bearing sacks on their shoulders, and began walking in the direction of the eastern flank of the village. There were three, four, maybe five men holding up hurricane lamps to light the way. Others were walking around, pacing or standing still. These men, I could just about discern in the darkness only fleetingly and partially dispelled by the light of the lamps, were in police uniform.

I don't know how long I stayed watching this shadow-show. Fifteen minutes? Half an hour? It certainly felt longer. I thought I saw more people leaving the warehouse with sacks, or maybe the same people who had gone out before came back in and then went out again, bearing more sacks, but I couldn't be sure of this. I heard the occasional shout, a raised voice, or the murmur of a brief conversation, an order, but only as noises; I couldn't hear any words.

Suddenly there was someone beside me.

I jumped out of my skin.

It was only Dhiren. He whispered very briefly in my ear – Let's go back.

We had seen enough. This time, returning, Dhiren and I walked more or less together, keeping each other in our sights. There was a figure walking ahead of us in the same direction; it was Samir. By some telepathic argument we ended up, without consulting each other, near the small pond beyond our end of the village boundary, the place near the bamboo grove where we usually gathered in the night to talk and plan.

No one spoke for a long time. Samir asked – But what were the police doing?

Was it a rhetorical question? Did he really not know? Still I felt the need to answer him – They were standing guard. They were protecting Basudeb Ray and his servants as they transferred rice to the lorry to be taken to Calcutta or to cities in other states, Bihar, Orissa, where it will be sold on the black market at prices much higher than the official rate.

Saying something as barely factual as that did something to me and I could not stop myself from saying more, spelling out the obvious – The police were protecting the rich jotedaar in his act of avoiding the state's procurement levy . . .

Samir cut me short – Protecting from whom?

There was another silence. Dhiren answered him – Protecting the criminals from the honest. Hasn't that always been the reason for the existence of the police? Why do you fall from the sky witnessing that?

Samir said impatiently – No, no, I know all that. I wanted to know if the Rays had called in the police to guard their smuggling because they know about us. I mean, not the three of us specifically, but our . . . our activities, the activities of our larger group in these areas.

This gave us pause. Who knew? It could well be true. Little, if anything, could be hidden from the eyes of the state and its biggest instrument of control and repression, the police.

CHAPTER SIX

As a girl, Chhaya was in the habit of visiting the roof after lunchtime and spending large amounts of time up there, an inexplicable thing in the long summer when the heat softened the tar on the roads.

Charubala had once asked her daughter, 'What do you *do* up there in this heat? Your blood will dry up.'

Chhaya hedged and gave vague replies: 'I want to see the mango pickle marinating in the sun', or 'I want to check that there aren't any crows or sparrows sitting on the washing.'

Charubala, relieved to have at least one of her charges off her hands for a little while, did not raise any objections, except for a grumbled, 'The sun will evaporate all the grey matter in your head if you're not careful.'

On those occasions, little Som, if he was around, pleaded to go up to the roof, a rarely visited and unexplored kingdom for him, with his didi. Most of the times Charubala said no firmly: 'You'll fall off if you go near the parapet', or 'Not in this heat, no; you'll get sunstroke'. Occasionally, if Chhaya added her voice to Som's, she relented, but with numerous riders – 'Only for fifteen minutes, no more'; 'Keep a sharp eye that he goes nowhere near the edge'; 'Don't let him sit or play in the sun'; 'Don't let him play with dirt' – and, only after Chhaya had given assurances, would he be allowed to accompany her.

Priyo, Chhaya's shadow, was not long behind. On the concrete roof, baking in the wood-splitting heat since seven in the morning, it was impossible to step beyond the threshold barefoot. Sitting on the landing in front of the prayer room, Priyo and Chhaya lured their five-year-old brother with sure steps.

Chhaya said to Priyo, pretending to whisper, 'Shall we play that game? The one that ends with the winner getting half a dozen New Market biscuits?'

The New Market biscuits were Huntley & Palmers', which were brought home by Baba from Hogg Saheb's Market regularly because they were Som's favourites. The boy did not much care for 'bakarkhani', the Bengali ones they were constantly being told they should eat because that would support the nationalist movement against the British, but the Ghoshes' weak sympathy for such sentiments never translated into action; not enough energy was present to bring that about. Someone, probably Madan-da, had started calling them New Market biscuits to distinguish the two classes, and the name had stuck.

Priyo answered, 'Shhh, don't mention it now, Som will hear us.'

'Oh, sorry, I forgot myself, what about . . .' Chhaya said, then proceeded to whisper in Priyo's ear.

Priyo's eyes lit up; he said excitedly, 'Yes, yes', then it was his turn to do the whispering, only letting the words 'game' and 'biscuits' become audible.

By now, all his attention focused on his elder siblings, Som cried out, 'Me too, me too.'

Priyo and Chhaya, now in unison, 'No, you're too small. It's a game for grown-ups.'

That reeled Som in. 'No, no, I play too. And I want New Market biscuits.' He seemed on the verge of kicking up a noisy tantrum.

'All right, all right,' Chhaya said, 'but on two conditions. One, you cannot tell anyone, not Ma, not Baba, not Madan-da, no one. If you do, we'll never never never let you play our nice games with us again. Okay?'

Som nodded his head innocently and eagerly. Secrets! This was getting better and better.

Priyo said, 'The other condition is this – you cannot give up on the game halfway through. You *must* finish it, otherwise terrible things will happen to you.'

'What terrible things?' the little boy asked, easily diverted by the more exciting part of the conditions.

Priyo extemporised, 'The ghost that visits you in your dreams will cut out your tongue and wear it around his neck. When you wake up in the morning you'll find that you cannot speak. Ever again. No sound will come out of your mouth.'

Som's mouth trembled.

'You'll cry out, "Ma, Ma", but there'll be no sound, nothing.'

Som whimpered, 'No!', about to start squalling. Chhaya, sensing its imminence, pulled him onto her lap, patted him on his head and said, 'Now, now. Nothing of that sort is going to happen. Just do as we tell you.' A few kisses were planted on his fat, dimpled cheeks and curls. 'You still want your New Market biscuits, don't you?'

The tears remained unshed. Som nodded again.

Chhaya explained, 'So this is the game. You run to that corner of the roof' – here she pointed to the area furthest from the attic – 'and start walking back towards us while we wait here and count up to one hundred. You cannot return to this point, where we are sitting now, before we reach a hundred. If you do that, you've lost. No biscuits for you. But if you get here on the dot of one hundred or after, a whole plateful. Do you understand the game?'

'Yes,' the child said, hesitantly.

Priyo now took him through the rules, more slowly this time, spelling out each clause for a child's understanding. It was difficult for him to tell if Som was absorbing and comprehending every little detail, including the sanctions that had been imposed earlier; his face had an unreadable expression, a kind of calm incomprehension mixed with wariness.

'All clear?' Priyo asked again.

'Yes.'

'All right then, we are going to start counting as soon as you have reached the far corner. You run to it but, remember, you have to walk back slowly, very slowly.'

The unshod boy ran swiftly to the north-east corner, which looked out towards Russa Road; he was in the full, blazing field of the early afternoon sun. He reached the corner, turned around to face Chhaya and Priyo, and then the effect of the three or four seconds of his feet remaining on the ground without being raised for shifting to a new spot hit him.

'Oooh, hot, hot,' he said, almost absent-mindedly, still registering the new sensation. He stood first on one foot, then on the other,

continuing the rapid exchange between the right and the left for a
good few seconds, then tried to stand on the outer edges of his feet.
He looked like a wobbly clown, performing antics, or an unsteady
toy, its clockwork mechanism gone haywire. Priyo and Chhaya giggled,
but their mirth was slightly adulterated by a squishy feeling in their
hearts – how unutterably sweet he looked, puzzled and in pain and
imprisoned by the rules of the game.

'My feet hurt,' Som cried out.

'No pain, no gain,' Chhaya called out. 'Just think of your plate of
crunchy, sweet, sugar-crusted biscuits and start moving forward. We're
going to start counting.'

Som's face was scrunched up with pain, or perhaps with confusion
and bewilderment at the experience of a game that had nothing of
fun in it, or pleasure; instead, it was a kind of agony. He kept hobbling
from one foot to another.

Priyo started counting out loud, 'One . . . two . . . three . . .
four . . .'

Som advanced, trying to keep as much of the under-surface of his
feet off the concrete as possible; he tried walking on tiptoe, then with
his instep curved in and only his curled-in toes and heel touching the
ground. All the positions were proving to be precarious and unstable.
He shouted to his brother and sister, 'I feel hot on my soles.' The
light was lacerating.

Priyo said, 'Twelve . . . thirteen . . . don't move too fast! Remember,
you have to last out until one hundred. Eight . . . nine . . . ten . . .
eleven . . .'

Som tried a few more steps. It was like trying to balance on a
pinhead. The only way to end the misery was to run back quickly,
but that was not a possibility.

Chhaya took over the counting, 'Thirteen . . . thirteen . . .
thirteen . . . fourteen . . . no, no, you moved too quickly . . . ten
. . . eleven . . .'

Som said, 'You said thirteen many times. It's fourteen after thirteen.'

'But you were taking very fast steps, so we had to adjust the counting
accordingly,' Chhaya said.

'On top of that you're cheating,' Priyo added. 'You're meant to
walk normally, not like a flittering sparrow.'

'But it's hot when I put my foot down,' Som protested.

'You'll get used to it if you let them stay on the ground for a bit. Try it,' Chhaya said.

'Go on, try it. We're older than you, we know better, don't you know?' Priyo said.

Som, suspicious now, paused to consider if this was to be trusted. The white heat of the sun had blinded him and he could not see his Bor'-da and Didi sitting in the darkness of the shade. The burning surface seemed determined to peel off the skin from the underside of his feet.

'Seven . . . eight . . . nine . . . ten . . .' Chhaya intoned.

Som shouted, 'But seven is finished, it is over, why are you saying seven again?' and exploded into the tears that he had been holding back.

Chhaya and Priyo heard Mamoni's-ma, the domestic who did the laundry, coming upstairs, with malign timing, to hang out the washing.

Unfazed, Chhaya changed tack seamlessly. 'Oh, you poor little cushy-cushy-pookie angel! Come running to me, come,' she said in her cutesiest voice, but stayed put where she was.

Som, blind now with tears, ran to the attic. Chhaya tried to pull him towards her to comfort him, but the boy stood there stubbornly, howling. He was on the threshold of a bitter knowledge, yet he did not know it, having only a cloudy intimation of some part of his life gone awry. Mamoni's-ma now reached the landing, two huge buckets spilling with washed clothes in each of her hands.

'What happened? What happened?' she asked, setting down the washing. 'Somu, why are you crying, my little one?'

Then she turned to Priyo and Chhaya and asked, 'What's happened to him? Did he take a fall? Hurt himself?'

Priyo rushed to answer. 'No, nothing of the sort. He was adamant about going out into the sun to play, Chhaya and I couldn't stop him. God knows, we tried! And as soon as he stepped out, he burned his feet, so he's crying now.'

Chhaya joined in the duet. 'This is what happens when you don't listen to your elders. We warned you,' she said.

The wailing doubled in volume.

Charubala called up irritably from the floor below, 'What's going on, eh? What's all that shouting and crying?' and started climbing upstairs. 'I knew this business of going up to the roof in pate-cracking heat would come to no good.'

Som rushed down to her.

Mamoni's-ma, with her grubby rag of a sari hitched above her ankles so that her cracked heels were all too visible, lifted up the buckets and, advancing towards the clothes line, said, 'He is only a little boy, he has delicate, soft feet, not hardened, calloused ones like ours. No wonder he's crying. This sun is a killing one . . . The clothes will be dry in no time at all.'

Charubala, intercepted by Som halfway up the stairs, paused in her berating to comfort the child – 'There, there, my golden one, hush, hush, it'll be fine' – then reached the attic to vent her anger.

It struck her immediately, looking at Priyo and Chhaya, that the time to give them a slap or two or wring their ears to punish them over minor things had long passed; they were nearly adults now. This took the wind out of her sails somewhat.

'Did I not tell you that it was all going to end in tears? Did I not?' she yelled at her stony-faced son and daughter. 'I want the two of you to go downstairs this very second, do you hear? Never a moment's peace in this zoo. Everyone's asleep in this heat, but only in my asylum do I have children who choose to play in the sun. How dare you disturb everyone's siesta? Downstairs, right now!'

Their ears burned with the shame of being scolded in the presence of a servant. Neither of them uttered a word. They stood up and made their way downstairs, letting out the breath they had been holding in for a long time. They did not look at each other, knowing that the imprint of relief that they had not been interrogated about the reasons for Som's crying fit would be all too readable on their faces; it would have bound the two together in too obvious a collusion, not least by bunching together related events from the past.

There was the time they had sat Som down, less than a year ago, when he was getting over a bad cold; they had made him pick his abundant nose and eat the pellets of snot, all of different consistencies and textures.

Such events were not regular; they were spun out on the spur of an inspired moment, and inspiration, or opportunity, did not cheapen itself by visiting too often. There was no intentional or premeditated cruelty in these games, not always; much of it had an anthropological interest for the perpetrators. Chhaya found her little brother between the ages of three and four so edibly sweet that she wanted to handle him much like a comestible, presented in portion-sized pieces to devour. She found her teeth clenching when she ran her hand through his curls; her hands itched with the desire to inflict pain; often she tightened her fist, his hair caught in it, one step beyond the acceptable boundary between petting and something murkier, more elemental. As soon as Som yelped, she retreated to cosier ground. How much could he take? How much could she get away with? Often, while squeezing his chubby cheeks, she would dig her fingers in so that she could feel his gums and the roots of his teeth through the intervening membrane of skin and flesh and fat, and Som would start crying. She would then spend a lot of time cooing and gurgling and kissing and consoling; a much paler time than the animalic excitement of the moments when her desire toppled into something else.

She squeezed cut hemispheres of lime into his open mouth just to have the pleasure of seeing him pull faces; her insides turned all woolly watching him. Then she forced his mouth open and rubbed the spent fruit against his teeth, witnessing his gradual working out of the unpleasant sensation of soured, tender teeth with something approaching a flailing inside her chest and stomach. These things were motivated not by an unperceived sadistic streak, but by a sense of curiosity; how would this beautiful, fair, curly-locked angel look and behave and sound when taken outside the matrix of his ordinary experience and transplanted into a new, unknown one?

Priyo, too, had this tendency towards experimentation. In winter, when oranges were in season, he convinced the boy that regular squeezing of the peel into his open eyes would guarantee perfect vision for life and offered to help him keep his eyes open and do it himself. The gullible child agreed. The citrus oil stung. Som blinked furiously, hardly able to keep his watering eyes open.

'Ooh, ooh,' he sang, 'burning, burning.' His eyes streamed.

'That's a good sign,' Priyo soothed. 'It means the goodness in the orange peel is working. Your eyes are going to shine like stars now.'

The tipping point came when Chhaya and Priyo lured Som to the terrace, grabbed his favourite toy, Teddy Tail, off him and hanged it, with much ceremony, on the clothes line, then amputated the toy's limbs. Som, unable to bear it, lunged at Priyo and sank his teeth into his wrist. Chhaya tried to detach the boy by catching hold of his abundant curls and pulling with all the force in her body. The ensuing commotion brought Charubala running up to the terrace.

Chhaya, never one to forget a slight or forgive anyone for having exposed her as being wrong and then for having punished her for it, more than two years later took a kind of revenge on her mother for the sound thrashing she had received that afternoon. She was helped in this by the coincidence of two events: the lead-up to the Matriculation Exam and her period that month.

On an oppressive summer late-afternoon, with the sky a livid violet-black, which warned of a thunderstorm, Charubala, finding the rooms prematurely dark, went around turning on the lights room by room. It was only after switching on the ceiling light in the sitting room on the first floor that she noticed her daughter lying on the low divan, almost at one with it.

Chhaya let out a 'tsk' of irritation at the sudden exposure and turned her face to the wall.

Charubala asked, 'What are you doing, lying all alone in a dark room? Why haven't you turned on the lights? To leave the house in the dark like this at dusk . . . it's not good, the goddess of wealth will run away. There's going to be the most almighty storm, just look at the sky.'

Silence.

'What's happened to you?'

No answer.

Then it fell into place. Charubala went over to her daughter, sat down on the edge of the divan and said to Chhaya's back in a more tender voice, 'Are you feeling ill? Is your stomach cramping? Shall I bring a hot-water bottle?'

Silence again.

Charubala touched her daughter's shoulder, only to have her arm batted away with a vicious swipe.

'What's happened?' she repeated. 'Why aren't you telling me?'

No answer.

Charubala persisted. Something about the girl's posture, all scrunched in on herself, the back of her head so eloquent with – with what? – indicated to Charubala that there was a different storm brooding, as if the weather outside were going to play out in Chhaya first. She pulled at her shoulders gently to make Chhaya face her and all she got was a tenacious physical resistance. When she managed at last to coax Chhaya to face her, she saw that she was not wrong: that dark face had in it a shadow of the livid blue of the clouds massed outside.

It felt as if years and years of something thwarted had banked up in the girl and was now going to overflow. For a moment Charubala felt something closer to fear than sympathetic worry, then tried to dispel its pressure by falling back on the more reliable emotion of gently badgering affection.

'Why can't you tell me? You should be able to tell me everything. I'm your mother, after all.'

At the word 'mother', Chhaya's mouth and face crumpled. 'No, you're not my mother, you're Somu's mother.' The words seemed to be excavated from some pit deep inside her soul. What agony and tamped-down anger burned in them.

The click of sudden knowledge in Charubala's head – how could she not have seen this coming? – was offset by the short falling feeling inside her. So this was what had been eating her daughter, causing her sulkiness, her mood swings, the cloud of pettiness and jealousy that seemed to trail her perpetually nowadays. It was only last week that she had come upon her and Priyo bullying Som, who was terrified of the dark, by shutting the boy in a totally dark room. Chhaya and Priyo had then shrouded themselves in long bedsheets and entered the room, impersonating ghosts, moaning 'Hooo, hooo, hooo', standing at the door to prevent the child from escaping. Children's games, yes, but ever since Charubala had discovered the blisters on Som's feet and joined the dots – some, if not all – together, she had been prone to sensing something unsmooth to these games and naughtiness, as if the nap of the fabric was not all uniform and comforting to the touch but had, instead, a tiny thorn here, a prickle there, to deliver an unpleasant surprise. Even this latest instance she, with her pragmatic mind and worldly-wise domestic strength, had been prepared to ignore as the inevitable process of siblings tussling with each other, something that would ease with time and the beginning of adulthood; but confronted now with those treacherous words, it was as if everything she had chosen to pass over in silence had found embodiment, a spectre transformed into a flesh-and-blood combatant that demanded reckoning with. Denial would no longer do.

She drew in a deep breath and began the job. 'Chhee, chhee, what inauspicious words! I'm as much your mother as Som's or Priyo's or Adi's. You are all my children.' Spoken out like that, the truth, obvious and axiomatic, acquired the falsehood of lines in a play.

A brilliant flash of lightning pushed the purple of the clouds to their most extreme, malignant shade for a second, then the darkening resumed. In the silence following Charubala's strained words, the drumroll of thunder sounded equally theatrical.

Chhaya began a low sobbing that was not so distant from retching.

Charubala tried again. 'Can you favour one finger over another? All of them make up the thing that is the hand. Each one is as important as the other.'

Chhaya's eyes streamed with tears.

'Don't cry. Please. I feel terrible watching you cry like this,' Charubala said. Her heart clenched with pity.

Still sobbing in that excruciated way, Chhaya brought out deadlier words. 'You . . . love . . . Somu . . . more . . . because . . . he's . . . fair . . . and . . . beautiful . . . and . . . I'm . . . dark . . . and . . . ugly . . . and . . . cross-eyed.'

With a dozen words Charubala's world lay cleaved. It was not that she had not known this; once again, it was the exposure of her unacknowledged fears, so indecently made incarnate to the open air, that caused this sensation of sudden terror. And yet she sat locked in her helplessness; how could she bring herself to leap over her embarrassment and say those words or act out those gestures that would wipe the slate clean for her daughter? Were love, compassion, pity expressible? How? Charubala certainly did not know. Love and affection were not particular instances of their manifestations, but rather the entire world one moved around in, an atmosphere. How could you isolate something so brutally flat and one-dimensional, such as words, from a kind of sky, which was intangible, both there and not there? The closest she had ever come to showing such feelings to her children had taken, typically in this world, the form of brusqueness or dismissal, a performance of irritation: 'Get off, get off, I have to go to the kitchen otherwise so-and-so is sure to burn the rice' to a child hanging on to her neck; 'Ufff, not a moment's peace in this home, you are burning me to death' to another, demanding to snuggle up to her during afternoon nap; or, delivered in a voice pitched halfway between mock-tartness and faux-scolding, 'Oh, melting over the sides with affection, I see. Off with you!' to another of her children perhaps wanting nothing more than a cuddle. These brush-offs, accompanied more often than not by the unlikely partners of a smile and furrowed brows, not dissimilar to a smile flashed through tears, were never meant to be serious. They were the array of masks that love wore, the only way it could be displayed and seen. Both parties knew this in their blood and their bones. It was in the very air they breathed. So being faced now with an imperative to leave that familiar set of comforting exchanges behind and take a leap into the unknown filled Charubala with a tense inertia. She had the sense that she had reached a crossroads and, whichever turning she took, she would do wrong, either by her daughter or by her world.

She made the boulder of her tongue move to bring out the words, 'Who has put such rubbish in your head? How can you say this?'

In desperation, she continued elaborating.

'Is skin-colour everything? You have so many talents – you are a prize pupil in Diocesan, and how many girls can boast of going to an English-medium school? And you sing so beautifully. Just the other day Arati-di from the neighbouring house was saying to me, "When your Chhaya sits down to practise in the evenings, we drop all our work, shush everyone and stand at our windows, drinking in everything. Will you ask Chhaya's music teacher, Shipra-di, to train my children too?" Beauty is skin-deep, you know that. What good is it to anyone? It won't quench your thirst, or cure a sick person.'

But already it was too late. Chhaya's cry had called for something instant, something headlong and impulsive. Instead, all she was able to return by way of a response was a cold, congealed thing, deliberated upon until its quick, fragile life had departed.

Around the same time Adinath made a strange choice, strange to his father, at least. Instead of joining Charu Paper immediately after he sat his Intermediate Science exams, he applied to read Engineering at Shibpur. At this juncture in Adi's life, his childhood love of the built structure had flared to something grander, more ambitious – he wanted to learn how to build houses. The arrival of Somnath had interrupted several things, one of which, not given much thought by Adinath, or at least not consciously, had been the gradual development of a bond between Prafullanath and his oldest son based on what father had assumed was an early grooming of the business sense and what son had taken to be the ordinary commerce of affection and companionship. But that undone drawing of the interior of a house, something that Adi later came to know was called something as simple as a plan, never found realisation in the expected father–son duet; it had to be learned, understood and executed as a solo. And yet Prafullanath's neglect – if that it can be called – of Adi after the birth of Som did not have the predictable effect of snuffing out the boy's interest in the area that had been so much his domain with his father, held pure and insulated from the interference of the world.

What happened was something else. The deepening interest in and fascination with houses, their depiction on paper, both stylised and representational, continued and expanded to take in harder questions that led to the study of the business of buildings and construction as a discipline. How did walls support a roof? Why did foundations not collapse? How could extra storeys be added to a house on the foundation estimated for a two-storey building? As Adi's interest gravitated towards the scientific and structural-engineering end of things, there was a concomitant diminishment of that part of his imagination that perhaps cooperated, unwittingly, with his father's desire to see this enthusiasm about houses and plots of land directed in one direction only: the growth and maturity of business sense, or 'material intelligence', as it was called, to the level needed for starting a construction business. Adi himself, as a boy, had never thought along those lines; it was an interest, a hobby; that was all there was to it.

To what use it could be harnessed, to which destination it was headed – these questions may have played in his father's mind, but never arose in the boy's.

Although the wish to study Engineering, inevitable if one gave it some thought, had been years in the making, Prafullanath had either been in denial about it or had not considered it worthwhile paying much attention to a trajectory that was in conflict with the design he had in his head.

He summoned his oldest son in an attempt to dissuade him.

'This was not the plan, this Engineering College business,' he said to Adi.

Adi, head bowed, replied with some trepidation, 'No, but, yes, but . . .'

'Stop but-but-ing – spit it out!' his father demanded.

'No, erm, you've known it, that I want to be an engineer . . .'

How could he not have known? Adi thought; his father had been the one who had ignited the flame, then held his cupped palms to nest it against anything that could extinguish it. All those drawings, those pencils and plans, interior and exterior – had he forgotten it all now? Now that his attention had moved elsewhere? Adi did not think about it in those terms, choosing instead to tell himself that in the effort and energies needed by his father to make a business thrive, this murmuring little dream, a secret between the two of them, really, first became inaudible, then, over time, as it no longer made its presence felt, was forgotten. Now that he had impulsively framed the answer to his father's demands in such a way that there was a possibility of Prafullanath being reminded of that forgotten secret and, worse, beginning to acknowledge a kind of abandonment, Adi felt panic creeping up on him. All he wanted was for the conversation to skirr off in another direction; he could not bear to have his father put form and substance in words to the one particular, vital loosening that had happened to their bond.

'Who's going to look after the business then?' asked Prafullanath. 'You are my eldest son, it's part of the order of things that you should take over from me.'

'I can do that as soon as I've qualified. It's only four years.' He felt a momentary reprieve, but also a shadowy disappointment, that the conversation had not gone down the feared path.

'No, you are going to start coming to the office with me regularly, not the two-days-a-week we've done so far. You've got to start learning the ropes. In business experience is everything.'

Adi bravely tried another argument. 'I thought engineering would provide a solid foundation for the manufacturing side of things,' he lied. But the relief had won out and he could not bring them both to the brink of a reckoning again by divulging that he was actually going to read mechanical engineering. In order to spare his father, he elaborated on the lie, 'It would be good to know how paper is made, how to improve its quality, the science and mechanics of it . . .'

Again he was cut short.

'We know how paper is made. There are machines to do it, people to run the machines. It's made the way it has been made all these years. Not much use, all this science and engineering and mechanics. No education can be a substitute for experience. What good is book-learning going to do? It's like teaching parrots to speak. Look at me: what harm has lack of education done to me? I left home at the age of nineteen, a year after my father's death. I worked my way up, beginning as a shop assistant, bundling paper, filling and emptying carriages, as an errand-boy. We did not have the luxuries of education and universities like your lot. We worked so hard that the sweat from our heads dropped onto our feet. Engineering was no help then . . .'

Adi's attention cut out at this point. He had heard the narrative many, many times before, the story of Prafullanath Ghosh, self-made man: his escape from his parental home; his rise from rags to riches; his resilience against the cruelties and injustices the world threw at him; his ultimate ascendancy; the shaky beginnings to the current solidity of his construction business, which he had started from scratch . . . not for the first time it struck Adi that clichés were clichés because they were truths that had been lived out by generation after generation of people before him. By the time those lived truths were inherited by him, they had become foxed, crumpled, brown and brittle with age. Through the entire discourse, however, Adinath remained still, his head respectfully lowered; he did not know anything else. It also served as a way of hiding the imprint on his face of the knowledge that he had just acquired: his father has forgotten that anything special had ever existed between them. He need not have feared, after all.

It may be said, not unfairly, that Prafullanath, having missed out on the experience of higher education himself and, therefore, to some extent, partly unsympathetic to it and partly unable to enter its potential imaginatively, had stumbled upon the business of educating his sons and daughter as an afterthought, extemporising on the basis of whim, or the chatter of other people, or the prevailing fashion in circles more elevated than the one to which he belonged, a familiar variant of the aspirational urge. So when the issue presented itself, the matter of convenience overruled all other considerations: Adi and Priyo were sent to Ballygunge Government High School on Beltala Road, a bare one and a half miles north-east from their home and, later, Bhola, to whom his parents gave the least attention, to the even nearer Mitra Institution. An unusual thing happened when it came to his daughter. It was only by a stroke of chance that the imminence of sending Chhaya to school coincided with one of Prafullanath's acquaintances remarking on the vital necessity of English education. The idea caught. In an uncharacteristic and momentary fit of daring, he had Chhaya admitted to an English-medium school, St John's Diocesan on Elgin Road. As if to atone for it, there was a throwback with Bhola, then again a reaching for the heights when it came to the jewel of his life, Somnath, who was sent to the highly reputed missionary school, St Xavier's, on Park Street.

In the twelve years between Adi and Somu, Prafullanath had felt, in every pore of his body, the toil involved in making a business stand on its feet, so he had banished, with wry casualness, the grand ambitions for several varied businesses that he had harboured for himself and his sons; in that sense, Adi was correct that his father had forgotten what it was that lay between them. While unable to acknowledge that the vastness of his earlier designs was linked in a straightforward if intricate causality to the life he had had before the great rupture happened, Prafullanath was steadfast in his aim of handing over the captaincy of Charu Paper in the future.

A new kind of knowledge surprised him as he looked at the dark hair, oiled down, combed and parted on the left, on his son's head. Did they all become their own persons, these creatures you gave birth to, these children whom you thought were an extension of your own self, endowed with your features, with aspects of your own personality and character, but who in the end came asunder and floated away from you, no longer like your arm or your leg, doing what you willed them to do, but puppets that suddenly became animated, only to rebel and set off on their own? Prafullanath felt a mild dizziness at the realisation; this was a parent's separation anxiety, the melancholy at the inevitable parting of ways. Why had he not foreseen this? Did one ever know the mind and soul and personality of one's child, even little segments of them?

The meditation only served to stiffen Prafullanath's spine. He said, firmly and with finality, 'No, I will have none of this newfangled college-going business. You will start coming to the office immediately.'

Adi's head remained bowed, as if receiving a sentence.

Adi never perceived when his indifference to taking over the reins at Charu Paper had begun to develop. But there it was, the apathy, like a tree one has uncertainly seen in a dream and in the morning it is there right outside, its branches brushing the window, impatient to get in. Adinath went through the motions on the six days of the week that he attended the offices of Charu Paper in Old China Bazaar Street. He listened respectfully to his father, in silence, talking about the advantages of the kraft process over the sulphite, the difference between internal sizing and surface sizing, how to avoid excessive rush or drag on the wire . . . Meanwhile, his mind wandered and took off from the occasional word of his father that would enter through his ears to spin elaborate, playful traceries of equations about the strength of materials or the number of beams required to hold together a room of dimensions $x \times y \times z$, when the other variables consisted of p = weight of roof, q = thickness of walls . . .

Khoka-babu, Prafullanath's factotum in the office and a kind of manager, always gave the impression of bowing low to Adinath during these occasional visits. He ordered tea and sweets from the nearby Annapurna Mishtanna Bhandar, made a fuss of the teenager, whom he called 'Chhoto-babu', partly as a joke, but partly also in earnest ingratiation because he knew that he would have to work under this boy one day. Adi smiled tightly, ignored him and waited for the whole thing to be over. That dream-tree gripped him tight in the embrace of its branches as he sat in a room on the ground floor of the building on Old China Bazaar Street and tried to focus his mind on files, papers, receipts, bills, challans, tenders, all of which filled him with a disaffection bordering on vague nausea.

Had he felt like this when his father had dragged him to Bardhaman and Hooghly ten, twelve years earlier, to ignite his interest in the business? Father and son had set out to visit the family mills in trains that moved slowly through the lush green countryside. Adi remembered the rice fields as parcels of bright emerald during the monsoon, and the flat land in late autumn all gold and green as far as the horizon, with patches of white cotton-clouds in the low blue sky, and the stubble brown in the red soil after the harvest in winter. He remembered his father pointing out to him the fountain-like banana trees, with their enormous, clattery leaves and their bizarre flower, a large inverted teardrop-shaped growth, maroon-black in colour, hanging solidly at the bottom of a long stalk. How could that be a flower? he remembered asking his father. The land had seemed so remote and uninhabited, full of trees and copses, the tight cover of vegetation everywhere. At the station, a car would be waiting to take them through dirt roads to a Charu Paper Mill. Prafullanath would point out to his son the various elements of the work-in-progress in response to the boy's questions.

'Why are there flowers on this machine?'

'The labourers have just done Bishwakarma puja. It's to consecrate the machine so that no harm comes to the production.'

'What harm?'

'Oh, just inauspicious things.'

'Why is that man loading rubbish onto that slope?'

'That's what is going to be turned into pulp.'

'What is pulp?'

'The stuff that becomes paper.'

'Why do you need so many machines to make paper into paper? Why can't you ask the men to stick the rubbish paper together?'

'Because we need to get rid of the impurities.'

'What is impurities?'

Thinking of those afternoons now, all the different occasions spliced together, the images appeared like mounted photographs in an album. The forceful gush of brown water into the open maws of huge drums and cylinders and churners, creating almighty whirlpools. The innumerable vats of dirty greyish-white chyme that floated up to the top as the raw material was subjected to dozens of chemical processes and churning and beating and swirling and sieving. The mounds of wet rubbish – plastic, buttons, bits of metal, straw, clips, particles of rags, unidentifiable coloured solids – left behind in the meshes. The tall, narrow, cylindrical cages of iron rods sticking out of the water at regular intervals, like the carpals of a futuristic skeleton. Shreds and scraps of wastepaper everywhere, in the walkways connecting the different units and on the ground, as if after a battle fought entirely with paper. A heart-pumping climb on a rickety ladder, supported firmly by one of the managers from below and his father from above, to the lip of yet another enormous drum; held in his father's arms, he had looked down on its contents of a kind of fleecy off-white foam circulated slowly by two huge rotating arms half-submerged in the substance, moving closer and closer towards him until he had cried out in fear. And pipes, pipes everywhere, in all styles of ribbing and all kinds of colours, straight and curved and curled and looped: the site was an eviscerated mythical beast and they its entrails. And that pervasive, wet, slightly suffocating reek of the forty chemicals – the figure had been proudly proclaimed by his father – that went into the making of an ordinary thing such as paper.

Where was he in all that excessive effort to produce something so common, so disappointing, after the massiveness of the process involved? Adi remembered being told off by his father for chucking stone chips, one after another, into the bore-well tank from which the mill drew its water, trying to make a bigger splash than the one that preceded it, or perhaps even trying out his recently learned trick of 'tadpole' – making one stone skim the surface of the water one, two, three, four times before it sank; the challenge here was to make it work in the severely confined space of the tank. Had he done all that out of boredom? He could not remember. And now, surrounded by the building blocks and tricky manoeuvres for making money, not bridges or roads or theatres, he could not map this more urgent boredom onto the lost memory of the probable one from his boyhood.

VI

They were not all innocent of what we had to teach them. When we began with our small evening meetings nearly five months ago, there were perhaps three or four farmers in attendance, the numbers almost totally made up of men from the three homes that had received the three of us. Then harvest was quickly upon us, and we hardly had the time even to breathe, and no energy at the end of the day either to explicate or to listen to Mao's theories. This was no bad thing: the situation at the end of the harvesting made it easier for us to spread our word. Then the numbers went up – six, ten, twelve, seventeen, at one time, even twenty-three, our high point.

At these meetings there were farmers who had no money to buy seeds for the next season, but without planting they would die, so they got deeper into debt. A few of them grew vegetables by the side of their huts; this was all the food they had in some months of the year. And when the season for waxed gourd and ridged gourd and bottle gourd was over, they would starve.

We told them that sacks of rice had been smuggled out at two in the morning.

We began by taking small steps: the reversal of 'the crop belongs to the owner of the land' to 'the land belongs to the cultivator of the crop'; the $\frac{1}{3} : \frac{2}{3}$ rule of harvest grain distribution. At night, Samir, Dhiren and I again and again debated the relative merits of economism versus militancy. We told the farmers about the uprising in Naxalbari last year. Without putting it in so many words, we knew we were moving towards militancy. The business of living with them, learning to be them, was not an end in itself, as we now began to understand. It had always been a stepping stone towards more radical action.

I knew from the moment that Dhiren brought out The Little Red Book, pointed to it and said – This man has freed eighty crore people from the noose around their necks, the kind of halter you have around your necks now – and I saw every pair of eyes in the room turn to look at the book, that we had crossed the line. Our work had begun. From the dissemination of the words of Chairman Mao and Comrade Charu Mazumdar, we will soon move on to squad formation and, from there, to 'action'.

As I was saying, the farmers were not totally innocent: Anupam Haati told the meeting – The city people who came here when we were sowing, they showed us a small red book too, they said the book will show you how to punish jotedaars.

Before coming here I had often wondered how difficult it would be to convince and mobilise villagers. I had made myself exhausted thinking about the months of talks and meetings, posters and expounding. It had felt, in my imagination, like the effort that would be required to move a giant crag by pushing at its base. Within a few days of our arrival, however, that sense of impossibility had become its opposite: an easy, achievable optimism.

Do you know why?

Because I saw the kind of lives they led: going to bed on an empty stomach for over half the year; drowned in debt without any hope of ever surfacing; their unborn generations bonded to service those debts; their blood sucked dry (talking of which, the Bengali word for 'sucking' and 'exploitation' is the same, have you ever noticed?); their children bony but with swollen bellies, arms and legs like reeds, hair bleached to brown with malnutrition; their lives shrivelled by worry. Because their lives were like this, I thought they would be simmering with anger and all we needed to do was a bit of stoking and there would be a giant conflagration that would bring down the blood-suckers and burn them to cinders. How hopeful it all seemed.

Then that hopefulness curdled: what I hadn't reckoned with was that decades and decades of this slow-burning flame of resentment and deprivation had burned them, not the perpetrators. The embers of anger we had thought of fanning had burned down into the ashes of despair. They were already dead within their lives. They had no hope, no sense of a future, just an endless playing out of this illness of the present tense until its culmination in an early death. In other words, we had to kindle a fire with ashes. Have you ever tried doing that?

Once again, the three of us by the pond near the bamboo grove at night. The cry of an animal in the distance is picked up, briefly, by more cries, all identical, then they stop.

– Jackals, Dhiren says.

– Nocturnal, like us, says Samir.

– Not quite. We work in the daytime too, we don't sleep it away.

– Tomorrow we have to walk thirteen miles in the dark.

We were going with eight farmers from Majgeria to Munirgram for a huge poster exhibition and mass assemblies organised by the Medinipur Coordination Committee. It was going to be a big day. Farmers and activists were coming from villages all over the western Medinipur region. Our aim was to educate them in class dynamics, arouse hatred in them against their class enemies, explain the events of Naxalbari and Telengana to let them know that they were not alone, that class uprisings were happening throughout the country, peasants were snatching their land and crops back from landowners, shaking off the yokes of their slavery. We were going to explain to them in simple, direct language that their lot would never be improved by the corrupt, slow process of parliamentary democracy and elections, that their freedom could only come about through armed rebellions of the kind that were erupting everywhere around them.

In Munirgram, endless prattle. Endless. Sometimes I felt I was chewing on sand. Should we work with ex-hooligans who had been the domestic pets of the Congress, but now wanted to join us? Were they motivated by ideology, as we were, or did they only want to settle scores, or an easy path to quick material gains? What if, under pressure, they betrayed us? For that matter, the exhibition and assembly were teeming with card-carrying CPI(M) cadres: we didn't know if they had made their break from the Party, or had been expelled, or were drifting towards the ideology being outlined by Charu Mazumdar and others. They were as dangerous as the paid ex-Congress criminals, if not more so. What if they betrayed us?

Jaw, jaw, jaw . . . my temples began to throb. I stuck to my line and quoted Chairman Mao: 'If you set a ball rolling, it will reach its target at some point. But if you keep being hesitant, and stop to discuss matters at every point in the trajectory, it means slowing down the ball. It may then never reach its destination.'

While writing all this I found myself hesitating at one point, the bit where I mentioned going to bed on an empty stomach. I saw your calm face suddenly worried by such a disarmingly predictable question – Did I too eat half-stomach?

I won't – I can't – lie to you. Yes, I did. Most days.

On some days there was nothing to eat, only water to drink, drawn from the well shared between this neighbourhood and the Maheshwar colony next to it. Most of the time it was not a fast, but a fraction of a meal: a plate of cooked gourd and mashed yam, once a day, not enough to fill your stomach, but just enough to see you from one day to the next. Nobody will die eating only this, because you're getting <u>something</u> to eat, but nobody will live either on this, only subsist. The picture of starvation here, the picture that we city-dwellers carried around in our heads when we thought of rural poverty, of bony, half-naked people withering to death, was wrong – that was what happened during times of famine. In ordinary times, like now, the truth was different: the boniness remained, but it was no longer day after day of fasting; instead, weeks and months of hunger, of not having enough to eat, of meagreness and undernourishment and weakness.

I remembered Mejo-kaki once commenting on the food eaten by the servants, Gagan-da and Kamala-di and Malati-di, and especially the temporary daytime staff – Look, just look at the amount of rice on their plates. It's a hillock.

The comment was mocking: it was a matter of amused condescension for her. I was too young then to read the observation for what it was; I too had giggled.

It is true that rural people eat a lot of rice, but not for the reasons she had assumed. They eat rice because there isn't much else to eat: the vegetables they grow; the roots and leaves they forage; the occasional fish from the ponds and canals; the even rarer duck, which sometimes appears on the flooded rice fields during the early part of the growing season. But that is the ideal, almost aspired-for, scenario. The truth is more naked: they eat so much rice because they are filling themselves up against the time they know will come when they won't even have this staple to fill their stomachs.

Dhiren laughed when I mentioned it to him – This sounds a bit like the camel theory of eating. Camels can store water in their humps, they're desert creatures, they don't know where or when their next drink is coming from. You think the same is true for farmers and rice? It's a nice, romantic kind of theory for someone so . . . so tough as you.

But how much waxed gourd and ridged gourd and bottle gourd can you eat? I have tried it, and I can tell you that it doesn't fill you up for long; in a couple of hours, even less, you are hungry again.

A thought keeps me awake. It's like a stubborn, delicate fish-bone stuck in your throat – it doesn't cause you any harm, but every time you swallow you know it's there, so you keep swallowing, hoping that it's suddenly going to happen cleanly, without that prickle. Nights when I can't sleep because of hunger, I wonder what Debdulal-da must have said or done to make these destitute Santhals and Mahatos, Kanu and Bipul and Anupam, agree that we could stay in their homes – after all, we were extra mouths to feed, one extra per household, even if we were extra hands during sowing and harvesting and, therefore, additional income. Did the two columns tally and balance each other? What was going through their heads when they said yes? Could it have been, besides all the calculation involved, also that our idealism about trying to be one with them sparked off a kind of responsive idealism, so that they thought – Yes, here was a chance to . . .

Chance to do what? Hard as I try, I can't answer their side of the issue, can't imagine myself into it. Instead of all this idealism of unity, did they not think – They've come from Calcutta, they have more money than we do, they live in brick and cement buildings, they get three meals a day (not true of Dhiren), they ride in buses and trams, they wear different kinds of clothes, so why are they going to bed with their stomachs half-empty nearly every night by choice? Which fool <u>chooses</u> to go hungry? Or could it be that they are eating secretly, meals they're buying elsewhere with their money? And if they're doing that, then why are they not doing that for us, buying <u>us</u> some food? They can see that we're getting barely enough to keep body and soul together, why aren't they doing anything about the burning in our bellies?

The logical progression of the thoughts I imagined for them, if indeed they progressed along that line, brings me to a disturbing conclusion: could it be that that particular endpoint of their thoughts, <u>why are they not ending our misery with their city money?</u>, could it be that it would become the cause of another resentment?

Now that I've thought that, I can't get it out of my head. Were we too going to be seen to be on the side of their class enemies, unable to cross a crucial dividing line? Would we too become yet another justified target of their hatred?

I don't want to think like this, but I find myself helpless to put a stop to it. Every little thing lifts the lid. Take, for example, Bijli sowing the seeds of various gourds and pumpkin in the tiny patch of dirt next to her hut. Who brought the seeds? Did she save them herself, taking them out and putting them carefully away when she cut the vegetables before cooking? Did she buy them somewhere? I asked Kanu. He said that his wife saved the seeds, everyone did it, so that they could grow a little something for their own use; the wealthier farmers grew cash crops, such as paan or sugar cane, because they had the land to do it, while people like Kanu grew edible stuff for their own use in a scrap of vegetable garden. In itself this fact was yet another of those little things that added to my growing knowledge of a new world. But it disturbed me because I hadn't noticed the process of retaining the seeds and drying them out and saving them. Did it happen while I was away in Chhurimara or Munirgram? Or did I simply overlook it? Whatever the answer, what stares me in the face is this: I'm failing to become one of them. A distance still separates us.

On some nights, I lie awake, trying to imagine being someone else, someone who has crossed my path that day, say, the man who was selling fritters at the mela in Munirgram, or the one selling hot gram, or the labourer whom I had noticed once, squishing all the fiery, tiny purple chillies into his rice first before beginning to eat, a thing that caught my eye for no reason at all . . . I imagine anyone, really, anyone who happens to fall into my mind as I wait for sleep to arrive. First, I concentrate to bring into sharp focus every detail of his face and clothes and bearing. When I get that, I move one step further and try to imagine his life in as much detail and minuteness as I can. Sometimes I arrange it on a time-axis: When did he wake up? What did he do then? What after that? I try to string out his day in hours and minutes.

Sometimes I use a different approach. I concentrate on one probable experience in his life and try to become him and live that experience in every single sensation and feeling. That wage-labourer mashing those blackish-purple scud chillies into his rice, for example – why was he doing that? It was obvious that he loved his food very hot, but when did he acquire the taste? Was he given chillies to eat from early childhood? Did his mother make very hot dishes? Could it be that in situations where there isn't much to eat, or not much variety in what there is, people eat more chillies as a way of adding some kind of zing to their dull food? Do they burn his mouth and make his . . . my eyes and nose water? Does the burn spread to my ears? Does it upset my stomach? What did I do when I couldn't get hold of chillies? The questions come thick and fast, each spawning five more, and those five, five each . . . until I find that I have squeezed my eyes so tightly closed that I see floating coloured shapes, like rotting fragments of dead leaves underwater.

I open my eyes. The centre of my head feels heated. And yet I'm no closer to that man. Most importantly, I haven't been able to answer that big question:

what idea did he have of the story of his life, not only of the past and the present, but also of what was to come?

There seem to be fewer stars; it must be getting close to dawn. No sign of your face or your name in the sky tonight. What is going to happen to the two of us? Doesn't that question haunt you, too, and keep you awake? It's eating me slowly from the inside. It's all impossible, everything between us, every possibility, imaginable or unimaginable, is impossible.

CHAPTER SEVEN

Many years later, as he faced his own dissolution, Prafullanath was to remember a distant afternoon when his father took him to see the Elphinstone Bioscope in an enormous tent on the Maidan. That same book of memories seemed to contain an infinite number of self-renewing pages; a well-visited one was the time when he had gone with his father to watch the IFA Shield match, which Mohanbagan had won. It was a book that Prafullanath forced himself to think he had erased successfully, but it was as if scraps of imperfectly rubbed-out writing, half a line here, a quarter-page there, still bearing the tiny worms of rubber-shavings and the impress of the letters wiped out, had cunningly revivified themselves and presented their taunting, undead selves to him, mocking, mocking his failure to annihilate them for ever.

Five years after Mohanbagan's IFA Shield victory, his father was dead. It was 1916 and the war in Europe had temporarily disrupted the passage of the ships that brought the medicines for his father's diabetes into India from the country of their manufacture. No amount of money, in which the Ghoshes were not lacking, could open this particular door.

When he was four, Prafulla had seen his brother, Braja, older than him by twelve years, celebrating British victory in the Boer War, and had joined him in running up and down the stairs, parroting his dada's 'The English have won! The English have won!' They were all supporters of the English then; victory for the English meant their victory. Who would have thought that a dozen years down the line the distant thunder of another war in which the English were again involved would descend so crashingly on their little lives? He had not, then or later, linked up the British with his father's death, stringing out the beads of cause and effect, in part because the rise in anti-British nationalism hardly touched the Ghosh family in North Calcutta. Four or five years after the child's jubilation at British victory in the Boer War, when the nationalist movement in Bengal was in full swing, the Ghoshes in their enormous family mansion in Garpar Road had not boycotted English goods, or given up their jewellery, like most patriotic families, to fund the nationalist cause, nor had they consigned their foreign silks and fabrics to the regular bonfires that the swadeshi revolutionaries organised.

Prafulla, Manmathnath's son from his second marriage, had lost his mother at birth. Manmathnath, cradling the motherless infant, had said to Braja, his elder son, 'This baby has never seen his mother's face. The two of us are his only world. We have to be mother and father to him, in the way I have tried to be both to you, after you lost your own mother. I married again so that you could have another mother in your chhoto-ma. That dream is now ashes. You are twelve years older than he, you must be not only a brother to him, but also another father.'

But it was the death of Manmathnath that was the true turning point in Prafulla's life; to speak of his world and his father as two separate things was meaningless. Manmathnath had established and run Calcutta's biggest and best jewellery house, Ghosh Gold Palace, and had lovingly explained to his younger son, without a trace of condescension in his voice, his innovations in the Bengali jewellery trade; Prafulla, despite himself, could still remember everything from those lessons, which he had absorbed eagerly as stories. He could remember the long, noisy, rattling trip in the Beeston Humberette to the huge showroom of the Great Eastern Motor Company in Park Street, where he was taken to feast his eyes on the steam- and motor-cars on display. The open-mouthed stares of people who stopped in their tracks to see that rarity, a car, phut-phutting down Circular Road. (The child Prafulla was not immune to this sense of wonder; he and his brother sat for long hours on the front balcony to watch motorcycles going down the street; when a horse-drawn brougham or a victoria or, better still, an Oldsmobile, made an appearance, the boys' day was made.) Much earlier, when he was a little boy carried in the tight embrace of his father's arms, the spectacular experience of watching the ascent of a gas-balloon carrying a man up-up-up from the Oriental Gas Company fields to the sky. The kadam tree in the garden that looked adorned with perfect spheres of creamy-golden light in the monsoon. The man who came around every evening, a ladder on his shoulder, lighting the street lamps. The unearthly rhythmic song of the Oriya palanquin bearers – *Dhakkunabor hei-yan nabor, dhakkunabor hei-yan nabor* – going about their business on the streets of Chitpur. Much later, the pale-brown-and-yellow trams with their many doors and their wondrous ting-ting-ting sound as they approached. The 'khut' sound as the conductor gave his father his ticket, which he handed to his son immediately. The priceless treasure of the Calcutta Tramways Company ticket, with writing in English and Bengali equally divided on front and back, which he saved in his little box of precious collectables along with pigeon and crow and sparrow feathers, coloured beads, pieces of shiny coloured glass, string, ribbons, buttons, a piece from a broken anklet, tamarind seeds, even a seashell. The drudgery of having to sit through Vidyasagar's *Barna Parichay* and Parry Charan Sirkar's *First Book of English* in the occasionally sooty light of hurricanes. Running his thrilled fingers over the tight and precise accordion of creases made by the servants, using gila seeds, on the sleeves of his father's panjabi. The pile of sitabhog, like heaped petals of jasmine, brought all the way from Bardhaman on the train, and he seated on his father's lap, being fed with a silver spoon from a silver bowl spoonfuls of that divine sweet. 'The Great Bengal Circus' one evening, once again sitting next to his father, his left hand clasped to his father's right throughout, the boy, enchanted, watching the Bengali strongman, Shyamakanta-babu, breaking enormous boulders on his chest.

This father, who had loved his motherless younger son more than the irises of his own eyes, more than the weight and value of gold and diamonds that passed through his shop every month, this man had suddenly died and Prafulla, completely orphaned, had found himself falling falling falling as if he had chanced upon the trapdoor that connected his life to the black infinity of space.

Braja took to heart their father's injunction, warming to the task, most enthusiastically in the disciplining duties of brotherly care.

Prafulla would never forget the day when Braja had summoned every single servant in the house and had belted him mercilessly in front of them for the misdemeanour of calling one of the servants a 'son of a pig', a filthy term in the mouth of someone so green. That hectic performance of tough love under the stairs might have established the credentials of Braja as an ideal elder brother in the eyes of the world, but in the boy's mind it planted the first seeds of the suspicion that Braja resented him for being the second wife's son.

In the months after their father's death Braja found a liberation, manifested in the frequent explosive flowerings of his cruelty. What shame and pain Prafulla had felt when he had been thrashed repeatedly without any reason, again in the view of everyone in the house who cared to see – and everyone did – and again without anything, or anyone, to restrain Braja. He knew then that nothing in his future could ever hold the terror of the prelude to these beatings: Braja taking off, one by slow one, the dozen or so rings that he wore to channel the propitious influences of the stars and planets, that warm-up exercise lovingly undertaken so that the metals or any protruding stone did not do any serious damage to his brother's face or mouth or eyes – such consideration – and Prafulla standing there, trying to control his pelvic floor so that he did not add the humiliation of pissing himself to the deluge that was about to break over him. A chasm had long opened up between Prafulla's public manner of respect and esteem for his dada, a mask that he put on every day and tried to keep firmly in place, and the private knowledge that the feelings which bound the brothers together were envy, rivalry, rancour.

First, there was Braja's great reluctance in having Prafulla continue to come to the shop in the mornings, as he had started doing in the company of their father to learn the ropes. 'In the jewellery trade,' Manmathnath used to repeat like a favourite chant, 'experience is *everything*, the first-hand, touched-by-your-skin, seen-with-your-eyes experience of handling gold and jewels – that is the greatest education.' Braja had benefited from it; now it was Prafulla's turn. While Manmathnath had been alive, Braja had had to keep a secure lid on his antipathy; now it became an open sanction against Prafulla coming in to Ghosh Gold Palace. Prafulla bit down on his indignation and acquiesced, but could no longer contain himself when his uncles and their grown-up sons started circling in the hope of rich pickings. His three uncles all had their own jewellery shops, all variants using the Ghosh name, but none a quarter as successful as his father's business; this added to the animosity that had already led to the brothers setting up separate businesses.

Days and nights of people, his relatives, going in and out of their enormous house in Garpar, relatives who had hardly shown their faces during his father's lifetime because jealousy and enmity ran so deep, now brimming over with solicitous tenderness for Manmathnath's orphaned sons. Soon, the eloquent sympathies were directed only at Braja, and Prafulla was ignored; the uncles had only had to sniff the air to work out who held the keys. All these uncles, at once frayed and battened by their perfumed lives of khemta dances, alcohol, the obligatory visit to the brother before returning home – when they did return home – to the ministrations of their cosseting, dutiful wives, these uncles who had lived off their family wealth and dissipated it in such sybaritic style, they had all come rushing to see if they could invoke family and heritability and loot more fuel for their finite fires and infinite appetites.

From his room Prafulla could hear voices raised, sometimes in altercation, sometimes in calculating cheer, as if it were not around a death that they had congregated, but a jubilation. Often this was accompanied by the sharp methyl smell of the spirits that lubricated the raucous proceedings. Forbidden from participating, Prafulla paced his room like a caged beast.

Braja's next step was to have everything transferred to his own name – the business, the house, the bank accounts, the assets and properties – effectively disinheriting Prafulla of his share of the patrimony and making him a dependant.

'I have done it for your own good, you'll come to understand one day,' Braja said to him. 'You will work your way up to the top. That training will be invaluable.'

Those who saw it as the barefaced robbery it was, most notably Chitta-babu, Chittadas Roy, the manager of Ghosh Gold Palace, and Manmathnath's friend and accomplice for decades, kept their mouths sealed.

Prafulla could not choke down his outrage. 'Why are you cutting me out like this? It's wrong. I am as much my father's son as you are,' he said.

This was exactly the opening Braja needed; if he played it carefully, Prafulla was going to do Braja's dirty work for him.

'Alas, I can't believe I've lived to see the day when I hear my very own younger brother talk of *my* father and *your* father,' Braja said.

'I have rights to all the things that you're denying me.'

Braja ratcheted up his display of hurt. 'Rights? I saw you being born, and you talk to me of rights? Has it now come to this?' His voice did an impression of a wobble. 'I feel I'm being called a thief by those very people for whom I do the stealing. This is all to protect you, and now you talk to me of division of . . . of . . .' He let this trail off for maximum impact.

Wrong-footed, Prafulla dropped the matter for the time being. It was raked up again, this time by a meeting with Chitta-babu, at which the elderly gentleman, clearly struggling to present a calm surface over the roil of things he could not bring himself to articulate in front of this young man, hinted darkly, 'If your father were alive, this . . . this sin would have been undreamt-of. One day you will understand all this. I can't say any more than that. But if you soon find yourself in need of help, I mean *any* kind of help, look at me, child, look at me; any kind of help, come to me and I'll see what I can do. More than this I cannot say. I hope you understand my constraints. But remember, He is seeing everything from above, He'll not let this pass.'

Prafulla, who had a reasonable idea of what the great unmentionable could be, confronted Braja again. This time Braja's wife, Surama, took a lead role. Speculation, not entirely baseless, had it that it was Surama who had poisoned her husband's mind against his much younger brother: it was she who had made a big thing out of the fact that the two brothers had different mothers, gainfully exploiting, if not initiating, a wild suggestion that Braja's mother, Manmathnath's first wife, had killed herself in mysterious circumstances, no one knew how. The propinquity of Braja's mother's death and Manmathnath's second marriage was a ready gift for this compulsive hyper-fictionalising tendency in Bengali culture; Surama was an exemplar. Yet Prafulla knew, even if he never gave it recognition in words, that Surama had had malleable material to mould.

'He is the son from the "second phase",' she was reputed to have said to Braja, 'he will usurp your place in your father's affections and you'll find yourself left with nothing. Act quickly.'

She had harped on the theme, with creative variations, for years until surmise and suspicion had solidified into truth; to Braja and Surama, Prafulla, a mere fledgling of ten when they got married in 1908, matured in their imagination into a raptor.

In the nine months since her father-in-law's death and, crucially, a year since the longed-for birth of a boy, Surama had amplified the behind-the-scenes attacks: 'You have to think about your son now,' she said, 'and secure his future. What if your brother takes everything away from us and lands us in the street? What will happen to your heir?'

The mask of filial duty had at last slipped at the final confrontation. Braja's calculated air of grievance got so much on Prafulla's nerves that he called his bluff.

'Stop your acting!' he said. 'I've had enough. The pain you say you're feeling, I know exactly how much that is. I want to go through all the property and shop papers. I want my name on half of everything.'

'I told you,' Surama said, addressing her husband, 'I told you that we were raising a snake with milk and rice. "Acting," he says. How can you swallow such an insult? We have practically brought him up, and this is our reward.'

Braja's practised lugubrious conduct now allowed a very slight tug of amused contempt at the corners of his mouth, but the words that emerged continued with pretend hurt.

'My heart feels ready to burst—' he began, but Prafulla cut him short.

'Why have you cut me off from everything?' he demanded. 'Going to the shop is forbidden, learning the business hands-on is forbidden . . . What else is out of bounds for me? This house as well? When I last went to the shop everyone was avoiding looking directly at me, all the salesmen, the craftsmen, Chitta-babu, Samar-babu, Ramaprasad-babu. What have you said to them? Why do I feel like a pariah? Even the servants in this house, my home . . . There seems to be something I'm not getting, I'm being left out of. What have you and Boüdi done to them?'

This was the opening Braja needed. 'You are overstepping some boundaries here,' he warned. There was flint somewhere in his voice now, so different from the faux-plush earlier.

'You are stealing everything from me and you sit here talking of boundaries? Yes, I have overstepped the boundaries of my patience,' Prafulla shouted.

The opera of Bengali life, already pitched so high, had begun.

'How dare you say that!' Braja said. 'Stealing? Stealing?'

'Yes, stealing. Baba said to me that half of everything is mine. You're trying to cheat me out of the business. Now I want to know what else you're cheating me out of.'

'*Baba said, Baba said,*' Braja mimicked the voice of a whining child. Then the flint returned. 'Can you prove what Baba said? Where is it written down that half of everything is yours? Go on, show me. And you're still a minor and a dependant.'

'No, I'm not, I'm nineteen. And you beat me like a dog because you are burning with envy, you have always known that Baba loved me more.'

From this point the escalation was linear, short and simple. Prafulla declared that he was leaving home for ever; it was not his home any longer, his brother was a snake, poison ran in his veins; he had betrayed their father and the trust that had been vested in him and the duty of care and responsibility; he had engineered to bring it to a state where Prafulla would be left with no choice but to leave . . . In this world of overheated reactions and hysteria, words spoken carried with them the unearthable charge of honour and insult; they remained crackling and alive for generation after generation. Another boundary was crossed, this time without the possibility of return.

Prafulla walked away from half of what was rightfully his, leaving behind a world of chandeliers, fleets of servants, the Beeston Humberette and a De Dion-Bouton, a world of diamond buttons on his panjabi, of womenfolk wearing fifty-bhari gold waistlets at ceremonies, of a 300-square-foot showroom on 130 Baubazar Street, which remained thronged with customers every single hour that it was open. He was never to return.

When Prafulla could bring himself to narrate these events in his later life, he would always include the sentence, 'The embers of my father's funeral pyre had hardly died out before my older brother and his wife booted me out of my home.'

It was to Chitta-babu that Prafulla turned after his dramatic departure from Garpar. Chitta-babu had put him in touch with Chunilal Saha, a paper merchant who owned a small shop in Old China Bazaar Street. Chunilal, an ageing, frail man, had long been looking for a reliable and hard-working assistant to run the business with, and possibly to include in a partnership – Chunilal was an only son and he had no male heirs, only a daughter – and the arrival of Prafulla appeared to be felicitously timed. That he was a scion of the famous Ghoshes of Garpar expedited matters greatly; questions about trust and reliability simply did not arise.

Prafulla, in two years, had mastered all there was to be learned about paper retailing. Business ran in his blood, Chunilal noted admiringly. The Great War had just ended when Prafulla joined C.L. Saha and trade was depressed. A lot of the paper they sold to the Bengali market was manufactured in Europe, but no entirely Indian outfit could directly import that paper; it had to be done through English firms that had offices in Calcutta. Besides, the war had put an end to any import from the countries that had comprised the Central Powers. Prafulla, a young man of growing intuitive skills, did a shrewd pincer movement. First, he concentrated on the indigenous side of things. The output of the native paper mills – Titagarh, Upper India Cooper in Mohulla-Masjidbagh, Bengal Paper Mill in Raniganj, the recently opened Indian Paper Pulp in Hajinagar – was very low and the quality of the paper they produced was erratic. Prafulla decided to make C.L. Saha an agent of these mills and push their products in the market; they would be priced significantly lower than imported paper. It kept down costs while creating goodwill with the mill owners, something that Prafulla was convinced would come in useful one day.

Second, in order to reduce overheads further, Prafulla threw himself into the business of establishing first-hand contacts with foreign exporters, bypassing the English companies, which had previously acted as intermediaries. In the teeth of fierce opposition from these interests, he managed slowly, over a period of nearly two decades, to build up a direct relationship with a fair few of these exporters.

Towards the end of 1919, Chunilal was diagnosed with lung cancer and given less than six months to live. He said to Prafulla, 'You were sent by Him so that my daughter doesn't find herself in deep water after I leave this world. I would like you to marry Charubala and take over the business. You were sent to me for this purpose, I know it in my bones.'

Two months after Prafulla married Charubala in February 1920, her father died. Chitta-babu, who had been fired from Ghosh Gold Palace shortly after Prafulla's departure, reminded the young man that he had two bighas twelve kathas of land in his name left to him by his grandfather, Mahendra Nath Ghosh, and which had been held in trust for him until he reached the age of twenty-one; it was now his, to do with it whatever he wanted. Prafulla sold the land and channelled the money into the paper business. He also changed the name: C.L. Saha became Charu Paper Company (Pvt. Ltd) on 29th January 1921, a date ingrained for ever in his memory because of the drama leading to the birth of his first son, Adinath, that very day.

Charubala had gone into labour the day before and although, as a man, Prafulla was not allowed anywhere near the delivery room, he remembered the anxiety caused by the inability that day to find a midwife or a doctor, or even a single vehicle on the roads to take her to the nearest hospital, should the need have arisen: the Duke of Connaught was visiting Calcutta to promote the Raj's idea of diarchy and the Congress had called a hartal; the city had been in absolute shutdown. He had fretted and bitten his fingernails and paced up and down, and prayed and made bargains with a whole raft of gods and goddesses; and, in the interstices of all this nervous vigour, imagining cloudily – he could not be said to have been very literate about natal matters – the rope of the umbilical cord coiled around his child's blue neck or his wife haemorrhaging to death, he had cursed the Congress, raged and stormed that it did not matter a jot, this business of freeing a nation and all such grand dreams and designs, if they put ordinary people in harm's way to get to their destination. After a long, difficult labour, mother and child had both survived and Prafullanath, in relief and joy, had come over all effusive, giving a name to his firstborn and his new company – all his now – in a purposeful act of joint naming; Adinath and the Charu Paper Company (Pvt. Ltd) were twins.

The new company was a new direction for him too. Prafullanath had been thinking seriously for a while, even during his father-in-law's lifetime, of moving the business away from being a paper agency into paper-manufacturing fully. He knew too that being both an agent and a novice owner of paper-making factories was an impossible exercise in acrobatics, like sitting on two horses; it would stretch him to the limit just to keep himself from falling. Now that Charu Paper was beginning to acquire power, it could suggest to the mills it agented that they should stop producing, say, four or five different kinds of paper in order to compete with the bigger mills and concentrate instead on the types of paper for which there was less competition among producers. If this should have the unintended consequence of making those factories uncompetitive and underproductive, creating losses and bringing down their value, then Prafullanath could snap them up at much-depreciated prices. It was in this way that he acquired, in 1923, his first mill, with a capacity of 75 TPD, in Memari in Bardhaman district. Charu Paper was no longer solely a paper agent. Two years later, Prafullanath bought what was to be the biggest mill of his business career, just outside the town of Bali, with an output that was twice that of Ghosh Paper Mill in Memari.

In 1927, the Ghoshes, now a family of seven (including Madan), too large to stay on in Charubala's childhood home in Jadunath Dey Road in Baubazar, sold the house and, in a move unheard of amongst North Calcuttans, moved to the southern area of Bhabanipur, to a four-storey residence on Basanta Bose Road. Prafullanath never mentioned it to anyone, not even to his wife, but he wanted to put as great a distance as possible between himself and the house where he had been born and where he had lived until the age of nineteen; if that meant moving to the newer south of the city, an area much looked down upon by the inhabitants of North Calcutta, then he was willing to do that too. The new house was enormous and he had acquired it quite cheaply from an acquaintance of a business associate because the family was in some hurry to sell; it obviated the need to buy land and the 101 problems attendant on building on it, which was the usual pattern. Besides, Bhabanipur was salubrious, leafy, wealthy – a lot of Marwaris were moving there – and was relatively distant from Muslim areas, which Baubazar was not quite. It was the southern edge of Bhabanipur, admittedly, almost shading into Kalighat, but at least it was north of Hazra Road, just; Bhabanipur was acceptable even to North Calcuttans.

Prafullanath had inherited his father's almost superhuman capacity for work; it was certainly of the order not seen or heard of among Bengalis. The mills that he had bought were weak creatures, stertorously gasping their way to imminent extinction. Their output was an ideal figure; in reality, they churned out around 125 TPD together. He worked out that one way to resuscitate them would be to have them make their own pulp, instead of buying their raw material from the pulp industry, a method that pushed up overheads. He installed hydrapulpers in both his mills and made them integrated factories. They bought wastepaper from the open market, made their own pulp and fed it to the cylinder mould or Fourdrinier machines to make the particular kind of paper that each mill specialised in.

The streamlining that had benefited him so greatly when he was an agent was also the central governing principle in his reform of the mills at Memari and Bali. One of the first things Prafullanath initiated was the trend in bleached paper. He remembered the Srirampur and Bali paper that he was occasionally forced to use as 'rough paper' for scrap work – a brownish, coarse off-white, as if it had sand in it. He had an instinctive dislike of that murky thing and used it only when he had to. Charu Paper Mill at Memari switched from the manufacture of several types of this 'dirty' paper to one variety of bleached writing paper. The factory at Bali had produced, before Prafullanath took over, four different kinds of duplex board and grey board and made losses on two of those. Prafullanath began by stopping production of the loss-making varieties. Bali was now going to manufacture only two types of paper: coated duplex and uncoated grey board.

The inevitable scaling back this resulted in throughout the rest of the 1920s brought focus and, with hindsight, it could be said that this retrenchment helped the Ghoshes to weather the global recession when it hit in 1930. They were saved, too, from the eventual financial ruin that reckless expansion would have brought. It was happening all around them: their friends, the Pals, for example, quickly consolidated their textile business, buying up factories, retail outlets, smaller businesses as if they were going to be asked to leave the planet tomorrow, and branched out into printing works, ink, a type foundry, only to be brought to their knees when the recession hit. They never recovered. It was only with Prafullanath's help that his friend Jyotish Chandra Pal could hang on to their first store on Harrison Road. Prafullanath noted the lesson carefully and stored it away; he was to remember Jyotish crying for help – 'I'm having to sell off my wife's jewellery now; if you don't help me, I won't know what to do' – for the rest of his life. Having to sell off the women's jewellery: now *that* was unimaginable, Prafullanath had shuddered. He deferred his ideas about shareholdings and directorships in other companies, postponed too his ambition of regional branches, and concentrated on strengthening what he had.

The '30s began with Gandhi's non-violent salt satyagraha. In College Street, people sat on the road, selling white piles of salt heaped on sacks in front of them, openly defying the Salt Tax. But Bengalis also answered with terrorism and a string of assassinations of high-profile British officials – the looting of the Chattagram artillery, the killing of Inspector General Loman in Dhaka, Binay-Badal-Dinesh's assassination of Simpson. Something was turning; the atmosphere, the very air, seemed cleft with fear and tension and something else . . . expectation, was it? In 1931, the District Manager of Medinipur, Peddy, was killed. The British retribution was brutal.

In 1932, one of Prafullanath's closest friends, Gyan Kundu, became the unintended victim of the second terrorist attack on Alfred Watson, the editor of *The Statesman*. The first one, only a couple of months before, had involved only one assassin; he had been stationed just outside the newspaper office in Chowringhee, waiting for the editor's car to pull up. When it did, he stuck a pistol through the open window and fired; incredibly, he missed. The subsequent attempt was a more elaborate affair. A carload of men pulled up behind Watson's car and showered it with bullets. Watson took two bullets, survived, but had to be retired because he was no longer capable of active work. Gyan Kundu, who was in the back, died instantly. Kundu-babu, as Prafullanath mischievously called him (they were peers), had been on his way to a meeting – an unprecedentedly rare one – with the board of the British-run *Statesman* as representative of the Paper Merchants' Association; the newspaper was looking to establish new connections with local newsprint, paper and ink suppliers as a way of cutting costs during this period of depression. It was the first time that Gyan Kundu had been invited to a mostly British gathering, especially of that echelon of British quasi-officialdom. The more nationalist-minded of the Bengalis could not refrain from pointing out that a freedom-fighter's bullet was the end that lay in store for Bengalis who colluded and cooperated with the enemy.

Prafullanath held no truck with such patriotic fools. 'Khaddar and charka and cottage industries are not going to feed us,' he said. 'We'll remain a nation of loincloth-clad, rib-showing beggars if we go down that route. The industries are controlled by the British and we should do business with them for our own good.' In this he had been indoctrinated by what he had seen in his childhood during the swadeshi movement in the 1900s. Back then, Prafullanath had noted and remembered his father's scornful words to a rich Bengali man; one of their customers, he supposed. 'All these calls to shut my jewellery shop, to stop trading in British gold . . . Well, I ask them, what are we going to eat if I close my shop? What are my children going to eat? And you, Banerjee-babu, how are you going to marry your daughter without jewellery, hyan? Have you heard of a wedding without ornaments? Besides, all this jabber-jabber about the country's economic development, how is the economy going to develop if we close down our small businesses?' It was an argument Prafullanath was going to use himself, copiously, when confronted with a similar moral choice during the turbulent decades of freedom-fighting.

In Gyan Kundu's death, Prafullanath, who had business in his genes, saw an opportunity. Within days he presented Kundu-babu's widow with an impeccably worked-out proposal, designed to hit all the right notes with a grieving woman left to look after her two small children, nine and six at the time. He offered to buy out Kundu & Co. at a substantial premium over the market value and invest the money for her, if she wanted, locking a percentage of it in a trust fund for the children so that Nirmala-boüdi did not have to worry about their school and college education and the girl's marriage; the children would even come into money when they turned twenty-one. A terrible bereavement such as this, and in such circumstances . . . surely she could not be asked to make difficult decisions requiring intricate financial and legal knowledge? If he could spare his best friend's widow the anxiety – and here he let his eyes brim over – then he would count himself a happy man. Besides, his business was the same as her late husband's; he understood this world, knew it as well as the back of his own hand. 'Look at your children's faces,' he pleaded, 'and do the right thing.'

He had pitched it perfectly. Nirmala Kundu agreed, partly in relief that someone was taking charge of the messier sphere, leaving her to get on with her grieving and bringing up her children, things to which she was more attuned than company finances. He had bribed the auditors of Kundu & Co. to undervalue the firm to a figure that he had set with the men, thus acquiring Kundu & Co. for something between 40 and 50 per cent of the company's true value. Crucially, he had known from his now-dead friend that two enormous contracts were shortly coming the way of Kundu & Co.

Prafullanath's own mills in Memari and Bali exclusively supplied the paper for these two contracts. With the financial muscle they brought him, he managed to stave off the worst of the recession. That year, in 1933, his youngest son Somnath was born.

VII

Scalp-splitting sun. It killed you. Darkness now came slowly, like a leisurely, majestic predator, unafraid of anything, swallowing the far things on the horizon first, then the near. You saw the line of trees in the forest in the distance go first, then the nearer trees, the palms and bamboos, then the fields became stretches of a featureless sea of black. After a while, you couldn't see your toes.

The soil had the surface of stone, punctuated with the stubble from last year's harvest. Kanu followed the plough hitched to the bullock – the plough was his, the bullock belonged to the man whose land Kanu was preparing for cultivation – and explained to me how I needed to keep the share steady in the soil and the bullock moving in a straight line. I was like a guttering candle turning to liquid. Kanu looked at me and asked – Are you suffering?

I was ashamed to be thinking of sunstroke when beside me Kanu, drenched, smelling awful, seemed indifferent to the sun. I looked at him and was struck again by how everything about him was wiry: his thin legs and arms, the veins on them bulging out like ribs; the dark, curly hair, like a dense pile of wire clippings. Where did this beaten physique, as if something carved in oily dark stone, come from, if all he and his kind got to eat was chhatu and rice and puffed rice once, maybe twice, a day? I couldn't even bring myself to ask if the sun didn't bother him. When I tried to do the third row myself, without his help, I thought I'd got it, until the bullock reached the edge of the plot and I had to turn it round and position the share so that the same line was furrowed again, but now in a different direction. I failed utterly. The bullock went off in a line at a thirty-degree angle to the one just ploughed.

By ten in the morning a nerve behind my left eye started jumping, I began to feel dizzy and, when I tried to get up, after sitting down to drink some water and catch my breath, I saw black and then some popping colours.

Samir and Dhiren were both working in plots to be used as seedbeds, but for a different landlord. We could barely talk at the end of the day after we had bathed in the pond and washed our clothes – we felt turned into something solid and inanimate with exhaustion. But even through that solidity something of the intricate nature of the timing of everything trickled through and amazed me. The plots that were right next to the landlord's house were generally used as seedbeds so that they could be kept under constant guard. The plot that Kanu and I and two others were working was going to be used to transplant the paddy saplings from the seedbeds one month into the monsoon. Kanu had explained the timing to us. And it all turned on the arrival of the rains.

The land was a stretch of huge, upturned clods. If I thought harvesting was difficult, I changed my mind when I began ploughing. Now I changed my mind again during this process of halui – churning those enormous clods into looser, smaller pieces of soil. Kanu said – The large boulders of earth, they keep soaking up the rain . . .

Here he paused and looked up at the sky. Would it arrive this year? his eyes seemed to be asking; would it be late? would it be enough? There was both anxiety and resignation on his face.

Kanu continued – These large chunks, they soak up the rain, they are greedy, but however much they drink, they don't seem to turn to clay easily. And we want this to be tight clay, so tight that the rainwater will stay on the surface. The plot must be underwater, here, see, this much water – he stretched his palm and marked off a point at the base; five or six inches, I reckoned – here, one hand of water, he said.

So the next ten days, twelve, passed in raking and beating and pounding the clods to dust. We kept ploughing the furrows over and over again, then the plough was replaced with a multi-toothed rake and we went through the same process again. The soil looked like red-black cottage cheese now. The June sun beat down upon us. The soil was hard and totally dry. When we brought out the sticks used to beat it to dust, it gave in and disintegrated. Then we needed to rake it up again to bring the bigger, more solid layers below up to the surface so that we could beat that to looseness.

Kanu has brought only his plough to the halui work. The bullocks belong to the landlord, as the seedlings, later, will too, so Kanu will get only 20 per cent of the crop produced. If he had been a bargadar, he would have got 40 per cent for the same work. I couldn't make any sense of this logic, that the better off got more and those who had little got less. The world ran on this law, and only on this. Some magnetic field began to develop around those who had a little something – power or money or influence or friends, you name it – and the more these things accrued, the more that magnetism increased (it was as if the things that flowed to them had attracting properties themselves), drawing more inside its orbit and away from those whose funds were already depleted, making them even more impoverished, depriving them of even more. It was like gravity: everything flowed, and could only flow, in one direction. Or a type of circularity: the more you had, the more will come to you, the more you will have.

Sometimes when my body simply couldn't move, when I was incapable of lifting even my little finger, incapacitated by the combined tyranny of the sun and the humidity, I forced myself to beat and rake and pulverise the clods of earth by thinking I was beating and raking and pulverising and eviscerating men like Bhaben Sinha, men like the Rays, who were smuggling rice at night, men like the police, who were standing guard over the operation, all the jotedaars and mahajans in this village. I wanted to stand outside the world, wielding a giant wooden stick, and use that to shatter the planet into tiny bits. I wanted to break the air, tear the wind, smash the water.

No nightly planning sessions during the sowing season; we were too exhausted to talk. I shall have to stop writing this and pick up at some point later when I have more time, more energy.

Kanu noticed my tiredness. He brought me a lipped, dented aluminium plate of chhatu kneaded with chillies and raw onions and some mustard oil, and asked – No more meetings for the city babus?

– No, Kanu, our bodies won't take it. You're talking to the others, as we asked you? They'll come once the paddy growing begins?

– Yes, Babu, they will. Those other two babus, your friends, they'll have a lot of work to do, just before the rains begin, to prepare the seedbeds. You'll work with them?

– No, Kanu, I'll be working with you wherever you get me work.

I knew what he was thinking: he was remembering closing his hand over the thirty rupees I had given him last time.

The monsoon didn't break crashingly one day. First, there was a light drizzle that barely wetted the soil, but it released that loamy-fresh-rotting smell. When the drizzle stopped, Kanu's face took on that constricted look.

– This little pissing, Babu, he said, it's not a good sign. It means something is holding back the water in the sky. It can be held back throughout the season then.

He was wrong. Two more days of dark, rolling clouds and another half-day of drizzling, then the sky broke upon us. Even his dying father-in-law seemed to register it: his face had an expression different from its usual one of resigned blankness, not far from a smile. The baby too appeared to be crying less. I had to move inside now.

– You'll get wet outside, Babu. And sometimes the water rises and floods everything around the hut and water comes into the room. No, no, Babu, you come inside now.

It was exactly as I remembered from childhood – sheets of water coming down for hours and hitting the ground with such force that you thought the road would dissolve – except that here the ground, which is earth, does dissolve.

The ploughed soil first turned dark with saturation, then became mud, a fractionally lighter shade than the wet soil. The mud started to retain water on its surface here and there. Then the watery stretches began to grow. Kanu said that the real work began now.

I laughed – What were we doing until now? Playing children's games?

He laughed too. – Preparation, he said.

Samir and Dhiren had been calf-deep in mud in their seedbeds for the last week, trying to keep them flooded. It was my turn now in the growing plots. I missed out on the sowing. When I mentioned this to Kanu, he said that it required years of skill to get the throwing of the germinated seed-paddy right; Samir and Dhiren wouldn't be sowing, only preparing the beds and perhaps guarding them.

I stepped into the mud, the mud that I'd avoided in the city all my life, that ever-present mud during the rainy season, which crept over the front edge of your sandals, seeped up between the toes, was lifted by the back of the slippers on every uplift of the feet and splattered all over the back of the legs of pyjamas and trousers; a thing that held only disgust, and a little bit of terror, for all Bengalis. So I had to leap over a mental barrier, erected through years of conditioning, to jump into a very sea of it. Silly petty-bourgeois things went through my head very briefly, such as how difficult it would be to get my mud-spattered clothes clean, get myself clean, in the pond at the end of the day, and would my clothes dry in the rain . . . Then I stepped in.

My feet immediately sank in to my ankles, then gradually to the bottom of my calf muscle. I clenched my toes. It was difficult to move: the mud embraced my feet and didn't want to let go. It was a slight wrench every time I lifted them up, as the mud slucked itself into the mini-vacuums my feet were leaving behind. There was a small danger of slipping and unbalancing on the tread down, but my feet adjusted. The clay felt velvety, then there was a strange sensation of it gently tickling and caressing my feet. I almost giggled out loud. I was, for a moment, returned to an elementary, tactile pleasure from childhood: playing with mud. What, a moment before, had held a small charge of something to be avoided had now become so desirable that I wanted to roll about in it.

There were sacks of cow-dung fertiliser sitting on the aal bordering the plots. We brought them into the mud and each sack was emptied at intervals of about five to seven metres along the area. I had to clamp down my jaws and swallow a few times because the pungent smell made me want to retch, but even this I got used to after a few minutes. But my joy in the mud abated – walking calf-deep in rainwater and clayey soil was one thing, doing the same in soil freshly enriched with fertiliser was another. Once again we directed the bullock, now fitted with a huge horizontal stick in place of the ploughshare, to flatten out the clay and make the earth level throughout. After the fertiliser had been spread evenly, the stick was replaced with that many-tined rake and the earth was ploughed again to mix the cow-dung thoroughly, letting it reach the bottom layers. The rainwater rushed squelchingly into the gaps in the raked soil. The skies opened again.

Herons and cranes did their old man's staccato walk through the fields, jerking their necks down to catch a worm or a fish, then resumed their odd gait – they seemed to lift their legs up a lot more than was necessary. They were intrepid, doing their thing cheek-by-jowl with our activities. As for the bullocks, they simply didn't care about the presence of the birds, not even when they perched on their necks.

The pond where we bathed and washed our clothes was full to the brim. That afternoon, during a small interval in the pelting rain, while we splashed about in the pond and beat our clothes vigorously against a stone ledge, Samir and Dhiren entertained me with their experiences of sowing that morning.

– They do a little ceremony before the sowing, did you know? Dhiren said.

– The usual stuff with new grass and blowing a conch-shell? I asked.

Samir said – No, different. The farmers' wives do it. They put on new clothes, it looked like. They carry a little quilt with germinated seeds on it, and a small plate with oil, and salt and sindoor. The farmers stand back, each holding little sacks of seeds. But the women have to consecrate the whole business first. They bend down, pick up a tiny bit of soil, touch it to forehead and then to tongue. Then they walk over the aal, along the full perimeter of the seedbed, singing a song and throwing a small handful of the seed grain mixed with oil and salt and sindoor at each corner. Do you remember the song, Dhiren?

– Not all of it, only snatches here and there.

– Sing it, I said.

– It's very elementary, there's no complicated melody or anything to it, it's more like a children's rhyme or a panchali, he said, and sang in a monotone:

Where are you, Mother Lakshmi?
Rise and show your face.
Our men are cultivating paddy
But there's no rice in the store-room.
What are we going to live on?
How are we going to get through the year?

I smiled, but a bracing thought went through my head: these lives had never been easy. From the very beginning, their core had consisted of a constant wrestling with dearth and want and, above all, hunger. All the so-called reforms brought in by the government in the twenty-one years of Independence, the Zamindari Abolition Act, the Land Ceiling Act, the Bargadar Act, they had not improved the condition of the munish one whit. The actors had changed; the play remained the same. That great magnetism was still at work: power spoke to and connected only with power; the government and its laws were for the benefit of the landlords, the powerful and the wealthy. Their interests were aligned: they looked out for each other, therefore they would always be looking after each other. That great circularity again.

It started raining, big, fat drops, slowly first, then faster, bigger drops, then a proper downpour. Samir raised his voice above the din of the water and said – Have you ever been underwater when it's raining? It's a beautiful thing.

He submerged his whole body, including his head, under the rain-strafed skin of the pond. I followed him. It was strange and unearthly. In the grey-green watery light just under the surface the sound was neither the 'tip-tip-tip' of raindrops hitting water nor the usual downpour sound that was like a large collection of little, dry seeds shaken inside a hollow rattle. This came muffled, and so changed by the intervening membrane of water that it sounded like the kind of percussion angels would use in their music, distant and dreamy.

I stayed under as long as I could, then I gasped out of the surface for air.

CHAPTER EIGHT

1969

Because he is so lost in imagining the intervals between primes, and visualising their distribution to the extent of the furthest number that his mind, using a rough-and-ready kind of modular arithmetic, will allow him, his heart nearly leaps out of his mouth when his wrist is grabbed by a grasping hand, accompanied by the words, 'There, caught you!'

He looks up to see the crazed smile of the neighbourhood's resident madman, nicknamed 'Mad Ashu', who lives somewhere on Rupchand Mukherjee Lane and is supposed to roam the streets at dusk, Sona had been told when he was little, and to catch hold of little boys and girls who were not safely inside their homes by then. What he did with those children after he put them in his sack was left to the imagination. At nearly thirteen, Sona is not quite a child, but he feels some of the residual thrill of fear from the stories that had so stubbornly rooted themselves in some cobwebbed corner of his mind all those years ago. Besides, the man, whose real name is Ashish Roy, does look menacing – staring eyes magnified to distortion by thick lenses, the earpiece of the spectacles broken and held together by filthy loops of red string; unshaven face, bristling with silver hairs halfway between stubble and short quill; drool at the corners of his slack, mobile mouth, now grinning, now grimacing; grubby, frayed fatua that comes down to just below his waist, and even dirtier pyjama, enormous, almost ballooning, with the drawstring hanging down the front, drawing attention to the unmistakable stain of dribbled piss on the area around the crotch. Sona shudders inwardly and notices the veined hand still clutching his arm; the nails of the man's hand are hard and have a yellowish tinge.

'There, caught you, where will you escape now, eh?' Mad Ashu says again, but the threatening tone is so exaggerated that it seems to be a broad-brushstroke performance aimed at gullible children. Before Sona can compose a suitable reply Mad Ashu says, 'Can you tell me which prime numbers can be expressed as the sum of two squares?'

Something opens up in the boy. The sound of rickshaw horns and the 'ting' of the tram bell that punctuates its groaning trundle as it makes its way up Russa Road and the sound of water from a burst standpipe and of evening puja from a house nearby all disappear in an instant, as if all this were happening in a dream. At discrete moments in his future Sona will invariably picture this instant as a differentiable point in a smooth curve, the point, that exact point, where the tangent grazes it; it is that one point of contact that will, in a long concatenation of events, change his entire life. The origin of it is this moment when Mad Ashu asks him a question about prime numbers.

When the sound floods back, Sona hears himself answer, 'All primes above 2 that leave the remainder 1 when divided by 4. So $4n + 1$.' He has known this from the age of seven: that all primes above 2 are odd; that they consequently fall into two categories – those that leave the remainder 1 when divided by 4, and those that leave the remainder 3; that only $(4n + 1)$ primes can be expressed as the sum of two squares, not the $(4n + 3)$ numbers. This had emerged as a branch-line while he was pursuing, at the age of six, a way of determining which numbers between 1 and 1,000 were primes. He wrote them down on pages and pages, then began to strike off 2 and every second number after 2, since they were all divisible by 2. Then he put a line through 3 and deleted every third number after 3. Then 5 and every fifth number after 5. And so on until all the remaining numbers were indubitably primes. He has favourites among them: 37 is one; $3 + 7$ gives 10, $1 + 0$ gives 1, which is yet another favourite number. (And also *interesting*; he has read the story of G.H. Hardy telling Ramanujan how 1,729, the number of the taxi in which he arrived to visit the ailing Indian genius, was a rather dull one, whereupon Ramanujan instantly replied that, on the contrary, it was very interesting for it was the smallest number that could be expressed as the sum of two cubes in two different ways: $1,729 = 1^3 + 12^3 = 9^3 + 10^3$. To which Sona found added glamour in the fact that the sum of all its numerals yielded 1, his favourite number.) These numbers come to him clothed in a beauty that surpasses everything in his dim, crumpled, shabby life. They are luminous, they speak to him in a way that gives him something precious, protected from the rest of his hours and days. They belong to a world that consists only of him and the numbers, nothing else, a world of absolute and utter perfection that cannot be expressed, and therefore debased already, by words.

The effect of his answer is equally unprecedented. Mad Ashu gives out a high, hiccuping giggle, poised somewhere between the gurgling of a baby, giddy with laughter, and a series of barks emitted by an imaginary animal. The lenses of industrial thickness flash, or are they his eyes?

'Bah, bah, grand! Grand. Now, can you prove it?' the madman asks.

Sona shakes his head. 'No, I've been trying, but I keep running into walls.'

'The proof is not easy. Do you know the Brahmagupta identity?'

Sona shakes his head again, but this time there is excitement and curiosity mixed with the admission of failure. He has got over the slurring way of talking that Mad Ashu has, as if his sleepy tongue is having trouble waking up to alertness.

'Proof is everything in mathematics. You know that, right?' Mad Ashu asks and peers at him as he would at an insect in his food.

Sona nods his assent.

'Listen, you come with me, I'll show you, show you the proof. I live right here, look, there's my house,' he says, pointing, and at that exact moment there is a power outage. A collective sigh from the whole neighbourhood goes up.

'Jaaaah, load-shedding. Load-shedding, do you see? Again,' the man says. 'But no problem, we'll work in the light of a hurricane lamp, we'll ask them to send one to the room. Come, come.'

Any other time this business of following a stranger, and not quite a normal stranger, home would have given Sona pause, not least by the promptings of his own shyness and solitary, reserved nature. But the lure of numbers has overruled everything; Sona is not even conscious of any such caution or deliberation. Maybe the bits of half-truths about Ashish Roy, those not to do with his apparent unordinariness, submerged under the more colourful gossip of insanity, played a part in this. Sona seems to remember, in shreds and patches, that Ashish Roy had been a much-respected professor in Presidency College; people used to call him interchangeably 'genius' and 'mad'; the terms, after all, could very well be transferable. Then something had happened – an illness, a stroke, an accident, a grieving? – something that Sona does not know, never knew; Ashish Roy had stopped being a regular commuter across the divide between 'genius' and 'madman' and had remained stuck on one side, unable to cross over to the other again. He had taken early retirement and was often seen walking along the streets of Patuapara or just north of Hazra Road with rheumy eyes, muttering to himself, sometimes laughing out loud, sometimes sighing, dressed in outsized, filthy hand-me-downs, a handy bugbear for mothers of the area to scare their children with. And yet, through all this open ridiculing, something of the awe at his former glory, something remembered, perhaps only through anecdotes at several removes, bubbles to the surface and mitigates what could easily have turned into naked cruelty.

Sona follows Ashish Roy to his dingy quarters on the ground floor of a decrepit house on Rupchand Mukherjee Lane. The falling dark and the power outage have not been dented in the slightest by the few hurricane lamps that are being lit; most of their glass chimneys are black with soot. A transistor radio is playing, in a room somewhere, a popular Hemanta Mukherjee song. An elderly woman's voice calls out, 'Who goes there?' No one replies. Ashish Roy mutters, 'So dark, can't see a thing, wait, don't move, you may trip over something', then gives a shout, 'Orre, bring some light here', which tapers to a thin cry towards the end of the call. No answer.

'Follow me, we'll get there,' he advises the boy, then begins his ill man's shuffle. Sona cannot see him very well, but does as he is told. A servant is complaining in shrill tones, 'The water's gone. If the pump had been turned on this afternoon, there would be water. How will I do the washing-up now?' There follows the clatter of stainless-steel plates and metal pots and pans.

When they reach what Sona assumes to be Ashish Roy's room, he notices that a hurricane lamp has been placed already on a wooden stool. It casts more shadows than it illuminates. The extreme shabbiness of the room is familiar to Sona – a wooden four-poster bed with greasy sheets and pillows, a large glass-fronted showcase containing scores of books, a wooden almirah, a cane stool, a diptych of framed photographs of perhaps his dead parents above the door-frame, a wall calendar from 'Basak Stores' with a picture of Kali.

The man plunges in straight away. 'Proof, proof, no proof, nothing. Have you heard of Euclid? The Greeks laid the foundations of math-ematics. Can you tell me how many prime numbers there are? Can you tell me?'

Sona knows this. 'Infinite,' he answers.

Ashish Roy cackles again, 'Correct, correct. Now, can you prove it? See here, see here.'

He limps to the bookcase, opens one of its doors, picks out a thick, battered volume, all the while muttering to himself, 'Nine twenty, nine twenty, nine twenty, infinity of primes'. He bends down towards the smoky light and locates what he is searching for. 'Here it is, here it is, look, look here: nine twenty, book nine, proposition twenty, *Elements*, Euclid's *Elements*, have you heard of it, the foundation stone of mathematics; here, look, the proof of the infinity of primes. Shall I explain it to you? It's very simple, you can see it in front of you as I speak, they'll appear in front of your eyes, the logical steps, shall I? Shall I?'

Before Sona has had a chance to leaf through the pages of this legendary book – his hands are a-quiver at the touch of Euclid – Ashish Roy has begun, falling over himself in his enthusiasm and child-like excitement.

'Let us assume that there is *not* an infinity of primes. So the series A, let's say, of primes goes 2, 3, 5, 7, 11, 13, 17 and ends with X. Are you following me?' he asks, then, without waiting for an answer, not because he does not care, but because something in the boy's wide-open eyes and half-open mouth, something approaching a trance-like state, tells him, this man who once upon a time made a living teaching and could work out by taking one brief look at a student's face whether he was with him or not, that the boy intuitively knows from this point on, from the finite set of $A = \{2, 3, 5, 7, \ldots X\}$ he has posited, that he will be able to construct the proof himself, so without waiting for a response to his rhetorical question, he continues, 'Now let us suppose, on the basis of our hypothesis, that there is a number Y, which is defined by the formula $Y = \{2, 3, 5, 7, \ldots X\} + 1$.'

Sona lets out an exultant cry, part one-note laugh, part shout – his magic number, his old friend, his saviour on the winged horse: one. Here too, in the proof, as in the geography of his mind, it is the key that will unlock, the hand that will guide him safely through the path in the dense, jumbly woods. His joy is at recognising his unfailing friend again. Yes, he knows how the proof will advance.

Ashish Roy has not been interrupted by Sona's ejaculation; if anything, it has spurred him on, because he has now received a sign that the boy's mind is flying along the beautiful arc of the proof, the mind at one with the path, indivisible. 'It is obvious that Y is not divisible by any of the numbers in the set A because it leaves the remainder' – in his excitement, not only at the elegant parsimony of the proof, but also at his certainty of the boy's innate under-standing of the steps to come, he trips over his words – 'onewhen-dividedbyanynumberbelongingtothesetAbutifitisnotaprimeitmust-bedivisiblebysomeprimeandthereforethereisaprimenumbergreater-thananyofthenumbers . . .'

Sona cannot sit still. He leaps up and shouts, 'That contradicts our hypothesis.'

Ashish Roy gives out his signature cackle, then the boy and man sing out in inseparable unison, 'So the hypothesis is false and so there are an infinity of primes.'

Then both of them simultaneously fall to a delighted laughing. It is the laughter, one imagines, of child-angels; the purest distillate of joy while contemplating some kind of immanent perfection. The shadows in the room, nearly totally in the dark, are tremulous. The hurricane-light flame, one side markedly higher than the other, is turning the glass blacker by the minute.

Ashish Roy says, 'Do you know what kind of a proof this is? It's a reductio ad absurdum, Latin, meaning, literally, to reduce to the point of absurdity, to the point of absurdity. Euclid loved this method. It is one of the finest weapons in the mathematician's drawer, one of the finest, the finest.'

Sona sees the glint of a thread of drool at the corner of the man's mouth catching the yellow light of the lamp and turning briefly golden.

'Beautiful, isn't it? What do you say, eh?' Mad Ashu asks.

Sona, still enmeshed in magic, can only nod.

'"A thing of beauty is a joy for ever",' the man says, losing Sona for a moment by this sudden switch to non-mathematical English. 'Have you heard this? "A thing of beauty is a joy for ever." Keats, John Keats. English poet, great English poet. Now do you understand how right he was?'

Because these are not numbers but words instead, with a fractious and slippery attachment to the meanings behind them, unlike numbers, Sona takes a while to work out the relation between the words of the great English poet and the reality they describe. He nods hesitantly, late with his reaction.

It is far too early to get hopeful, but Ashish Roy, after what seems like an entire geological era in which he has been crushed and atomised and obliterated, after that oblivion and erasure, feels an unforgettable tug, an imprisoned tiger glimpsing, for the briefest dart of thought, a chink showing the wide open, before it closes again. Or rather, he sees himself as the tiger that has a flash of its freedom; it comes to him with shocking visualness, the black-streaked yellow, the white between the nose and mouth, even the suffocating odour of the big cat. Then it is gone. The dust settles, a heavier patina than before. He does not know how to feel after this – what was it? unexpected vision? intimation? of what could be potential renewal? Pain that it could be a teasing, lying illusion? Hope that it may be real and true? Dread that it could be, as so many times before, true for a while, then turn out to be a cul-de-sac? That pendulum-swing between the two extremities had ruined him. So why is he being tortured with it again? He is finished, he has nothing to give, nothing can be extracted from him any more. But this lanky, underfed, big-eyed boy . . .

'You come here when you can, and talk mathematics with me. How does that sound?' he offers with utmost tentativeness, his voice disappearing as it progresses.

Sona nods avidly again.

Encouraged, Ashish Roy continues, 'Nowadays I have no one to talk to. There were many in the past, many. My world was full of talk of mathematics, was full of it, loud with it. Now . . . all gone. All finished. There was a time when I was even forbidden to talk or think about numbers.'

A long pause. Sona is mystified, but does not ask any questions. He has been trained not to ask anything unless it is in a mathematics lesson, only to listen and watch. Listen, watch and keep oneself invisible, absent. Pagla Ashu, mad Ashu, is rambling.

'I couldn't do it myself. I thought I came close, several times came close, but the next morning, or the next week, I'd discover a mistake, a mistake, a mistake. Everything would come crashing down. Jah, all over, all over!'

Another long silence. A cockroach flies from the space between the almirah and the bookcase and lands whirringly next to the calendar. Sona flinches. The pervasive slippage in the professor's speech, mannerisms, physical demeanour, as if all were sliding away between intention and its correct manifestation, may be the effects of some illness, but it is not madness, Sona decides. Maybe the higher reaches of mathematics have curdled his mind. The dividing line between genius and madman is hair-thin, he has always been told. Turned mad while walking around in the world of numbers – Sona cannot imagine a greater pleasure. With the fingers of his mind he caresses the *reductio ad absurdum* proof again and again.

A middle-aged woman enters the room. Dishrag of a block-printed sari, burdened looks as if she were a pack animal not a long way off from the knackers' yard. She adds to the shadows in the room.

In a tight voice that people adopt when they do not want their words to be overheard she says, 'Again? Again? You've brought someone back again? How many times have you been asked not to do it? How many times?' The fury in her words belies the partially hushed delivery. Sona fears that she is going to explode any minute, but the low hiss continues. 'You clearly haven't learned your lesson. How much lower do you want to pull us? You may not have any shame, any repentance, but you could think of us. Or is that too much to ask? To replace some numbers with humans? Mathematics has eaten not just you, but is devouring us alive too.'

Ashish Roy sits through the tirade blinking and drooling like an idiot. He does not look particularly embarrassed or mortified. What is going on in the prickly thickets of his unknowable mind, Sona has no idea. Sona himself wants to become inanimate, like the Basak Stores calendar, something outside the horizons of human address.

She turns to him and spits out, barely bothering to change her tone, 'And you. You go home now. Don't come here again.'

This Sona understands – it is plain, unclothed rejection. Scampering off through the gap between the scolding woman and the door, he cannot turn back to answer Mad Ashu's desperately slurred shout directed at his fleeing figure: 'Ei, wait, stop, where do you live?'

Running back home in the dark, with a thudding heart and flaming ears, past Pandey's cowshed and its attendant smell-cloud of cow-dung and hay, then the corner shop with its one weak taper and strings of peanut brittle hanging from an open shutter, Sona sees old Panchanan, with his cheeks sunk in on his toothless gums, sitting behind the grubby glass jars of sweets and savouries. In the daytime he would perhaps have called out to Sona, 'Ei je, mathematics-moshai, where are you headed?' but it is pitch-dark now. Sona is often sent to Panchanan's tiny shop to buy four-annas' worth of puffed rice or a candle or a box of matches or a plastic bottle of kerosene for the small stove that his mother had lately started using to cook on. He runs faster, knowing his mother is going to be worried.

At home, the usual rusty clockwork of festering days. Mejo-kaki is shouting at a maidservant because the stairwell and the inner veran-dahs, the courtyard, are all utterly dark and the servant has failed to dispel it quickly enough. From their room Sona can see the weakest illumination of candlelight. Madan-da can be heard muttering to himself as he emerges from his room near the back garden and goes upstairs; from his tone it seems that he is none too pleased with something or the other.

Purba asks, 'Why are you so late?'

Her son lies, 'I had to do some extra work with Sougata.' In that moment of involuntary lying he understands that he is going to find ways to circumvent the stricture forbidding him to visit the professor.

Purba asks, 'Did they give you anything to eat?'

Kalyani, sitting on the floor, doing nothing at all, turns to him, all attention.

'Yes, rice pudding,' he says.

'Rice pudding?' mother and daughter ask together. 'What was the occasion?'

Sona, face averted from them, mumbles, 'I think it was Sougata's birthday a couple of days ago.'

Here too Sona has something to hide, but it belongs to a different order of privacy. This afternoon, while he was doing his usual three-times-a-week English tuition, Mala-mashi had brought in, halfway through the tutorial, three bowls of chilled rice pudding, one each for the two boys and one for Sanjay Banerjee, the new English tutor. (Dibyendu-da had left after six months, to become a Naxalite, it was rumoured.)

'It was Bumba's birthday on Wednesday,' she announced coyly while handing out the bowls.

Sanjay-da had wished Sougata happy birthday while the boys concentrated furiously on the bowls in their hands, hoping to avoid any excruciating social small talk.

Ever since Sona had moved to St Lawrence School last year, his status in the Saha house had changed, but not entirely for the better. On the one hand Mala-mashi was clearly impressed, expressing a hooded admiration: 'Now that your skill in mathematics has taken you to a better school,' she said, 'you must make sure that some of your cleverness rubs off on Bumba.' Sometimes she operated through coiled locutions where occluded envy and a calculating expectation fought a tug-of-war: 'A tiny bit of credit for moving up must be given to all the help Sona has had with English, his weakest subject, in the tutorials at our home,' she said to the neighbours, 'let's hope he remembers that'; obligation can loop more complicated knots around the giver than the receiver. Occasionally something boiled over in her and she said to Sona, 'You've reduced coming here to three days a week instead of the usual five, now that you're in a better school. So be it. But you're not the type to become arrogant. We, on our part, are happy to do the little that will help you along, regardless of five days or three.'

She stretched to identical cups and bowls for tutor and both students now – previously Sona had been given stainless steel while Sougata and the tutor got china – but took away with the other hand: she exited the room with a comment that left no one in any doubt that she grudged the little good she had done this neighbour's boy. Couched, of course, as caring affection.

Today it was a different variation. Today the rice pudding was laced with: 'Just because you've now moved to a big school, it doesn't mean that you can't have some of the rice pudding I made for your not-very-clever friend's birthday.'

Sona, cocooned for the most part against this kind of poison, stayed silent and ran his spoon through the rice: it was a luxurious version with sultanas and cashews. He put a spoonful in his mouth. It was so delicious, coating every millimetre inside his mouth with its silky richness, that he closed his eyes. On his birthdays, his mother struggled to make him the obligatory rice pudding; she had to make do with broken rice, rather than the expensive gobinda-bhog, while raisins and nuts were beyond her imagining. He felt almost physically swayed by a wave of pity for his mother. His eyes prickled and the rice pudding, now bitter in his mouth, refused to move down his obstructed throat. In fierce defiance he thought that his mother's rice pudding was the best in the world; this one in his wretched hand could not even begin to compare with it.

Now to be asked a direct question, albeit in all innocence, about something that had nearly unseated him from his studied indifference seems like the resurgence of a newly anaesthetised pain. So he treads with the utmost caution while answering, refusing to give out any signal of weakness. Besides, he is itching to have another go at trying to prove $p = x^2 + y^2$ if (and only if) $p = 1 \pmod 4$. That Brahmagupta identity, so teasingly dangled in front of him, could well be the key to unlock it, but it is unattainable, at least for the moment, from Pagla Ashu, so he will have to figure out a way of finding it.

Sona knows who he can ask. The mathematics teacher in the senior school of St Lawrence, Swapan Adhikari, is a legend. He has a reputation for being fierce and bad-tempered. It is said that he pulls up lazy boys from their seats by their sideburns and is the acknowledged master of the 'double slap', a strike to the face so forceful that it flings aside the first boy to be hit and lands resoundingly on the cheek of the boy sitting next to him, taking care, with great efficiency, of two boys sitting on the same bench and talking, or not paying attention, in class. He is impatient with, and frankly not interested in, those who have no aptitude, instead choosing to concentrate on the one or two who are gifted. Given that he neglects nearly all his students and can't be bothered to follow the rules set by the syllabus, it is surprising that he has been kept on as senior (and only) mathematics teacher. And this despite a growing clamour from parents that Mr Adhikari is responsible for their sons' underwhelming performance in mathematics, their being 'unripe in maths'.

Mr Adhikari has a degree in pure mathematics; that alone sets him apart from most school teachers. He thinks differently and discourages all his students from the learning by rote that is the basic, dominant and only model of education. Ingest and vomit – that is the order of things; you learn by heart reams and reams, and then regurgitate it all during examinations. Everything – History, Geography, Bengali, English, Science – is dealt with in this one unchanging way. It develops only one faculty, memory, and atrophies everything, most of all thinking. You can see the results of this in the teachers themselves; there is a blankness, something of a ruminant's absence of thought about them.

But the dangers of not toeing the line are serious: you fail an exam if you don't do as you have been told, because you create extra work for a teacher by asking him to think instead of letting him continue on autopilot and, if you fail an exam, it decreases the chances of getting out of the system that will slowly crush you to a flat piece of cardboard.

So Sona does what he has perfected: he becomes two persons, an outer one that goes through the motions required of him, and an inner one that is the true, pure he. The shell does the rote-learning, the core attends to his current obsession with even perfect numbers and how, and if, they relate to the universal set of his greater obsession: primes.

In the almost daily updating of his long list of primes, there were only five Mersenne primes so far (3, 7, 31, 127, 8191), and he had quickly established three obvious things: one, not all $2^n - 1$ numbers were prime; two, not all primes could be expressed as a Mersenne number; three, for $2^n - 1$ to be prime, n should be a prime number. No sooner had he arrived at those generalisations than fissures started appearing in the structure: while the intersecting set of his first and second conclusions needed to be explored further, he found that the third was no guarantee of primality. $2^{11} - 1 = 2047 = 23 \times 89$, to take one such crack running along the edifice. Since he had not found a way of tackling this head-on, he thought that perhaps approaching them from the beautifully contiguous territory of even perfect numbers, numbers whose total factors (including 1, but not the number itself) added up to return the original number, could yield some point of entry.

Faced now with all this unwelcome prying that could very well lead, at least himself, if not his mother and his sister, to the dangerous swamp of emotions, he falls back on his version of thumb-sucking – he teleports his mind to the larger latitudes of numbers, leaving the shell behind.

He says, to no one in particular, 'I need to do my homework now.'

Of course, he knows Euclid's proof of the infinity of primes; he kept quiet because that was what he did, what came best to him, but also because he wanted to see how much the mad professor knew, if he really was a professor who knew a few things about mathematics. Who knows what attributes rumour can give people? It's the volume of Euclid he had held in his hand less than an hour ago that has raked the burning coals of even perfect numbers in him, for who doesn't know his proof connecting primes and perfect numbers through $2n - 1$? If $2n - 1$ is a prime, say P, then Euclid's proof could be rephrased to state that $\frac{P(P+1)}{2}$ is always an even perfect number.

Purba looks at the bowed head of her son, rummaging in his tattered school satchel – an old hand-me-down from Suranjan – for his books and pen. The way the loose curls on his head catch the feeble light of the candle makes them look like the cloudy bloom of a drop of ink the moment it hits a bowl of water. It takes her a fraction of a second to work out who he reminds her of.

As far as his intuition leads him, he feels that the converse must be true, that is, if an even number is perfect, then it must conform to the formula $\frac{P(P+1)}{2}$ where P is a prime of the form $2^n - 1$. Yet intuition will not do; all this while he has not seen in the eye the centrality of proof to his hunches and feelings. That encounter with Pagla Ashu this evening was one of those moments when chance spoke with pointedness, with almost a design. He will have to prove the hypothesis.

Sona looks exactly like his father. The equivalence Purba has just drawn winds her. Why has it eluded her so far? Whoever said that time blunts all pain did not quite understand that bluntness can wound as grievously as sharp points and edges; Purba finds herself rooted to the spot.

He writes out on a clean sheet of paper: 'Let N be an even perfect number.

∴ $N = 2^{n-1}(2^n - 1)$, where $2^n - 1$ is prime.' The next step is crucial. He stakes everything on it. He has carried it in his head for months now, shuffled it around, waiting for the right pattern to emerge. What if he substituted $2^n - 1$ with an odd number, m? Then $N = 2^{n-1}m$, and since m is not divisible by 2, it is relatively prime to 2^{n-1}, so that

$$\sigma(N) = \sigma(2^{n-1}m) = \sigma(2^{n-1})\,\sigma(m) = \frac{(2^n - 1)}{2 - 1}\,\sigma(m) = (2^n - 1)\,\sigma(m).$$

The inspiration with the fourth step, the trick – what a brainwave! – of using $2 - 1$ as a denominator comes easily, but he does not know its source. The series of equivalences look like elementary parsing when written down, but each step is an advancement in terms of shape, of design. It is like an explosion in reverse motion, where all the parts come together to cohere into the undiminished whole as if the shattering has never been, yet it is exactly this process of detonation and watching the debris with unblinking attention that yields up the secrets of the architecture of things.

Kalyani asks, 'What, aren't you going to give us anything to eat?'

Purba does not hear.

'You are going to get a haircut this Sunday,' she says to her son, steadying her voice. 'You look like a ghost,' she continues, making her voice stern, almost rebuking, in case he or Kalyani hears any tremulousness in it, 'with all those curls falling over your forehead and eyes. Like a ghost.'

He barely hears the order. He shifts the forms further:

$\sigma(N) = 2N$ because N is perfect, so $\sigma(N) = 2N = 2(2^{n-1}m) = 2^n m$. But $\sigma(N) = (2^n - 1)\,\sigma(m)$ – as above – ∴ $2^n m = (2^n - 1)\,\sigma(m)$.

He feels that familiar yet rare sensation of his insides going into free fall, that slight loosening of his sphincter, and knows that he will reach the end of the proof successfully.

A few hundred yards away, Ashish Roy comes to a clearing in the impenetrable forest of his mind. A shaft of light pours in. Several questions fly out in a swarming buzz from the undergrowth. *Eeesh, I forgot to ask the boy his name, his address. Now how will I find him?* Navigating the thorny brakes and tangles defeats him at the best of times. The medication he was given after his breakdown was not to cure him, to help him find his way to order and method again, but to keep him quiet, neuter, chained. They are heavy muggers, which silence him with their repeated blows. Who around him wants to see the eked-out, expensive process of becoming better, a path riddled with switchbacks, reversals and doubtful probabilities of success, when one can have the far more convenient option of an end to the thing that bothers everyone around him most – his occasional lapses into shouting fits and violence? Hanging above the pathless and dark forest is the heavy, unlifting pall of haloperidol and quietiapine fumarate. The beast has been muzzled.

But occasionally, very occasionally, there are patches of illumination when he can follow a path from one point to another without being swallowed by the surrounding darkness. It is only a temporary reprieve, given, it seems to him, to taunt him with what he has lost. *But, first, that boy. I must find a way of tracking him down. If I stand where I found him today, exactly at the same time, would that work?*

He wants to know which school the boy attends. In the rare gift of intermittent clarity given to him nowadays, something had passed from the boy to him that evening, an electric current, the conduction of some knowledge. He could read what was going on behind the boy's expression of guarded, private wonder. The boy *knew*. He knew Euclid's *reductio ad absurdum* proof, he knew Fermat's two-square theorem. He said that he had got stuck trying to prove it, which meant that he did not know the proof, but – and this causes Ashish Roy's hobbled mind to exult and soar again – *he was trying to prove it himself.*

How many boys of his age – twelve? thirteen? fourteen? – have enough number-theory to even know that theorem, leave alone want to prove it? But, wait, if he doesn't know it is a theorem, how has he arrived at it? Could he – here Professor Roy's hairs stand on end – could he have worked it out by intuition, or as a by-product to something he is toying with? No school in Calcutta teaches this kind of mathematics. Does he have an exceptional teacher who explores these topics alongside the dead and boring school syllabus? It all comes down to that crucial question: which school does he go to? He looks . . . looks . . . grimy, meagre, except for those large, slow eyes lit up with curiosity and a special kind of intelligence. I have to find him, I have to find him . . . This boy could . . . could . . . could . . .

He has reached the end of the clearing. Beyond it waits the hulking blackness, forever present. It crackles, shifts and leaps on him, obliterating his whole being. He falls down from his bed on to the floor, thrashing and thrashing, as the darkness inside lays its claim on him once more.

VIII

The sound of rain on straw-and-coconut-leaf roofs all night long. And, drowning that, the non-stop croaking of hundreds of frogs, calling out across fields and ponds and the dirt lanes that have all dissolved into runnels of water the colour of milky tea. If you woke up in the middle of the night for some reason, you wouldn't be able to go back to sleep again because of their varied cacophony. The intervals, rhythms, identification of different types of croaks, perhaps even going so far as to imagine individual frogs each emitting a particular and recurrent line in this mad music – all these sounds and pauses would enter your head and you would be anticipating it, and it would drive you mad.

And it was not just water coming down from the sky. It seemed there was a rain of insects too. I didn't know the names of half of them. You had your common centipede and millipede and black ants and flying ants that you get in the city, but there were armies of other kinds. When I was small, Mejo-kaka once told me that centipedes could enter your ears while you were sleeping, then they made their way through the ear canal into your brain, where they nested and bred and created a huge colony, which then proceeded to eat up everything inside and then you died, thousands of the creatures leaking out of your nose and ears and eyes. I knew what that typically colourful story by Mejo-kaka was worth now, but it had made a deep impression on me when I was a child. I believed it for a long time and it created a tiny corner of horror mixed with repulsion in my soul. I found that I hadn't managed to wash it out of myself completely; a mark still remained. Sleeping on the damp floor of Kanu's hut – I called it a floor, but with rain coming in through the gaps in the thatch it was becoming more mud than floor – the sight of a centipede sent that shudder through me before my rational mind took over.

In this poorest of all the sections of Majgeria the collection of twenty or so huts arranged in a tight huddle with only narrow spaces of dirt and earth separating them seemed ready to dissolve into the water and mud that now filled the spaces in between. I tried to think of my instinctive distaste as the last vestiges of my reactionary upbringing, something almost counter-revolutionary.

Samir, meanwhile, revelled in it. He pointed out — Look! The whole picture has changed. It was all brown and grey and white in the summer, and red earth, with only a little bit of green. Now the entire canvas is like a study in hundreds of different shades of green.

I said — Yes, only if you forget the mud-brown and mud-grey of the bottom of the canvas.

He laughed and said — You, mairi, will remain an urban soul for ever.

— Urban guerrilla, if you don't mind.

— You really don't like this eye-soothing, eye-filling riot of green all around you? It's what Bengali poets and singers have gone on and on about for centuries.

— Perhaps that's the reason.

— Now listen to this: *I have seen the face of Bengal, that is why I I do not want to see the beauty of the world.*

I cut him short — All this Jibanananda and Rabindranath will be the end of the Bengalis. I expect you to break out, any minute now, into *Again the month of ashad has come, filling the sky.*

Kanu and Bijli's son got a bad cough. They gave him a paste of tulsi leaves, but this did not have much of an effect. The old man and the baby were now a hacking duet at nights.

Three weeks after this I saw the paddy saplings and I felt an exaltation take hold of me. That green! How could the chemistry of brown seeds and grey-red-black mud have produced this green, which seemed almost boiling up out of the earth? I too felt like reciting the lines that had Samir's heart, but I restrained myself. It was enough that I knew that my soul sang, I didn't have to break into minstrelsy.

I noticed two kinds of clouds. The first was the obvious one — dark rain clouds. These brooded sometimes; sometimes they slid along slowly. Behind them, the backdrop to their stately movement, was not the sky, but the matrix of another kind of cloud — a uniform, dull expanse of a bright grey you could be fooled into thinking was white.

I watched the transplanting process, hypnotised. Kanu told me that I should study it carefully. It was not something I could be taught hands-on because there was no margin for error here, as there was in ploughing the soil. It was mostly women who did the transplanting. The uprooted saplings, all about four to six inches high – Kanu said 'one-hand tall' – and bundled into bunches of a dozen or so, were dotted all over the plots that we had prepared. Then it began. The women, their short saris hitched up nearly to their calves, stood ankle-deep in the mud in the inundated plots, bent low from their waist, leaned down, picked up a bundle, separated it into individual saplings, then fixed each in the mud, making sure the roots remained underwater. The next one was planted about four inches away. The women worked with speed, precision and what I could only call a kind of choreography – the whole thing looked like a disciplined dance. And then it struck me that it was probably as physically trying; bending down so that your top half made, at the waist, a variable angle between forty-five and sixty degrees with your bottom half and maintaining that for hours without interruption was a visual illustration of the process that had given us the term 'back-breaking labour'.

The world outside had changed subtly. Where there was the ugly monotony of mangled mud before, now that wet, grey broth was transforming itself into a lush, velvety green carpet, patch by patch. This was a green I'd never come across in my life before. You could look and look at it, thinking it would satiate the hunger of your eyes, but the more you looked, the more that desire increased at the same time as soothing you. How could this be?

Two weeks later Samir was still quoting lines from <u>Beautiful Bengal</u>. Dhiren joined him now. Seeing an insect poised on the edge of a leaf, he quoted – *On a leaf in Bengal, the glass-insect has gone to sleep.*

So I said – That's not a glass-insect, you fool, it's a dung beetle.

He said – Really, you have no soul, no . . . no finer juices in you.

– The first requisite of revolution: evaporate your finer juices.

– What about soul then?

I quoted Mao – That is for the 'concrete analysis of concrete conditions', the very soul of Marxism, according to Lenin. Not for empty and superficial aesthetic pleasures. This beautiful green in front of you is an instrument of the oppression of the masses.

That shut him up.

There was a breathing space after the transplanting. After the burst of intense physical labour, we were back once more in the old, eddying whirlpool of talk, going round and round in circles.

I worried that so much thought – and so much talk – was making the action become insurmountable. Perhaps the first step, the first stroke, that was what was difficult.

Dhiren asked – Do we have the movements of everyone on the list? We have to get that absolutely right: their movements during every day and every evening of every season of the year. Where they go, whom they see, their habits, the places they visit, the roads they take . . .

I said impatiently – Not everything in that calculation will be perfect. There will be variations and changes and interruptions. Do you do the same thing every day, or every hour of the day, or every, say, 12th August?

– No, no, but there are patterns.

– Yes, patterns. We have to get the patterns of their movements correct. But we can never eliminate chance. Your moneylender, Nirmal Maity, for example, does not go to Medinipur Town or Garhbeta every ninth day of the month, setting out of his home at midday, then returning at eight in the evening. You have to accept that if we lie in wait for him when he's alone, based on previous instances, we may well be disappointed. He may not be going to Medinipur Town that day, say.

– I understand, but the opposite strategy, attacking on the spur of the moment, seems riskier. What if we're not prepared? What if he's prepared instead?

– The guerrilla should <u>always</u> be prepared, because he doesn't know when an opportunity is going to present itself.

Samir intervened – What about a median way?

– That would mean being armed all the time?

– Exactly my position: being prepared all the time, I said.

Samir said – No, I meant something slightly different, something more spur-of-the-moment, something that happens as the consequence of a flashpoint . . . We take advantage of a heated moment and push things forward. Once one action is under our belt, the second one will be easier, the third easier still. And we'll be able to increase our numbers, if the munish see that we mean business, that our hands are already bright with blood, like a true communist revolutionary's. I have the Chairman's words to support me.

True, he did.

The paddy plants will grow, bear flowers and then the grain, the grain will ripen, finally they will be harvested. It rained and rained and rained. Mosquitoes, dense clouds of them, kept us awake with their biting; their whining was even worse. Kanu's child slept badly and cried a lot. It kept Bijli and me awake for a large part of the night.

The weeding began. I leaped towards it greedily: it was something to do for a small period until time froze again and we went back to the endless waiting.

Large groups of munish, we among them, spread out over the aals, about twenty to twenty-five munish per bigha of land. We wore a toka on our heads and carried a small, sharp sickle, niraani, in our hands and went about uprooting weeds and the different types of grass – durbamukho, moina, shyam, an old Mahato man told me as I worked alongside him – that had sprung up on the aals and were creeping along, extending their long, tenacious roots into the green felt of the paddy fields they bordered.

We squatted and moved forwards and sideways slowly. It was impossible to do this job standing up and bending down; I felt my back and neck were going to break if I did that. The squatting motion was better, but only marginally, I soon discovered. At least I should be able to sleep better at nights. In the intervals between the rains, the cooling effect disappeared instantly and the land seemed to exhale its warm breath in the form of an invisible vapour . . . It was impossible to do anything more than breathe, and even that seemed strenuous, so you can imagine what the weeding did to me. No amount of gritting my teeth and murmuring the Chairman's words about discipline was going to lessen the immediate pain of this work. Would I come out of the other side, stronger? Would it make me steelier, more disciplined, the ideal guerrilla? I didn't know. There were frequent days when the answer was a very straightforward 'No'.

CHAPTER NINE

Who would have thought that when the toddler Somnath had been inconsolable after the brown mynah had snatched a dragonfly out of his fingers' grip he had been reacting not to loss, or to the knowledge of the mercilessness of Nature, but had really been giving vent to frustration at an impulse thwarted? That inclination found its full flowering as Somnath grew older. He became adept at catching alive all kinds of flying insects – mosquitoes, flies, butterflies, moths, cockroaches – without squashing them, tore off their wings or legs with the utmost delicacy so that their bodies were not damaged in the traction produced by the pulling, and then set them free and watched them unblinkingly. He took immense delight in their limbless writhing, short-lived sometimes, but not always. At other times he left on a couple of their legs and watched them hobble and skitter. That sent him into fits of clapping and hopping about; joy was such an easily attainable thing. After a heavy rain-shower, when the big, black ants came out, he dripped hot wax from a burning candle on them and achieved a kind of instant embalming; this was a special thrill.

'O ma, how clever of you to think up this one,' his mother said.

'But it's so cruel!' Chhaya protested.

'What's cruel about it? He's doing us a favour by getting rid of these pests.'

At the apex of this pyramid of pleasures was the setting of larger insects on fire. Stealing a matchbox was not difficult. It was tougher to go about the business of immolating insects without anyone discovering it; the house was full of people and he could be spied all too easily. His favourite creatures for this purpose were the shiny, rust-brown centipedes, which were quite common, especially on the ground floor, during the monsoon. Somnath loved the way they curled up into a tight spiral as soon as they were touched. He spent hours trying to stretch them out to their natural length, once they had rolled into themselves, by impaling them with safety pins or needles to isolate their two ends and then pulling on both simultaneously. Without being formed in so many words, the thought went through his head that if the touch of any object was so inimical to their uncoiling, what would happen if they were exposed to another kind of stimulus, one that would force them to unfurl? The answer appeared almost instantly to his budding pyrophile's brain.

It was in this act that he was caught by Charubala one afternoon: the inert coil of the centipede first doused in a few drops of kerosene filched from the kitchen, then a lit match held to it, causing instant ignition, the flames hardly visible in the strong sunlight, and the insect leaking a yellow-orangish fluid. He was given a resounding slap to his face, the first ever in his life. Uproar followed. Madan and the servants were rounded up and scolded for neglecting to catch the child getting his hands on something as forbidden and dangerous as kerosene ('What if he had mistakenly set something bigger, or even himself, on fire?'), then reprimanded again for leaving matches lying around. Somnath went into a sulk that kept the whole family dancing for two days. And yet it was clear to Charubala, torn between chagrin and pique, that she had slapped Som not to discipline him and deter him from unhealthily cruel activities, but out of protectiveness, so that he did not injure himself playing with fire. It was not a lesson in morality, but in self-preservation.

Nineteen forty-three offered Somnath's particular brand of creativity a broader array of opportunities. Madan began to save the starch-water from the drained cooked rice for the skin-and-bones beggars who had gradually proliferated all over the city in an attempt to escape the famine in the countryside. They came begging throughout the day, these cages of bone covered in loose folds of skin. They could not bring themselves to ask for rice, begging for the cooking water instead. Ten-year-old Som, standing at the front door, fascinated, watched them drinking the lukewarm starch-water from dented aluminium bowls. His mother called from inside, 'Come in, come in right now', an angry panic in her voice. She could tell by the clothes they wore and the way they spoke that this shrivelled mother and her two little daughters who had come begging were not the indigent poor, but came possibly from the rural lower-middle classes.

Som watched them lap up the gruel. The sound it made was subtly different from sipping or slurping.

'Come inside,' Charubala ordered and tried to move him physically by force.

The boy, not used to having his will opposed, refused to budge, but his mother, bigger than he, tried again, this time nearly lifting him up in her arms. Som fought back, throwing about his arms and legs. In the tussle, he kicked the half-empty aluminium bowl, which one of the little girls had set down for a minute to watch the struggle, and sent the gruel spilling in first a swift then a slow, broad lick across the top of the stairs where the woman and her girls were sitting.

A short, sharp cry came out of the woman's mouth, then silence. The older-looking of the two girls went down on all fours, prostrated herself on the floor and started to lick up the spill. Transfixed, Somnath and his mother looked on. Charubala returned to life quicker; as if they had witnessed something unspeakable, she and Somnath, now more pliant, left for the interior of the house swiftly, silently.

The incident, played out for, it seemed, a few infinitely elastic seconds, caused a certain calculation to go through the boy's head. When another set of starving beggars turned up at their door, two or three days after this, Somnath was ready. He knew that he was not supposed to be around, staring at them, so he waited until Madan-da had gone into the kitchen, then sneaked downstairs, ran stealthily to the man – a shadow of a man, really – and his stick-thin daughter, snatched the bowl out of her hands and dripped the remainder of the cloudy liquid onto the rags the girl was wearing. Then he stepped back and said, 'Wring your clothes and drink what comes out.'

Father and daughter stared at Somnath, their breathing seemingly suspended. What meekness and subordination differences of class and wealth had hard-wired in them were consolidated by hunger and debility. They got up from their sitting positions slowly. The man pulled his daughter close to him, as if wishing to protect her and, without turning their backs to Somnath, they climbed down the four steps and reached the front gate backwards, the entire while keeping Somnath pinned with their eyes. At the iron gate they turned their backs to him, facing the street at last, but then the father spun very slowly around to look at Somnath one final time and said, 'May god keep you well', and shuffled away with his daughter.

Around the time Somnath turned twenty, his childhood mischief had become the stuff of local anecdotes, recounted over and over, as if in celebration, by Charubala mostly, but certain incidents had either been forgotten or were never mentioned. The story that was retold frequently was the one involving a cat.

It was a white animal with an orange tail and an orange sock on three of its paws, the right front leg missing out on the droll detail. Madan-da used to say that the creature had used that paw to swipe so much food, stealing into the kitchens of the neighbourhood, that the sock had fallen off. The explanation was not entirely without merit: in the year of famine, when the corpses of emaciated cats and dogs and humans could be seen lying around the city, this cat seemed to have miraculously avoided that end. It was notorious in Basanta Bose Road – a fish head, waiting to be cooked, would go missing; cooked fish, left uncovered and unsupervised in the kitchen while the cook had her back turned for only a few minutes, would be attacked brazenly, the cook returning to find a piece gone or fish bones sticking out from the bowl. The cat clearly knew where fish was being cooked and when; it lay in wait nearby, endlessly patient, for it knew an opportunity would come along soon. Its reputation had reached such a height that it was shooed off energetically whenever anyone saw it loitering with intent, and children threw stones at it or hid behind doors, their breaths held, a big stick in their hands, waiting for the cat to enter so that they could bring the stick crashing down onto their unsuspecting adversary's back. Somnath, now nearly eleven, loved this game of guerrilla attack, but the cat proved wilier after a couple of occasions of being taken by nasty surprise. When the animal got swifter in its evasion of or escape from Somnath wielding a lathi, the boy became more determined to do it real damage; his blood was up.

He had a foolproof idea. He stole a couple of his father's Valium pills from the medicine box in his parents' room, crushed them to powder, mixed them in warm milk in a shallow bowl, left this by the steps to the back garden and waited, this time not armed with the stick, but watching only. Soon enough he was rewarded with the sight of the cat lapping up the milk in one go. The question now was this: would the cat oblige by falling into a stupor right in front of him or would the pills take some time to work, during which period it would lope off goodness-knows-where and sleep off the effects of the drug? Somnath was faced with a dilemma; he did not know which would give him more pleasure – the drug-induced death of the cat or beating it to a pulp with the lathi, once the tranquillisers had kicked in and it was incapable of escaping.

As it turned out, the cat sat down to wash itself after the milk, then began to have trouble getting up. It tried, failed, tried again, and stumbled after the first couple of steps. Then it stood still, swayed for a few seconds, tried to move forward, now in a kind of drunken uncoordination, and toppled over sideways. It stood up again and shook its head, as if trying physically to shed the veil of confusion and sleepiness that had descended, suddenly and heavily, upon it. Its normal gait now became a loopy, erratic curve for a while, then it fell again, unable to keep its head up. Som, his heart hammering, watched with joy. Now that the cat was so obviously powerless to run away, he emerged from his hiding place. The cat took no notice. It did not try to raise its heavy head to look at him. Som took the lathi, moved towards the cat and brought it down on the nearly comatose animal with all the force in his body, but the lathi was bigger than he and he had misjudged how close he needed to be to the animal to maximise the force of the long stick, so the blow came as an anti-climax, at least to him. The cat tried to yelp and move, neither of which it could achieve. Som remembered someone mentioning that the best way to kill a cat was to hit it hard on its head. He moved back a few steps so that he could have optimal leverage.

Before he could raise his arms a second time, Madan-da appeared from the house and called out, 'What are you doing with that lathi, what are you doing?'

By coincidence, Charubala too appeared on the scene. She repeated Madan's cry, took in the scene and added, 'What's happened to the cat? Why is it lying down like that?'

'I gave it Valium mixed in milk. Now I'm going to beat it to death. Look, it can't move. What fun! No more stolen fish.'

'Where did you get your hands on Valium? How?' she demanded, panic making her voice rise.

'Where else? From Baba's medicine box,' he said, contemptuous that she did not know something so obvious. 'I know where it's kept. Baba told me he takes those tablets at night to help him go to sleep, so I gave two to the cat. Then I can beat him and beat him and beat him.' The contempt modulated to pride; he was clearly expecting to be praised for his cleverness.

Charubala reacted quite differently. She flew into a rage.

'What nerves, taking Baba's medicines! Don't you know you're not supposed to touch that box? Those medicines are strictly forbidden to children. What if you had taken some by mistake? Valium is poison, don't you know, poison,' she screamed. 'What if you had come to some harm? My hands and feet are turning numb at the very thought. You need to be taught a lesson. You were sent into the world to turn my flesh and bones black . . .'

Leaving them to carry on, Madan discreetly picked up the cat in his arms and took it to his room. He got some warm milk from the kitchen, dipped a clean piece of cloth in it and squeezed slow drops into the sleeping creature's mouth when he noticed it beginning to stir. Would it live? At least it was still breathing. He put the cat's head on his lap and covered the lower half of the animal with a sheet so that it did not get cold. Was it only last year that he had stayed up two nights in a row, putting cold-water compresses on Somnath's forehead when he was burning up with fever? Ma's face had been thin and desiccated with worry. The doctor had said that the boy should be given cold sponges every hour and monitored throughout the night to ensure that his temperature did not shoot up. It was nothing for him to obey those orders, to see Somu-babu returned to health again. His Dulal, whom he got to see only once a year during the month-long visit to his village, was just under a year younger than Somu-babu. For the eleven months of the year that he was in Calcutta, Somu-babu was a substitute Dulal; Madan held little distinction in his head between the two boys.

Chhaya carried tales, not all of which were innocent. She got a thrill out of poisoning people's minds and playing them off against each other. 'Bhola's digging dirt in the garden, you asked him not to,' she said to her mother to try and get him into trouble; she snitched about Adinath: 'I saw Dada going to the terrace in the afternoon sun and he told me not to tell you.' She expected to be rewarded for all this. When the kulfiwalla went down the road in the late afternoon, with his terracotta pots, covered in woven jute, full of ices and kulfis, Chhaya kept an eye on who among the four siblings got ordinary kulfi (two annas), malai kulfi (three annas) or double cream (four annas); god help Charubala if her daughter thought she had been fobbed off with the cheapest.

It served Charubala's purpose on occasion that her daughter acted as an extra pair of eyes and ears, and she knew that children love to tell on each other and squabble among themselves, but all hope she had that Chhaya would outgrow this unpleasant trait proved to be in vain when it continued, unabated, as the girl turned twelve, then thirteen, then fourteen . . . By the time Chhaya sat her Matriculation Exams, Charubala had stopped noticing that her daughter's childhood habits were still present, still strong. Now, without a child's innocence to lighten it, the full unsavouriness of the personality revealed itself.

Servants regularly found themselves to be the focus of Chhaya's malignant attention. From overt accusation ('I saw the dish-washing maid eating off our brass plates in the kitchen' or 'Madan-da was in Baba's room this afternoon when he should have been having his nap'), meant mostly for her mother's ears but often mentioned in the presence of the servant concerned to cause maximum discomfort, she became a mistress of the art of insinuation. Those childish tags, 'You told him not to', 'He swore me to silence', were now dropped. She had an unerring knack of sniffing out the balance of power between people and she played it for all she could. Her veins and arteries ran with a bitter fluid, not blood, Adinath exclaimed in fury one day.

Just one glance a fraction longer than the ordinary duration of a casual look would be construed by Chhaya as being a look of derision or revulsion because she was dark or cross-eyed. Slights were imagined and built upon with creative architecture. Anything could become mined in her imagination. It had the effect of a kind of psychological terrorism – people around her became hyper-conscious of what they were saying or doing, or not saying and not doing, because Chhaya's susceptible, paranoid mind could alight on anything she chose and make it into a cause for war.

The exception, of course, was Priyo. It sometimes appeared that Chhaya distinguished insufficiently between her person and Priyo's to the extent that she often did not communicate with him verbally or through signs, assuming that the unity of their minds did not necessitate such things; unity in the strictest sense it was, a oneness, an indivisibility. When Chhaya enrolled in Bethune College to do her Intermediate and then a BA, it was Priyo who frequently accompanied her there and brought her back home. (One of the family cars – there were two – could always have been at her disposal, and sometimes she availed herself of this service, although never unaccompanied; someone from the family had to be with her in the car.) Although buses were now seen frequently on the city streets, the idea of Chhaya boarding one on her own, or a tram, to go back and forth between home and college, was unimaginable. Bethune proved to be convenient for such arrangements involving decorum and social rules: Priyo, who was studying Commerce in City College, could chaperone Chhaya a bit further north of College Street to Cornwallis Street and then retrace his route south to go to his own college.

Sometimes they took the tram, changing at Esplanade. At other times they took a bus, which reduced the journey time by half. What no one knew was how often Priyo and Chhaya played truant from their respective colleges to take in a matinee at a cinema together.

This was a fun time for Priyo and Chhaya. War had broken out in Europe, but at first the flames were so far away that no one felt much heat. A small item in the papers, about a warship making its way towards Bangkok from the Far East, seemed like someone else's story. Bhola said it was a Japanese ship, and Japan was on the side of the enemy – Britain's enemy, that is; it was customary to see enemies of Britain as enemies of India and the ruling power's allies as the colony's friends. Then the rumour began that because Calcutta was on the eastern flank of the country, it was in real danger of being bombed by the Japanese. Prafullanath came home one day with blackout shades for the lights at home.

'One and a half rupees I paid for each of these, one and a half rupees,' he grumbled. 'Now there's a ban on car headlights. Neon lights, signboards – all off. The whole place has turned into a ghost city.'

Every single light in the house was shrouded in black paper. The effect was eerie, much like an eclipse; only the area directly under the shaded bulb remained in a small circle of light. Black curtains on doors and windows, black paper gummed onto skylights – all added to a depressing subfusc air. The objective was not to let a single crack or hairline of light be detected from outside. The Air Raid Patrol checked on this with the vigilante's zeal.

'O moshai, I can see a line of light under your door,' came the holler from an ARP going about his rounds.

The Japanese will strike on a full-moon night, the rumour went. The first bombs fell just before Christmas. The city emptied like a bottle with a large leak. Adi and his father, who had to go near Sealdah on work, complained about the seething throng of people at the railway station trying to flee the city.

Prafullanath said, 'The station is thick with people. We bumped into Chatterjee-babu and his family. He was sitting on his holdall, surrounded by luggage and people streaming everywhere, holding two cauliflowers, one in each hand. So we asked him what on earth he was doing carrying cauliflowers around in an emergency. Do you know what he said? "Arrey, moshai, don't ask. On our way here I see this woman selling cauliflowers by the roadside. They were so fresh, so tight, I couldn't resist, so I bought a couple. We have to eat wherever we go, no?" We didn't know whether to laugh or to cry.'

Huddled in the big sitting room now, with the six other members of her family, all wrapped in shawls and sweaters against the cold January night, Charubala began her predictable harangue.

'I don't like this one bit. How can you live with your life in your hands all the time like this? What if we get bombed? The whole city is empty, everyone has escaped to the country. Why are we still here?' She whined at no one in particular, but it was obvious that her husband was the target of her complaint. 'This maddening sound of sirens and all-clear and the drone of planes overhead – I feel these are going to finish me off well before a bomb. Why have we not left the city?'

Somnath, meanwhile, was so beside himself with excitement that on blackout nights he invariably threw a tantrum about not being allowed to go up to the roof to watch Japanese aircraft dropping bombs onto the city; nothing could be more spectacular in his imagination: bombs! explosion! fire! Forced to stay in the sitting room with everyone else, he ran about singing the playground doggerel he had recently picked up: 'Bombs, bombs, bombs / The Japs have dropped bombs, / In the bombs there is a cobra, / The snake-charmer says "Abracadabra".' Charubala thought she would go mad.

In the middle of all this Priyo and Chhaya sat, usually sharing a large duvet, breathing noiselessly in rhythm, reduced to such a concentrated stillness that the charge around them somehow kept everyone at bay. Their minds emptied and in this eternal present tense everything fell away except the perceiving pores of their skins, intensely alive, intensely open. Even the sense of touch of their linked hands seemed unphysical, almost spectral, compared with this communion. They heard each other's blinks, the sound of blood pumping in and out of their hearts, they heard the strangely lit darkness shift and change shape; that was all. The controlled chaos of the stir-craziness in this imposed house arrest glanced off the surface of the sphere that sealed them from the rest of the room. Only when the 'All Clear' sounded and the shades were removed were they discovered sitting like inanimate objects on the sofa, their sides glued to each other.

At the next raid Charubala saw to it that it was she who shared the big duvet with her daughter.

By the end of the month it was evident that the air raids were decisively over. Somnath had switched allegiance by then and was zipping around chanting the name of Maurice Pring, the British pilot who brought down three Japanese bombers in as many minutes in the mid-January raid.

Priyo and Chhaya saw *Bahen* in Chitra in North Calcutta slightly over a year and a half after it was released. This was a turning point that they did not understand as such, but this film, about a possessive brother plotting to have his sister remain dependent on him for her entire life, entered the dark of their souls. The grief of the brother at her eventual marriage, his machinations to prevent her from going away – the themes seemed to leap out in an invisible lasso from the screen and bind them tightly together, sitting in two balcony seats high above, in an unknown complicity. It was like the first diffusion of a drug through their blood; in years to come they would seek out all films that centrally featured the adoring relationship between a brother and a sister. A little more than a year after this they were rewarded with *Meri Bahen*, in Chitra again.

Other films brightened their lives for the space of the two-and-a-half hours of their running; the afterglow, which lasted much longer, offered them a more bittersweet pleasure because they knew it too would diminish, but more slowly, over time. They went through a Kanan Devi phase: *Parichay* in Rupabani, *Shesh Uttar* in Uttara, *Jogajog* in Sree. Then a Chhabi Biswas period: *Garmil* and *Samadhan*, both in Chhabighar. They had to keep it very quiet, particularly Chhaya; Charubala would have had a fit if she discovered that her daughter was going to the cinema. She suspected the medium and was convinced that it corrupted, even going so far as to proclaim that 'Hindi films ruin your character'. Only films on devotional themes, or centred on characters from the epics or legend and mythology, passed muster, but not without some initial reluctance.

It was a strange time for the city. For months it felt like the deserted simulacrum of Calcutta; so many people had fled in fear of Japanese air raids that streets, buildings, shops, houses were all like something in a filmset before the crew and actors entered to populate it. Then, in no time, it seemed to them, military vehicles were everywhere. A traffic block one afternoon in Chowringhee made them late for *Shahar Theke Dure* in Chhabighar on Harrison Road. The roads were suddenly full of white soldiers. American troops, Priyo pointed out to Chhaya; not English soldiers, as she had thought. They saw Chinese troops, as well and men who were the black of ablush wood, who looked as if they had been carved out of coal, then had had life breathed into them.

'They're from Africa,' Priyo said.

'Look at their fleshy lips!' an amazed Chhaya said. 'Ufff, I feel scared just looking at them. Think what would happen if you ran into one of them in the dead of night! I'd immediately get heart-fail.'

Although the city remained mostly intact, they saw a couple of devastated buildings on the southern end of Harrison Road where the Japanese bombs had fallen at the beginning of the year – carcasses of houses standing amidst rubble, not unlike a construction site, but at the other end of its destiny.

'Just think if these bombs fell on us in South Calcutta,' Chhaya shivered.

Priyo soothed her, 'No more raids, I think. It's been over three months and there's been nothing.'

Bombed-out buildings and Africans were not the only frightening sights. Thick clusters of famine-struck people sat or lay on the roads, dying like insects. She could not tell from looking at them whether the prostrate people were dead or still through starvation-induced weakness. From the middle of August, the stench of rotting corpses, or a stiffness in the odd angles at which a woman or a child lay on the side of the streets, gave them a more certain clue. On Amherst Row one afternoon, as they were taking a shortcut to Maniktala Road, they saw a dead woman – mouth open, the body all vertices and angles like a collapsible contraption – whose eyes were being pecked out by a crow.

Chhaya lifted the aanchol of her sari to her mouth, but too late; she turned away and stooped forward to throw up. She had seen the gelid opaque-grey custard quivering out of the eye socket that the shiny black beak of the crow was worrying over and over with staccato pecks. She was never going to forget the image.

A boy, maybe six years old, maybe ten, it was difficult to tell, for extreme malnourishment had simultaneously added to and subtracted from the real number of years, leaned against a wall eight or ten feet away from the scavenged woman, a stone in his hand, perhaps in the process of aiming it at the bird, but the arc of the action had been frozen at its starting point; he had no energy to fling the stone. He sat there, a fossil within his own life, helpless in the face of the intrepid crow's desecration of his mother.

They backed away on to Upper Circular Road, shortcut abandoned.

There had been talk, of course; where would this world of theirs be without it? There was talk of the price of rice rising like the wind – from seven rupees eight annas per mon to twelve rupees eight annas in two months, then through twenty rupees to over thirty in another six. They vaguely remembered worried conversations between their mother and Madan-da about last year's killer cyclone in Medinipur right after Durga Puja; about the rice shortage and corresponding inflation in rice prices beginning from the winter of the year; about hoarding and government confiscation of rice stocks . . . All these excerpts from conversations seemed to float up like murky and slippery remnants of obscure dreams and then got submerged again. Chhaya remembered a maid-of-all-work who serviced four or five houses in their neighbourhood, telling her mother about starvation deaths in her village not that long ago; maybe a month, or less?

Even Baba had mentioned then, on hearing it reported to him by his wife, that he too had heard rumours of such deaths in the eastern districts of Chittagong and Noakhali. 'Yes, the people in the mills there . . . The manager had heard,' he said; he was vague. 'But we should be more worried about cholera doing the rounds. This heat has sparked it off, I tell you,' he observed, suddenly alert. 'Careful, we have to be very careful. People like us don't die of starvation, but no one is immune to cholera.'

Charubala, easily panicked, harped on disaster, always imminent for her. 'Do you know, Madan was saying that he had heard of people dying like flies in the countryside?'

'Hang Madan! I can't figure out how long I'll be able to evade all this government requisitioning, and you talk to me about deaths in the countryside. Tell me when the deaths come to the city.'

Prafullanath had not exactly laughed it off, as he had laughed derisively at Gandhi's twenty-one-day fast around Saraswati Puja that year – the Mahatma had sipped sweetened lemonade throughout the hunger strike – but he was not far off from his usual snorting contempt. This time it had been tempered by the sure knowledge of cholera.

But, really, death from hunger was such a remote possibility in their lives – no, impossible. It was not their situation, never would be; they were not in any danger; it was only a changeable backdrop to the drama of their lives. Later, they would collectively complain about how useless Sir Azizul Haque was, sitting in Viceroy Lord Linlithgow's Executive Council, in charge of food – more crucially, a *Bengali* in charge of food in a state ravaged by famine. And they would murmur about how stealthily the famine had come, like the sound of dewfall, like the sound of evening descending at the end of the day. And that would be all.

Maane Na Mana was one of the last films Chhaya saw with Priyo before his work at Charu Paper became too demanding for him to carry on playing truant. To cut lectures was one thing; to disappear from work in the middle of the day, right under the noses of his Baba and Dada, would be quite another. As if he had foreknowledge of the end of his film-going days with his sister, Priyo bought Chhaya a *maane na mana* sari, a fashion trend inspired by the film; it was a souvenir to mark the close of a giddy time, of a secret in more ways than one. Or perhaps that was the way it appeared to her in hindsight, after Priyo stopped accompanying her regularly to the cinema.

For a few years Chhaya went with her college friends, sometimes in groups of three or four, occasionally larger. To *Naukadubi*; *Neel Kamal*, the first Raj Kapoor–Madhubala film; *Raamer Sumati*; *Suhaag Raat*, with its captivating Geeta Dutt songs. With two Raj Kapoor–Nargis films in two consecutive years, *Aag* and *Barsaat*, Chhaya discovered something else: even without Priyo sitting by her in the balcony high above the mass of the common audience, that familiar smell of his skin – something she felt she had known since birth, the smell slightly similar to gunpowder or the combustible material they packed inside fireworks – arriving to her nose in legible wisps, even without that physical proximity Chhaya found that she could insert herself and Priyo into the silver screen, superimpose his and her faces onto the protagonists' and *become* them, *become* the two points of the romance; it was *their* story the film told. Her whole body thrilled so to this fantasy of substitution that at every musical love-sequence she felt a delicious wringing-out of her insides.

The holiday from life did not continue for too long. Prafullanath sounded the warning at home one evening in late 1946.

'The Muslims are getting ready to riot,' he announced. 'The Muslim League is busy stoking the fire. We'll all burn. Ghosts have possessed them, the Congress is powerless in front of their might. The ghosts are not going to leave them until their demands are met. The country will have to be divided, there's no avoiding that. Look where Jinnah's "direct action" is going to take us. To hell, to hell!'

When the idea of partition had bedded in, Prafullanath did not seem to be too unhappy about it. 'Everyone here seems to want this partition,' he said. 'Well, we'll be shot of the bloody Muslims for ever.

Good riddance, I say. They can leave for wherever they want, as long as they leave us Calcutta.'

Bhola, who was studying Commerce in Ripon College, provided daily bulletins on how the large Muslim population in Sealdah and Entally and Beliaghata was getting restive; you could smell the gathering storm in the air. There were frequent strikes in college. Bhola was not very interested in his degree and moreover found the dense, suffocating 'cattle-market' atmosphere of Ripon College enervating, and so was relieved at these increasingly regular halts. One hundred and fifty students in each class; seething crowds of students on the balconies, in class, on the staircases; the jostling and pushing to enter the classroom, then the jostling and pushing to exit again, this time five minutes before the bell rang to announce the end of class, otherwise the tide of incoming students for the next one would clash with the flow of the egress; the unbreaking tide of sound from traffic on Harrison Road and Baithakkhana Market, above which you could not hear a word that the professor was droning – Bhola sometimes felt like a riverbank being eroded by forces rubbing against him continuously; strikes were heaven-sent. By the time the college closed for the summer, streets and roads had begun to resonate to the slogan 'Ladke lenge Pakistan' – 'We'll go to war to get our own country'.

Processions of hatred and anger along Harrison Road, Mirzapur Street, Amherst Street became a daily occurrence; college was not going to reopen anytime soon. Then, as soon as the monsoons were over, the Hindu–Muslim riots and killings began. For days in August no one left home. Charubala sent up hourly prayers of thanks that they lived in a Hindu neighbourhood. Prafullanath, Adi and Priyo, who had recently joined Charu Paper full-time, sat at home, relaying news, gossip, rumour and statistics to each other and everyone else who cared to listen. Hordes of Muslim men, armed with sticks, shovels, spears, knives, axes, kerosene and matches, were slaughtering Hindus on sight, entering Hindu homes to kill, loot and burn. The city became a warren of no-go zones. People said, 'Rivers of blood are flowing in our streets.'

Prafullanath paced about and complained bitterly.

'Four of our mills in the countryside have had to be shut down, Ilam Bazar, Chalna, Meherpur, Nalhati, because of the riots. Apparently the Muslims are beheading Hindu men like you cut the heads off fish,' he said to his wife, 'and all you can think of is petty rubbish like not leaving home.'

Prafullanath himself was half-frozen with fear at the killings – he had expressly forbidden anyone to leave home – but he had other fears to contend with too. They made him tetchy. His wife's nagging gave him an excuse to vent his irritation.

'There's a war on, in case you'd forgotten. Everything is in short supply – food, kerosene, newsprint, paper – and the price of everything has touched the sky. The government is requisitioning whatever it can get its hands on. I thought if we could keep production going at slightly over our usual output we could sell it elsewhere and make a neat profit, but sand has fallen on that bit of molasses.'

He meant, of course, the plan that he and Adi had hatched of hoarding paper and selling it on the black market, an idea sparked off by the hoarding of rice three years ago during the famine.

'Business wasn't going too badly, then the famine came and now the riots . . . I blame everything on my burnt forehead,' he said.

'But, Baba, worse could be in store for us,' Adi pointed out. 'Think what will happen if the mills in the Muslim-majority areas go to Pakistan after the division. What are we going to do then?'

'Yes, say all this,' Prafullanath hissed with irritation, 'and make it easier for fate to bring it to pass! I weathered the recession in the Twenties, even made a profit in the last recession in '36. But this . . . this' – he was at a loss for words – 'this will bring us to our knees.'

'I don't understand all this ree-shey-shaan thi-shey-shaan,' Charubala hit back. 'I want to see all of you safe from harm and I'm going to keep on praying for that. Is it too much to ask?'

A frenetic accounting of acquaintances, friends and relatives in Muslim-dominated areas of the city began. Chhaya pointed out that her erstwhile music teacher, Shipra-di, lived in Moulali. Somnath, on the other hand, could only wish the rioting would continue so that he would not have to go to school – close enough to Muslim-heavy Park Circus to be out of bounds now – for the foreseeable future.

The foreman in the mill at distant Chalna, a Muslim man, was killed by rioting Hindus: his head was bashed to a pulp. His relatives had to identify him by a birthmark on his back. The Ghoshes sat at home and wrung their hands. They feared that all their factories were going to be set ablaze; the news from the countryside left them in little doubt that the nation had turned into an abattoir: Noakhali, Bihar, United Provinces, Delhi . . . an endless cycle of revenge, a snake swallowing its tail.

Shipra-di's son turned up at Basanta Bose Road, unclothed to the waist, unshod, unshaven; his father, missing for nine days at the height of the carnage in the city, had been discovered, both his arms hacked off, blocking a drain off Muchipara Road. The son had come to invite them to his father's sraddha.

'I know people who've lost everything – family, home, the roof above their heads – in these riots. They only have the clothes on their backs to call their own. But I keep thinking: buildings, property, savings, all these one can accumulate again . . . but you can't get back the people you've lost' – his voice came out stifled – 'especially in . . . in this way.' Then he whispered, 'I'll remember that corpse forever.'

Chhaya and her mother wept silently. The men in the house were horrified into silence. Prafullanath knew that the man was going to ask for money sooner or later.

Fretting about the mills kept him awake at night. When he thought how much money he was losing, his heart started hammering. How was it all going to end? He fingered the rings on his hands – sapphire to avoid the wrath of Saturn, coral to appease Mars, topaz for Jupiter – and wondered, not for the first time, about the astrologer's warning that a tricky phase involving Saturn was about to begin, but prescribing the wearing of sapphire was a decision that he could not take lightly. So what did these bad times tell him: that the phase of the destructive reign of Saturn over his life had begun, or that wearing the sapphire to mitigate the planet's malign influence had been ill advised in the first place? His heart thumped away faster and faster.

When the Ghoshes started venturing out again, elaborate plans had to be made to share one car; the other two had to be kept in the garage because of the petrol shortage. Avoiding Muslim-dominated areas necessitated convoluted detours. So in order to drop off Prafullanath, Adi and Priyo on Old China Bazaar Street, Niranjan-da, the driver, had to avoid the area north of St Andrew's Church; most of the route was straightforward and safe, but after Old Court House Street it got tricky;

the Muslim spread south of Harrison Road began. Chhaya was not allowed out of the house for months. Bhola, who had to negotiate the most perilous route from Bhabanipur to north of Pataldanga, talked to a couple of his Muslim peers at City College who, appalled at what was happening, had decided to speak up for unity; these Muslim students banded together and began to accompany their Hindu friends and colleagues along the dangerous stretch from Old Ballygunge to Wellesley Street on journeys both to and from the college. Bhola did not breathe a word of this arrangement to anyone at home.

With news of the ways in which the subcontinent was going to be carved up between Hindus and Muslims coming in on a regular basis, of the squabbling and negotiations and fiats between their British overlords, the Congress and the Muslim League, Prafullanath's worries now came to rest wholly on how the manufacturing plants he owned would be distributed along the dividing line. Would Calcutta at least remain a part of India? Anything else seemed inconceivable to him. And not only to him – in an echo of the slogan that had ignited the riots last year, there were now processions shouting 'Ladke lenge Calcutta.'

The Boundary Commission's decision just before Independence came as a shock: the Ghoshes were to lose the mills at Chalna and Meherpur to the new country, East Pakistan.

Charubala said, 'Arrey, Baba, at least Calcutta will remain ours. We won't have to move with our belongings or become refugees. So what if a couple of mills have gone? Buy another two here.'

Prafullanath said, 'It's a bit too late in the day to explain business to you. We've been running well below optimal output for over two years. Then for one year the mills have been closed because of all this rioting. Now two of them have gone to another country overnight. If I had known this was going to happen, I would have sold them years ago, like all these East Bengali families who have been selling all their possessions and land and houses for decades and decades now.'

Charubala fell back on her old reasoning. 'I don't understand all this output-foutput. That we are all alive and safe in these times is enough for me.'

'There'll be riots again, you mark my words. Otherwise why would Gandhi come to the city again? Precious little he could do last year, wearing his loincloth and walking barefoot – all this unbearable rubbish! – and talking to villagers. The riots and killings went on erupting here and there: Calcutta today, Noakhali tomorrow, Bihar the following. Ashes and cinders he could achieve! I hear he's going to set up camp in Rash Bagan with the Muslims. This sucking-up to the Muslims will be the end of the Congress. At every stage, sitting up, standing down, they are appeased. Could the Congress do anything to Jinnah, who is about to take away half the country for the bloody Muslims?'

Charubala muttered, 'Ufff, all this politics . . . it's eaten your head.'

Listening to Nehru's speech on the radiogram at midnight of the 14th August, with the set turned up loud, all of them stoked up, for once, in the patriotic blaze sweeping the country, Charubala came up against the limits of her understanding again.

At the stroke of the midnight hour, when the world sleeps, India will awake . . .

Charubala, who had sat through the *Vande Mataram* and the speeches of Chaudhry Khaliquzzaman and Dr Radhakrishnan grumblingly – 'Ufff, why they decide to do all this so late at night, don't these people need to sleep?' etc. – could no longer check herself.

. . . A moment comes, which comes but rarely in history, when we step out from the old to the new . . .

'Oh, I can't bear this prattling in English any longer! Why isn't anyone speaking in Bengali?'

'Will you be quiet for just a second?' Prafullanath cried.

At this point Somnath piped up, 'But the whole world is not asleep! He's wrong. Everyone in Japan is awake because it is morning there, and everyone in Britain and America too, because it's evening and afternoon there. We were taught this in our Geography class, time zones and time differences.'

He looked like a puppy who expected to be patted on the head for mastering a new trick.

The achievement we celebrate today is but a step, an opening of opportunity, to the greater triumphs and achievements . . .

There was news of the outside world occasionally. (Look, look, how odd that I used the words 'outside world'. When I used to live at home, I considered the villages, deep in the heart of rural Bengal, the 'outside world', or even, the 'real world'. But away from home, the city and everything elsewhere, even other villages or another part of rural Bengal, became the 'outside world'. Does that mean that the world is wherever one is? Is that not the most accurate and strictest of all definitions of self-centredness? Does that mean that there is no escape from the self? After chanting to ourselves millions of times, Change yourself, change the world, is this the outcome – failure?)

Yes, people from Calcutta showed up sometimes, bringing copies of Deshabrati, Liberation; we pounced upon them. It was only on reading those papers that we realised that our people had fanned out into the rural heartlands of at least three states: West Bengal, Bihar, Orissa. I had no idea that the spread was so extensive, that we had so many in our team. My spirits lifted.

The news items obviously did not report setbacks, such as our people not being allowed to work in a village and being chased out, or comrades going to hamlets and not being able to last the race because of the hardships that such a life entailed.

I can hear you asking if it was truly so hard. Yes, it was. Rats bit us – some of them could be as big as kittens – while we were asleep; the rice fields were full of them. In desperate times, I was told, the Santhals caught and ate them. Snakes came into the huts during the monsoon. Upset stomachs and a mild dysentery were our doggedly faithful companions – we knew they would go away, but also that they would be back before we could fully appreciate their absence. Then there was the business of eating once a day, if you were lucky (rice, a watery dal, a little bit of fried greens of some kind); of days of eating puffed rice only, or water-rice with chillies and salt; or not eating, days of fast followed by a half-meal, that instantly set you running into the bushes. There was the lack of bathrooms or any kind of sanitation. Above all, there was the slow pace of life, with nothing happening and nothing to do for enormous chunks of time, nowhere to go, nothing to read, no one to speak to.

I try not to write about these because I can hear you taunting – Aha re, my cream-doll! Besides, I feel ashamed to admit to feeling the bite of those hardships; really, a middle-class cream-doll, that's what I am. It hurts to acknowledge this.

I worried about how swiftly this catalogue of difficulties and woes could descend into an easy horrorism; I have always wanted to avoid that. What use did it serve to emphasise the unbridgeable gap between the lives of these people and people of our kind? It only consoled and comforted the middle classes that their lot was better. They will tell you that they want to know the details of the daily hardships of rural life in order to be <u>aware</u>, in order to be moral, but the appetite really was for propping up their idea of themselves as people with sympathetic souls and sensitive social consciences. It was not awareness they were after, it was the reinforcement of the separation between 'us' and 'them'.

Did you see how easily I fell into ranting again? I must stop.

But one aspect of the hardship of life in the villages I must truthfully confess to you – the thing I found most difficult to bear, much more than going hungry or the absence of toilets, was the solid weight of time. That had the potential to crack me. The books we had brought with us had been read over and over again. We could recite <u>The Little Red Book</u> backwards. We talked until our tongues felt loosened from inside our mouths. We instilled Mao's words into the farmers and wage-labourers like teaching a parrot. Yet we didn't manage to budge that solid sphere of time even a little; it was always there. There were long evenings and nights when there was nothing to do except listen to the din of crickets. Sometimes I thought people in these parts went to sleep early not because of their days of bone-breaking work, but because there was nothing to do. Sleeping was an activity. If you could manage it, it made you forget the stasis of time, its sheer, pressing weight on a life. Much like work did.

The measure of time too was different. I asked Kanu how far it was to Titapani. He said – Far, quite far; then – Very far. I persisted in nudging him to be more accurate, expecting an answer in terms of hours and minutes. He finally came up with – About six bidis can be smoked easily on that walk.

Later, I began to notice this subjective, if picturesque way of measuring cropping up everywhere: short distances by the number of paces, length by the number of hands, even growth of paddy by the number of fingers. You had to get a feel for it otherwise a lot of basic communication was doomed.

And when you let yourself down into this different stream of time, you had no choice but to align yourself to its flow. In the lull between weeding, removing snails from the fields and the ripening of the paddy, I followed Kanu and the other Santhals and Mahatos as they went about other jobs that brought them a little bit of money or food – erecting woven-cane barriers, catching fish in the ponds (but not in the private ponds of the jotedaars, or the ones in the upper-caste sections towards the interior of the village; they were not allowed to do this; if caught, they'd be beaten mercilessly), growing vegetables next to their huts, repairing straw roofs.

Dhiren said that a group of a dozen or fourteen had set out with their ploughs to look for potato cultivations in places as far-flung as Nadia and Murshidabad and Bankura because they couldn't find enough work locally to feed themselves and their families.

At least they were not migrating to cities. I had seen for myself how the migrant workers were slowly extinguished, crushed to death by the jaws of the city; working, yes, but in such jobs that we would have to find a word other than 'life' for what they had. Very few of them got lucky and found a better life.

Madan-da would be one such fortunate one. Ma and Thakuma were not exactly forthcoming or clear with details about Madan-da's life before he came to us, and I had never asked Madan-da myself, but from what I could piece together, he was from a tiny village in a particularly impoverished district in Orissa. The same story: drought, famine, death, failure of crops year after year, no hope, nothing. The lucky ones were those who escaped this, found a better kind of job in a city, sent money home, moved their families into a brick house. In that scheme of things, Madan-da had been the luckiest; or, if you prefer, he sat right on top of the ladder of people who sought a livelihood in cities.

But nine out of ten of those leaving their villages in the hope of making a better life for themselves faced exactly the opposite fate. After having lived in Majgeria for a while, I was no longer sure if migrating to urban areas was such a terrible thing.

The tufty fronds of the grain-heads had begun to show. We were being steam-cooked in the humid heat of late September.

The weaver-birds were beginning their plunder again. Harvest soon. This time I hoped to be less of an embarrassment to myself and to others.

It's been a year since I left home. You are a constant presence in me, so I won't ask after you — it feels like I'm talking to you inside my head all the time — but I also think of Ma, Sona and Kalyani. I dreamed of Ma the other night. In the dream I was famished, craving food, and she was serving me dinner, but when I looked down at the plate and the bowls I found only ashes, heaps of black, burnt scraps. I looked at her with confusion and I saw her laughing, as if in contempt. I was seized by a great anger then, my heart was hammering away, and I began to shout at her, and the more I shouted, the more defiantly amused and uncaring she became. She was laughing at me. I wanted to be violent, to do some harm to her . . . and then the mad thumping in my chest woke me up. I could hear the beats in the first sweaty moments of wakefulness. Above that thudding rose the billows of my anger still. And then shame, deep shame and confusion at the content of such a stealthy revelation: did I really harbour such resentment towards someone who loved me so vastly and unconditionally?

And what news of Sona? Yes, he does look like Chhoto-kaka, but that's where the similarity ends. How detached he is from everything! Occasionally I used to think that there was something not quite right with him, but most of the time I was envious. That resilience to the outside world, that capacity of not being damaged, even lightly scratched, by it — what wouldn't I give to be blessed with that? Although you've often complained that I am like that, indifferent to the world, hard, stony. Did you mean that seriously? You know that I'm not. Not to you.

We were in the middle of harvest when Dhiren informed us that Bipul's brother, Shankar Soren, whom we had assumed was slightly better off than Bipul because he had a tiny plot, had had to give up his entire harvest to Senapati Nayek, a small landlord who owns about twenty-five to thirty bighas.

This was the story. There was a drought in '65, then a mini-famine in '66, and Shankar's plot lay empty for those two years. Then his wife fell ill and he had to borrow money from Senapati — it was an informal side-business that most landlords had, to earn a little extra something, or to manoeuvre themselves into ever more powerful, ever more advantageous positions — for buying food and for his wife's treatment. Senapati, instead of asking Shankar to mortgage his little piece of land, which was the usual practice, gave him 400 rupees; Shankar would have to pay him back nearly 600 rupees by the end of the year. It was impossible for Shankar to do this because his plot had produced nothing for two years running. If he could grow something there and sell it (instead of consuming it, as he normally did), he thought, perhaps he could pay some of the loan back, so he borrowed more money from Senapati to buy a bag of seeds to sow in his plot. The repayment of this loan was to be the amount of paddy cultivated that would theoretically pay off the loan <u>and</u> the interest, but Senapati had done something wilier than that straightforwardly exploitative arithmetic. He bought up Shankar's harvest at half the market rate, thus alienating the poor man of his entire produce while giving him the illusion that he was repaying the whole sum he had borrowed.

Senapati then reminded him that there was still the interest on the loan of seed-grains to be serviced; his harvest had only paid off <u>part</u> of the loan, not to mention the principal, plus the accruing interest on the previous loan for food and medical bills for his wife's illness . . .

This year Shankar woke up to the fact that while the interest on the loans, both money and seed, would go on increasing, his crop yield and his labour were both finite and would never be enough to clear his debts. He would be nibbling away at it for his whole life, then one day he would die, the size of the debt <u>greater</u> after a lifetime of trying to bring it down to zero and free himself.

The realisation led him to vent his anger and frustration on the nearest person – his wife. He beat her regularly, blaming her and her illness for landing him in this situation, with this mountain of debt on his shoulders, until things got out of hand and Shankar's wife threw herself into the well in the Muslim neighbourhood and killed herself.

The story was common and universal. The Bengali novel had played its part in making it a matter of common and universal knowledge to the literate middle classes. So no surprises there. But the twist appeared at this point.

Dhiren said – A dry-as-stick figure, this Shankar, you know. He looks like a shrivelled broom. You realise he doesn't get enough to eat the moment you set eyes on him. Do you know what I did when I heard the story, when I saw that all the grain he was standing in, literally, was not going to feed him, or get him money, and the wages from his work too were not going to come to him, but be deducted by Senapati, do you know what I did?

Even through our exhaustion the tale had filtered through, I didn't quite know why: there was something in the way the story had been told, in the sixth sense we had that Dhiren was withholding something that he would spring on us towards the end . . . We were sitting up, quiet as children being told a ghost-story, almost unable to breathe, with Dhiren asking repeatedly – Do you know what I did?

He answered himself – I moved close to Shankar; there were so many people around, I moved close to him, brought my mouth near his ear and whispered: What if we finish off this Senapati man?

We were still holding our breath.

– It took a long time to get the real meaning of this through to Shankar. He began by saying: If I could, I'd tear out his windpipe . . . But he said this as part of the twist-and-turn of conversation, responding in kind to what he thought was just a way of speaking . . .

I couldn't bear it any longer. I leaped up and asked – What next? What next?

– I said to him: We can tear out his windpipe, truly truly, it can be arranged. Shankar then started to put two and two together and asked: You are the men from the city who our people have been talking to? Saying that we can have our land back? Not be slaves any more? Eat two full-stomach meals every day? So I said yes, and I told him that we were going to plan this seriously, he needn't fear, no one would know . . .

CHAPTER TEN

1969

Suranjan slumps slowly sideways like a timber pillar showing the first gentle sign of collapse. His chin almost touches his chest. The crumpled rectangle of the silver foil, blackened now, from the Wills Filter packet, the short straw made out of rolled-up card, the match burned to a long black curl with a tiny pale end, a minute ago all bound to him in such a fierce concentration of unison, now fall from his loosened hold; the cohering force keeping human and object together has been suddenly dissipated. His eyes too have shut. The brown sugar will keep him in this trance for a good couple of hours, but this calibration of time means nothing to him in this state; it could be two minutes or two years. In the beginning he would have marvelled at identifying the perfect fit between the act and the term, 'chasing'; at how the tiny heap of brown powder placed on the flattened-out piece of foil and heated from below with a match became a smoking trickle of liquid running down the length of the silver or gold paper and how you had to 'chase' the smoke down the course of that miniature rivulet on its silver lawn; he would have wondered with awe at the inherent poetry of heroin, at the deep wisdom of those who were the drug's acolytes and servers.

But those days of child-like wonder are behind him now. The poetry has been parsed, the mythologising has become a bit passé; they had been shiny sweeties to lure the child in. Now he has come of age. The first few times he had taken smack, all in the company of Bappa-da and his friends, he had been sick; not the racked-with-convulsions kind of vomiting, but a really easy sort, as easy and natural as breathing or seeing or hearing; just lean over sideways and throw up, then let the opiates suck you into their vortex. He had also felt his face itch agonisingly.

'It's the impurities in the smack,' Bappa-da had said. 'Don't worry, it'll go soon. Soon you won't feel anything but perfect, unending bliss.'

He had been right, certainly about the 'perfect', though not the 'unending'. The bliss is becoming increasingly mortal, its life-expectancy inside him decreasing with a frightening exponentiality. Time is such an assassin. How fugitive all the pleasures of the world are; so much to hold on to, so much transience, he had begun to think a while ago, but had never managed to get to the end of that philosophising. That was the other thing about smack – it did not allow you to finish things. Everything kept hanging, his days and hours and thoughts all an agglomeration of loose ends like an amateurish piece of knitting unravelling.

In the beginning brown sugar offered him the cushioniest, velvetiest ocean of support; instant relief from the multiplying anxieties of his life in the form of oblivion. And there were so many. He had felt lost in a labyrinth of those jagged edges of reality – a missing brother; a father sinking into alcoholic inertia every day; a mother who had checked out of life; escalating squabbling between his aunt and his grandmother. Then there was the diminishment of the family's source of prosperity (now firmly erstwhile): the destruction of Charu Paper in slow degrees, for which his grandfather and his father and uncles blamed each other. He had known only this falling-off, an inexorable downward slide, each year of his advancing life measured by shrinkage, by more bitterness amongst the family members, more economising, more tension.

Bappa-da had once explained Marx to him. 'All superstructures, including the family, rest on the base of one thing, and one thing only – economics. The family is the first and the primary unit of oppression and exploitation. Freud too agrees with this, although his take on it is different. From what you've told me about what's going on in your home, we have living proof of Marx's theories. You take away economic security and the whole pack of cards collapses. Everyone is at each other's throats. All these vaunted bourgeois values that prop up society – love, duty, honour, respect – all rest on power-relations lubricated by economics. They are the gloss people put on the naked truth: self-interest. Hypocrites, the lot of them, fucking hypocrites! Here, have a toke, you'll feel better.'

And he did. But, of late, that ocean of comfort had shrunk from a sea to a river to a shallow brook; a stream of piss seemed not so unlikely in the near future. The only way back to keeping afloat in that ocean he had experienced in the beginning was through more and more frequent hits. So here he is, slumped on the bathroom floor, his back against the wall opposite the tap. His temporary, small ocean. Not brown sugar, not only that, but disappointing sugar, betraying sugar.

He has no idea how long the sound has been going, but it hauls him up to the shore ultimately, a dull banging first, then, quickly, not so dull; someone is hammering on the bathroom door. Is he imagining it? His eyes close again and there is such a forceful tug away from where he has been beached back to the shallows. But the banging will not go away.

Now he hears a vocal accompaniment too. It is his father, he identifies eventually, shouting outside the bathroom, 'Open the door! Open up immediately!'

There are several stages beyond exhaustion, beyond complete, meltdown fatigue, for which there are no words. Or at least not any known to Adinath. Contrary to the images and vocabulary of dullness and extinguishing, he feels it as a malignant incandescence. The click inside that whisky brings him, the click that presages the eventual falling into a feather bed, has become elusive; it is deferred further and further to a shifting point that Adinath fears he will not reach any longer. The journey to that click has become fearsome because of the uncertainty in ever reaching that destination.

He can even pinpoint the turning point in that journey: ever since Superintendent Dhar from Bhabanipur police station had informed him that they had evidence Supratik was a Naxalite, and that he was somewhere in Medinipur, engaged in terrorism – that was the word the Superintendent had used, 'terrorism', that and 'extremist' – and things were going to move outside the Superintendent's control soon.

'I shall no longer be able to . . . how should I put it . . . keep an eye on him, Ghosh-babu,' SP Dhar had said, exuding a novel mixture of power, arrogance and ingratiation. 'You can see how tottering the United Front government is. The last one survived less than a year.

God knows who's going to come after Ajay-babu. He's back again after President's Rule, but for how long, do you think? The communists are the ones pulling all the strings now. And in power . . . What I'm saying is this: it's going to be difficult to . . . to . . . er . . . shield your son. Playing with fireworks on College Street, shouting slogans, that's one thing, but going on a killing spree, taking out policemen and landlords in the villages . . . well, that's a big boy's game, wouldn't you agree? A completely different thing.

'And we, the police, seem to be the targets in the city too. Not a day passes when there isn't a bomb thrown at us by these good middle-class, fish-and-rice-fed boys who have turned terrorist,' he had said with a different tone to his voice, as if through clenched teeth. 'We won't tolerate this state of affairs for too long. Something's got to give, and give soon.'

Over the years, the Ghoshes had tried to cultivate and maintain a good relationship with the police; gifts, not all nominal or token, sweeteners, things to keep them happy and on their side. It was Prafullanath's old advice: 'It is important to be on good terms with them, because you don't know when they're going to come in handy. They say, "Eighteen sores when touched by a tiger, but fifty-eight if by the police." Don't forget that.' They started with their local police station and made their way up to Lalbazar and the CID. At no time had that piece of wisdom seemed more pertinent than in the last few years. What would they have done without friendly policemen in the first gherao at their factory? One manager, Ashoke Ganguly at Bali, had had to leave. It was only the arrival of the police that had broken the gherao and saved Ashoke-babu's life.

Now SP Dhar, a significant portion of his oily jowls and distended belly caused by the Ghoshes' contribution to them, had told Adinath – and there was no reason to doubt his words – that his eldest son, the scion of the family, was a Naxalite. Or had he been asking for his palm to be crossed with more silver? The policeman had tiny eyes, the eyes of a hippopotamus, eyes that looked minuscule in the animal's leaking-out-of-its-frame build. They were eyes that even his own shadow could not trust.

The tricky business had been to keep the news from the women and children in the house. Priyo could be trusted to keep it to himself, but Bhola was the loose cannon. No information was safe with him. What Adi could count on was the power of denial: the word 'Naxalite' was like leprosy; it turned you into an untouchable instantly; no one would want to come anywhere near it.

The whisky has begun to give him sour eructations. It burns slightly as it goes down and sits, tingling, somewhere behind his sternum. A Naxalite son. There is no recovery from that. The shame . . . they will have to move from Bhabanipur to a place where no one knows them, where rumours and whispers cannot reach their new neighbours. It feels like he is standing at the edge of an ocean and must swim across, beyond the horizon, to the other side that cannot be seen.

How can he bring himself to tell his parents of SP Dhar's visit? The last time Adi had to confront his father with something unpalatable, it had all blown up in Adi's face.

Adi will never forget the evening, just under a year ago, when everyone had heard his frail father berating him viciously after the closure of Basanta, the spin-off publishing house that Bhola, useless as the finance director of Charu Paper, the parent company, had been entrusted to look after.

'It took me twenty-five years to build, twenty-five years of every drop of my blood and sweat to set this up, and from the moment you joined the company you let things slide. I should've known better. I should've trusted my instinct that you were useless, totally worthless. Not an ounce of business nous, not a whit of interest. This was all written on my forehead.'

His mother had interrupted him, 'Don't shout like that, please don't, your heart, your heart! Go inside now.'

'What can I do if Bhola ruined the whole publishing venture by backing those unsellable poets and novelists, which was tantamount to standing on a street corner and giving money away?' Adi bleated. The feeling of emasculation was intolerable: at the age of forty-seven he was being upbraided by his father for that quintessentially childhood thing – the faults of his younger siblings.

'Giving money away,' his father mimicked. 'How old are you? Four? And how old is Bhola? Are you toddlers squabbling over who is taking whose sweeties away? *Standing on a street corner and giving money away . . .* you stupid, ineffective eunuch!'

No one had heard his father like this, not in public.

'Why are you shouting at me for Bhola's failure?' Adi had fought back. 'He held soirées and adda sessions instead of working and gave money away to people he called "promising young talent", basically, to anyone who came asking. Do you know how much he has frittered away like this? Do you know?'

A devil had possessed Adi; the streamer of retaliatory rage coming out of his mouth seemed unstoppable. 'And what gives you the right to talk about eunuchs? You are responsible for driving Charu Paper into the ground. You, you,' he had accused, stabbing the air, with his finger pointed at his father, with each 'you'.

Charubala's attempt to calm matters came out as highly pitched. 'How dare you?' she said to Adi. 'Don't shout at him, can't you see he's ill? Can't you see he's shaking? Something terrible will happen now.'

The hysteria had only encouraged Adi: 'How long will he hide behind his illness? The illness was two, three years ago. We're cleaning up *his*' – the pronoun spat out, like venom – 'mess now, the mess *he* created with *his* project of modernising the factory at Memari. That was the beginning of our end. And he has the cheek to blame me and Bhola for it. How dare he?'

The new machines for the aged and nearly obsolete units arrived at Kidderpore Docks seventeen months after their order, in 1958: a turbo separator; a huge new drying section to replace the dying dinosaur that was holding everything back at Memari; a new press section that would supposedly create a seamless join between the mould and the Fourdrinier parts; and, finally, the drives arrangements to bind old and new together. They had reached the end with their standard practice of replicating parts for the cylinder-mould machine, and anything else that required replacement, in what they grandly called their 'Research & Development Wing', a large, corrugated iron-and-asbestos barn. For ten years, the head of R&D, Prajwal Sarkar, some kind of a wizard of make-do, had visited mills more modern than his own workplace to spy and copy their machines, or had prevailed on the Ghoshes to pay for information from people who worked in these factories. It didn't take anyone of exceptional business nous to see that this method, while ingenious in the short term, could not be relied upon indefinitely. Prafullanath wanted to upgrade the technology of the smaller mill first and, depending on how things went, eventually turn his attention to the far bigger project of modernising Bali.

Quite apart from the enormous investment needed for this, there was the great labyrinth of regulation to negotiate first. The new foreign-trade laws of the country meant that a licence had to be obtained to import the machines and they could only be imported as prototypes to be used to construct, by imitation, similar models with home technology and home resources. 'Licence' was, of course, a euphemism for bribing a chain of employees in the bureaucracy juggernaut set up for issuing these permits. The cost of greasing the requisite number of palms was a not inconsiderable percentage of the expenditure in buying and importing the machines, and businessmen were beginning to get into the practice of factoring this into their informal accounting, for whatever licence it was they wanted, be it the import of foreign technology or sanction to run a transport or liquor or retail business.

But this bribe was a fluid, moving, protean creature: the number of people with their palms open to receive first and facilitate afterwards always increased, so that the figure factored in, even if it was thought to be overestimated, was found to be, in reality, always short. The Ghoshes had begun the conversation about technology in 1950 and then spent six years obtaining a permit to import, despite spending a fortune in bribes at every step during this period.

It had taken over a year to settle on two German machines from Nettlinger-Kilb in Hamburg, and two from W.H. Cottrall in England. The managers of the state-owned banks that the family used had long been friendly with the Ghoshes, but even they baulked at the sums involved in the purchase and shipping. Adi and Priyo had signed off on the relevant papers, but they were soon to find out exactly how the complex and huge loans had been secured. In this, their inattention to detail had allowed Prafullanath to circumvent any theoretical opposition from his sons.

The new machines had the power and design to stay ahead of the competition in the Indian market for the foreseeable future. Or so Prafullanath had said; otherwise, Adi would not have known a thing about it.

Those endless evenings at home over dinner, with their father droning on: 'You know, this new turbo separator, the drill screen is between 1.8 and 2.8 milimetres. Ours belong to ancient times, we really need to get a new one to deal with all the new impurities. How long are we going to carry on with that relic? What do you say?'

Adi's eyes had closed with boredom as he clamped down his jaws on a yawn. He had said something cursory, like 'Yes, you're right', or some such.

The notification for the arrival of the imported machines at the docks came through. After more bribing, the machines were released; it took a year between their arrival at Kidderpore Docks and their transportation to Memari. From this point, Adi firmly believed, a particular alignment of planets and heavenly bodies occurred to cast maximal malign influence on the Ghoshes. It began with Prajwal-da informing them that a sectional drive had the wrong gearbox and helical parallel shaft, so the revolution systems of two of the units, instead of being synchronised, were slightly off. Work stalled at Memari for a year while this was fixed. The plant couldn't carry on using its older machines and continue production, since they had been dismantled to allow the fitting of the new.

The foreign machines had been ordered in 1956, just before the family tragedy, a piece of timing that was to prove crucial in the undoing that followed. Prafullanath's rapid deterioration in health following the tragedy meant that he was laid up in bed, having survived what the doctor's called a 'massive cardiac arrest', and everyone was under strict orders to protect him from trouble, anxiety and stress. The whole mess was left to Adi and Priyo to sort out, a thing they did not succeed in doing with any degree of competence or even a thin, superficial professionalism.

Prafullanath, his sons discovered, had not done a rigorous, watertight and airtight costing for the upgrade to new technology, and the cost-benefit analysis, or what there was of it, was so far out, in both columns, that their heads reeled. Who would have thought that this had emerged from the head of someone who had been a successful businessman for thirty years? It did not, for example, take into account the substantial amount of money that had to be paid by way of bribes to acquire a permit. More critically, there was no accounting for the interest on the loans during the period of stasis, from the time of ordering to the beginning of enhanced production at Memari, a period of five years; the enhanced production still remained a mirage, having gone up by only 20 TPD. Why had Baba not thought of something as elementary as a risk calculation, assuming a fixed period of servicing the debt while the plant lay idle? How had he arrived at those hugely inflated production figures? Adi and Priyo would keep returning to those questions.

Two things with the power to scrunch Prafullanath's plans into a shapeless paper bag had not occurred to his myopic mind. First, there was a thriving market in second-hand parts and units for existing technology – they did the job – so importing the latest machines at such cost seemed criminally profligate. Second, the well-established paper manufacturers in the country – the competition, that is – had played the game with older machines for so long that there appeared to be no clear advantage to what Prafullanath was setting out to do. The projected benefits column alone was a staggering piece of wishful thinking, on a par with fairytales and children's stories. In it, Prafullanath had fantasised that a loan of the size they had taken out could be repaid in seven years.

Seven! Adi had gaped at the number; it wouldn't be possible to dent appreciably the compound interest alone in that time. The returns should have been realistically projected so far into the future that they wouldn't begin to break even in Baba's lifetime, perhaps not even in his and Priyo's. Besides, Charu Paper was too small, almost a cottage industry, to have the capacity or the capability to manufacture replacement sections for those machines. Who was going to do it? Prajwal Sarkar was a man of the past; manufacturing parts belonging to machines he had dealt with for three decades was an activity that belonged to the backward past. How could he bring that same inventiveness to the latest technology from Germany and England, to the objects of the future, in what he affectionately called his 'machine kitchen'?

Adi and Priyo on their own would have been unable to parse the situation in its full complexity, but in a year when their only income was from the Bali factory, they were compelled to sit down at separate meetings with Samik Mitra, the head of the eastern region of the State Bank of India, and Barun Chatterjee, his counterpart at United Bank. It was only when the directors of the bank gradually elucidated the details of the structure and the fine print on the loans that the sky fell on the brothers' heads: Prafullanath had offered up Bali as collateral, concentrating risk on one factory. It became ever more imperative that Bali shouldn't fall behind, otherwise the Ghoshes would be unable to honour their debts. Four years into living with this dangling terror, the sword fell on their heads: Bali closed down.

This is how it all ends, Adi thinks; a slow erosion, beginning with lethargy, then . . . then what? Nothing except the hoeing of the same row by a yoked man over and over again, until the attrition of days eats into you and you are just a bit of chaff, obedient to the wind. He doubts even the wind will be able to lift him off. A scrap of elementary physics flits in and out of his head – what if the force of gravity brought about by his inertia is so great that the force of the wind is unable to lift him? One weighty husk, that. The bladder presses. His mouth is sweet-sour-furry with the whisky. From Johnnie Walker Black Label to Diplomat; what a fall. With unionisation going the way it was, and the communists flexing their muscles and grabbing key portfolios in the state government, things had become so bad that they had had to close down the Bali factory indefinitely. It had produced, at its peak functioning capacity, before all the troubles hit, 125 TPD and had formed three-fifths of the Ghoshes' business. If it didn't start functioning soon, the last one standing, at Memari, would have to be sold to pay off the debts. Then fragments from the other bit of arithmetic, still elementary, that has built a permanent residence in his head (he can almost feel it, as a tumour): a mill with a production capacity of 100 tonnes of paper a day costs eighteen crore rupees, give or take, to set up; desirable annual production capacity of a mill if it is not to go under = 30,000 tonnes; at the current rate of government tax on paper, which is 35 per cent, plus the freeze on the retention price of paper since 1962, while the government allowed the increase of prices of vital items such as iron, coal, cement, etc., this means that for every 300 working days a year (with closures, strikes, holidays, walk-outs, union activity all factored in, in the conservative remainder of sixty-five days), the factory would have to produce . . . Other variables present themselves now – the retail price of paper produced by the said factory, the interest on the bank loan for setting up the same factory – and increase the pressure, oddly enough, not in his head but inside his bladder.

At this point Adinath topples over into superstitious territory: if he can solve the equations mentally, it will signify that he will be saved, that the Ghoshes will not be ruined; if he cannot do it before he has to go to the toilet, well . . . defeat. That is the sign he signifies for himself. The bet taken, something else instantly breaches his attentive-ness to the self-imposed arithmetic problem. A wave ripples through his insides. It is caused by a sudden image of Supratik flashing through his synapses: a little boy, concern and curiosity battling to take control of his face, looking up at him, asking, 'But what if the orange pip I've just swallowed grows into a tree inside me? Will I die?' At that remembered word – he will not repeat it to himself – something breaks; his mouth contorts and he feels a heat in his eyes. Only by concentrating on his urgent need to piss does he return himself to some semblance of control. And yet, the exhaustion will not let him get up to go to the toilet.

By the time he gets there he has already let out a small dribble. He contracts all his pelvic-floor muscles; the effort could be defeated in a breath. He pushes the bathroom door; it is locked.

Swapan Adhikari recalls, with great deliberation, every detail of the events over the last month, to savour them almost, before he sits down to write the letter to his friend Ayan Basu.

●

It was an ordinary day in school: the usual boredom, the usual predictability. He was introducing cosine curves to Class Seven. Half the class was numb with boredom, some switched-off, some insulated by stupidity from what he was trying to teach. The borderline delinquents, sitting right at the back of the class, had begun to show signs of their usual restlessness. Two of them, sitting on the same bench, were nearly choking with the effort of suppressing their giggles. He was certain they were cracking up over dirty pictures that one of them was drawing. Not for the first time an intense sense of waste gripped him briefly and then let him go, but not before it had managed to make him feel reduced.

He had been one of the prize pupils in Ashish Roy's stable at Presidency, all set to go to ISI, at the very least, for a PhD in number theory, maybe even Cambridge or MIT or Stanford . . . but his father's untimely death had meant that he, as the eldest son, had to shelve all those lofty ambitions instantly and find a job to support his mother, and his two younger brothers and one sister, all three of whom were at school. It had been impossible to find a job for which he was not overqualified; shocking, a starred first-class Mathematics (Hons) degree from Presidency and no employment after seventeen months of application and job searches. Without his friend Samiran's help this humiliating position of mathematics teacher at St Lawrence – a school – would also have been a mirage.

'Take it,' Samiran had advised. 'In this current climate, how are you going to hold out for what you call a "proper job"? Did I tell you that last week I got an interview letter from the Geological Survey of India? They were interviewing applicants for the post of assistant field researcher. One post, a single one. Guess how many applicants? Four hundred. I'm not joking. They were giving two minutes to each candidate. Eight hundred minutes, so over thirteen hours. Which meant that they were not going to be done in one day: the babus doing the interview needed their breaks, of course, tea break and snack break and lunch break. There were candidates from parts of West Bengal you have never heard of. You think they were going to give the job based on those two-minute interviews? They had picked the person beforehand, someone's nephew or son; this was just a show. And you're still chasing a "proper job", you crazy fool.'

Swapan had been in similar situations over the last year and a half. Still, that childhood indoctrination in the moral principle of just deserts – that the right and the deserving always win at the end of the day – was a terribly tenacious thing, difficult to shake off.

'Listen, don't be stupid,' Samiran had advised. 'Which college is going to give you a lectureship? Are you a Party member? Even then, you'll have to serve time in Siberia – in those appalling colleges in the sticks: Bardhaman, Kalyani, Jalpaiguri . . . are you prepared for that fate worse than death?'

So St Lawrence it was, to stave off debts, rent and bills in arrears, the shrinking of days through squalor. Every day now, work on Riemann's zeta function seemed more and more like the depleting memory of having had a dream, not even of the dream itself. His reality, instead, was a bunch of slothful, slow-witted, smelly idiots, not one of whom, not a single one of them, was destined for anything higher than a nine-to-five job as a low-to-middle ranking manager in a local bank. And that was the destiny of the best of the lot.

Well, maybe there was one exception, that eerily quiet and shy new arrival, Swarnendu Ghosh, whose sole aim in life, it would appear, was to make himself invisible. That boy, he knew, was gifted; not only full marks in mathematics in the few exams and class tests he had taken, but also something about the *way* he did mathematics had alerted him to this boy's talent. It was not the standard cud-chewing ease with set questions and exercises that came with regular practice and drill, but something far deeper, something to do with an effortlessness of movement in the world of abstraction. The boy *thought* mathematically.

But he too seemed to be paying no attention that day, staring at a small collection of paper on his desk, so still that he appeared not even to be breathing. Right, time for some order.

'Swarnendu,' he called.

The boy remained shut in his world.

'Swarnendu!'

No reply. No change in posture.

'S-W-A-R-N-E-N-D-U!' It was a bit mean to pick on him when dozens of others would have done – every one of them was inattentive

– but something about the paradox of the boy's seemingly endless drift, yet brutal concentration, caught his interest.

Now the class was focused on this diversionary drama, a welcome relief from the impenetrable talk of horizontal and vertical axes and anticlockwise movement of a circle and intersection with the positive horizontal axis. A tiny choir of tittering and whispering had erupted.

Swapan Adhikari stepped off his dais and strode over to Swarnendu.

'What is keeping you from paying attention? Let's see,' he said and pulled the sheaf of paper away. The boy involuntarily tried to protect it by bringing down his arms, but too late; he had been taken by surprise.

'Since you're such a whizz at mathematics that you think there's no need to listen to what I say in class, why don't you tell us about the cosine curve? And stand up when I'm speaking to you.'

It was cruel, Swapan Adhikari thought, but he had the right to make them take notice. The boy stood up, his eyes fixed to the ground at his feet.

'Go on, then, tell us something about the cos curve.'

Silence.

'I see you're not with us yet. Can you tell us the relationship between the sine and the cosine curves?' That'll teach him.

The boy looked up at the board, then down again.

'Here, go up to the blackboard. Take this piece of chalk. I want you to explain to the class.'

He had pushed the boy too far; he looked as if he was going to burst into tears. Instead, he obliged. He stood facing the blackboard, his back to the class, and held this pose for a minute, two minutes, absolutely still. Then he started writing:

$2\pi = 1$ *complete revolution of circle.*

He drew the x and y axes afresh, showing all four quadrants, and marked off equal intervals on the x-axis: -2π, -1.5π, $-\pi$, -0.5π, 0, 0.5π, π, 1.5π, 2π. Then he plotted a sine curve on it, beginning at $(0,0)$ and marked it, accurately, $y = \sin x$. Even the sound of ordinary susurrus had been hushed in the classroom. Swapan Adhikari felt the beginnings of what he could only think of as an effervescence somewhere in his throat, trying to move up and out, as he watched from the side

Swarnendu plotting a cosine curve, again with cast-iron accuracy, on the same axis and naming it y = cosx. He mumbled something. Swapan Adhikari asked him to repeat it.

Sona mumbled, 'The cosine curve is to the left of the sine curve by a distance of $\frac{\pi}{2}$.'

He wrote on the board again:

$cosx = sin \left(x + \frac{\pi}{2}\right)$ or $sinx = cos \left(x - \frac{\pi}{2}\right)$.

He stopped for a bit, looked at his teacher for an instant, immediately looked down again, then once again faced the board. He wrote:

From the above, $sin^2x + cos^2x = 1$.

Again he glanced briefly at Mr Adhikari. This time he gathered up enough courage to ask, 'Shall I prove it?'

Swapan Adhikari shook his head and said, 'No. Go back to your seat now.' He was going to add, redundantly, he felt, 'Pay heed to what I'm teaching next time', but decided not to.

The boy meekly returned to his bench, his expression of desired erasure unchanged; not an atom of triumphalism or self-satisfaction anywhere. But that was not what was going through Swapan Adhikari's mind at all. What dazed him was the clarity of the boy's mind, of his impeccable return to first principles and proceeding from there. This new pupil in Class Seven had just elucidated a topic that he was three years away from being taught in school.

At home he looked at the bundle of papers he had confiscated: a collection of different kinds, ruled, plain, of different sizes, quality and colour, all held together by a rusty safety pin. The first ten or twenty seconds of browsing was a blur of numbers and alphabets and faux-equations, and then it hit him with a force that could have lifted him clean off the ground if it had had a material correlate – the boy was trying to prove Fermat's two-square theorem. First, over several sheets there was an ultimately successful attempt to prove that the set of all sums of two squares was closed under multiplication. Using that as a starting point, he had embarked on a proof of $p = x^2 + y^2$ iff $p \equiv 1 \pmod 4$. There were shortcuts the boy clearly did not know about, so he had spent a lot of time reinventing the wheel. Shorn of the circularities, the reiterated steps, the occasional cul-de-sacs, he had been engaged in working out from scratch Euler's proof by infinite descent. The notations were unconventional, there was a lot of chasing of his own tail, but there it was: a messy proof, not parsimonious, not austere, but a proof nevertheless, one even assuming a knowledge of relatively prime and – miraculous, this – a feeling for the notion of finite difference.

On another page there were series of numbers, written one after the other, line after line. A few minutes' contemplation of those revealed that the boy was trying to feel his way towards prime gaps and twin primes. On yet another, an innocently formulated: 'if a $>$ 1, then a . . . P . . . 2a?'; the boy did not know that he had stumbled upon Bertrand's theorem. Swapan Adhikari had to prove it in his final exams for the BA (Hons) degree. There was a long-winded working-out of the binomial theorem – he must have had access to some kind of intermediate mathematics books to symbolise binomial coefficients correctly as $\binom{p}{n}$ and even a knowledge of combinatorials in his use of n! – and its correct proof using induction. Buried deep within was some incipient thinking about asymptotic equality leading on from logarithms and the prime counting function.

Swapan Adhikari had never felt such a sustained sense of disbelief. Question after question rose and fell in him like the peals of giant bells – Was this all intuitive? How could it *be*? Was someone, a relative, a maths professor, guiding him? If so, why the idiosyncratic language? The symbols were all wrong, the competence in mathematical notation and the sequentiality of steps amateurish, as if a child were trying to build the engine of his car with the pieces of his Meccano set. Where did he live? Where was he before he came to St Lawrence? Could it have been a preternaturally gifted teacher at that school? What else had he been feeling his way towards? How could someone like this, with such an innate understanding and feel for the music of abstraction, be untrained? Yet untrained he seemed to be. Where had he got hold of books on algebra? This boy was thirteen years old . . . the fact was like repeated socks to his jaw. This was not possible. There was something under his nose that he was failing to notice, that would clear up the mystery, and he would be left feeling a bit foolish at his incomprehension.

But with every nugget of meaning that Swapan Adhikari scooped out from the mess, one thing only stood out with the incontrovertibility of a basic axiom – he almost did not dare think it – this boy was a

. . . genius. The slightest touch of hysteria brushed against him. Then it seemed to intensify – he flipped again through the pages and found his eyes welling up. Something from the magic world of childhood reading reappeared: the story of Byangoma and Byangomi, the bird-couple who knew the fates of the princes and men who fell asleep under the tree in which they lived, the birds who talked about the future of those mortals, alerting them to what was to come. It seemed to him that those magical creatures had guided the boy through these matters that should have been beyond him.

He could not tell why he found it so deeply affecting that Swarnendu had tried to go back to first principles, at almost every step of the way, in order to prove the theorem. It was so pure, so innocent. It was like watching a child, except this child was touched by a kind of divine fire, a child in whose presence you felt like bowing your head.

The room was densely blue with smoke: he had made his way through two packets of Charminar.

That was when he decided to drop in on his old, now nearly demented, professor, Ashish Roy, the man who had come close to solving some of the open problems in number theory, including the $n^2 + 1$ conjecture, only to have a series of nervous breakdowns take it all away from him. The rumour within mathematician circles in Calcutta was that he had had a glimpse into the mind of god, into god's book of numbers, and had been driven insane as a result.

Then came the second attack of incredulity. Ashish Roy not only knew Swarnendu – Sona, he called him – but they were near-neighbours. At the time Swapan Adhikari had briefly wondered about the statistical probability of the joining of three random dots – Ashish Roy, Swarnendu Ghosh and himself – distributed amidst a dense scatter, seven million to be exact, but non-mathematicians never believed you if you said there were more coincidences in life than in books, concurrences at which they did not bring illogical charges of 'Oh, that's unbelievable!' that they reserved for the fictional variety. Why would there be saws such as 'The world is such a small place' and 'What goes around must come around' if coincidence did not form a regularly occurring part of life?

Ashish-da had leafed through Swarnendu's workbook. The silence in the room had been punctuated by the wonderfully aleatory music of a brief giggle; an 'eeeesh-tsk-tsk-tsk' of regret, the kind that resulted from watching your favourite candidate in a race falling slightly behind; a long rumble of laughter; a deep 'ooooh'; several 'a-ha-ha's of admiration – all widely spaced from each other. Behind the random soundtrack had been his ever-present anxiety that Ashish-da's wife, who blamed mathematics for the dark pit into which their lives had fallen, could have entered the room at any minute and broken up their mostly silent meeting. She kept her husband under continual surveillance, forbidding any of his mathematician friends, ex-colleagues or students from visiting.

'Have you seen, have you seen, a list of arithmetic progressions, he's on the brink of Dirichlet's theorem.'

Long silence.

'I saw the proof first in '37, Harding-saheb drew my attention to it. Oh, Harding-saheb, what a nice man he was. A giant moustache. You could hardly make out the words behind it. He missed out key steps in a proof, assuming that you'd know it, or that it was too obvious to be spelled out.'

Another pause, this time dotted with odd snuffling and guttural noises.

'Jaaaah, it slipped my hands, it slipped.'

A huge sigh followed by another protracted lull.

'I thought you and that other young man, the one who left, what was his name, I thought you would go too, but . . . yes, you two could see if the first and second Hardy-Littlewood conjectures could . . . could . . . nah, the bell rang.'

Then the closest Ashish Roy came to the nub, a one-point touch like that of a tangent to a curve, then off and away again: 'Maybe we could all pass the baton on to this boy. Invest him with all our hopes. But we need to help him. Ufff, if he arrives at Dirichlet by pure intuition' – here he rubbed his hands the way a miser would, contemplating his hoard of gold – 'you could talk to the student who's abroad, what's his name? I can't remember anything nowadays, my brain is a sieve, sieve ha-ha-ha-ha-ha, a sieve for primes like that Greek had, a sieve ha-ha-ha-ha-ha, that was a good one, no? What do you say, eh? But some books may tide him over the short term . . . Hardy & Wright, maybe . . .'

Swapan Adhikari had got what he had wanted. Something had been clarified for him.

●

Finally, after weeks of mental preparation, Swapan Adhikari sits down to write to his friend Ayan Basu, now an associate professor of mathematics – 'the one who left', the one he was supposed to join, until fate dealt him a crippling card . . .

Dear Ayan, he begins:

I hope this finds you in good health and spirits. I have no excuse for the large gap that has fallen between this and your last letter to me except to cite the usual mess that is life. But I'm writing to you with a request you may well find a bit unusual. A little bit of the back-story, first. You may find it unbelievable too, as I did, but please be patient. There is a boy in my school, a Swarnendu Ghosh, thirteen going on fourteen, in Class Seven.

He stops there. How can he take it forward, short of sending Ayan the boy's exercise book for him to experience it first hand? What else can he add about Swarnendu? The gentle questioning of the boy in the staffroom and outside the school yielded up very little. He had the strange capacity of returning pure silence to direct questions in a way that made the interrogator feel intrusive and, ultimately, embarrassed. It was Swapan Adhikari who had felt flustered and discomfited, as if the ordinary power dynamics between teacher and pupil had been reversed. About the mathematics, the boy had not been able to say anything at all except to confirm that it was his own work, done unaided in his private leisure time.

'I . . . I think . . . and then . . . then the numbers take me from . . . from one step to another,' he had said haltingly, struggling to put words to experience.

Other information too was minimal; he had refused to talk about his parents or any other members of his family, but had told Swapan Adhikari which school he had attended before he came to St Lawrence. Now, writing about him to Ayan, he realises that the boy is an absence, a geometric gap bounded by the facets of the different elements of analytic number theory that he had tried to think about.

A tiny spark at lunch. The family has long stopped sitting down together to eat, a result of the absence of Sandhya's kind, superin-tending eye. Purnima and Charubala, not on talking terms for a good while now, go through the motions of sitting at the same table around half-past one or two every afternoon, even though they do not speak to each other directly. If this non-communication was a cause of active tension when the hostilities began, now it has calcified into something inorganic, like a darkening water mark down an external wall, that can be ignored; it seems the natural course of things. The age-old oppugnant relationship between mother and daughter-in-law in this instance is an apparently paradoxical variant: Purnima feels she has failed to elevate her husband to the top position in Charubala's regard. After years of jockeying, the accreted failure, by now densely settled into a stratum of fury and resentment, could not be checked and has started bubbling up under the increasingly flimsy superstructure of family unity and its foot soldiers – respect, obedience, love.

How like that Geography chapter on volcanoes, thinks Arunima, as she picks out tiny bones from her piece of fish, a time-tested strategy for deferring the act of eating until so late that her plate is eventually cleared away, saving her yet again from eating the rubbish that gets served day after day, unchangingly, for lunch: rice, dal, a mushy medley of vegetables, a watery fish stew, the fish chosen deliberately, she felt, for maximum boniness; it is an invitation to starve yourself, that fish.

Her mejo-jyethi calls out, 'Madan-da, bring me some of the rice left over from last night.'

Madan says, 'But there's fresh rice, just cooked, here, on the table.'

'But I don't want the leftovers to go to waste. Why don't you reheat it and bring it?'

Madan does as he is told. Charubala looks at nothing in particular, her eyes stony. Something is coming, Arunima knows. Her pishi, Chhaya, has that look on her face, the one that presages warfare.

The tiny spark comes from Purnima. 'We can't afford any waste nowadays, what with the recent state of things here,' she adds as a coda to her request. 'Someone has to start paying for the years of kingly behaviour of others.'

She is in a fiendish mood.

Arunima notes that she is taking on the collective might of her grandmother and her pishi; no mean feat. She feels vicariously afraid.

Madan brings in the reheated leftover rice. Charubala says, 'Madan, pass the *fresh* rice this way, will you? It wouldn't do to mix the two', and moves the bowl of fresh rice far away from the old one, as if the grains had the agency and ability to mingle on their own.

In one surprisingly agile movement, Purnima gets up from her chair, carries her container of warmed-up rice to the receptacle containing the new, spoons the old into the fresh, gives a few thorough stirs, picks up the full bowl and moves back to her place, where she serves herself some rice. All this before Charubala and Chhaya can open their mouths to cry out in protest.

The very air seems cloven. A shiver of terrified delight goes through Arunima.

Charubala responds first. 'Madan,' she calls, her voice almost a high, quavering trill with the effort to keep clutching onto dignified behaviour, 'take the rice away and throw it out.'

Madan comes in from the kitchen. He has the cultivated detachment of someone who has long experience of being used as a device by warring parties. But he is pushing sixty now, no longer a green boy who could be shouted at, punished, for not doing anyone's irrational or machinating bidding. Besides, he has been with the family for longer than anyone at the table except Charubala, so he knows where his loyalties lie. He begins to do as he has been told; he picks up the rice and asks Charubala, 'Ma, what will you eat if I throw this out? I can put on some rice for you now, but it'll take some time.'

Unwittingly Madan gives Charubala a bit of fuel. 'No need to, Madan. Bin it. If it's been willed that I won't eat, fine, so be it, but I'll make sure that those who have willed it don't eat, either.'

Arunima, wise to the ways of quarrels among people who refer to each other in the third person, now begins to get interested in how sustainable the trope can be in this particular flare-up.

'Yes, Madan, do take it away and throw it out,' Purnima says. 'How else to show one's empty snobbery? Cutting off the nose to spite one's face – if, at the age of seventy, one doesn't understand how stupid it is, I wonder when one will.'

Madan leaves for the kitchen; it is best not to offer himself as a conducting rod.

Chhaya butts in and addresses her mother. 'I warned you many, many times not to bring this . . . this creature into our house.' The claim is not true, but she has said it so often over the years that it has become the truth. 'She'll burn it down,' Chhaya says. 'It turns out you have nurtured a snake on milk.'

'At least I was lucky enough to have the option of marriage and of going to another home to live, although it turned out to be a pit of vipers. Some amongst us are so ugly and so venomous that marriage has passed them by,' Purnima says.

Chhaya sits there, shaking, then manages to bring out a strangulated, 'Ma, my heart is hammering again, I think something's going to happen to me.'

'About time,' Purnima says.

Charubala rises to the challenge. 'It is imperative that one behaves in a civilised manner in a civilised house, regardless of one's background,' she begins, addressing, it would appear, the framed black-and-white photograph on the wall opposite her, of her husband receiving a prize at the Bengal Chamber of Commerce nearly twenty years ago.

'Civilised!' Purnima says. 'Show me where civilisation is in this house!' She breaks the unwritten third-person rule and attacks Charubala directly now. 'I can see father and favourite son skimming off money from the business and pretending that it's going down the tubes. I suppose someone like you, in cahoots with them, would call that civilisation.'

In the time that Charubala takes to draw breath, Purnima charges again. Today she is indefatigable; if at this point, when Adinath is at his lowest, losing control of the business, haemorrhaging money and reputation, if now she cannot strike to dislodge him and make her husband usurp his position, they will never get another opportunity again.

'"Bad times, bad times",' she mimics the dominant line that has been the unremitting background noise in the house for several years.

'I ask you, who is *responsible* for those bad times?' Her voice rises to its extraordinary pitch, that split-toned duet caused as if by a cracked voice. Madan cringes in the kitchen, but cannot help soaking it up. He stops clattering about with pots and plates and glasses.

'Now that you've feathered your nests, it's up to us to make the economies. Thieves, that's what you are, low, common thieves,' she shrieks.

Charubala finds her tongue. 'Careful, very careful now,' she warns. 'You are no longer in the house of riff-raffs and common scum that you came from. If you are to stay on as a daughter-in-law here, you have to abide by our rules, otherwise . . .'

'Otherwise what? Are you threatening me? Are you?' Purnima, already standing, tucks the end of her sari at the waist, prepared even for physical conflict.

'Yes, I'm threatening you. You will have to leave. I will not put up with this kind of behaviour. This is *my* house and you will learn to know your place in it and behave accordingly.'

'*Your* house?'

'Yes, it's in my name.'

'Well, you won't be around for ever. What'll happen then? Oh, don't tell me, it's going to be equally divided among your children. Not for a moment in your shitty little life have you done anything governed by equality. I know you're going to leave it all to your eldest son. But I'll see how you do it. We'll talk to lawyers and pursue litigation until you will beg, beg to be forgiven.'

Chhaya finds her voice again. 'Ma, you mustn't shout, you'll fall ill. Let's leave her to stew in her own poison.'

'Did you hear what she said?' Charubala asks. 'Lawyers, litigation . . . Is this what has been lurking in that cesspit of your venomous mind?'

'Cesspit? Poison? Looks to me like a case of the sieve saying to the colander, "Why do you have so many holes in your arse?"' Purnima modulates her tone to fit the glory of her colloquial style. 'Your daughter could give a snake a few lessons in "poison" and "venomous mind".'

Another frisson of shock goes through Arunima.

Chhaya says, 'You are shameless, *shameless*. An animal, a greedy animal out to devour us. I warned everyone about you, the moment I heard your vulgar voice during the matchmaking. This is all so predictable.' She pauses for breath, already aware that her hits lack the force of her sister-in-law's earthier words, her more skilfully targeted darts. The knowledge makes her even angrier, but a secret anxiety, just beginning to whisper inside her head, leaches it away somewhat: does she . . . could she *know*?

Purnima fires her final shots. 'I'm telling you this now, this is your last chance to come to a settlement, otherwise I'll have walls erected to divide the house.'

A common enough story in joint families, the threat has not been defanged by the frequency of its occurrence; it curdles and slows the hot flow of anger in both Charubala and Chhaya.

In the kitchen Madan thinks: How did it come to this? Will the family really break up into smaller units? Where will I go if that comes to pass? What's going to happen to me in my old age?

Charubala can only return a few feeble words to this incendiary thrown at her: 'It will not happen while I am alive.' But, she thinks, to announce in public such an enormous intention to rive must mean that Purnima has discussed it with Priyo; the thought is like thunder. How could *her* son have colluded with this woman against his mother, against his father and his siblings? No, no, that is unthinkable, unnatural. So what gave Purnima the power to utter such a thing? Does she really hold so much sway over her son? Division of the house . . . Her head is reeling with the reverberations of those unspeakable words. It is true that the situation with Priyo and Purnima has not been ideal for a long while; tension in the air, an undercurrent of animosity rippling through all the time, congealing silences, avoidance or minimising of contact, a coldness and formality in the ineludible conversations and interactions that one was forced to have because of living in the same house. But whose fault was it all?

Priyo is not the most intimate among her children, or the most expressive with his affections and emotions, he never has been, but ever since he married this woman, who did not think anything of using the language of the gutter in front of her elders, something befitting slum-dwellers, ever since then there seems to have been a gradual swerving away from all familial bonds. Yet Charubala has never noticed Priyo to be uxorious, or even minutely different from his usual phlegmatic and detached self in his deportment with his wife; he has behaved towards

everyone with a total democracy of what she could only call indifference. And she is convinced that it is not the split between his public
and private faces; living in one house together means that all the things
one imagines are private are not really so – the walls and floors have
eyes, ears and interpreting minds. Charubala knows that Priyo does not
possess a secret self for his wife's consumption only.

As she sits feeling humiliated in front of her granddaughter and in
the hearing of a servant, an idea takes shape in Charubala's head.
Before it has fully formed she blurts out, 'All right, if dividing up the
house is what you've been plotting, I hope you will remember that I
too have some say over the division of other things. It's Baishakhi's
wedding later in the year. She won't even get the dust from the jewellery I've been saving up for her.'

This has the effect of a forest fire reaching the line where all the
trees have been felled to contain it.

During the matchmaking leading to Priyo and Purnima's marriage,
the bride's family had quickly discovered that the groom's father was
the younger son of *the* Ghosh family, which had made its money and
name in the gold business. Jewellers were thick on the ground in
Calcutta, but the Ghoshes had long attained the electricity of legend,
helped generously by rumours of family dissension, dissolute living,
all manner of excess, even rumours of a suicide and gunfire in their
family seat in North Calcutta long ago. Didn't someone kill herself?
Poison or self-immolation? Didn't they regularly have to bring back
one of the sons or brothers, unconscious with drink, from the brothels?
The risk of becoming a daughter-in-law in a family tainted with scandal
was heavily outweighed by the possible riches, in the form of gold
and jewellery, that would accrue; this was Purnima's parents' sharp
reasoning. Besides, wasn't the groom's father a breakaway who had
reinvented himself in a new business and had nothing to do with the
decadent main line any more? Purnima herself had been dazzled by
the idea of gold; the lure of metal made her forget that she was actually marrying into paper; forgotten too was the fact that the connection of her husband's family with gold was historical, not real.

Yet Purnima had not been deceived in her acquisitive ambitions,
not totally. Although he never talked about jewellery, certainly never
within Purnima's earshot, Prafullanath had a secret obsession with it;

or so she speculated. It gradually emerged, a few years after she had taken up residence in Basanta Bose Road, that her father-in-law bought gold ornaments, almost ritualistically, about three times a year and kept them in a State Bank of India vault in his wife's name. The jewellery he bought was not trinkets like rings and thin gold chains and bangles, but of the heavier, showier and more intricate kind, the kind that would be worn by the women of an extremely wealthy family on the big social occasions, a wedding or a family puja. Some of them could not be worn, in public or private, any longer; the era of gold hair pieces, tiaras studded with gems, drooping and baroquely decorative chains linking nose to ear had probably passed.

Rumour within the family – a word slipped into conversation by her jaa, Sandhya, an unguarded comment by Priyo, evasive answers given to her dogged and strategic questions about the existence, nature and exact content of this jewellery vault – had convinced Purnima that a far bigger hoard lay beyond the usual loose change of necklaces, rings, bangles, earrings and chokers that the women of the house, herself included, kept in the steel lockers in their bedrooms. There were stories about the Ghoshes of Garpar, with whom her father-in-law had had no connection for nearly fifty years, of how they wrapped their daughters in so much gold at the giving-away ceremony of their weddings that only their eyes could be seen, two quick, black holes in the dull yellow glitter. But she had never known her mother-in-law to wear such stuff, not even when she went to attend upper-crust weddings. Where was it all then? How much jewellery did Sandhya have? Did she have her own private locker in a bank? And what about Chhaya? Traditionally, most of the jewellery would have been saved up for her, a gift from her parents when she got married. Now that that possibility had been ruled out, where was her share? In a bank? In her almirah? What good was it going to do Chhaya? It was like a feast of pork for a starving Muslim.

The only time Purnima got to see what the other women in the house possessed was when they dressed formally to go out. She strewed seemingly innocuous questions in their way, hoping to elicit information about how much more they had beyond the fraction they chose to display.

'Oh my, what a beautiful emerald set, Jayanti,' she flattered her younger sister-in-law once. 'It goes so well with your green benarasi sari. Where did you get it?'

Jayanti shyly parried the question. 'I've always had it,' she said.

'Oh, I see. You got it at the blessing before the wedding, didn't you? It's just that I don't think I've seen it before. What about the pearl set you have' – this was a shot in the dark – 'that would go really well with the green too.'

No reply from Jayanti, only a coyly perfunctory smile before she stepped into the car to be driven off to wherever she was going that evening. Purnima remained ignorant of her treasures.

Purnima's own cache was not inconsiderable, a lot more than that of other women she knew. Not everything had been given to her when she got married; she insisted Priyo bought her some jewellery a couple of times a year. In this way she had built up quite a collection, but all these imagined old-world splendours of baju, tagaa, hanshuli, mantasha, shaat-lahari-haar, chik, chur, ratanchur, gold combs and hairpins with floral ornamentation to make the bun above the neck look like a miniature garden of jewelled flowers, all this she imagined was in Charubala's trove and she wanted some to be bequeathed to her or to her daughter, Baishakhi, when the time came.

Now that the time has arrived for Baishakhi, this skinflint mother-in-law of hers has just announced her decision not to part with anything. In Purnima's mind it is indubitable that this is what Charubala has been waiting for all along: to grab any excuse to hang onto her hoard and gloat over it in private.

Purnima pounds out of the room, leaving a shaking, tearful Charubala trying to swallow her humiliation and channel it to appear as the onset of feeling ill.

Very belatedly attention falls on Arunima. Chhaya is the first to realise that the girl has witnessed everything. Her frustration finds an easy target; she starts scolding her niece – 'What? You still here? How many times have you been told not to remain sitting in a room when the elders are discussing something? How many times?'

Kalyani mashes up some hibiscus leaves – they exude something sticky that forms thin threads – and then apportions equal amounts onto three tiny dented aluminium plates.

'Here you go,' she says. 'Mutton pulao with cashews and raisins. I want you girls to finish every last bit, no leaving something on the plate.'

She places the plates in front of three dolls propped against the trunk of the guava tree. One is plastic, the painted dress and eyes and lips and hair on its nearly neon flesh-coloured body erased in patches after years of handling so that it looks like it has a radical case of vitiligo. The terracotta one, also with flaking paint and one arm and a foot missing, was a present from Madan-da, brought back from one of his yearly visits to his home up country. The red paint on its inscrutably smiling lips has flaked off in one corner; Kalyani thinks it looks as if a morsel of rice is permanently stuck there, an instance of slack hygiene on the part of the doll, something for which she never fails to tell her off.

Sitting in the shade of the guava tree, she proceeds to cook the second course for the reception of her dolls' wedding, a rich mutton kaliya made from dust, torn-up bits of grass, some shredded guava leaves and a couple of broken twigs, all stirred with water to a textured, heterogeneous paste.

'Right, I'm about to serve the kaliya,' she declares. 'Sromona, careful, the edge of your benarasi is touching the gravy, you'll ruin the expensive sari and then where will we be?'

At the age of eleven Kalyani is too old to play 'cook-and-serve' with her dolls, but there does not seem to be anything better to do. She has failed her annual examination in school and been made to repeat the year. Not that anyone is greatly perturbed by it. Her brother is so obsessed with his fat books of numbers and his continual scribbling – head down, uncaring about whether he has had any food or even about a decent place to sit and write – that getting a word out of him has become impossible, while their mother seems only physically present, her mind and spirit, like her son's, somewhere else; they are both hollowed-out.

Malati-di had once told her a story about nishi, the ghost who moves by night and calls out your name, assuming the voice of someone you know, and if you answer that call, the nishi traps the sound in a box and with that she has got your soul too, for her to call in as and when she wants; you are her creature from the moment you have replied. It seems that the nishi has sent for the souls of her mother and her brother; her dolls have more animation, more life. She even misses her mother's scolding. Now that seems so much more preferable to the distraction and melancholy and secret bouts of silent weeping, checked, as soon as Purba is caught out, with a pathetic, 'I always cry when I'm chopping onions' when there is no onion anywhere in sight. It is as if she just is not there. Flanked by these two people, who are all that her life contains, Kalyani's days have fallen into a kind of dispersal, a diffuse structureless nothing that slips through her fingers like smoke.

She reprimands another doll: 'There'll be no mango chutney and papad for you if you don't clean your plate. I can't stand waste, you know that.'

From the second-floor window, Baishakhi has been watching her cousin muttering to herself. She calls and asks her to come up. A leap of excitement in Kalyani – something at last, something different from the viscous drudge of her days – almost instantly moderated by the training of years of cautiousness and inhibition about the 'upstairs people'; it is noticeable in her walk from the garden up to the second floor: three skips, then however many measured paces with head held down, eyes downcast; not sullen, but just quiet.

Her eyes become as large as cottage-cheese balls when she enters her cousin's room. Fanned out on the bed are what she takes to be the entire wealth of Baishakhi's wedding saris, dozens of them, silk and benarasi and tangail and jamdani and others she does not know the names of, but all gorgeous and dazzling, filling every sense.

'Wedding saris,' Baishakhi says redundantly. 'Do you like them?'

Kalyani can only nod.

'I'm trying to decide what to wear on which day.'

Kalyani nods again.

'Do you know how many days the whole ceremony is going to take?'

This she knows. Three days: the smearing-with-turmeric ceremony followed by the actual wedding in this house; then the bride leaves her father's home for ever; then boü-bhaat at the groom's. She also knows that although the formal talks have happened, the ashirbad ceremony will be next month, and the wedding at the very end of December.

Baishakhi picks up a comb and runs it through her long hair, but gives up after a few strokes. She goes to the window, looks out at nothing in particular, returns her attention to the saris and Kalyani. She seems on the verge of saying something, but thinks better of it and starts desultorily going through the saris again, gets bored with this too and walks up to the window again.

'Are you excited that there's going to be a wedding in this house?' she asks Kalyani.

This time Kalyani nods with more vigour.

'Do you want to know what each sari is called?'

'Yes.'

But Baishakhi loses interest as soon as the question leaves her mouth. Instead she says, 'Do you know, Baba has chosen a cook recommended by Debu-kaka to do all the catering? Debu-kaka owns Bijoli Grill, he and Baba are friends.'

Kalyani, who does not know about professional caterers, has been awed into silence; awe at the spectacle that this, her first ever wedding, is going to be. All this opulence of saris and caterers serves to intimidate her.

'What? Why so silent?'

'No, nothing.'

'Do you want to see some of the ornaments I'm going to wear?'

'Yes, yes,' Kalyani says, her habitual wariness at being upstairs cast aside at last.

But Baishakhi makes no move to show her anything. She asks, 'Listen, do you know who I'm getting married to?'

Again, a brief nod.

There is a brief flare of irritation from Baishakhi – 'The cats' got your tongue or what?' – then subsidence into alternating between distracted fidgeting and aimless inertia. 'What have you heard about him?' Baishakhi asks her cousin.

Kalyani, so unexpectedly put on the spot, becomes even more tongue-tied than usual. She cannot read the question at all, but feels under pressure to answer it, otherwise she may be told off again. But what can she say?

'What? Why aren't you saying anything?'

'I . . . I haven't heard anything about . . . about him,' Kalyani manages to bring out.

'Why such hesitation? Tell me the truth, what have you heard? You clearly must have heard something, otherwise why did you stammer and halt?'

This has the effect of terrifying the girl, so her stilted reply – 'No, no, I'm telling you the truth, I've heard nothing, I was thinking, that's why I paused' – comes out all wrong: hesitant, deliberated, protesting too much.

Baishakhi uses some false logic to trick Kalyani. 'You live on the ground floor, so surely you hear a lot of stuff that people say, coming and going. Downstairs is full of people all the time. Tell me, tell me what you've picked up.'

'Nothing, really, I'm touching you' – here she moves closer and places her hand on Baishakhi's arm – 'and saying, "I've heard nothing".'

'If you've lied while touching me, you know I'll die, don't you?'

'But I'm telling you the truth,' Kalyani insists again.

'All right, just tell me one thing: do they say good things about him or bad things?'

'Good things, good things only.'

'Aha, caught you, then they do talk about him *and* you know what they say. You lied. Which means I'm going to die. On the second night of my wedding I'm going to die.'

Kalyani nearly shrieks, 'No-o-o-o-o', then remembers just in time where she is, so it comes out low.

Baishakhi changes the subject suddenly. 'Listen, will you be my nit-bou at the wedding?' she asks.

'What's nit-bou?'

'A kind of bridesmaid. You'll have to accompany me to my in-laws' and return after three days.'

Kalyani, now wide-eyed, takes some time to process this utterly unexpected gift. Then she nods energetically.

'Then you could wear one of these saris,' Baishakhi says, adding to the giddiness.

A cold thought strikes Kalyani. 'What if my mother says no?'

'Tell Kakima that I suggested it.'

Kalyani is now all assailed by doubt; this is not going to happen, her mother is almost certain to veto it and, if not she, then her grandmother, definitely.

Just as suddenly as the beginning of her flash of generosity, Baishakhi's interest in her cousin switches off, before the girl has had time to work out fully the treat that has been handed her.

'All right, you go back downstairs now, I have lots to do,' Baishakhi says.

Kalyani lowers her head and leaves the room, but not before stealing a final glance at Baishaki, who lies reclined on the bed, squashing some of her new clothes, chewing her nails and staring at the ceiling, looking both languid and restless, her pose not that of someone who has just announced that she has lots to do.

X

Dhiren tracked Senapati's movements. Somehow the fact that it was winter seemed to be significant – it would have to be done now, when the dark came early and stayed for long.

Who would have thought that something as thickly crowded and public as the annual winter mela in the neighbouring village of Gidighati would present us with the opportunity? We did not go following him there; that was a matter of chance. We went to the mela to meet other activists in the area, mostly AICCCR members, formally or informally, and to discuss strategies and update each other with news of our respective villages. It was a good place for such things: we wouldn't stick out as strangers; there was a sea of men, women and children in which we could become invisible. It was here that we learned what was going on in other villages, in other districts (24 Parganas, Hughli), even in Muzaffarpur, Darbhanga and Champaran in Bihar, Koraput in Orissa.

There were couriers and Communist Revolutionary members here. There were rumours floating about of the formation of a new party, cleansed of all revisionism, bringing together all ex-CPI(M) members, some AICCCR people and the CR group, under one umbrella.

The din of the mela was somehow comforting: local drums; palm-leaf flutes; wooden flutes; performing singers; people talking and shouting and laughing and haggling; squealing and crying children; calls advertising wares; a horbola, mimicking all kinds of bird calls and animal sounds; several bahurupis, each performing dozens of roles and changing his appearance accordingly . . .

I recognised several farmers from Majgeria. At one point Dhiren gripped my arm and said – Come.

I went with him, pushing through the crowd. We stopped at what seemed a random spot. I could see a line of people selling things: toddy, fritters, dried chillies, pinwheels, painted terracotta toys.

Dhiren said through his mouth firmly pressed – That fat man, bending down, buying toy bow-and-arrows, that's Senapati Nayek.

I nodded very slowly.

– How are we going to keep an eye on him in this mela?

– Follow him until he leaves.

– All of us?

– Yes, otherwise we'll lose each other.

– But . . . but . . . we have nothing with us.

I knew what he was saying. I couldn't answer him. A wasted day when the target was so near, when the causes were so immediate: that would not be good. Yet an impromptu individual action – but how? where? with what? – seemed dangerous and could set us back in Majgeria for ever. Besides, we needed the farmers with us, we could not be an assassination squad of three acting on their behalf. Everything about this looked, felt, smelled wrong. And yet that prodding inside, that we were letting an opportunity slip, wouldn't leave me. Us.

It remained this kind of welter until sundown. We were tense and bored at the same time, a dangerous combination, as we tailed Senapati for what felt like hours and hours. He met a lot of people he knew. Sometimes he became one of a group of three or four or five. Sometimes he was alone. He watched a bahurupi performance, alone, for a while – we too caught it, although on the margins of our concentration; the bahurupi was enacting Hanuman setting Lanka on fire – then moved on to the corner where the local liquor was being sold. We looked at each other with despair.

Samir said – He could be here for ever. Especially if it leads on to visiting a prostitute, as these things do.

The gap between sunset and darkness was short. It would be the easiest thing in the world to lose him to the night now. Bands of people were leaving, the mela was breaking up. There were no lights in the eight-mile walk to Majgeria. An idea had been going through my head ever since Senapati had sat down to drink. I outlined this to Samir and Dhiren, then we looked for holes in it. There were many, but we had progressed from the anxious chaos and flailing around that had held us when we first spied the moneylender.

Dhiren began to walk back to the village while Samir and I moved closer to our drinking quarry. There were enough people for us not to stand out. I was thinking of how wrong I had been to believe that taking a man out was a matter of swift action, impulsive, done on the crest of a wave of great passion.

And there I was, stalking someone, and it felt like the growing of paddy from seed to harvest.

We whispered about the possibilities that could throw us off-course. What if Senapati did not return to the village, but went off somewhere else? What if we lost him in the dark? Or on the long walk back? What if he realised he was being shadowed? What if he was accompanied all the way to the village, all the way to his home? We drove ourselves mad with the chatter of doubts and possibilities.

But luck or chance – same thing – dealt us one good hand after another. First, Senapati left early. He didn't seem drunk: he hadn't forgotten the set of bow-and-arrows he had bought for his children or the other assorted things that we had noticed throughout the day: glass bangles, a big aluminium pot, paper bags of snacks, a disc of solid molasses. He would normally have brought a servant along to carry everything, but he appeared to be on his own. Had he sent for a cart or a rickshaw?

I was now certain that we would lose him on the way back, or be discovered ourselves. As we walked over aals and through fields, I noticed that we were not the only people headed towards Majgeria. It was impossible to determine how many, but I knew there was a group of four between us and Senapati, and a few people behind us. There might well have been several ahead of Senapati too. The cold began to bite in the open country through which we made our way. What if Senapati recognised friends and fell in with them? Our heads and most of our faces were covered with chadors. I found myself thinking random thoughts, skittering about from one worry to another.

Then luck handed us our next two breaks, one after the other. Samir and I noticed that everyone else appeared to have peeled off somewhere, absorbed by the dark. Maybe they were somewhere out there, but we could neither see nor hear any of them. We could not make out Senapati, either. He too had disappeared into the night. My big fear was that if we tailed him too closely he might turn round and notice us or want to talk to us, since it would be apparent to him that we were all headed for Majgeria together and he would want to be friendly and would want to know where we were going and whom we knew and what we did . . . he would probably recognise one of us. But the flip-side of maintaining a safe distance was losing sight of him. I felt I had made one error after another and I was thinking that the whole plan should be aborted, and how best to get the message to Dhiren, waiting back at the village with Shankar for our arrival, when the second piece of good luck presented itself: the unmistakable sound of a man pissing and humming to himself.

If that was Senapati, we were still on track. Yes, it was. My ears picked out the sound of objects being handled – all the stuff that he had bought at the fair and had had to set down to relieve himself. Not a minute passed after I thought this before I negated it: it could be anyone. I knew Samir was even jumpier than I was because he hadn't had a single bidi in this endless walk in the dark.

We were close to the bat tree, near what everybody thought of as the mouth of the village – it was here that a path forked, the left one going to the lower-caste, poorer section of the hamlet, the right to the landlords' and upper-caste neighbourhoods. I counted fifty paces, then ten more, then another ten – he was in front of us, there was no mistaking that now – then I nudged Samir and we broke into the song that one of our comrades back in Calcutta had devised out of the story, in The Little Red Book, of the foolish old man who tried to remove mountains. This was our signal to Dhiren and Shankar.

We were loud, as we had agreed to be, and the words – Boka buro, o you foolish old man / What a cretin you are! / With two mountains in your way / How are you going to go far? – rang out clean and clear in the quiet, cold night. Senapati wheeled round and took a step or two towards us, calling out – Who is it?

Then we were lifted up by the wave I had always thought was the shape of this kind of event and it happened very quickly, all the actions fitting into a portion of time that had itself become compressed into a hair-thin sheet. Senapati turned and started to walk towards us. He could not make us out in the dark. Samir handed me his chador and stepped further away so that Senapati wouldn't be able to see his exposed face.

I had only one chance at this. Only one.

I replied to Senapati – No one. No one you know.

I could tell that he was suspicious – it gave off like an odour, or maybe it was my self-consciousness – because he could instantly tell by my accent that I did not belong here. I moved closer and furled Samir's chador over his head and clamped my hand onto his mouth with all the force in my body and soul and nerves, and whispered in his ear – One little sound from you and you're finished.

The aluminium pot containing the wheel of winter jaggery, the bow-and-arrows, the paper bags of nuts and sweets, all hit the ground and I sensed more than saw everything spill out. Dhiren and Shankar leaped out from where they had been stationed, in the bushes behind the tree, just beyond the fork in the path. They held a tangi each in their hands. Only their eyes were exposed.

I didn't know who drove the tangi into Senapati's chest first, but I heard it – felt it more – as a thud with the hint of a crack somewhere in it. It transmitted itself through the mass of Senapati's body that I was holding so tightly around the mouth and neck. He bucked once, twice, and I had trouble holding onto him. He was trying to lift his legs off the ground to shake me off and ward off his attacker at the same time. Even through the clamp of my hands, an 'aaak' sound leaked out; it did not originate in his throat or mouth, it seemed to issue from where the tangi was buried in him.

Then the second tangi – I didn't know, again, who wielded that one – was lodged in his fat, springy stomach. I was wet with a warm liquid. There was a metallic, peculiar smell that I would only later understand was the smell of blood. I wanted to let him go, but I couldn't. He seemed cemented to me. I tried to push, but it felt as if I'd forgotten how to execute that basic little thing. The more I tried, the more I grasped him to me. We had become one. Then I physically sensed a slackness in his body. I simply lifted my hand from his mouth and loosened my arm around his neck, and he fell to the ground in a sacky heap. He didn't move. It was over for him. My knees gave and I too fell down. Dhiren and Sankar were nowhere to be seen.

Samir whispered very close to my ear – Move!

He put his hands under my armpits and tried to get me to stand. I could discern something in the dark, something on the earth. It felt like a long time before I could identify the toy bow-and-arrows Senapati had purchased a few hours ago at the fair.

This was a beginning.

Later, I didn't know how much later, Samir led me to the pond so that I could wash the blood off my clothes and myself. As I lowered myself into the freezing water, my teeth chattering, my heart beating so fast because of the shock of the cold water that it hurt, Samir recited from memory:

– All men must die, but death can vary in its significance. The ancient Chinese writer Szuma Chien said, 'Though death befalls all men alike, it may be weightier than Mount Tai or lighter than a feather.' To die for the people is weightier than Mount Tai, but to work for the fascists and die for the exploiters and oppressors is lighter than a feather.

A half-moon, slipping closer to the horizon, blackened the trees in front of it.

CHAPTER ELEVEN

Once the complaints began, Charubala found herself facing a flood of them from boys and parents she did not know, had not heard of, did not know where they lived. A bespectacled woman, accompanied by a thin, fair boy who seemed to want to hide behind her, knocked on the door of 22/6 one afternoon and asked to speak to 'Somu's mother'. Standing outside the threshold, the lady, clearly belonging to a different order from Charubala in the way she spoke, the kind of words she used, some of which were English, which left in no doubt that she was one of those educated 'mod' women that Chhaya spoke about – who otherwise would have had the nerve to defy social rules and call on a stranger? – this intimidating woman very politely but sternly pointed out that her son had been coming home lately covered with bruises and nicks and scratches, and on being asked their cause had reluctantly admitted that an older boy called Somu had been bullying the younger boys, hitting and terrorising them. Charubala, cowed somewhat, hardly took in what she said. So great was her relief after the woman had gone and she had shut the door that the substantives of the complaint were forgotten and the accidentals that remained – something blurry about Somu being a rowdy boy – did not deserve to be made a big deal of, so she neither told her husband nor questioned Somnath; it was hardly an important matter.

Then, over time, more evidence began to pile up. Another complaint, this time from a man to Prafullanath; he said that he spoke not only for his two sons, who had been beaten ruthlessly by Somnath, but also for other boys in the neighbourhood. If Somnath was not disciplined, he threatened, then he was not going to be allowed to play in Diana Club any more.

'A bunch of Brahmo ninnies,' Prafullanath said. 'If his sissy boys can't put up with some natural, healthy rough-and-tumble, they should stick with their singing assemblies and other effeminate stuff.'

It was true that Diana Club was a predominantly Brahmo organisation and the boys and young men there, while very good at sport, especially cricket and football, did have the refined genteelness of the community to which they belonged, but this was only an excuse for Prafullanath.

Charubala agreed with her husband's reasoning, but she was reminded of that first complaint; now she was left in no doubt that that fiercely intelligent-looking and eloquent woman was a Brahmo too.

Somnath, never a good student, failed his Class Six exams lamentably; not in one weak subject, as the mitigating case could be, but in all the major ones – English, Bengali, Arithmetic, Science. Despite the indulgent affection lavished on this boy, his worsening performance in school seemed not to have come to his parents' attention at all. When the red-mark-filled report card arrived at the end of the year, there was a little bit of tut-tutting and his father's usual 'It doesn't matter, it's only book-learning, real knowledge is in hands-on experience of the real world.' If Charubala thought this was the last thing he should have been saying, especially within Somu's hearing, she did not bring up the matter with her husband.

While Somnath repeated Class Six, she began to notice other things about him: a certain insolence in his manner, an open defiance of his elders, spending a lot of time in front of the mirror doing his hair, growing it long and combing it over his ears . . . the answering back to his elders and the disobedience seemed so much a continuum of the kind of child he had always been that Charubala would have failed to notice them particularly, had it not been for these other telltale external manifestations of a boy becoming what was known in the culture as 'spoilt', much as one would use the term of milk that had gone off. As if she had invoked their presence by thinking about these attributes, they began to show up. Somu was rusticated from school after being caught smoking in the toilets. Prafullanath raged and ranted, but fell well short of any of the fearsome disciplinary measures that were the common currency – taking a belt to the boy, imposing a curfew; he had never been one for corporal punishment, not because of any high liberal principles, but because his private experience of what went on in the name of disciplining made him unable to mete it out to his own children.

Somnath scraped through the repeated year, just about, then failed his Class Seven annual exams. He was now the oldest boy in his class by more than two years. Over and above the stigma attached to that, there was the burgeoning physical evidence of him belonging to a world beyond a boundary – nascent moustache, broken voice, disparate colonies of acne breaking out on his chin, forehead, cheeks. He hung out in bad company, with similarly overgrown boys who had something of a sullen uselessness about them. Some saw in them a foreboding of a blasted future of mediocrity and misdeeds. When Somnath failed the Class Seven exams a second time, he was asked, as the school rules dictated, to leave St Xavier's. Prafullanath, who did not nurture any great hopes of his youngest son becoming a doctor or an engineer, thought twice about forcing Somu to run the entire gamut of secondary education – better to have him start learning the ropes in the business now – and then reluctantly decided to have him admitted to another school, this time to the downmarket Ghosh Institution, where Bhola had been sent as a child.

Somnath fell into worse company here. Reports of the boy spending most of his time with the futile, unemployed young men who sat on the stoops of houses, killing time chatting and smoking and ogling women, reached his parents' ears. He seemed to be some sort of hero to this group of wastrels because of his prowess in football and cricket. He was indispensable when local teams were formed – Bhabanipur XI or South Calcutta Football Federation, teams of amateur enthusiasts who dreamed of joining at state- or even national-level. 'Somu's leg-spin is a killer,' they said. 'No goalie I know has been able to obstruct his penalty kicks,' they said. But in this world talent did not lead, through intensely hard labour, to the slow scaling of the ladder of achievement; instead, it took the easy lateral route of chatter and talk, and found itself shrivelling more or less exactly at the point at which it had begun to bud. His local fame, confined to about fifty or, at most, a hundred people, pleased Charubala enough. 'At least he's good at something,' she thought.

Somnath stayed out in the evenings well past his six o'clock curfew hour and once or twice returned home long after everyone had gone to bed, sneaking in and going straight up to his room, hoping he would not bump into anyone. He was nervous about the alcohol on his breath, and other signs that he had been drinking. His absence at dinner cast a shadow over the assembled family: not only was he breaking a cardinal rule, but he was also too young to be doing so.

'He's going to the dogs,' Charubala said.

'Not a surprise, considering how you have raised him to your heads,' Chhaya commented tartly.

'Yes, really, he's turning into quite a handful,' Priyo added.

Prafullanath, in thundery mood, took it personally, as a slight to his parenting. 'I'll show that boy today what's what. Let him come back.'

The clouds passed. It was Chhaya who ferreted out the reason for Somu's occasional late, furtive returns. She stayed up, ears pricked, and when she heard the slow creak-and-clang of the iron gate, then the muffled, over-careful opening of the front door, she came downstairs, as if by accident, pretending that she had some business in a room along the path that Somu would have to take to reach his room. She saw him taking one step at a time, very, very gingerly. He looked at her, his eyes bloodshot. He tried to hold onto the banister, but could not manage it in one attempt. Even Chhaya, whose experience of drunken men, swaying in front of her on the balls of their feet, was not frequent, could tell what was going on. The spirituous reek was unmistakable. She pressed herself to the wall as she passed him, as if he were a pool of vomit that she was avoiding stepping on.

The next day, when he surfaced around noon, Somnath found himself facing walls of brooding silence wherever he turned. Charubala, usually persistent with queries about his whereabouts the night before if he had been late returning home, was noticeably absent from his room and then silent as stone when he saw her in the dining room.

'Can one get a cup of tea in this house?' he said, attempting to cover his guilt with a forced light-heartedness.

Charubala, grim-faced, lips squeezed to a thin line, stormed out of the room, her swishing sari and jangling keys tied to the end of her aanchol, sounds that Somnath, throughout his life, had found to be the very definition of a cocooning security, now somewhat like the music of war. Chhaya walked into the room and pointedly walked out again, she too silent. In a trice Somnath understood what had transpired.

No tea from Madan-da, or from anyone, was going to be forthcoming. He noticed that his dinner from last night, usually cleared from the table in the morning if he came in too late to eat, had been left standing, the plate and the small bowls ranged along one-third of its circumference all sitting in a bigger container filled with hot water, a bath to keep his dinner warm, the whole thing covered with a big mesh dome to keep out flies and insects. The warm bath had obviously cooled in the last fourteen hours. It was a still life of the great wrong he had committed.

After fielding this emotional boycott from his mother and his sister, a harsher reminder of the gravity of his misdeed arrived when his father returned home. Before he sat down in the living room downstairs to go through the daily routine of tea and snacks and the solicitous attention of Charubala, Prafullanath summoned Somnath to the boy's room, shut the door, bolted it, took off his belt in a baleful mimicry of an action from another life and brought it down like a whip, over and over and over again, on his son's shocked body. And yet this was no punishment that he was giving out, but an act of revenge; that trembling, crouched figure on the floor was his elder brother Braja; the tables had turned after all this time.

An overindulged, unruly son who had fallen into bad company and had started coming back home drunk, at the age of sixteen: is this what fate had kept in store for him? Prafullanath had turned the thought in his head all day long as he had smoked one cigarette after another in his offices in Old China Bazaar Street. The distance of more than thirty years between that chapter of his past and the present suddenly seemed foreshortened to nothing; the bad blood was flowing in the new one too, no escape was possible. Inheritance was everything, and he and his had got nothing except the negatives: cheated out of wealth and property, stalked by decadence and bad character.

As he lashed his youngest son with the leather belt, that zero distance became real and material to him. *Take that* – the belt came down on the back, curling around to the ribs and upper arms – *and that* – back and bottom – *that, that* – shoulders, arms . . . the cracks were like the air sundering. *At last. I have dreamed about nothing but this moment when I could pay you back for all that you've done to me. This is a beginning. Remember this? Remember thrashing me under the stairs in front of all the servants, thrashing me until I had no breath left inside me to ask you to stop, to ask for water? Remember? Remember?*

Somnath felt more confused than terrified: why was his trembling, spitting, crying father, transformed into a frenzied animal now, repeatedly shouting 'Remember? Remember?' at him? Had he forgotten something his father had enjoined him to keep in mind? Was it some moral lesson about transgression and its consequences? Was it specifically about alcohol? For the life of him, Somu could not remember.

Outside, Charubala hammered on the door, wailing, 'Stop it! Stop it now! Let him go!'

'I've written another short story. Do you want me to read it out to you?' Priyo asked his sister.

Chhaya said, 'Yes, yes! Read it out right now.'

Priyo paced his reading slowly. It was a story about a woman who leaves her husband of forty years because every night he washes his feet and goes to bed while they are still wet, despite her entreating him, every single night of those forty years, to dry his feet before he gets into bed. One day she has had enough. She walks out of their home, saying to her baffled husband, 'I cannot bear you clambering into bed with your sopping-wet feet any more. I'm leaving.' Those words were the last line of the story.

'Bah!' exclaimed Chhaya admiringly. 'Very modern. Like Buddhadeb Basu, or Premen Mittir. I feel like applauding. You know, you will be famous one day, like Rabi Thakur.'

Priyo, basking in her enthusiasm, made a show of deflecting her appreciation. 'Ufff, you and your Rabi Thakur! His days are over. How behind the times you are. It's the age of the ultramoderns, don't you know?'

'That's why I mentioned their names. You will be a star along with them.'

He lapped it up a bit more. In the entire world, only she seemed to understand him and regard his talent truly, to 'get' his work. Everyone else was unresponsive, rejecting. He had been trying for so many years to get a story or a poem published in the cutting-edge literary journals, but they seemed to be staffed by donkeys. Each generation seemed to get stuck on its gods, refusing to move on: first there was Tagore, now there were these modernists, Bishnu De, Buddhadeb Basu and others, territorial dogs guarding their patch from interlopers. Did people really *read* Sudhin Datta's poetry? Did they understand all those teeth-hurting words?

Ultimately, in a backward-moving procession of causes, he blamed his father – he was finding it so difficult to get a foothold in the world of Bengali letters because he had not been immersed in arts and letters from birth, as his father had no truck with the business of culture and literature. He had been born into a family of philistines, and this was his undoing. Take, as a counter-example, his friend from his school years, Susobhan Ganguly. Susobhan had not been demure about recounting his famous grandfather Dwarik Ganguly's exploits at every opportunity he got, and then some. There was one story that had caught Priyo's imagination. Dwarik Ganguly had been, along with luminaries such as Debendranath Tagore, John Elliot Bethune and Vidyasagar, at the forefront of the female-education revolution. On reading a nasty, innuendo-filled editorial against the education of women in a conservative Bengali daily, he had torn out the relevant piece, marched into the editor's office and asked him to confirm that he had written it. Then Dwarik Ganguly had said, 'Right, I have come to make you eat your words', crumpled up the cutting and handed it to the editor with a glass of water, standing by him, his walking stick in hand, until the offending editor had swallowed the ball of paper. Then Dwarik Ganguly had said, 'If I do not see a retraction tomorrow, I will come again.' There had been an editorial the next day, taking back everything written in the earlier one.

This was the family he should have been born into, Priyo thought with a lurch of envy: fierce reformers; progressive, educated people; men whose fathers and elder brothers had been published in *Bichitra* and *Parichay* and *Saturday Letter* before those magazines became defunct. Instead, he had been forced by his father to do a degree in Commerce, then join Charu Paper. While he was competent enough, he assumed, looking after the production side of things, Priyo also held that if you did not love what you did, love it so much that it took up permanent residence in a protected corner of your mind so that you were never without its company, if that kind of love was not there, then you would never be any good at it. You would forever tread the path set down by others, by books, and never advance the subject and extend its horizons. Priyo only felt that kind of love for his literary efforts, not for the business of subjecting the output of the plant in, say, Memari to quality control. Every day he felt let down by what he had inherited and wished for another history, an alternative life.

Only Chhaya understood his soul's very fulcrum, the thing around which all his thoughts and energies turned.

'Tell me, have you written any more poetry?' she asked him now.

Oh, for a poem, a luminous vitrine for his talents, a new, transparent shape in the air through which a different kind of light shone. 'Not for a while. I'm thinking of concentrating on the short story for a bit,' he said instead.

'Wonderful! You too will have a *Galpaguchho* to your name.'

'Ufff, Rabi Thakur again! Can't you think beyond him? People are writing short stories now too – Manik, Buddhadeb . . .'

'All right, all right,' Chhaya said hastily, trying to deflect Priyo from thinking she was backward-looking. 'Where are you thinking of publishing them? Why don't you ask some press to bring out a volume? That'll be fantastic!'

Priyo shrank at Chhaya's move from literary-critical appreciation to the depressing business of, well, business. How much, or what precisely, should he tell her? That he had been trying for the last ten years without getting anywhere? That his writing was for an audience of one: her? That he had never thought of publication – now there was an idea she had given him?

'We all thought Bhola was going to turn out to be the writer,' she said, 'given the way he used to chatter away all the time, creating all these ridiculous tall tales, but it turned out to be the quiet one, you.'

Priyo flinched inwardly at the comparison with Bhola. How distasteful that even Chhaya should bring them together in her head, using the common bond of storytelling. But Bhola was only someone who was afflicted with logorrhoea, and his chatter was just that, chatter; whereas he was the true writer, literally so – he wrote his stories down on paper, they had shape, a design, a *selection* of things from life, a gathering that imposed a paradigm on the formless wash of time and reality. But Bhola? Priyo immediately felt disloyal, thinking this line of thought; Bhola was his brother, after all; a simpleton maybe, but still, connected to him by blood.

And yet, sitting here, talking about Priyo's literary efforts, both brother and sister unspokenly conspired to ignore the loud, pervasive ticking of the clock in the background.

The same ticking was, like the slow rise of an inundation, filling Charubala and Prafullanath's lives. Lying in bed, under the white canopy of the mosquito net, the ceiling fan turned on at full volume to battle the almost-solid presence of June heat, their conversation came back to that unchanging centre.

'The lecturer's family has said no,' Charubala said to the roof of the net.

'Oh,' Prafullanath replied, looking up at the ceiling too. There was enough in that one syllable.

Silence.

'Did they say why?' Prafullanath asked at last.

'The usual excuses: horoscopes not matching, girl too educated . . .' she said.

She imagined the futile beating of the fan's blades, a fast, blurry whirr in the dark. It was going to be another of those long nights.

'Did you tell her?' he asked. They had long reached the stage when they had stopped referring to her, or could no longer refer to her, by name.

'No. What's the use? I can't bear to see the disappointment on her face,' she answered. She paused to steady her voice, then continued, 'At least they didn't, like last time, that engineer, write back to say she was too dark. Or like that family where we had to keep chasing them and they came back with, "She doesn't seem like a home-maker."'

There was real anger beginning to taint her tone. Prafullanath remained silent.

'This business is putting an end to all my nights' sleep,' Charubala declared.

'What if we step up the amount of dowry?' he suggested.

'You have done that on two occasions now, but nothing has come of it.'

'Yes, but what if we increased it further?'

'All is fate. How can we ever go against what's written on our foreheads? I fear . . . that . . . that . . .'

Prafullanath reached out sideways and tried to clamp his hand on her mouth. 'Chhee, don't say inauspicious things like that.'

The sanction made the unsaid even more palpable, as if the thoughts had been waiting outside the room and had at last been given permission to enter; now there was no denying their presence.

Prafullanath and Charubala circled around them in a quaint dance.

'Achchha, what if we got a new set of photos? Got a really good photographer and asked him to do some top-notch studio portraits?'

'How is that going to help? They will eventually have to come here to . . . to see her.'

They had come face-to-face with the unacknowledged party in the dance. They started again.

'What about those families who don't bother to get back after they've visited? Are there any of those still left that we're waiting to hear from?'

'There can be only one meaning to their silence, don't you think? What's the use of contacting them? They'll only come up with the usual excuses.' Pause. 'Or tell us the truth that we all know.'

There, the presence again, unignorable.

Charubala broke part of the taboo.

'Achchha, don't dark girls get married? They are becoming brides by the hundreds, thousands, every day. Our Chhaya is hardly the blackest imaginable,' she said.

In through the opening Prafullanath went, somewhat reluctantly. 'Y-y-yes, that's true. But . . .'

'But what?'

'But . . . I mean . . . her . . . her blackness is a . . . is slightly different, no?'

Silence again, which was answer enough.

Now that the breach had been made, it seemed to hurt them less to widen it.

'Then there is the other matter.'

'I did look into it . . .'

'We should have had it done when she was small.'

'But who could have predicted at the time that a slightly lazy eye would have become so prominent? I suppose others see it more than we do. We live with her, we see her every day, we don't even notice it any more.'

'Yes. Do you remember, one family wrote back to accuse us of lying by omitting to mention it? They were really nasty about it, all respectability thrown to the winds. Thank god our Chhaya didn't end up at theirs.'

'Yes, small mercies. Do you think we should seriously start looking again into the eye-operation business?'

'We must. She's not getting any younger, you know. As it is, she's marred her chances by doing an MA. I told her then, what's the need? Isn't a BA enough? I reminded her that it would be difficult to find a match for her, if she kept doing one degree after another. Do you know what she said? "You seem to be in one hell of a rush to get rid of me. Am I such a burden to you? I am happy to go out and look for a job so I can earn my keep." Can you imagine? I could hardly speak, I was so upset.'

'She has a dangerous tongue, like a knife.'

'She's twenty-six this year. Soon she'll be over the hill. We'll also have to start thinking of Priyo and Bhola's marriages.'

'We haven't been able to get Priyo to renege on his foolish oath of not marrying until Chhaya is married off. Do you think he'll budge?'

Charubala was again on the brink of thoughts she had managed to keep unthought, just about, for many years. She looked into the whirlpool briefly and felt dizzy with . . . with what? Fear? Or shame? She looked away quickly and decided it was a matter of the greatest imperative that either Priyo or Chhaya, and preferably both, got married as soon as possible. This winter, she decided. It had to be.

Why Priyo agreed – on a whim, it appeared to his mother – no one knew. Charubala did not dare ask him in case he went back to his previous position of intransigence. Maybe he had forgotten his foolish pledge, she thought; and let it rest at that. The wedding was rushed through, even though Charubala had her doubts about the girl. Priyo's 'yes' had such immediate weightiness that she did not think about speculative and lighter counterweights on the other half of the scales. It did not occur to her to ask her son why his choice had alighted on Purnima – the caste, the family, the woman herself, everything was a fraction of a degree off – when she, Charubala, had preferred at least three or four of the matches that had come in. There was that shy, modest Datta girl who had so decorously kept her head down throughout the first meeting. The family was not well-off, but that had seemed a small blot. Then there was the pretty, smiley, child-like Das girl; lower-caste, yes, but such a sweet disposition; she would have been such a radiant presence in the house. And she had been as fair as the dawn too. But no; Priyo had to go for a dark, coarse girl, with a voice that could curdle milk instantly. But hers was not to reason why or question; it would not do to look a gift-horse in the mouth. So on a cool February evening Charubala and Prafullanath ticked yet another box in their long list of responsibilities towards their children; two down, three to go. Only Charubala knew that she had ticked her box feebly, with fading ink, for could it be that Priyo unmarried but Chhaya stable was a more desirable option than a married Priyo with a sister who was becoming more intractable by the day?

How much Chhaya had relied on Priyo's rash oath – taken by everyone else as frivolous, as a kind of performance of solemn intentions – became apparent during the days over which the knowledge of Priyo's assent percolated down to the core of her understanding. The occasional match presented to Priyo by their mother: this Chhaya had learned to bat away, for she knew Priyo would go through the motions and then come up with a final 'no'. That the game would change she had no idea. Through all the early stages of the matchmaking, Chhaya had been genuinely unbothered, even, initially, by the news that Priyo had said 'yes'. It could have been disbelief, it could have been denial, but the first contact with the truth was like a stone flung at delicate, innocent glassware. The reassembling took an effort that was hundredfold the energy of the shattering: it was her abnormally pitched voice as she pulled out the trembling words 'What good news! It's time for celebration' from inside her, when she was informed that the final talks between the two families had begun; the way her face seemed so frangible, so effortfully held back from disintegration; the way she seemed scrunched up on herself, but bravely trying to go through the ordinary motions and reactions of life; a smile that never reached her eyes, a mechanical answer, a choked muffledness sometimes at the edge of her voice when she spoke – it was all these that pierced Charubala at the same time as chilling her soul.

Fear. That is what Charubala felt in the presence of her daughter. Ordinary conversations felt like booby-trapped enclosures.

'Have you decided which saris you're going to wear?' she asked her daughter, instantly regretting missing out on articulating the occasion she meant.

Chhaya called her on it; the time for sensitivity was long over. 'Wear when?' she said.

Charubala made her second mistake. 'You know very well when.'

'If you know that I know, then clearly you do too. Why such difficulty in spelling it out?'

Terror had emptied Charubala's mind; she had no response. In any case, Chhaya did not wait for one.

'Yes, of course, I have been thinking a lot about *Priyo's wedding* and what I should wear at *Priyo's wedding*,' Chhaya said, that raggedy edge to her brittly-pitched voice. 'Tell me what to wear at *Priyo's wedding*, on the different days of *Priyo's wedding* – one for each day and another for each night of *Priyo's wedding*. What an auspicious occasion.' Her voice rose higher and higher at each recurrence of what her mother had thought it tactful to leave out.

Charubala cried out, more in fear than anger, 'What's happened to you? Why are you behaving like a madwoman?'

Unnervingly, Chhaya did not snap. Instead she gave a high, unjoyous laugh and turned her back to her mother. Charubala thought that she had turned away to avoid being seen to cry, to appear weak. A long-buried memory shifted in her mind, of an afternoon when this daughter, then much younger, had looked into her soul and confronted her with an insuperable choice. It was too much for her. She would have to ask Sandhya to deal with this, but what precisely was she going to say to her daughter-in-law? She fled from the room, from the sight of that dangerous suppuration.

In the four-month lead-up to Priyo's wedding, Chhaya's behaviour became more and more erratic. She secluded herself in her room, pleading some kind of illness or the other. At times she appeared for dinner wearing stale clothes, her unwashed hair all over the place, looking the picture of wildness, not far from an incarnation of the goddess Kali. At other times she showed up wearing what seemed like a shopful of heavy ceremonial jewellery – bangles up to her elbows, chokers and necklaces, earrings that covered the entire ear – looking even more precarious, her face a mask of a sick excess of powder and snow and lipstick. She resembled a malignant, bloodthirsty goddess even more. On these occasions, with everyone else around her walking as if on eggshells, she asked her rhetorical questions, 'How do I look? Good, don't you think? At least I don't look so dark with all the make-up. What do you think? Why aren't you answering me? Tell me, tell me, why aren't you answering me?' And, poised teeteringly at that pitch, she took off her ornaments, piece by piece, and dashed them onto the floor, against the furthest wall.

Sandhya gently said, 'Chhee, such expensive stuff, and sacred to Lakshmi too, it's not good to hurl these things onto the floor.' She almost crooned the words, as if lulling a child to sleep. 'Give them to me and I'll pick out the ones that will look best on you and match your sari and blouse, come now.'

Charubala thought of the imminent wedding and her hair stood on end; what unknown heights would Chhaya ascend on those climactic days? It did not bear thinking about.

Sandhya suggested, 'Ma, I think Chhaya may be feeling left out. It'll be all right if we involve her in more things. What if we asked her to sing on the evening of boü-bhaat? Such a wonderful singer. She just needs to feel that she too has a role in all this.'

Sandhya was a year younger than Chhaya but relationally her senior, since she was married to Chhaya's elder brother; Charubala had always thought this was a felicitous combination – Sandhya could be a mixture of sister and friend for her daughter and still have a kind of gentle, subtle command over her. In the six years that Sandhya had been in the family, she had taken on more and more responsibilities and become a solid, reliable, gentle sanctuary, but she was also efficient and hard-working. Even with two little sons to look after, she worked in tandem with her mother-in-law as the core that held the Ghosh household together, its central nervous system, its head factory. Charubala foresaw a day in the near future when Sandhya would be running, with her blessing, the entire show, so that when she suggested something, such as this solution to the problem of Chhaya, Charubala was always willing to heed it.

Pointedly Chhaya did not go to the bride's house in Behala for the main wedding rituals; she said she was too ill to move out of bed: nausea, head-spins, high temperature, a throbbing inside her head, palpitations, extreme weakness. A doctor was called. Charubala was torn between extreme irritation – what a fine time to fall sick! in the middle of a frenetic circus at home, with scores of people, decorators, caterers, guests milling around, everyone rushed off their feet – and the need to put on a mask of caring sympathy. Yet something inside her also registered relief. Chhaya was a loose cannon nowadays, and who knew what she would do at the bride's house during the wedding? Best that she remained at home, even if that meant wasting precious time trying to organise people to stay back to look after her and, vitally, to act out, with tears and theatrical excess, a drama of trying to persuade her to come to Behala; she was safe in the conviction that Chhaya would not budge. It set back the wedding by three hours; there was hysteria in Behala that the auspicious hour was passing; Chhaya extracted a tiny morsel of satisfaction from the compounding wreckage of her life.

Purnima arrived that evening to take up residence in her new home. Chhaya did not come down to join the throng of women welcoming bride and groom at the threshold, showering them with paddy and new grass, blowing on conch-shells. Her face was not at her window upstairs, furtively feeding her curiosity about her new sister-in-law. Sandhya found time to visit her, sit on her bed, give a short account of the wedding. Chhaya lay on her bed, silent and somehow abbreviated. Then Sandhya asked, 'Will you be well enough to sing tomorrow? We're all counting on it.'

Chhaya nodded. 'Of course. I'll be fine,' she said. The words, the tone, her expression, all pulled in different directions.

Number 22/6 Basanta Bose Road had turned into a fairground. The 400 invitees were going to be fed in batches on the roof, which had been covered in coloured fabric and lights for the purpose. Long trestle tables had been set up. Flowers, fairy lights, a specially constructed eyrie of bamboo and cloth and planks twelve feet above the front door, to house the shehnai-player and his accompanists as they played one raag after another through the evening, the aroma of pulao and mutton curry and fish-fry and women's perfumes and tuberose – in the midst of all this Chhaya seemed the unappeased wraith who had come back to haunt and curse.

In the big room on the first floor, where the newly-weds sat, receiving guests and the presents they had brought with them, Sandhya ushered in Chhaya. She had suggested this odd thing, that the groom's sister was going to entertain the guests coming in and going out of the room with her singing, but now she was doubtful about the appropriateness of the idea. Charubala had called her aside and confessed her misgivings about it too. But it was too late to go back on the plan. That Chhaya, who was ordinarily so reluctant to perform in public, seizing up with shyness and inhibition when asked to do so, had readily agreed in the first place without any cavilling should have alerted both her mother and Sandhya, but there was a wedding celebration to organise, they had a hundred other things to attend to.

As Purnima was introduced to Chhaya, she got up and then bent down to touch her sister-in-law's feet. Chhaya graciously played the game of coy reluctance, followed by the inevitable giving in. Guests milled around. There were so many people that it did not seem unusual that Chhaya did not once look at Priyo. On Prafullanath's insistence, the house had been turned into a blazing core of light. There were no shadows in that cruel room. The chatter and laughter of people rose and fell like spume on grand waves, swelling and partially disappearing, then appearing again. Word quickly went around that Chhaya was going to sing. Someone was sent off to fetch the tanpura from her room.

Chhaya began with the love-songs of Tagore. Glances of approval were exchanged; her choices were fitting for the occasion. 'I haven't seen him yet but I've heard his flute', 'I yearn to speak what's in my heart but no one wants to know', 'Clouds covered the stars at dusk', the difficult 'What radiance is this that fills my soul?' As so often with Tagore, it was difficult to separate cleanly the spiritual from the romantic, and Chhaya leaned with the full force of her considerable talent on this chord of blurring and made the songs speak with unexpected luminosity. The chatter had ebbed away.

Purnima, looking appropriately bashful, was doing the usual bridal thing of keeping her eyes downcast in a show of modesty. God, she sang well, Purnima thought, but was it one of those families that was all Tagore songs and effete poetry quotations and literature-grazing? Her heart sank.

In Priyo's roiling mind a clear photographic memory bobbed to the surface. A little boy singing, 'I am a lost traveller. O flowers, you, night-blooming jasmine, mallika of the morning, do you recognise me?' And a little girl singing out in joyous affirmation, 'Yes, yes, I know you, new traveller, I have seen the edge of your colourful clothes in the forests . . .' His chest was a tight band. Did betrayal feel like this then?

Now that she knew she had her audience captive, Chhaya began the crossing-over. With two mournful, almost unredemptive songs, 'Both banks of my heart flood over, alas, my companion' and 'There is a thirst in my eyes, a thirst across my entire chest', both more straightforwardly from the 'Love' section of Tagore's songbook, she flicked the mood. No one seemed to notice it, no one registered that something about those two songs sounded some off-notes in a celebratory gathering. But her audience was of one. She knew for whom she was singing and she knew, with the knowledge of someone who has thought another's thoughts, that a meaning occluded from the perception of everyone else was hitting its target with lethal accuracy. But it was not an audience of one, as she assumed; in a corner of the room Charubala wanted to be swallowed up by darkness, to disappear entirely. The meanings that were forming and disintegrating inside her could not be tolerated; she had to turn her mind away from them.

Chhaya moved on to the kirtan-inflected, 'You appear only occasionally, why do I not get to see you for eternity?' At the words 'It's as if clouds move over the sky of my heart, preventing me from seeing you', Priyo felt the bitter taste of treason in his mouth again: it was like cinders, ashy one moment, burning the other. Out of the corner of his eye he saw his mother bring her aanchol to her mouth and hold it there. Nothing could have prepared them for this. Was it revenge, or was it the cry of a fatally wounded animal as it ran around in pain?

And then Chhaya twisted the knife in the final movement. She began by singing the compassion-drenched, minor-mode song that her mother had sung to her as a child to console her when she felt small in the eyes of the world because she was dark: 'Clouds are black, the darkness is black / And scandal too is black / Black is the sin that caused Binodini to be cast out / But blacker than all these, my daughter, is the hair on your head.' In one neat bundling, Chhaya threw back onto the face of the world, like spit, all that it had arrayed against her. She had been born into a melodramatic world; melodrama was the tool she used to banish it from her.

Meanwhile, to Bhola's room on the second floor – Bhola, like everyone else, was mingling with the crowd of guests, friends and relatives – Somnath had succeeded in bringing the housemaid, Meera, on some pretext or the other. He had not only been eyeing up her healthy, curvy, nineteen-year-old's body for some time, but also making sure that she knew he held it in admiration. The lightest of touches on her shoulder, a feathery and seemingly accidental brush of his arm against her breasts, a casually engineered, and equally debonairly executed, full-frontal bump into her while turning a corner – Somnath had played this with the subtle surety of an old rake, as if what he lacked in experience he made up for with the natural expression of something that was coded in him, something that ran in his blood. He did not know what Meera thought about his creeping advance, but she had appeared to be receptive enough, not pushing his hands away or making excuses not to be in his vicinity.

He had clocked all her movements and knew that she had her bath in the afternoon, then went up to the roof to hang her washed clothes out to dry. A fortnight ago he had timed his entry to the roof to coincide with this and had been rewarded with the sense-filling sight of her ripe-fruit breasts brimming out of her blouse as she had tried to put it on. Masturbating himself dry while fondling the memory of that image, Somnath had come to the conclusion that it had not just been a matter of serendipity, that there had been something deliberate, almost provocative, about the way those breasts had spilled out before she, taking all the time in the world, had tucked them in. The whole incident occupied barely five seconds, but it stretched itself in Somnath's mind, adding to his perception of it as pointed, calculated. Over the next ten days or so Somnath planned furiously. He tried to catch her on her own, but was foiled by something or the other. The wedding preparations had made everyone so breathlessly busy that a snatched moment or two of privacy had become even more difficult to come by than it normally was in this populous, ever-public home.

He could hardly lock himself in a bathroom with her; even that would be discovered – somebody was bound to come along and hammer on the door, wanting to use it, halfway through.

And then, amusing Somnath, the opportunity to hide presented itself at the moment of greatest publicness: there was so much going on elsewhere that no one was going to discover them in his brother's room. But he had to hide his embarrassingly obvious erection from her first, so he asked her to fetch a glass of water.

'Come straight back here, don't get roped into doing other stuff on the way,' he said.

Meera shook her head and ran off to do the errand. Somnath reclined on his brother's bed and arranged himself and his clothes to hide his arousal. An odd thing occurred to him: he addressed Meera customarily using the lowest of the three forms of 'you', as everyone in the house did, but he could not think of a single instance in which Meera had spoken directly to him, either using the highest version of 'you', which would have been normal, or the middle one, which would have been disrespectful and impudent for a servant to use with someone of her employer's family, even though he and Meera were more or less the same age. Had she always found ways of speaking to him in such a way that the 'you' had been avoided? How was that possible? The conjugations of the verbs would have given the game away instantly. He had to make her say something now and find out the answer.

Meera walked in with a glass of water. She advanced towards Somnath, he reached out his hand for it, she extended hers to give it to him, then he did not know how it happened, perhaps because of his awkward angle of repose on the bed, perhaps because the timing of the transfer of the glass was a whisker off, but it slipped in the moment of being passed, spilling its entire contents on Somnath's lap.

'Eeesh, jah, it slipped,' Meera exclaimed. 'Let me do it, let me do it,' she said and before Somnath could move or react Meera had whisked off some piece of cloth from somewhere and begun to rub his crotch and lap vigorously, the area drenched by the water, in an effort to soak up part of it. In a dream Somnath watched and felt her rub his rock-hard penis as if it were the most natural action in the world. Was she doing it purposefully? Or was she just dabbing at the wet patch? Did she know, feel, that he had an erection? Why was she continuing to touch his cock as if by accident, if she knew what it was exactly? Or was she so innocent that she had no idea? The swarm of questions came like a trick of light or air, here one moment, absent the other, so that he had no idea, in the giddiness of his sensations, whether he had thought them at all or had retrospectively appended a kind of cerebration to what at the time was only an undifferentiated wash of sense-data. Swelling the excitement was the fear of discovery. He seemed incapable of asking her to shut the door.

Over the drumbeats of his heart he heard his voice whisper from very far away, 'Take it out. Take it in your hand.'

He reached forward to touch her breasts, then, encountering no resistance, pushed his hands inside her clothes to feel them naked against his fingers and palms. Meera deftly exposed his aching cock from the covering of his dhoti and underwear. In the space of two strokes, maybe three, Somnath juddered and came all over her hand. She contemplated the mess for a fraction of a second, then carried on with her earlier wiping as if she were still mopping up the water from the previous spillage. Her face was unreadable. Somnath, released by his orgasm, noticed for the first time that she was wearing new, dressy clothes, probably given by his mother on the occasion of the celebrations. Without a single word Meera finished her business of cleaning up, then left the room with the cloth and the empty glass.

Somnath put his detumescing cock back in place. He would have to put on a new pair of underwear and dhoti; these were too wet to be worn. Or maybe he could stretch out on the bed and contemplate this new milestone in his life. He would have to tell Subir and Deepak and Paltu that he had had his first fuck – the exaggeration was obligatory – that he was not a virgin any longer. He was first off the mark in his group of friends. But now that a barrier had been crossed, would he really get to go the whole distance and fuck her? He felt confident that it was going to happen soon. The idea of it made him begin to get aroused again. Had she deliberately spilled that glass of water? Who was in the driving seat, he or she? Then another thought struck him – he had totally forgotten to test her on how she addressed him.

Six weeks later Charubala discovered her youngest son taking the maidservant, Meera, from behind in the attic prayer room. Its instantaneous effect was the firing of the girl. Horrified by what she had seen, Charubala felt herself incapable of acting in the right way. What were the correct measures to take in a situation like this? The dismissal was a natural beginning, but she could not bring herself to face that filthy creature ever again. So after some deliberation about what kind of loss of face and honour was involved in confiding in Madan – after all was said and done, he was still a servant, on the other side of the line – she got him to do her dirty work, but not before some recalibrating of the scales of power in order to remind him that she, or her side, was not weakened by this. Or perhaps she needed to convince herself.

'It is your responsibility to engage the temporary servants in this house,' she told him off. 'How could you have made such a mistake? You've been in this home for nearly thirty years, you are like one of us.' She did not exactly reveal to him what had brought this on, only giving some vague hints within the general hand-wringing about 'fallen girls' and 'loose morals', leaving Madan to read between the lines. He would, in any case, find out in the servants' quarter what had happened.

'The shame, the shame!' Charubala raged. 'What entered your head that you allowed a . . . a growing, young girl like her to come into a house where there's a boy who's turning into a man? She must be out of this house before the day is over, I don't want to have to tread even on her shadow. Chhee, chhee! And in the prayer room too . . .'

Madan hung his head lower. In the prayer room! They *were* daring, he thought; that at least must be said about them.

'I can't begin to think of what will happen if the news gets out. The whole neighbourhood will come and spit on us. Madan, let no one find out a word about this. Promise me!' Her tone changed to pleading. 'The shame, the shame,' she repeated. 'How much I must have sinned in my past life to have given birth to a son like that!' And at this she gave in to the tears that she had kept in check in front of Madan.

XI

Only he who has dipped his hands in a class enemy's blood can be considered a true revolutionary.

The police did not know where to begin. We feared that they would suspect one of Senapati's debtors. If that crossed their minds, it was not acted upon. I thought this was because there was little by way of formal records of the loans he had given to farmers. We feared a rounding up of the poorest of the village, a raft of trumped-up charges, imprisonment and beatings – but none of these came to pass. Not this time. We were baffled by this quiet indifference on their part.

Meanwhile rumour did its work. Senapati's wife was having an affair, and her lover did it. Senapati had made an enemy of the powerful Sinhas, one of the biggest jotedaars of the area – they lived in Jhargram, but owned about 300 bighas of land around here – and they had had people kill him. Some said the enmity was with the local Rays, another big landowning family. They meant to get the more powerful man whom Senapati was accompanying (no one knew who that was), but got the toady instead. Some unappeased ghost had done it. Senapati had got into a fight about debts with someone drunk. He had tried to have his way with some farmer's wife and the farmer saw it and dispatched him. In twenty-four hours the village was humming and buzzing with stories.

And with fear. You could feel it in the air, a sort of invisible mantle that had come down over everything. The place seemed even more deserted in the evenings. People stayed in because they thought they might be next. A strange sensation had us in its grip – not quite ennui, or quite inertia, but the lull that sets in after you think you've achieved what you had set out to do. I realised how dangerous this feeling was: we had removed one tiny, very minor class enemy, a little minnow in a sea of sharks. Our warfare had only just begun. If we slackened now, we were going to be extinguished in no time at all.

In the bamboo forest at night, Dhiren asked – Have you noticed any change in Kanu or Anupam?

Samir – What sort of a change?

Dhiren – You tell me?

I – No . . . nothing . . . nothing that I can tell.

Dhiren – Maybe it's to do with the rest of the Sorens then. They seem more . . . more daring, less cowed by the people who've been sucking their blood for centuries. I heard Bipul say, Now for a few more to send down Senapati's way. So I said to him, We can do bigger things if we combine our forces, all of you, hundreds of you. They thought – I don't know, this is all speculation on my part – they thought that we were going to egg them on and then disappear, leaving them to do the hard work and face the music afterwards. Now they see that's not the case. And that's what they're talking about among themselves. What do you say?

I – Very possible. And if that's true, we need to capitalise on this trust and sense of unity.

Samir – So all these months of talking Mao to them, it's had some kind of an effect. That, combined with our guerrilla action.

I – So let's make the most of it.

Dhiren, Samir and I, Kanu, Bipul, Shankar, Anupam: seven in total. Shankar said – We can bring more, many more. All the wage-labourers will come. You want?

I – Not now. We may need them later. But no one must know that we're together, otherwise . . .

Kanu – Even if they hack us with tangis, we won't talk, don't fear.

We worked systematically, enjoining them to secrecy at every turn, pointing out the consequences if they opened their mouths even to their wives. First, we made a note of all the jotedaars in the village, where they lived and who their men were. I told them, again, that if even a whisper of this reached the ears of the jotedaars' flunkies . . .

The web was deeply complex. Landlords were also moneylenders; flunkies doubled as pawnbrokers; middlemen and yes-men owned small parcels of land; anybody who owned more than two or three bighas called himself a farmer; on bad harvest years middle peasants rented out their labour, becoming munish for a season or two; big landowning families used the same families of wage-labourers whose earlier generations had been engaged to work for them by their grandfathers or great-grandfathers, making the connections of obligation more intricate, both formal and informal. The landlords had their fingers in other pies too — retail, cement, jute factories, clothing — and ran shops from which the villagers bought some of their basic things . . . All this scratched only the surface. And everyone knew everyone else, so the prospect of secrecy was not very likely. We had had more than a year to think about this, but in a theoretical kind of way. Now that it was crunch time, we found it impossible to draw clear lines of demarcation. A rule of thumb would have to do, so I suggested one, a simple one that everyone would understand and agree on: who was the most hated jotedaar in Majgeria, the one responsible for the maximum misery and injustice and anger? That was as good a metric as any.

Four names emerged: three jotedaars, one overeager toady. The jotedaars — Dwija Ghosh, Haradhan Ray, Kanai Sinha — we had known of before, as we had about the toady, Bankim Barui, himself a small landlord, owner of about seventy-five bighas, a not inconsiderable amount. Bankim had featured in our calculations from the moment we came to Majgeria — Nitai Das used to work for him. Then one day Nitai was dead. Who knows what happened on that last day of Nitai's life? That was unknowable, but what was beyond doubt was the role Bankim must have played, directly and indirectly, in driving Nitai to his destiny.

The shortlist was deceptive. It lulled you into thinking that you had a manageable job ahead of you. We had been lucky with our first attack; that was certainly not going to be repeated.

Then there was the issue of weapons. Because Kanu, Anupam, Bipul and Shankar were adept with lathi, tangi, hashua, daa, spears and javelins, it was best to stick with those. The question no one was prepared to voice was this: what if the people on our list owned guns and were all too ready to use them?

Samir quoted Mao at length — All the guiding principles of military operations grew out of the one basic principle: to strive to the utmost to preserve one's own strength and destroy that of the enemy. How then do we justify the encouragement of heroic sacrifice in war? Every war exacts a price, sometimes an extremely high one. Is this not in contradiction with 'preserving oneself'? In fact, there is no contradiction at all; to put it more exactly, sacrifice and self-preservation are both opposite and complementary to each other. For such sacrifice is essential not only for destroying the enemy, but also for preserving oneself — partial and temporary 'non-preservation' (sacrifice, or paying the price) is necessary for the sake of general and permanent preservation.

Explaining these concentrated ideas in simpler words, I had to grasp that big thorn: what happened if one of us died in action?

Samir said — We knew what we were letting ourselves in for. If we wanted jobs, money, ease, power, influence, we could have stayed on in the CPI(M). When we decided to follow the Chairman and Comrade Charu Mazumdar, we knew we could pay with our lives, become martyrs.

Are you flinching reading this?

Our four new comrades pledged their lives. Anupam said – This is not life that we have. This is a kind of death. If we die fighting so that our children can have better lives, we will die fighting.

He was echoed by Kanu, Bipul, Shankar. There was no reaction that could measure up to this, so we let the silence fall. But not a total silence: there was the sound of bamboo leaves shivering in the occasional breeze.

But this guilelessness – I've wanted to tell you about it for some time. How easily these Santhals and Mahatos had made us one of them. They still fell into the bad old habit of addressing us as 'Babu', but if they had only one plate of rice between five of them, they made sure to share it with us. They seemed to be governed by a 'what is mine is also yours' principle, especially when it came to food and shelter. Selflessness and generosity – that's what I'm trying to say. But also, beyond those, a kind of simplicity, a unity between what they said and what they felt and meant. There was no dissembling or contortion of feelings. I felt as if a kink inside me, one that I was born with, had been smoothed out. Now that it wasn't there, I knew that the knot had bothered me and scrunched up my soul. Yes, these people had filthy mouths and they swore colourfully and imaginatively – I've been busy censoring their speech while reporting to you – but this was of a piece with the simplicity of their hearts.

We banged our heads against that old problem: how to go about mobilising hundreds of farmers without anyone on the other side becoming any the wiser?

Samir offered a line: each guerrilla attack would bring us ten or twenty farmers, so we needed to mount another two or three before word spread to the optimal number of people that we wanted to attract for a bigger squad action. They would come and offer to join us because it would be clear to them that we were doing something. That was Samir's reasoning.

This sank in and seemed sensible. It would be foolish to fritter away time. The police were going to be here sooner rather than later, so why not take advantage of the lull?

Bipul said that the easiest home to raid would be of Bankim Barui because it was in the middle of Majgeria, whereas the really big landlords, the owners of hundreds of acres, didn't live in the village proper. They had large, concrete homes in bigger villages or small towns in Binpur or elsewhere in the district, mostly in Jhargram. Those could be target projects for a later phase of the revolution, not now, Bipul added.

Crucially, there was his connection with Nitai. It was odd that although we didn't speak about it, all of us knew that there was an inevitability about picking on Bankim. We went through so many planning sessions to settle on the most appropriate person to attack, but that choice had already been made for us by history.

So Bankim Barui it was. We knew he had about seventy-five bighas of land, most of which had been acquired by evicting farmers who had been poor tenants. He was up to all kinds of tricks: falsification of deeds of lease to facilitate his land-grab; being aggressive about letting the police loose on farmers who were protesting at his crimes and also slapping trumped-up charges against them . . . The usual, then.

Bankim's house was two-storeyed, built of brick and cement. There was a courtyard at the back; unenclosed land to its west; another, smaller tract of land enclosed by a woven-cane barrier to the south of the garden; a front door set in a box of a balcony, and a back door leading to the courtyard; about six rooms in total on both floors, not including kitchen and bathroom. There was also an outhouse in the south garden and two golas for grain storage. It was surrounded by five similar houses and about half a dozen much smaller affairs. Kanu and Anupam provided us with other vital pieces of local knowledge: Bankim lived there with his elderly mother, his uncle (late father's brother), his wife, their three children (all under twelve or ten), two servants and his uncle's son, who had a job in another village, Barashal, and visited frequently but was away at the moment.

We decided to strike around 2 a.m.

Shankar, Samir and I, faces covered, broke down the front door with a spear and a tangi. It gave after about six to eight blows, then we rammed it, all three of us, with our shoulders, and got in. The other four were stationed at the back door (we were certain that Bankim was going to try to use that route to escape). We heard the terrified screaming even before we entered. What if the cries for help brought people running, armed and ready to defend Bankim? Villagers were known for the closeness of neighbourly ties, unlike cities. Too late, it was too late to worry about that.

No one in the front room. We moved to the next one. An old man in a vest and a lungi was trying to hide under the bed. This, we assumed, was the uncle. A punch would kill him. We dragged him out by his feet and pushed him into the dark kitchen, but just as we were about to lock him inside we noticed a boy, maybe fifteen or sixteen years old, the servant, probably, cowering in a corner but with a lathi gripped in his hand. The screaming from upstairs, a chorus of women and children, was now in full swing. They were standing on the front verandah upstairs, shouting – Help! Help! Robbers! Robbers!

The servant boy couldn't decide between trembling like a leaf and attacking us. I decided for him: I brought my tangi to his neck and said – Sit quietly here, one word or one move from you, your head will be rolling on the floor – and pushed him to the corner. Then I got out of the kitchen and fastened the chain on top of the door to the hook on the lintel post. I felt I'd done all this in the space between one inhalation and one exhalation. And there was an odd sensation: my heart was beating so hard and so fast that it seemed it had actually slowed down to those few beats in between that knocked against my chest. The rest I could not feel, but I knew they must be there.

We rushed into every room downstairs – three in total – and scanned every possible place that could be used for hiding: behind an almirah, under another bed, under a divan. Then we stormed upstairs. This was what I had been waiting for. The screaming people had barricaded themselves inside the front room, the one connected to the verandah. I had a feeling Bankim was hiding there too. We needed to get in there to shut them up. What if Bankim managed to climb down and escape from the front while we had our comrades waiting at the rear? We forced open the door – the screaming had stopped – after hacking it with tangis, then pushing a spear through the crack to make out what it was that they had pushed against it. The big bed. How on earth did Bankim's wife and children manage it? Bankim <u>must</u> be in there. It would take some time to push it away, so we splintered the door to pieces and stepped on the bed to enter the room. No Bankim, or not obviously, but a boy of ten or so, a younger girl, their fat mother and an old woman, all squatting or crouching in the furthest corner, some squeaking, some frozen.

Samir shouted at them, much the same words that I had used in the kitchen downstairs. Bankim's wife gave out a shriek, which she had the good sense to cut short, knowing that more screaming was not going to be doing her any favours. We ransacked the room. When Bankim's wife refused to hand over the keys to the big almirah, Samir grabbed hold of the girl (more shrieking, ear-splitting this time), pulled out the hashua he had had Kanu tie around his waist with a gamchha and held it against her neck. The keys were produced before we could blink.

At this point a huge commotion began outside. It came from the back of the house, drowning out the racket the stray dogs were making at the front. I ordered Shankar and Samir to search the room and the verandah and ran to the back through two rooms, both empty. I couldn't see what was happening in the dark, but there were shouts of – Beat the ***! Beat the ***! (unspeakable abuse, not for your ears) and there were far too many people. I couldn't make out how many, but many more than the four from our squad. Before I could understand how foolish it was to make myself known (they could be paid guards, neighbours trying to fight us, people otherwise in the pay of or obliged to Bankim, even the police), I shouted – What's going on down there? What's happening?

Dhiren answered – Come down. We've caught the ***.

My head reeled. Who were all these people then? If our squad was under attack, how come Dhiren was in any position to reply? Wouldn't he be fighting, or running away, hiding?

The action was happening in the courtyard, spilling out into the adjoining land. Two brands had been lit and in the meagre, flickering light of these, I began to discern what was going on. A tight circle of fourteen or sixteen men, all holding some kind of weapon, had surrounded Bankim, who was now a corpse. He looked like a bulging sack of grain that had fallen out of the back of a truck. There were two spears through him, one through his neck, another through his shoulder and upper chest.

– Shala was trying to escape around the back; poor *** didn't know we were waiting for him in the dark. Trying to escape leaving the women and children to face the music. Didn't have a chance, the dog. We didn't even let him finish his miserable begging – Forgive me, forgive me, I've done a great wrong, it'll never happen again, forgive me, I'm falling at your feet – but beat him down to the ground and then whack, whack, two javelins straight into him. All over.

Dhiren was at my side, saying – The noise brought other farmers over. They came to help us out. Look, they have lathis and tangis and spears . . .

I felt dizzy. Was this true? Had the unthinkable, something we hadn't dared hope for, something that was the acme of all our striving and actions, had that come to pass with such ease, without us being even aware of it?

I was still in shock. My heart was rattling, but it was a different kind of motion and sensation now, much closer to those moments of intense joy of childhood. I wanted to shout and embrace everyone and tell the whole world that revolting against oppressors was the natural state of man.

There were two golas in the courtyard, one much larger than the other. The smaller one housed seed-paddy, the larger husked rice – for consumption, or selling, or for the other purposes to which it was unfailingly put: smuggling, lending it to extort interest or bind the farmer into ever greater ties from which he would never be able to free himself. The grain that gave life and took it away too.

I said to Dhiren and Kanu — Distribute everything. Equal amounts to all.

In the main bedroom, which Samir and Shankar had turned upside down, Bankim's family was still cowering. I whispered to Samir — Good news.

Bankim's wife cried out — Please let us go, spare us, spare the little children, they've done no wrong . . .

I took an instant decision not to tell her about her husband. She would find out soon enough.

I rapped out — Shut up or I'll slit your throat. And your children's. Where's all the money and jewellery? Where?

She quaked and wept, a ham actress in a bad film. Even in this moment of great danger, faced with such a threat, she was reluctant to reveal the whereabouts of her material possessions. For a second I toyed with the idea of giving her a few blows with a lathi, but instead I got Samir to try out the keys on the huge wooden almirah in the room. Everything of any value was bound to be in there. It took some time, but we got there in the end: 3,000 rupees in cash, a fair amount of jewellery, no guns . . . but that wasn't what I was looking for.

— Listen, take all that stuff, everything you can get your hands on. But look for documents: loan documents, stamp paper, lease deeds, deeds of sale . . .

They were not in the almirah. Samir said — We turned up a wooden box. It was on the verandah, with a pillow on it, pretending to be a seat. Then I noticed it had a keyhole and hinges . . .

We broke open the box. There was no time to fiddle around with keys. Yes, a loose stack of papers, some with revenue stamps on them, some with thumb imprints.

We took it down to the courtyard and set the whole thing on fire. The papers in it caught instantly. The box took its own time, but eventually it too went the way of the documents.

The farmers downstairs were busy filling sacks and clothes and gamchhas with grain from the storage rooms.

CHAPTER TWELVE

Madan timed it well. A month after he sacked the maid Somu had seduced, he came to Charubala with his petition.

'Ma, my son is growing up. He's a year younger than Chhoto-babu. It's not a good idea to keep him in the village any longer.'

'Why, what's wrong with your village?' Charubala asked.

'There are no jobs to be had. Everyone says that now that the sahebs have gone, they are giving jobs in the big cities to our own countrymen.'

'Yes, everyone says it, so you believe it. What sort of a naïve man are you? So, what will your son do? Be a cook like you? I can ask around.'

'No, Ma, not a cook. I was thinking of some kind of a job in Calcutta, like an electrical shop . . .'

'Electrical shop?' Charubala seemed surprised. 'How on earth are we going to find him an electrical shop? And what do you mean: working in someone else's shop or setting up his own?'

'No, no, not his own,' Madan replied hastily. 'Where's the money for that? But if Baba can find him something – he knows so many people . . .'

'So talk to Baba then. You see him every day, you live in the same house. What's the big deal?'

Madan looked abashed. 'No, Ma. If you mentioned it first to him . . . then maybe . . .'

'Ah, I see,' she said. Now that she understood what it was Madan had in mind, it became easier for her to talk it through with him.

'Yes, of course, I shall mention it. Have you given much thought to what it is that you want your son to do? He's only sixteen years old. Will he finish school this year?'

'Yes, Ma, this year. He can read and write. If something were to come up . . . If something could be found in one of Baba's mills or factories . . .'

More and more of the picture was beginning to get illuminated for Charubala. Yes, what a good idea, why had she not thought of it herself? This would be a good thing for Madan; she would make it her business to intercede. She performed a rapid calculation in her head, a piece of arithmetic that she has done without thinking an uncountable number of times over the years; a number, which never failed to amaze her despite its familiar and clockwork changeability, presented itself at the end of the process: next year Madan will have been with them for thirty years.

When Charubala's children were grown-up she used to remark frequently, 'It is Madan who has raised them, on his lap and his back.' Prafullanath and Charubala guessed Madan was about ten years old – his birth was not registered, so neither he nor his family knew his exact year of birth – when he started working for them in 1922, while they still lived in Baubazar. Adinath had just turned one and was crawling everywhere on his hands and knees, trying to lift himself up and start walking, putting every bit of rubbish he chanced upon into his mouth first. Madan had come from a tiny village in Nuapada in the province of Bihar and Orissa, led by his uncle, who was the cook in a neighbour's house. He began as the general dogsbody, helping Charubala around the house: he ran errands, swept and cleaned the rooms, did the odd task that was required of him at any given moment – carrying the bags of shopping in from the car, fetching a glass of water, making tea, bringing food from the kitchen to the table, moving a chair; he was the beck-and-call boy of the house. He looked after the children for short periods when Charubala was engaged in other things. He picked them up and carried them around, singing to them and rocking them if they grizzled or cried. 'Careful, careful,' Charubala laughed. 'You're leaning sideways under the weight of the child, you're hardly any bigger than him.' Like Prafullanath and Charubala's children, he too called them 'Baba' and 'Ma'.

Charubala, whether in shrewd speculation about the future or out of the compassion in her soul, also started giving the illiterate young boy, a year or two after he came to them, lessons in Bengali and basic arithmetic.

Prafullanath teased her, 'Good plan. When he's totally competent, I shall give him a job at the office and you'll have to find another servant.'

'Stop joking,' she said. 'I have my misgivings: I hear so many stories of people educating their servants and then the upstarts leave their homes and go and get a better job elsewhere.'

Still, Charubala managed to bury her qualms and be generous; she felt a tug in her heart when she saw the motherless boy's shrunken little face and rickety arms and legs. Slate and chalk were bought for him and she wrote out the Bengali vowels and consonants on the slate and asked him to trace his chalk over each of those at least a dozen times, while saying aloud the sound of the letter at each repetition. They progressed slowly to *Barna Parichay* and numbers, elementary addition and subtraction, then to multiplication and division. Madan was given paper and pencil, but he struggled to find the time to do his lessons in the erratic and increasingly rare lulls between his duties. Sometimes he tried to put in an hour at night, after everyone had gone to bed, but failed to keep his eyes open after the first ten minutes. He tried to make use of the afternoons, when everyone had a nap and he had his first uninterrupted break for the day.

'Orre, where's Chhaya gone? See if you can find her,' a cry would reach him. Or 'Where's Bhola? I don't see him. Quick, quick, he's learning how to climb the stairs, see that he doesn't go up to the roof.' Any call or order without a name was for him to answer. It was this fragmented miscellany of tasks that ate into his studies. The enthusiasm and desire to learn, always there, saw him through. Despite the fitful application, Madan could read passably well and even write by the time Adi and Priyo were initiated into the 'chalk-in-hand' ceremony, although his spelling was parlous and his letters uneven, crooked, amateurish. When Bhola reached school-going age – they were ensconced in Bhabanipur by that time – Madan was not just functionally literate but fluent; he read the books the boys read: the illustrated children's *Ramayana* and *Mahabharata* by Upendrakishore, Tagore's

Katha o Kahini. He even started on English, but never progressed much beyond the alphabet and 'cat', 'bat', 'sat'; lack of guidance and time, increasing responsibilities, a whole household on his shoulders, all put paid to that ambition.

By now, Madan's Oriya accent had been almost totally leached out of his Bengali. But when he was younger, and for quite a few years after the family moved to Bhabanipur, Charubala and Adi and Priyo loved to poke fun gently at his accent; it was one of their occasional and reliable entertainments at home. It had taken him a while to work out why they so frequently asked him to sing songs that he had picked up in his village.

'Go on, Madan, sing that one you sang last week, the wedding one,' they implored.

The innocent seventeen-year-old, in the clutch of shyness, demurred but ultimately had to oblige. 'Girl's wedding, girl's wedding / Everyone is crying silently on the wedding day / Their eyes are streaming with tears,' he sang, his voice nasal, the melody plangent, wailing at regular intervals, and oddly pitched, the lyrics impenetrable, 'The wedding sari was chosen after looking at fourteen markets / It was one hand long, wide from thumb to little finger / The bride wore it in pleats.'

At the Oriya expression for pleating, *kunchi-kanchi*, so primitive to their refined Bengali ears, Charubala and Adi collapsed, shuddering uncontrollably with laughter.

Priyo, all of seven years old, was too young to know what was going on, but he could read that it was ridicule, albeit affectionate, that was making his mother and Dada double up.

'Did you then "doonce" at the wedding?' Adi asked, trying, and failing, to keep a straight face as he picked out Madan-da's Oriya inflection of the word 'dance'. 'Come on, do a doonce for us.'

Priyo pranced about, addressing him as 'Udey', the pejorative term for people from Madan-da's province, and mocking, 'Udey babu, udey babu, doonce-u for us-u.'

Madan knew that he was being laughed at and felt an inchoate sense of humiliation, which did not, could not, grow, because they were his masters who were making fun of him. What could he do, except join in with them, laughing along aimlessly, a bit foolishly, with their more pointed laughter directed at him? But he really did not mind; he knew he had come from a backward village; these were city people, born and bred, they knew better; he too laughed at his backward ways of speaking.

Charubala put Madan's preternatural affinity for cooking down to his Oriya origins. She taught him the basics – which spices went with which dal; that hilsa was never cooked with onions, ginger and garlic; shukto was flavoured only with mustard seeds and ginger – and he consolidated that with an ease and talent that showed he had the real 'cook's hand'. He never burned the rice, oversalted or undersalted the food, made the staple fish stew too watery. Charubala did not have to guide him through every single step of a dish; a brief set of instructions before he began was sufficient. He did not make any mistakes or forget the recipe when he prepared the dish the next time. He introduced them to new tastes, new dishes that he picked up from his more experienced uncle or brought back, when he was older, from his annual trip back to his village; they were things unfamiliar to the Bengali palate.

Charubala tasted the dal at lunch one day and said, 'What's this? I don't think I ever taught you to make this.'

Madan, nervous, almost hiding behind the door, answered, 'No, Ma, this is biri dali.'

'Oh, you mean biuli-r dal. It's delicious,' she exclaimed. 'What did you do?'

'I toasted it first,' he said shyly, 'then I fried panchphoron and chopped garlic and whole dried red chillies in mustard oil and added it to the boiled lentils.'

'I've never had it before. Is this from your "country"? You must cook this more often for us.'

It became known as 'Madan's dal'. Over time, things came to be called 'Madan's stem-vegetable fry' or 'Madan's fish' (fish cooked with curry leaves and mustard and garlic paste with lime juice added right at the end, an unconservative way of cooking something, over which Bengalis thought they had a monopoly of inventiveness).

He even made thrift inventive. After squeezing out the milk from grated coconut, instead of throwing away the grounds, he mixed them with sugar and cardamom powder and set them in lightly oiled stone moulds in the shape of fish or abstract patterns. He fried up the gills and fins and bones of fish with garlic and chilli powder; this became so popular with the servants that Charubala heard of it, tasted it herself and became an instant convert. In later years Chhaya, as a young girl of twelve, developed a mild addiction to it. Madan firmly set his signature to dishes that one could get only in 22/6: fritters of mutton fat served during teatime at 6 p.m.; banana-flower croquettes; stems and buds of pui cooked with tiny whitebait. Charubala sent up thanks for his Oriya blood and never forgot how lucky she had been in finding Madan. Neighbours told her, only half-joking, 'We'll steal him from you one of these days . . .'

Because Madan came to run this vital segment of the household – grocery shopping, cooking, suggesting what should be served to guests or at events such as birthdays and pujas and celebrations – he became not only indispensable but also, over time, someone whose say on certain domestic matters carried some weight, whose opinion was frequently consulted. For example, the maids who did all the menial jobs in the kitchen – cutting vegetables, cleaning and gutting fish, doing the washing-up – were engaged only after they had been approved by Madan. Even the maids-of-all-work, responsible for the laundry and sweeping and swabbing the floors, were hired with Madan's consent. In time, as the household grew and more servants had to be engaged, Madan came to be a sort of housekeeper in charge of all of them.

As if this level of correspondence with culinary matters – and, later, the business of domestic staff arrangements – were not enough to make Madan a great catch, there was his wonderful way with the children. As with the kitchen matters, Charubala found him such a safe pair of hands that she left a substantial part of the childcare to him. Madan would be asked to keep an eye on the crawling babies or the unsteadily walking children – for several years Priyo, Chayya and Bhola formed one continuum of that – so that they did not fall, bang their heads, injure themselves or put dangerous things in their mouths. He would be asked to distract them when they refused to eat. Before long, he was asked to spoon food into their mouths as well. He helped Charubala when she bathed, dried and put talcum powder on them before easing them into their clothes. In winter, he massaged them with mustard oil, left out to warm in the sun, before they had their baths. When the four-year-old Bhola tried to pick up a caterpillar from the trunk of the guava tree in the garden, it was Madan who comforted the bawling child and extracted the barbs, one by one, from his forefinger and thumb. When the children were naughty or recalcitrant, and distracting or bribing with toys and games and goodies did not work, Madan tamed them with the thrill of fear.

'Don't go near the guava tree after dark. You see those big branches' – here he pointed out the limbs of the tree – 'those are actually the legs of the she-ghost who lives there. At night the branches move in the wind, but they are really her legs and hands that are moving, beckoning naughty children, so that she can wring their necks and drink their blood.'

The children's eyes widened with terror. Chhaya was too scared to cry out. They huddled closer and avoided the garden after dark. They sat at the windows at the back of the house and willed themselves to see the she-ghost's dangling limbs. Charubala's wish that the children stayed indoors after nightfall was effected in one neat stroke.

At other times Madan got carried away by the momentum of his tales. One autumn afternoon, when the six-year-old Chhaya was picking shiuli flowers fallen on the grass to use the saffron stalks to dye the clothes of her dolls, Madan said, 'Don't pick those flowers. Don't you know why the plant sheds them? L-o-n-g before you were born, a little girl used to live in this house. When she was six she died of the pox. Her family buried her in the garden and planted the shiuli on her grave. In autumn, which was when she died, the flowers are shed on her grave as an offering.'

For a few minutes Chhaya remained transfixed. Then her lips quivered, her chin wobbled; a bout of weeping followed. Madan, who always brought a bag full of toys for the children when he returned from the annual visit to his village – tin whistles; little figurines made out of sal-leaves, fragile and ephemeral in the hands of the children; apple-seed necklaces; gaudy plastic objects such as toy maces, rattles, dolls – came back with extra toys for Chhaya later that month: a pair of clay dolls, Radha and Krishna, with their features and clothes and ornaments painted on them in garish colours; a bheesti with eyes drawn in black ink and lips in the deepest shade of red.

Imitating their parents, Adi, Priyo, Bhola and Chhaya had all begun by calling Madan by his first name, but Charubala had firmly seen to it that they always addressed him as Madan-da. She never ceased telling her neighbours, 'Our Madan is part of the family' or 'He is like our eldest son.' But despite all this apparent oneness between servant and master's children, an invisible membrane separating the two worlds never got breached. It was as if a supra-surveillant intelligence, invisible itself but ordering all and keeping everything within the design of things, which was meant to remain unchanging, ever so, was ceaselessly invigilating a flexible barrier that could be moved only so far and no further. Without ever being instructed on what he should call his master and mistress's children, Madan fell to addressing the boys as 'Bor'-da', 'Mej'-da', 'Shej'-da' and Chhaya as 'Didi-moni' from their infancy, breaking a lesser law, of chronology and seniority, in order to honour a superior, overarching one of social hierarchy. While singing to them, when they were still babies, a traditional children's rhyme, 'Come, come, o long-tailed bird / Come and play with ——', in that blank space where he should have inserted the name of the child he was singing to or distracting, Madan invariably inserted the relational status.

And this man now, his son older than he, the father, was when he came to work for the Ghoshes and stayed on for a period longer than any of her offspring, except Adi, has been part of Charubala's life, has brought himself to ask her for a favour, possibly for the first time.

She smiled and said, 'But there are no factories or mills in the city itself. It'll have to be in a town elsewhere. Then we've lost two or three factories to East Pakistan recently . . . On top of that, there is this wave of refugees swamping us. All of them want jobs in the city. From what I hear from your baba and Adi and others, there are really no jobs to be had. But let me ask. Will a small town do? The Calcutta jobs are all in offices . . . he'll have to be a peon somewhere.'

'Yes, Ma, small town will do very well. It's just that the villages in our place . . . there's nothing there. If you don't have land to farm, then the prospects are really nothing.'

'All right, I'll talk to your baba and let you know.'

She was true to her word. Prafullanath put the matter to Adi and Priyo.

'Well, there's always the need for another pair of hands in a mill,' Priyo said.

'We can find him something in Bali,' said Adi.

'Yes, that's what I was thinking,' said their father. The mill at Bali was their biggest possession. In a depressed post-war market, the Ghoshes had not done too badly. From Prafullanath's export-market contacts they had picked up rumours of an imminent shortage of grey board and had hoarded it. Then, through the war years, they had released it very cautiously – they did not want the King's government to requisition their entire production and their private properties too – but with the condition that for every unit of grey board purchased, a stipulated number of units of paper would also have to be bought. This paper was supplied, of course, by the Ghoshes' mill at Memari. So when the recession of '46 began the Ghoshes were better placed than most. While the mills at Ilam Bazar and Nalhati continued to lie shut, the loss of Meherpur and Chalna in '47 was at least offset.

'Let Dulal work in Bali for a while. We're stepping up production there, so we'll need to hire more workers. Depending on how he does, he could keep an eye on the labour situation for us,' Prafullanath said. 'I trust you know what I'm trying to say.'

'Yes, he could be our inside man, as long as no one else finds out how he came by the job,' Priyo said. 'We'll have to ask him to keep his mouth shut.'

'All right, it's agreed then. Madan will be happy,' Prafullanath said.

So it was that Dulal, Madan's sixteen-year-old son, joined the Ghoshes' paper mill at Bali as one of the several labourers who worked 'on the floor', drawing water to feed the pulping pits, stirring the vats, laying out the pulp in frames. Later, because he had the advantage of literacy and numeracy over most of the other workmen at his level, he was put in charge of the electrical equipment. In two years he had moved up to the rank of unofficial head of the workforce of 250 that kept the mill operating, then, in another year, to de facto manager of the Bali outfit; still under a formal manager, appointed by Priyo on one of his visits to oversee the company's production units. It was becoming a matter of tacit knowledge that Dulal was the man who, at twenty, understood every nut and every bolt of the actual work done at a paper-manufacturing factory.

In the thirty years since Prafullanath had set up Charu Paper, a kind of moderate success had come his way, although he would have been the last person to see it like this. Caught in the daily battle of making his two factories cleave as closely as possible to their maximum yields, he had only just let the niggle of continuing to produce on average 180–200 TPD, instead of the perfect 250, become consciously negligible. Still, it was a 45–60 per cent increase on what he had started out with; not to be sniffed at, although it had taken the best part of seventeen years to get to this point. In moments of self-doubt and anxiety, however, the debit column seemed to be endless. Two factories, albeit fallow, lost to East Pakistan, the money written off. Two more factories yet to be repaired, refitted and reopened; the investment required was too huge to contemplate. The fluctuating nature of the output at Memari and Bali, never a steady average of 200 TPD every year: issues of quality control, a late delivery of some chemical, a roller malfunction, a mistake with the metered amount of lacquer entering the Fourdrinier machine, minor accidents with careless and unskilled labourers who didn't understand the basic functioning of electrical equipment . . . the list was dizzyingly proliferating. After all these years Prafullanath was still occasionally thrown by an error he hadn't encountered before. At least the appointment of Dulal could theoretically troubleshoot some of those minor problems that had such a disproportionate effect on production.

And yet Prafullanath couldn't cavil with the real benefits that he and his family had cumulatively begun to enjoy: three cars, more money to spend on household expenses, servants to take care of the running of such a big house and the needs of the people who lived in it, frequent purchases of gold jewellery, a growing portfolio of land, swelling savings accounts and fixed deposits and life insurances. They were comfortable. Prafullanath hadn't let the spectre of daily economies and cutting corners, always such a threat, ever materialise. Now that the domestic front had been secured, it was time to turn his attention to the consolidation that had long been his dream. He had laid a strong foundation and brought in his sons to the business. Now it was up to this family team to work together. What were they going to do with the profits?

While Adi, conservative to the core, asked his father to hold on to his gains, Prafullanath was all for using them to modernise the factory at Memari. 'Money begets money,' he had always maintained. 'If you can't make it work to breed, then you'll end up consuming it. We can double the TPD of Memari with new, imported machines. Triple it, even.'

'I think it may be best to sit on our war chest a bit longer,' Adi suggested. 'What's the harm? The interest will not be inconsiderable. What if trying to step up production turns out to be the wrong strategy?'

Prafullanath said to his son, 'Listen, I hear Nehru is going to announce the first five-year-plan next year. Where our sector is going to be in the scheme of things is anybody's guess. I would imagine not very high up. Now is the time to modernise. There will be a whole new set of regulations to deal with then, a new regime of subsidies and taxation and duties. I have a feeling it's not going to be rosy at all. Besides, we know all the middlemen in these deals, we know what they want, they know how reliable we are in keeping them happy, we know how reliable they are in expediting matters – why not take advantage of this comfortable set-up? Who knows when it'll all be gone?'

'All right then,' Adi conceded. 'But why not think of other interests? Not big ones, such as mines and minerals or the heavy industries – these would be state-owned, in any case – but what about something related to the line we're already in, like publishing?'

'Publishing?' Prafullanath and Priyo asked in unison.

'Yes, publishing. Why don't we start a press? Under these five-year-plans education will emerge as an important sector, don't you think? We already have a kind of "in", being paper men.'

Prafullanath and Priyo absorbed the new idea in silence. A thought was forming in Priyo's mind.

'Yaaaairs,' said Prafullanath slowly, mulling it over. 'Not a bad idea, not bad at all.'

Priyo played his card tentatively. 'Actually a good idea, I think. We solve two issues together – lateral expansion and . . . and Bhola. He can look after the publishing house. I think it would be more his kind of thing than straightforward business.'

At the mention of Bhola's name a fidgety embarrassment descended on the three. He remained the strand of hair that did not fall in to lie down with the rest, when oil and water and comb were rigorously applied. There was the periodic turning-on of the great fountain of words and fabulism, then there was that undimmable, slightly simple smile, the ever-present suggestion of imminent drool at the corners of his mouth, the spiky hair, the infinitesimally awry movements and physical awkwardness – they all added up to a person who gave the impression that he had not received enough nourishment in his mother's womb and had come out semi-formed. And yet there was nothing medically or physically wrong with him, only a kind of off-centredness and a touch of the holy fool. All the Bengali terms used for him – 'grinning idiot', 'not quite there', 'otherworldly', 'like Shiva' (alluding, of course, to the god's playfully child-like aspect) – were at once pejorative and not inaccurate. He was twenty-four and, now that Priyo was married, Prafullanath and Charubala would have to start thinking of finding a wife for him, but who was going to marry a simpleton? Prafullanath would never admit this, but Charubala knew that he looked upon his third son as a kind of personal failure, much in the way a poet knew, in the innermost cloister of his soul, that one poem in his collection did not quite deserve to be made public through the medium of print; it was a shame felt at his deficiency in the making, not at his son's apparent defect.

Bhola, on the other hand, seemed oblivious to how he was perceived. A certain percentage of the shares of Charu Paper was in his name, but he did not bother about it, nor was exercised about the fact that, unlike Adi and Priyo, he did not have a fancy designation to go with his decidedly unfancy job in the family firm, a mere bookkeeper, a director only in name, not in practice. It could be said of him that while others chased the mirage of happiness, he was happy with being content. And it appeared this was not something that he had arrived at after strenuous meditation or struggle, or application of scrupulous moral principles; it was an ease and carelessness he had been born with. At times Charubala thought that it was Bhola's armour against the world; if it was, it had not been donned consciously. But there he was – a creature who moved a few inches above the ground on which everyone else walked.

But this very unworldliness proved an impediment to the plans Prafullanath had for Charu Paper and the ancillary companies he hoped his sons were going to own and manage. Bhola was crippled by a blind trust in people. He smiled too much, too often, and told them things that should never have left the office. He worked well enough when he was set a task, but had no initiative and, worse, no capacity for thinking creatively about business. Initially Prafullanath had thought that Bhola could look after the company accounts and be guided by him and his older brothers in the more creative aspects of company accounting, but very quickly he realised that even that called for sharp thinking, the capacity for which Bhola lacked.

Last year Adi had discovered a one-lakh-sized hole in the company accounts. When he had asked Bhola, his brother had pretended not to know anything about it. After a day or two of ferreting, the truth had been revealed: Bhola had simply forgotten, in the beginning, to chase up invoices and then this matter of overlooking had become active avoidance, settling ultimately into a gelid lack of interest. When his initial reminders to the agents about outstanding payments were met with the usual 'Yes-yes, we'll pay you tomorrow' and 'Of course, next week, definitely' and 'The cheques just need signing', the deferrals fitted in like cogs to the grooves of Bhola's laziness, his endless capacity to put off until tomorrow what could effortlessly be done today. The agents, sensing a weak spot, delayed payments to see how much they could get away with; as it turned out, a lot. The three agents in question worked out that they could probably get their consignments of paper for free, certainly in the short term. In several instances, when invoicing, Bhola actually forgot how much was owed by whom and when.

Prafullanath had tried to console himself with the thought that a weak son did not seriously jeopardise his grand plans because he had three others; Bhola needed an eye kept on him, that was all. Now he was being presented with a graceful solution, a foolproof get-out clause.

He was instantly imagining complex scenarios: a publishing house kept deliberately small – small outlay, small educational books, small profits – with Bhola as its head . . . But, wait, if it was an educational-books publisher, it would be taxed at a different rate, lower than the tax on paper, so a simple bit of transfer-pricing could shift most of the profits from Charu Paper onto the books of the publishing house, which would mean losing much less profit to tax. Or if the publishing house could be shown to be perpetually making a loss, which wouldn't be difficult to do, since Bhola was going to make sure that was going to be the case . . . he had it. It was going to be easy to effect; not so his bigger dream of modernising the plant at Memari.

'I want to begin a costing of a technological upgrade of Memari,' he began. 'Foreign machines. Latest things from Germany and England and Holland. It's not going to be cheap, but in the long term it is going to be more costly carrying on with below-par production.'

Two days after New Year, in mid-April, Priyo took his wife out for their first evening outing, the 6.35 p.m. showing of *Jogan* in Rupali, followed by dinner at Firpo's in Esplanade. It was something that Priyo had read about in a recent novel and the idea had caught; it was modern, new, with just the right touch of adventurous daring about it, a slight defiance of middle-class conservatism that he felt all writers should take it upon themselves to push against. There were two more visits to the cinema – *Babul* and *Tathapi* – before news of Purnima's pregnancy was announced to the family on a blustery monsoon evening in July. Eleven days after this, in the bathroom on the first floor, Chhaya slit open the veins in her wrists with her father's straight razor, appropriately called 'Bengall', manufactured by Luke Cadman, Sheffield, England, a simple and dangerous item of luxury that he had bought himself in 1930, following his father's habit of spending occasionally on small, private pleasures to remind himself, in his father's words, 'that you have worked your way up to a world where you can afford these things; a treat from you to you'.

The Ghoshes tried hard to control the information from becoming public knowledge, tried to hide it even from the younger members of their own joint family, but how could they ever have contended with the supreme acoustics of Bengali life?

Their first recourse was to lie and spin the news: they gave it out to be understood that an ambulance had to be called that monsoon evening and Chhaya rushed to hospital because her blood pressure had dropped dangerously low and she had fainted in her bath. But the servants had had to clean up the blood from the bathroom floor, and hushing them up meant appeasement and bribes and playing a very long game whose dynamics and balances, bound to change with time, meant that the Ghoshes could not staunch that particular flow. Besides, the bandages around both her wrists, when Chhaya returned home, were not easily explained away. So people talked with jubilant ferocity and, as they talked, the Ghoshes changed the story to something involving broken glass from the bathroom window that Chhaya was trying to open when she slipped on the wet floor. That was concession enough. The whole neighbourhood pounced on it, feral beasts fighting over the meagre meat on a bone. This taint, it was later whispered, had ruined what little remaining chance she had had of finding a husband. Overnight, she became untouchable; it was as if the sharp razor she had used so imperfectly on her arteries had at least shredded, with hideous efficiency, both her marriageability, already attenuated, and her social standing.

By the time Baishakhi was born in late February of the following year, Chhaya could still be considered as recovering. Madan took it upon himself to serve only convalescent food to his Didi-moni for this period. All the dishes that he cooked when they were children, suffering from measles or fever or chickenpox or tonsillitis, he revived for her. Pish-pash, bone-marrow soup, gentle mutton stew with carrots and green beans and potatoes, soft kedgeree with an omelette on the side and that staple – magur or shing fish (both were supposed to aid the production of red blood cells) cooked with ginger. It was as if Didi-moni had regressed to childhood and needed all over again the things that a child required: nourishment, pampering, care. She had lost so much blood. The very thought turned him to cold stone. What was in his capacity to give her so that she could be whole again, except what he had given them for the span of their lives until now – his food? Would that bring her back from death's door? That is where Chhaya had been, everyone whispered: death's door. He heard other things, such as a figure (she had needed six bottles of blood in hospital) or a medical prescription (she had to have her wrists bandaged for two months), and pity reduced him to nothing. Random memories played through his head as Charubala spooned food, which he had brought in, into her daughter's mouth and he stood in a corner of the room, watching, ready to obey Ma's orders before she had even finished saying them. A six-year-old girl crying because she had chipped the paint off the clay figurine of a flute player that he had bought her from the Chadak Mela in his village. He trying to coax an obstinate girl, ill with chickenpox, to eat the incredibly bony pholi fish that was thought to help against the illness. A girl of twelve stealing into the kitchen and saying, 'Madan-da, quick, give me a little bit of that spicy dried-fish fry-up, quick, quick, before Ma comes and catches me.' A broken seed-necklace, the tiny seeds scattered all around it under a flowering bush and a little girl saying, 'Madan-da, pick them up for me, won't you, I'm afraid to go near that bush, you said there's a girl buried under it.' Was that girl and this bandaged, semi-conscious, broken woman on her bed the same person?

When Charubala was sure that Chhaya had mended, she moved her up from the first floor, which she had so far shared with Priyo and Somu and now Purnima, to the second floor. Whatever anyone felt for Chhaya, and this was different for each person, although it was a difference of degree rather than of kind, pity was a dominant emotion. This pity curdled partially to what could only be called fear.

When even Bhola, who was also thought to be unmarriageable, got married three years later, to a 'nice, simple girl from a nice home', as Charubala described Jayanti to everyone, they gave up trying to find someone for Chhaya. A worm of regret wriggled through Charubala, especially when she found herself sleepless during the small hours, but nursing and feeding this almost-grief seemed to consume less of her energies than the continual waging of what had become a battle, a battle she knew she had lost. Occasionally a small hope flashed in her, she scurried around for a day or two chatting to matchmakers, making enquiries, a kitten amusing itself with falling leaves; then the true nature of the deceiving glimmer made itself obvious to her and she subsided into a tearful inertia.

Chhaya took a job at a new school, Ballygunje Shiksha Sadan on Gariahat Road, in an attempt to start afresh; rumours had insinuated themselves into her previous workplace at Beltala Girls' School, much closer to home than Gariahat Road. Every summer when Chhaya went on a school trip with her new students to Puri or Digha or

Ghatshila, Charubala imagined her daughter was going to her husband's home and her in-laws'. A week's holiday elastically stretched itself in Charubala's mind as a lifetime, then snapped back with the slap of limitation when her daughter returned; the whole episode had just been a cheap toy of her mind.

As Chhaya stepped outside the front gate on her way to work one morning two women came up to her. One of them asked, 'That Ghosh house, aren't you the sister?'

Belatedly Chhaya understood that they were talking to her; she had never set eyes on them before. Maidservants, she could tell immediately, but she was certain that neither of them had ever worked in their house. Unless it was during the time when she was in hospital and then, later, too sunk in slow recovery at home to take notice of temporary staff.

'Yes. Why do you ask?' Chhaya replied hesitantly.

'Somnath your brother?' The tone was harsh, aggressive.

'Y-y-yes. What do you want?'

'Your brother has a friend called Paltu, in that neighbourhood?' she asked, pointing somewhere vaguely west with her left hand.

Chhaya was beginning to get irritated by this rude inquisition, so she said tetchily, 'I don't keep a list of Somnath's friends. And, anyway, what is it to you? Now move out of my way, I'm getting late for work.'

'No, we won't. Take us to your mother, we have things to tell her,' the woman insisted.

Chhaya, taken aback by such impudence on the part of a servant, tried a new tack. She said, 'You think my mother has nothing to do except meet riff-raff all day? Think again. Now move.' That note of command in her voice would ensure that these two women backed down.

The woman who had remained silent so far now spoke. 'Your brother and Paltu have been frolicking with my sister. She works as a maid in that Paltu's house. She's with child now. People at your home know about this?'

The words had the effect of a furious slap across Chhaya's face. She edged backwards and ran into the house. She wanted to shout,

'Lies, lies, all filthy lies', but this would have been too feeble. She ran up two flights of stairs, found her mother on the first floor and panted, 'Ma, there are some people outside . . . servants, servants from another neighbourhood . . . Filthy stuff, filthy . . . Somnath and his friend, Paltu, all lies . . . They're outside and want to see you. Don't go, don't listen to what they have to say. Send Madan-da to deal with them – throw them out.'

'What is wrong with you?' said Charubala. 'Sit down. What are you babbling on about? Which servants, what filthy stuff?'

'There, outside,' Chhaya could only point weakly.

Charubala got up to go to the front balcony. Chhaya said, 'Don't listen to them!'

From the balcony Charubala looked down onto Basanta Bose Road, noticed nothing special and half-turned to Chhaya, still inside, to say, 'Where? What am I looking for? What women?'

'Two maidservants. They're standing outside.'

'Oh, maids. I see. Where . . . I can't . . . oh, those two? Come here and point them out to me.'

Chhaya quailed at the prospect of facing them. She let out a brief 'No', then began to think whether it was not better that her mother heard from her, Chhaya, what she had been told than from those strangers. But how was she going to bring herself to say it? Even thinking about it made her feel polluted. How could people have such cesspools inside their heads? How typical of that class of women.

She heard her mother call out, 'You, what do you want?' The reply was inaudible. Then her mother again, 'You want work? We have all the people we need. You should go elsewhere to look for work, there's nothing here.'

A pause again, this time followed by an impatient outburst from Charubala, 'Yes, yes, I am Somnath's mother. Say what you have to say from there, and be quick about it, I don't have all day.'

At the mention of Somnath's name some familiar dread in Charubala was beginning to sound a warning that an ill-humoured attitude was probably not the wisest one to take, especially standing on the balcony, in view of the whole wide world. She gripped the balustrade tightly. She was glad of the support, because what the women then proceeded to say made the ground beneath her feet move as if to dislodge her. She squeezed her eyes tight shut and opened them again; the women were still there, this was not a dream; the snaky trails of poison were still streaming out of their mouths. The brief vertigo over, Charubala now felt seized by anger.

She found her voice and shouted down at the women, 'Don't you feel any shame, coming here and spouting these unspeakable lies? Who has put you up to this? I know my son, and I'm not going to stand here listening to all this sewage. Get out of here, get out now!'

She turned around, expecting to find succour from someone in the house, but realised that all the menfolk had left. There was no one she could ask to take charge of things except Madan.

'Madan,' she called, going back inside. 'Madan. See to the women outside. Two maidservants. Get rid of them immediately.'

Charubala sat down on the edge of her bed, panting. Chhaya was in the room too; neither could bring herself to look at the other. United in humiliation, each felt as if she had done something wrong and was being silently judged by the other person. Aeons passed as Madan went down, spoke to the two women, clanged the front gate shut and came upstairs. They strained to hear what was going on. Sounds of vehicle horns; people passing, talking, calling out; more people; a utensil-seller calling out her wares; a man selling toy flutes made out of bamboo and palm-leaves.

Then the screaming began. Not every single word could be heard from indoors, partly because of the way sound travelled through a competing wall of other sounds, partly because of a willed underhearing to protect themselves, but what filtered through was enough.

'. . . didn't care much about filth when fucking maidservants . . . may be poor, but we don't have to put up with . . . go around from street to street, telling everyone . . .'

The woman shouting was on the further side of Basanta Bose Road; she had clearly been asked by Madan not to hang around outside the house. She raised her voice as she progressed through her litany, the escalation in volume and the accusations feeding off each other. Within minutes a small crowd had gathered: what could be more interesting than other people's lives?

Charubala sensed rather than saw the people – strangers, neighbours, acquaintances, passers-by – assembling in a wide, loose circle around that vile, shrieking woman and felt that whirling dizziness again, this time accompanied by a spreading heat in her ears, her face, neck and arms. Chhaya seemed to have turned into stone.

Purnima came to the front room and asked, 'Ma, there are some women standing outside, shouting. Is there some problem?'

Charubala shrank. A fantasy of disappearance pressed urgently against her.

On the third floor the two little boys, Supratik and Suranjan, attracted by the noise outside, ran to the verandah to see what was happening.

'Look!' Supratik said to his younger brother, 'people are gathering around in a circle. A monkey-dance. Or maybe travelling players. There'll be a circus.'

'Where are monkeys?' Suranjan asked.

'Ufff, wait, they'll come. That woman is announcing their arrival,' Supratik replied, impatient at his five-year-old brother's obtuseness.

But, wait, something about the pitch, the tone . . . He felt something was not quite joyous and entertaining here. There weren't going to be any monkeys, or madaris setting up a tightrope and swinging their toddlers in a sack in huge, heart-dropping arcs. There was also something of the forbidden going on down there. Some of those words . . .

'. . . think we don't know why she tried to kill herself' – then some incomprehensible word – 'that's what the lot of you . . .'

Sandhya rushed out to the verandah, swooped down on her two sons and shooed them inside, barking, 'Go inside, you two monkeys, go on, go inside, nothing doing standing out here, listening to that rubbish.'

'. . . see to it that the son of a whore is sodomised on the streets and left bleeding . . .'

Before the two boys ran inside reluctantly, Supratik took one last look at the street below: the number of people seemed to have swelled and everyone was looking at their house.

Suranjan was about to start bawling. 'No, no, I want to see monkey-dance, I want to go downstairs and see monkey-dance.'

Sandhya turned and smacked him. 'Not one word from you,' she said.

The wailing burst like a ripe cloud. Supratik felt intimidated; it was unusual for his mother to be so short-tempered. He had better slink away and sit with his books to mollify her by pretending to study.

Drifts from the theatre downstairs were still audible: '. . . don't think we don't know . . . know it all . . . son of a pig . . . the whole lot of you will . . .'

Supratik felt a guilty thrill at the term of abuse he could recognise, 'son of a pig', but also, simultaneously, a tense deflation – were they the target of all these bad words?

In the front room on the first floor Charubala had started shaking.

At last Chhaya spoke, her voice emerging in a croak, 'We should go to the back of the house.' She leaped up and called out, 'Madan-da, Madan-da. Shut all the doors and windows on all the floors right now.'

But the damage had been done. The great, roaring world outside – against that, what match were these transient bits of straw?

— The Baruis haven't seen your faces, Kanu said, trying to allay our fears. Or his own.

Then Shankar threw the bombshell. He said — Those farmers there tonight, they're all friends, they won't blab.

— How do you know? I asked, beginning to suspect something.

— We told them to be ready with weapons. And hide nearby. What if we needed help?

I was stunned into silence.

— You . . . you . . . told others? Dhiren managed to get out.

All those meetings in the still heart of the night in which the need for absolute secrecy was every other sentence spoken — all that had come to naught.

Kanu read our dismay and said — They're our people, they're one of us, they won't tell anyone.

This was not the time to get into an argument, so I accepted their reassurances on the surface. I said — You shouldn't have done it. Maybe we got lucky this time. We'll see. What are we going to do when the police arrive? Or the men of the landlords?

Kanu — Don't go out of the house. Hide inside. We'll protect you.

At any other time I would have laughed at his naïvety, but instead I said — These are the police, Kanu, they can come inside any time.

Kanu pondered this for a while, then said — You guys leave the village now.

— What will happen to you?

— Two or four thwacks from the police's lathi are nothing to us. But you need to leave now, light will soon begin to show in the sky.

They gave us beaten rice and cane molasses wrapped in a cloth bundle.

— Go, go, go now, they urged.

*

We tried to run – impossible to do this through stretches of bamboo groves – but once we reached the fields, we took long strides towards the jungle, hurrying in the direction from where we knew the police from Jhargram were going to enter Majgeria. But we were miles away from the road, on a parallel outlier, protected by trees. I didn't know if I imagined this, but just as we made the edge where the trees began to get denser I heard the distant sound of motor-cars. The sky was pink and orange and pale yellow.

As we moved deeper into the forest, Dhiren said – I think I'm going to collapse, and he did exactly that, bending down to the forest floor and stretching himself out fully. Before Samir and I could say anything he was asleep. Looking at him, we realised that this was what we wanted to do too, immediately.

I didn't know what woke me up. I had no idea what time it was and I could not see the sun in the sky. Sunlight only made it down through the tree cover in patches. I was cold and itching all over, I had the beginnings of a headache and I was completely parched. We had no water to drink, it dawned on me. I turned to Samir and Dhiren – they were curled in on themselves, snoring away. Mosquitoes had formed a flying colony above each of them. There were insects in Samir's hair – not ants; I had no idea what they were – and Dhiren, still asleep, brushed off something annoying him in his beard, then around his nose, then again his beard, followed now by his ear . . . until he awoke, red-eyed and thrashing, swearing at the disturbance – Shala, killing me, these bloody insects . . .

I waited for him to ask the inevitable question before giving him the bad news.

Dhiren – Ufff, my chest is cracking with thirst.

– No water. They forgot to give us some and we forgot to ask.

– What are we going to do?

– Unlikely we'll find water in a forest.

– But . . . but we'll die!

– Don't be silly. No one dies of thirst in twenty-four hours. We'll be at Debdulal-da's at night. If we set out as soon as it gets dark, we'll be there in six to eight hours, maximum.

– But . . . but . . . we can't walk for that length of time without any water!

– Here, have some of this, it'll make you feel better.

I gave him the cloth bundle in which Kanu had given us molasses and beaten rice.

– Don't devour it all. It'll have to last the three of us until we reach Belpahari. Which is twenty hours from now, or thereabouts.

He began to swear, but gave up. There was nothing to be done.

When Samir woke up we made a half-hearted plan to go looking for water. He said – I'm sure there's some stream or fountain in the forest.

There wasn't a trace of hope in his voice. He said it because he felt he had to say something. Nobody got up to go on the water-finding mission.

Samir tried again – Listen, trees need water to survive. How can there be a forest without water? Elementary biology.

Dhiren said – Trees have deep root systems to draw water from the ground. Elementary biology, level two.

My headache was like somebody poking around in the soft tissue behind my right eye with a hot knitting needle. Samir said that he too was getting a headache.

The heat increased. We sweated and scratched and slapped the insects sitting or trying to land on us. Then we sweated and scratched our itches some more. Seventeen months in a hole of a village, where we had spent at least half of that time simply waiting for time to budge, had evidently not been entirely successful.

I said – Listen, guns or tangis or bombs won't kill us, this waiting will.

Dhiren – It's only time. It kills everyone.

– Yes, but eventually. This is slow, concentrated time, a huge dose of the poison in one go. It'll kill us all soon.

Before long all this aimless conversation petered out. We tried to talk about important things, chief of which was the big problem facing us now: how to work in Majgeria from Belpahari. To walk for eight to nine hours from Belpahari at night, hide in Majgeria for the day, do a guerrilla action at night, hide in the forest, walk back again under the cover of night through the forest to Belpahari – this hardly seemed a feasible way of going about it. It would put paid to both revolution and revolutionaries.

Samir punctuated the half-hearted discussion at regular intervals with – I think I'll die without some water.

I didn't have the energy to move a finger, but sitting here, sweating and getting eaten by insects and thinking obsessively about the impossibility of moving forward and failing to come up with any solutions would make me go mad, so I began the search for water.

Dhiren said – We have to be careful with directions. We don't want to set out on the wrong route after we come out of the forest at night.

It was this that constrained our search; not that we would have found a stream here. The thirst was not helping us think clearly. At some point we sat down and ate some more jaggery and flattened rice. My mouth was so parched that I had trouble swallowing the dry mass of chewed stuff. Dhiren became fixated on direction, not allowing us to move in anything other than a straight line headed one way only.

He said – Too many turnings and we'll lose track of where we have to exit the forest to get to the road that takes us to Belpahari. He kept repeating this like someone demented.

Samir stopped complaining. The dehydration had ground us down. The food was over too. We had no idea how long it was to nightfall. Then I added eight hours to it, eight hours at least. It seemed an unpassable piece of time. I wanted to scream. Knowing we were going to get to its end didn't make the process of getting there any more bearable.

We got to Debdulal-da's at around two in the morning. I noticed later that this was not the kind of tiredness that I felt after a day's harvest or halui, but the effect was the same – I felt inanimate, a machine with moving parts. There were lessons to be learned in this, but I couldn't think of any that didn't include the image of a water container. We couldn't eat much of the rice and dal that Debdulal-da gave us – halfway through the night's walk I thought I could easily manage to eat every brick of his house – but we drank three kunjos of water between us before we fell into a sleep much like I imagine death must be.

When we woke up it was around noon. Yesterday seemed insubstantial, something that didn't happen, but was only thought. With that was gone the feeling that all the things we had gone through – exhaustion, hunger, thirst, despair – were of any moment at all. It all felt so trivial that, if the same were expected of me on that new day, I would do it in so far as my body would allow.

The dissection and analysis began in the evening. There were people present whom I'd never met, four of them, all from the AICCCR. I was amazed to hear how far the struggle had advanced in Mushahari in Bihar – apparently, responding to the AICCCR's call given on 15th August last year, hundreds of peasants had seized the autumn harvest and fought pitched battles for days with the police and the landlords' men. I asked about the ultimate outcome – who won? how? what was the casualty on the side of the peasants and their leaders? – but the talk moved on to the even greater success story of Lakhimpur in Uttar Pradesh and, of course, the beacon of our movement, Srikakulam: mass actions, creation of bases, dozens of landlords annihilated, land reclaimed, crops seized . . . my head reeled. They had managed to move on from isolated, small guerrilla incidents to full-blown peasant uprisings. How, how, how? I knew that some of the retelling was a bit optimistic; I'd done it myself when writing reports for Liberation and Deshabrati. I felt a flash of envy burn quickly thorough me.

Then I pricked up my ears: rumblings amongst the ranks of the AICCCR. They would have been easy to dismiss as ideological jaw-jaw about the Lin Biao line and Soviet revisionism and the usual topics, but this time I heard something else. There seemed to be serious dissension in the AICCCR, and the talk of a new party was not all chatter. I listened for a while. There was an argument about what our movement should be: the Charu Mazumdar line was that it should be centrally an uprising by the peasantry to eradicate feudalism, while the Nagi Reddy line was that it should aim to be a broader, more inclusive workers' anti-imperialist struggle against the two imperialisms trying to dominate the world currently: US imperialism and Soviet social imperialism. This led naturally to the difference in the tactical lines: while Charu Mazumdar held that we should keep it as an underground movement, the trade-union leader Parimal Dasgupta thought that was just a kind of 'Che Guevaraism' and favoured a bigger mass movement, involving not only farmers but trade-union activists too, opening up the revolution to the whole population of people who could be described as workers.

I said a word here or there, but mostly absorbed in silence. There was much talk of who would leave the AICCCR to join the new party, but everything was under a cloak of speculation and secrecy, lending our normally secret meetings an even sharper edge. After a while I switched off. That envy was still there, or its embers. What was it about Bengalis that made them want to talk and talk and talk until their ghosts came out of their mouths? Was it a way we had found of never having to do anything?

A small man – Anjan Roy Chowdhury – with a round head and radically receding hairline, although he could not be more than five or seven years older than me, said – Why did you come all the way to Belpahari? Didn't you know that we have over twenty villages in that corner of Binpur covered by our people? You could've hidden in any one of those?

Samir sounded as surprised as I was – No one told us.

Anjan-da said – Squad action has begun in those villages too. A courier sent to one of them would have prevented all this hiding in the forests and coming all the way here. But all this is necessary training. I think one of the three of you should become a courier between these villages; the closer ones, certainly.

I was afraid of this. We formed a good unit of three and I would feel the loss of either of them, or become the isolated courier myself, a vagabond. I'd held my tongue so far, and now I found that someone else had exposed me to those possibilities. I couldn't object; individuals were nothing compared with the movement. Charu Mazumdar had written in <u>Liberation</u>: 'At the present time we have a great need for petty-bourgeois comrades who come from the intelligentsia. But we must remember that not all of them will remain revolutionaries to the end.' That possibility, that shadow of doubt that would come over everyone, were I to acknowledge my reluctance for the three of us to be split up – I wouldn't be able to live with that. I wanted to remain a revolutionary to the very end.

Debdulal-da added his voice to Anjan-da's – Yes, which one among you?

Dhiren volunteered.

I kept looking at the floor. A wrench went through my heart.

Over the next few days we talked strategy endlessly. It was a badminton of book-learned wisdom. Or parrot-learning, as you would no doubt call it; and rightly. My heart wasn't in it – I kept wanting to know what exactly was going on in Majgeria. We had left the village before we had had the time to organise protection squads, groups of informers who would give advance warning of a police raid; a mass mobilisation, in short. I thought of Kanu lifting up his perennially ailing son, and instead of the delight and playfulness that should have been his expression, I saw his creased brows, and worried eyes, dark with the clouds of anxiety and helplessness. Was he even around to do that?

Majgeria was like a crematorium. The story Bijli told us turned my blood to ice. An army of policemen had raided the village. She said they had come in droves, ransacked their homes, charged at them with batons, hitting whoever they could find – men, women, children, old people, they hadn't discriminated – and then taken almost everyone from this neighbourhood and the next one away to jail.

– But . . . but . . . that's over a hundred people, I said.

– All of them, she said, everyone. Said they'd leave us as corpses if we stepped out of our homes.

It took me a while to get any sense out of Bijli's story. She fell into weeping intermittently and scrambled up the sequence of events, so that I had to ask frequent questions to make a straight line of it. Often she blazed with anger, cursed . . . Her anger was directed at me. She left me in no doubt that I was partly to blame for the current state of affairs. There was no reasoning with her.

– And the child's sick too. Who'll take him to the doctor?

I tried to offer to help, but she gave me an earful: what was going to happen if I got caught by the police on my way to hospital with the child, because they were looking for us, looking for 'outside men', as they had said, 'outside men' who had come to the village to cause trouble.

I felt guilty and ashamed, my face was burning, but my distress was a luxury compared with the seriousness of the situation, now that the police had moved their repression up several notches.

– You should be hiding, she said, softening a bit. Not walking around in the open like this. Their people are everywhere, they're watching us. They'll come again, they said. You go now.

I asked her for only one thing: water to take into the jungle. She went away and came back after a few minutes, with a clay pot and a small cloth bundle.

– There's nothing at home to eat, she said, except for some puffed rice. No molasses to go with it. I've given you some salt and chillies. That's all I have.

I kept my head bowed as I took the water and the food.

We hadn't progressed much. According to our plans, which had seemed so smooth and free-flowing during the talking stage, our next step would have been to seize the lands of the killed jotedaars and their toadies and hold the hundreds of bighas long enough to claim the next harvest on them. If things had gone according to plan we would have done that with the '68 winter harvest, but we were only just beginning to get into the groove then. But now, with all our friends herded into jail like cattle, what were we going to do with just two people? I remembered that we referred to our groups as 'cells', and one of us as 'commander', and now those words, applied to two thin, ragged, hungry, dirty, cold men, almost turned to stone with exhaustion, made me want to laugh at their absurd bid for a kind of glamour. What were we going to do now? Hide in the forest, come out at night and take down one or two minor people – a manager walking past, a flunky on his way home?

Samir was as clueless as I.

– I think we should join the cell in Gidighati and strengthen our numbers there, he suggested. That was the line given to us in Belpahari, we mustn't forget that.

Line, cell: I could tell that the old fearfulness in him was stirring and the use of those words was a way of trying to keep it at bay.

I asked — And leave these poor villagers here to be tortured?

— Well, that's a problem . . . What's going to happen to them?

— The police will press charges against whoever they feel like harassing. Or whoever their paymasters ask them to victimise. They'll torment them until they fall into line. Kanu and Bipul and others don't have the money or the connections to fight their cases in court.

I felt that old simmering in my blood again as I tried to outline what lay in store for the farmers. I couldn't bear to think of the conclusion to that story. I said — Didn't you hear how Bijli was blaming us for their situation? To abandon them now means that we'd never be able to show our faces here again. And that's the least of the problem. It means we're letting this village go, creating a chink in our area-wise seizure of power. Remember the Chairman's words? This will become the gap in our armour.

— No, no, I understand, but I can't think of any way to move forward.

It hit me then: the beginning of the recognition of the holes in our strategies, the insufficient manpower, the lack of planning for the worst 'what if' scenarios, the medieval networks of communication (if any). It was the first of many such waves to hit me.

We set out for Gidighati. Because we tried to cleave to the cover of the forest, the route became two long, angled sides of a triangle — going up only to come down — instead of the easier, shorter straight line.

Gidighati was a bigger village than the one we had just left, but not by much. It wasn't difficult to find the Santhal neighbourhood — as always, on the periphery and, here, almost within the forest. There was a main road on the affluent side, which made our work that much more dangerous. I longed for the relative seclusion and inaccessibility of Majgeria.

Babu Mandi's hut was not difficult to find. We stood out so conspicuously that people came to us, asking who or what we wanted, effectively doing our work for us. The questioning was touched with suspicion and aggressiveness: how could they tell that we weren't working for the landlords or the police? The city guys, our comrade counterparts in this village, came out from their huts and everything was settled. Samir was going to stay at Babu Mandi's, and I in the hut of Bir Mandi, his cousin, three doors down, a new-looking hut, the last one before the forest took over. The others, Ashu, Debashish and Dipankar, were none of them more than two or three huts away. Five of us here – I began to take comfort in this increase in our ranks.

We were led into the jungle by Ashu, Debashish and Dipankar. (Dipankar was slightly older than us, just over thirty, I'd say. He had read Mechanical Engineering in Jadavpur University, then briefly joined a private firm before giving up. Of the three of them, I got closest to him.) I was entranced, suddenly, by the forest. It was indistinguishable from the one we had hidden in before going to Belpahari, but now, I didn't know why, it absorbed all my attention, so much so that Samir quipped – You're getting a bit besotted by it. Could it be that the innate poet in you, dormant for so long, is waking up at last?

Maybe there was a little bit of an aesthetic awakening. Maybe it was because we were almost <u>within</u> the jungle in Gidighati, whereas in Majgeria we had had to walk a mile or two to enter it properly. But most of all it was to do with another kind of growing revelation: how well it could serve our purposes. Our comrades here had worked it out: Ashu and Dipankar said, for example, that it was possible to walk to the nearby villages, even most of the distance to Belpahari, without leaving the forest. A whole green corridor that could afford us safety.

The jungle could be our shelter, but in this arid corner of Binpur, far away from rivers, how were guerrillas going to survive in the forest without ready access to food and water?

I said – If we begin to live in the forest instead of a village, the poor villagers won't be at the receiving end of police repression.

This had been weighing on my mind a lot. I had had a glimpse of the kind of hell that the police had unleashed over powerless people.

Ashu spoke my unsaid thoughts – Where are we going to get food and drink? What are we going to do in the monsoon?

– Couldn't we visit the villages periodically and stock up?

– That would still leave them open to police brutality. They would be terrorised by the state into not cooperating with us. At least if we stay in the villages, our presence there keeps them militant.

And so it went, round and round and round. In any case, a mass action was deferred until just after harvest, so Samir and I were grounded here for the next seven months at least.

Ashu, Dipankar and Debashish had already undertaken two guerrilla actions in Gidighati in as many months. One was a standard stabbing, they said and, by the sound of it, it didn't seem to be very different from our job on Senapati: waylaying first in the dark, then the quick business with a hashua (they cut his throat). The second one was more interesting. I'll write down Ashu's words as closely as I can reproduce them from memory. (Full of swearing, which I've cleaned up. If you heard him speak, you wouldn't be able to tell that he used to be a medical student. You'd mistake him for one of those wastrels who stands in a small gang at paan-bidi shops on street corners in South Calcutta and makes catcalls to every passing woman.) Here is his account.

– Name: Harekrishna Das. Walks around as if his father's bought the whole place for him. We've had our eye on him ever since we came here after the Chadak Mela last year. He's got his filthy pig's snout in every trough of shit: moneylending, pawnbroking, smuggling . . . everything you can think of. A week after we send Haren Patra over to the other side in two halves, head first, body later, this Harekrishna begins to walk everywhere with a guard next to him. Our eyes pop out on stalks. Can you believe, a personal bodyguard in tow, going wherever he goes, sitting when he sits, running when he runs? What if we attacked Harekrishna while he was shitting, eh? The bodyguard would be there too? Anyway. The fat, greasy fool goes around twirling his umbrella and saying smugly, No one can touch me, I have a guard to protect me, look, he's following me. That expression on his face alone would make you want to relieve mankind of his existence. Anyway. So we hide behind a bush and leap out one evening. The guard, who's armed only with a lathi, tries to put up some sort of a fight, but we can tell that his heart is not in it. He sees we have knives and axes, so all he wants is to run away and save his own life. We say to him, Aren't you ashamed to be in the pay of a dog like this? This dog is your class enemy, generations and generations of these dogs have exploited generations and generations of your people, and will carry on doing so eternally, so why would you want to serve him? We snatch his lathi off him and say, We'll let you go because you are a poor man and we're fighting for people like you, we're on your side, but don't let us catch you working for dogs like this again. Then we give him a few blows with his own lathi and he runs off over the fields so fast you'd think he was late for his own funeral. Harekrishna, meanwhile, is pinned to the ground by Dipankar and this Santhal lad, Babu's nephew. We have him well and truly in our clutches now, there's no way that fat corpse of his can move, he knows this too, so he starts begging for mercy. What sweet music. We know we're going to slit his bloated stomach, pull out his guts and stuff his open mouth with it, but we let him sing for a while. He believes that if he pleads and begs we're going to relent and let him go after a few slaps. We let him believe that – it was hilarious. The usual, you know: I have a wife and three small children, an ill ageing mother, they're going to land in deep water if something happens to me, who's going to look after them? We remind him, Did you think of the little children and ill ageing mothers of the destitute men, broken by your torture, their blood sucked dry by you? His stomach was so fat that the hashua sprang back when I tried to stick it in. Then I thought it would be more fun to slit his belly open only a little bit, like surgeons do during an operation. He was squealing like a sacrificial goat, so we couldn't carry on with our games for very long, people would come running. How I wish we could have let him squeal for longer after I made that big, curved cut on his pot-belly. It looked like a smiley face. Then Dipankar says, Okay, we need to finish this and go. I think of slitting one of the veins in his neck and letting him bleed slowly to death, as they do in Muslim abattoirs, but in the end I show him mercy, find his jugular and, sataak! He really looked like a slaughtered fattened-goat.

The rhythm of life that I had had in Majgeria reasserted itself; the ancient, unchanging acts of ploughing and tilling and sowing and weeding and watching the paddy grow. I seemed to have exchanged one village for another. Memories of Kanu and Bijli could turn me still and silent for hours. I had no way of finding out what had happened to them, no means of helping them without endangering myself. Would we repeat our mistakes here too and expose this lot to the same fate? I couldn't bear to think of it.

Almost as if in atonement, or in a desire to write a different kind of story with the new set of villagers, I tried to get to know Bir in the time available, that slow time between weeding and harvest. Unlike Bijli, Bir's wife, Bela, sat with us as we talked and didn't hurry away with our empty plates to begin the washing-up or continue to hide herself behind domestic duties. She didn't come with us on the evenings when Bir, some other Santhal men and we 'city boys' went into the luxuriant, rustling forest in the dark, but in the hut she was an active participant in whatever conversation was struck up.

The Santhal men, Bir, Babu, Bimbadhar and others, came up with a plan that I began to see more and more as a kind of gift. It was the gift of protection. Individually and together, they suggested that they would protect us in the event of a police raid, smuggling us out if things got too bad, providing us with shelter in their own homes and, if that proved unfeasible or dangerous, arranging for our shelter in the homes of their trusted friends, in other villages nearby or, if it came down to it, in the jungle. They didn't have a raft of set plans and strategies, and much of this emerged in conversation, through thinking aloud, with many crossings-out and reinstatements, but the upshot was this: the poor, landless farmers of Gidighati had decided to look out for us. The implications were enormous: instead of letting the status quo settle again over the surface of their lives, they had decided to be inspired by our teachings and actions. Armed rebellion it was going to be. They had made their choice.

Dhiren arrived, on a passing visit, halfway through the monsoon. It was from him that we heard of the formal establishment of the CPI(M-L) by Charu Mazumdar and Kanu Sanyal at the May Day rally in Calcutta Maidan. He wasn't there, he had heard from someone else, but he recounted the story – the speeches, the torchlit procession, the songs, the slogans – as if he were talking of his own memories. The final news had taken nearly three months to reach us, although at Belpahari we had listened in on the ructions going on inside the AICCCR. Dhiren had come on other work: first, to give us the names of farmers in three neighbouring villages in whose homes we could stay should the need arise; and second, to bring us a pistol and a box of bullets. But I couldn't help thinking about the celebrations marking the formation of the CPI(M-L) and, for a while, wished I had been in Calcutta then.

I realised I must have gone all quiet and distracted because of what Dhiren said, much later, when we went down, the Majgeria threesome, Samir, Dhiren and I, to the pond at the end of the day, for old times' sake, to have a splash while it was raining. That same rattling, dissolving music on the green surface, changing to something so different just under it, and the shiny green shields of the banana leaves on the bank and scores of lush trees and plants I didn't know the names of and wanted to ask my friend Dhiren, who had now become a visitor to these parts instead of a resident . . . His appearance now, as a courier bringing news from elsewhere, unsettled me by the strength of how much I missed him.

– You mustn't feel left out because you weren't in Calcutta for the May Day rally, he said.

– No, no . . . not really, it's nothing.

– Listen to me: don't you think it's better to be in the thick of action than in city politics, which is all talk anyway? You got sick of all that, remember? You couldn't wait to get out and do what you called 'real work' rather than 'armchair politics'. Remember?

He was right about that.

– So why this backward glance now? Aren't you happy here? Do you want to return home?

The word 'home' did the trick. I said – No, I don't want to return home, but sometimes I think I'm missing out on the action . . .

– But the action is all here, in these villages!

– I know, I know. It's just a grass-is-greener-on-the-other-side feeling, it's a momentary weakness, it'll pass. In fact it's already gone, talking to you. Anyway, are you finding this vagabond's life to your taste?

He made a face, then said – I keep telling myself that I'm the revolution's eyes and ears . . .

– Don't forget legs, Samir quipped.

– Yes, the transport and communication service, true. But it needs to be done until safe corridors are established. The things I had to go through to bring you this one pistol. Often there are no safe houses on the way, so you have to take your chance . . .

– And all this walking, hundreds of miles cumulatively, does it not tire you out? You look like a broomstick, Samir said.

– Sometimes . . . sometimes I wish I could fall into a sleep from which I'd never wake up.

– That's called death, stupid, Samir said.

– Yes, yes, but you know what I mean; a long, long, long uninterrupted rest.

– And would you go to Calcutta? How many times do you think that would be? I asked.

– Don't know. I know I have to, at some point, but so far there hasn't been an occasion.

He gave a pause, then asked – Why do you ask? Do you want something from there? Or do you want anything done while I'm there? Easily done, if we can get the timing right, because I don't know when I'll be in Majgeria again.

– No, no, just asking, nothing particular . . .

Bir and his family had not always been so poor. He used to own a small plot of land, about two bighas, but he had been finding it increasingly impossible to grow enough on it and so, on the advice of one of the village officials, he decided to lease it to someone the official recommended. Bir, an illiterate man, had put his thumb impression on the lease deed. When the rent fell overdue and Bir called to collect it, he was told by the lessee that Bir had sold the land to him. The plot belonged to him, the lessee, now; the deed on which Bir had put the imprint of his thumb was a sale deed, not a deed of lease. The village official, it turned out, had been in cahoots with the lessee or, more likely, had been handsomely bribed. Bir Mandi's plot had been sold to Nabin Sarkar for a sum of 1,500 rupees, less than one-fortieth of the value of his land.

Once again, no recourse to redress: the village official in question was the person through whom such complaints were made. When Bir started complaining, he was told to leave off if he valued the honour and life of his wife. Bir threatened to go to the police in Jhargram. The police said they couldn't do anything because Bir had signed away his land. In any case, the police wouldn't do a thing because Nabin Sarkar had the wherewithal to grease their palms, Bir didn't. Two months after this, Bir's hut was ransacked and destroyed by a group of men; he had been living, as he had always done, in the hut at the edge of his (now Nabin Sarkar's) land. This time the police told him that he was on it illegally and, if he didn't move out, or if he attempted to build again on the same spot, he would be thrown into jail. And who knew what could happen to his defenceless, protectorless family, they added, when he wasn't around to look after them?

That was how he came to build the hut where we were now, in the poorest circle of Gidighati, almost where the treeline of the forest began.

I did something that I wished I had thought of in the first place. But in this imitation of the words and action of a friend there was more admiration than envy, and also a kind of invoking of his presence, a wish that he would materialise in front of us. I leaned forward and uttered a variation of the words that Dhiren had said to Shankar – Bir, tell me, what if we remove the village official and Nabin Sarkar? Silently. No one will know a thing. And we'll burn the sale deed that has your thumb impression on it . . .

Thirty of us raided Nabin Sarkar's home on a late November night. Harvest was just in, so we got Babu to organise twenty men as backup, to wait, with sacks and whatever they had to hand, to empty his granaries as soon as it was safe to do so.

On Dipankar's suggestion, we did a pincer-movement on the house: fifteen men entering from the front, fifteen men leading the rear action.

We broke down the doors and the noise alerted the men inside. They got their act together fast, so that when we entered they were waiting. We were at close range and they charged at us with axes and knives and sticks and spears. I heard a cry of pain: one of the Santhal men had been hit. I thought we were facing sure death. At no such action in the past had we encountered fully prepared men waiting to engage us in pitched battle. I was right at the front, abreast with three other men, one of whom, I thought, had been struck.

Were the dozen men behind me still there? Had they turned tail and run off?

Nabin Sarkar's men were shouting, baying for our blood in the filthiest language imaginable. I had no idea whether to advance or retreat when the decision was made for me. Our rear flank had entered the house from the back and, swinging their tangis, spears and lathis, the men were hacking their way through Nabin Sarkar's men, now caught in the middle between our two groups. The man who had got one of ours with his tangi turned to see what was going on. I seized my opportunity: I aimed my axe, with all the force in my body, at the back of his head, missed, and got his neck and shoulders instead. He fell. At that very moment the men behind me surged forward, shouting too, expressions of pure hatred and rage.

It was a messy battle, our most difficult so far. They were not that many in number − I initially thought about five; it turned out to be eight − but they fought back instead of taking fright and escaping. When we thought they were running away, we discovered shortly that they were trying to fool us into dropping our vigilance. They <u>were</u> fleeing the immediate fray, yes, but they were doing this to hide behind doors, in other rooms, under the stairs, and catch us by surprise and hack or stab us.

We had caught them on a night when four guests were staying overnight. We put this together much later, only when we asked ourselves why there were so many of them, and especially what two village officials, one of them the man who had duped Bir, were doing there. Someone got that evil official in the back with a tangi. (When Bir discovered this, he ran to the fallen, dying man and decapitated him.)

I took out a man as he was tiptoeing out of the pantry to escape into the courtyard. It took me two attempts. The first blow caught him in the shoulder. He fell, screaming. I moved closer and finished him off. He didn't even get a chance to plead for his life.

The search of the house began. Ashu had already given the green light for the redistribution of grain to proceed. The farmers, who had come prepared for this, were waiting outside.

Nabin Sarkar's men had all turned, unknown to themselves, into guerrillas, but they had got a very fundamental principle of that kind of warfare wrong: you didn't turn to the guerrilla mode in an enclosed space with an enemy who was more numerous than you. We won ultimately only because they were outnumbered.

With much misgiving (and dread), I was the first to enter each of the rooms. We got one more of theirs: he had positioned himself behind a door off the landing on the first floor, tangi poised to get one of us the moment we entered, but we rushed in, more than eight or nine of us, in such a fast torrent that he missed and the blow landed on the floor, unbalancing him. A farmer sent a spear through his chest. The force sent him across the landing and halfway down the staircase. The skewer held him at a strange angle to the stairs so that he looked like a piece of bad workmanship, a rejected clay effigy with one oversized bar of his framework showing.

We found four others, hiding, armed, dotted around various places in the house. We rounded them up as we went about searching for money, jewellery and documents. Apart from the walls and other concrete structures, we took everything apart; no Nabin. He had fled. I looked down from the first floor at our ring of men outside and said – No sign. He's gone.

Babu shouted back – We haven't seen him. He can't avoid us. They smuggled him out before we arrived.

– Send a few out to scour the gardens and grounds around us.

But I had little hope: burning torches and hurricane lamps only dazzled the eyes of the person holding them, making the larger surrounding darkness much darker; they didn't shed any useful light. Who knew in which of the neighbours' houses he was hiding, or to which nearby village he was running, as we picked apart his home?

Dipankar discovered money and jewellery stuffed inside pillows and in mattresses, some also in the main almirah. We took what we could use, burning the documents as usual.

As we were getting ready to leave, I managed to put a name to the anxiety that had been tightening around me: I hadn't seen Samir for a while.

After three-quarters of an hour of frenzied searching, Dipankar and I found him on the roof. A tangi driven through his left shoulder and neck was making his half-lopped head lean at a strange angle, a branch of a tree both attached and loosened from the trunk. His eyes were still open to the world, but now they saw nothing.

CHAPTER THIRTEEN

'He must be married off immediately,' Charubala said.

'Yes, that much is obvious,' her husband replied. 'But who will marry him? He's brought our name so low, to dust, which sensible father is going to want his daughter married into a family like ours?'

Charubala heard the rare note of resignation in his voice; she had temporarily lost the will to rally him.

'True, all too true. Was this written in our fate? Who would have thought? Chhee, chhee . . . what humiliation!' The memory of it brought on a strange kind of nausea, one that seemed to come from the neck, not from the pit of her stomach. That blood-pressure business again, she thought; the doctor had asked her to be careful and avoid situations of stress and anxiety. He might as well have asked a fish to avoid water.

'One cannot discipline a man of twenty-one,' Prafullanath said. 'In any case, he has gone beyond the reach of any kind of control or punishment we can impose on him. You stop eating for three days and sulk, I become like a storm cloud for a week . . . do you think these things have any purchase on him? I used to think that putting him to work in the office would do him some good, since he was never going to finish school or go to college. At least he would have to account for his time there; he'd be out of mischief for seven to eight hours a day. He used to show up late, spend an hour adjusting his clothes and hair, then pull rank over the rest of the workers, shout at a few, crack jokes with others, chat, disturb others' work, sing, then leave around two and not show up for the rest of the day. Then he wouldn't turn up for the next two days and would show his face briefly again on the third. To tell you the truth, we reached a point where we were relieved that he didn't come to the office. Six, seven months of this and we discover that he has been taking company money from Ashim-babu, the head clerk, then from Bhola, from the publishing house. Do you know what he does with the money, do you know?' Prafullanath's voice rose dramatically.

Charubala instinctively began to flex an inward defensiveness; *she* could say what she felt like about Somu, but the slightest shadow of criticism from someone else, even from his father, made her feel uneasy. She was his mother; she had rights that no one else did.

'You're right,' said Prafullanath. 'Everything was ordained by fate. Or it is all in the blood. Bad blood will tell one day. All those things I thought I had left far behind . . . I was so wrong. All that depravity and excess, they've all been passed on by me to my children. I feel I have just been a conducting pipe between the bad in the past and the bad in the future.'

Charubala had to staunch this immediately. Very soon, she knew, the self-excoriation would turn sickly and maudlin and, who knew, even into some real threat against Somu.

'There's no point punishing yourself like this. What has happened has happened. We should think about what to do now. I think we should find him a wife immediately, a nice girl who'll set him right, reform his ways.'

'Easier said than done. Besides, we've already had Bhola's wedding this year. It'll be a big financial hit to have another one so soon. He's our youngest son, everybody expects that his wedding will be a big affair. It's not as if it can be a registry-office thing, in and out, then a reception at home.'

Charubala mulled this over and said, 'Why not? He has thrown quicklime-and-ink on our faces, let this be the price he pays for that.' She found herself still caught up in the rapid pendular arc of hating Somu, wanting to punish him severely, and feeling protective towards him. All she wanted was a respite from that constant motion, some resting point.

'No, no,' Prafullanath said. 'How can that be? Everyone will then say that it was a marriage for *our* convenience, to mend his ways. Will you be able to live with that?'

'People can't be saying anything worse than what they're saying now.'

'What is your point?'

There was steel in Charubala. She said, 'Marriage at any cost, that is my point. No point going to a matchmaker this time around. We should look amongst people we know.'

'People we know?'

'Yes. Listen: you, Adi, Priya, all of you know a lot of people through your work in the big world outside. You will have to put your heads together and find a girl soon. Leave the social side of things, reception and ceremony and invitees, leave all that to me.'

In less than three months Adinath found a girl for his younger brother, which led to a regret-filled, jokey aside from his mother: 'You should have been engaged to find a husband for your sister.'

Prasanta, one of the clerks at the office, had come to Adi to ask for an advance on the following month's salary. Eyes fixed firmly on the floor somewhere a few inches away from Adi's feet, he poured it all out. 'It's not for me, sir,' he said. 'One of my uncles has fallen on hard times. He worked as the postmaster in Ranaghat: comfortable government salary, family house with some land around it. There were fruits and vegetables in the garden, even fish in a pond. They weren't well-off, but they got by well enough. But eight years ago they closed down the post office and he hasn't been all right since. Soon after that my grandmother, his mother, that is, died after a long illness. Then the four brothers squabbled over the land and the house. What can I say? I'm ashamed to say that my father was one of them, fighting over inheritance and property and how to divide the garden, the house, the pond. To cut an ugly story short, my uncle was left with hardly anything except two dingy little rooms. He seemed to have lost all will and the brothers exploited this. His wife fought back, but she didn't have a chance. Anyway, since losing his job he has lost all interest in everything. Caught in the middle of all this, suffering the most, is their young daughter, about to sit her secondary-school exams. I feel most for her' – here his voice caught and he had to gulp a few times before he could continue – 'she's sixteen, only four years younger than me, and we grew up together, she's closer to me than my own siblings. I also feel doubly bad because my father is involved in all this. He's responsible, to some extent, for their awful situation.

And I don't want to have any part in it. I help them secretly whenever I can: a sack of rice, a few kilos of lentils, cooking oil, salt, whatever. If they can't pay Purba's school fees, which have been in arrears for a few months now, they'll deregister her and she won't be able to sit her exams. Her parents don't have the wherewithal to get her married; at least if she has a matric to her name, maybe . . .'

The words dribbled to an end. But no, not yet. 'Forgive me, sir,' he added, 'I've taken up a lot of your valuable time with my personal troubles. It's not your business to listen to all this petty rubbish. But, sir, I . . . I didn't know who . . . who to turn to . . .' Here his voice cracked again.

Adi knew in his guts that the man was not spinning him a sentimental tale, one told by so many so often that it had calcified into a giant pillar of cliché, one of those load-bearing struts that held up the structure of Bengali life. But perhaps it had become a cliché because it was a truthful situation for so many people: stretched lives, limited income, indigence, debts, the scrabbling and fighting of dogs replicated by humans. Could he deny that these were not true?

'Don't worry, this is not a problem,' he said. 'Just tell me how much your cousin's school fees are and I'll pay them all – it needn't come off your salary.'

It was only in the small hours, tossing and turning in bed, sleepless with anxiety over the correct structure of the loan for the new imported machines, that a hidden hook, which had caught in the shallows of his memory, revealed itself in a scrap of sentence he had heard earlier in the day. A scheme was murkily outlining itself in his mind; he would have to test the waters first.

The next day he summoned Prasanta and said to him, 'So Ashimbabu should be retired, we think. I was also thinking that maybe you could take over from him. Your salary will go up, of course, and that may help you with the situation in your uncle's family. Talking of which, weren't you saying yesterday about the trouble you will have getting your cousin married? Well . . . what does she look and sound like?'

In a month's time Somnath was married to Purba. Neither of them had much choice in the matter. The Ghoshes withheld from Purba's parents the reason for the haste, and the true nature of their youngest son. Here was a beautiful girl, who looked like the goddess Lakshmi, as Charubala remarked on seeing her picture; surely she would be able to reform Somnath? The Das family, for their part, could not quite believe their luck: the disparity in class (and caste) was so huge as to be unbridgeable, but bridged it was. It never occurred to them to dig deeper or to question why; one doesn't look a gift horse in the mouth.

Prasanta, who was later going to be sorry to see Purba go, experienced the dazed detachment someone feels when events they ignited go far beyond any reasonable trajectory they had imagined. From a request for a loan against his salary from his boss, a trifling piece of the shabby everyday for his class of people, to the marriage of his cousin to the youngest brother of the boss, all within the speed of one month: he will later think that it left his imagination so far behind that he wondered if a faculty that could not imagine things should deserve that name. And there would be something else too, a cloudy suspension in all that clear amazement and disbelief that could only be called envy, as if a fellow prisoner had been released and he left behind to serve his indefinite sentence.

Purba tripped on the edge of her red benarasi sari as she crossed the threshold of her new home. Charubala, Chhaya, Sandhya, Purnima, Jayanti, all the women of the house, were waiting at the doorstep to welcome the new bride with paddy, sandalwood paste, new grass. They bit on their tongues, swallowed their premonitions and got on with blowing on the conch-shells and making the ritual sound of jubilation, *ulu ulu ulu ulu ulu*.

Because there was to be no wedding ceremony on traditional lines – there was a reception in three days – Charubala had decided to treat the day of Purba's entry into the household as an informal boü-bhaat for the family only; she made Purba serve rice to everyone. Purba, transplanted overnight, it felt to her, from a tiny, homely back garden to the immensity of a cultivated steppe, started her new life with all the animation of a machine.

By the time she was shown to her room, where the huge bed, of a size she could not have contemplated previously, had been strewn with flowers and the posters around it decked with hanging curtains of tuberose and tinsel, studded with red roses, it was four hours past her bedtime. She took up one corner of the vast land in front of her and sank instantly into an all-obliterating sleep. Her last thought before shutting down was: 'It's like the field beside the Double Pond back home, this bed, it will take me a very long time to roll from one end . . .'

The nightmare was of a hot, heavy, unidentifiable weight, which seemed to surround her, at once over and around her, something bearing down to crush her ribs and all the breath out of her tiny, squeezed lungs . . . and she could not breathe . . . breathe in . . . brea— She woke up to find a huge animal on her.

She screamed, or tried to. She tried again, but terror seemed to have removed her vocal cords. It was a man wrestling her down, kneading her breasts, tearing at her red-and-gold benarasi, her matching red silk blouse, trying to flip her over and keep her pinned down on the bed at the same time, a man trying to climb her as he would a ladder. She could not even begin to fight back, she was too small. The man was breathing heavily and a terrible smell was issuing out of his mouth, a smell that caught at some corner of her memory. Then, in absolute fear, she began to piss on the bed. No sooner had she finished than the man put his hand between her legs to check on the enormity of what she had just done. As soon as it was verified she was punished for it: briefly, first, with the fingers, then a cracking rod of pain fissured her in half. This time the scream emerged, but a hand was quickly clamped over her mouth as the chastisement of fire continued. Just when she thought she was going to pass out, the man spasmed and grunted, as if seized with a great pain that was going to fell him, then that too stopped and she felt the point of her bisection flooded with a momentarily warm liquid; she knew it was blood; she was going to bleed to death on her wedding night. Her husband rolled off her and fell asleep, it seemed, before the movement had come to a halt.

All she could think about was not her blood leaking out onto the flower-strewn bed, but how it would be discovered tomorrow that she had pissed on it and wet the mattress. The fear, a new kind now, and the shame released the flow of tears at last and she wept and wept, silently and motionlessly, at her absolute incomprehension of why she had been singled out for such searing pain. How long was this punishment going to last? That smell coming out of her husband's open, snoring mouth hit the side of her face in little gusts. She suddenly knew what it reminded her of. Two years ago, just after Kali Puja, in the field beside Double Pond she had smelled something similar to this. In a corner of the grounds, loud with the buzzing of fat, blue flies, lay the blue-red entrails of the goat that had been sacrificed on the night of the puja; the meat was cooked and served to the people of the neighbourhood at a communal lunch the following afternoon. The smell of the rotting intestines had made her retch then. Now, too, she turned sideways and threw up onto the floor, her head leaning out of the side of the bed.

XIII

On our first afternoon hidden in the jungle we heard the sound of conch-shells, one after the other, until there was a kind of chorus of disharmony. Then it stopped. We knew that the police had arrived in Gidighati. The Santhal men had said that was how we were going to be warned.

Nothing happened for a good few hours. Darkness fell. We secreted ourselves deeper into the trees in a fanning circle, so that if they sent the police to the forest, they would be surrounded by us regardless of the point at which they entered. We had only one pistol, the one Dhiren had brought us, a small packet of bullets, nine tangis and three spears (none of us, the city boys, could use a spear, which required years of practice; its weight alone dragged down one side of my body). The rest of our weaponry, sickles and daggers, could only be used in close combat with an unarmed or disarmed enemy, or by stealing up from behind.

Our ears were strained so intently that we could hear every falling leaf, every scurry of a small bird or animal. Later, we picked up on raised voices, a cry or two, but maybe we imagined these. Bir had a pile of kindling ready to carry into the village so that he had a ready excuse if anyone asked what he had been doing in the forest. No one came for us. Bir left in the morning.

Dipankar and I whiled away the hours in the forest, talking about the route we were going to take to Majgeria. I didn't know why I persisted with what I thought of as 'one last visit' to the village I had left behind. Part of it was, of course, the way the fates of Kanu and Bijli haunted me. But part of it was also because I couldn't let a silence descend on us in the daylight, when I felt so naked and exposed, my face and expressions so visible.

I asked – How did you know to look for money and jewellery in mattresses and pillows?

Dipankar said – I saw a pillow leaking some cotton stuffing. Then something, I don't know what, maybe I had felt the corner of something hard while I was tossing the pillows onto the floor, maybe I had noticed a rough line of stitching in the middle of the mattress, something made me feel the pillows again. Bundled paper, I thought. The rest you know.

Yes, the rest I knew. Suddenly, it was the word 'rest' that redistributed an unknown internal system of weights, hardly ever perceived, and brought an enormous heaviness to my chest that rose like a column and tried to escape through my throat and mouth, and I was sobbing like a beaten child, crying helplessly and without shame in front of someone else, my first time since the age of six or seven.

– What am I going to tell Samir's mother? I said through my tears. How am I ever going to be able to show my face to her? We've left him on Nabin's roof, there won't even be a body to return to her.

Dipankar sat me against a tree and let me cry. He said – Be strong.

That was all he said and I was grateful to him for that.

Bir returned at night with food and water and news. The police had come to their corner of the village, rounded up about twenty men and taken them away to Jhargram. They said they were going to come back. Apparently nobody had opened his mouth, when asked about 'some men from outside this village'.

– But the men they've taken away, what's going to happen to them? Ashu asked.

Bir said – Lock-up for a few days, a little bit of beating to find out who was behind killing those dogs. The police are in their pay, so they'll make an effort. If the dogs are all killed, who'll pay them bribes?

– And if the men talk?

Bir laughed – No one will. Not a single one. They want to get rid of the police too. Let them come here, we'll see to them. Not many policemen came. Before, there used to be more.

I had a sudden revelation. I said – They're short of manpower because all these actions in dozens of villages all over Binpur have had them running from one place to another. They're stretched thin. This is our moment.

And the moment arrived the very next day, heralded once again by the discordant and staggered chorus of conch-shells. Minutes passed, or it could have been hours, as we waited, spread out in a wide circle according to our formation plans. My pistol was with Dipankar – he was a far better marksman than I could ever be – and I felt a bit helpless without it. Then the unambiguous sound of humans walking on a dry forest floor: rustling, snapping, an occasional split-second crackle. I peeped from behind my tree with the utmost cautiousness. Nothing except sprays of green and brown vegetation. I was suddenly conscious of how denuded the forest was in winter, how much more cover it would have offered us in the summer and during the monsoon.

The dry rustling stopped. Or maybe it left my field of hearing. I couldn't see any one of us to my left or right. I tried to visualise the path that the policemen – how many of them were there? did they have guns? – would take through our circumscribing circle, and the image of them as a moving diameter came into my head. It was absurd. But what if they were nearer one arc than another? And what if they were out of range for Dipankar? How could he take aim with the trees and bushes and branches in his way, intervening between him and his target? My heart was beating so loudly that I turned round again, stupidly, to check if anyone had heard it. I had a sudden desire to pass water, but I knew I didn't have that luxury.

The noise began, a kind of distant susurration in the undergrowth. There was no breeze, so it could only have been the police. Why weren't they talking or whispering? Were they moving in single file or spreading out? Did they have a plan?

Time trickled like something so viscous, almost solid, that I had to ask myself: was it even moving? Then the report of a gun, followed after the space of two speeded-up thumps of the heart by another. A cry, a burst of rustling followed by voices, then the sound of human chatter, the tone of panic and distress. I bent down, flattened myself against the ground and tried to move like a snake until I came to the next big tree behind which I could stand up. There was a closer, longer outbreak of rustling and movement, and then a brief blood-curdling cry that came to an abrupt stop with a thud. There was the sound of running; how many pairs of feet, I couldn't tell, but they seemed to be coming from all directions. I stood up, forgetting all my training and caution, moved forward from one tree-trunk to another, stopped at an arbitrary one and peeped. I saw Babu and Ashu emerge from the thicket and run past me, tangis raised. I followed them. Soon there was Bir running after me too.

I heard another cry from deep within the thicket where Bir and I were headed, following Babu and Ashu, whom we couldn't see any longer. At a small clearing a sight met my eyes that made my head swim. Debashish was trying to release his tangi, which was lodged in the back of a fallen policeman. Dipankar was removing the gun from yet another policeman, this one with half his head missing. Giri was holding two guns, one in each hand.

– There were six of them, Dipankar panted. One got away. Not into the village, but deeper into the forest. He has a gun.

– Where are the other three? What were the gunshots? Were they firing? I asked.

– No, I sniped two of them, one after the other. I saw their heads above the bushes and fired. I was lucky to get them, very lucky. Then they started running.

– Then? My heart was still hammering.

– Debashish and Giri moved closer to me after they heard me fire. We started chasing the policemen at the same time. They were fleeing us, they didn't turn around to see that we had only one gun and there were only three of us chasing four of them. Giri got one with his tangi. The remaining three scattered. We followed the two that kept together and got them. The other one's gone in that direction.

He pointed with his hand somewhere to the west of where I was standing.

– But we have five rifles now, he said. And also their clothes, it'll help camouflage.

– We'll have to take them to the village to wash off the blood, Babu said. Some will be ruined, anyway.

– Let's see what we can salvage, Dipankar said. Then to Babu – Wash and dry them stealthily, see that no one notices you have police uniforms with you.

We located the fallen policemen in reverse order of their killing. There were flies buzzing above them already, some clustered in the centre of their fresh, wet wounds. Of the two Dipankar had shot, one wasn't dead and had dragged himself into the bushes, leaving his rifle behind. We saw to him with his own gun, there seemed to be some kind of poetic justice in that. Then we set about disposing of the bodies.

Babu and Bir and Giri kept us supplied with food and water. We were anxious about the inevitable, terrible repercussions that this execution of policemen would have. There was no turning back from this point. But we didn't hear cars or vans, so we assumed . . . well, we assumed a number of things, each as theoretical as the other: they didn't know about their dead comrades yet; they were in the planning stages of an all-out revenge attack; they were still trying to work out what exactly had happened; they were trying to lull us into a false sense of security so that we would emerge from the forest and then they'd strike.

Meanwhile, our three Santhal friends brought us something that was situated somewhere between news and speculation. The police had not been to the village, or to their neighbourhood, and there was talk that even armed members of the force were refusing to enter the forest to flush out the 'police killers'.

Could this be true? We debated this for hours, turned it this way and that to see if we could extract any hidden meaning from it. Was it a good thing that they were afraid? Did it mean we could have a clean run at our revolution? Was this going to be the pattern everywhere: the police taking fright and ceding the ground to us, leading to our victory? No obstacles, no warfare, no bloodshed, no toil . . . No, no, it sounded too good to be true.

The debate changed direction at this point. We fell over each other trying to point out the legion instances of the police <u>always</u> acting against the people and for the state. They were the guard dogs of government: they were let loose on a state's own people every time there was a move towards greater equality or fairness or justice, and they obliged without fail. Every time. They had no morality, no principles; only a slavish obedience to whoever paid them any money. (There is a precise word for this profession, but I won't offend your ears with it.) Throughout history, in every single nation in the world, this class of paid servant of the state has turned against its own people, terrorised them, beaten and tortured them, unleashed untold misery and repression, like those illnesses where the body's own immune cells have gone so horribly wrong that they whip around and attack the harbouring body itself.

Our Santhal comrades kept us alive and hidden. They taught us to read the direction of the wind; the nature of tracks in the forest when none seemed visible to our urban eyes; under which trees we shouldn't sleep in the night; which insects were poisonous; how to identify holes where rodents and snakes could be living; which dried leaves to use and how to layer and line them in order to make a kind of 'bed' at night, so that the moisture from the earth didn't make us cold or damp; the leaves of which small bush to squish into a paste and apply to cuts and insect bites; what it signified when the red soil paled into a browner shade; which wood didn't smoke when burned; how to use a line of trees to orientate yourself; how to leave a track of markers for someone in the group who might get lost; the way to weave a zigzag track among the trees, avoiding hitting them, as someone chased you with a bow-and-arrow . . . I focused on each lesson with a concentration that sometimes made me feel that the soft bits behind my eyes had been brought to a point of white heat. It kept my mind off other things.

All this talk of Santhals – I suppose I keep skirting around the issue that's uppermost in both our minds. Does the word 'Santhal' make you quail? Still? Every time I use the word I hesitate, thinking of what kind of reaction it'll spark in you, reading it. And I'm also conscious of the fact that I'm not very far from the Chhotanagpur Plateau area, where Chhoto-kaka died: it's only a short hop away across the border into Bihar. Our Santhal friends, while they cannot possibly be related to the Santhals Chhoto-kaka and his friends encountered all those years ago, must be part of the lateral spread of the same people. I remember a story from childhood in which they were referred to as 'people of the red soil'. The image stayed with me, dormant, until it germinated when I first came to these parts and saw those words in my memory given life and reality in the world.

Is it fanciful of me, do you think, to imagine the reason for the colour of the earth of this region – that it is red with the blood of its exploited people? Do you remember a story you told me when I was little ('prancing around in silk dhoti and silk panjabi', as you put it, on the day of your wedding)? Chhoto-kaka had just died and you had had to give up eating meat and fish and eggs, when I noticed one day that there seemed to be a sanction on eating mushur dal, red split lentils, as well? (I've never asked you this before, but I must now: all these intricate and punishing sumptuary laws, were they imposed on you by my grandmother? Or did you invite them upon yourself?) Yes, the innocent, obviously and purely vegetarian red split lentils – what wrong had they done? You explained that a god had once fought an evil demon above a plantation of pulses, and the god had slain the demon and the demon's blood had stained the grain indelibly. This was the origin of red split lentils, in bloodshed, and so it was not as strictly vegetarian as I had assumed it to be, you said; there were things that a boy, regardless of his knowledge of stories about the Buddha, didn't know, so there.

I was eleven years old at the time and you were eighteen.

The night was very cold. I could see torn scraps of the black night sky, almost smoky and milky with the dense scatter of stars, through the gaps in the tops of the trees, but no longer your face or your name; I couldn't see a stretch of the sky big enough for that. When it wasn't the cold that kept me awake, it was the continual sounds of the forest, the rustling and scraping and murmuring, as if a furiously busy world, unseen by the human eye, was going about its stealthy activity. Often, when the sounds got a bit louder or more sustained, I thought it was the escaped policeman who had come to look for us, to slaughter us in our sleep. And whenever I shut my eyes I could see Samir's in death, open, unseeing, the whites disproportionately larger than the pupils.

Before I fell asleep I had this thought: forests, wherever available, could be profitably used for the purposes of our revolution. Our armies – no longer two or three or five guerrillas – could hide there; food, water and other supplies, including an advance warning system, could be provided by the inhabitants of whichever villages the forest skirted; the forests could be taken over completely and become no-go zones for the state and its organs of repression . . . Very quickly, in my mind, the dream became swollen to something almost real. To deal with our future armies they would have to cut down entire forests, and how were they going to do that? I fell asleep to the imagining of an imminent new dawn.

Next day, Dipankar and I set out for Majgeria. We took the pistol with us. It was just a precaution – Dipankar swore blind that the journey was going to be entirely through the forests, so we were never going to be in a position to be discovered.

Before we left, Babu handed me a bundle of chhatu and what looked like a cloth side-bag.

Babu said – That friend of yours, that babu who . . . who didn't return, it's his. I'm giving it back to you.

I didn't know why I took so long to recognise Samir's bag. His meagre belongings were in it: a short-sleeved shirt, musky with his odour; a pair of pyjamas; a box of 777 matches; a copy of The Little Red Book, almost every single line underscored in pencil and dot-pen, with notes written in the margins. There was a Collected Poems of Jibanananda Das, with lines from some poems marked. The book fell open at the poem 'Wristwatch'; I noticed he had glossed a difficult word in it – he had underlined it and written 'lust' in the margin. I too hadn't known the meaning of that word. There was a notebook too. My hands were shaking as I swiftly thumbed through the pages: drafts of poems that blurred and then became illegible because of my tears.

Dipankar and I stopped to eat from our bundle of chhatu. It was late afternoon. I felt tired and my eyes kept closing. From far away came the sound of the whistle, long and melancholy and pleading, of a train. I didn't know why, but the lonely sound had sleepiness associated with it, and the promise of an untethering, as if the sleep it induced would liberate me from the here and now and set me afloat on some infinite ocean of peace and silence and calm.

My eyelids grew heavier. Dipankar must have seen me nodding off, so he tried to engage me in conversation. He too had heard the train's whistle. He asked – What train do you think that is?

– Don't know, I mumbled.

– How far do you think the nearest railway track is?

– No idea.

– Near Gidhni or Tatanagar and Jamshedpur, no? Do you think the sound's coming from that far away? Impossible.

– Who knows?

– I should know, I think it's the train route I used to go down as a child to visit a distant uncle in Giridih every year during the puja holidays. The uncle's still alive, but we haven't been for so many years . . .

He seemed almost to be talking to himself. I felt unmoored from the ground I was sitting on, about to levitate.

Suddenly Dipankar's momentary lull of introspection snapped and he turned his attention to me – You're almost asleep. We need to get going. Come on, come on.

It wouldn't do to nod off now, so I forced myself to make conversation.

– I've heard Giridih is a nice place.

He said – Yes, it is. Clean, and a nice dryness to the air. I loved it as a child. There are little hills dotted around the place. The city boy in me found that exciting. There are waterfalls and little streams and forests. It's very pretty. And quiet. Do you want to come with me one day?

– That would be nice, but when?

– I would say as a holiday from all this, but maybe it's more likely that we'll need to go there to hide. Kharagpur, Jhargram, all the Calcutta stations, they're bristling with policemen. They're watching the trains and the stations in this area like hawks.

The thought of hiding in a calm, pretty corner of Bihar, away from all this action, was so appealing that my eyes began to droop again. A brown kite was wheeling above us, its squealing whinny working on me like the far-away train whistle.

Dipankar noticed and gamely made another attempt to engage my interest. He said – Let me tell you an interesting thing about railway tracks. Did you know about fishplates? They're metal bars that are bolted to the ends of tracks to make them one and continuous.

Only an engineer would think he could keep someone awake by talking about engineering. Silly, innocent man.

All I wanted to do was find out about Kanu and Bijli, but I couldn't risk being seen walking around in the familiar village even though the gapless dark of the rural night had long fallen. It was Dipankar who would have to be my eyes and ears in Majgeria. I had been repeating to him the detailed directions to identify Kanu's hut so often that he asked me to shut up. He could tell I was on edge; I was behaving like a nervous mother seeing her son off to battle.

I paced the jungle while he was gone, possessed of a fiendish energy that I had been lacking all these days. Mind you, the energy didn't seem to affect the slothful nature of time; that ticked on slower than ever. I convinced myself that Dipankar had been gone for hours. Over and over again I did the calculation for the time to walk there + time to investigate + time to walk back, and under different conditions imposed on each of those variables, so that the numbers themselves started getting distorted.

By the time he returned, I was standing as much outside the jungle as I dared, reduced to what felt like a state of instant combustibility.

– Put on the police uniform, he said. Come with me. Very, very quietly.

Dressed in a khaki outfit we had taken off one of the executed policemen in Gidighati, I followed him but, surprisingly, deeper into the jungle, eastwards.

– What's up? I asked.

– The sound of our feet on these fallen leaves is very loud. I'm always scared that people outside will know there's someone moving around in here.

We were speaking in whispers.

I said – It sounds loud to us, but no one outside can hear it, don't worry.

– Listen, bad news. I think they're deploying the military police here. A group has set up camp in a building on the other side. It'll be impossible to go through the village, that's why we're doing it the long way.

Thunder fell on my head. So the ordinary district police couldn't cope with the number of actions erupting around the place and were stretched so thin that the military and the reserve police forces had had to be called in. Did we ever factor this into our equations?

Dipankar didn't remember discussing it with anyone. Neither did I. How could one fight the army with a toybox-worth of axes and spears?

He spoke the words of the man who knew his side had lost everything

– Listen, I may be wrong. Another pair of eyes is always a good idea.

In any case, it was a bit futile to try and spy on them at night, at least from that distance. We could see nothing for a long time as we stood behind the trees. Then we moved out of the cover of the forest and advanced closer, across open fields, towards the building that was the village school. A dog barked. It could have been any of the strays in the village, but to me it sounded more aristocratic, the sound of the military's guard dog. We edged back into the protective cover of the trees, rewarded only with the silhouette of a man who crossed the dimly lit square of the window a few times. Did I imagine an odd outline humping his shoulders into a strange shape, something added to the human form and sticking out above the side? Did I will myself to see a rifle strapped to his back?

A tuneless snatch of melody reached us. One of them was singing. It sounded as if the singer was Bihari.

It was only the next morning, in daylight, that we were able to establish more. A uniformed military policeman was sitting on a chair in a patch of sun outside the entrance to the school, rubbing tobacco on the palm of one hand with the thumb of the other. Like the seven other men we could count, he indeed had a rifle strapped to his back and a belt of live rounds around his waist. Dipankar was correct in all his assumptions: they really had set up base in the school.

The two of us would be routed in a matter of minutes if we took them on. My own death I could be stoical about, after much training, but I did not have the stomach to see yet another friend killed. We debated, but very briefly, the possibility of a guerrilla attack at night. There was no hope for it. We had to leave Majgeria, perhaps to return in the near future with reinforcements, but for now it looked hopeless.

To have shared what Kanu and Bijli were most probably going through now, the hell of police-beatings and incarceration, would have been better than this limbo of darkness and ignorance and amateurish planning and laughable resources.

It's not possible to tell, once inside a forest, how far from or how close to your destination you are; everything looks the same. Only the time elapsed is a marker. As agreed, we were going to sing well-known revolutionary songs as we got close to our comrades' encampment so that they could tell we were approaching, not strangers or enemies; Comrade Subbarao Panigrahi's composition 'Tell me, can you prevent the sun from shining with your tiny hand?' and 'We advance towards the edge of life to pluck light from the stalk of darkness'. I say 'encampment' but it was no such thing, of course. Besides, there was the very real possibility of our comrades having moved on to another patch of the forest for reasons of security. There was no spirit in us to sing the songs with any degree of interest or tunefulness, so they came out like badly recited poetry.

Ashu and Debashish came out of the jungle, one by one, from behind trees and bushes, to meet us. For a few seconds I couldn't recognise them, I was so shocked by their appearance – thin, reedy, dark men in dirty clothes, unwashed, unkempt, puffy eyes with dark circles under them, looking like a bunch of beggars afflicted by chronic starvation . . . Then I thought that they must be thinking the same about me.

Then, making my heart come out of my mouth, Dhiren emerged from the jungle: they had been hiding him so that I could be given a surprise. I embraced him.

— At least starvation and all this vagabondage have brought out your tender side, he quipped, returning my embrace.

It was as if we had never parted. We went to a clearing marked by a little black patch on the ground where they had clearly burned wood and leaves to keep themselves warm. I noticed that they had been careful to leave the fire small and contained.

After the beautiful surprise came the nasty shock: troops from the Eastern Frontier Rifles had set up camp in Gidighati. Dhiren, who had been out in the wider world, brought us news that was both dispiriting and blood-boiling. The Home Minister, Jyoti Basu, apparently at the request of the Chief Superintendents of the police forces of the 'districts afflicted by terrorism', had given orders for the EFR and military police to be deployed. The big landlords of the area, who had the police in their pockets, and most of the politicians too, had got together, both in public and in private, and used their combined power to pull the levers at the topmost level. None of the process and reasoning behind it was surprising, only the fact of the outcome. But we were beginning to get used to that, too.

When I asked where Babu and Bir were, they looked away. Ashu said, after a bit of hesitation, that they had returned to the village, worried by what their families were facing during the crackdown, and hadn't come back.

— What are you eating then? I asked.

— We can't stay here any longer, Ashu said, we'll have to go back to Belpahari and rethink.

— And the military camps are everywhere here? I asked.

Dhiren confirmed — In all the villages that have seen action. If not all, then soon it will be all.

I could tell that a strange battle was playing out inside all of us, a conflict between despair and anger. Which would win? The endpoint of a course of action (or inaction) led by either was unclear, but if we could do something, anything, to dent some of the might of these EFR bases, then they would know at least that we meant business, we were not going to slink off like frightened dogs. Besides, we had pledged our lives to the revolution.

I said as much, but failed to ignite any spark, only distracted murmurs from averted faces. Everyone seemed to have fallen into a small, private pit of blackness.

We went back to Belpahari and returned, one day before a new-moon-night, to Gidighati, all five of us, armed with home-made grenades. Not everyone returned for further action willingly. Someone suggested that one way of staying on in the forests was to force the villagers to provide us with food and drink and other necessities, using the same method that the police were using to discourage them from supporting us. There was some indecision initially about which of the military camps to attack, the one at Majgeria or the one at Gidighati. Ultimately the decision came to hang on the most important factor: which one was closer to the forest so that we would be least on open ground, fully exposed and in the line of fire? Gidighati, therefore, it was, although I still tried to push for Majgeria even while I knew that it was a lost cause. It was a place close to my heart, since I had spent over two years there. But Party always before individual . . .

It all went horribly wrong.

Because the policeman on guard was dozing in his chair we thought we'd creep up on him and get him first: either finish him off or use him as a hostage. Ashu, Dipankar and I were moving very carefully for a frontal attack – Dhiren and Debashish, both in police uniform, were approaching the back of the school from the village for a rear attack – but we knew that we couldn't nab him. There was too much open ground to cover and we would be exposed on all sides. I was surprised that no one was looking out of the first-floor windows at regular intervals. I hoped we were not visible if they did decide to scrutinise the surrounding darkness periodically. There was a bad feeling looping inside me, something coiled and heavy, taking in my heart and stomach. It was not the mixture of fear, exhilaration and anger that I had felt during the earlier actions. This one was dull, blunted, something that weighed me down and pushed me towards a kind of lethargy.

A dog, which had been asleep and making tiny squealing noises in its dream, woke up and started sniffing the air. Then everything happened together, so that writing it down as a string of events, one after the other, somehow falsifies the reality and the experience of it. The dog stood up and began to bark. The man started, woke up and, in the time that he took to work out that the dog had reason to be barking, all three of us were upon him. Ashu drove the tangi straight through his chest and I shot the dog, both at the same time. There was an explosion – clearly either Dhiren or Debashish had lobbed a grenade into the building – then another, followed rapidly by the sound of shots and men shouting. We crouched low and waited for someone to come out of the front.

The sound of confusion from the back of the building had reached a peak now. We couldn't make out a word. The shooting continued, but there were no further explosions. This could only mean one thing: that they had got Dhiren and Debashish. Between them, they had ten bombs. We could see the light from the flames where something had caught fire. As Ashu was ridding the dead guard of his bayonet, two men charged out. One instantly bayoneted Ashu through his stomach. Before they could act further, Dipankar and I let out a roar and hurled two, three, four grenades into the building behind the men. We got one of the men on his thigh with a tangi while the other ran off sideways, presumably to get more men, now that he had seen only two of us. The building was burning. There was nothing to do except flee into the forest.

We ran in short zigzags, as we had been taught. Then we heard the sound of two more explosions behind us. At least one of them was alive! I expected to be shot at as we were escaping, but nothing; the soldiers were concentrating on bombs being hurled at them. Which meant that Dhiren and Debashish's lives were going to be the price for ours, unless we were caught too.

I was panting so much that I thought I was going to have a heart attack. Once inside the brush, the running got difficult; we were nearing dense cover.

Dipankar's words came out in small bursts, almost incomprehensible – Not towards Belpahari, no. Bihar. Bihar. Giridih, we'll try Giridih, not very far . . . My uncle, we could . . .

– Can you lead?

They did not have enough numbers to mount a search in the forest, not that night, so we had to get out before they called up more troops and surrounded the forest, locking us in there with no hope of escape.

CHAPTER FOURTEEN

1969

Increasingly nowadays Prafullanath finds himself dividing to become two persons. One of those detaches and watches the old, nearly crippled, broken fool lying on his high bed, sometimes even unable to wipe the drool threading out from the corner of his slack mouth. It has not always been like this. The feeling of doubleness, of being a spectator in his own life, is new. What does one do with one's own life but live it? Now, to watch what little there is left of it from the sidelines makes Prafullanath wonder – has he stopped living? If there are two of him, as he so strongly feels, which is the real he: the one who watches or the one who is embodied, on the bed, afflicted by the needles and rods of gout, by the creeping solidification of arthritis, by the capricious fluctuations of blood sugar and, reigning above, the omnipotent emperor of them all, the deadly, yet silent heart disease?

He can tell from the muffled noises that the final preparations are under way for Baishakhi's wedding. She is the first of his grandchildren to get married and he will be lucky to be supported in a chair and wheeled out for a few minutes before being sent off to bed again. Both families will do a token obeisance to him as head of the family, blessings and all that rubbish, then will be relieved to carry on with the real business of celebration, away from his orbit of illness and senescence. No full-blown participation for him. Besides, what is there to participate in? It is not as if this wedding, in this falling time, is going to compare with the grand three-day events, loud with people and music, glittering with gems and wealth and opulence, that he had arranged for each of his sons. Well, for most of them, anyway. At each of those weddings he had insisted on a small projecting enclosure, much like a miniature balcony, to be constructed above the doorway for the musicians to sit in, so that guests could be welcomed with shehnai-music. At Adi's wedding the terrace where the guests had dined had been wrapped in maroon velvet, and the maroon-velvet carpets on the stairs leading to it sprinkled with rose petals and rose-water. For Priyo, Prafullanath had had fifty-lamp chandeliers installed in every room. The finest caterers, four fish courses and three meat, and five types of sweets at the banquets – these were the luxuries to remind you that you had worked hard to get here, a private treat to yourself and to the sons who were going to carry on your line.

But something about that phrase 'private treat' brings on an anxious confusion . . . some . . . some search for an answering image that will explain this sudden unease but he can grasp at nothing nothing except for the idea of a sharp edge or maybe an image could that be an image of a sharp a sharp a sharp something and then blood . . . oh god, it is best not to go there so he shuts that bad window because he has been warned by his doctor not to dwell on things that make him anxious or unhappy. But he has now lost the bookmark showing where he was before the intensification in his heartbeat began and cannot move back or forward from the bad thing that has cast its shadow over him but refuses to show itself.

The clatter of crockery, the busy feet up and down the stairs, electricians and decorators and catering staff and servants hollering and talking, children shouting, women chattering – does he hear it all or does he imagine them happening outside his door? One generation builds, the next generation consumes it to nothing; that is the abiding truth of life. That is the abiding law of *Bengali* life. Look at the Marwaris; they come from villages in Rajasthan, stick together, work together and build family empires in business that subsequent generations consolidate. Their wealth, power, dominion – everything expands. They buy up everything and keep it in their family concern because they know that the family is going to be the driving power, the unit of cohesion and commercial force. In his life, his family has been the eroding power: he built, his sons ate. His heart races again. He has exchanged his earlier bad place for yet another, as if each square on the snakes-and-ladders board he is traversing has the head of a snake on it.

Then the biggest head appears, its flickering forked tongue reaching out over several squares to get him. Those words again, those words that could have only been said into the darkness, not when light made faces and expressions perceptible, when one had to look at people to talk to them. How like a child's terror it had been, a child admitting a misdeed to a savagely strict parent, that same sweatiness under questioning, that identical trembling and pummelling in the chest, as he spoke those shameful emasculating words to the darkness in the room, to the walls of the mosquito net, those words fearfully testing what Charubala thought of giving up some of her gold to . . . to . . . to help them out after all it was not for his own benefit but for the good of all of them and maybe it was all a temporary arrangement these switchbacks happened in any business and when times were good again just round the corner there would be restitution he knew there would. All the while a childish superstition tugging away like a stealth current under the churn of his words and thoughts – someone who gave something and demanded it back was reborn as a dog in Kalighat crematorium. Worse still, the foggy wraith from an early chapter of his life: Jyotish Pal crumbling down while telling him of that great unthinkable, selling off his wife's jewellery to keep rack and ruin at bay, and he, Prafullanath, so moved by it that he had helped his friend with money so that he could hold on to his store on Harrison Road. He has now become what he was most terrified of.

Priyo feels the diminishment as pity in his soul. What anger there was that his daughter has chosen a callow, flashy ne'er-do-well for a husband instead of dutifully allowing her parents to find her the right kind of man has now burned itself out; the residue in the crucible is resigned pity. Pity because her wedding is going to be so much more restrained than his own or his brothers' had been. What had been a river in spate runs as a contemptible trickle now, like a baby's piss-stream. His daughter's in-laws had not noticed; the dowry they had demanded had been pegged to a public idea of the Ghoshes' financial might and standing. It had been far-sighted of Priyo's father to have bought so much jewellery during the days of plenty. Garlands of gold guineas; armbands of solid gold studded with emeralds and rubies and diamonds; lurid tiaras – what was he thinking? or, more pertinently, of *whom* was he thinking? – encrusted with gems; sometimes even plain solid-gold bricks. There was no way the family could have lived up to what had been expected of them, had it not been for his mother's jewellery hoard: it had helped them save face. The outside world has so far been kept from noticing that family jewellery is being sold off or pawned to surmount liquidity problems. Or so he thinks. The fear that others may have an inkling sends a familiar feeling in to his guts, a feeling that he needs to evacuate immediately.

He tries to dispel the sensation by dwelling on how he is literally going to cover his daughter in gold, for everyone to see, at her wedding. No one outside need know that his mother has only loaned what is left of her jewellery to prop up the illusion of family wealth; since his wife and his mother had so recently fallen out with each other over the contentious issue of ornaments, his mother is in no mood to part with any of her belongings to help Purnima.

'Take them to deck Baishakhi. But I want them back, each and every single one of them. I'm counting out the pieces, so I'll know if anything goes missing. It was an evil hour when I gave my blessings on your marriage to that woman,' Charubala said.

The situation is not ideal, far from it, but averting this public loss of face somehow compensates for the private shame he feels at being unable to give his daughter the kind of wedding that people in Bhabanipur would talk about in years to come. They will say, 'He covered his daughter in gold' and that will be consolation enough, for satisfaction is not going to come from the number of guests (limited to 150 only), shehnai-players sitting in a temporary Juliet balcony (they were going to play records of Bismillah Khan and have a loudspeaker to broadcast the music) or posh caterer (merely a hired cook). Yes, he feels sorry for Baishakhi. Then he begins playing the game, comforting and incendiary in equal measure, of casting about to blame someone, something . . . Today, the long shadows thrown by his father's stubborn insistence on a radical technological upgrade at the plant at Memari would do.

When Priyo began to discover how much Baba had exposed to risk for the sake of the modernisation of the plant at Memari, the offering up of the Bali mill as collateral seemed the most breathtaking. At the time the other detail, that the larger part of Ma's jewellery in the locker, and all of the family's investment in gold, had been bound as security

too, had seemed trivial, a matter of the private domain, easily contain-
able. Now that petty subclause raises its head to bite him every day as
if in punishment for being written off as harmless. Over the last ten
years choice bits and pieces, mostly the pure-gold biscuits, had been
sold, sometimes to pay the pressing interest on a loan, sometimes to
nibble away at the principal of such a loan from the bank. When those
gold ingots were all gone, it was the turn of his mother's jewellery.
One evening, in the immediate aftermath of the disaster that was the
upgrade of Memari, he and Dada, seeing no way out, had broached
the topic of needing a lump sum of ready cash in front of their mother.
The money was required for bribing customs officials to release the
imported machinery from Kidderpore Docks. They had perhaps not
initiated the conversation pointedly, with the implicit purpose of asking
their mother to release some of her ornaments. They had not even
known, if he remembers the evening correctly, that she was participating in this men's chat, so that the words she had used to enter the
discussion had felt like a slap to their faces.

'Sell my garlands of guineas,' she had said. 'They've already been
pledged to the bank as security, your father has told me. What difference does it make if what almost belongs to the banks becomes totally
theirs? At least it'll save us from shame.'

The brothers' burning faces had felt too heavy to lift up to look at
their mother, or at each other. Priyo can close his eyes now and
summon up exactly the configuration of the residual grains of rice
on the plate, the wipe-marks of his fingers on the central smear of
drying yellow gravy, the vertebral column of the fish picked clean and
its head chewed and the fibrous bits rejected in a compact grey bolus
on one side.

Their mother had filled the silence with words meant to soothe
and salvage. 'What's the big deal?' she had said. 'What's mine is yours,
you're my sons. Money, gold – these things come and go. It's not
good to form attachments to these things. I'm selling off my gold
today, it'll come back to me tomorrow, I know it.'

But Priyo thinks of it as the beginning of the long plunder. He has
no idea what she makes of the business of having to sell off most of
her valuables to pay for the mistakes of her husband, and it is not
something that can ever be talked about, but now, seeing her sudden

parsimony at parting, even temporarily, with what little she has left, it is her generosity that lashes him, and the curdling of that largesse because of the conflict with his wife is a reduction of his spirit, not his mother's.

And Baba? What had he made of his shame? Conveniently enough, he had still been on his protracted recovery arc after his first heart attack in 1957, the one nearly two years before the new machines arrived, so not much could be raised with him, most definitely not in any accusatory or angrily remonstrating ways. The potential confrontation would itself then have become the excuse for another bout of illness, possibly even another heart attack. Priyo and Adi had struggled on as best as they could, coping with nearly six years of zero output at Memari. When, at last, the new machines had started working, the TPD had increased by a risible twenty, not the 125 that Baba had hoped for and shown in the applications for the bank loans. It was going to be a long drought, with all the profits going to offset the crippling loans, but at least the mills, or – unthinkable – their house, wouldn't have to be sold. The factory at Bali had continued to be their saviour. Some sadistic god must have laughed at this: within twenty months union trouble began at Bali. Two years later, the factory shut down. The full implication of putting Bali as collateral revealed itself.

When Prafullanath had been inflexible about pushing ahead with his deranged idea of a face-to-face with Dulal, Priyo and Adi had said, over and over, 'Baba, this is madness. You are the arch-enemy for him and his CPI(M) paymasters, why would he even want a meeting with you?'

Rage, lidded down for months, had turned Prafullanath into a creature that was not quite he, but an approximate simulacrum. Ever since he had come to know of Dulal's mischief-making, he had wanted to use the most aggressive strategies to deal with the man – having him beaten up, even eliminated, by goons; firing his father, Madan; bribing powerful people who could pull strings for him at the CPI(M) headquarters on Potuatola Lane to have either the union defanged or the police ordered to act. Not for the first time Priyo had wondered if he shouldn't have immediately told his father and Dada about that meeting with Ashoke-babu instead of sitting on it for over a year. Would Dulal have reached this stature if he had addressed the issue then? Would they ever have reached this point?

There was a short interim when Prafullanath was prepared to rehire the same workforce in its entirety, even pay them their salaries for the duration of the lockout, if they were willing to drop their intransigent demand for the reinstatement of Sujan Hazra, the man who had been dismissed after he had lost his hand in an accident. The issue became circular and, for Prafullanath, it was a matter of honour not to capitulate; he had made enough concessions. So this new tune, of a direct meeting with the man they considered to be the central nervous system of all their woes, was not born out of a mood for compromise and conciliation. That would be like a lion lying down with a lamb although, in Priyo's mind, the roles of predator and prey kept shifting. He had the presentiment of something coiled and dangerous, something that could only end in terrible things, and said as much to his father.

'I have a better business head than you,' Prafullanath had shot back. 'In ten years you and your brothers have turned to dust what I built up from nothing. Now you're asking me to pay heed to your old woman's fears?'

This was of a piece with Prafullanath's recent attitude towards all his sons, so Priyo had merely clenched his teeth and wished, for more than a fleeting moment, that serious ill would really befall his father during the confrontation.

And so it had.

Red pennants, bearing the sickle-and-hammer insignia, planted for a good half a mile along the stretch of road leading to the factory, squashed any residual doubt that this was an isolated incident at one factory. When the request for some policemen to escort them had been turned down, Prafullanath had insisted on having a carload of paid local Congress goons to accompany them in case the laid-off workers got violent.

'The CPI(M) will have planted anti-social elements among the picketing workers there. We'll be murdered without protection,' Prafullanath had said.

'But only the police can deter them. They'll know you've come looking for mischief, that you want confrontation, if you turn up with the neighbourhood tough guys,' Adi had argued. 'Then there will certainly be violence. Whereas now there's only a very slight possibility.'

Adi had prevailed, but it took only the sight of the little flags fluttering in the breeze to unnerve him. Had he made a mistake? What if something happened? They wouldn't dare, would they? It's one thing to gherao a manager, but to rough-handle the owning family? No, no, that couldn't be; they had the invisible aura of protection that royalty and god-men had; they couldn't be touched.

They had kept their visit secret for several reasons: chiefly, they wanted to catch Dulal off-guard, but equally important was their fear of a crowd of more than 200 people barring their way, shouting slogans, trying to intimidate them with sheer volume of noise, or standing on the margins, silently watching them with a kind of simmering and vengeful alertness, waiting for a signal to be let loose.

But there was only a handful of people squatting outside, six or seven at the most. The rusty red iron gate of Ghosh Paper Mill now had more locks and chains than its security had ever needed; that shameful, mocking excess marked its descent into a more permanent state of closure. Posters obscured almost its entire surface. There was no GHOSH PAPER MILL, painted in an arch, followed by the smaller BALI, DISTT. HOOGHLY, to be seen, but instead: *We're fighting for unfairly dismissed Sujan, we'll keep fighting; Owners, answer why you shut down a profit-making factory! The pending salaries of the fired workers must be paid without delay; Workers of the world, unite,* among scores of others.

The presence of a car outside the gates seemed to rouse the men. Adi rolled down a back-window, pushed his head out and asked, 'Is Dulal here?'

He thought he would be recognised instantly, but clearly these stragglers didn't know who he was.

'Dulal-da's not here. Who are you?' a man asked.

Before Adi could answer, Prafullanath intervened. From the front seat he said haughtily, 'I'm Prafullanath Ghosh, the owner of this mill. Bring Dulal.'

In the back, his sons, expecting contempt and defiance, clenched themselves, but were wrong-footed by that ineradicable tendency towards the bent knee in the labourer-class of people. The man bowed his head, lifted up his joined hands, but before he could settle into full servility, Prafullanath got out of the car and repeated, 'Send for Dulal. Tell him Prafulla Ghosh has come to see him.'

Priyo croaked, 'Baba, what are you doing? Have you lost your mind?'

The man ran off, whispered with the others, then came back to the car and said, 'It won't be possible to get hold of Dulal-da now. He's not around. What do you want? Maybe someone else . . .'

Prafullanath cut him short with, 'What do you mean by "not around"? Where is he then?' The hauteur was now mixed with irritation.

Two men left the symbolic picket and started making their way across the fields in the direction of the town.

The sun climbed the sky. Prafullanath, a bent, desiccated figure, barely managing to steady his bony grip on the silver lion's head that topped his polished black cane, tried to pace hobblingly outside the car. All he managed was an impression of an old, injured crab. Then he got in, slammed the door, got out again, paced a while longer, re-entered the car . . . It carried on like this for an hour, maybe two.

'This is *my* mill and *I* and *my* sons can't enter it,' Prafullanath spat out the words. 'It's my last standing mill and I'm not going to die before I modernise it. I'll not let another Marwari swallow this one, too. If I have to shoot every single one of these striking beggars, I'll do it, but I'll see my mill opened.'

A trembling took him as he spoke these words. Adi and Priyo shook too, inwardly and with terror; their father seemed like someone possessed. This unbending mood of confrontation was not what they had bargained for when they had so reluctantly given in to their father's determination to face down Dulal.

More people arrived and joined the four or five still standing near the gate. They stood at a distance, staring at the Ghoshes. It was here, Priyo later reminisced, that some kind of slippage in perception or memory took place, a kind of foggy passage between the before and after. When they next noticed, more staring men had gathered, and they weren't positioned only at the picket lines in front of the locked factory gate, but were on both sides of their car, and in front of it, and at the back: Prafullanath, Adi, Priyo and Gagan were being slowly ring-fenced. It didn't occur to Priyo even then that something was afoot, that this staring was anything other than the customary curiosity of provincial people who had never seen a car, who had so little excitement in their lives that the arrival of city-folk in an Ambassador was a spectacle.

The Ghoshes got out of their car, leaving Gagan inside. It was only then that the pattern began to acquire significance: the Ambassador had gradually become an island, surrounded, after a clear ring of fifteen feet or so, by a thickening circle of people. Beyond them, Priyo saw more coming over the fields, crossing culverts, emerging from behind banana trees. Who were they? They seemed to be rising out of the earth, like in that story he had read as a child, in which demons sprang out of teeth sown in the ground.

The signal for what happened next remained unseen and unheard, but not the result. A chant went up: *Why was Sujan Hazra fired? Owner, answer us! Answer us!* Then, two different ones, old, reliable mainstays: *Grind and crush the black hand of the owners. Grind! Crush!* and *Our agitation is continuing, will continue.* Priyo located and recognised the man who was leading the chanting. His name was Ashish Majhi. He worked in the boiler room and the Foudrinier room. That recognition released something, for Priyo now began to identify more and more of the faces in the crowd. They were surrounded by their former employees or, more accurately, the whole workforce that they had fired ten months ago. A current of fear thrilled through him.

Prafullanath, however, seemed to be buoyant on rage. With the demeanour of an emperor facing down a peasants' revolt, he roared, 'Where is Dulal? Bring him to me, bring Dulal over right now.'

Priyo, whose memory of a public mauling in the red-light area of Sonagachhi was still fresh, wished he could become invisible. He shut his eyes, opened them again; the labourers were now accompanying their chanting with determined forward thrusts of their arms, the textbook gesture of revolution. He was not confident that Dulal's presence was going to ameliorate matters; quite the opposite, probably. He closed his eyes again. It had all appeared so benign fifteen years ago, the business of Dulal pouring balm over everything and bypassing all potential confrontation – what a picture of amity and harmony it had been. It had taken nearly a decade to see it for what it truly was:

a long, wickedly misleading dress-rehearsal for the real play unfolding now.

Answer us! Answer us!

Where did all this fury, all this hate, come from? The strikers possessed the terrifying beauty of a fully reared-up snake, hood engorged, waiting to attack. Could he use that metaphor in one of his stories?

Prafullanath tried to shout down the men with his obsessive call for Dulal. The veins in his throat and forehead stood out. Standing on his left, Priyo could see the throbbing purple-green worm in his temple.

'Baba,' he said into his ear, 'please calm down. Please. They've sent for Dulal, he's going to come. Just calm down.'

Prafullanath had gone past the stage of turning to his son and shutting him up with a few forceful words. His focus was entirely on his elusive nemesis. Defying everything, Prafullanath advanced in his slow, limping, half-broken manner towards the crowd.

'Baba!' wailed Adi and Priyo together. They couldn't bring themselves to move.

The sea of agitators inched nearer. The island containing the Ghoshes and the car and Gagan shrank.

The Ghoshes found themselves facing Ashish Majhi and Bijan Hazra. The chanting of slogans had given way to the ordinary, incomprehensible chatter of a crowd.

Prafullanath asked, 'Where's Dulal? Where's your ringleader?'

Ashish said, 'There's no ringleader business. He's not here. You speak to us.'

Adi called out, 'Move back, move back' to the nearest group of faces pressing in on them. The words had no effect.

Prafullanath said, 'I head this factory. I'll speak to no one but your head.'

Bijan Hazra said, 'When will we get our salaries? We haven't been paid for a year. What will we live on?'

'I'm not going to negotiate with you,' Prafullanath said, his tone falling back to the kind that a man of his class reserved for pestering beggars. 'I want to see Dulal, he's the man behind all this. Who are you?'

'My elder brother lost his hand. You threw him out because he was no longer useful to you,' Bijan said.

Adi intervened, 'Move, all of you, move, give some space here. We've been through this before, hundreds of times.'

Priyo felt the refractory mood coming off the crowd as touch on his skin. He was appalled that these labourers were daring to answer back, and in tones of such disrespect, too. Then the distaste swiftly transformed itself into fear.

Ashish was so close now that Priyo could smell his sharp breath when he, startling the Ghoshes, gave out what seemed like a battle cry: 'You must listen to our demands.'

You must! You must! went up the answering chorus.

Priyo wanted to tear out the windpipe of the snake. He could certainly see a long way towards his trachea through his wide-open mouth shouting out the slogan – the crooked yellow teeth, the furred pinkish-grey tongue, the stubby pink worm of the uvula.

Prafullanath was now visibly shaking.

Priyo whispered, 'Baba, you must get into the car right now. Come.'

Adi shouted ineffectually above the din, 'Move away, move away.'

Crush! Grind!

The inner ring of men shuffled, but didn't move back. Prafullanath felt a squeezing in his chest, a slight thickening of the air that he was breathing. He inhaled more deeply and said, 'Move your men, I've come to talk. I have no time for a CPI(M) pimp like you', but it came out in a whisper.

Priyo, sensing something, took him by the shoulders.

Adi now tried to reason with the men. He pleaded, 'Ashish-babu, Bijan-babu, please, look at him, he's an old man, he's feeling ill. If you could just move back a little bit . . .'

Priyo heard his brother's wheedling tone and hated him.

Bijan snapped back, 'We're ill too. We haven't eaten for ten months, we haven't been able to feed our wives and children for *ten months.*'

As if on cue, another cry went up: *We're not listening to the false promises of the owners. We shan't listen.*

Not listening! Shan't listen!

The people churned. Ashish whispered something to a man standing next to him. The man turned and pushed his way into the throng behind him and disappeared. The meaning of this emerged later, when Gagan poked his head out of the car and called out, 'Babu, Babu, come inside, come and sit in the car.' Priyo looked quickly behind him and saw an incipient spar of men forming, trying to come between the Ghoshes and the car, cutting off their access to any form of safety. The men were spoiling for a fight and, if it came to that, it would later be reported that the Ghoshes had initiated it, that they had come to the locked factory with hooligans, despite having been warned by the police not to show up, with the express purpose of demoralising the sacked workers and sabotaging their just revolution. Nobody would listen to the owners' side of things; they wouldn't even have a side then.

Priyo looked at his father; Baba was dripping like a tree after an hour of uninterrupted rain.

From this point, things accelerated.

Prafullanath said, 'I know Dulal is behind all this. I know you're all in the pay of the CPI(M). That's why the police didn't come, they're in the pockets of the CPI(M) too.' With each word a wheezing racked his frame. Again the words, which were meant to be thundering, came out hoarse and whispery.

Our demands must be heeded, must be heeded.

Adi and Priyo each held an arm and started moving their father gently towards the Ambassador. It was a distance of only a few feet.

Prafullanath's chest had become an infernal anvil. He could barely bring out the words, 'Chest . . . my chest . . .' The light around him seemed to buckle like a rod.

Gagan, who had noticed the beginning of a kind of loss of rigidity to Prafullanath's frame, now saw him gulping for air and Adinath and Priyonath trying to prop him up. He started the engine, found a gap between the men trying to cut him off from Boro-babu and his sons and edged closer. Perhaps this move on Gagan's part had not been foreseen by the playscript: the men, moving in discrete groups of one and two and three, trying to impose a wall between the Ghoshes and the car, were thrown by this unrehearsed bit of stage-direction. Gagan kept the car moving. Survival instinct, deeper than revolutionary strategies, forced the men to swerve aside. By the time they woke up to what was happening, Adi and Priyo had succeeded in bundling Prafullanath into the back seat.

Adi, shaking in the passenger seat beside Gagan, said, 'Drive. Drive now!'

Gagan said, 'But how?'

The Ambassador had finally been cordoned off by the workers.

'Drive,' Adi cried.

Gagan moved the car gingerly forward until he was inches away from the ring of men. A noise of great confusion spread among the crowd, submerging the now half-hearted *Crush! Grind!* The men surrounding them didn't move. The car was like a flimsy boat in the moment before the waves closed in on it. Gagan swore filthily, backed the car, engaged second gear by mistake, made it give out an almighty revving sound, then jerked it forward at speed, hitting two, three, maybe four of the workers. A cry of astonishment, then pain or rage. Disbelief at this breaking of such an inalienable rule froze the men for a few moments, then that primitive coding for self-preservation again asserted itself. The crowd fell back and Gagan drove the car, without stopping or slowing, through the furrow that was opening up. The passage was narrow and people continued to press against the sides of the Ambassador, and Gagan didn't know, didn't care, how many men he was knocking down. That whimpering wheeze from the back seat had become the only point on which his world was concentrated.

As they reached the periphery of the crowd, where the dense clot had thinned out to a few stragglers and the road out was in clear view, Priyo looked out of the rolled-up window glass and caught a flash of Dulal, a dark, thin man but now with a moustache and a paunch, flanked by several men, all of whom were caught by surprise by the steadily accelerating car, staring at it, momentarily frozen in their behind-the-scenes commanding of the action.

Lately his father has taken to trotting out the old mantra: 'One generation builds, the next generation sits on it and consumes it to nothing.' How Priyo would like to turn that against him. The generation that builds is also the generation that destroys; the next generation is only the audience outside the invisible fourth wall, watching the antics of its elders puffing themselves up with hubris then getting deflated, like balloons four days after a child's birthday party. For a change, Priyo can draw a clear, linear map of causal links: his father lies half-dead in his bed upstairs because he disregarded everyone's advice and visited the factory at Bali in 1966 because it was so important that Bali became functional as quickly as possible because the survival of their business depended on it because he had pledged it as collateral to the banks because he had had the brilliant idea of wanting a complete techno-logical overhaul of their other plant at Memari. That flare lights him up inside again. Baba built the business; he started to extinguish it too.

The thought of upstairs drags Priyo back: if he does not rejoin the company of his wife and restart the supervision of caterers and elec-tricians and decorators, she is going to give him hell. As he climbs up to the terrace, taking two steps at a time, he sees Bhola, in a hurry too, coming downstairs.

'Mej'-da, listen,' Bhola says, 'the electricians seem to be having some problems with the decorators, something about how crossing the bamboos one way and covering them with cloth will prevent extra lights from being placed on the façade of the house. I didn't quite understand. You need to tell them what you want, otherwise they'll make a royal mess of it.'

'Come, let's see what's up,' Priyo says, then adds, despite himself, 'So, which of your literati luminaries are coming to grace us with their presence?'

Bhola, as always, does not get it. He laughs his signature silly laugh and, glowing with pride, says, 'A young man called Sunil Ganguly's coming, you may not have heard of him.'

Priyo ignores the jab and asks, 'You mean *the* Sunil Ganguly, the poet?'

'Yes, the very same. He's written four fine novels too. Do you know them? *Exposure, Young Men and Women, Days and Nights in the Forest* and *The Exiled Heart*,' he reels off their names.

Priyo swallows this presumption of ignorance, too. A childhood feeling visits him briefly: his right hand itching to give Bhola a resounding slap. He asks through clenched teeth, 'And any of the authors you so generously supported?' He was going to add 'with family money', to leave Bhola in no doubt that others could respond to his barbs with sharper quills, but restrains himself; he has more information to winkle out.

Bhola looks crestfallen for a second or two, then recovers his foolishly grinning self.

'Just one or two, one or two. Not very well known, not yet, but one day they will be, mark my words.'

'But of course!' Priyo says. 'If *you* have foreseen their fame, not even fate can stop them.'

Shocking Priyo, who has always taken his younger brother's impermeability for granted, Bhola looks stung. He goes quiet for a bit. Then, the habitual ebullience gone out of him, he says, 'Yes, I'm not very good, am I?' Pause. 'This business-thisness, not my thing, you know. I know everyone's disappointed in me.'

Priyo feels as small as the nail on his little toe. He interrupts his brother with a faux-gruffness designed to hide his own shame at causing distress: 'Enough, enough. No such talk on an auspicious day like this. Only good things today.'

Bhola immediately reverts to his cartoonish smileyness. 'Right, right, you're absolutely right. No such talk. You go upstairs, let me go and make myself useful with the catering staff.'

Really, that man is a yo-yo; Priyo nods, turns away and continues climbing upstairs, now one step at a time.

Bhola calls out to him: 'Mej'-da, do you know if Didi will be singing this evening?'

Priyo freezes. Nearly twenty years have not bleached his wedding evening of its full horror. His heart does a fierce dance of shame. He turns around slowly, composing his face first, he hopes, into a perfectly affable mask of normality, and says, 'I haven't been told anything. Why don't you find out and let me know?'

Bhola bounds down the stairs, giddy with joy: he has managed to throw some ink on Priyo's unblemished day. And today of all days. That foolish fucker.

It could easily have been Purnima's week – it is *her* daughter who is getting married – but instead she feels an ambivalence casting shadows in corners. She feels she has not won the jewellery war, although Priyo has told her a dozen times what her mother-in-law had apparently said when he had broached the prickly subject: 'All this is for my eldest granddaughter, I've been saving them up for this day.' Purnima does not quite believe this; it is simply not in her mother-in-law to give away her life's treasures like so much puffed rice. Even if that had been the case, in some counterfactual supposition, it certainly would have been negated by the argument they had had recently. Lest she come too close to conceding her own role in that clash, she quickly chases away any rerun of that memory – it is ever so slightly different every time she lets it play inside her head – and wills herself to concentrate on the real thing: the spoils. But that too is not an entirely happy rumination. How typical of Priyo to think that he could 'cover Baishakhi in gold' with the pieces he has been fobbed off with. A few bangles and armlets (a pair of kankan, yes, but no chur or mantasha), four necklaces (only a thinnish five-stranded one among them, not the seven-stranded one she was hoping for), two chiks (both grudgingly admitted) and a miscellaneous category in which she lumps what she considers the loose change of jewellery – earrings (no kaan), rings (no ratanchur), chains and other sundries. Taken together and adorning her daughter, you could say – and it cost her to admit this – that she is not being sent off too badly, at least loss of face has been avoided, but 'covered in gold'? No, no, no, no. Purnima has made Baishakhi do several dress-rehearsals wearing every single piece of jewellery given by her mother-in-law and she could still see large windows of her daughter's clothes and flesh behind the sparse covering of gold and jewels. What to do? She has had to part with some of her own stuff to hide those shameful gaps. Her mother's heart burns with shame.

Baishakhi enters the room with a jewellery box in her hand. 'Ma, I have something to show you, I'm shutting the door.'

Before she can sit on the bed Purnima says, 'What's that? What's that? Show me' and reaches out her hand.

She opens the long red box. Nestling in the red velvet inside is a gold shaat-lahari haar, the seven-stranded necklace of her dreams.

Her eyes widen to cartoon Os. She whispers, 'Where did you find this? Who's given this to you?'

Baishakhi says, as if it is the most expected and ordinary thing in the world, 'Pishi gave it to me just now. She asked me to wear it for boü-bhaat, not the wedding.'

Purnima's hands clutch the bedclothes ineffectually. She can only let out a 'Jah!' of profound disbelief. Chhaya? The queen lioness in the valley of lions where she, Purnima, is a calf? That . . . that walking capsule of poison? Why would she give *her* daughter this amazing heirloom piece of jewellery?

'You're not lying?' Purnima asks. 'Is it true that your pishi's *given* you this?'

'Why would I lie?'

'Was she smiling when she gave you this? Or muttering with anger?'

'Why would she be muttering? She said it was best to have the gift-giving within the family out of the way and not done in public. So I bent down and touched her feet and she said that she was blessing me with this necklace. "Go, go adorn someone else's home, I never had the chance," she said and then her eyes filled with tears and she turned her head away.'

Purnima can find nothing to return to this. She feels odd, as if she has been caught doing something wrong and been chastised by someone much younger; a mixture of shame and indignation. In its peculiar way it seems to be a version of the loss of face she had been so keen to avoid by making up the shortfall in Baishakhi's wedding gold. But it is not in her nature to sit with an ambiguous feeling for long, not in front of her daughter.

She takes out the necklace, its several strands spilling and now entangled in her nervous fingers, and says, 'Yeeees, remarkably weighty.' Then, after a pause, 'Looks like real gold all right. Just checking, it's good to make sure about these things. After all, you can never tell with this family. Or with your aunt.'

Purnima untwists the strands of the necklace, pats smooth the bedclothes and spreads it out. There is no denying it is a beauty: seven lines of thick chains, each with a decorative centre pendant in graduated sizes, the pendants getting smaller towards the neck as the chain-length reduces with each strand. It is not something that Baishakhi's generation of women can easily pull off. Besides, where would she wear it? Purnima lifts it up gently, with the delicacy one would bring to a newborn's fragile head, and slips it carefully over her own neck. It is a tricky thing to wear and needs disentangling again while resting against her chest, flowing down nearly to her navel. There, done now. She stands up and turns to the mirror on the steel wardrobe. Oh, my. The sheer weight of the thing is its signature; it is a presence that cannot be forgotten for a single second, as you can a ring or a bangle. You feel slightly bowed by it, as if in reverence. A tiny burr of envy catches at the admiration: really, shouldn't her in-laws have given it to her when she came to this house, rather than giving it to her daughter now?

Much better, much more satisfying to think of what this beautiful thing has been doing in her sister-in-law's clutches, immured in the depths of a bank locker or the darkness of a steel almirah. Had it been given to her by her mother? When? When they expected Chhaya to get married? How galling to learn that that ugly smudge of a woman was in possession of such amazing old-school masterpieces, while she has had to make do with attenuated chains and earrings. Her only truly heirloom piece is the ring that her aunt gave her as a wedding present, a gold ring with a pigeon's-blood ruby at the centre, its deep, discreet fire set off by the showier sparkle of the twelve small diamonds surrounding it.

Many years ago, shortly after coming to live in Bhabanipur, Priyo had given her what he had called a shaat-lahari haar, but that was a crow compared to the peacock of this real thing on her chest. Had she really believed hers was the seven-stranded necklace of Bengali jewellery lore, or had she pretended to believe in order to please her husband? Its chains were like cotton threads, weak and tangly; these were curved strips of pure metal, each the width of two fingers.

But there is a dissonance somewhere that she cannot quite put her finger on. She cannot fully immerse herself in the predictable pleasures of acidulous speculations about Chhaya. She feels she has been trumped. Who would ever have thought that Chhaya was capable of such generosity? In fact, the idea is so unfeasible that she is certain there is some kind of a cunningly secreted catch involved and keeps hunting for it. She *wants* to trip up on a snag planted by her sister-in-law; that way comfort lies. She remembers a conversation with Priyo well before things curdled so irreversibly between her and her in-laws that she feels under siege in this house now.

Priyo had come home from work one evening and ushered her into their room. 'Look what I've got for you,' he said, extracting a bottle from his briefcase. Perfume! 'Intimate', it was called; she can still recall the ridged glass of the bottle, the sharply pointed cupola of its scarlet cap, the gold-coloured liquid.

'O ma,' she had said, 'shall I try on a squirt now or leave it for a special occasion? It's Tapati's wedding next week, I'll wear it then. Where did you get it?'

'On the black market. You can't get foreign scents in shops.'

'O ma, foreign! I shall have to be careful with it.'

'No, no, no need for that. It's there to be used, not kept in storage and admired. When you finish it, I'll get you another one.'

Later that night, when she opened the wardrobe, she saw her bottle of 'Intimate' on a shelf inside. But had she not put hers on the dressing table? She wheeled around; yes, there it was, where she had left it. There was a second bottle, then, which Priyo had hidden, without her knowledge, in the almirah. Some planning must have gone into it: how had he got hold of the keys? They were tied, in a bunch with other keys, to a knot in her sari and tucked in at her waist; he could not have had access to the shelf inside the almirah without her knowing. But these were children's games beside the spectre of the second bottle of perfume and the meaning it radiated, the only meaning it could possible have.

After three days of fielding an armoury of sulking – curt replies to his questions, a face like thunder, sudden exits from the room when he appeared – a baffled Priyo asked, 'What's up, can you tell me?'

Several hours of tears and indirectional talking and heavy hints and mystification later, Purnima had, to her shame, to spell it out: that second bottle of 'Intimate' in the wardrobe.

Priyo's face fell. Purnima knew that she had caught him out. But it was bathos that had flitted across Priyo's expression and, if there was any guilt in it, it was not the kind that Purnima had been preparing herself for.

'Yes, you're right, I bought a second bottle,' Priyo confessed. 'But it's not what you think. That second bottle is for Chhaya.'

'Chhaya?' Purnima echoed.

'Yes, Chhaya. Sit down, I think it's time I told you about this.'

Purnima, stunned, sat down. Priyo began, 'Chhaya is over thirty years old now. It's safe to say that she won't get married. The shame and agony of it lashes her, can't you see? She thinks that everyone is pointing at her and whispering, "Look, look at her, a spinster for the rest of her days." She's not totally wrong about that. And she is, how should I put it, not the easiest of persons, as you well know. She looks at you and Boüdi and Chhoto-boüdi and thinks all the time that these are things that she is never going to have: a husband, children, in-laws. She will have to remain in her father's house for the rest of her life. When Dada and Boüdi go somewhere, or I buy you a sari or some cosmetic, or when we go to the cinema or a restaurant – I've seen her face become so small. I can see the thought inside her head: "There's no one to bring these little treats for me, no one for me to go out with." I feel sad when I see her . . .'

There was a long pause.

'I feel sorry for her,' he continued. 'I thought I should try and make life a little bit happier for her, so I decided that whenever I buy you something, I'll buy two of it and give her one: face-cream, lipstick, scent, sari, whatever. If these little things can make her happy, can make her feel less left out, then . . . Besides, it's not as if the cost is a consideration for us. Please think about it,' he had pleaded. 'It brings a smile to her face.'

It is a conversation from fifteen years ago, from a time when she had found it easy to accede to her husband's requests without a thought. Things are so different now that it feels they were all different people then, like characters you read about in a book, not the younger version of your own self. A different thought occurs to her now: did she ever ask Priyo whether Chhaya had been given pieces of the jewellery identical to those that he had bought her over the years before the wealth trickled away? The thought of duplicates of her rings and bracelets and necklaces lying in another almirah in the same house, but on a different floor, makes her feel slightly queasy. And all the saris given by Priyo too? She has lost count of them. Did he give Chhaya the same seven-stranded chain, calling it a shaat-lahari haar? Did she fall for it? Especially, it turns out, when she had a genuine one?

There is no vantage point opposite the house where he can station himself and spy on 22/6. He could hardly perch in one of the windows of the neighbouring houses, or on the stoop of number 14/6/A, which is directly opposite 22/6. The Basaks live there. Vikramjit used to be his childhood playmate. They went to manimela together and sang 'Touch my soul with the touchstone of fire' in a chorus of about a dozen boys. Where is Vikramjit now? He does not know; he has fallen out of touch, drifted apart from these childhood affinities and friendships. He wraps a part of the gamchha over his head, making sure that at least half his face is covered. They would not recognise him, not unless they were specifically looking, but it would be foolish not to be vigilant. Some busybody is bound to notice him if he stays in one spot near 14/6/A for a long time, most likely someone from the Basak family or one of their servants, and then where would he be? Not that the chance of being discovered reduces to zero if he keeps walking up and down the street; there are so many people, with dead, empty time on their hands, who sit at a window or on a verandah all day, watching the traffic of people on the streets, with nothing to do with their hours and days, nothing. There is old Bhadra-babu on his balcony, biding his time until the final call comes. There will inevitably be a maid hanging out the washing who will notice him, then mark him again when she comes out to check if it is dry, then again when she gathers the dry clothes . . . This is how this world runs, a small group of people who know each other, a closed world of intense curiosity in other people's lives because your own is just empty, dead time.

There is Pintu-da, stepping out of his front door to go to the Writers' Building, where he works as head clerk to the transport secretariat, cloth bag hanging from one shoulder; rickety arms and legs, but with a paunch straining at the lower buttons of his tucked-in shirt and the top hook of his brown trousers. It is eleven o'clock; by the time Pintu-da makes it to his desk it will be around twelve-thirty. He will chat to his colleagues for an hour, drinking tea and snacking on wedges of cucumber dipped in rust-red chilli-salt. Then they will have a lunch break for two hours. At three-thirty, it will be time for tea. He will move a pile of files from one side of the table to the other, feel exhausted with the pressure of work, gossip for a while longer with his co-workers. Then, at five, it will be time for him to leave his office and head back home, where he will complain about his gruelling day, and everyone else around him, his wife, his children, the servants, especially his wife, will run about doing his bidding, trying to make the last hours before he goes to sleep easy and comfortable.

The bile rises to his throat. He swallows it, because hawking would draw more attention.

He stands for a few minutes gazing at the house, slightly defamiliarised now that he is looking from the outside at a structure whose inside he has known since his birth; he has never had the opportunity or the inclination to scrutinise the exterior with such intensity of concentration. Four storeys, with the date of completion of construction, 1921, in bas-relief plumb in the horizontal centre of the façade, right at the top, just under the parapet.

It was a solid if unoriginal, and now ugly, edifice, with a deeply recessed balcony, on the left of the main door and the staircase, on each of the four storeys. With the exception of the balcony on the ground floor, which was completely enclosed in iron grilles, each of the three on the upper floors had a stomach-high wrought-iron railing, intricately carved and dense, prone to rust and flaking. 'Don't go to the balcony, you'll fall over the edge' was a standard refrain from adults when he and his cousins were growing up; no one seemed to have taken into account that a child would have to climb over the railings to achieve that mishap. In his lifetime the building had been painted twice, the first time white, with the balconies, windowsills and the edge of the parapet picked out in green; the second time, a shade of dull yellow and the contrasting colour, an equally dull brownish-red. It stands cream and green now, this house which is asymmetrical, he notes with surprise for the first time, along the vertical plane. If one were to draw a longitudinal line dividing the building into two halves, they would not correspond to each other; the balconies would be to the left, the two windows of one of the front-facing rooms, used as bedrooms on all four floors, would be to the right. There are four rooms on each floor, the one leading out to the front verandah the largest and meant to be used as the living room on that floor, but on the top two floors they are used as bedrooms: his grandfather and grandmother's on the third floor, and his aunt's on the second.

Long L-shaped corridors open to the back courtyard ran along the entire inner side of the house, facing away from the road, the ones they had always called the back verandas; each floor had one. These were the verandahs where the children had had their birthday parties: banana-leaf plates had been set down on the floor in a row and the invitees, all children from the area, sat with their backs to the walls of the rooms, eating off the plates in front of them. The large court-yard had a pump room, which housed the electrical pump, the reser-voir on a raised bank, and a small enclosure with a simple hand-pump, where most of the washing-up and even some of the washing of the house was done. The courtyard was slightly sunken, two or three feet below the corridor of the ground floor. Madan-da had planted dahlias, chrysanthemums, marigolds, roses, chillies, impatiens of several strains, a blue aparajita and a white one, and god knows what else in terracotta pots and tubs, row upon row, in an effort to beautify the frankly squalid, wet, dark, slippery place; somehow there always seemed to be a big fat tongue of slime and water, edged thickly with green, in one corner. The ersatz garden had worked for a while and then, after decades of a forced and reluctant kind of flourishing, the plants had mostly died or become shrivelled and spindly because Madan-da had lost the energy that he had lavished on them for so long.

Through a corner of the courtyard, one entered the most surprising bit of the house, a back garden; surprising because it was a rare thing in this part of the city, but also because it was hidden and one could not tell from the layout of the courtyard that there was a garden tucked away behind it. It was not visible from the ground floor because the mess of the courtyard and the rooms that had been habitually used as the servants' quarters towards the back of the house got in the way, but if you stood on the back verandahs of the first, second and third floors, or at the back windows of some of the rooms upstairs, you could see that scrap of land – it was not big – with its guava tree, the oddly bent jackfruit tree that never bore any fruit, the shiuli bush, the jumbly tagar tree, all in an erratic arrangement on the grassless earth.

Again, he is thrown by an observation that had never occurred to him while he was an inhabitant of the house that he watches now from the outside: why had Madan-da never tried to elevate the garden to his aesthetic standards, channelling instead all the relevant energies into improving the blighted concrete courtyard? Is it the lot of the insider to be marked, always and predominantly, by a kind of absence of thought, a bluntness of perception?

Apparently, his grandfather had bought this huge house for cash in 1926 or '27 or thereabouts. The story went that the three brothers who had had the house built towards the end of the First World War went out of business overnight sometime in the mid-Twenties; his grandfather had saved them from destitution by buying their house; the original owners had moved, with their wives and children, to quarters somewhere else in the city. In keeping with his scrutiny of the building with new eyes, he now turns that childhood tale around, lifting it up to see if he can discern what lies underneath. Too much time has passed; the dead grass buried under it would be that unnatural shade of mutton-fat white. Besides, he had never really paid much attention to that story; which child is interested in the history of his parents and grandparents? The adults too, sensing this, perhaps concoct an easy formula that barely touches the true, and therefore complicated, history, choosing a short, convenient fiction over the dense adventitiousness of fact.

But now, as he stands watching the house that has become a separate, independent entity for the first time, detached from him, something in the outer world, he speculates: is the story true, that emphasis on his grandfather's philanthropy? Isn't a more credible story one in which his grandfather had seen an opportunity to acquire a large house cheaply from people who had backed themselves into a corner; that he had exploited them at their weakest moment, agreeing to save them from bankruptcy and ruin by giving them money with the house as collateral? That collateral had never been released, so maybe he had formally bought the house; the money given to the three brothers had been used by them to save their skins from their creditors.

The house seems to shift shape minutely for him and become subtly different, a bit more hostile and forbidding, its shameful history giving it an aggressive aura as if it has become defiantly shameless. From all the things he has bothered to find out about the way the Ghoshes ran their business – planting lumpens within unions to spark off violence so that all the union workers could be sacked; an old story of buying off a business from a friend's widow, who did not

know any better, for a fraction of its real value; using the Hindu–
Muslim riots the year before Independence, the year he was born,
to shut down mills, regardless of how many workers were deprived
of their livelihoods, and buying up factories in areas emptied by the
migration – all this immorality and opportunism, this was what
characterised them, not altruism, as the stories they had spun would
have you believe. But then, this is a world whose running fuel is
anecdotes and stories, he reminds himself. The anecdotes need not
be first-hand; in fact, better if they are not, better if they are repeated
across several degrees of separation, because that proves how potent
and pervasive they are, bringing everyone together in one huge,
collusive matrix. A legendary lecture given by so-and-so in Presidency
College in 1926, its iconic status relayed by a nineteen-year-old in 1965
with the words 'You needed to be there to feel the goosebumps'. The
memory of a martinet kept alive by stories recounting his disciplinary
measures from fifty years ago, handed down a dendritic chain of
people across the generations. This is the way this world runs: self-
mythologising through anecdotes proliferating like a particularly
virulent strain of virus. Chatter chatter chatter, always the chatter
of what others did and others said in a golden age of an unrecover-
able past.

He feels his blood flowing more quickly. The gamchha around his
head and part of his face is making him steam. All the while, the
building opposite him remains resilient, unyielding with the information he seeks from it. The slatted wooden shutters in the windows
have been opened, an unchanging morning ritual, before he arrived
on the street; but no one on the front verandahs as of yet. No sooner
does he think this than a maid – a new one, it seems; he does not
recognise her – appears on the second-floor balcony with a broom,
gathers up all the dust and fluff and rubbish that she has swept and
tips it out onto the street. That floor is Pishi's and Mejo-kaka's. How
uninhabited the house seems – no one coming out onto the balconies,
no one peeking out over the parapet, no face at any of the windows,
no one coming out of the front gate. The new lick of paint it has
had earlier this year, on the occasion of his cousin's wedding, is
already beginning to get stained and tarnished. How odd that the
painters had not uprooted a couple of bat or ashwattha plants that

have taken root in the cracks, one along the top left, near the roof, and the other on the low wall of the parapet itself. Everything needs a toehold here. The tenacious plants will grow and their roots will crack open the building like a butcher cleaving a joint of meat. He visualises a huge yawn running through the middle of the house, as if someone has taken hold of the two sides along a fissure and prised it open like a mouth, its deep insides exposed – the rooms, the furniture, the people, their lives. His heart thumps with the angry euphoria of retribution.

The house still appears devoid of people. What are they *doing*? It is quarter-past eleven, the men must have left for work and the children for school, but what about the servants? Why is no one coming out to go to the market or the shops? Where is Madan-da? It is impossible to glimpse the person he really wants to see because she lives on the ground floor; she does not use the barred and grilled dark cage of the front balcony, which, in any case, is blocked from view because the iron front gates are shut. Suddenly he feels deflated; the waiting outside is hopeless. What is he really expecting to see? And if he does catch sight of that, what is he going to do?

On the top floor of 22/6 Sandhya gets out of bed, ignores her head-spin, comes out of her dark bedroom and goes in search of her mother-in-law. There is a great turmoil in her, as if of dead leaves skittering around in a stiff breeze, about to be lifted clean off the ground in a mighty, sustained blast of gale. She feels a premonition of that particular kind of levitation that can only be effected by a force of Nature.

She announces to her stunned mother-in-law, 'Ma, Boro will return today. I feel it in my bones.'

Looking at this woman with dishevelled hair, the inky shadows under her eyes, about to disappear into their sockets, the dull skin, Charubala wonders briefly if her eldest daughter-in-law has finally toppled over into madness, but the magnetism of sixth sense is stronger, especially if it is, as in this case, felt by a mother. She dismisses her suspicions of insanity and says, 'What are you saying!'

'Yes, I feel it. The goddess has at last smiled on me. Ma, I think this may be the day.'

'Don't say that, you'll tempt fate. Let's just wait and see what happens. Why don't you have a bath and go to the prayer room?' Charubala advises.

He can feel an intense impatience and longing breaking up his hard, silent core. He is beginning to fragment at last. No, this will not do. If he has put up with the unspoken rules for so long, reined in his feelings, been as careful as a predator stalking its prey, it will not do to ruin everything now by giving in to impulse, however strong that may be. To have the boat capsize so near the shore – no, no, it cannot be. He can feel his jaw muscles and the vein at his temples throb with the force of determination, so hard has he gritted his teeth to will himself to stand steady.

Kalyani freezes with fear. She knows she should scream but she cannot, her tongue and throat will not move. The man, his head wrapped in a filthy gamchha, holds her arm in his grip. She cannot see his face, only his huge, coal-black eyes, blazing with menace. There are threatening noises coming out of his mouth, but they are muffled by the red-and-white chequered cloth. She shivers like a leaf. All those warnings about kidnappers on the prowl in the streets, waiting to pick you up and put you in their huge sack and take you away and sell you into beggary after blinding you and chopping off your arms and legs so that you could not run away, so that you could extract more sympathy from passers-by as you begged, all those warnings were not tall tales but true, and now they have come back to bite her: a kidnapper is about to whisk her away. A tumble of thoughts tries to go through her fear-paralysed head: can no one see what is happening to her? Why are they not intervening? Why can she not produce any sound? How is she supposed to know that kidnappers loiter just outside her home? They are supposed to hunt in dark alleys and outside school gates, lying in wait for children to come out after classes are over. She had only stepped out to buy a ribbon for her hair from old Panchanan's shop with the four annas her mother had so unexpectedly given her.

The kidnapper shakes her arm. With his other hand he removes the covering from his mouth. His face is covered with the most foresty beard she has ever seen. His lips move, but she does not hear a word.

The man's hand now takes hold of her shoulder and shakes her gently. 'What, you don't recognise me?' she can hear him say at last, but she can only look at him with terror.

'Kalyani, what's happened to you? You don't recognise me through my beard, is that it? Look, look at me carefully! Tell me – who am I?'

The man is staring at her and laughing. Yes, laughing. He is not a kidnapper then, he knows her name; he is looking at her and asking her to identify him and laughing . . . He is . . . he is—

'Listen, where's your mother?' he asks.

She has it: this is her missing Bor'-da! She screams it out – 'Bor'-da' – but it comes out as a grating whisper.

'It took you so long? Have I changed so much?'

Kalyani nods and manages to sound the first audible words: 'Such a bushy beard! And you're so . . . so thin, like a skeleton. Where were you?'

'Where's your mother?' he asks again.

'Inside. Shall I call her? When did you come back? Won't you come inside?'

'Yes, I will. But, first, go and tell your mother that I'm back and whisper it to her. Don't tell anyone else, all right? No one, not even my mother. Did you get that? Go on.'

Kalyani does some kind of calculation in her head and asks him, 'You've not been to the house yet? Does no one know that you've returned?'

At that moment the front door opens and Purba looks out, first left, then right, searching for her daughter who has been gone longer than she should have. She does not, at first, notice them standing directly opposite her, about fifteen or twenty feet away. Kalyani shouts, 'Ma!'; Bor'-da's grip on her arm becomes a vice, Purba looks at them, a quizzical expression on her face, then her eyes widen.

Unlike her daughter, she recognises Supratik instantly. How could she not?

CHAPTER FIFTEEN

'Did you know that sal forests have their own music?' Ajit said.

'Music of the forest? What've you been smoking? You must have started early today,' Shekhar mocked.

'Can you drop your poetry rubbish now that we're on holiday?' Somnath joined in with Shekhar. 'It's made you soft in the head. All this poetry business hasn't landed you the big fish yet. And we all thought chicks like that kind of stuff, you know, the sensitive-romantic drivel.'

'Is it open season on me?' Ajit protested weakly. 'Do you guys ever think of anything other than women?'

'Who do you think you're trying to kid, eh, pretending that it's moonlight and birdsong and flowers that goes through your head, and sewage through ours?' Somnath said. 'You think we didn't see you unable to take your eyes off the ripe tits of these Santhal women?'

Shekhar said, 'Ufff, those tits! You're absolutely correct, Somu, they're exactly like ripe fruit. The only thing you want to do when you see them is pluck and shove into your mouth. Mairi, my hands are itching at the very thought.'

Ajit, to fend off accusations of being cerebral and effete, joined in with extra zeal. 'They fill every single sense. But not only tits, have you noticed their waists? The way they wind that cloth around themselves, it hardly covers anything, leaves nothing really to the imagination. High-blood-pressure stuff.'

Now it was Somnath's turn. Ajit and Shekhar deferred to him with something approximating reverence: Somu had a reputation as a ladykiller, an experienced kind of guy who had started the business of sexual liaisons at an early age and had continued with unimpeded ease, so much so that he had had to be married off unusually young, in the standard attempt to have his ways mended. Had it reined him in, a wife and a one-year-old son, had it thrown cold water on his libidinous impulses, focused, like a pack-animal's blinkers, his permanently roving eye? Ajit and Shekhar scrutinised surreptitiously for signs, but found none. The desired gravitas that marriage and fatherhood were thought to bring seemed to have omitted to visit their irrepressibly priapic friend. Somu was ragingly horny, and infamous for it in their circle of friends in South Calcutta, but that very ill-repute gave him a sheen of glamour; he had ranged freely as a guest in the room they had wanted access to for so long, but had only succeeded in getting in a few toes so far. There was a grain of envy in this, but the larger part of it was awe, admiration. How did he do it? When he had come to invite them to his baby son's rice-eating ceremony he had said, 'Listen, I've just had an idea. If I were to invite loads of people, in the inevitable crush on the stairs and the roof where the eating's going to happen, we could brush against women's tits, even elbow them, as if by accident. What do you guys think? Brilliant or what?'

It was not a new idea: ever since they had been friends, Somu had suggested the same thing to them every year; to go to a public ceremony of the immersion of the goddess Durga at the end of the five-day festival at some huge ghat or lake and there, in the thick of the milling, crushing crowds, feel up, to their hearts' content, the breasts of women they would engineer to have pressed against them.

No, becoming a regular family man was not going to uncrease his soul; in him was invested the ineluctability of the shape of a leaf – no amount of doctoring was going to change the paradigm of that shape Nature had so forcefully wrought.

The defiantly unreformed Somnath now said, 'Yes, those maddening tits, the narrowing at the waist, the cleft where their thighs join their upper halves, all just delicious. But do you know what I like best about these tribal women? They look at you in this completely uninhibited way as if they have never known how to be shy. Have you noticed that? They stare at you and smile and giggle. Do you think that's a come-on?'

Shekhar said, 'City girls would never, ever look at you like that in their entire lives. Would not look at you, full stop. After two films, four outings for ice-cream and spicy puffed rice, half a dozen walks and more expenditure, they may just about allow you to hold their hand for five minutes.'

Ajit assented vigorously, nodding his head. 'These tribals don't appear to have any inhibitions or boundaries – the men and women hug and touch each other and hold hands openly, the girls hang out in groups and are constantly giggling and falling over each other, have you noticed? And that outfit of theirs, that short cloth! I love the way they put flowers in their hair – just one flower or a head of blossom. It makes their dark skin glow.'

'Here we go again,' Shekhar sighed, 'flowers and radiant skin . . . Man, you're such a loser.'

Somnath laughed and said, 'Did you notice yesterday at the market that the women were drinking?'

'Really?' Incredulity in Shekhar's voice.

'Didn't you see? The men and women were all sitting in a loose circle on the ground, passing the bottle around. Mahua or fermented-rice haandiya. Drinking and leaning against each other and then falling over.'

Ajit said, slightly tangentially, 'Shall we go for a walk in the forest? We'll have light for another four hours or so . . .'

Surprising him, Somnath and Shekhar agreed.

It took them less than ten minutes to reach the edge of the straggle of small, ramshackle, dirty buildings that was the mining village of Patratu. Most of them had tin roofs and only a few were built out of bricks. The shops looked as precarious as if a child had drawn them. They were stained with darkness, dirt and indigence. Everything was covered with a patina of red dust. The air was dry, and the clear late-April heat too. The occasional bicycle, ridden by a man carrying a huge, unbalancing sack of coal tied to the pannier rack, probably on his way from the mines to sell the coal at Ranchi, twenty-five miles to the south, trailed a low cloud of this red dust as it made its way. The three holidaying friends too had this dust-swirl following their feet, like a pathetic little pet, as they walked the village's only tarred road to the end. But everything was about to change. A big thermal power station was being constructed with Russian money. This sleepy little village in the Pithauriya-Patratu valley, surrounded by lush green hills and forests, criss-crossed by streams, rivers and waterfalls, was going to get a lick of developmental paint. Residential colonies were being purpose-built for the workers at the power station and the dam; the village was transforming itself into a small town. These newly arrived residents would join tourists, especially from the big town of Ranchi, for picnics in the surrounding forests and to the dam, while the more adventurous ones would head out westwards to the nearby Chatra forest. Already there was a small holiday lodge halfway towards the reservoir. It was this that they had luckily stumbled upon, looking for a place to stay. Patratu was within spitting distance of the more famous McCluskiegunj. It was only on a whim that the three friends had got off at Barkakana Junction instead of staying on the train for another hour for the Anglo-Indian colony.

Walking towards the forest, which was everywhere and within reach, they felt that they had come, if not to the middle of nowhere, certainly to a place remote enough to allow them that superficial illusion, the surrounding scenic beauty providing a sufficient dosage of the untampered Nature they desired.

Where the tarred road gave out the tribal women sat with their baskets in the early morning, selling what little they had to sell – vegetables, eggs, bidi, unidentifiable leaves. It was near this spot that Somnath had seen Santhal men and women drinking their home-brewed liquor. Now the young men walked close to the edge of a field. There were little brown hillocks undulating the middle distance, while on the far horizon a large green-brown range camouflaged itself in the haze by looking as if it were three-quarters of the way through a very slow disappearing act. There were a couple of better-heeled detached bungalows now, freshly painted and set within their big, gated front gardens, clearly the holiday homes of wealthy city people. Then the human habitations ended. Beyond another field on the other side, the forest lay like a dark-green, almost black shawl, extending from the dissolving hill in the distance. It appeared to be a repository of condensed dark, the vessel from which evening and night leaked out at a certain hour and covered the land and sky. They made their way towards it.

Once inside, the darkness proved to be a trick that the forest – assuming its magician incarnation, like its companion, the hill, which was trying to become invisible – habitually performed for everyone outside its boundaries. The light, so flat out in the open, became dramatic and mobile: it seemed to have somersaulted up high to form a canopy over the heads of the trees, but even that, after a few minutes of advancing inwards, turned out to be an illusion. Instead of the white uniformity outside, it had broken itself up into legion entities, all different: shafts and beams entered the middle heights, some breaking against and streaking the tree-trunks, some coming to rest on the ground, so miraculously free of undergrowth, in stippled pools of light and shade. The forest floor, of the same red soil, was dry; large leaves from the sal trees, which largely constituted the forest, lay here and there like brown plates with curled edges; occasionally a branch or some twigs. The hide-and-seek light, the unending series of sal, a whole different world hidden so openly within the shell of the soiled one they knew – all the things these city boys had never experienced before – silenced even Shekhar and Somnath.

Their ears opened not to silence, but to what they had derided a few minutes ago: the music of the forest. An unknown bird sent out an atonal *tu-tui-tuiieeee* at regular intervals. With a papery rustle a leaf dropped somewhere. Crickets vigorously churned out an unremitting background of their anthem. Now that the men's senses had opened to this secret world, they heard all kinds of things: a clatter of wings accompanied by the swishing of the displaced air; a brief tap-tap-tapping; a whirr and click repeated in a monotonous cycle for a few minutes, then nothing; the repeated one-note of a string being plucked, most probably a hand-held cotton-carder, far, far away. They walked as if in a trance, spellbound in this kingdom of magic, until, with a snap up above and then a fluttering descent, a small, flowering branch landed near them. They stared at it as if it had come from outer space. Ajit broke the silence first.

'Did you know the sal tree bore flowers?' he asked no one in particular.

Shekhar and Somnath shook their heads, still too enmeshed in the spell to make a sound or to indulge in their mockery of Ajit's inexplicable fascination with Nature. Ajit lifted up the branch from the ground and all three looked at the cluster of flowers in silence; an inflorescence of fully bloomed, small, coral-pink flowers, with a contained explosion of anthers in the middle and, under them, alternate rows of greenish buds that looked like fruits, invisible when on the tree except as a spray of hazy yellowish-orange tint on the canopies, so easily ignored or not noticed but now, on closer inspection, a dense, intricate miracle.

Then the spell broke and Somnath said, 'Isn't this the flower the Santhal women had tucked in their hair when we saw them dancing yesterday evening?'

No one could answer the question, but Ajit hazarded a guess. 'No, I think that was the mahua flower, the one from which they make their alcohol.'

'How do you know?' Shekhar immediately countered. 'Have you ever seen a mahua flower in your life?'

The brief brush with the sublime was over. The world outside, the one they knew, had entered the forest.

Ajit now put up a small fight. 'How do you know that I do not know? Have *you* ever seen the mahua flower?'

Uncharacteristically, Shekhar withdrew. 'No, it's just that I thought you were again beginning your flower-fuckery poetry shit.'

Before Ajit could retort, Somnath said, 'Will you two cut it out, squabbling like dogs in a beautiful place like this? I feel like staying in this forest for ever.'

Shekhar and Ajit burst out laughing.

Somnath smiled and said, 'No, really, I'm serious. Sometimes . . . sometimes' – a different tone crept into his voice, something at once serious and tired – 'I feel responsibilities have been piled upon me as you'd burden a load on a donkey. I can't move with all that weight on my shoulders.'

What could he be referring to, wondered Ajit and Shekhar silently. Surely not his beautiful, curly-haired boy, whose first birthday was celebrated last month? Or his meek, silent, beautiful wife? They could not find a suitable response to their friend's abrupt introspection, but just as suddenly as the brief cloud had cast its shadow, it quickly flitted past. The sun shone unobstructed again. Somnath wiped his face with his hand, once, twice, as if he were brushing off cobwebs that he had accidentally walked into, smiled with the full force of his radiance and said, 'Where were we?'

Relieved at the passing of the unexpected, and unwelcome, sounding of a minor key, Ajit and Shekhar plunged, with somewhat excessive zeal, into the safer music of laddish chat.

After a little bit more wandering Somnath observed, 'Listen, guys, don't you think it's darkened a bit in here? Shouldn't we be heading back to the bungalow?'

Shekhar agreed, 'Yes, darkness comes down suddenly in these upland areas. It wouldn't do to get lost in the forest at night. And the bungalow's right at the other edge of the town.'

The light outside the forest had indeed changed. That white glare, which had seemed to cast no shadows, had now become golden air, present in that it tipped everything with its hue, but itself absent. There were shadows nestled against the hillocks and against the sides of all physical objects. The light turned orange, then pink. At the open area where the market sat, stray groups of Santhals congregated. And there, at the edge of the road, the young men instantly spotted a group of half a dozen Santhal women sitting on their haunches and doing what they did best – nothing. They whispered to each other, giggled, fell over laughing at some imperceptible jest, stared at nothing in particular, giggled some more . . . They lacked the discipline of works and days.

Ajit said, 'Look, that woman in the middle, look at her hair! Have you seen? Mahua blossom! We can ask them and settle the issue once and for all. Ei, Somu, you go and ask them, you are the least shy among the three of us.'

Somnath did not demur. He bounded off and stood in front of the circle, pointed to the blossom stuck in the young woman's hair and asked, 'What's the name of that flower?'

The women stared at him, then began their laughing and falling-over routine as if this urban stranger had told them the most cracking joke they had ever heard. Somnath remained unperturbed. All these girls swaying like reeds afforded him an almost licensed opportunity to feed his eyes on their bodies. They wore no additional garment to cover their breasts, only the parsimonious piece of cloth they wrapped around themselves, leaving so much of their lower legs, waist, back, neck, throat, shoulders exposed. In this tawny light of dusk, their black skins shone as if each had just emerged from a vat of oil.

He repeated his question. The same reactions were re-enacted. This time, however, the girl in question turned coy and shy and tried to hide her face on her friend's shoulder. Soon Somnath established that this was nothing but coquetry, for the girl kept peering at him like a child playing peek-a-boo.

Then, stunning him, for he had mentally prepared himself to have this game played, unchangingly, for a good while longer, the girl asked him directly, 'Babu, you give me money if I tell you the name of the flower?'

Somnath felt unstrung. That use of *tui*, the 'you' reserved for close friends, peers and intimates, or for juniors and servants: it was unthinkable for him to be the subject of that mode of address from a person of her standing. A squeezing sensation went through his insides. Trying hard to steady his voice, he too replied with *tui*: 'How much money do you want?' How could he be so unmanned by her language, an extraordinarily musical mixture of Bengali and Hindustani, by the lilt that animated her looks, her every gesture, her diction, her tone?

'You give me one rupee?' she sang.

One rupee! He would give her one hundredfold to have her continue speaking, calling him *tui*. An earlier incipient plan suddenly consolidated itself in his head. He asked, 'Will you be dancing tomorrow in the market place?'

'Why? You'll come and join us?' she asked in return. A peal of laughter rippled through her friends.

Somnath turned to his friends and said, 'They are inviting us to dance with them tomorrow', then, without missing a beat, his usual confidence restored to him, he addressed the girl, 'Yes, I will, but only if you' – here he pointed to her emphatically – 'if you dance with me.'

Once their eyes became adapted to the near-total lack of electric lights outside, Shekhar, Ajit and Somnath found that the low orange moon, like a large dinner-plate in the sky, gave so much light that they could see the garden with ease. The moonlight did queer things to objects. The shadows it cast looked painted; they lapped and hugged their parent objects in such a way that their inkiness leaked, as if by capillary action, back into the buildings or shrubs or humans and cloaked them in that same unreality. If you looked at them long enough, they, especially the rose and dahlia bushes and the grass, appeared not black, but a green or blue iteration of the dark. This light was not meant to illuminate; it was meant to create its antithesis, shadow; even the stretches in broad moonlight looked secretive.

Ajit said, 'It's like daytime. So much light! You don't get to see this in the city.'

'On a full-moon night during a power outage, if you walk the streets of your neighbourhood in Kankurgachhi, you will get the same effect,' Shekhar quipped.

Ajit replied by breaking full-throatedly into a Tagore song: 'On this full-moon night, everyone has gone to the forest . . .' The bottle of rum they were sharing in the garden of their guesthouse had not yet begun to tell in the melody. Whatever his friends made of Ajit's aesthetic impulses, they always fell respectfully silent when he sang; he had a beautiful voice and had had singing lessons throughout his childhood.

Faint drumbeats, sometimes near, at others distant, carried over in the air in a way that confused the men about their source and direction. When the percussion became more pronounced, it created such a rhythmic dissonance with the song that Ajit stopped before reaching its end.

'What do you think they are celebrating?' he asked.

'Who knows?' Shekhar said. 'Do you think this is a regular thing with them?'

'No idea,' Ajit said.

Were they dancing? Was that woman part of the carousing? That was Somnath's only thought. The caramelly taste of the rum turned to a sourish sugar in his mouth.

'I know you're going to disagree with me,' Ajit now said, 'but I find these tribal people really innocent and pure. Qualities we city-dwellers have lost.'

'No, mairi, you're totally right,' Shekhar said. 'They have no money, no jobs, no solid houses, yet look how happy they are. They sing, dance, laugh all the time, drink alcohol, all as if they didn't have a single care in the world.'

'And we, who have everything, are weighed down with anxiety, illness, tension, worry, from cradle to grave,' Ajit finished his friend's thought.

Shekhar asked, 'Really, you have everything? *Everything?*'

'You know what I mean.'

'But *everything?*' Shekhar persisted.

'Ah, I keep telling you, it was a way of putting things. Stop harping on that one note.'

Shekhar would not be budged. He had caught something between his teeth and he would not let go now. 'But *everything?*' he repeated. 'Do you have a girlfriend?'

Ajit tried to ignore this; best not to encourage Shekhar, who was probably well on his way to getting sozzled, which would explain this resurgence of the bullying. 'The less one owns in life,' he said, 'the happier one is. Santhals = few worldly possessions = happiness. Ajit & Shekhar & Somnath = family and friends and home and expectations and responsibility = sorrow. Straightforward equation.'

'Don't forget Santhal women = beauty,' Somnath interjected.

'Do you have a huge family house like Somnath does?' Shekhar asked. 'Three cars? A fleet of servants?'

Ajit clenched his teeth. 'Has the rum gone to your head?'

'A wife? A son?' Shekhar continued, following his own train of thought as if the aimless convivial chit-chat had turned into a monologue; his interlocutor had disappeared.

Ajit returned to his old tack. 'Innocence belongs to these tribal people,' he said. 'They are closer to the pure state of mankind than we are, less corrupted, more noble.'

Somnath had only a small part of his mind on the increasingly drunken conversation of his two friends, participating absent-mindedly. He heard the splattering stream of one of them pissing against a bush, so loud in the surrounding stillness that it felt slightly obscene. He wanted to concentrate solely on the sound, which was no longer dispersed in the night air in intermittent shreds and patches, but was continuing louder, he felt, in his pumping heart.

The air was mazed again with that very rhythm the following afternoon. In the market place there was a sizeable crowd – where did so many people come from? – that seemed to swell as the afternoon deepened from white to gold. In a clearing at the edge of a field, where the human habitations gave way to open space, a circle of Santhal men and women, linked to each other with their arms across their neighbours on either side, expanded and contracted to the unerring rhythm of a drum, with the grace of a dream. On the red soil they formed at one moment a small ring, then, at another moment, obeying the syncopations of the drummer, a larger one. Somnath thought of a bud blooming into a day-long flower, then collapsing into a shrivelled prepuce at the beginning of nightfall. Expanding and contracting, expanding and contracting. The men and women bowed as they moved inward, then lifted their heads up on the outward move. The effect, unfurling to the repetitive drumbeats, was hypnotic.

He wrenched his eyes off the collective harmony of the dance to search for his Santhal girl, but had trouble picking her out – all the women were wearing flowers in their hair. And then he saw her, an ebony figure of perfect grace and form, her skin strangely luminous in its contrast with the dark-red cloth that she had wrapped around herself, leaving so much of her legs and body unencumbered. The thuds in his heart outpaced the drumbeats. He followed the circumference of the dancing circle until he stood diagonally behind his girl at a distance of a few feet, part of a looser circle of the audience gathered to watch. Then, suddenly, the mesmeric hold broke, the harmonic duet between the drum and his heart snapped. An immense hunger seemed to be devouring him, a hunger exacerbated by all this nibbling away at the scene in front of him with only his eyes; he wanted a different kind of assuaging.

Someone was shaking him by his shoulder, offering him something. He turned around. It was Shekhar, holding out what looked like a pint-bottle.

'They're selling mahua,' he said. 'Have some. It's killer stuff, not what I was expecting it to be.'

Somnath took a swig, swallowed and nearly choked. The liquor had a burning, laboratory quality to it. It tasted of putrefaction. He grimaced and asked, 'What were you expecting?'

'Well, doesn't the name lead you to believe it will be something fragrant and honeyed?'

'*Fragrant and honeyed*,' Somnath mimicked. 'Man, you've been infected by Ajit's poetry bug. Come on, give us another swig.' It was a desperate attempt to swagger and fall into the comfortable macho camaraderie of their usual intercourse; he felt he had to keep his distracting, consuming hunger sheltered from the gaze of his friends.

The drumbeats stopped; the dance had ended. There were hundreds of people jostling and milling around. A man was selling tin whistles, another one pinwheels, yet another gaudily painted bamboo baskets. Somnath noticed at least two groups gambling. Ajit seemed to have been swallowed by the crowd. Somnath turned to Shekhar and said, 'Do you think you can get me another bottle of mahua?'

'Yes, no problem. They're selling it in that shack over there.'

'Why don't you give me this bottle and you go get a new one? I'll be right here. Here, take some money,' Somnath said, pulling a few crumpled notes out of the pocket of his trousers. 'Will you be able to find me? It's so bloody crowded, people are eating each other's heads . . .'

'Of course. But don't you move from here, otherwise I'll lose you,' Shekhar said, handing Somnath the pint-bottle, still nearly half-full of the fiery liquid.

As soon as Shekhar's back was turned Somnath wheeled round and lost himself in the crowd. He had to find her; this was not even a village, more like a hamlet; he could find her without any difficulty; she would still be with her tribespeople, for the dance had ended only a few minutes earlier. After a few restless minutes of pushing through the press of people, he discovered her, sitting with other Santhals. It took him some time to work out that they were getting drunk in a silent and focused way. That aimless mirth, the inexplicable, fluid joy, were all gone, yet the concentration seemed desultory. There was a core of hopelessness to it, even perhaps of despair.

Somnath stood beside her and said, 'Ei, ei, are you listening?' to draw her attention; he did not know her name and it embarrassed him.

She looked up, smiled sleepily and turned away, her attention engaged more by the bottle doing the rounds. In the final blaze of twilight the flower in her hair glowed. Soon it would be dark; he found the thought oddly comforting. Run through with that thought, indivisible from it, were the words he spoke next, almost in a whisper, to her, 'Come with me, I've got more of the stuff with me, you don't have to share with anyone.'

The man and the woman on either side of her turned round along with her. This time her smile had a little bit more interest in it. She tried to stand up, failed, leaned against the man, who continued to stare at Somnath. Somnath knelt down to be level with her.

She giggled and asked, 'You give me liquor? Where is it? Show me!'

Somnath brandished the bottle and said, 'There's more.'

The staring man now said to Somnath, 'You bring the liquor here, she won't go with you.'

Somnath looked at him with contempt and said to the girl again, 'Come.'

The man answered, 'No, she won't.'

Showing some spark for the first time, the girl let loose a shower of incomprehensible words to the man. He retorted with equal eloquence. This resulted in a veritable fusillade from her. Somnath watched with bemusement; even the seemingly heated exchange appeared to him to be oddly dotted with their habitual languor. Or was that the effect of the stuff they were drinking? A fair few of them seemed to be half-asleep, some swaying gently, others with their drooping heads nearly touching the earth. No one seemed to be paying much attention to this corner where a sudden display of energy was playing out. Except for the woman who was sitting on the other side of the girl. She called out to someone and said something that led to another woman, on the opposite arc of the circle, letting out a titter, then a few slurred words, and finally a giggle, before she fell back into the doziness that had taken over the group.

Then, surprising Somnath, the girl got up, teetered for a bit, steadied herself and said to him, 'Let's go. You buy me some liquor.'

Somnath leaped up and handed her his half-empty bottle. She took a swig, two swigs, passed the bottle back to him and in the same forward motion her upper body keeled towards him and fell against his chest. His free hand instinctively reached out to steady her. He held her elbow first, then her arm. Her warm skin was like an electric shock through his fingers. She disengaged herself, or maybe he foolishly encouraged her to do it; the contact was all over in a few seconds, but Somnath felt feverish from it. Was that moment of unbalanced lungeing a calculated move or was the unsteadiness an effect of the drinking? He would never know. She kept drifting in and out of a mild trance, not far removed from her slow, wakeful manner. This made it easy, even imperative, for Somnath to keep touching her so that she would not fall.

He finished off the remnants of the mahua in one big draw from the bottle and winced; it was not as bad as the first time. The thought of touching his lips to the rim of the bottle that had just been in her mouth mitigated some of the rotting taste. He felt a momentary quickening that was at odds with her swaying lethargy. He was trying to lead her to the forest he had walked in yesterday.

Suddenly the dark came down, swift as the falling of a mantle. Somnath had a brief sense of being caught in a wildly erratic flow of time, scrambled into sudden, unpredictable elongations and compressions, then that feeling left him too; he fell into a warp. How long had she been saying to him, 'Ei, babu, the forest is in that direction, you said you give me liquor. That is in the other direction'? Then he was almost dragging her to the sheltering dark of the trees. Was he? Was he not simply supporting her in her inebriated condition? If she did not want to go with him, why was she not resisting? Why did *he* feel pulled along? How pliant she seemed. There was a moon now, low in the sky, again an enormous orange coin with a tiny, tiny bit from one side pared off. Was it waxing or waning? He felt puissant like a nocturnal predator. And then he sensed that the forest was around them. When had they entered it? How much time had elapsed? He thought of the mahua – his first time ever on that strong stuff, no wonder it had so gone to his head.

She said, 'Ei, babu, you take me to Calcutta, give me a job?'

'A job? I'll make you my queen!'

She giggled and asked, 'You speak truly?' Then, again, 'Where is the liquor? You said you give me some.'

He would never tire of the meandering lines of her speech, the way she elided Bengali and Hindi together.

'Babu, the forest is dark. You come back with me.'

'No, let's stay here. My eyes have got used to the dark.' He pulled her close to him. He felt her resist him, first weakly, then with increasing force. She was no meek, wilting flower, she was a tribal woman; these people had the strength of wild animals. It excited him, this promise of a tussle first.

The forest floor was crackly under their feet. They had entered a new world, where a wholly different order of sonic smudges brought it into its eerie being. It had the temporary effect of diverting his focus away from the demands of his pounding blood. A small creature went scurrying, setting off a series of rustling noises as if it were moving under an armour of dry leaves worn over its body. There was what he took to be the call of a night-bird, a long whirring ending with a *tick-tick-tick*, an unnerving sound. Its very unearthliness underscored the immediate matter; he was returned to the business at hand again. He had his hand on her arm like the grip of a feral beast's jaw. Some atavistic instinct had perhaps warned him that she knew the forest much better than he, was its denizen and, if released, could run away, never to appear within his orbit again. His dark-adapted eyes could make out the trunks of trees, as darker pillars embedded in the matrix of the dark of night, then understood there was enough diffuse moonlight breaking through the cover of the forest to enable a form of night-vision.

The girl had stopped speaking. He had heard that these promiscuous tribal women had insatiable desires; they were at it all the time, with whoever approached them. The moment was now. As if on cue, a night-bird, a different one this time, emitted a loud, metallic *chaunk, chaunk, chaunk* in an unstoppable run and startled him out of his skin. He tried to ease her to the ground, but she was having none of it.

'Babu, let me go, babu,' she kept pleading. The counterpoint of the birdcall and her unvarying words flashed off a quick irritability; he barked, 'Shut up!' The game had changed. Why had she come so far with him if she wanted him to let go of her? It could only be a part of the performance that wily Santhal women put on to make keener the edge of desire.

Her motions and behaviour, which had so far seemed as if taking place under water, suddenly speeded up, the drunkenness dispelled. She tried to twist her arm away, but Somnath now held her with both hands. She shouted out a string of words, presumably about how much he was hurting her, but this was only the first act of the tussle she so wanted. He pushed her against a tree and tried to keep her pinned against it using his whole body, but she kept twisting like a collared cat. It would have been so much better if they were on the ground, but he was now caught between making the most of their standing positions and wanting to bring them both to lie down; the two involved different actions and he tried to find some intersection between them.

A larger rustle rippled through nearby: the presence of humans had clearly alarmed some bigger animal. Holding her against the tree with his waist and legs, he slightly leaned his upper half back and tried to get his hands everywhere, to free her from the cloth wrapping her. She cried out a couple of times in between heavy snorts and panting. A brief thought flitted through Somnath's mind, that perhaps she was earnest in her resistance, and exited just as quickly, his concentration now wholly on groping and squeezing and subduing. There was a flapping of wings and a shrill *kri-kriii-kri* that ended with a muffled abruptness as if the bird had fallen asleep before finishing its cry. The rustling was getting louder.

Then, shocking Somnath, she bit his hand; sank her teeth in with all the strength she could muster. He cried out and his unaffected hand went up, almost involuntarily, to slap her face, once, twice, three times. This time her screaming emerged unimpeded, with the full force of her lungs. Suddenly the rustling was all around them – they were surrounded by people.

Things moved very fast. A man spoke out some sharp words, the girl ran towards him, wailing; the sound of angry words from the same man, another couple of slaps, then silence from the girl. A torch was shone on Somnath's face, blinding him. Other men now started speaking. He had no idea how many men there were; at least three. Then the first blow fell before he could think of running away. It hit his side and was swiftly followed by several more, on his legs, back, neck, ribs. He let out a cry and collapsed. The torchlight had gone off. They were beating him with long sticks. A voice rasped out a string of urgent, angry words. Clapped in the stocks of pain and fear, Somnath began to discern Bengali abuse being fired at him – 'Lowlife! Dog! Son of a sow! You think you can come from the city and do anything you want with our women?'

He curled up, trying to protect his head with his hands and arms, reduced to the fragility of a foetus. Then another set of harsh words that sounded like a command. The torchlight went on and raked him in swinging, jerky arcs. It fell to the ground from the hand of the man who was holding it, its cone of light pendulating a few times before it came to rest. In that ghostly terranean light the men aimed their blows with greater precision. They tried to get to his skull in the way they killed a snake in these parts, by crushing the head with the blows of their sticks, for bringing them down on the body would not do, even if they damaged it and turned it to pulp. They knew that the snake could regrow its body and, once revived, it would come back for revenge, so you had to get the head and beat that into a paste to make sure that you had not just maimed it, but killed it properly.

Later it was said, because Purba did not visibly erupt into the hysterical grief that was expected of a woman widowed two years into her marriage, that she had a heart of stone, but that was only the beginning, and a clement one too, of the weather that was coming.

They tried to keep her from seeing Somnath's corpse, but only half-heartedly. *An accident in the forests of the Chhotanagpur plateau,* someone had said. *A road accident,* said another. A whisper, quickly suppressed, that Santhals may have been involved in some way, but no one was talking about it, definitely not to her or in front of her; she could not ask anyone, she did not dare ask. How could she? This was not her family, but her lifelong exile among strangers. She saw the room on the ground floor, in which the body had been laid out, thronged with people at all hours, saw the brass vases full of cut stalks of green-tinged white tuberose, its smell mingling with the smoke from the continually burning incense sticks, and felt only the cold clutch of fear.

She took in the clotted black jam that had been his head and tried to turn her face away, but was transfixed by a small line of ants leaving the mess and beginning a march in the opposite direction on the white sheets on which he had been placed. She wondered, sacrilegiously for a time like this, if the ants had been picked up in the forest as he was lying dead in the thick of trees and bushes or if they had come in search now, attracted as they were by rotting organic matter. Then she had thrown up right there and was rushed out of the room; her second great error, a defilement of the sacred room of the dead.

The doctor who had come to write out the death certificate, and give Prafullanath and Charubala a sedative, looked in on her on his way out; she was pregnant with her second child, he said. She had cried then; the doctor had taken it to be for her great misfortune. And yet the tears had not been for her, or for the new child beginning inside her – that was not incarnate yet, only an idea – but for her son who would never know his father. Watching his curly head and his dark, innocent eyes, she felt something like a smashing of everything that was held behind her chest. In a household where she was the youngest adult, who had to defer to the wishes and commands and whims of her seniors, she deferred too on the matter of sorrow and grieving – Somnath's death was a greater loss to these others.

The little boy, Supratik, whom she had seen prancing up and down, wearing a child's silk panjabi and a child's dhoti, when she had got married two years ago, the child who had seemed like the principle of irrepressible energy and was only about seven years younger than she, now slipped into her room and announced sombrely, 'This is the first death in this house.' He was only eleven.

Purba lifted up her head. She did not know what to say.

Supratik said, 'Do you know that story about the Buddha?'

'No.'

'A woman's child died. She was very sad and crying, all the time. She went to the Buddha and said, "Buddha, Buddha, please bring my son back to life." And she was crying, crying. So the Buddha said to her, "Go bring me some mustard seeds from a house in which there has been no death ever and I'll bring your son alive." So the woman went around from house to house, begging for mustard seeds, crying. But she couldn't find a single house in which there hadn't been a death. For days she went looking and crying but no one could give her those seeds. So she returned to the Buddha, fell at his feet and said, 'I couldn't find the mustard seeds. Every house I went to has had a death in it. What will happen now?' The Buddha said, 'I asked you to do the impossible. Every mortal is marked by death. No one can escape it. That is why you couldn't find a death-free home. This was my lesson to you – death is universal, all of us have to die.' So the mother, crying, crying, still crying for her dead son, went away. And that is the end of the story.'

She could not bring herself to speak.

The boy let the silence tick for a little while longer, then said to the floor, 'Don't be sad', and left the room.

Several years later she would keep turning the little incident this way and that in the hope of discovering an answer to the question: could this have been the beginning?

The day after Somnath's cremation at Nimtala Ghat, Prafullanath, who had spent most of his time under sedation since the corpse of his youngest son had been brought back to Calcutta, woke up from the obliteration of his drugged sleep with a strange pain up his right arm. It was not very bad, but neither could it be ignored. He called out to his wife – where was she? – but his throat was too phlegmy for the call to carry. What time was it? There was so much light in the room, he had never known the room to be flooded with so much sunlight. Why had they opened the windows and the door if he had been sleeping? Where was all this light coming from? He got out of bed, felt for his slippers with his feet and managed to kick one under the bed trying to get his feet into them. He bent down to retrieve it. The room canted around him. The light exploded.

After three weeks in PG Hospital, twelve days of which were in the cardiac intensive-care unit, Prafullanath returned home not as himself, but as his beaten shadow. Only one thought, sometimes murmured aloud to himself but overheard gradually by others, kept wheeling and turning in his head: 'It's against the order of Nature for a father to mourn the death of his son. What wrong did I commit that I am being punished in this way?'

The efficacy of the sedation was variable. Charubala had sat beside her dead son's mangled corpse and, dry-eyed, begun to bang her head against a wall, the force of impact increasing with each ramming as she settled into the consolation of a distracting pain. She had to be forcibly removed and restrained in her bed as the doctor gave her an injection. On regaining consciousness she showed no grief; she did not wail, cry, speak – she became instead a stone. If everyone had been horrified by the brutal expression of her sorrow before, now they were even more alarmed. They set about to draw some kind of emotion from those frozen depths. Over days they tried. They cajoled and suggested and tried to make her afraid. News of Purba's pregnancy could not lance the boil, nor could showing her photographs of Somnath and asking her to choose which one should be blown up, framed and hung on a wall. In one extreme instance Priya tried to describe his brother's body in gory details and speculate about his final hours, hoping that cruelty would bring about the thaw; his mother remained petrified.

Sandhya suggested that if Purba sat beside her mother-in-law, the sight of her son's widow might break her heart and release her. Purba, now in her widow's white, the vermilion line in the parting of her hair permanently removed using the big toe of her husband's corpse before it was taken away for cremation, complied with her habitual meekness. For unknown reasons, a murky sense of guilt made her want to be overobedient, overbiddable; it was as if she had brought her in-laws to this pass and there was nothing she would not do to atone.

But her mother-in-law, still suspended in the limbo of her shock, read these murky, unplumbed deeps of Purba's soul with ease. On the third day of Purba sitting at her vigil, Charubala surfaced from wherever she had been drowned and uttered her first words. She looked at Purba and said, 'You have brought this great misery upon our heads. You are ill-starred, evil.'

The effect of her resurgence momentarily shrouded the meaning of her words. Chhaya shrieked, 'Ma's speaking! Ma's speaking!' and ran up and down the stairs summoning everyone. In that room, now full of people, Charubala arraigned her youngest daughter-in-law. 'You have brought this misfortune to our house,' she repeated. 'You're a burnt-faced woman, it is because of you that my son died.'

Sandhya tried to interrupt, 'Ma, please, this is not . . .' but the words shrivelled and died in her mouth. A great pall had fallen over the house. The silence in the room was that of unspeakability. A magic circle had been drawn around Purba; locked inside it, she instilled fear in everyone outside that malignant aura of the cursed one. Superstition did the rest. Purba found herself to be the weak animal that the rest of its own kind attacked and drove outside the fold.

From this point the culture of strictures governing widowhood will settle on Purba's life like the clanging shut of the immensely heavy metal lid over a manhole. She will eat only strictly vegetarian food, all manner of protein forbidden in case it inflames her blood, leading her to any kind of impropriety in her thoughts and actions. She will observe strict fasts every eleventh day after the full moon. In a previous generation they would have had her head shaved and made her wear a piece of coarse, white, handspun cotton cloth that reached only down to the top of her ankles, but some grudging acknowledgement had to be made to social progress. On the excuse of some long-overdue rearrangements in domestic space, Purba and her two children will be asked in a year's time to move from the first floor, which she had shared, when her husband had been alive, with Priya, Purnima and Baishakhi, to the ground floor of the house.

The apportioning of space and the layout of rooms on this floor followed a pattern different from the architectural interior regularity of the other floors. It was a mess: a sitting room that was never used; a kitchen with an adjoining enclosure for washing-up and cutting fish and meat; a room at the back that could have been a bedroom, but had been used as a pantry and storeroom from the early days of the building's history; a couple of dingy rooms, their space eaten into by the need to accommodate, a few steps down, the garages and the entrance. In one of these rooms Purba will be asked to make her quarters with her son and daughter. Her exile will begin to take on its physical lineaments.

CHAPTER SIXTEEN

1970

He scintillates with the glamour of terror. Or so it seems to him. Only now, a month after his return, do the children of the house, his cousins, bring themselves to talk to him; initially, during the first weeks, it would be a lightning peep from the corner or behind doors, then a quick scampering off if he caught them at it. Sometimes he called out – 'Ei, Arunima, come in, come inside' – but she was gone, too frightened to think of him as her eldest cousin. What have the children been told? Supratik wonders. There is so much unsaid that he feels the air shimmer. Everyone avoids his eye; when they think he is looking elsewhere, he catches them stealing quick glances at him; the Ghoshes' very own resident cicatrice. He is beyond indifferent.

But his mother dents this carapace. Watching, when he can bear to, the three-way pull between relief, fear and curiosity on her readable face, her fear barely winning out over her indestructible love, something goes through the rickety cage of his chest, but he stops it there. Emotion is a luxury, he knows; like all revolutionaries he cannot draw the correct line between emotion and sentimentality. He reminds himself of a story that had made a deep mark on him as a child – the man who had been following the Buddha around for years and years, in the hope that he would be accepted as a disciple, one day breaks down, falls at the Buddha's feet and declares, 'Master, I have nothing!', to which the Buddha says, 'Give that up too.' That temporary tightening he feels behind his eyes when he sees his mother looking at him with the devotion of a dog – that is his 'nothing'; he will have to learn to give it up too.

She has Madan-da cook him all the dishes she thinks he loves, five different things at every meal – bottle-gourd with poppyseed paste, green papaya with little shrimps, parshey fish filled with roe, lentil cakes cooked in sauce, white egg curry – and hovers around while he toys with it with the tips of his fingers.

His father dares to confront him one day, soon after he returns. Supratik knows the calculation that has gone behind this: if he does not do it quickly enough, he will never be able to speak to his son with any authority. Pity battles with antagonism, as Supratik watches his father hem and haw and stammer pathetically before he can even begin. In fact, he has to help him out with the opening: 'Do you want to say something to me?' he asks.

'Yes, no, yes . . . yes, I do, actually. You've blackened our face,' Adinath launches in. 'You've brought down so much shame upon us that we cannot show our face to the outside world any more.'

What does his father know of the 'outside world' that he cannot bring himself to name any longer? It is Supratik who knows about it: he has loped in and out of that demesne with the cautiousness of a preyed-upon animal. And fear? Yes, that too; he knows he is going to be hunted down. There is an inevitability about it that he finds oddly liberating, even euphoric at times. Yes, he knows that outside world.

The world, say, of his Badal, who had lived with a tuberculotic, unemployed father, a mother and two younger sisters in one room the size of a cardboard shoebox in a bamboo and tin shack in a slum in Santragachhi; Badal who had dreamed of a better life for his parents and sisters and no doubt for himself too, a better life that consisted of living somewhere with brick walls, not the insubstantial, bendy partitions made out of gunny-cloth and thinly beaten woven canes, a life in which he could get some kind of job that would provide two meals a day for his family of five and perhaps, if he got lucky, a couple of eggs for his father because the doctor had prescribed proteins for him, but protein had seemed as unreachable as the moon when every other day his mother had been unable to light their little mud-and-brick oven because there had been nothing to cook on it. The loose change Badal had earned, walking the streets twelve hours a day, peddling jam, jellies, pickles made by a cooperative, had not stretched to proteins. It had been commission work and there had been days when he had failed to push even one measly bottle on any household.

That had been the life of his comrade Badal, who had tasted, daily, hourly, the bitter grit of humiliation as door after door had been shut in his face, and the children and servants who had answered his knocks, he had been able to tell instantly, had been instructed to lie and say that there was no one at home. Badal, whose anger had bubbled and spilled over like the foamy starch of boiling rice, watching everyone he loved desiccate as if their life-spirit was being sucked out, little by little, until one day they would all turn into husk. He had rebelled against that imminent state of huskness and had thrown in his lot, his anger and his dammed-up frustration and energies and his human capabilities of thinking and working, with the party he had thought could bring about some change in making the world a less hostile place for him and his own. For which he had been smoked out of his slum by the police, who had thrown a Molotov cocktail on the street outside – it was President's Rule in the state now, the second time in as many years; the police could do anything now, not that they couldn't when there was a government in place, mind you, but they could do it with the *overt* blessing of the state machinery now – had thrown a Molotov cocktail, then entered each shack on the excuse that some slum-resident was doing his usual terrorism stuff, and had rounded up about fourteen young men. Badal had tried to escape by running out of the back, through the mazy warren of the narrow space between the rows of shacks, a two-foot-wide zigzagging line, really, of compacted earth and mud and the estuarine trickles of washing-up and used bath water and liquid sewage, all trying to merge into one or two open drains, but he had been surprised by the policemen waiting on the other side of the woven-cane boundary wall he had so easily climbed over, thinking, while surmounting it, that he could run away and lie low somewhere else for a few days and then return after things had calmed down and Calcutta Police had transferred their attention to some other hapless place where they thought they could trawl successfully for Naxalites, but, no, that was not to be. The slum had become, in a matter of a few seconds after the raid began, an eerily silent, abandoned hive; those who had doors to their shacks had slammed them shut and the rest hid inside, pretending not to exist, praying that their hovel would not be visited and turned upside down by the police. Badal's bullet-riddled body had been discovered, minutes after the black vans had left, lying on the outer edge of the boundary wall, where the police had shot him. Later, Supratik had been told by Subrata, another comrade, who had gone to visit Badal's parents, that Badal's mother had spat on his face and tried to scratch his eyes out. 'You boys are responsible for my son's death,' she had howled at him, 'you boys taught him to play with fire with your politics. I wish my fate on all your mothers.' On his mother, too, Supratik had not failed to note. For it was he who had taught Badal first how to grind finely potassium nitrate, sulphur and charcoal, then mix them in a ratio of 2:1:1 very carefully into clayey balls with water, sometimes with nails or screws or ball-bearings as shrapnel, then tie them up even more carefully with jute threads, dry them overnight, ready to be carried in jute side-bags and lobbed where they saw fit; it was he who had directed Badal where to get hold of pipe-guns and ammunition on the black market or, better still, the cheap and easy Sten guns that had started making an appearance from 1963, not long after that ridiculous border skirmish with China; he had educated Badal in all this and more – target practice; dismantling and putting back together a Sten in order to work out if they could manufacture it locally; how to absorb the recoil of a gun and steady oneself during and after firing . . . True, all too true, literally, that he had taught Badal to play with fire.

Now that he is facing his father, who speaks of his confected luxury of shame, his inability to show his face to the outside world, Supratik is reminded of a more authentic, more painful variety of it, in his unwillingness to visit Badal's mother after Badal's murder. Could *that* be described accurately as shame, the real, soul-staining thing?

Or was it the feeling that went through him when, just before escaping from Majgeria, he had seen Kanu and Bijli's ill two-year-old son squatting on the hut floor, unable even to cry out for his mother, and shitting his guts out, the ground clearance between his arse and the floor not big enough so that the virulent chemical-yellow, clayey stuff that came out of him was continuous between arsehole and floor, gluing him almost; and Supratik had seen the vermicular seethe of that infected shit and wondered if, by the time Kanu took him to Medinipur Town, to the abandoned ghost house that was the public hospital with its absent doctors and staff and nurses and the few medical supplies that came through stolen and resold on the black market by the staff, by the time he got lucky enough to have a doctor see the child, perhaps after days of waiting, he wondered if the child would be alive.

It struck him again, with vivid force, that all this talk of 'the outside world' turned round one thing only: what the outside world made of your own life. You were forever at the centre of things, the subject of the sentence; it was not the outside world you were thinking of, but where *you* stood in the regard of that world. He wanted to say to his father that others thought of their own lives too, perhaps more often, more deeply, than they did of his father's. The assumption that his father would always have some sort of a privileged access to that outside world, much more so than his son, by virtue of his age, grated Supratik's nerves raw. He wanted to quiz him, firing one question after another to this ridiculous man about the world outside. How much did he know about, say, the lives of those students who were being rounded up by the police in raids on neighbourhoods, men's hostels of universities, taken into cells and tortured until they gave up names and whereabouts of their Naxalite comrades? Of those boys broken by beating and electric shocks, for whom betrayal was an abstract noun in all senses when placed beside the very real and immediate pain of a nail being uprooted with a pair of pliers? He, Supratik, had seen the blue-black stub of a comrade's finger, not quite a human appendage, and the shadows under his eyes which looked as if they would never smile again. But it had been shame, that easily bandied-about emotion, that had cast its shadow on the comrade's face: shame that, under torture, he had given the names and addresses of his comrades and was now an outcast from the Party; shame and fear, for if the police had not got him, then his comrades, whom he had thrown to the lions, would. The prospect of that punishment corroded him daily into a whittled-down version of his previous self, smaller, more frangible, as if that ruined finger had become, by some synecdoche, his entire soul.

He, Supratik, has witnessed all this, not the emasculated, pompous fool in front of him, making grand claims about the world outside. He can ask his father, for example, how much he knows about the nearly daily occurrence of bombings in the city, bombings that Adinath

terms, with derision, 'playing with fireworks' in the same breath as
he expresses relief because he occupies the third floor of the house,
far above the 'mosquitoes and the bombs that those dangerous
Naxalites have taken to hurling', as if the Naxalites are spoilt children
with expensive toys? 'Hurling'! Does he know that in at least half of
these incidents explosives are being targeted *at* Naxalites by Congress
and CPI(M) goons? Does he know that Naxalites are now caught in
a pincer movement – if the bombs and guns and knives of the enemy
parties do not finish them off, then the police will be only too happy
to oblige?

This is going to be the next phase of their revolution now: the
urban side. Supratik has been entrusted with drawing up the strategies
for action in the city. But in all the operations that he has so far thought
about, the line between offensive and defensive ones, already delicate,
has become blurred: so much of their city activism originates in the
need to defend themselves from the trident of Congress, CPI(M) and
the state. And, as always, it boils down to a bare economics: if they
cannot find enough money to finance their defence, they will be wiped
out without ever managing to reach the proactive attack stage. It's a
question of survival now and that is the most ruthless question of
them all. Us or them?

Us versus them.

It gives Supratik a little thrill to witness his father going to considerable lengths to avoid the word 'Naxal'. He tries to manipulate the
conversation so that he can get Adinath to bring himself to utter the
word.

'And how exactly have I brought so much shame upon you?' he
asks calmly. That is another thing – the great effort he puts into
appearing so placid is repaid, with interest, in the way it makes his
father more and more turbulent.

'Y-y-ou . . . you know it yourself, how dare you ask? Don't you
have any shame?'

'How can I? You've just told me it's all yours!'

'If you're to stay in this house, you have to obey the rules,' Adinath
splutters.

'Otherwise?'

'Otherwise . . . otherwise . . .'

'Otherwise you'll throw me out, am I correct?' In his smoothest, most unruffled manner Supratik carries on, 'You don't have to go through the trouble of doing that. Perhaps you've forgotten that I had left of my own accord.'

Sandhya, who has eavesdropped on most of this exchange, confronts her husband at night. 'What do you want?' she cries. 'That he goes away again? Do you want that? Do *my* wishes mean nothing to you? If he goes away this time, you'll see my dead face, I'm warning you.'

Supratik does not know of this. He thinks his father is off his case because he has been defeated by his son's cold contempt.

One lunchtime Madan lingers on, annoying Supratik with his usual 'You didn't touch your food, look what you've made of yourself, all skin-and-bones, this is what happens when you eat like a sparrow, did they not give you enough to eat where you were', until Supratik realises that this mantra is only an excuse; Madan is stalling for time, waiting to have a moment in private with him.

He tries to make it easy for the old man. 'Do you have something to say to me?' he asks gently once the servants have departed. How old is he? he wonders. Pushing sixty? Older? He cannot think of a time when Madan-da has not been there. He remembers Madan-da reading aloud to him from Tagore's *Words and Tales* when he was little. Or could that be a scene from his father's life, told to him when he was young and now appropriated by him as a kind of false memory? Madan-da does little, if any, of the cooking nowadays, delegating it to a younger fleet of servants, whom he orders about and directs, but nobody has found it in their heart to let him go, certainly not while Supratik's grandmother is alive, or indeed his mother.

Madan stands apart, at a distance from him, and says, 'Boro-babu' – Big Boss, that only half-ironic term of affection from his childhood has fused to him; there is no hope that Madan-da is ever going to call him by his first name – 'your mother has survived a lot of pain.'

Supratik does not, cannot, say anything.

'We are poor people, Boro-babu, what do we know? You and your lot are educated, you've read books, been to college, will you listen to what we have to say?'

'Why don't you try?'

'Boro-babu, the world does not change, you destroy yourself trying to change it, but it remains as it is. The world is very big, and we are very small. Why cause people who love you to go through such misery because of it?'

Once again, what response can he give to this?

'Your mother took to her bed after you were gone. At first she wouldn't even touch water until you returned. I've made a bargain with god, she said. She was shrivelling up like leather in the sun. I've known her ever since she came to this house as a daughter-in-law, it burned my chest to see her like that' – his voice breaks.

Supratik looks up sharply. Madan-da's eyes are red with unshed tears. Supratik turns his face quickly away.

But Madan reins himself in. 'What good will come of all this that you are doing?' he asks.

'What is it that you think I'm doing?'

Madan answers tangentially, 'Being kinder to your near and dear ones – isn't that a bigger thing than doing good for the unknown mass of people?'

A switch is flicked somewhere. It sends through Supratik a surge of cold fury that he is being given a lesson in political morality by the family's cook. His answer is like the crack of a whip: 'Was that what you were doing when you prostrated yourself in front of my grandmother after Grandfather's heart attack, and wept and begged her to forgive you for your son's part in gheraoing him? You asked her to mete out whatever punishment she thought fit for your betrayer of a son. *Let loose the police on him, let him go to jail*, you said. Was that kindness to your near and dear ones?'

Madan looks as if he has been slapped. The lower half of his mouth goes slack for a moment or two before he can begin to assert some kind of control over it.

Supratik is not done. 'Remember? You told her that you wouldn't see your son's face again, he had destroyed your honour and dignity with the family who employed you, who had given you a home for decades? Do you remember?'

Madan looks at Supratik with the unblinking gaze of an idiot; Supratik expects the corners of his mouth to start dripping with drool any minute. His own initial reluctance to engage is gone. In its place is that familiar saw-toothed hardness.

'What? Have you forgotten? A CPI(M) stooge, that's what you said your son was. You were right, as it turned out. But what did you think was more important – that he served your petty interests in not rocking the boat for you or that he fought for the rights of scores who have nothing?'

Madan begins, 'Boro-babu . . . where did you—'

Supratik cuts through his feeble words: 'It's irrelevant where or how I came by all this. You were looking after yourself when you were grasping my grandmother's feet and wailing, *your* self-interest. But it was all couched in the language of feelings for your near and dear ones, as you are doing now. *Punish him, he's done great wrong, but don't abandon me*, you said then. Did you ever think of Dulal? The factory's been shut down, possibly for ever; your son's out of a job, struggling to set up an electrical-goods shop. All the men who worked at that mill are jobless now, thanks to the people you work for, the people you are now pleading on behalf of. In these times of shortage, of hundreds and thousands of unemployed and no jobs to be had, how are these men going to eat? How are they going to feed and clothe their families and keep the roof over their heads?'

Madan now visibly flinches as the hissing, which is what Supratik's words have become, hits him. Supratik knows that somebody who is not a servant in their home can easily retaliate with the argument that Madan's advice to him, that one must pay heed to the private over the public, otherwise one is inviting disaster in, is coherent for both situations, Dulal's and Supratik's, but he also knows that Madan-da will not answer back because his station in life has not taught him how to. Besides, as Madan himself pointed out, Supratik has had the benefit of higher education while the cook is, at best, someone who learned how to read at home – how could he ever have the competence to mount an argument exposing holes in Supratik's logic?

And, predictably enough, Madan looks routed, as if he is staring at some devastation wrought by a natural calamity or war. He opens his mouth to try to speak, but thinks better of it. If Supratik feels a quantum of regret, it is because of the party Madan-da has been speaking up for – his mother – but that too vanishes almost as soon as it appears.

Only Sona seems to be unaware that Supratik has been gone for two and a half years, that he is now, like a circus lion, enclosed by a ring of fire.

Supratik catches hold of the boy downstairs in his quarters one day and asks, 'What's going on in the new school? Your mother seems unable to report anything to me.'

Purba, flustered at this direct reference, absents herself for a while. Supratik has forgotten the difficult trick of getting Sona to talk or, when he does, of extracting the real meaning from the little that he says.

Sona mumbles something; Supratik does not quite catch it, only half his attention is on the boy. He knows he must ask the boy again, so he dutifully poses another question.

'Are you facing any trouble with English? What are they teaching you now?'

'Agreement of prepositions with verbs,' comes the succinct reply.

'Difficult?'

'Yes, very. You learn by heart things like "prefer to" and "abide by", so if you don't know the meanings of "prefer" and "abide" then things get quite tricky.'

'Don't you ask your English teacher for the meanings?'

Silence.

'And how is the mathematics going?' Supratik asks.

'It's going well. The maths teacher says he wants to see someone . . .'

'See someone?'

'Someone from here, from home . . .'

But before Sona can finish his sentence Purba enters the room and Supratik is all a-scatter again.

'Get moving, get moving,' she tells her son peevishly, 'you can't be sitting here all day, chatting away with anyone who gets it into their head to drop by to waste time.'

Sona does not bother to respond.

Supratik, his heart thumping, asks Purba, 'How come I've become "anyone" suddenly?'

Purba turns her back to both of them. Her heart pummelling against her ribs, she scrapes up enough daring to reply, 'If someone disappears for so long, sends no news, no nothing, no sign to let anyone know whether he's dead or alive, yes, then he becomes just "anyone".' The last few words are bright with the smoulder of real anger.

'To you too?' Supratik brings himself to ask. Something has happened to his gullet. He feels the need to swallow repeatedly. It's a feeling familiar from those sneaked moments on the terrace when he used to time his visits there to coincide with her routine of hanging up the washing in the afternoons. They had had to be so careful, even to the excruciating extent of him deliberately missing some days so that no one suspected anything. On those days, Supratik imagined the twenty minutes of Purba upstairs with such force of concentration, hearing every footfall, every wet slap of the washing, that he felt drained and weightless when he heard her footsteps going down the stairs back to the ground floor. And on the days they met in the sun-baked terrace, they went through an unvarying miniature drama.

'You hang the clothes, I'll peg them to the line,' he would say, hardly able to bring out the words, or hear them himself over the roaring in his blood.

She would nod, her face flushed.

And then their hands would touch on the clothes line, the length of rope and a wet sari or shirt between them. He hadn't trusted himself to speak then, for he had needed every particle of energy to prevent his teeth from chattering. He had clasped her hand with such ferocity, to steady as much himself as her.

She breathed the words 'Someone will see us' and held onto his hand even more tenaciously.

The kind of trembling that this memory ignites in him is much like the one he had felt in a tiny, injured sparrow he had once cupped in his hand. The pages and pages that he has written for her, the pages that have kept him going because through the faithful scribbling he has imagined her as their sole recipient and dedicatee, imagined her as the source of light, as if in a painting, illuminating his writing as she reads it – he has not found the courage to give them to her. What stays his hand, he now wonders? Fear? Fear that he has shown her too much of the flow in his heart that cannot have a destination, that can only eddy around endlessly inside him in an arid circle? Fear that she may be baffled by it or, worse, repelled?

It is true that he has not had the opportunity to bring the account up to date. The fraught experience of his own and Dipankar's deliverance – that final disastrous action, which had culminated in abandoning Dhiren and Debashish and becoming fugitives for days, hiding out in patches of forests, in little villages and towns, until he and Dipankar reached Giridih, feverish with fear, exhaustion and starvation – remains unwritten. The two months in Giridih were spent lying low in Dipankar's uncle's home, writing the larger part of the account of the time in Majgeria and Gidighati, picking up from where he had left off, at the beginning of the first sowing season. The other substantial occupation was learning, with furious concentration and intent, the engineering of railway tracks and fishplate joins from Dipankar. They had walked for miles at night, for hands-on lessons – Dipankar called them 'practicals' – on far-flung railway tracks running through land that was so devoid of human habitation for miles around that they had sometimes felt they were on the moon. All that is yet uncommitted to paper. But it is truer that the incompletion serves as a convenient excuse not to give her what is already written; the writer's timeless self-acquittal – 'Oh, I need to write just the last couple of pages . . .'

Or is it another kind of fear that has been the cause of the procrastination, fear that he may be exposing her to knowledge that will make her vulnerable, put her in harm's way? Several times a day he swings between cursing himself for leaving behind the pages in Giridih because of this particular variant of fear, the fear that they may compromise her if the house is searched by the police – he is, after all, in their cross-hairs – and thinking that he has done the prudent thing by not bringing his incriminating account back home.

Would she have called him 'anyone' if she had known what he had been up to in the last two and a half years? Or would it have pushed her further away?

There is no answer from Purba. Everyone in the room is pointedly looking at nothing in particular; a calculated indirection. Even Sona, who is impervious to ordinary reality most of the time, feels something in the air has thickened and acquired a quality he can only think of as waiting, expectant. Like the atmosphere in the vicinity of a bomb, seconds before it explodes.

'Your maths teacher has sent for me. Do you know why?' Supratik asks Sona.

'No,' is Sona's brief reply. He seems to be taken aback by the contents of the letter that sir has given him to deliver.

The letter had surprised Supratik so much that he only has occasion to think much later about the implications of Sona handing it to him. An ordinary handwritten letter on a piece of paper torn neatly out of an unruled exercise book; the envelope has been addressed, in an upward-sloping hand: 'The parents/guardians of Swarnendu Ghosh'; its contents brief: could the parents/guardians of Swarnendu Ghosh come to the school to see me, the senior school mathematics teacher, any weekday between the hours of eleven to one, signed Swapan Adhikari.

So Supratik is not prepared for what's waiting for him. Why could Swarnendu's parents not come? is the first question. Because his father had died when he was little, and his mother, well, she would be uncomfortable, out of place in this world, Supratik answers, leaving Mr Adhikari to fill in the gaps; he says that he is Swarnendu's cousin and can be trusted with anything that requires looking into.

Nothing that needs looking into, Mr Adhikari assures him, but something quite different, something bigger. The boy is preternaturally talented in mathematics, a prodigy really; he is working on things better suited to the postgraduate level and is thinking about some crucial open problems in the subject of number theory, things he has never been taught, it all seems to come naturally to him; and the teacher has spoken to a close friend who is an associate professor at a university in the USA and has sent some of the boy's work to him, his notebook and papers, and he too thinks this is no ordinarily gifted boy who is good in maths, but someone rarer, someone very special, and this friend is of the opinion that a place can be found for him in the mathematics programme of the university, right now. Swarnendu need not go through the business of completing school and sitting school-leaving exams and American university-entrance exams, the professor has spoken to his Faculty members already, the other professors in the department, the Dean and the Chair, showed them Swarnendu's work, and he seems to be of the opinion that a place can be found for the boy, a fully funded place, on full scholarship; the university would like to welcome such prodigies and mature their talent, so will the family, the boy's family, be willing to consider this? It is a chance in a million, so he would strongly, very strongly, advise them to think . . . to think, erm, positively and purposively about the whole business. It could all be arranged in six months, or maybe nine. A year, maximum. He, Swapan Adhikari, is, of course, going to do everything in his power to push things along.

That torrent of information – each point so unthinkable and, therefore, unimagined by Supratik – has exactly the opposite effect of drowning with confusion and surprise; yes, his hands shake a bit and turn cold and clammy, but the revelation also gives him such a sudden, brief burst of sharp-edged clarity that he thinks for a moment it is the opening chord of something like a seizure or a stroke. And in that extreme lucidity he thinks first of Purba, then, almost simultaneously, how odd it is that he does not any longer think of her as his aunt, Chhoto-kakima, that he thinks of her as her unadorned, naked name, not what she is relationally to him. Will she be happy, share his sense of levitation? Will she even understand? Here, at last, so close to home, *at* home in fact, is the first proof of that wishy-washy, folksy, superstitious hypothesis, that good things happen to everyone in equal measure, that the great distribution system in the universe sends down sweeties to everyone with a blind and stringent even-handedness. Cock, total and utter cock; it has been his long-held conviction that only shit happens to the world's have-nots and no good ever comes their way without radical intervention; good things only happen to those to whom good things happened. Here, suddenly, mockingly, is a hole in his conviction. Here is something beyond good happening to someone in whose way nothing good has ever come in his small life. Will Purba understand at least *that*?

On the way back home he asks Sona, 'Are you happy about this?'

Sona, who seems very far away inside his head, does not answer. Then, much later, entering Basanta Bose Road, he says, in a small voice, 'Bor'-da, will you tell Ma?'

And Supratik does; first, to Purba's complete incomprehension, then to one question only, asked quaveringly, 'You mean Sona will leave us and go abroad?'

Over the next few days he tries to explain to Purba, with what partial and imperfect knowledge he has of the matter, the process of going to study in a country far away, only to be returned, time and time again, to that insurmountable issue – her son leaving home at the age of fifteen. It is only after he is forced to resort to a low kind of senti-mental blackmail – 'You do not want your son to do well? Do you want him to stay here and fester? Become a servant like you, sitting and standing to the demands and whims of everyone in the house? Don't you want him to *escape* this? Don't *you* want to escape all this? Do you not have in mind a future for him that is better than your past and present?' – it is only after this barrage has reduced her to tears that he has the first stirring of hope that Sona may leave with her blessings.

But this chapter has just begun. Supratik has to tell his mother the news about Sona and wait for her to inform the rest of the family. It is best done that way: the messenger's good standing amongst everyone would cast the message as inherently positive and somewhat mitigate the poisonous reactions of envy that Supratik is fully expecting to be unleashed tricklingly over time. Purba may have slipped from being the target of active hostility, through a long state of being passively considered a pariah, to becoming, along with her two children, mostly a kind of forgotten outpost now, related to the main house in a vague, historical and dusty way, but Supratik knows the milieu, knows that nothing swells and replenishes their poison sacs more than the success of others, especially those whom they have consigned to a different kind of destiny. Happiness for Purba and her children meant rebellion, it meant trying to break the walls of the prison they had been immured in, it meant unconscionable acts of defiance, and how could that be tolerated?

But he must not derail himself with the old animus today. Today he must answer the question Purba had asked him when he was arguing for Sona, a question that will leak its destructive half-lives into their own, and one day they may discover that they have been made irrecoverably ill. When he had asked, carried away by his rhetoric, if Purba did not imagine for Sona a future better than her blighted past and equally rotting present, she had looked up at him and said, 'But what about *my* future? What about *our* future?' That commute from singular to plural pronoun had felled him. How can he answer the question that is like a vortex inside him? That it is easier enjoining others, in distant villages, to break the walls of their historical conditions than to do the same violence to the fabric of his own social conditioning? Or can he bring himself to do both with equal ease? Can he?

Purnima is first heard screaming, then rushing around from floor to floor. 'My jewellery's gone! All my jewellery's been stolen – all. Clean missing from my safe. All gone, disappeared!'

It is difficult initially to get to the facts behind the nearly solid wall of hysteria, but the small crowd of family and servants that swiftly coalesces around her manages to put together some basic things: Purnima had come out of the bathroom after her midday bath, gone to her almirah to take out some clothes, discovered it was not locked, which made her suspicious, so she had unlocked the drawer in which her jewellery was kept, only to discover that it was staring at her emptily like the eye-sockets in a human skull. The story changes elastically according to who is narrating it to whom; sometimes the almirah is locked, and not the jewellery-drawer inside it, while sometimes it is the other way around. There are divergent accounts involving keys, and others about the value of the jewellery – some put it at one lakh rupees, some at ten. Purnima herself cannot give any fixity to these stories; she is too much in shock to make much sense of the events and, for a start, she cannot make up her mind if this storm of attention centred around her goes a little way, a very little way, towards compensating for the great loss.

Priyo is incensed with her. 'Why did you leave the stuff lying around in the house when it should have been in the bank locker?'

Purnima bleats, 'I brought my precious things home for the wedding, then . . . then I didn't find the time to return them to the bank. Or the chance.'

'You didn't find the *time*? Who do you think you are? Empress

435

Victoria? The president of this country? Couldn't you have even *found the time*,' he mimics savagely, 'to ask me to do it?'

'So much gold and jewels! Worth such a lot of money. All gone, all gone' is all Purnima can bring herself to say in between bouts of crying.

A repeated chord resonates in 22/6: 'Who could have burgled us?' The suspicion alights automatically on the servants. But which one of them can it be? Everyone in the house is an old and trusted hand and the newest of the lot, Kamala, the helper cook, has been around for nearly six years. The temporary staff – Usha, the maid who comes to clean every day; Reba, the washerwoman, who has been doing their laundry for the last twenty-five years – have been irreproachable so far. What about the revolving staff, usually three or four early-adolescent boys, none of whom stays for more than a year or two before moving on to another job, the ones who help out with the dusting and cleaning and miscellaneous duties? Surely it must be one of them. They are new, they have access to the rooms, they are not as melded in with the rest of the household as the other servants.

The police are called. The three boys are questioned, threatened, slapped around a bit. They are in tears, they deny everything. Their bodies and clothes are searched, then the room in the servants' quarters where they sleep. Nothing. Someone comments, 'They're hardly likely to stash it in their rooms. The loot's been taken away, they came to the house just to do this, their job's over now.' The boys plead for mercy, they protest their innocence, they wail like little children, but to no avail – they are beaten, then hauled away to jail. Their very profession has incriminated them. If they haven't done it, who has? There is much tearing of hair over the question of how they got hold of the keys to Purnima's almirah. Could she have left it open by mistake? Could she have mislaid the keys? She cannot remember.

Chhaya says, 'Just because someone has been in the family for ten years doesn't mean that they are honest or above temptation. Maybe it was part of the plan to stay so long, to lull us into a false sense of security and trust.' Everyone understands to whom she is referring. Malati is questioned; she and her room, which she shares with Kamala, are searched. Neither of them is very happy about it. Kamala, a placid, slow woman, goes about her business with furrowed brow, a sour frown on her face. Malati, more volatile, can be heard complaining loudly to an invisible adjudicator while going about her duties: 'Ten years I've worked here, ten years. In all that time I haven't helped myself to a single glass of water without asking. And now this. Because we are poor people, we are all thieves? We have no honour? No dignity? Being searched like this, as if we have stolen . . . chhee! Chhee!' Then, louder, as she wields that old, reliable filleting knife, the second-person singular, which is actually an unnamed third person: 'It's clear who is pulling all the strings. This is what happens when you do not have any happiness in your life; you try and stick your nose in other people's business to bring them down to your level of unhappiness. Book-learning is no substitute for honour. We may not be lettered but we're not in the habit of putting a stick in others' arses.' Every one of the Ghoshes pretends not to hear her, but the wrung, dyspeptic look on their faces betrays the strain of this performance. Sandhya, for instance, feels that familiar boiling of anxiety, for it is she who will have to do the smoothing and mending afterwards. Besides, over the last week, Supratik has been staying out a lot, leaving home in the morning and returning after everyone has gone to bed. She has a vertiginous sense of déjà vu, a premonition manufactured out of the memories of the recent past; she would not be able to survive his vanishing again.

An inventory is made of all the missing items. It is doubtful how stable Purnima's accounts are, but it turns out that not all her jewellery is gone; the safety-deposit locker at the bank had not been totally cleaned out; not *all* the ornaments had been brought home. Once again Purnima is torn between relief that at least some of her treasure still survives and a sense of bathos that this puncturing of the story of being robbed of *everything* brings about. The inventory keeps changing until the officer in charge of drawing up the FIR, the First Information Report, his patience frayed, barks, 'Listen, Mrs, you have either lost one choker or you haven't, there's no "maybe" or "I think" about it. If you can't be accurate about this, it becomes that much more difficult to find them.'

Purnima has to collect her thoughts, concentrate and collate her holdings with their different storage spaces, and then work out which ones she gave away to Baishakhi. Then she has to describe the missing jewellery, its weight and monetary value; the monumental project defeats her. As if this were not enough, word has reached her of some of the comments being made in unsympathetic quarters. 'If you look hard enough, you'll find that she has had the stuff removed herself so that replacements can be bought. A time-tested way of getting more, when the usual methods have run dry,' her mother-in-law had apparently said. And Chhaya, 'It's just a ploy to get her hands on some money. She's passed it on to the folks in her father's house and she's now crying "Thief! Thief!" to save face. And, of course, she needs to be the focus of attention again somehow, now that Boro-boüdi is back at the helm.' Purnima can hear the perfect punctuation of the petulant sigh as a full stop after the words.

The police eventually undertake a search of the house. No one asks what good this is going to do, a week after the burglary; the question does not seem to occur to anyone. Seven constables turn the house upside down. Some rooms are spared, Prafullanath and Charubala's, notably, out of deference to the elderly and invalid. Not every member of the family is accorded this special treatment: Supratik and Suranjan's room, for example, is ransacked, every article of clothing from the cupboard and on the clothes horse unfolded, the two beds turned upside down, the books and papers in the room painstakingly scrutinised. Both brothers are out during this act of sanctioned and official vandalism. As storey after storey is turned over, some more than others, following an opaque and arcane logic that the Ghoshes are unable to read, everyone at home seems resigned to this undignified upheaval, but not without murmur. That old saw, 'If a tiger touches you, you get off with eighteen sores, but if it's the police, you're lucky to escape with fifty-eight', is repeated more than once. Even Sandhya is heard to grumble, 'It's not they who are going to put everything back in its place after they're done. We'll have to do it ourselves.'

Bhola dares to ask a constable, 'What use is it to search the rooms of the family members? It's not we who have stolen our things. It's really inconvenient . . .'

The constable replies, 'We are doing our duty. If you do not like it, speak to Inspector Saha. We'll lose our jobs if we don't follow orders.'

Simultaneously with the searching, people are interrogated. The tone and style of the questioning are tailored to fit the subjects: threats and accusations for the servants, unctuous deference for the Ghoshes. In the middle of this bedlam, a ring is found and brought over to Purnima to establish if it is hers; a gold ring with a large ruby at its centre, the red gem surrounded by a circle of twelve tiny diamonds.

'Yes! Yes!' she cries, 'It's mine, mine. Oh god, I didn't know that this had been taken too. My aunt gave it to me when I got married. Where did you find it?'

'In Madan's room,' comes the answer.

Purnima looks as if someone has suddenly shifted the medium of conversation from Bengali to Finnish. First she stares with incomprehension and then, after a good few minutes, she shakes her head in disbelief. 'No, no, this is a mistake' – she can barely speak.

As if by an instant osmosis of thought, the news percolates down to every corner of the house almost as soon as the words are out of her mouth. The chorus of 'No, this must be a mistake' is shell-shocked, unanimous.

Charubala, supported by Sandhya, descends the staircase slowly, her voice raised in anger. 'Who has alleged this?' she asks. 'Who, I want to know? Madan is one of ours. He has been at my children's births, he has been with us longer than some of my children. I will not have these things said about him. Who has said this? Bring him to me.'

Charubala squares up to the constable who has discovered the ring and repeats her words in stronger terms.

'The ring was found in his room,' he says. 'There must be an explanation for it. We will have to take him in for questioning, those are our orders.'

'What questioning?' Charubala retorts. 'Question him in front of me. I don't believe you found the ring in his room.'

Adinath says, 'And you can't take him away without a warrant. Bring one first.'

For the Ghoshes some fundamental law of Nature has been bent out of shape; they go about as if they are underwater, their thoughts and movements and reactions viscous and slow. Before they have collected their wits about them sufficiently to talk to Madan first, Madan comes into the room where most of the family is sitting, congregated in incredulity. He too looks puzzled, like someone lifted up and set in a new world; the wordless staring between the two parties ticks on and on until Charubala's words, 'Madan, what is all this going on? Where have you been? Have you heard?', all in an elided stream of nearly one continuous word, break both the spell and something in Madan. He begins to answer; his mouth moves, but no words come out of it. Then the ordinary speech-movements of the mouth become somehow more elastic, the mouth contorts and, to everyone's spellbound horror, this man of sixty, this old man who has brought up Charubala's sons and daughter and her grandchildren on his lap and his back, presses his fists against his cheeks in an effort to stop his mouth twisting and begins to weep with the silent shameful-ness of one not used to crying.

Instead of congealing the horror to embarrassment, Madan's tears move all the women in the room – Charubala, Sandhya and Chhaya – to a similar point of release. Dabbing at her eyes with the end of her sari, Charubala finds it difficult to speak without giving in to the tide of emotion within her. It is Chhaya who breaks the silence.

'Madan-da, what is going on, can you tell us?' she asks.

Madan's account, in a brittle delivery, is stitched through with sobs: 'Ma, what can I say, what's written on the forehead will come to pass . . . Was this what was in store for me in my old age? I can't show my face anywhere any more . . . the shame, the shame! . . . The police say I've stolen Mejo-boüdi's jewellery . . . You tell me, is this possible? Do you remember the time, Ma, when I found your diamond earrings in the bathroom, I brought them over to you straight away . . . and that other time, when you couldn't find your gold ring, who was it that found it hiding behind the gas-cylinder in the kitchen? And now they say I'm a thief, a thief . . .' He is like a plaintive child in the middle of a long protest, having just bruised himself against the essential, indurate unfairness of the world.

'No, Madan-da, it is unbelievable that you are a thief,' Sandhya is moved to intervene and console, 'but we are at a loss to understand how it happened, we cannot believe our ears.'

Madan pauses, maybe to draw some succour from this, then continues, 'They came to search my room, so I said search away, I have nothing to hide. They begin to look, sweeping things aside, turning everything inside out, upside down, but what possessions do I have, nothing much, they knock everything down and . . . and suddenly one of them . . . the small, dark one with the pot-belly, he says he has found something, it was under the brass statuette of Krishna in my room . . . Boro-boüdi, I had forgotten that it was hollow inside, the thought never crossed my mind in all these years that something could be hidden there . . . god is punishing me, I know, he's punishing me for I don't know what, but for some sin, otherwise why would that ring be hidden under his statue? The policeman shows it to me and asks . . . asks what else am I hiding and where have I hidden everything, then . . . then he slaps me . . . he hits me and shows me the ring and asks do I recognise it . . . ? And I say that I don't, it's not mine, how can I afford such a thing and he says, Oh, I see that every joint in your body is aware of the price and value of such things; he taunts me . . . Ma, what can I say?'

He stops to draw breath and the reactions to his words all rush to crowd into the vacuum of that lull.

'Purnima's ring in your room? This . . . this cannot be believed,' Chhaya says, only now beginning to let the fact permeate her understanding.

'But how did it get there?' Priyo says rhetorically.

'Who put it there?' Adi asks.

'Did they find anything else? Not in your room,' Chhaya hastily adds, 'but elsewhere? Have all the rooms been searched?'

'My head is reeling,' Charubala says feebly. 'Purnima's ring in our Madan's room,' she keeps repeating, as if articulating the words will give the scarcely credible occurrence the solidity of fact.

'Where are the police?' Adi demands.

'Yes, why have they not notified us of anything?' Priyo says. He feels oddly polarised; on the one hand, it is his wife's jewellery that has been stolen; on the other, the sympathies in the room are all directed at the man accused of the theft. Should he be angry with Madan-da and break the solidarity that has developed in the room? But how can he will himself to side with the accusers of this man who is part of his earliest memories, a man who has never been anything but upright and honest, who has treated him only with affection and indulgence? But then why is he pricked by this sense of betrayal towards his wife when he acknowledges his natural feelings for this man? It is just as well that Purnima does not form part of the parliament to which Madan-da has brought his supplication.

When the constables enter the sitting room, all four of them, they are adamant about taking Madan away. 'For questioning,' they say.

'What are these questions that have to be asked in the police station?' Charubala asks. 'Why can't you question him in front of us now?'

'We have orders,' one of them answers.

'Who has given the orders?' Adi is on a roll now that he knows he is dealing with minions. 'Ask your inspector to come and talk to me.'

But the roar behind the words is half-hearted and the constables on duty, bred to detect, because their livelihoods depend upon that talent, the tiniest movements in the hairsprings that drive power, know instinctively that Adi is not the one calling the shots, not in this particular game; his roar is of the child wearing a lion mask on stage.

Madan prostrates himself at Charubala's feet and howls, 'Ma, I've eaten your salt, I would never do something like this, I'd much rather take poison than steal from you, Ma, Ma, please tell them they're making a mistake.' Then, in his fear and anguish, he turns erratic with his targets – he clings first to Adi's feet, then to Priyo's, crying, 'Bor'-da, Mej'-da, I'm telling the truth, I'm touching you and saying this, if it's a lie, god's going to bring down endless punishment on me, I didn't take Mejo-boüdi's ornaments, I swear I didn't. Please save me, save me!'

Sandhya turns to her husband and says with something approaching anger, 'Why can't you do anything? Why are you sitting there silently?'

No one moves. The despair has turned everyone to stone; Adi and Priyo seem unable to move their feet away from where Madan is writhing.

As he is hauled up and pushed out of the room he turns to the ineffectual gallery one last time. Something has changed. The tears on his face are not yet dry. His mouth is now twisted not with agony, but with contempt. He snarls, 'This is how it ends, I should have known. The milk and the mango-flesh mell, the mango-stone is always rejected.' He tries to laugh mockingly, but it comes out as a short, acid bark. There is a disparate crowd outside, people in the street,

outside the houses, faces at windows, figures standing on their verandahs, all feasting on the unexpected treat of a man's supreme public
humiliation; fodder for conversation through the shrivelled days of
dearth.

An ashy gloom descends on the house; its grasp is tight, but the effect
it has on the Ghoshes is one of slackness. Even the recurring and
compulsive discussions are underlined by tiredness, resignation. The
questions go around in a barren loop: how could the burglar have got
hold of the keys to Purnima's safe? It must be an inside job or else
how could he have known which was the right key? How could the
heist have happened right under their noses? Where was Purnima
when the theft was in progress? How come no one had noticed
anything? It had to be an inside job, in that case. But who on the
inside? They chase their tails, but like clockwork toys whose wind-up
energies are coming to the end.

Charubala has to explain the events to her husband, now slow-witted
with illness, several times before he can comprehend the narrative.
He says, 'The police are right. Never trusted that man, especially after
he put his son up to all that union mischief. The enemy inside is far
more powerful than the enemy outside.'

Charubala retorts sharply, 'If all fathers had to suffer for the deeds
of their sons, you wouldn't have been here to make these tart
comments.'

Supratik is back home well before dinnertime. Sandhya hovers around
in his room, trying to help him put his things back in their place while
simultaneously keeping up a running commentary of the day's events,
which her son has missed. Supratik goes through the usual motions
of a periodic 'Hmmm' or 'I see' or 'Really?'

Sandhya asks, 'You are the clever one, can't you shed some light
on this?'

He answers, 'If Madan-da has really taken Boro-kaki's jewellery, all
power to him. They are poor people, the stuff is going to be useful
to them. Your lot have more than enough already.'

It is not until later, not until she is in bed, picking over the day,
knotting and reknotting all that has happened, unable to sleep, that

his outrageous words return to her and she notices, for the first time, that he said 'your lot' and not the usual, expected 'we'.

Inspector Saha comes along the following day and attempts to convince the Ghoshes of Madan's culpability. 'Who else knows the ins and outs of the family, the smallest details?' he asks. 'Who is in charge of what set of keys, which key opens which safe and which almirah, who comes in, who goes out of the house and when, the routine of every single one of you – who knows all this? We have ruled out the others. Gagan, your driver, doesn't stay in the house overnight. Besides, he hardly ever comes inside. Malati and Kamala – well, they would have needed a man's help to do it. The day-maids who do the cleaning and the laundry, likewise. Who does that leave?'

Sandhya says, 'But . . . but he is like one of us. He has been with us since my husband was one year old.'

'Look, I'll hope you'll pardon me for saying this, but this is how these people operate. We've been seeing cases like this crop up all over the city. They play a very long game, get your trust completely, then one day' – he claps his hands – 'all into thin air, both servant and jewellery. For what is he doing it? What is the motive?' the Inspector continues, saying the word in English, *moteebh*, and repeating it with pride – 'What is the *moteebh*? You know all about the problems with his son, Dulal; they happened at your factory, union leader and all that. Did you know that Dulal set up an electrical-goods store in Jadavpur after he lost his job at Bali? The shop's not doing well, he's drowning in debt. Where do you think the money to set up in retail business came from? There was no way out for Madan but to get his hands on some money quickly. Hence the burglary.'

Sadhya and Chhaya exclaim in concert, 'What? What are you saying? We didn't know all this . . .'

Neither did Adi, but he is not going to let his surprise show. He is the one who asked SP Dhar and Inspector Saha for a favour – to 'talk' to their colleagues in Bali and enlist their 'help' when union troubles were beginning to get out of hand – and he cannot give the Inspector the pleasure of showing his amazement, if the SP and the Inspector have made Dulal's subsequent business a matter for their interest. The Ghoshes have not forgotten that the police refused to come when Prafullanath went to confront Dulal, but they can do little in retaliation. In the coalition government the issue of labour unrest had been moved, in a shrewd manoeuvre by the CPI(M), from a law-and-order issue under the Home Ministry, a Congress portfolio, to the domain of the Labour Minister, a CPI(M) man. Or so SP Dhar had said then, his voice dripping with well-honed regret and affront at such political football. It strikes Adi again that it had suited the police very well to say that their hands were tied. But why then this ongoing show of concern, of consultation and democracy, with the SP coming to inform him about Supratik, and now the Inspector being all solicitous and chummy and a bit too forthcoming with explanations over Madan-da's arrest? Atonement for that error with his father? Or, more likely, that they do not want to burn the bridge, however unimportant and small, with the Ghoshes?

He recoils inwardly at the man's professional mixture of authority and ingratiation, but brings himself to look at the Inspector's face to be reminded of those shifty eyes again; yes, they are the same if tinier than last time because the Inspector's face is puffing up as if in geometric progression with age. Inspector Saha turns to Adi, to appeal to a man about matters of the world that men understand better, and catches Adi looking at him then averting his eyes instantly as their gazes meet, but not before Adi has noticed the Inspector's recognition turn into something that Adi cannot quite put his finger on, something truculent, something that resides more in the territory of power than obsequiousness.

Inspector Saha continues as if nothing has passed between them: 'And, of course, we have cast-iron proof: we found the ring in his room. How else would you account for that?' he asks triumphantly.

Purnima echoes him, 'Yes, how else? How else?'

Chhaya cannot let this pass, so she begins, 'Oh, I'm sure there can be many explanations for that—' but stops abruptly because she does not have a single one handy and it would not do to be asked and have nothing to show; such loss of face in front of Purnima.

Sandhya, suddenly mindful of the fact that the Inspector has not been offered a cup of tea, leaves the room to direct the staff in the kitchen; there is no Madan-da to look after these things any more.

Inspector Saha says, 'The big question facing us now is how to recover the items? Has he sold them? Is he using someone as a fence? We're questioning him to see what we can unearth.'

Priyo flinches; he has some understanding of the exact nature of this 'questioning' business. It would have been preferable to follow the kind of natural unspooling of these things that happened in more common, lower-middle-class neighbourhoods – a hue and cry raised after the accused, a ragtag bunch of people gathered to beat him in public into confessing – rather than have the police question him in jail. At least with the method where people took the law into their own hands, they, the Ghoshes, could have been witness to the rough justice of the crowd, they could have *seen* the worst, they could even have intervened. They would not have had to speculate about what was being done to the unfortunate old man in the foetid privacy of prison.

Inspector Saha says, 'You understand we're living through difficult times. President's Rule again, twice in as many years. Governments rising and falling as if they're doll's houses, terrible law-and-order situation, getting worse by the day. Heh-heh-heh-heh, who knows what lies in store tomorrow?'

There, that fawning laugh again, Adi thinks, as he suppresses a shudder; the SP had clearly trained his junior well. Hearing it is like having a bucket of cold snot thrown on you; you want to rub yourself with a loofah afterwards for hours. As if in rhythmic response, the fan flutters the pages of the Charu Paper calendar on the wall; it sounds like mockery.

Sandhya comes in with a tray of tea and snacks – only Marie biscuits; no Madan to direct the rustling-up of delights – and sets it down on the coffee table. She says, 'Ma wants to come downstairs.'

Adi says, 'Let me go up and help her' and leaves the room with his wife. *Who knows what lies in store tomorrow?* Could the Inspector have been trying to send some kind of message to him? Why the prefix of that insinuating laugh otherwise? Could SP Dhar have sent Saha for that very purpose?

Inspector Saha is still distributing meaningless reassurances like cheap boiled sweets at a children's party when Charubala comes into the room, supported on one side by Adi and on the other by Sandhya. The Inspector does not stand up.

All through the previous night Charubala has lain awake thinking of the configuration of words she would use to tell the policeman several things: how wrong he was, how one could trust Madan blindly, how they were not going to tolerate this terrible error of their Madan being in jail . . . She had driven herself to a keen point of agitation, even anger, but seeing the Inspector sitting right in front of her, slurping tea noisily from his saucer, dunking biscuits into his cup, that anger somehow dissipates. He is, after all, a policeman of senior rank, not a constable, but a powerful, well-connected person, and Charubala has never been able to shake off an early fear of both policemen and Englishmen.

All the impassioned speeches in her head fade to a meek, plaintive, 'Inspector-babu, Madan is innocent. You must kindly release him. I give you my word that he hasn't done this.'

Inspector Saha pulls off the difficult trick of looking concerned, condescending and respectful all at once; a miracle, Adi notes, given that a complex of emotions would find it tricky to play quickly through all that flesh and adipose tissue. Then he is gone, with an ominous, 'Not everything is in our hands, as you think. Some things are in yours too. Also' – here he pauses at the threshold of the living-room door, turns round, flashes his yellow teeth in a way that makes Adi wonder how a smile so greasy can have such a sharp, dangerous edge – 'we don't usually come to people's homes to update them on the state of an investigation, they usually come to the police station. I came as a personal favour to Adi-babu. After all, Boro-saheb Dhar, Adi-babu and I go back so many years, we have so much history between us, heh-heh-heh-heh.'

Much like the iron grilles on the Ghoshes' front balconies, poxy with rust under the recent new coating of paint, the steady conviction that Madan is innocent begins to corrode under the acid that the Inspector's words have sprinkled on it during his visit. Purnima, loyal primarily to her material possessions, is the first to be swayed. 'The Inspector is right,' she says to Priyo. 'Who else could have taken it? Madan-da knows the ins and outs of everything, the routines of everyone. Only he could have burgled us with such ease and with no one being any the wiser.'

Priyo too teeters: 'I'm finding it difficult to get my head around it.'

'He's been nursing a grudge. It's that business with his son. I think he has been biding his time.'

'A long time to bide. But I cannot think of anyone better placed than Madan to burgle us, you're right. Still, I find it difficult to believe. He has been with us since before I was born . . .' Priyo's words tail off. The worlds of reasonable doubt and dogged faith have never seemed more incommensurable.

Bhola consoles his mother with equally empty words. 'Ma, what good is all this crying going to do? The Inspector can't be lying. If he says Madan-da has stolen, then he must have reason to say so. We couldn't counter any of his arguments.'

Charubala is heartsick. Memories play like clips from old films inside her head and she relays them weepily. 'How can it be?' she cries. 'Do you know, when he and Adi had very high fever at the same time – Adi must have been around six or seven then – I put them on the same bed and stayed up all night, putting cold water compresses on their foreheads.' What she wants to ask the world is whether that act did not fasten him to her and hers for life, but she cannot find the words, or perhaps the courage, actually to say this, because to embody it in words would be an acknowledgement of a sort of fissure between them that had been eternally present. She dwells on details that sieve through her soul, leaving behind both purified object and unwanted residue: Madan bringing her children gifts every time he came back after his annual visit to his home in the village in Orissa; Madan lying to protect the children from her anger when she knew they had been up to mischief; she and Adi making fun of Madan, affectionately, by asking him to sing Oriya songs, then cracking up at the outlandish language; Madan tripping over his reading from *Shahaj Path* in the early stages of his education at her hands . . . How could those instances, so funny or ridiculous or endearing at the time, have been sifted to become only repositories of pain now?

Sandhya is no better than her mother-in-law. Things are at sixes and sevens without Madan-da's cohering presence. She finds herself lacking the energy to be the girder around the house; it has had to do without her for two and a half years, it will no doubt survive the two days of looseness brought about by Madan-da's arrest. Yet this very pragmatism is the result of inertia. So many details were taken care of by Madan-da that in less than twenty-four hours of his absence cracks are proliferating everywhere. Did she then do nothing worthwhile? Or was Madan-da the real energy behind the scenes and she only a titular supervisory figurehead? Thoughts along these lines are interrupted by the appearance in her room of Chhaya and Jayanti. Without saying anything, they need, it is clear to Sandhya, some principle of reassurance from her in the middle of this unravelling.

Even Chhaya has no appetite for this particular spectacle of someone else's unhappiness. She says, 'Who would have thought . . .' and stops. Previously those very words would have been the prelude to a ripe thrill of a conversation saturated with cheerful malevolence; now the words are only doleful.

Jayanti echoes her sentiment – 'Yes, truly . . .' – and brings the aanchol of her sari to cover her mouth.

Sandhya, attempting to emulate the rationality of her elder son, says, 'Wait, wait. Nothing has been proven against him yet. They still haven't found the missing jewellery.'

Jayanti says, 'But they took him to jail. Would they have done it if he was innocent? Then there was all that business with his son . . . We didn't know a word of that, did we?'

Sandhya cannot answer this; neither can Chhaya. There is a long pause marked by the same looseness, the same unbinding that has begun to rear its head everywhere. It manifests itself as a lack of energy in everything; this twilight gathering, with the darkness falling outside, is no exception. It is a testament to that dispersion of focus that no one gets up to turn on the lights, despite everyone's firmly held belief, particularly Sandhya's, that dark interiors at dusk drive out the goddess of wealth. Now if Madan-da had been around . . .

Madan has become, overnight, a ghost in the midst of the living.

CHAPTER SEVENTEEN

1970

Only three months since the news about Sona has broken and already a different order is beginning to set in. Like the camouflaging of an insect, one saw the before and, with great effort, the after, but never the process in between. So how and when exactly, and in what degrees, the new dispensation arrived no one could tell, only the fact of its dawning and its presence afterwards. Purba, in turmoil, notices, but does not give it much thought. As for Sona, it is impossible to tell if he perceives at all in the first place, or if he senses and understands but will never bring himself to comment on it, or if he is simply above it all in the world of numbers.

But nothing escapes the fine sensor of Kalyani's attunement to the unstable connections, forever careening, sometimes this way, sometimes that, between people. It is she who notices the increasing frequency with which food is sent down to them from upstairs, and although Madan-da's recent departure has led to a lot of things beginning to fall to rust, this is one area that has, shockingly, improved. Then she notices that it is not stale food, on the cusp of turning, that is being sent to them, but freshly cooked marvels – any number of vegetable dishes, cabbage or bottle gourd with small shrimps, egg curries, yellow split peas with raisins and fried coconut, rui fish in yoghurt sauce, mince with peas and potatoes, mutton curries . . . This is what heaven is in her imagination – delights being sent down from up above. They even take care, she regards, to send her mother's vegetarian food separately from Kalyani's and Sona's non-vegetarian dishes to avoid contamination, but she does not move one step further from observing to pondering on the reasons for this sudden newly-found consideration for her mother.

Purnima comes one evening, bearing a box of classy sandesh from Ganguram.

'Baishakhi's had a son,' Purnima says, giving the paper box to Purba, 'so I'm distributing sweets.'

Purba smiles and receives it with her usual, 'Oh, really, there was no need . . .'

'I'm giving it to everyone in the family, so why should you be excluded? You are family too,' Purnima says. 'Besides, *you* have your own reasons for eating sweets now, Purba, don't you? All this wonderful news about our Sona . . . who would have thought that a boy from this house was a hidden genius? Really, unthinkable for stupid people like us! Anyway, some goddess is sure to be smiling on you now, things are beginning to look up, good news is beginning to come in . . .' The tone for noting good tidings modulates to faint regret by the time she reaches the end of the sentence.

Purba only smiles wanly; it is left to Purnima to fill the silence.

'Kalyani, why don't you serve your mother some sandesh and help yourself to some, too?'

Kalyani runs out to fetch a small plate, picks out three pieces of sandesh and offers it to her mejo-jyethi first.

Purnima cries out, half in jest, 'Oh god, not three! If you give three, you make an enemy of the person you're serving. Hasn't your mother taught you this? Here, why don't you take one? Go on.'

Kalyani catches her mother's expression of peeved strickenness and demurs. Purnima blithely continues, 'You have to learn these things now, now that you're growing older. What will your in-laws say about us, if you make these mistakes? What kind of a home has this girl come from, they'll say.' She laughs at her own witticisms as she polishes off all three pieces of sandesh on her plate.

Bholanath comes downstairs one evening, all booming camaraderie and jollity. 'Here now, where is the boy? Where is the genius who is going to brighten the name of the Ghoshes? Here you are, sitting in a dark corner, head buried in a thick book. No doubt thinking grand mathematical thoughts. But your stupid uncle will say this to you: you've got to look after your eyes. If you can't see the numbers, what proofs can you do? Ha-ha-ha-ha-ha! That was funny. What book is it?

Oh, let's see – *An Introduction to the Theory of Numbers*. Ufff, too much for my little brain, too much. And such strange symbols in it, can't understand a thing. And such tiny print, Sona-baba, you'll really ruin your eyes. Just the other day I was telling someone, "This nephew of mine, all of fourteen years old, he's some kind of prodigy, an American university is trying to snatch him away from us, like one would something precious, such as a gold chain; this nephew, we've always known that he was going to do something very big one day, something that would make us all so proud, and this boy is being offered a full scholarship to go to university before he has finished school. A double-double promotion." Can you beat that? A double-double promotion, ha-ha-ha-ha. See if your silly uncle has been right with his arithmetic, you are the maths brains, see if he has calculated correctly. One double promotion – Class Ten; second double promotion to Class Twelve; so you skip two years, Nine and Eleven. What? Am I right? See, your mathematical gift must owe something to the blood that flows through your veins. It's the Ghoshes' blood, after all.'

Arunima fails her final exams in arithmetic and has to repeat Class Six. Jayanti is aghast.

'I had no inkling that you were struggling in these subjects,' she chides, 'otherwise I would have asked your father to find a private tutor for you. Why didn't you tell us earlier? Why? Oh, the shame, the shame!'

Word gets out that Arunima has to repeat a year. It is Chhaya, as always, with her infallible talent for neatly isolating the afflicted nerve and aiming for it, who gives voice to the greater shame: 'How strange that our recently discovered mathematics genius should be helping out other boys in the neighbourhood and not his own cousin. If he can go to Mala-di's house and give mathematics tuition to her son, can he not do it out of charity for our Arunima? They are cousins, after all.' Then she twists the knife – 'Perhaps Mala-di gives him a little something? Jayanti, maybe you could ask Bhola to give Sona some money?'

Chhaya announces this, like all her calculatedly murderous comments, loudly and in public, as if addressing the air, for maximum dispersal. Even Supratik, who has long cultivated a stony indifference to dirty domestic politics, is jolted out of its armour enough to say directly to her, 'Pishi, you'll find that it was I who arranged, through Ma, to have Sona give maths lessons to Mala-mashi's son in exchange for Sona receiving English lessons from their private tutor. Chhoto-kaki cannot afford private lessons for Sona, as you well know, and it would have been a great shame if that bright boy fell behind because of the one handicap of knowing no English.' Behind his back he twists his right thumb as far as it will go without snapping, so that he can channel his anger into that small act of violence, leaving his voice and tone and delivery imperturbably steady.

'Oh, you were behind it,' Chhaya says, sounding disappointed, but she is not to be outdone. There is a final flick of the scorpion's tail: 'How charitable of you to have done that! All these inexplicable generosities – these are what make men noble. I'm slow on the uptake, so I'm still left behind, trying to figure out the reasons behind these selfless acts.'

Supratik's insides turn to ice with fear.

A conversation between mother and son late at night; she has waited up for him and is fussing about while he eats his dinner, kept warm, around midnight. He has given up asking her not to do it; it's futile; not a single note of the endless variations he has constructed of that wish of his has ever entered through her ears, let alone reached her brain. He knows that it is the only time she can seize to talk to him, to find out what he is thinking, what is going on in his life, and he grudges her that, although it is beginning to settle into a kind of edgy toleration. The sense of déjà vu in this repeated business of being confronted by her late at night over food has become, like a familiar and predictable scratch on a record over which the stylus keeps slipping, one of the more dependable things in his life at home.

'Your father was saying . . .' she begins with trepidation.

When he does not respond, she continues hesitantly, '. . . he was saying that . . . that you have turned your face away from the . . . the family business, and you are . . . you are . . . you are the eldest son of the family.'

Silence flowed between the chewing sounds, the occasional clink of a small bowl being set down, the sound of fingers on china plate.

'Your aunt was saying,' she says with the quick volubility of the nervous, 'that you told her . . . that you arranged for Sona's tuition at Mala-di's. I didn't tell anyone anything, mind you. You made me promise at the time that I wouldn't breathe a word about it to anyone and I didn't.'

At last Supratik breaks his silence: 'Yes, I had to divulge the whole business. You know Pishi, there's toxin in the very breath that comes out of her. She was up to her usual stirring. If Chhoto-kaki had heard what she was insinuating, she would take out her humiliation on poor Sona.' Pause. 'Also . . . also . . . I didn't want Chhoto-kaki to find out I was behind it, but it's too late to undo that now.'

'Yes, you know what your pishi's like . . .' Sandhya says resignedly.

Supratik is suddenly touched by the bigness of his mother's soul; it would have had been so easy, so convenient, for her to fall in with the general viciousness of the Bengali middle-class family, its compulsive drive towards contraction of the spirit, yet she had never strayed into it.

In an effort to be kind to her he says gently, 'Besides . . .' He halts, not sure whether he should be saying this at all.

'Besides what?' she asks.

Oh, what the hell . . . 'Besides,' he says, 'I feel bad when I see them, Chhoto-kaki and her two children. They're as much part of our family as Boro-kaka and Baishakhi and Mejo-kaki and Arunima, yet they live in a kind of exile, confined to one small room, existing on the charity of Baba and my uncles, the handouts you secretly engineered with Madan-da' – he flinches inwardly when uttering the cook's name and watches its refraction manifested in his mother's face – 'and the other servants to send down occasionally. What kind of a life must it be for them, have you ever thought?' His voice hardens halfway through. Reciting the catalogue of their miseries has swiftly scorched with a June sun the sympathy for his mother that had been beginning to germinate.

Sandhya says, 'I used to think about their tragedy a lot. I talked to your father in the beginning about it. But . . . but I don't know how how . . .'

'How this apathy became the order of things,' he completes her sentence. 'Is that it?'

'No, not that, not exactly. Things were somehow . . . difficult to change.'

'Difficult to change the darkness of superstitious rubbish willed on all of you by an old, tyrannical woman?' he hisses.

'Chhee, chhee!' is her involuntary response. 'She is your grand-mother, how can you say such things about her?'

'Which is worse in your opinion: obeying without question the blind superstitions of a hardly literate old woman or condemning three members of your family to shame and penury for ever? Which one?' his voice rises.

Her voice trembles as she says softly, 'I understand what you're saying. But do you understand my position? How could I, as daughter-in-law, have challenged her rules? When you marry, you'll understand that, you're still too young.'

'But you took over from her,' he argues back. 'In the beginning, perhaps, yes, she was the head, and she couldn't be challenged and all that, but five, seven, ten years down the line?'

'You won't understand it,' she repeats helplessly. 'It's not how things work. I tried. At least with those two children, Sona and Kalyani, I've tried to show them the same affection in which I hold all my nephews and nieces.' Pause. 'And my own sons.' Her voice catches.

Here we go again, the old waterworks. His fury is still coursing through him. He says, 'Yes, but, at the end of the day you came down on the side of the one who was powerful, against the powerless side. Everyone can anoint an already anointed head, don't you know?'

Sandhya cannot check her tears any longer, but these are tears of frustration. 'Stop giving me lessons!' she cries out, restored for a few moments to the time when this son of hers was a child and she could rule and discipline him as a mother should her son. 'Enough of this book-learned wisdom. If you are so full of kindness and sympathy for the powerless, why don't you look closer to home, instead of running away and playing at dangerous politics with farmers and beggars?'

Her tears are unimpeded now. It transports Supratik from anger to shame in the space of no time and lands him with a bump: his mother is crying yet again and he has been responsible for it. And all she had wanted was a few minutes of his company, perhaps a show of some fondness; not much, just a little bit.

'Someone who can't look after his own cannot look after others,' she announces indignantly. 'Did you know that your brother is going to the dogs? He returns very late at night, sleeps until noon, hardly eats anything. He's losing weight. He looks like a beggar on the streets. Do you notice? Do you care? Did you know that your father discovered him, drunk out of his senses, passed out on the bathroom floor?'

No, he didn't know; he is surprised, but not at the facts, only at his overlooking of them.

'When did this happen?' he asks.

'What good is knowing that going to do?' Sandhya cries, seizing the sliver of opportunity that has opened up in taking the high moral ground. 'What do you care? Did you bother keeping us informed about your whereabouts, whether you were dead or alive? If you can do that to your mother, you're clearly made of stone, and no amount of information about these little things, like a younger brother losing his way or falling into bad company, is going to make you care.' She knows she is squandering the capital that has come into her possession for such a tantalisingly small duration, but the accumulated force of culture is too mighty to resist.

Supratik wonders at the coincidence of three people at home, Purba, Madan-da, and his mother now, voicing identical thoughts to him in the course of as many months. Why did they all think alike? Typical bourgeois brainwashed homogeneity? How else could this unvarying calculus about the worth of one's own kind measured against the lives of others have come about? Could he allow himself a few moments of entertainment considering the possible truth-value of that insane thinking? And here is his mother, parroting the same lies in the same, worn-to-dust mode of lachrymose blackmail, trying to rouse him to shoulder some kind of adult responsibility. What prevents her from asking directly, 'Could you talk some sense into your brother? We think he's straying' or some such, rather than resorting unfailingly to these circuitous dramas, all womanly wiles and manipulative strategies?

He gets up to wash his hands, lashed with self-loathing.

Supratik, sitting on his bed, notes that Suranjan does not arise before noon and as soon as he wakes up he goes to the toilet for what seems a long time, so he lies in wait and catches his brother as soon as he comes out of the bathroom. The signs are all there, so how has he failed to read them? It's not as if they are the uncials of a foreign script he is unable to understand and, therefore, is excused from deciphering any meaning out of them; the acrid blast out of the bathroom after Suranjan emerged from it is transparently readable. Could it have been a willed ignorance on his part? Or – and perhaps their mother was right in this all along – his indifference to those to whom he is attached by ties of blood? Or even his deep distraction, for Supratik has his sights set on the shiny moon of a new, ideal order, not on the soiled coin, which can be scrubbed to a gleam, lying at his feet?

He makes a stab at some sort of a beginning: 'Don't you have classes to go to?'

Suranjan does not reply, as if he has not heard, so Supratik repeats it.

'Oh . . . yes . . . classes,' Suranjan says so vaguely that all this talk of attending classes may be as alien and distant to him as manned interstellar travel. 'Classes,' he says again. 'Hmmm. Well, there aren't any until exams, it's revision time.'

This is such a ridiculous lie – college exams in early September? – that Supratik feels pity for his brother.

'Oh, I see,' he says. 'So why aren't you revising then?'

'I shall, I've only just woken up.'

'Why are you waking up so late nowadays? Is everything all right? Are you ill?' Supratik looks elsewhere while asking the questions; he cannot bear to look at those signs facing him, cannot bear to be right about their meanings. The diminishing weight, the sallow complexion, those coal-dark rings under the eyes which are devoid of any spark, that waiting lassitude . . . No, unthinkable.

'No, no, why should I be ill? Do I look ill?'

'Yes, as a matter of fact, you do. You look as if you're doing some kind of drugs.'

Suranjan freezes, then tries to give a cool, contemptuous, dismissive laugh, but he can get only a quarter of the way there, after which it comes unstuck and sounds like a written-down onomatopoeia of laughter, dead letters on a page.

'What nonsense!' he says hoarsely.

'You think I'm so naïve that I won't be able to identify the smell of charas drifting out of the bathroom? The room stinks.'

'I smoked a cigarette in there.' He tries another laugh, this time to make light of things. 'Actually, without a cigarette in the morning nowadays – you know . . . motions and cigarettes, really, impossible without them.'

Something about the lie piques Supratik. 'I see. The burnt foils from cigarette packets lying around are also to aid you with your bowel movements? And the clutter of burnt matchsticks around the burnt foil? The puncture marks on your left arm? You think all of us move about with our faces to the grass? You can fool Ma and Baba, they have no idea of the poisons of our generation, but you thought you could fool me too?'

The waxy-yellow pallor of Suranjan's face glistens with sweat. Supratik does not miss the shiver; so his brother *is* afraid. Afraid of what? Of being discovered doing drugs? Or afraid that Supratik will tell on him and have him punished? He cannot distinguish the two questions in his mind. All his life he has been blessed, or maybe cursed, with the ability to separate himself out of his own self, move away from any scene in which he is involved and watch himself acting out the moves, speaking the lines; the doubleness has conferred a rare lucidity on things. But the duality fails to kick in, where his brother is concerned.

An old discomfort resurfaces: he is bothered again by how few memories he has of Suranjan, or of he and Suranjan together, growing up, sharing the same room for nearly all of their lives. Did they read the same books and talk about them? Did they have different approaches to eating their food, one of them saving the best bits for the end, and the other gobbling them up right at the beginning? Had they ever fought over trivial things – who would go first with a detective novel, who had received more on a plate, whom Ma was perceived to be favouring, who bore the brunt of the blame when Ma disciplined them for some mischief? He cannot remember anything. How could his brother be just a hole in his life? How could he account for this absence? Purba has recently told him that her first sighting of him was on her wedding day: a little boy, dressed in silk dhoti and panjabi, with sandalwood buttons, prancing up and down the stairs, beside himself with joy. He had felt a mild sense of embarrassment, shame even, at this memory of hers. Now, if he asks himself whether Suranjan was dressed identically, whether he too was jumping around the place, he cannot come up with an answer; there is only a dark lacuna there. Would Purba have noticed and remembered? He would have to ask her.

Suranjan has transferred his fear to aggression. He snaps, 'You are hardly the one to give lectures on how to behave.'

'What do you mean?'

'Big words about the *poisons of our generation* don't suit you. Your terrorism, your poison, is not without its side-effects.'

'Don't you dare talk about things you don't understand!'

'How dare *you* talk about pulling the wool over others' eyes? What have *you* been doing all these years? Playing at revolutionaries, terrorism, killings, bombings – you didn't do it exactly openly, did you, with the full knowledge of Baba and Ma?'

Supratik is amazed, not so much at the extent of his brother's half-knowledge as at the intransigence of his speaking out with such vehemence. When did this kitten grow up into a snarling, clawing cat?

Suranjan takes advantage of the resultant pause to press ahead. 'Keep your big talk to yourself, I don't need any lessons from *you*,' he says, his voice rising. 'You've forgotten that I've grown up. Or not quite "forgotten" – when did you ever *know*? You haven't been around much to know.'

Supratik can only say lamely, 'What are you saying?'

'Only this: keep your hypocritical talk for your Mao-reading comrades.'

'Hypocritical?' His hand is itching to slap the cur. 'Your druggie friends have taught you some big words, it must be said.'

'At least my druggie friends don't go around killing innocent people.'

'Killing? Innocent people? Do you have any idea of how little you know about such things?' Supratik says, trying to keep his voice level and low. All he wants to do is to repeat those words to the rhythm of banging Suranjan's head against the wall.

'Much more than you give me – or, for that matter, anyone – credit for.'

A sharp stab of anxiety goes through him: does Suranjan know about the stolen jewellery?

'The word "revolution" should not pass the lips of an idle, parasitic, basket-case like you,' Supratik begins, but is cut short by Suranjan, who becomes unrecognisable in the escalation of his rage.

'Shut up!' he shouts, 'enough of your moralising. Enough! What you do is revolution, of course, what others do is idleness and wastage. This is the problem with fuckers like you – you are unable to understand anyone else unless they fit into the standard-issue mould you have made for them. Chairman Mao! My cock!'

Supratik leaps off his bed and slaps Suranjan with all the force he can bring to his assaulting right palm, once, twice, three times across his face. While delivering the blows he tenses his body, fully expecting to be hit by a retaliatory punch, but what happens wrong-foots him again: Suranjan folds over, almost daintily, like a decorative collapsible chair, and falls to the floor. Supratik watches, unable to move a finger, as Suranjan, lying down, begins to cry, slowly at first, snifflingly, then with huge sobs racking his body. Supratik loses all track of time, all ability to react, until god knows after how long their mother enters the room and panics. 'What's happened? What's happened? Why are you lying on the floor? Have you been fighting? Aren't you too old for this kind of thing?' Then she turns to Supratik and berates him, 'Don't you have any shame, hitting your younger brother like this? Do you think you're both still little children?'

No, he does not, but he feels as emasculated and powerless as one.

Suranjan goes out some time in the afternoon and does not return home that night. Supratik, his insides tense as a taut bow, lies awake, debating whether to tell their father the truth about his younger son. Supratik does not know much about heroin addiction – it has not been around for long – but all that he has heard has come wrapped in a fog of hush-voiced fear. *You can never recover from it, the addiction is so strong it's irreversible. One hit hooks you for ever, and then your life as you and others around you know it is over. It sucks you out from the inside and finishes you.* Not for the first time he thinks of how the Bengali word for 'suck' and 'exploitation' is the same. How typical of an exemplary specimen of the petite bourgeoisie to get hooked on a destructive drug that is an import from the decadent, evil, capitalist West. The predictability and the perfection of the fit would have elicited a contemptuous chuckle from him at any other time, but this illustration is too close to home. He finds this business of the micro-depredations of capitalism, one where the effects are felt on the smallest units, such as the family, and not just perceived as giant historical phases and on the masses, an interesting new direction in which he can take his dialectical thinking. Or is that only an illusion? Could that too be subsumed under the paradigms that had already been set down in the key texts? How would Charu Mazumdar dissect this fashion of killer recreational drugs amongst the middle classes and link it to historical process?

But what is he going to tell his parents? *Would* he tell them? *Just a skirmish with words*, he had said tersely to his mother when she had demanded an explanation. Those few words had damned him into an impromptu collusion with his brother; they both knew, after he had spoken them, that he was not going to tell on Suranjan. It had not led to a truce, but it had bound them in an unspoken conspiracy, an adult variation of a children-united-against-parents kind of scenario. Again he returns to that sticking point about memory: did they have such affiliations and groupings when they were children, brothers protecting each other from the prying, censorious regard of parents instead of snitching on each other? Was this the usual situation in other families where there were two brothers? Did his father and his uncles close ranks against his grandparents?

How clean he thought he had kept his life, unblotted by the inev-itable stain of private life; and now that too is traduced. He wants to eat his pillow whole, shred the bedsheet into thin ribbons. How did this come to pass, especially when he had been so assiduous in standing away from it all? First Purba, now Bhai. Then there is the ticking time-bomb of the jewellery theft. Why does he feel both snared and duped? He cannot put a name to what or who has tricked him; maybe, when he was still trapped in the old, pre-dialectical ways of thinking and knowledge, he would have called it heart or emotions, but he has seen through that bit of politics a long time ago, so there is nothing to fall back against. There is only a void and himself.

Over the next three nights, Supratik watches his brother travelling into the land where no man can be his companion, where he is alone with himself, or a version of himself, in a solitude magnified and distorted so extremely that that reality seems as impregnable as death itself. In that aloneness, Suranjan, his eyes closed, his chin nearly meeting his chest, cannot even bring himself to stretch out on his bed; he is arrested in the position he is in when he begins his journey, the unmistakable debris of burnt foil, thick straw made from rolled-up card, black, curled stubs of spent matches littered around him. Every day Supratik has enjoined himself, *I must catch him at it this evening*; every day he has missed it and failed, partly because Suranjan has mastered the self-protective stealth of the addict, but also because Supratik himself has been away – and, when not away, distracted – working out the great plans regarding an imminent action in the city.

Seeing Suranjan nearly unconscious in that awkward position, leaning at an impossible tilt and yet not falling, not jerking awake when his head has reached an excruciating angle with his neck and shoulder, fills Supratik with such a fury of protectiveness that he has to stop staring at his brother and force himself again to go over all the steps, written out in his head, as it were, in numbered points, leading to the big event planned for Monday night. It has the effect of counting backwards to induce sleep; it does not achieve the desired result, but it calms him somewhat so that when he looks at his narcotised brother he feels something slightly different, the same realisation one has of the limits of human understanding when faced with someone asleep, because one can never enter that insuperably private world of the sleeper, regardless of how inter-twined the lives are of observer and observed. The melancholy is sharp and bitter; it makes him despair about being able to do anything about the hell Suranjan has got himself into. They have not managed to come out of the castles of their dented egos and wave a white flag since they fell out three days ago; they have stopped speaking, even looking at each other. Except for now, when Supratik allows himself to gaze unrestricted at Suranjan because he knows no one is looking. He cannot shoulder this burden himself, but he already knows what Purba, the only person he can think of confiding in, will say. He can hear her voice in his head this instant – 'It's not a good thing, this falling-out between brothers, and then this business of not being on speaking terms. He's your younger brother, it is your duty to love, protect and forgive him, whatever he does.'

He makes up his mind. He will not tell Ma and Baba the truth, not now; he will act on it himself first. His initial port of call will be Suranjan's friends, to attempt to establish the exact nature of his addiction. From there the subsequent course of action will follow. He will start the ball rolling the very day after the big event. He reads Chapter 23, 'Street Tactics', of Carlos Marighella's mint-new mini-manual again:

> When the police troops come wearing helmets to protect them against flying objects, we have to divide ourselves into two teams – one to attack the enemy from the front, the other to attack him in the rear – withdrawing one as the other goes into action to prevent the first from being struck by projectiles hurled by the second. By the same token, it is important to know how to respond to the police net. When the police designate certain of their men to go into the crowd and arrest a demonstrator, a larger group of urban guerrillas must surround the police group, disarming and beating them and at the same time allowing the prisoner to escape. This urban guerrilla operation is called 'the net within a net'.

The opportunity to get to the bottom of his brother's drug problems never arrives. At three o'clock in the morning on Tuesday, four black police vans enter Basanta Bose Road. About twenty policemen get out, break down the front door of 22/6 and enter the house. The noise of the wood splintering, the men shouting, 'Police! Police! Open up!', wakes everyone in the house. Purba, Sona and Kalyani are affected first; on the ground floor, they are nearest the breach. They lie frozen in the dark as the noise increases. Then their door is kicked in. Several policemen with torches almost fall into the room in a heap, the light is turned on, a voice commands, 'Look everywhere. Under the bed, inside the almirah, everywhere.' Another voice, now inside, raps out, 'Get out of bed, all of you, get up and get off the bed, onto the floor. And don't move.' Before they have woken up properly, their room is turned into something on the route of a cyclone. The bed is partially lifted and set down on the floor with a crash. The almirah is opened, everything inside is flung out, then they kick its door and crack it. They knock and kick things over, trample on everything that is on the floor and exit.

They are everywhere at once. In the pantry on the ground floor they lift up the large glass jars, the utensils and earthenware, the pots, pans, tins, skillets, and fling everything down. In Purba's dark cubby-hole of a kitchen next to the pantry they run their arms across every jar, bottle and tin standing – not many – and leave them broken or lying on the floor. They kick the small mud oven into small clods, leaving behind the heavy, worn disc of its iron grill. They enter the seldom-used living room on this floor, tear down the curtains, upend the coffee table and chairs, slit open the cushions, tear the stereo and the sound-boxes from their wires and hurl them, smash the impassive and inert terracotta Bankura horses and then do the same to the glass front of the bookshelf by throwing the two heavy ashtrays at it, pull out the books and hurl them too. A nearly empty bottle of whisky falls and smashes; the resinous smell of spirit from that small amount is surprisingly strong. No, they cannot find what they are looking for. 'Not here, not here,' someone shouts, 'Will be upstairs, no doubt.' They have smoked out Kamala and Malati from their room behind the pantry, down the short, narrow passage in the warren of outhouse-coops towards the garden. The women stand rigid with fear, speech-less, as the police carry on their rampage. There are no more servants for them to flush out – the men and boys have already been hauled away.

But the ground floor is a picture of still-life compared with what is going on in the upper storeys. Heavy footsteps, an army of them, thudding up the stairs; men shouting, 'Get out of our way, this is a police search'; the sound of things crashing, breaking, being kicked in. In the chaos, Chhaya's hysterical, 'What's going on? What's going on?' is drowned out. The Ghoshes are all awake now, but the last few threads connecting them to the world of sleep are still not torn: they stand confused, terrified, their voices dead in their throats. A general ques-tioning cry of 'What is happening?' rises and then that too dies. Jayanti tries to shield her daughter from the stampede, but their room too is vandalised. The words, 'She's a child, please leave her alone, why do you need to go into her room?' resonate in her head, but fear prevents them from becoming sounds and emerging. A similar thing happens to Chhaya's wail, 'Priyo, Priyo, what's going on? Someone tell me, please, please', doomed to circulate only in the prison of her mind.

The police enter rooms simultaneously, in groups of three or four, and smash and break and ruin; they cannot find what they are looking for; they know they will, but none among the Ghoshes seems to know, or acknowledge in their souls, what it is. The police go into bathrooms, drag in chairs and stools, climb on them to reach the high cisterns, remove their heavy iron tops and fling them down, then run their hands through the water in the reservoir – nothing.

'Not there, not there, how can you have a grown-up man in there?' a policeman comments.

'You can't trust these fuckers,' someone replies. 'If not a person, then maybe explosives, bomb-making masala, guns – who knows?'

A scream comes from someone on the top floor; it is impossible to say who it is. There is a surge in the thudding and crashing; several voices scream in a hell's chorus of atonality. Within that the shouted words, 'Found him! Found the bastard! Here, here. Come, come quickly, we need a hand' can be discerned in shreds, as Supratik is dragged out by his hair by two policemen from his bedroom.

'Hold him tight, be careful! See that he doesn't escape.'

'Where's he going to go? Every single lane and by-lane is blocked by our men outside.'

'Hiding under the bed, he was. Fucking around with bombs outside, a mouse at home when the police come knocking – typical! Where's all your Naxalite courage now, eh?'

Inspector Saha, who has been directing the raid, says to Supratik, 'You think we're so stupid that we don't know who is the mastermind behind the bombing in Shyambazar tonight? You think, if you do your terrorism far away from home, we'll not know who it is?' He slaps Supratik across his face; Sandhya flinches and tries to cry out; Inspector Saha orders, 'Take him away', then, as a coda addressed to the assembled wax-dolls that the Ghoshes have turned into, 'The game's changing, these sister-fuckers are going to be hanging from every lamp-post in town.'

The disappearance of the ingratiating Inspector – three months ago, when he came to arrest Madan, he was bowing low and doing his 'We are your servants, it is for you to command us' patter, punctuated by the laugh that was both oleaginous and menacing – and his replacement by this obscenely swearing, disrespectful dog has been so swift that it is on this that the Ghoshes focus their attention. Their momentary outrage about superficial points of conduct offers a respite from the far greater upheaval playing out in front of them. Another thought briefly fans open in their minds: every single person in every house in the neighbourhood must be awake in their beds now, or peering from behind their windows, all ears pricked, the frisson of this undreamed of drama right outside their front doors galvanising their lives. The thought allows, yet again, the welcome postponement of the taste of ruin.

Sandhya whispers, almost to herself, 'Please leave him, please let him go.' This is ignored; it is not even clear that anyone has heard it. She turns to her husband and implores, 'Why are you standing there? Why aren't you doing anything?'

Adinath remains impassive, frozen. Three months ago, during another search-and-arrest scenario at home, the Ghoshes had been aghast, but not so much that they had not been able to point out, with the confident arrogance that comes so easily to people of their kind, that the police had been mistaken in their arrest of Madan. Now fear has devoured them; it is only their shadows who stand and watch. It is one of their own who is in trouble now, not an adopted servant. Angry remonstrances, their easeful way with giving out orders, could make the situation irredeemable, with consequences they cannot bring themselves to think about, but know on a level deeper than thought, in their cells and blood. The only performance they can put on is one of placatory, undignified begging.

But something gives and the person who has most to lose by not playing it cautiously liberates herself from this mummery of fear and calculation: Sandhya repeats her earlier whisper, but this time it lets itself loose as a scream, 'Please leave him, please let him go! Why do you have to hold him like this? Can't you see you're hurting him?'

In response, two of the four policemen manhandling Supratik twist his arms, already pinned to his back, to the very edge of dislodging them from their sockets at the elbow and shoulders.

Supratik cries out in pain, the sound more animal than human.

Bhola, rooted halfway up the stairs, watching the proceedings like a child peering over the height of a wall at something terrifying and forbidden, tries to intervene with 'Stop it! This is cruel', but it emerges as a phlegmy clatter. The string of his blue-and-dirty-white-striped pyjama is hanging down the front of his flies to his knees. A segment of his hairy pot-belly, displaying the navel, is visible between the bottom of his vest and the crinkled circumference of the top of his pyjama. An officer dawdles up to him, as if this were a picnic and he is moving with dozy contentment to the basket that holds the oranges, and kicks him down the stairs. Chhaya and Charubala gasp audibly. From this point on, what little decorum there had been in the proceedings evaporates completely.

'Shut up!' growls the Inspector. 'One more word or sound from you and I'll have all of you arrested. You'll see what it feels like to breathe the air in the lock-up.' He turns to his men and says, 'Take him to the van.'

Supratik tries to stand up from his kneeling position. Immediately the four officers surrounding him pounce and, before further orders can be given, drag him by his overgrown hair down the stairs as they would the carcass of a huge, butchered creature. Supratik roars in pain again and lets out an unearthly elongated call for his mother – 'Maaaa!' Or so it sounds to Sandhya. She has turned insane. She runs to the Inspector and entreats, 'Take me away instead of him. I'll answer for him. Take me away.' At every iteration of the word 'I' or 'me' she brings down her clenched fist on her chest with a thump so loud that everyone shudders each time it occurs. She falls down to her knees and grasps the Inspector's legs, sobbing, 'Please let him go, I'm falling at your feet, please let him go.' She has transformed everyone into stone figures in a tableau.

The spell is broken by a thin wail coming out of the bedridden Prafullanath's room: 'What's going on? What is happening? Where's everyone?'

The Inspector takes this as a kind of permission; he disengages himself roughly and bounds down the stairs.

His men have only just reached the ground floor with Supratik. That young widow is standing outside her room, weeping, her aanchol held to her mouth out of habit, or perhaps out of the usual sense of decorum. The Inspector is familiar with enough of the family's history to know that she and her two children form a detached unit, a sort of dispensable parenthesis to the rest of the Ghoshes. It is odd for someone of her position to be standing outside her room, listening to the circus upstairs; much more normal for her to be inside, gripped by curiosity and yet hiding, unable to eavesdrop with any ease, because of fear. It is certainly unusual enough for the thought to occur to him at this time of such intense turbulence. Then he notices what it is that has made him pay any attention to yet another weeping woman in a home being raided – she is clawing the air around her waist with her free hand as if bidding him and his men to stop, but fear and inhibition have not allowed it to be expressed in its fullness. The aborted gesture has instead become diverted to a tic, the kind one would see in an old, ill man afflicted with some neurological problem. It gives him the strange impression that she has the edge of her sari clamped to her mouth to stop what she wants to say from getting out. A remarkably attractive woman, he notes, giving her the once-over with his eyes; she is at the apogee of her ripeness. How old could she be? Thirty, at the most? He files away the thought, of half a mind to return to it later perhaps; something has caught at the peripheries of his consciousness and he needs to bring it to the light. But this is not the time.

Then he and his men are out of the house. Sounds of climbing into vans; the brief burst of a conflicting set of instructions about which van to bundle Supratik into, quickly resolved; the police watching the possible exit points in the vicinity returning to the vehicles; van doors slamming shut. Not a single light has come on in any of the doors or windows of the houses on Basanta Bose Road, yet each has a covert and intense quality of watchfulness, of absorption, about it; eyes and ears, stretched to their maximum sensory capacity, seem to have transferred their biological qualities to the portals behind which they are hidden. The silence itself is suspect, too silent. Then, cutting through that tense quietness, the vans leave, with the knock-and-rattle of running engines, one after the other.

CHAPTER EIGHTEEN

1970

The room Supratik is taken to is bare and ordinary: whitewashed walls, the white turned to a tallowy grey; a table with two chairs on either side; a naked bulb hanging down a dusty plait of red, green and white wires from the centre of the ceiling; a rusting steel almirah; no windows. It could be anywhere. Although he is handcuffed, this is not a prisoner's cell; maybe an administrative room, someone's office, a meeting chamber. The two policemen who have brought him in here leave without a word; he can hear the door being bolted and locked from the outside. He knows it will be a long while, maybe even a day, before anyone comes down, knows that this is the stage they call 'pickling', where they let a suspect sit in total isolation and silence so that the speculation of what awaits him can loosen the tight coil of what is a human mind or soul. Often it is easy, this undoing; knowledge helps nothing. Or, rather, the knowledge helps the other side in doing half its preparatory work for them, which is why Supratik decides not to allow his mind to stray into the territory of what he has heard of the ways people such as he are dealt with by the police; he is not going to make their work easier by presenting them with the unravelled weave of himself when they walk in.

But the mind is the most impossible thing to empty and Supratik runs up against the obstinately contrarian will of his the moment it thinks its strategy of resistance: he can think of nothing other than what lies in store for him. Quite aside from playing its treacherous, self-consuming game of dividing itself into two camps and pitching them in battle against each other, his mind – a different creature, really; embodied inside him but a separate presence – introduces yet another combat. He thinks of the recent 'shoot to kill' orders given to the police, the military and the Central Reserve Forces across seven states to deal with his kind. But, surely, if they take him not in action in the field, as it were, but from home, that diktat does not apply? Perhaps they will let him go, after roughing him up a bit to extract any information they think will be useful? From second to second the answer flicks between yes and no, yes and no, a mad, manic child playing with toy light-switches marked 'Salvation' and 'Despair'. In some ways he is immaterial to this conflict. It is as if two abstract principles are locked in their gladiatorial confrontation in a morality play, and he is just the stage on which they perform their encounter.

The rattle of the bolt and lock outside returns him to the solidity of the room. The door opens. The man who is shown in by two uniformed flunkeys is not someone who answers Supratik's mental image of an interrogator, or even a policeman. This short, shy-looking, middle-aged man, with his salt-and-pepper hair and moustache, his jowls beginning to sag, his eyes hidden and distorted behind the powerful bifocal lenses of his thick black-framed glasses, could be anything from a college lecturer to the manager of a local branch of the State Bank of India. The utter ordinariness of the object that he is carrying, and then sets down on the table, adds to this impression: a tired, much-used brown paper file. He moves the chair and sits down, facing Supratik, but somehow managing to keep his face in the penumbral region that the almirah creates on his side of the table. Throughout this meeting Supratik will never properly get to see his expression, the changeable meanings in his eyes.

The voice too, when it issues out of those grey lips, could be a bureaucrat's: cultured, impassive, bored. No leading up gently, lullingly from the margins; it launches headlong into the middle with, 'Achchha, besides Debdulal Maity, you, Samir Ray Chowdhury and Dhiren Chatterjee, can you tell me who else was at the meetings in Debdulal-babu's home in Belpahari in March/April last year? I mean, '69?'

Two immediate things strike Supratik, although he does not acknowledge the surprise to himself, let alone betray it by any visible signs: he is being addressed respectfully with the highest form of 'you'; and, second, they have a lot more on him and his comrades, even 'micro' details, as he would have once put it, of their whereabouts and activities than he would ever have given them credit for. The surprise is at the galling admission that he will have to make, shedding his condescension, of their nous and perspicacity. Supercilious hatred is easy; hatred tempered with the beginnings of respect – but in no way denting the antagonism – is much more difficult, Supratik finds. Or is this called fear?

He has no idea how he is going to play this. After all, he has only a limited range available to him: lying, denial, inability to recall; and those are intersecting sets, too. Where is he going to begin? Denial of the meeting? Denial that he knows, or ever knew, any of the people named? A brazen feigned surprise and ignorance, even outrage, that he is being questioned? It is a crucial question, for the response to it will set the parameters for everything that is to follow. He has to be as careful as a stalking cat.

The reply from his long-unused voice comes out all catarrhal, weak and risibly unconvincing to his own ears: 'I don't remember.'

There. He has gone down one path of the several available to him and foreclosed all other possibilities. He is now doomed to stick unveeringly to it and follow to its particular end, and who knows if that is not a destination more baneful than the others would have led him to? Besides, those three simple words have opened up other exposed flanks: that the meetings took place and that the meetings took place between the people named, in the place and time mentioned. He has, after all, not specifically denied them.

The man does not seem interested in attacking those weaknesses. Instead he asks, 'And the tactical line of' – pause – 'of killing in small groups, "guerrilla action", I think you call it? Who was the brain behind it in Jhargram and Belpahari? You?'

There is nothing that he can say to this. Is he expected to reply to every question? If so, is he allowed to ponder it as one would a chess move, expansively, with all the time in the world? Or would that be damning? Would swift, rat-a-tat replies be rewarded with a better conclusion?

Again his inquisitor does not prod, letting the silence lengthen and become the third voice in the play. The State Assembly has been dissolved and it is President's Rule again in West Bengal, the second time in two years, but Supratik feels in his bones that this man must be someone high-ranking in the CPI(M) Politburo, the erstwhile Home Minister Jyoti Basu's right-hand man, even.

'What about the people you saw during the times that you returned to Calcutta' – here he consults some papers in the open brown file on his lap – 'let's see, um, here, you visited Calcutta three times between February '68 and January '70? Or was it five? Before you returned . . . returned for good in March this year? Or are you thinking of going back to Medinipur again?' The man's voice remains steady and polite, even sympathetic, but this casual little question he has just lobbed freezes Supratik's blood and lique-fies it, all in one instant, so that he suddenly feels light-headed, about to levitate. It is one of those few things that he has refrained even from writing down in his diary to Purba. He knows they have not got hold of that – they cannot . . . But a few things become clear to him. Has Dipankar been caught and made to – here his thoughts buckle into performing an elision – made to give up some information or or or

'You have always been the quiet one, haven't you?' the man says, not really asking a question, but giving voice to an idle, fleeting impression. Then something approaching intent shows itself in the next few words – 'You know what they called you? Your nickname, because you are so silent most of the time?' – before the refusal to reveal the answer leaches it away. Or perhaps that is the intent – the dangling question that will goad him to ask for an answer. But he is not going to oblige.

'It's not as if you have been conducting all your . . . er . . . your business in complete secrecy,' the interrogator continues. 'All these farmers, hundreds of them across dozens of villages . . . and then boasting about it in your papers, *Liberation* and *Deshabrati*, although those reports are slightly wishful, don't you think? The *vast* numbers of people joining you, the *enormous* impact your group's actions have, the great success of all this squad action and annihilations, the Red Party inexorably exercising its hold village by village – these claims were always a bit hopeful, a bit exaggerated in your reports, no?' His voice is apologetic, as if he is slightly distraught at having to point out the gaps and the errors and the abridgement that ideology inev-itably demands.

'But very little reporting, I see, of your retreats and losses and setbacks. Those are dealt with' – pause – 'hurriedly. If at all,' he adds as a coda. The tone remains regretful.

The greater part of Supratik's mind is too busy whirring away elsewhere to heed these ant-bites. Could this man be from the *Congress*? If so, there is some hope of escaping lightly: did his grandfather not have some Congress connections, or even his father? Did they not know anyone high enough up the ladder to put a few words in the right ears?

This time the man reads Supratik as if his head has become transparent glass and the thoughts inside it a lean procession of simple, large words. 'It must have occurred to you, once or twice, that you could have been arrested earlier had it not been for the, uh, police connections that your family has maintained for many years?' he asks, but the interrogative tone at the close of the sentence is so attenuated as to be almost absent; he does not require an answer to this one, either. That vertiginous feeling revisits Supratik. Could that be why he has not been banged up with other prisoners in Ballygunje police station – so close to what he still thinks, perhaps with renewed intensity at this moment, as home – but instead held alone in a cell for three days, or was it four; not penned and beaten up with other political prisoners, which is, he knows, a matter of routine occurrence? Again, that near-instantaneous reversal: it could equally be because they have different plans for him; that specialness could only contain a terrible meaning.

'We are just trying to establish,' the questioner says, 'how much of a linchpin you were. Or were you one of the members of the high command?'

Despite himself, Supratik is impelled towards an answer. 'Since you know everything, why go through this drama of questioning?' he asks. He had meant it to sting, a retaliation perhaps for the barbs his questioner has been aiming at him, but only manages a petulant tiredness.

'We *do* know a lot of things,' the man admits, somewhat disarmingly, then flicks the tone like someone tossing a coin. 'Which is why it may not be such a good idea to remain silent. Or to lie.'

The silence seems to be emanating from the interrogator now, not imposed by Supratik on the proceedings. He controls its flow according to the rules of the game, which only he knows, then cuts it out with unusual garrulity: 'The members who plan and give out the orders, that's what that's what, um, interests us. The fingers of your hand pick up something, but the command comes from the brain. The central nervous system. That's the goal. Not the ideologues, mind you, those we know; not even the foot soldiers, but the generals. And you are one of them, am I right? The stealthy nights of planning in, here, let's see' – that show of consulting papers again – 'oh, let's choose any three from this long list, quite long, 23A Satgachhi 2nd Lane in Tiljala, 76/2 Dihi Entally Lane, 17/B/2 Bechu Chatterjee Street in Kalabagan . . . what? Am I right?'

Supratik makes fists of his hands under the table to steady himself. The sudden change in the man's persona, from a mild, laconic nobody to this spitter of absolutely accurate facts, like your pot-bellied, rice-and-fish-eating next-door neighbour turning out to be a supreme assassin, getting his bullets unfailingly into the plumb centre of his target time after time, sends Supratik's whole being careering. Yes, they know everything. There is no hope; and yet that great deceiver taunts him with the meagre residues – look, it says, they do not know about X or Y. And only X or Y it will be, since they have made it their business to know the entire alphabet bar those final two or three letters. Which they may very possibly know about, anyway.

The man now asks his first direct and pointed question: 'Who are the city guys still in Medinipur?'

Silence. Do they really want to know, fill a gap in their knowledge, or are they trying to catch him out?

The man persists: 'Did you not like the question? What about a different one: name me some villages that your groups, ah, penetrated. Not only in Bengal, but also Bihar and Orissa. I read in your papers how your spread is now over a hundred districts. The figure in that boast – is that wishful?'

'I don't know,' Supratik replies; so lame even to his own ears. He has the sense that the man is looking at him fixedly, but he cannot be certain of it because of the combination of the thick glasses, the shadow in which he keeps his face and the cone of light under which Supratik sits directly. A worrying thought darts through his mind – how can he not see the face of a man sitting three or four feet opposite him? – and slips out again.

'I have a different matter to sort out with you, it's been worrying me for a while,' the man now says. 'Something private, something more about me than you. I want to understand something. A lot of these young Naxal men, both activists in Calcutta and in the rural districts, they come from poor families. I can see how they would want to . . . to to throw in their lot with a, ah, movement that promises to be of the poor, for the poor, by the poor.'

Supratik knows so well where this is going that he finds himself nodding as if to encourage the man.

'But . . . but so many of you, the boys from the city, I mean, what your Charu-babu calls "the urban intelligentsia", so many of you come from well-off, middle-class homes, in your case an upper-middle-class home, am I right? You boys have been educated in good schools, you've had enough to eat, enough to wear, comfortable homes to live in, the benefit of college education, not a day's want in your lives . . . What made you leave that that that comfort zone to risk your lives?'

How amazing the transformation is, Supratik thinks: you scratch the surface of a serious-seeming, important apparatchik, all silences and measured reserve, and out comes the loquacious Bengali soul; no less a performance, that incessant chattering, but a thinner mask, all too easy to come by, and easily wearable.

He is not done: 'Putting yourselves in such danger . . . bombs, guns, knives, axes and whatnot?'

He makes it sound like sweeties that will give you a sore stomach, if you indulge too much.

The man continues, 'And life in the villages could not have been a bed of roses, right? Especially for people from your kind of background? The rough food, the discomforts of daily life, no electricity, no sanitation. Did you boys get diarrhoea and stomach upsets a lot? Surely you must have.'

A swirl of amazement at this catalogue, absurd coming from such a source, injects itself into the stream of Supratik's fear and anxiety. He was prepared to tackle the questions straight on, but now he feels he is being ridiculed, that their revolution is being attacked not only in the usual way, with the police and military and the machinery of state power, but also with comic derision. The immediate sting of this is more irritating.

'What? Am I right or not? What a terrible time you must have had. And if you fell ill, what then? The nearest hospital would have been in Jhargram or Medinipur Town, no? Long walk from where you were, very, very long. Days, right? Trains were out of bounds, weren't they, because of increased police presence in the stations? But you boys had a lot of practice in walking, walking from one village to another in the night. What? Am I right?'

Before Supratik has had a chance to stifle his pique and subject his words to a measure of control, they rush out – 'Yes, you are.'

The man seems taken aback by the simplicity of the admission, and the ease with which it appears. There is a pause to accommodate the unexpected before he resumes, 'So why did you young men do it? You had the whole world to look forward to. Such bright futures, now, now all . . . all . . .' He leaves out the culminating word point-edly, maybe out of an incongruous sense of politeness.

Supratik does not know where to begin; the profusion of the points of entry stump him. Are the questions in earnest or a form of entrap-ment that he has not been able to decode? Surely this man is not really asking for a lesson in politics; their individual sides have been chosen a long time ago, and each is settled into his own with the inextirpability of giant trees. Whatever he says now in response will be, on several levels, an exercise in futility. Or is the man extending a covert invitation to help him mitigate his own circumstances of impris-onment, and worse, by mounting an ideological plea? Since when did that work, Supratik asks himself, incredulous that the absurdity of thought has infected him too.

'I keep stumbling over that bit. Not so much on why you went to the villages, not so much all that, that's easy to understand – your brains were washed by this this this propaganda, and you are all young, your blood is hot, you are restless and and, if I may say it, a bit reck-less, a bit of adventurism, it's natural that that runs in all your blood; this, after all, is the age for doing, not for sitting still or thinking deeply about things. What I cannot understand is why you didn't dabble in it briefly and then return home to your books and your comforts. A lot of your, ah, comrades did that.'

Supratik decides to steer clear of sarcasm. Instead he says, 'Because who else will be the defence counsel for humanity?' He has to do his old trick of twisting his thumb to its most extreme possible to prevent himself from adding, 'Not you or your type.'

'Eh?' Not the more polished 'What?' this time, but a shortcut into the rustic interjection.

'Who will fight the corner for those who have nothing?' Supratik elucidates. 'For those who don't even know that something can be done? That they can fight back? That their expendable lives needn't be fodder, generation after generation?'

'Whoaaah. Stop stop stop stop, my head hurts with all these big words . . .'

Supratik marvels again at the man's chameleon-like capacity for seamless transition, this time into feigning to be a simple-minded buffoon; how many skins does the man have? Is he going to be entertained with all of them, one by one? But on no account must he be drawn into talking about the moral basis of his politics; that would only serve to make him outraged, lose control, go down the road of vicious sneering attacks, all of which would not do him any favours. He feels small that such a self-serving calculation has entered his head; has he fallen so far, become so emasculated, that, when called upon to defend the revolution, he has traded off his possible personal safety against it? Is this how it all ends?

'All this bleeding-heart sensibility,' the man says, 'not really very sensible. If you feel so much for the poor and the needy, why did you let your cook, Madan, take the blame when it was you who had stolen your aunt's jewellery?'

The mood and tone, chameleons themselves, have shifted their colour and shape. There is cold metal in the man's voice. The recent clown could have been imagined by Supratik.

'You stole her jewellery to finance your terrorism. You think everyone moves with their faces to the grass? The "urban intelligentsia" is not so intelligent, after all. Or perhaps it doesn't credit others, of different political stripes, with much intelligence?'

So the police know: Supratik feels the shock as a moist heat that suddenly wicks into his face. It enters his ears, from the inside, as a ringing, and as the droning din subsides he can hear the man saying, '. . . not know that? So clearly no fighting Madan's corner, for you? His life was not fodder, as you put it, to you middle-class boys playing around with some dangerous fireworks? Tsk-tsk.'

Supratik can hear the hiss-and-burn of acid as the bass to his questioner's words; the sarcasm, now no longer his prerogative, is not another colourful skin the man has stretched over his personality. Supratik thinks that some residue of dignity – that word will have to do – prevents him from answering the questions. Shame consumes him. He tries to think back to the moment when he had hatched the plan to steal his aunt's jewellery and have Madan-da framed for the burglary, but he seems unable to return to that point of origin. What had he felt during the planning? Excitement that he had found a way of injecting easy and substantial funds into the urban side of his party's ongoing revolution? Had it been mitigated by at least a tiny blot of pity for the old man he was offering up as sacrifice? Had there been any guilt? Shame? He keeps returning to that word and, like a giant landslide blocking the way, it won't allow him to get to his destination; he will have to reckon with it first.

The ruin of a kind, loving, innocent old man in the evening of his life against the money necessary for reaching the next stage of the revolution's city-based operations – the exchange reveals itself with such starkness now that he feels the shame as a bloom of terror right in the centre of his body. Could it be that he felt no dilemma, no queasiness, at all about it when the idea first began to germinate in his head? Could he not have engineered the theft in such a way that his pishi, Chhaya, was suspected for the deed? That would have seemed so natural, a public culmination of the two women's decades-long animosity. Instead, he had deliberately and carefully placed his aunt's ruby-and-diamond ring under Madan-da's hollow statue of Krishna, hoping that it would be turned up during the ensuing raid, leading to the old man's arrest.

The calculation at that time, he remembers, had been strictly mathematical – if one have-not had to be sacrificed so that fifty have-nots could be benefited, nothing trivial such as emotions could stand in the way. He had chosen accordingly and, now, that arithmetic, for which he and Madan-da have paid such an unthinkable price, will not provide him with a crumb of comfort. The questions of feelings and principles and inhuman betrayal that he has had to wrestle with surge back, this time without the soul-destroying arithmetic to balance them out: did he . . . did he go down that route because of reasons of class, because a servant stealing is so much more credible, so much more *natural*, than a member of the family? Was it to make the theft believable to the police that he had framed Madan-da, or was it because it had cost less to betray a servant than one's own kind?

The questions are so unbearable that Supratik's mind throws him toys and baubles to distract, and one of them is a memory of himself as a four-year old riding his red tricycle in the garden and suddenly finding that he was unable to stop and crashing against the trunk of the guava tree.

Madan-da had come running to pick up the bawling child in his arms and had put Mercurochrome on his skinned knees and elbows.

'Eeeesh, eeeesh, poor little baby' – Supratik can hear Madan-da's voice in his head – 'it'll be all right, all fine. Here, look, here's the magic red medicine, I'll put it here, and here, and there, look; I can see it healing as we speak, the red medicine is spreading its goodness all over the little cuts, eeesh, eeesh . . .'

Red medicine. At the age of nine or ten, Supratik had discovered that Madan-da couldn't get his tongue round the complicated name, Mercurochrome, so he called it 'red medicine' instead. He had tried to teach Madan-da, but the hilarious attempts had come out repeatedly as 'Mar-coo-kom'.

He feels as if a careless hand has swiped through a shelf of delicate china in his chest. The sobs emerge from him as a series of retches.

The man mocks him, 'What? Feeling uncomfortable? Did part of the jewellery you stole fund the Shyambazar bombing?' he asks.

From the strangely sliding territory of the irrefutable accusations of a few minutes ago, these straightforward questions return Supratik to more comfortable land; he begins to feel steady, solidity under his feet again. He does not have it in him to put on a drama of denial – 'What on earth are you talking about? I don't understand at all' kind of rubbish – so he suffers the questions in silence again. That is a kind of answer, he knows, but it is the best he can do; he does not hold many cards in his hand.

'And what will it finance, the loot?' His voice has the serrations of a knife in it. 'Home-made bombs and pipe-bombs, maybe a gun or two? But those you'd rather steal from the police or from others, given that stealing and looting form such pillars of your Charu Mazumdar's politics lectures, right? How long will it sustain your revolution, this petty thieving?'

With that, he suddenly gets up and leaves the room, unusually quickly for a person like him, before Supratik has had time to process what is happening. He will never see him again, never find out who it was that subjected him to such an oddly formal two hours.

Three more days in solitary confinement with his handcuffs removed and then the regime changes. Two khaki-clad policemen enter his cell, start to taunt and abuse him – the terms deployed are standard currency among the lower classes – and, when he does not rise to this, beat him with their regulation sticks with a kind of mindful randomness, letting the blows fall anywhere except on his head or neck, then depart, still swearing. Supratik uncurls himself and, through the blanket of pain, finds himself thinking that if this is going to be the level of mistreatment involved before they let him go, he will take it in his stride; this much is endurable.

But he is wrong.

The following day four policemen enter his room. One holds him down by his hands, one by his knees, the third one keeps his feet straightened, while the fourth man beats the soles of his feet with such concentrated energy and vigour that he can hear his screams punctuated by the policeman's panting. He thinks, in so far as the pain has left him any capacity for thought, that he will never walk again. Later, much later, after the sharp but localised agony has become dully pervasive, creeping up from his feet to his knees and, oddly, his testicles, his lower abdomen and head, he will remember from somewhere that they beat you on the soles so as to leave no bruising on you.

No less than the Senior Superintendent is sent to look in on him the next day; Supratik has long known how to tell their rank by reading the insignia on their shoulder-flashes.

He launches directly into business. 'What? Do you think you will talk now?' he asks Supratik.

Supratik, lying down in the cartoon shape of a lightning bolt, turns his head and looks at him, then goes back to his original position, head bowed and nestled against one side in the crook of his arms.

'These are not good signs,' the SSP says opaquely. 'We have ways to make you talk.'

It seems to Supratik that they forget about him for days, he is not sure how many. In that time he can only think and dream about the purple-bordering-on-black butt-end of one of his comrade's fingers.

When they come next they are prepared; and they come as if sent by a malignant god who gives the heft of physical reality to dreams and thoughts. The panting man who beat him is there along with one, maybe two, of the posse attending on him that day; he cannot clearly tell. Their ranks are swelled to six now, but, it is obvious from the moment they enter, that this Superintendent – only one metal star this time, as if he, Supratik, has been demoted in their consideration – will not be participating; he sets himself slightly apart. The reason for this emerges soon enough. A policeman grasps his right wrist, another his left, two hold down his legs, one each; all of them grip like a vice winched to breaking point.

The remaining man, kind-looking, almost fatherly, with chubby cheeks and a luxuriant ink-black moustache, turns to the SP and makes a querying motion with his head; the SP nods, once, calmly, then moves to stand behind Supratik's head, from where he cannot see him. Chubby Cheeks takes out a short length of what looks like a nylon rope and a pair of pliers from the pocket of his voluminous khaki trousers and advances towards Supratik. It takes a while for Supratik to extract the meaning from what he sees; there is no space or time between that comprehension and his involuntary, hoarse cry, 'No!' It comes out so low that he could have been mistaken for expressing disbelief in a session of gossipy chit-chat.

But the SP has heard him all right. His voice says, 'Who planned the bombing in Shyambazar?'

'No,' Supratik says again, this time in a whisper. Chubby Cheeks looks beyond him for a signal, asks the policeman holding his left wrist, 'You're sure you have it all right?', then brings the pliers near his fingers.

Supratik closes his hand into a fist, as much as the grip will allow; his bladder gives at the same time. Chubby Cheeks taps sharply on the knuckles with the pliers; he instantly unclenches his hand for a moment; in that brief second, his longest finger, the one next to his index finger, is held in the jaws of the pliers. Gently.

There is a question again, but Supratik does not hear it, so he does not answer. The pressure on his finger increases infinitesimally; maybe he imagines it. His eyes are wide, unblinking.

'Where are Tapan Mukherjee and Ashim Mondol? Where are they hiding after the bombing?'

Chubby Cheeks presses down on the short curved handles of the pliers, the blunt jaws bite obediently, Supratik screams and screams and his body tries to buck up and out, but he cannot, he is being held down at exactly the points they know he is going to rear. The jaws unclamp. His screams turn, with a will of their own, into a whimpering. He sounds like a dog.

'Do you now remember where your friends are?'

The whimpering continues, but it is not a response to the question; that was inserted as if aimlessly into the flow of the sound coming out of Supratik. It is posed again. Supratik does not even try to shape into intelligible words the unmanning, acoustic flux he is producing; he has no will. This time he imagines the sound of the crack of bone; it is the crack of a pistol shot giving the 'Go!' signal to the run of his animal scream as the pliers press down and press down and press down, wishing to obliterate the obstruction of the tip of his finger standing between the perfect union of the two metal jaws. His screams end in billowing sobs, one after the other, unstoppable.

There is an amused, avuncular twinkle in Chubby Cheeks's eyes. One of the restraining policemen says, 'A squealer, this one. He'll drive us crazy, the fucker.'

'And this is just the beginning,' another policeman observes.

Chubby Cheeks gives a resigned smile.

The voice from behind Supratik's head is terrier-like with its query. 'Tapan Mukherjee and Ashim Mondol?' it echoes itself.

There is no available cell or nerve inside Supratik's head to deploy in conjuring up a lie or a diversion; everything has been conquered by the sensation of pain – it fills his entire being. But he finds that he cannot utter the simple words required of him, or bring himself to lift his head and look at his hand, which they have now released, although he is still held down by the other hand and at his knees and legs. If he says something, anything, there will be an end to this; all he wants to do is buy his reprieve with a few words, but he has lost the capacity to form them. At last, when he can, they come out as a sobbing croak, which he has to repeat three times in order to hear it himself – 'Don't know, they've run away. Don't know where.' How could he ever have imagined that ideology, revolution, the needs of others, abstraction, all these, combined or individually, could have been weightier than the simple business of self-preservation, of the sheer physicality of pain?

'Lies, all lies,' comes that voice.

'No! No!' he says with as much strength as he can gather, because if he fails to convince them . . . His mind refuses to go there.

Chubby Cheeks speaks for the first time. 'Get on with number two?' he asks. His voice matches his face: it is kind, purring, the sort of thing one imagines as part of the arsenal of the ideal doctor's perfect bedside manner.

The voice from behind says, 'Where are they? We want to know, before the trail goes cold. Then there are other questions. Such as the addresses of all the places where you make your fireworks.' Supratik takes a while to work out that the question is addressing him and not replying to the short question Chubby Cheeks asked.

The answers tumble out of Supratik without a whit of thought. 'Don't know where they've gone, I swear, this is the truth, I'm telling you the truth,' he manages to say, haltingly, in a groan. 'Bombs – in Kankurgachhi, Motilal Basak Lane, right after the jute mill, number seventy-six, you have to go through it to the back, there's a tiny alley. Then in the Kasai slum, off Potopara Lane in Narkeldanga, 15/1, between the Canal Road and a lane in the slum. It's not easy to find.'

The pain stops him there. He feels hot, malleable rods shooting up his arm, in his armpit and elbow.

Another question: 'The numbers again?'

Supratik obliges.

'That can't be all. Where are the others? What are the names of the people in these places?'

'Can I sit up?' he entreats.

There is a short pause. The policemen holding him down let go of him. He lifts himself up from his neck and shoulders, then tries to sit up; all he wants to do is see what they have done to his finger. But the sight of it – the nib of a strange pen, dipped in dry blue-black ink – draws a howl from him. It sets him sobbing again, tears, snot, saliva, all running down his face and chin; the time for dignity or maintaining a hard, impervious front is long over. He trots out the names, matching them with the addresses; gives them more names, more locations; pain is everything. They ask him to repeat; he obeys like a good little child. Suddenly, without any warning, they grab hold of him again, but leave him sitting up. He cannot feel the grip restraining his left hand. Chubby Cheeks draws a different pair of pliers, one with thinner, more pointed pincers, much like tweezers.

Supratik screams and sobs simultaneously, 'No! No! NO! I've told you everything, everything, all true, every single word, let me go now, please, let me go, I've told you all that you wanted to know.'

Matching the decibels of his plea, the policemen enter into a chorus of yowling:

'Squealing before anything's done! A precious prince, do you see?'

'Put something in his mouth, stuff something in.'

'Gag the foolish fucker!'

'Hold him tight, hold him tight!'

They unleash a pandemonium of noise, as if the auditory energy will galvanise them into executing their task; they shout themselves into action. Chubby Cheeks grabs hold of the overgrown nail of Supratik's big toe with the thin pliers while Supratik, prevented from writhing, screams himself hoarse, so that when the toenail is first twisted and then uprooted, like a fish-scale, and before he passes out, the sound from his vocal cords comes out as long arcs of a breathy, grating rasp.

The SP says, 'That'll teach him to go around killing policemen.'

Chubby Cheeks laughs and says, 'Did you see how I got it in one go?'

'No wonder they call you Doctor-babu. You should preface all this with, "It won't hurt at all, trust me, I'm a doctor, I've been doing this for decades, just trust me." What about it, eh?'

They burst out laughing. The SP adds, 'He'll think twice about lying when we come back next. The beginning of a meal should always be memorable, don't you think?'

★

When Supratik comes to, he is alone; he has no idea how much time has elapsed. All day and all night, for an ungraduated period, he flickers on and off like a light with a faulty connection. In his lucid moments, his thoughts appear like weak, wiggly stripes on the black matrix of pain. They will not find anything in most of those addresses; they have left it too late. Had they extracted the information from him hours after he was brought in, yes, then they could have turned up people and things in their trawl, but now? The news of the raid on his home and his arrest would have spread immediately; they will have known to vacate and go into hiding.

He looks, desultorily, first, then with more intent, for his ripped-out toenail, but cannot find it. In any case, he is hardly mobile enough to search for it properly. He pities himself for ever having harboured ideas of what police torture entailed; they have all been proved wildly incorrect. He does not have any sharp memory of it, the real having supplanted the imagined, and so recently too, but he had thought it involved beatings with sticks, a broken rib or two, punches to the face, broken teeth, a black eye . . . The imagination mostly deals with the permissible. He had imagined the pain all those relatively large-scale, crude things, such as mass beatings, assault with sticks, could cause, but who knew that this miniaturist's art, concentrating on tiny areas, working with instruments finer and more delicate than the stick or the fist, could make all the unsubtle, old-school acts that he had contemplated seem like children's games – amateurish mimicking of the real things, endearing in their predictability and harmlessness, ultimately preferable.

Then fear begins to eat at his soul: what if they think that he has lied and led them up the garden path, when they go to all the locations he has given them only to find out there is nothing or no one there? For the first time those rust-coloured splatters and drip marks that he has seen distributed sparsely on the walls, in corners and where the walls meet the floor, change their meaning from 'paan stains' to something else. The urge to piss is suddenly uncontrollable, but his bladder is dry. It is only then that he notices his pyjamas are damp and the faint whiff of ammonia is coming off him.

A square of black jelly marks where his toenail has been.

*

He has become clairvoyant: they come for him engorged with anger, not in the diffuse spirit of an idle reconnaissance that they had begun with on the previous occasion. There is the SP again, some of the lower-ranking policemen from earlier, but no Chubby Cheeks; instead a thin broomstick of a man in civilian clothes – seven men in total. The repetitious nature of it all, as if the ordinary sequential flow of life has become circular in his case, makes him feel dizzy; is he hallucinating it all? The five khaki-clad policeman fall on him in a riot, like a pack of starving dogs, the moment they enter; the dream-like feeling ends. The beating is accompanied by rousing shouts and abuses, all in a continuous stream, drowning out his pitiful mewling. He reacts in the usual human way, by curling up into a ball, but this time there are no niceties observed by the assailants; the blows land everywhere, back, rump, hip, arms, head, shoulders, legs, neck, thighs. He is an open receptacle.

The preamble over, they lift him up and throw him on his cot, then tie his arms and legs together, much as hunted animals or animals about to be sacrificed are bundled up for ease of carrying.

'Stop shouting!' the SP orders Supratik. 'Stop your screaming right now. We'll teach you how to scream, you lying motherfucker. So forward with the addresses, so helpful and willing. Now we know why: there's no one fucking there. No one! The birds have all flown. And no bomb-masala either.'

Supratik begins to explain to the ceiling from his supine position – 'Listen to me, please, listen' – but a slap across his face shuts him up.

'You will talk now. We'll make you talk now. Every name that you know, including the names of your fourteen forefathers, will come fucking out from you.'

They untie his pyjamas and draw it down to his ankles. He cries out, 'I'll tell everything, don't do this, please don't, everything I know.' His sobs are now racked by hiccups, so his words come out oddly syncopated. Still he tries: 'They got news that I had been arrested, so they ran away. You would have found out if you had gone earlier, I'm telling you the truth . . .'

'So it's all our fault? Is that what you're trying to say?'

'No!' he shouts.

The policeman holding him down at his knees, obstructing his view of what they are going to soon begin doing to the lower half of his body, says, 'The fucker will sing, sing for his life. There will be a lot of noise. Shall we tie his mouth?'

'How are we going to get things out of him if he can't speak, you foolish arse?' one of his colleagues notes with mirth.

A sudden silence descends in the room. In that stillness Supratik can discern something that he can only think of as the sounds of preparation – the rustle of clothing, a click, a suggestion of small, hard objects coming into brief contact with each other . . . His mouth and throat are completely dry. If he could only see what it is they are taking out, what it is they are planning to do . . .

The thin man in plain clothes says, 'Hold him down really hard. He mustn't move' and sits down on the bed, next to Supratik's naked thighs. He touches the inner left thigh and brushes it, as if smoothing down some paper before bringing his pen down on it. Supratik screams.

The SP says, 'Now for some answers.'

Supratik cannot control the sounds coming out of him; they control him, not the other way around; the notion of agency has been inverted. He feels a prick on the skin where he has just been touched, like a hypodermic needle entering.

'Nooooo! Noooo!' Tides of screams break over him.

'Don't move. The more you move . . .'

Then he feels a series of those pricks, slow, methodical, closely spaced, along a long curve on the skin of his thigh. With each insertion of the needle, his whole body tries to jerk; after half a dozen of these pricks he begins to find the pain not totally intolerable. His mind begins its habitual trickery, starting with salvaging the memory of a childhood game he used to play with Suranjan: they used to spell out words, letter by letter, on each other's backs, using the tip of one finger, and they had to guess what the word was.

'Names,' the SP says. 'Every Naxal you know in the city, I want to know their names. We'll impale all of you fuckers.'

Supratik cannot think of a single name. He feels yet another curve being tattooed into his skin, this one close to and following the first one. It hurts more.

'What are you doing? What are they doing? What are they doing?' he begs.

'Shut up!' the SP commands. 'The questions are ours to ask, you son of a whore. Names, I want names.'

'Ashu Chatterjee, Ramen Niyogi, Debashish Ray Chowdhury, Debdulal Maity, Ashish Mukherjee,' the names come out, as if from a tap; Supratik has no idea if they are real, or fabricated, or semi-fictional hybrids where the surnames and forenames, both tethered in truth, have become mismatched.

The needle is now picking out a line that feels as if it is running perpendicular to the curves just executed. He has no idea what is happening and the ignorance corrodes him into nothing. It feels less painful than what he has already been subjected to, unless . . . Unless this is a throat-clearing before the real singing begins.

He lets out an involuntary cry, this one of fear, but it is indistinguishable from a cry of pain.

'Again,' the SP orders.

He recites a list, not congruent with the one he has given before.

'Lies, lies!' the SP shouts. 'How did Ramen Niyogi become Ramen Mukherjee? How?'

The needle-artist has dotted out a pretty outline of a sickle and hammer over an area of nearly twenty square inches on Supratik's thigh in pinpricks of blood. He pokes a sharp knife at one corner of the sickle and with a quick, sharp dig-and-twist movement loosens a little bit of skin, enough so that the pinch formed of his thumb and forefinger has a purchase on the flap.

Supratik howls as the pain reams his entire being.

'Names and addresses and whereabouts,' the SP demands.

How can he speak?

'Names,' comes the order again.

With one graceful movement of the point of the knife, the tattooist cuts along the dotted line of one curve of the sickle, then proceeds to do the same along the other arc. The craftsmanship is so fine that it takes a tiny fraction of time for the blood to bead along the bend of the line. He then begins to pull the skin, held by the corner that he has loosened, along the crescent of blood, bit by slow bit. An old-fashioned flaying is in progress.

'Fucker's screaming as if he's being slaughtered!'

Another policeman suggests to the SP, 'He could be gagged now and the questions could be asked after it's over. He'll know not to lie after this.'

As if to test the robustness of this hypothesis, the thin man pulls off the strip of skin that forms the metal blade of the representation of the sickle, in one quick tug. The sound from Supratik is indescribable. The peeled skin, a thin strip of wet, red rag, is attached to the bit where the joined-dots diagram of the sickle-handle begins.

The SP roars above this, 'Taking out policeman, eh? Killing policemen. This'll teach you, you son of a whore; this'll teach you to stab and shoot and bomb the police.' His delivery is a mixture of exultation and admonishment; he is delighted that policemen have been assassinated, otherwise how would this opportunity have come his way? 'Cover up his mouth,' he orders.

After silencing their subject, they continue with their exercise: the life-sized, live, tear-along-the-dotted-line game extends to the handle section of the sickle and, after that, the head of the hammer. Muzzled now, Supratik finds it difficult to breathe; respiration through his mouth has been made impossible – screaming in pain also doubles as a way of breathing, he understands now – and his nose has been given over to becoming predominantly a channel for leaking mucus. He will have to wrest away some of the energy in feeling pain to concentrating on the instinctive, unthought business of exhaling and inhaling.

Creating a distributary like this for his thoughts and senses, away from the main flow of the pain, however feeble this side-channel may be, brings him to a new understanding: that he can exercise a small amount of control over the pain, that it need not drown and erase him so completely.

The SP appears to be unaware that Supratik cannot answer his questions. He positions himself beside Supratik's twisting, jerking head and keeps thundering, 'Names, names of all the fuckers. We'll eliminate them all, their family lines will end with them. We'll show them exactly what fucking around with bombs leads to. Names, all the names, we'll pull each and every letter out of you.'

Now that Supratik has learned to bifurcate his concentration, the referents behind the SP's words once again begin to become legible and the relentless interrogation makes his mind, in its own peculiar state of fugue, wander into bizarre, aberrant territories. He thinks, for example, about that standard first question asked of a child by any stranger – 'What is your name?' Faced now with a different kind of query about names, his own disintegrates into nothing. Who is he? Is he his name? Could the two be uncoupled? What would he see in that gap?

Then there is a particularly grievous rip on his thigh. His constrained mouth, deprived of any freedom of movement, transmits the action of silent screaming into such a contortion that it is forced to bite down on his tongue. The cloth binding his mouth, already wet from leaking saliva, begins to turn pink, then red, as the salty, metallic taste in his mouth expresses itself visibly. The air curves in front of him. His mind, flirting with derangement, now brings to him, following its helter-skelter illogic, lines from the closing song he used to sing as a boy of eight in chorus in manimela: 'Lift up this body of mine / Make me a burning lamp in your temple . . . / Touch my soul with the touchstone of fire / Sanctify my life with this burnt offering.'

They bundle him – he is not capable of much movement on his own – into a black police van in the dead of night.

'We're going to let you go,' he was told; no reason was given, but he assumed it was because he had given them enough useful leads.

A dark shadow, of what lies in wait for him around the corner as a consequence of singing to the police, has briefly flitted through his mind, but immediate pain, and relief and incredulity at being released, have held that in abeyance.

He has no idea where they are taking him and he knows better than to ask. They are probably not giving him a lift back home, that much he can safely assume. The pain-induced hallucinatory darts-and-tumbles of his mind keep revisiting him. Now he has a gratuitous vision, no longer yoked to the dry words of propaganda, but something akin to a thing half-dreamed, half-experienced in the raggedy borders between sleep and waking – a vision of a near future, maybe fifty years, maybe seventy-five, a hundred, when the seeds that he and his kind have been busy sowing have grown, hidden from the human eye, or denied until unignorable, into forest cover for most of the country.

It brings tears to his eyes and, for the first time in his life, he cries moved by the possibility of fulfilment; not tears of joy, but of a kind of proleptic hopefulness.

The van stops and he is ordered to get out. It is slow, painful going. Four policemen get out of the van too, as if concerned about his impaired ability to stand, move, walk. Again that playful deception of the mind: is the wood before him real or is he seeing things from the metaphors in his very recent thoughts fleshed out in the real world after a time-lag? Has he gone mad? Where is he?

'Where is this?' he asks.

'Go. Walk. Go home,' comes the answer.

What was it that his mother used to say about such situations? *Don't spurn the goddess of wealth, waiting and ready at your hand, by pushing her away towards your feet.* The thought of his mother brings a sudden constriction in his throat – have they robbed him of any kind of self-control, of masculinity?

How will he ever find the words to ask her for forgiveness?

He hobbles, stops, limps a bit more; no, he really cannot move. The policemen are watching him in silence. Should he crawl on all fours? He would be much faster if he did that. He tries walking on the sides of his feet; it is impossible after two steps. An axis of pain has brought together, in one rod, the discrete epicentres of where he has been worked upon – the right big toe, the soles of both feet, his raw, bloody left thigh – and is driving that into his entire body, from toe to head. He takes another couple of steps.

'Run,' comes an order.

How can he run? He can hardly breathe.

A shot rings out, then another. The first bullet gets him in the back of his skull, the second in his back, under his left shoulder blade. He falls to the ground face-down.

CHAPTER NINETEEN

1970

A week of mild, half-hearted beatings, followed by three months of being left alone in his cell with other criminals, then suddenly Madan is set free; no explanations, no threats, no reasons, only the mocking, harsh words from the minion who unlocks his cell and leads him to an officer on the ground floor: 'Freedom. The effect of some good deed by your dead forefathers trickling down to you.' He is given papers to sign and finds himself surprised at feeling insulted, after all that he has been through, when the officer barks at him, 'Are you lettered or will it have to be a thumb impression?' When his effects are returned to him, Madan discovers his watch is missing, and the twenty-rupee note he had taken out of his pocket before being ushered ungently into his cell. The loose change, assorted keys, two pieces of folded-up paper, the folded picture of Ma Kali, they are all there. He wants to ask about the watch, but stops himself; what if they use it as an excuse to keep him inside for longer?

He comes out onto the confluence of Anwar Shah Road and Gariahat Road. Although it is past dusk, the residue of daylight in the sky and air hurts his eyes for a few seconds. Instinctively he crosses over to Gariahat Road and starts walking north. The missing watch silently nags at him until he thinks about how he came by it – it was his wedding present from Charubala nearly forty years ago; it was the most precious thing he possessed, a Citizen watch – and that little pleat of history transforms his minor irritation into something else. He sits down on the lowest of the three steps leading to the hardware shop just before Selimpur crossing because he suddenly feels weightless, a thing about to be blown away by a breeze; perching on the edge of concrete may moor him for a while.

There is a new branch of Carmel High School opposite him, right beside the petrol station. Didn't Arunima go to that school? At that thought he presses both his fists against his cheeks so that the roaring inside cannot escape his mouth, but they are already wet. He gets up and resumes his empty walking northwards because he does not want people to take him as a blubbing drunken fool. There is nowhere to go. He had heard Shej'-da once explaining to his children, when they were little, how birds made their way home to their nests at sundown: apparently, a small but very powerful magnet at the bottom of their nests navigated them back surely. At which point Arunima, after a moment's thought, had asked, 'If each nest has a magnet pulling birds to them, why don't they end up in each other's homes?'

A similar invisible thread of attraction is leading him, almost unawares, towards Bhabanipur; but that story had been Shej'-da's usual high nonsense. To Madan, home has always meant Basanta Bose Road, not his village, Amlapali, in Orissa.

Everything had seemed so small, so bare, when he had first returned, on his two weeks off, to the village, five years after he joined Baba and Ma in Calcutta. People had come from every single hut – everyone, men, women, children, old people – to see, even touch, 'our city boy', expecting whatever transformation they had imagined to touch their lives, too. Some of them had hung around for days, expecting something of him: a rupee or two, a shiny coin, a used shirt, a rubber ball, marbles, anything. On future visits he had remembered to bring little things – baubles, really – to distribute. Yet another feature that had remained unchanged for long was his parents' home (his mind had, unknown to his conscious self, already begun the process of stopping to think of it involuntarily as his own): one small room that housed anywhere between six and eight people; the needs of Nature answered in the open air in the fields around them. All these things that he had never noticed, or thought of as anything particular to be taken note of, had gradually become marks of difference. There was his father's back-breaking work growing onions on his tiny plot; his increasingly despairing complaints about how he made no money selling them to the middlemen and merchants who made all the profit; his wish to go and sell his crop on the open market himself. But how could he go to the nearest market in Tarbod with his sacks of onions without a cart? There was his mother, a silent, dark woman, thin as the kindling she collected from the forest. He wanted his parents' lives, and his two brothers' and sister's, to aspire to the conditions of his own in the city. He sent them money so that they could move up from one meal a day to two. He sent them shawls; the after-effects of malaria, contracted when they were children, made them shiver even during the summer months. Two of his brothers had died of the disease when he was little.

Over time, the dream of building a part-concrete room or two for his family had begun to be realised. He had paid the dowry for his sister's marriage, and for a bicycle for one of his brothers so that he could migrate across the border to Madhya Pradesh for short-term jobs, which brought in more money than scratching the arid land would ever do.

But that feeling of contraction never left him: every year that he visited, life in the village where he had been born and raised felt smaller, the people stunted, the country empty, sleepy and abandoned. There had been quite a competition among parents to bag him as a son-in-law, for his city job made him a good catch. He had picked Banita, the daughter of a local shop-owner.

He saw his wife, and subsequently his children, once every year, during his month off from Basanta Bose Road. Perhaps it was the short time that he spent with his biological family, perhaps it was something else, but he had never felt properly and tightly sewn into that life. His real life was elsewhere, in Calcutta, with the Ghosh family. The feeling of elsewhereness began to haunt him about one week into his month's holiday in Amlapali every time. Playing with his children; maintaining healthy conjugal relations with Banita; taking Dulal to the dissari, the local healer-man, when he had a particularly long-lasting case of stomach upset at the age of five; watching his children's faces light up as he brought them marbles and the Ghosh children's discarded toys and cast-offs – all these seemed like the intermittent illustrations in a children's book from which the words had disappeared, so that the pictures alone didn't cohere into a story. Those illustrations were strays and strangers in the book, as he was in Amlapali for a month, longing to be united with the thing that provided his life with the spine of meaning. That word 'holiday', for his time in his village, summed it all up: he was a tourist passing through the place inaccurately called home.

The terms 'people you call your own' and 'family' always conjured up for him, instantly, as they do right now, the faces of Ma and Baba and Didi-moni and Bor'-da and Mej'-da and Shej'-da . . . not the faces of his wife or Dulal or his two girls, Kanak and Prabha. Is this a mistake, like birds ending up in the wrong nests because each one has a magnet pulling the birds in the sky indiscriminately? Now that he remembers something trivial he didn't know he had stored away inside his head, it is like the discovery of something hidden long after the hiding place, and even the act of secretion, have been forgotten. Then he wonders if shame and humiliation are curdling his brain, making him go mad. He knows when it all went wrong: when that son of his turned ingrate dog and started biting the hand that fed him. Another question bubbles up in his murky soul – could Baba and Bor'-da and Mej'-da have silently orchestrated his arrest as a way of punishing him for Dulal's role in Baba's second heart attack, the one that broke him?

At the highest point on Dhakuria Bridge, he looks down and sees the railway tracks. He turns back a few metres and uses the staircase along the side of the bridge to descend to road level. Rickshaw stand; sweet shops; puffed-rice seller; narrow, dense lanes; people, hundreds of people, going about their lives, lives with a destination, a nest with a magnet pulling them. A young beggar is working his way through the crowds slowly, singing that song, 'Roop tera mastaana', from the hit Rajesh Khanna film last year. He's not doing a bad job, but the present appreciation brings to mind his bemusement at recently finding that the regular beggars on Basanta Bose Road, a blind man and his daughter who appeared early in the morning, had switched from their devotional 'Let my soul blossom like the hibiscus at the feet of my mother-goddess' to this very Hindi film song, 'Roop tera mastaana', a number touched somehow by vulgarity. He remembers, too, complaining about it to Charubala, that there was nothing reliable – everything derogated, and all change was slanted downwards. And here he's at it again: how all thoughts and memories lead back to that unchanging centre of Basanta Bose Road, of Charubala. Home.

On one side towards the end of Dhakuria Station Lane the evening market is setting up. Gas lights, tapers and kerosene lights are being lit and set beside mounds of vegetables, sacks of rice and lentils and dried red chillies, precarious piles of ripe limes, hillocks of glistening green chillies. There is even a short row of fish-sellers, baskets at their side, the plastic spread out in front of them containing small piles of minuscule shrimps; thick, red cross-sections of steaks of katla, two big fish-heads on one side; a tin bucket of something kept alive in soapy water. He did not know that there was an evening fish market in Dhakuria and the knowledge fills him with a tiny thread of excitement. He wants to check out how fresh the fish here is, compare rates with his regular fishmonger in Bhabanipur; Ma would be curious to know about it too. Then that weightlessness seizes him again as he laughs at this old mental habit of wanting to report everything to Charubala, because this time, this last time, there will be nothing to tell her.

When he hears the wailing sound of the level-crossing coming down to bar people and traffic on either side of the tracks, at the imminent arrival of a train, he stops loitering around in the market and quickly heads towards the end of Station Lane. A huge, solid mass of people waiting on this side; he has to jostle and push to get himself right to the front so that there is nothing between him and the tracks, right to the narrow opening between two metal posts, one of them part of the gate that has bent down and stopped at a right-angle to the post to form the barrier. Even now one or two swift daredevils are leaking out from either side and crossing the tracks hurriedly. A magnet is pulling them; they have to get to their nests quickly.

The tracks look enormous. He hears the rails, or maybe the wires above them, humming and zinging, then the hum magnifies to a metallic rattle. The world is only sound. He is perfectly weightless now, like air.

Epilogue I

Bay Area Professor Gets "Mathematics Nobel" Prize

A reclusive Indian mathematician, who was a child prodigy, has won the Fields Medal, the highest honor given to a mathematician under the age of 40. Professor Swarnendu Ghosh, a Professor of Pure Mathematics in Stanford University, is 30 this year. He came to the USA when he was 15 years old, before he had finished school in his city of birth, Calcutta, and was awarded a PhD at the age of 19.

The Fields Medal, widely regarded as the "Nobel Prize for Mathematics," is awarded every year to between two and four mathematicians by the International Mathematics Union at its Congress. Professor Ghosh shares the 1986 prize, given at the International Congress of the International Mathematics Union at Berkeley this year, with Professor Martin Freedman, who holds the Charles Powell Chair of Mathematics at the University of California at San Diego; Professor Simon Donaldson, the Wallis Professor of Mathematics at the University of Oxford; and the German mathematician Dr Gerd Faltings, Professor at Princeton University. Professor Ghosh did not attend this year's Congress.

He was offered a teaching job at Stanford University, his alma mater, at the age of 20, thus becoming the youngest-ever faculty member in the history of the university. His work on prime numbers—numbers divisible only by themselves and 1—has garnered him this year's Fields Medal. He has provided the solution to a 137-year-old problem called the de Polignac's conjecture, named after the Frenchman who first proposed it in 1849.

This conjecture states that every even number appears as the gap between two consecutive primes, infinitely open. A generalization of the still-open problem of the 'twin primes conjecture', which hypothesizes that there may be an infinite pair of 'twin primes'—pairs of prime numbers which are 2 apart (such as 5 and 7, or 17 and 19)—Professor Ghosh's proof that there are infinite pairs of consecutive primes which are 4 apart, infinitely many that are 6 apart, and so on, marks a great step toward solving some of the most celebrated unsolved problems in number theory, notably Goldbach's conjecture.

In a correspondence between Leonhard Euler and Christian Goldbach in 1742, the latter asserted that every even number from 4 onward is the sum of two prime numbers. So $4 = 2+2$, $6 = 3+3$, $8 = 3+5$, and so on. No full proof of this conjecture is known.

Prime numbers are a valuable tool in encryption and are considered by mathematicians and scientists to provide the underlying design of many things in Nature.

Renowned for his shyness, the attention-avoiding professor, who was a child prodigy when he arrived at Stanford University at the age of 15 from his native Calcutta in India, has not returned calls by this newspaper.

His thesis supervisor, Professor Alan Pfeiffer, said, "It is fair to say that the entire math faculty here in Stanford had rarely seen anyone the like of Swarnendu when he arrived here. It is impossible to convey the sense of excitement, the sense of great possibility that we felt, when he started his graduate work. We are thrilled to have those hopes and promises fulfilled. It is a day of great joy, both for him and for us, and, of course, for the University. We feel very, very proud."

The professor responsible for bringing the 15-year-old over, Ayan Basu, also from Calcutta and now at Caltech, said, "I couldn't believe my eyes when this boy's math teacher at school, a childhood friend of mine, sent me some of Swarnendu's stuff to look at. He was sure this boy was special, that he was onto something. And he was right. When Swarnendu arrived at Stanford, the faculty had only one thing on its collective mind: here was the next Ramanujan."

Ramanujan was the most famous Indian mathematics prodigy of the twentieth century. But it looks as if his reputation could be eclipsed by Professor Ghosh. While still a graduate student, Professor Ghosh published a paper, at the age of 18, that stunned the mathematics world. It moved the world closer toward a solution of the famous Goldbach conjecture, which, as yet unproven, states that every even number can be written as the sum of two primes. Professor Pfeiffer said that his former student's proof, running to over twenty-five pages, had to be simplified and the young student cajoled to have it published. "You see, he came to us without any training in the conventions of mathematical language. What he had was an innate understanding of the world of numbers, of abstraction and reasoning and intuition," said Professor Pfeiffer.

The following year, at the age of 19, he published yet another theorem that took the mathematics world by storm. This time he showed that either a prime number or a semiprime (a number which is the product of exactly two primes, such as 6 = 2 x 3) always exists between any two square numbers. As Professor Basu said, "This is one of the most famous, and most famously stubborn, unsolved problems, called Legendre's conjecture, in number theory. And Swarnendu's proof, worked out while he was still at his PhD, is the most promising progress on that problem that has been made so far."

Almost as famous as his skills in solving difficult math problems is his reclusiveness. He never gives interviews or appears at public functions, not even departmental ones. Archishman Chakraborty, one of his graduate students, says, "His classes and seminars make you feel as if you're eavesdropping on a private conversation with himself. He is hugely inspiring, not because he reaches out to encourage you, but because you get a glimpse of this focused, brilliant, obsessed mind. It is as if you've walked into a room where he is sitting with god's book of numbers. You too want to enter that room."

Professor Pfeiffer confessed that it had been an uphill struggle to draw his erstwhile student, and now colleague, out of his notorious introversion. 'Well, most mathematicians, you'll find, are creatures somewhat dissociated from the real world,' he said. 'The abstract matters to them much more than the concrete. Swarnendu is a very pure example of that. There is an innocence about him which the world has not been able to touch. He still lives with his mother, who came out to join him shortly after he was offered his teaching position in the Faculty. As far as I am aware, no one from the Department has ever visited him at home.'

Calls to try and contact Professor Ghosh's mother at their home have not been returned.

San Jose Mercury News, August 27, 1986

The reply from Dr Leif Carlsson of the Classics Department has arrived. He takes out the medal and places it next to the letter. The gold medal's rim bears his name, Swarnendu Ghosh. On the reverse side the inscription CONGREGATI / EX TOTO ORBE / MATHEMATICI / OB SCRIPTA INSIGNIA / TRIBUERE means, Dr Carlsson writes, 'The mathematicians, having congregated from the whole world, awarded [this medal] because of outstanding writings [ie., outstanding work].' There is a branch of leaves behind the inscription, and then, behind that, mostly obscured, some etched curves and lines. He turns to the obverse side: a profile of Archimedes's head – he can read the Greek letters that spell out his name – and an inscription running along more than three-quarters of the circumference of the medal. This one says, TRANSIRE SUUM PECTUS MUNDOQUE POTIRI. In Dr Carlsson's translation, 'To rise above oneself and to master the world.'

He looks at the medal for a while, turning it to one side, then the other. Suddenly the etched lines and curves on the reverse, the face of Archimedes, all relate into meaning. The diagram obscured by the branch of leaves is nothing less than an illustration of Archimedes's own proof, which he considered his favourite: the volume and surface area of a sphere are two-thirds that of a cylinder (including its bases) circumscribing it, or a cylinder of the same height and diameter. Sona smiles; yes, of course. A voice inside his head, a voice from another country, says, 'The Greeks laid the foundations of mathematics.'

Then he reads again, '*Transire suum pectus mundoque potiri.*' To rise above oneself. That will do. That is enough.

Epilogue II
September 2012

They come out of the dark forest as if spawned by the night itself;
the trees sending out their new kind of children. A single file of
people, perhaps about a dozen or fifteen of them. They are silent like
the scrub that surrounds them, or the red, dry earth out of which
they have sprung. Each one of them is carrying something in his hand,
or hoisted on a shoulder. It is a new-moon night and they need to
walk for three miles or so in the breachless dark to reach their destination. They have torches, but it is part of their plan to do the walk
without turning them on. In any case, they know where they are
going: the railway line that cuts through Latehar district, nearly
hugging National Highway 75 right after McCluskiegunj, then cleaving
away from around Kumendi, through Gotang and Betla forests, via
Chhipodohar and Barwadih, until it rejoins Highway 75 at Chianki
and Daltongunj. Between Barkakana Junction and Daltongunj, the
Kolkata–Ajmer Express passes by, without stopping, twenty-one towns
and villages; their job is between Kumendi and Kechki, the last third
of this sector, a distance of just over thirty-five kilometres. Four of
them are going to get to work near Hehegara Halt, the rest are going
to fan out after Barwadih Junction, near Mangra and Kechki, before
the express starts to slow down towards Chianki for the stop at
Daltongunj.

They have been trained in what they are about to do. They have
maintained their individual jobs and other responsibilities within the
Party, coming together only for the purpose of training for tonight's
action. They have been selected not merely on the basis of their
military abilities, but also according to their political level and discipline. Tonight's squad is under the leadership of Sabita Kumari.

Sabita Kumari, twenty-eight, a graduate from a tiny college in Daltongunj, has never dreamed of this role. Her parents expected her to become a school teacher. But that seems to her a half-remembered page from a book of someone else's story. Her two younger sisters were killed eight years ago – the sixteen-year-old beheaded with a machete while her parents, tied to the bed, were forced to watch; the youngest sister, fourteen, gang-raped, her eyes gouged out, her tongue cut out and then her neck stabbed. Their crime? The family had tried to resist the moneylenders' attempts to take over their land in the village of Pabira. The police at the nearest station, in Ranchi, refused to issue an FIR in response to Sabita's complaint unless she fellated the duty officer; more action would be taken according to the escalation in services she provided. That, too, seems so long ago, from a different life.

People talk of rage as something fluid; it boils, flows, spills over, scalds. For her, it is not any of these things. Instead it is a vast, frozen sea, solid as rock, unthawable. She has never seen the sea, but she knows it wraps around three-quarters of the world. All her anger is that and more. When she joined the Maoists she was twenty. Within two years she had killed five officers at Ranchi police station, all those who had leered and asked for sex when she had gone to complain. When the little of her life had been reduced to nothing, the Party had held and rocked her in its iron cradle, told her that the nothing of her life could become a path, a straight, narrow, but tough one, at the end of which was a destination worth reaching.

She has repeated the same words, almost without change, to her comrades who are silently marching with her now to their business of the night. She has picked them with great thought and care. Underlying her choice had been one immutable principle: they must be people who are nothing too, whose lives are nothing, who have nothing. No recourse to any form of redress or justice. Revenge was their last roar. And what was justice but revenge tricked out in a gentleman's clothes, speaking English? She knows the relevant section of the recruits' histories like she knows the back of her hand.

From Simdega district have come two tribal brothers and their sister, Subir Majhi, Deb Majhi and Champa Majhi. The Majhis, members of a tribe who lived along the edge of Saranda forest, had been told that the land where their ancestors had lived from as far back in the past as the human mind could see is no longer theirs, but the state's to do with as it wanted. They did not have a patta to prove ownership; the state did. Soon afterwards, policemen, contractors, officials spread out over it; their land was going to be mined; the earth there contained metals. A group of people from the city came and told them they would get compensation. But the forest was their home; what compensation would return that to them? Would they give them another forest somewhere? The compensation turned out to be 5,000 rupees per head, not exceeding 25,000 rupees for each family. The CRPF forces, with their AK-47s and metal breastplates, posted in the forest to deal with the Maoists, got 4,000 rupees a month. The tribal people knew what fate awaited them outside their land – daily wage-labourer in the city, maidservant in someone's home, prostitute.

When the Majhis joined forces with the hundreds of forest-dwellers who were also being driven out, their land no longer theirs, the state deployed the military police. The police were protecting the lawful property of the mining companies, the property that had been the tribal peoples' last year or the year before; they had a right to use force against the tribals, for they were trespassers and outlaws now. The campaign of intimidation began: a house looted and then razed to the ground; someone maimed for life after being hauled off to prison on the flimsiest of excuses and beaten in lock-up; a girl raped; a well poisoned; a man shot; food shops destroyed and supplies cut off, so that the jungle-dwellers could be starved into submission.

This had all happened before, their father said to them; it had happened in neighbouring districts, in Chiria, in Gua, when he had been a young man. The same story – forest-tribes banished after their land was sold by the state to mining companies; those meant to protect you turned into your attackers. Imagine coming home one day to find that your parents were waiting with knives to slaughter you. That is what the Maoists said when the tribes escaped into the forests to protect themselves from the military police. They had a choice: to be snuffed out overnight by the world or take on the world and wrest something from it; not very much, just a little, just to survive and live like a human, not an animal. This is the hope the Maoists offered, the hope of dark clouds gathering over parched, fractured soil; it could rain or it could not, but they brought something new into their lives: possibility.

Sabita has planted IEDs in the forest and blown up military vehicles, she has raided outposts of the Indian Reserve Battalion and blown up their buildings, she has burned security vehicles sent to protect the Prime Minister's village road-building programme, the Gram Sadak Yojana, in Belpahari in West Medinipur; she is itinerant, like the rest of her kind, through several districts in several abutting states: two nights in Saranda forest, three nights in Dandakaranya, a week in Karampada, constantly on the move, bringing to the country their promise of a mobile war. But the end of tonight's action is unknown. None of them is going to be there to witness it. Were her thoughts in the past, before doing something terribly beautiful like an action for the first time, was her mind then like it is now, all a-whirl? They would all die one day – and it will come a lot sooner in their lives than in others' – but it was better to die fighting, like a cornered wildcat, than crushed underfoot like an unseen worm. You kick a dog, it will run away, but you keep kicking it and kicking it, it will have no option but to bite you back just to stop being kicked. How could you want to live a life that makes you yearn for one thing only – its end? Every human being in this world wants, strives for, a better life, but they are deemed to be below that wanting and striving. Their lives are nothing, less than nothing. They are lower than animals. How has this come to pass? Is it true of everywhere in the world that some people are just fodder? Or has their country taken a wrong turning? She does not know.

Her subgroup of four reaches the point near Hehegara Halt while the rest carry on towards Mangra. Not a whisper is exchanged. Even their breathing is cautious. A torch is produced, its light covered with a thin cloth before being switched on. They bend and squat and go down on all fours on the railway track, shining the torch close to the ground, until they find what they are looking for: the fishplate joining the ends of two rails to form the track. They are careful about not stepping on the stone chips between the rails; the crunching sound it produces is too loud. Sabita stands guard with her AK-47 removed from her shoulder to her hands, turning 360 degrees every eight minutes in four slow ninety-degree sweeps of two minutes each, with clockwork precision; the human equivalent of the swivelling turret on a tank. The night needs watching; she knows that the darkness skitters and slides between being a friend and an enemy with alarming unpredictability.

While she keeps watch, her three comrades bring out medium-sized wrenches, wire-cutters, jacks, industrial pliers and screwdrivers from their bags. Each instrument has been carried separately and individually to prevent clanking during the walk. They lie flat on the tracks, one on each side and one on the stone chips in the centre, and begin to dislodge the fishplate holding the rail-ends in perfect alignment. The trick is more than forty years old, she has been told during her training. Someone had come from Chhattisgarh to show them the ropes, and he had mentioned that according to local Maoist lore it was a Bengali invention, the work of a man known as Pratik-da in the late Sixties in some district bordering West Bengal and Bihar. Or was it West Bengal and Orissa? Pratik-da was no longer alive – he had been tortured and killed by the police in the notorious Naxalite purges in 1970 and '71 in Calcutta – but his gift to his future comrades survived and, for those who cared to or were old enough to remember, he lived on in his bequest.

It is not easy work – their necks have to be held at an angle of forty-five degrees to the ground while their bodies are stretched out flat – and their hands have little purchase because of the limited freedom of movement. The sounds of creaking and clinking, of the tinkle of metal on metal and of metal on stone, of the occasional crunch of the loose chips, are too loud to their ears. They cannot concentrate fully on their work because a part of them is forever listening out for the slightest whisper of something awry, something outside the ordinary. But they are lucky. Their chosen area is nowhere-land, between two tiny stations in the middle of such abandonment that people talked of the place as being in the blind spot of even god's vision; the nearest station is nearly ten kilometres away on one side and seven on the other. Besides, the fear of Maoists means that no one ventures outside after darkness falls. There are no vehicles passing on the dirt road running mostly parallel to the railway line a few hundred metres away, but at this time of night that is normal.

When at last they are done, they put the fishplate away in a shoulder bag, first swaddling it tightly in clothes. Then they try to wedge a jack in the tiny gap between the two rail ends, but this defeats them. They are not surprised; they had discussed this during training. They had decided not to leave anything to chance, which is why they are taking out fishplates at more than one point along the same track; one of them is bound to work; the average speed of the train is between 70 to 80 kilometres per hour on their chosen stretch. They strain a little bit more and ultimately leave the end of a curved machete wedged in the crack. They pick up their instruments and turn off the torch. Then they cross the tracks and disappear into the night and into the forest, these new children of the trees. Their work here is over. They will leave the forest now and never return to this region again.

In three hours, well before dawn breaks, the Ajmer–Kolkata Express, carrying approximately 1,500 people, is going to hurtle down these tracks.

A NOTE ON NAMES AND RELATIONS

In any Bengali family the members address each other relationally. Only children's first names are used; also, a husband addresses his wife by her first name (but not the other way around). These four prefixes show the relative seniority of a person being addressed:

Boro-: eldest

Mejo-: middle

Shejo-: between middle and youngest

Chhoto-: youngest

So if your father has three older brothers, you would call the eldest Boro-jyethu (jyethu being the term for father's older brother); the next one, Mejo-jyethu; and the youngest, Chhoto-jyethu. The prefixes can be added to all the relational terms listed below:

Bhai: younger brother

Boüdi: brother's wife

Dada: older brother, often shortened to –da

Didi: older sister, often shortened to -di

Jaa: husband's older sister

Jyethima: Jyethu's wife; sometimes abbreviated to 'Jyethi'

Jyethu: the older brother of your father

Kaka: the younger brother of your father

Kakima: Kaka's wife; sometimes abbreviated to simply 'Kaki'

Mama: maternal uncle, brother of your mother. The same term is used of uncles older and younger than your mother, unlike paternal uncles, who are classified as Jyethu and Kaka based on their ages relative to your father.

Mami: Mama's wife

Mashi: mother's sister

Pishi: father's sister.

The relational terms can also be appended to names outside the family, thus: Mala-mashi, Namita-di, Rupa-boüdi, Sunil-mama.

These are some other terms used in the book:

Boro-boü: the eldest daughter-in-law of a large, extended family

Thakuma: paternal grandmother.

GLOSSARY

aanchol = The 'n' is nasal. An entire cultural complex resides in this part of
    the sari, the endpiece, which hangs over the shoulder at the back (mostly;
    it can sometimes hang from the front, depending on the way in which it
    is worn). Because it can be used to cover the back, arms and shoulder, it
    is the 'display area' of the sari, its peacock's tail, as it were, for which the
    craftsman or mass-manufacturer reserves the showiest of embellishments.
    Its uses are legion, from wiping tears to drying plates; from tying keys
    to draping it around the arms and shoulders to feel less exposed; from
    covering the mouth and/or nose to fanning oneself in the humid heat.

ablush = Ebony.

achchha = Literally 'well' (ejaculative, not adjective), 'okay', 'right' or 'I see',
    the word can denote assent or stand as just a filler.

adda = A Bengali institution. It consists of long sessions of aimless
    conversation, mostly between men. Bengalis try to give it a high
    intellectual gloss, believing that it is the soul of life and productive of great
    breakthroughs in the arts, sciences, politics, etc., but don't be fooled – it's
    classic Bengali idleness, a way of wasting, cumulatively, months and years
    of one's life in procrastination and ridiculous self-importance.

anjali = Prayer.

aparajita = *Clitoria ternatea*, or butterfly-pea, or blue-pea. A perennial climber
    that bears strikingly blue flowers singly (white variants obtain, too). The
    fruit resembles a smaller, narrower, flatter, downier sugar-snap.

arrey = Very difficult to translate, this could mean 'Hey', or express surprise,
    or simply act as a filler, a kind of cultural verbal tic.

ashad = The first Bengali month of the monsoon season, usually mid-June
    to mid-July.

ashirbad = Literally, 'blessing'. In the context in which it is used in the story, it
    is the formalisation of a nuptial match by the visit of the groom's parents
    to the bride's home to bless her, usually with a piece of gold ornament.

ashtami = The third, and grandest, of the five days of Durga Puja.

ashwattha = *Ficus religiosa*, or peepal tree – an iconic tree, because the Buddha obtained enlightenment under one.

bahurupi = An itinerant folk performer with a wide repertoire of roles and corresponding disguises. He assumes several forms and wholly inhabits the identities, which are dizzying: gods, goddesses, demons, tradesmen, conmen, animals, children, professionals – nothing is potentially outside his reach. An endangered species now. For an adequate overview, see www.tribuneindia.com/2008/20080308/saturday/main1.htm.

baju = An ornament for the upper arm; a gold armband.

bargadar = Sharecropper.

bat = *Ficus benghalensis*, the iconic Indian banyan tree. Enough said.

benarasi = A type of silk sari, named after the city, Banaras (or Varanasi), which is the centre of India's *zari* figured-silk weaving industry (*zari* is gold-wrapped thread). Benarasi saris are rich, gorgeous and usually feature intricate floral and foliate patterns. Considered de rigueur for Bengali weddings.

bene = A class of trader who deals exclusively in jewellery.

bhari (weight) = Generally used of gold, 1 bhari is 11.664 grams.

bheesti = Water carrier. A person, not an object.

bidi = The native Indian cigarette, small and thin, made of tobacco wrapped in kendu leaves and tied at one end with a string. Very cheap, it is considered the poor man's cigarette.

bigha = A measure of land. In West Bengal, the bigha was standardised under British colonial rule at 1,600 square yards (0.1338 hectare or 0.3306 acre); this is often interpreted as being one-third of an acre (it is precisely $\frac{40}{121}$ acre). In metric units, a bigha is hence 1333.33 square metres. See also **katha**.

bijaya = The last day of Durga Puja, the conceit being that after her sojourn in her parents' home, Durga returns to her husband, Shiva.

bonti = A sharp, curved blade, fixed perpendicularly to a horizontal wooden stand, and used in the kitchen for cutting fish and vegetables.

boü-bhaat = Literally, 'bride-rice'. The wedding proper – that is, the rituals that bind bride and groom together as man and wife – is held in the bride's home, after which she leaves her father's house and comes to her in-laws'. The man's family now throws a reception, a complement to the wedding, if you will; mass feeding invariably characterises it. The new bride is supposed to cook for her husband's family and serve rice to her in-laws and the guests on this day, hence the name.

Brahmo = This entry is going to be kept deliberately short. Interested readers can go to www.thebrahmosamaj.net. Brahmoism is an early nineteenth-century reformist movement within the Hindu religion that tried to free itself from cant, rituals, superstition, idolatry and all kinds of social ills that had come to plague the practice of Hinduism. Socially and doctrinally progressive, Brahmos had a central role in the Bengal Renaissance of the nineteenth century. The starriest of the two Bengali families, the Tagores and the Rays (Upendrakishore, Sukumar, Satyajit), were Brahmos. In some current, colloquial usage of the word, 'brahmo' can mean, slightly pejoratively, over-refined creatures floating a few inches above the vulgar, unwashed masses. As with all such colloquial usage, there is a small grain of truth in it.

chador = A length of cloth, usually to cover oneself at night. The same word is used of bedsheets or cotton shawls.

challan = Invoice for goods sent.

charas = Hashish.

chhatu = Flour made from roasted chickpeas or barley. Can be eaten uncooked and usually is, kneaded rigorously into a dough with oil, water, green chillies, salt, chopped onions, etc. Considered to be the poor man's food.

chhee = This is the exclamatory word to express shame mostly, but also sometimes distaste or disgust.

chhillum = A small, simple, trumpet-shaped clay pipe for smoking marijuana. Often called chhilim.

chik = Vernacular for choker.

chur = A flat decorative bracelet of varying width, usually in filigree, but also in floral chasing; mainly a marriage ornament.

crore = Ten million.

dhaak = A kind of drum slung over the shoulders in a sling and played with sticks. The man who plays it is a dhaaki.

eeesh = One of the most eloquent words in Bengali, it can express – depending on context and the tone in which it is said – disgust, distaste, wonder, regret, sympathy, revulsion, and no doubt a few more feelings.

fatua = A short-sleeved, shorter version of the **panjabi** (q.v.).

gamchha = The poor man's towel, very thin, coarse, and invariably chequered red-and-white.

ghaghra = Long, flared skirt, colourfully, often garishly, decorated, common in north-western parts of India.

gherao = The practice of aggrieved labourers surrounding members of the management (or the owners) and creating a wall of humans through which the encircled persons could not escape until the workers' demands were met.

gola = Barn for storage of grain.

hanshuli = A stiff sickle-shaped hinged necklace that derives its form from tribal Indian jewellery; the equivalent of a collar.

harijan = Literally, 'people of god'; this was Gandhi's term for the class of people considered as untouchables in caste-based Indian society.

hartal = Strike.

hashua = A knife with a curved, crescent-shaped blade, not unlike a sickle.

horbola = A professional performer who mimics all kinds of sounds, chiefly bird calls and animal cries. The horbola used to be a regular fixture in village fairs, but is now an endangered species.

hyan = Yes; okay. Often an interjection standing for 'What?'

jah = Yet another eloquent ejaculation, this is an intensifier that can denote regret, contempt, dismissal or disbelief.

jamdani = The most exclusive and expensive of Bengali muslin saris (or Dhaka muslins, as they are called), jamdanis feature a distinctive style of supplementary-weft work woven into the fabric.

jhalmuri = A spicy snack made with puffed rice, finely-chopped onions, spices, peanuts, mustard oil, chillies etc.

kaajol = Kohl.

kaan = Literally 'ear', this is a formal, dressy genre of earring, which covers the entire ear, hence the name.

kaash phul = The flowers of *Saccharum spontaneum*, a perennial grass, which grows up to three metres tall.

kadam = *Neolamarckia cadamba*. A large deciduous tree, capable of growing over 30 metres tall, bearing the most amazing flowers during the monsoon, which resemble perfectly round, dusty-orange or yellow woollen balls. They are fragrant, too.

kaliya = A gem from Bengali cuisine, this is a rich, fragrant, spiced fish or meat dish. The basic spicing is bay leaves, ground onions, ginger paste, yoghurt and Bengali garam masala (a mixture of equal amounts of cardamom, cloves and cinnamon).

kankan = An elegant conical bangle of repetitive motifs, once obligatory for married women.

katha = $\frac{1}{20}$ of a **bigha** (q.v.), so, in metric terms, 66.66 square metres.

kendu = *Diospyros melanoxylon*. A deciduous tree whose leaves are dried, then used to make the outer wrapping of **bidi** (q.v.), the poor man's cigarette.

khemta = A type of dance. Derives its name from a particular rhythm structure. In Bengali culture the dance is associated with dissolute lifestyles.

khichuri= A dish of rice and lentils cooked together with spices. The English word 'kedgeree' derives from this; the dish is some distance from the original.

kirtan = A very Bengali stripe of devotional music in which the songs describe the acts of Krishna's life. Listening to them uninterruptedly for any length of time requires particular tenacity or strength of character. However, most Tagore songs where the idiom of kirtan is used in the melody are beautiful.

kota = Named after the original home of its manufacture in Rajasthan, this sari has an open weave of alternating cotton and silk threads.

kunjo = A round earthen vessel for storing drinking water.

lakh = Hundred thousand.

lathi = A wooden stick, usually bamboo, used as a weapon.

lungi = Cloth worn by men, wound around the waist, to cover the lower half of the body.

madari = A class of travelling player.

mahajan = Moneylender.

mahua = *Madhuca longifolia*, a rapidly growing deciduous tree that can attain a height of up to 20 metres. It bears creamy-white flowers in dense clusters through most of April. The flowers are sweet and edible and have a distinctive smell. Pradip Krishen writes in his wonderful *Trees of Delhi*: 'Arguably the most valuable of Indian trees because its flowers are a nutritive lifeline for millions of poor people. In season, the succulent flowers fall to the ground just before dawn. Deer, monkeys, wild pig, jackals and bears compete to gather them. A large tree bears up to 300 kg of flowers in a season. They are eaten raw or sun-dried and are distilled into a strong country spirit with a smoky, nutty flavour ... The extremely hard, durable timber has a dark, reddish-brown heartwood, but is seldom used because the tree is too valuable to be felled.'

mairi = A mildly vulgar swear-word.

mallika = *Jasminum sambac*, also known as Arabian jasmine, and as *bel* in Bengali. A small, woody shrub that bears small, white, gorgeously perfumed flowers. Like all jasmines, it is powerfully indolic, with that characteristic back-of-the-throat rasp.

manimela = Literally, 'a fair or gathering of gems'. A kind of informal and local children's club, with most neighbourhoods boasting a couple, where boys and girls of the area get together in the afternoons, after school, to sing, play, do light drills, practise an instrument, rehearse a play. A bit of a pious and goody-goody kind of outfit with sound intentions – that children don't fall into bad or idle ways – at its heart.

mantasha = A fitted gold cuff worn unaccompanied around the wrist.

mashima = Aunty. A generic term used to address senior women not known to one. Also commonly used for friends' mothers.

mastaan= Hooligan.

mela = Fair.

mon (weight) = An old weight measure, anglicised to 'maund' in British India. The maund was first standardised in the Bengal Presidency in 1833, where it was set equal to 100 Troy pounds (or 82.28 lb). This standard spread throughout the British Raj. After Independence, one maund became exactly 37.3242 kilograms.

moshai = Mr, but more respectful than that sounds in English. Probably from 'monsieur'.

muri = Puffed rice.

orre = A more polite (and rather endearing way) of saying 'Hey, you', and not only to call someone.

panchali = A melodically simple, droning, sometimes long piece of narrative song in rhyme.

panchphoron = A five-spice mixture unique to Bengali cuisine. It consists of equal amounts of fenugreek, fennel, cumin, nigella and mustard seeds.

panjabi = Bengali word for a kurta – a loose collarless shirt, coming down to just above the knees.

pantua = A type of sweet. Cottage cheese and thickened milk-solids mixed together, flavoured with black cardamom, shaped into patties, deep-fried and finally soaked in sugar syrup. Sublime.

papad = A spiced wafer made out of lentil flour. Usually served fried or, sometimes, grilled/toasted. Inexplicably (and wrongly) called 'poppadum' in Britain. Why?

patta = Literally, leaf; in the context used, a piece of paper, title-deed.

pui = A green vegetable, often called Malabar spinach, with waxy, shiny, rounded leaves and smooth stems, both edible. The stems have a slightly viscous texture when cooked. Usually prepared with potatoes and pumpkin and sometimes lifted to another plane by the addition of tiny shrimps. Only obtainable in Bengali homes, it is considered, wrongly, too simple and frugal to be served to guests.

ratanchur = An elaborate ornament that covers the wrist, hand and all five fingers.

sal = *Shorea robusta*, a hardwood tree that can grow up to 30 metres, with trunks as wide as 2–3 metres. Its broad leaves, when dry, are used to make leaf plates and bowls.

sandesh = Bengal's signature sweet, made out of sweetened and flavoured ricotta-type cottage cheese. The varieties are legion.

ser (weight) = One-fortieth of a **mon** (q.v.) or maund. In Raj India it was written as 'seer'. One ser is just under 1 kg (exactly 933g).

shala = A mild swear-word; it originally implied sexual relations with the addressee's sister.

shataranchi = A thick woven cotton rug, traditionally of many colours.

shatta = A gambling game, played with cards.

sheel = A large slab of flat stone used as a mortar to grind spices.

shingara = Bengali word for samosa – tetrahedral parcels of pastry, stuffed, most commonly, with a potato filling and deep-fried.

shiuli = *Nyctanthes arbor-tristis*. A deciduous bush or small tree that bears beautiful clusters of night-blooming, fragrant white flowers. The petals occur at the end of a small, brilliantly orange tube.

shukto = Of the many jewels in the crown of Bengali cuisine, this surely must rank as one of the most prized – a bitter vegetable dish, made with bitter gourd, green papaya, green banana, sweet potato, drumstick (the long, ridged, stick-like fruit of *Moringa oleifera*; not chicken) and dried lentil croutons, that usually opens a multi-course meal. It is delicate and subtle and you get it only in Bengali homes.

simul = *Bombax ceiba*, or red silk cotton, is a glorious deciduous tree, which stands bare in the winter, then explodes into deep-red or coral conflagrations in the springtime, while still leafless: the large flowers have five leathery, fleshy petals. The fruit is a large brown capsule that splits open in the early summer, dispersing masses of white silk cotton along with the seeds.

sindoor = The 'n' is nasal. Vermilion powder worn by married Hindu women in the parting of their hair and, sometimes, as a decorative circle, in the centre of their forehead.

sitabhog = A kind of white Bengali sweet. It resembles long-grained rice.

sloka = Verse(s) of prayer.

sraddha = The Hindu religious ceremony that is the culminating point of the obligatory period of mourning after the death of someone in the immediate family. It is supposed to release the soul of the dead to wherever it is that souls go after the last rites have been performed. As always with these things, it involves feeding of the masses.

taal = Rhythm or beat.

tagaa = A kind of ornament for the arm.

tagar = *Tabernaemontana divaricata* is a pointless, overcultivated, straggly evergreen bush that bears small, white, pinwheel-shaped flowers. In *Trees of Delhi*, Pradip Krishen calls it 'a downmarket jasmine'. The description cannot be bettered.

tangail = A class of **jamdani** (q.v.) sari. Although jamdanis were traditionally woven by Muslims, Hindu weavers who moved during Partition from Tangail, now in Bangladesh, developed India's modern jamdani industry. West Bengali jamdanis are often called Tangail jamdanis, and they typically have many *buti* (small, usually floral motifs, created as a repeat against a plain ground) woven throughout the field, often diagonally.

tangi = A kind of (lethal) axe.

tanpura = A long-necked plucked lute. Its body shape slightly resembles that of the sitar, although it has no frets – and the strings are played open. It has four or five (occasionally six) wire strings, which are plucked in sequence in a regular pattern to create a harmonic resonance on the basic note. It is exclusively an instrument of accompaniment, usually to a vocal recital.

tashar = A type of 'raw' silk. The entry in Hobson-Jobson is 'tussah, tusser'.

toka = A wide-brimmed hat made of dried palm leaves.

ufff = Most commonly an expression of irritation, this can be an intensifier in contexts that express admiration and even fear.

ACKNOWLEDGEMENTS

This book could not have been written without the generosity of the Free Word Centre and the Belgian literary organisation Het Beschrijf/Passa Porta, which gave me a six-week residency in the Passa Porta writers' apartment in Brussels in autumn 2011. Passa Porta also gave me a crucial three weeks in the apartment in summer 2012. I am very grateful to them for their support.

I would like to thank the following people for all their help and support:

Penny Hoare.

Peter Straus.

Clara Farmer, Poppy Hampson.

Suzanne Dean.

Sudeep Chakravarti, JM Coetzee, Judy Corbalis, Mahasweta Devi, Jean Drèze, Damon Galgut, Grant Gillespie, Michelle de Kretser, Dominic Leggett, Vestal McIntyre, Alison Mercer, Anuradha Roy, Amartya Sen, Rose Tremain.

Sreyashi Dastidar, Devashri Mukherjee, Tushita Patel, Deeptanil Ray.

Sumanta Banerjee, Arpita Bhattacharjee, Krishnendu Bhattacharjee, Kate Bland, the late Satyesh Chakraborty, Swapan Chakraborty, Ashim 'Kaka' Chatterjee, Sukanta Chaudhuri, Supriya Chaudhuri, Soumitra

Das, Kanchan Datta, Ilke Froyen, Anik Ghosh, Shreela Ghosh, Meru Gokhale, Mandy Greenfield, Durgapada Hajra, Jenny Hewson, Ieuan Hopkins, Ian Jack, Seema Jayachandran, Pradip Krishen, Udayan Mukherjee, Amiya Nayek, Basudeb Nayek, Susannah Otter, Rohini Pande, Nicci Praça, Ritwik Rao, Debdulal Ray, Saktidas Roy, Chiki Sarkar, Malabika Sarkar, Sudipto Sarkar, Sumit Sarkar, Tanika Sarkar, Ruth Warburton.

Richard Elwes, Tim Gowers, Christian Lübbe.

For giving me a home away from home: Anubha Das, Bulbul Mitra, Devashri & Udayan Mukherjee, Brinda Sirkar.

PERMISSIONS

Parts of the descriptions of saris in the 'Glossary' are from *The Sari: Styles, Patterns, History, Techniques* by Linda Lynton. © 1995 Thames & Hudson Ltd., London. Reprinted by kind permission of Thames & Hudson.

Some of the entries on trees and flowers in the 'Glossary' are from Pradip Krishen's *Trees of Delhi* (Dorling Kindersley: Delhi, 2006), by kind permission of the author.

The lines from Daniel Kehlmann's *Measuring the World* (Quercus, 2009), translated by Carol Brown Janeway, appear by kind permission of author, translator and Quercus Books.

The sentence from James Salter's *Light Years* (Penguin Modern Classics, 2007) is reproduced by kind permission of Penguin Books UK.

The sentence from *War and Peace*, translated by Richard Pevear and Larissa Volokhonsky, and published by Vintage Classics in 2008, appears by kind permission of Random House UK.